CELEBRATING HOLIDAYS

Diwali

by Rachel Grack

BELLWETHER MEDIA • MINNEAPOLIS, MN

Note to Librarians, Teachers, and Parents:

Blastoff! Readers are carefully developed by literacy experts and combine standards-based content with developmentally appropriate text.

Level 1 provides the most support through repetition of high-frequency words, light text, predictable sentence patterns, and strong visual support.

Level 2 offers early readers a bit more challenge through varied simple sentences, increased text load, and less repetition of high-frequency words.

Level 3 advances early-fluent readers toward fluency through increased text and concept load, less reliance on visuals, longer sentences, and more literary language.

Level 4 builds reading stamina by providing more text per page, increased use of punctuation, greater variation in sentence patterns, and increasingly challenging vocabulary.

Level 5 encourages children to move from "learning to read" to "reading to learn" by providing even more text, varied writing styles, and less familiar topics.

Whichever book is right for your reader, Blastoff! Readers are the perfect books to build confidence and encourage a love of reading that will last a lifetime!

This edition first published in 2017 by Bellwether Media, Inc.

Library of Congress Cataloging-in-Publication Data

Names: Koestler-Grack, Rachel A., 1973- author.
Title: Diwali / by Rachel Grack.
Description: Minneapolis, MN : Bellwether Media, Inc., 2017. | Series: Blastoff! Readers: Celebrating Holidays | Includes bibliographical references and index. | Audience: Ages: 5-8. | Audience: Grades: K to Grade 3.
Identifiers: LCCN 2016033347 (print) | LCCN 2016046193 (ebook) | ISBN 9781626175938 (hardcover : alk. paper) | ISBN 9781618912725 (paperback : alk. paper) ISBN 9781681033235 (ebook)
Subjects: LCSH: Divali–Juvenile literature.
Classification: LCC BL1239.82.D58 K64 2016 (print) | LCC BL1239.82.D58 (ebook) | DDC 294.5/36–dc23
LC record available at https://lccn.loc.gov/2016033347

Editor: Kari Schuetz   Designer: Lois Stanfield

Printed in the United States of America, North Mankato, MN.

Table of Contents

Diwali Is Here!

Fireworks explode in the night sky. Children wave **sparklers** in the streets below.

sparklers

Mumbai, India

India is bright with light and color. It is Diwali!

What Is Diwali?

diyas

Diwali is the biggest holiday in India. It is often called the **Festival** of Lights.

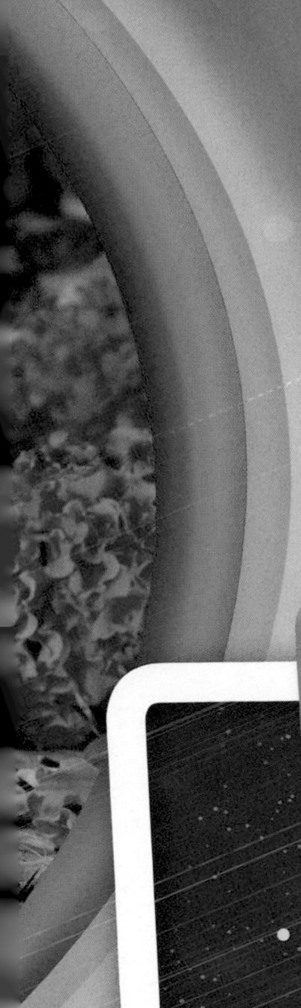

For the celebration, people light rows of clay lamps called *diyas*.

How Do You Say?

Word	Pronunciation
Diwali	dee-WAH-lee
diya	DEE-yah
Lakshmi	LAHK-shmee
puja	POO-jah
rangoli	rahn-GO-lee

Who Celebrates Diwali?

Diwali is a **Hindu** holiday. However, it has spread to other faiths.

Hindu Diwali celebration

Around the world, people celebrate the power of good over evil during Diwali.

Diwali Beginnings

Diwali started as a **harvest** festival in India. Farmers gave thanks for their crops.

They wanted the Hindu **goddess** of wealth, Lakshmi, to bless them.

Today, people also remember other **gods** and goddesses during Diwali.

Ravana

Many tell the story of Rama.
He saved his wife and kingdom
from a **demon** called Ravana.

Time to Celebrate

Diwali lasts for five days in October or November.

The dates change with the Hindu calendar. They depend on the position of the moon.

Taj Mahal
in Agra, India

Diwali Traditions!

People clean their homes for Diwali. They open their windows and doors to welcome Lakshmi.

They light lamps to keep evil away.

People decorate floors and pavement with *rangoli* art. These beautiful designs are often made of colored sand. People also hang flower **garlands** in doorways.

Make a Rangoli Lotus

People often show lotus flowers in their rangoli art. In India, the lotus stands for beauty and life.

What You Need:

- piece of cardstock paper
- pencil or marker
- glue
- colored sand

What You Do:

1. Use the example below to draw a lotus flower on cardstock paper.
2. Trace the lines in glue.
3. Sprinkle colored sand on the glue. Let dry.
4. Tap the picture over a garbage can to get rid of loose sand.

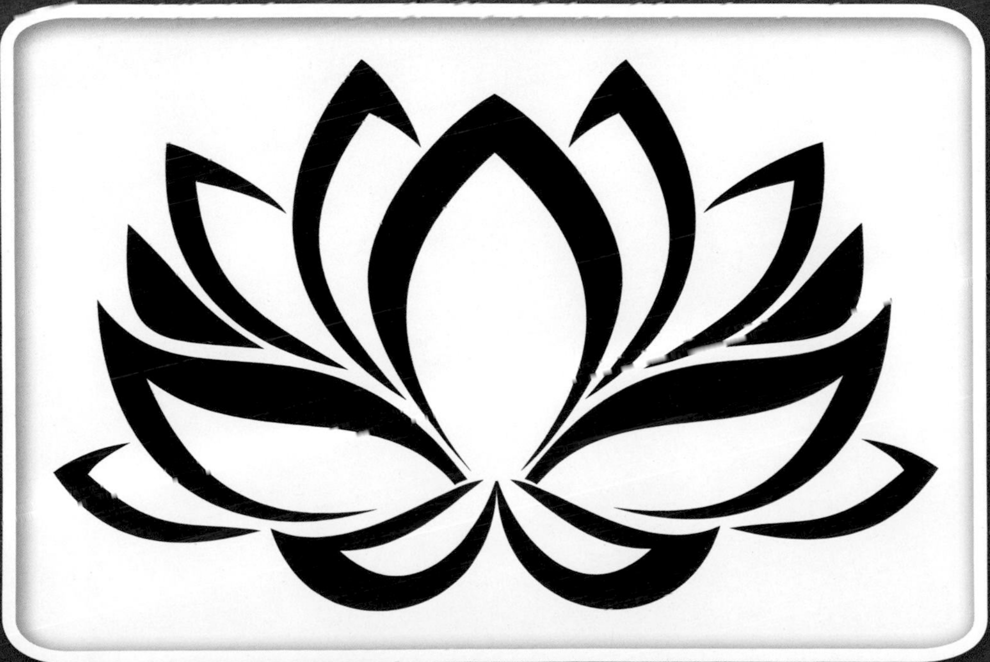

For many people, *puja*, or **worship**, is a **tradition**.

Families also gather to share sweet treats and gifts. Some gatherings have dancing. Diwali is a joyful celebration!

Glossary

demon—an evil spirit

festival—celebration

garlands—long strings of flowers used for decoration

goddess—a female god

gods—holy and supernatural beings

harvest—a time to gather crops

Hindu—related to Hinduism, a religion practiced in India and other parts of the world

sparklers—fireworks that people hold

tradition—a custom, idea, or belief handed down from one generation to the next

worship—to show respect and love for a god

To Learn More

AT THE LIBRARY

Amstutz, Lisa J. *Diwali.* Mankato, Minn.: Capstone Press, 2017.

Murray, Julie. *Diwali.* Edina, Minn.: ABDO Publishing Company, 2014.

Ponto, Joanna, and Michelle Parker-Rock. *Diwali.* New York, N.Y.: Enslow Pub., 2016.

ON THE WEB

Learning more about Diwali is as easy as 1, 2, 3.

1. Go to www.factsurfer.com.
2. Enter "Diwali" into the search box.
3. Click the "Surf" button and you will see a list of related web sites.

With factsurfer.com, finding more information is just a click away.

Index

The images in this book are reproduced through the courtesy of: JOAT, front cover; espies, p. 4; HIRA PUNJABI/ Photoshot/ Newscom, pp. 4-5; Rakshashelare, pp. 6-7; Mohd Samsul Mohd Said/ Getty Images, p. 8; shylendrahoode, p. 9; CRSHELARE, p. 10; Dipak Shelare, p. 11; Luciano Mortula, p. 12; flocu, pp. 12-13; uniquely india/ Getty Images, pp. 14-15; age fotostock/ SuperStock, p. 15; Umar Qayyum/ Zuma Press, p. 16; Hindustan Times/ Newscom, p. 17; PhotosIndia.com LLC/ Alamy, p. 18; Naddya, p. 19; szefei, p. 20; picture alliance/ Marco Becher/ Newscom, pp. 20-21; Karve, p. 22.

HOW TO PLAY LIKE A PRO

SOCCER SKILLS

BY J CHRIS ROSELIUS

Enslow Elementary
an imprint of
Enslow Publishers, Inc.
40 Industrial Road
Box 398
Berkeley Heights, NJ 07922
USA
http://www.enslow.com

Enslow Elementary, an imprint of Enslow Publishers, Inc.

Enslow Elementary® is a registered trademark of Enslow Publishers, Inc.

Library of Congress Cataloging-in-Publication Data
Roselius, J Chris.
Soccer skills : how to play like a pro / J Chris Roselius.
p. cm. — (How to play like a pro)
Summary: "Readers will learn how to control a soccer ball, play offense and defense and defend the goal like their favorite players"—Provided by publisher.
Includes bibliographical references and index.
ISBN-13: 978-0-7660-3206-4
1. Soccer—Juvenile literature. I. Title.
GV943.25.R64 2009
796.334'2—dc22
2007048516

Credits
Editorial Direction: Red Line Editorial, Inc.
Cover & interior design: Becky Daum
Editors: Bob Temple, Dave McMahon
Special thanks to Amy Pettibone, girls' soccer coach at Cinco Ranch High School in Katy, Texas, for her help with this book.

Printed in the United States of America

10 9 8 7 6 5 4 3 2

To Our Readers: We have done our best to make sure all Internet Addresses in this book were active and appropriate when we went to press. However, the author and the publisher have no control over and assume no liability for the material available on those Internet sites or on other Web sites they may link to. Any comments or suggestions can be sent by e-mail to comments@enslow.com or to the address on the back cover.

Enslow Publishers, Inc. is committed to printing our books on recycled paper. The paper in every book contains 10% to 30% post-consumer waste (PCW). The cover board on the outside of each book contains 100% PCW. Our goal is to do our part to help young people and the environment too!

Photo credits: iStockPhoto/Jana Lumley, 1, 27; iStockPhoto/Alberto Pomares, 4; AP Photo/Pier Paolo Cit, 7; iStockPhoto/U Star PIX, 8, 17, 38, 41; AP Photo/Luca Bruno, 9; iStockPhoto/Brandon Laufenberg, 10; AP Photo/Paulo Duarte, 11; AP Photo/Hans Pennink, 12; iStockPhoto/Alex Nikada, 13; AP Photo/Denis Poroy, 14; AP Photo/Ivan Sekretarev, 15; iStockPhoto/fabphoto, 18; AP Photo/Steven Governo, 19; iStockPhoto/Michael Flippo, 20; AP Photo/Greg Baker, 21; AP Photo/Bernat Armangue, 22; iStockPhoto/Jim Kolaczko, 23, 29, 30; AP Photo/Khue Bui, 25; AP Photo/Ahn Young-joon, 26; AP Photo/Nam Y. Huh, 28; AP Photo/Stephan Savoia, 31; iStockPhoto/Eric Hood, 32; AP Photo/Michael Sohn, 33; AP Photo, 34; AP Photo/Fernando Bustamante, 35; AP Photo/Greg Wahl-Stephens, 37; AP Photo/Paul Connors, 39; AP Photo/Martin Meissner, 40; AP Photo/Julie Jacobson, 42; AP photo/Sara D. Davis, 43; iStockPhoto/Jani Bryson, 44; AP Photo/Paul White, 45.

Cover Photo: iStockPhoto/Jana Lumley (large); AP Photo/Ahn Young-joon, 26 (small).

CONTENTS

SOCCER PREGAME

The sport of soccer requires a variety of athletic skills. Players need to be coordinated and able to endure long stretches of running without a break. They need to have leg strength in order to kick the ball far. Soccer players must have the proper touch on the ball in order to make accurate shots and long, booming passes.

The sport's creativity also makes it appealing to the millions of players who take to the field every year. Players can dribble the ball by themselves, look for a teammate on the receiving end of a pass, or kick a long cross to try to create a scoring opportunity. The different ways to create and defend plays are endless, which makes soccer such an exciting sport. Whether you're a beginning or advanced player, it's always a good time to learn more skills.

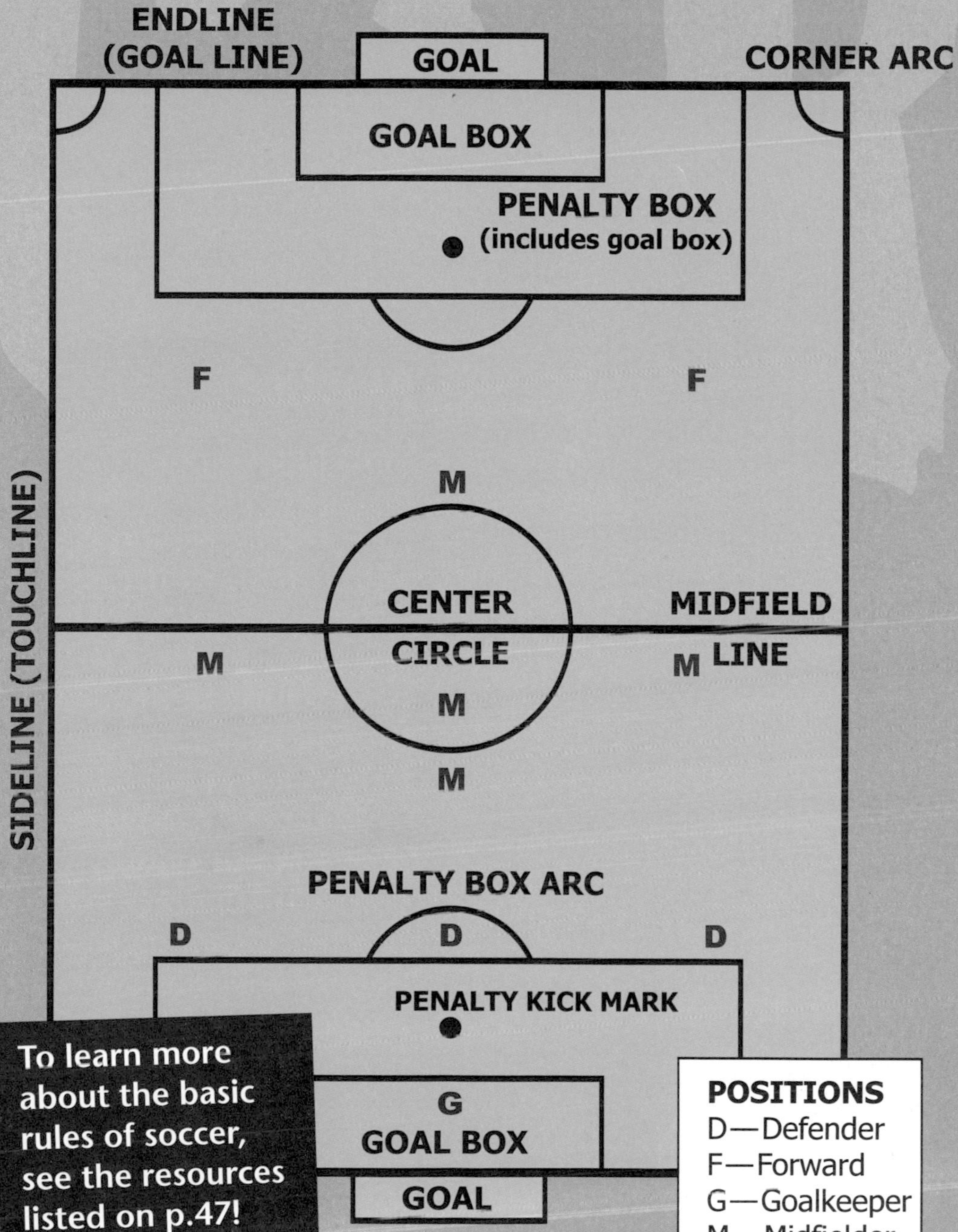

To learn more about the basic rules of soccer, see the resources listed on p.47!

POSITIONS
D—Defender
F—Forward
G—Goalkeeper
M—Midfielder

BALL CONTROL

In the sport of soccer, a successful team must be able to defend and score to win. Just as important, however, is the ability to control the ball. Often, the team that possesses the ball the most in a game wins.

A player who has good ball control can watch the field and not the ball. Learning ball control is one of the first skills a player should learn.

Juggling is one of the best ways to get a feel for the ball and learn how to control it. The goal of juggling is to keep the ball off the ground by using any part of the body other than the hands and arms.

Practice

Start juggling by dropping the ball on the ground, kicking it with the top of the foot (where the laces of the shoe are), letting the ball bounce on the ground again, and then kicking it again.

From there, a player may attempt kicking it two or three times in a row before letting it bounce and then continue to progress from there.

Good ball handlers are masters in a variety of skills. They must be able to dribble well and make on-target passes to teammates. Players also must be able to receive a pass and head the ball.

Key Ball Control Skills

- Develop a feel for the ball
- Learn to juggle
- Use all parts of the body
- Use all areas of the foot
- Be able to control a bouncing ball

The Brazilian striker Ronaldo is considered one of the best ball handlers in the world. He is a talented dribbler but also has good passing and receiving skills.

A striker is a forward who plays closest to the opposing team's goal.

DRIBBLING

It is important to be able to run, or dribble, with the ball at your feet. The best way to keep the ball away from an opponent is to control the soccer ball, even while being closely defended.

Good dribbling skills allow a player to advance the ball past defenders, set up good passes to teammates, and create open shots on goal.

The goal of a good dribbler should be to stay close to the ball when defenders are nearby. If a dribbler has space, he or she should kick the ball forward at the same speed he or she is running.

The best way players can learn to dribble is to simply run up and down a field with the ball at their feet. A good soccer player can control the ball with both feet.

Practice: Finger Game

This teaches players to dribble the ball while looking up. While players dribble the ball around the field, someone stands in the middle and puts a hand in the air with either one, two, or three fingers showing. The players dribbling call out the number of fingers being flashed.

Forwards and midfielders usually possess the best dribbling skills because they often touch the ball the most. All players need to practice the skill.

A good dribbler is able to look up while dribbling in order to see where teammates and opponents are on the field.

The arms help provide balance while dribbling. They can also be used to fend off a defender.

The upper body can be used as a way to fake out a defender while dribbling. A subtle move made with the shoulders or torso can force the defender to one side to create space.

Juninho, a top Brazilian midfielder, is considered one of the top playmakers in soccer due to his fantastic dribbling skills.

Balance is important when controlling a ball. Both feet should be under the body. Often, the balancing foot can be used to protect the ball from opposing defenders.

RECEIVING

Receiving is the ability to quickly stop and control a ball that has been passed in the air or on the ground. This is a very important skill to learn. The faster a player controls the ball, the more time he or she has to decide what to do with the ball.

When a ball comes to a player on the ground, the foot should be used to stop, or trap, the ball. The easiest way to do this is to "step" on the ball with the bottom of the foot. Toes should be pointed up.

Practice

Stand five yards away from a wall. Kick a ball against the wall. When it bounces back, try to receive the ball with the foot and control it. Bend the knee of the leg that will receive the ball and "catch" it with the side of the foot.

When chesting a ball, the shoulders should be squared up to the ball to have it fall straight down.
The upper body should lean back slightly while the shoulders are thrown forward.

Go For Gold

Abby Wambach (20, above) is an Olympic gold medalist and plays for the United States women's national team. She has become one of the top women's soccer players in the world.

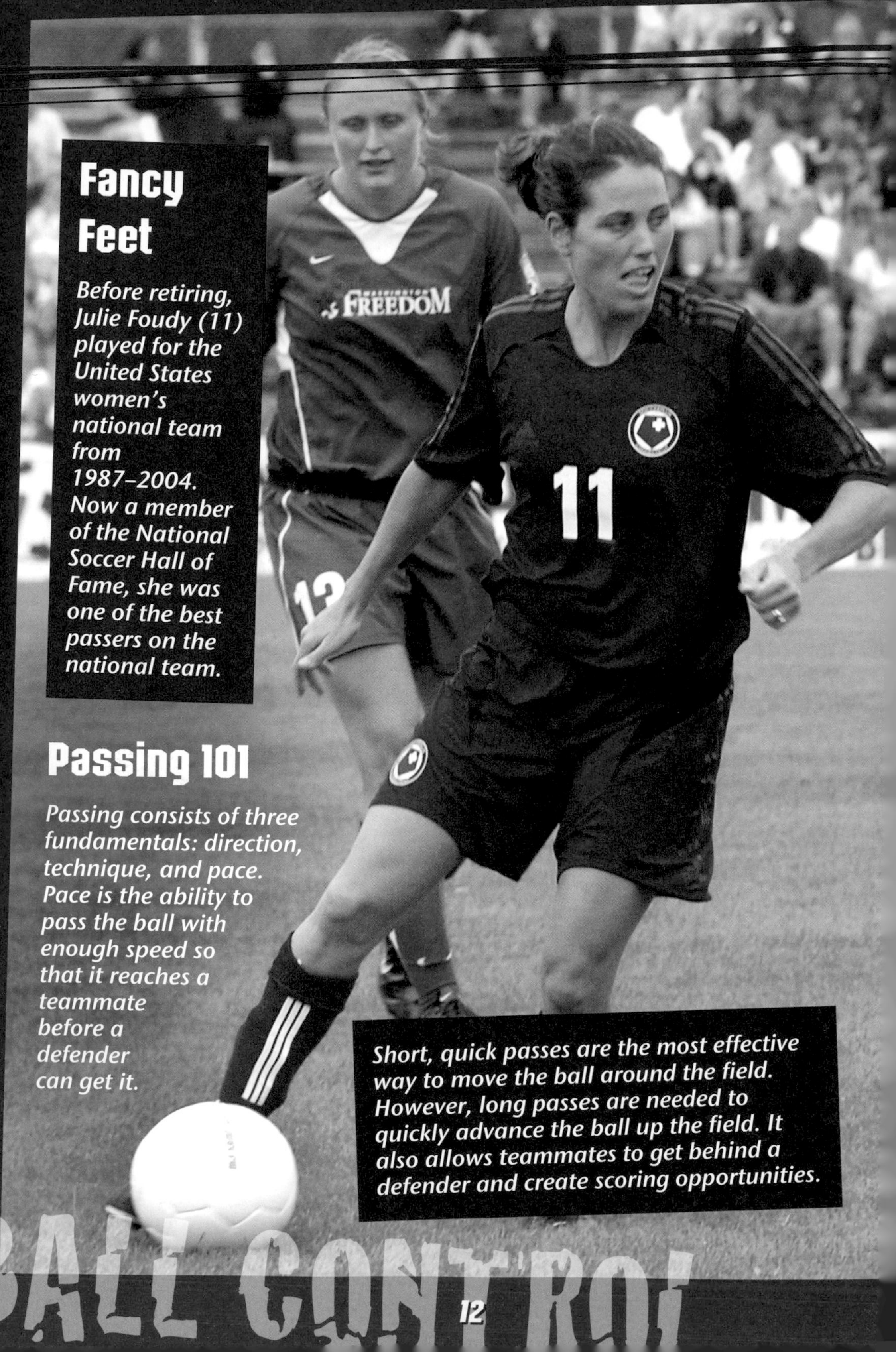

Fancy Feet

Before retiring, Julie Foudy (11) played for the United States women's national team from 1987–2004. Now a member of the National Soccer Hall of Fame, she was one of the best passers on the national team.

Passing 101

Passing consists of three fundamentals: direction, technique, and pace. Pace is the ability to pass the ball with enough speed so that it reaches a teammate before a defender can get it.

Short, quick passes are the most effective way to move the ball around the field. However, long passes are needed to quickly advance the ball up the field. It also allows teammates to get behind a defender and create scoring opportunities.

PASSING

Over the years, passing has become a key fundamental in soccer. One of the best men's teams in the world is Argentina, largely because of its ability to pass the ball around the field. This helps maintain possession and create scoring opportunities.

Passing can be done with the head or chest, but using the foot is the best method. A long pass up or across the field is usually done with the top of the foot. The inside and outside parts of the foot are used for shorter, softer passes. Always try to pass to a teammate's foot.

Midfielders

Midfielders are often the best passers on the team because they usually have the ball the most. They are expected to start the offense by passing to the forwards. They also play a role on defense by passing a ball back to a defender.

HEADING

The foot is the part of the body most used in soccer. The head, though, is also important to use when controlling the ball. The head can be used to pass the ball, receive a ball, or shoot the ball on goal.

While any part of the head can be used to strike the ball, most players try to use the forehead. A player can suffer a head injury using the side or back of the head if not using the proper technique. When heading a ball, always try to keep the neck as stiff as possible.

Heading can be broken down into four main categories. The defensive header is used to clear the ball from opposing players. The attacking header is used to score. The glancing header is often used to pass the ball but also as a way to score. The backheader is used to keep the ball going in its original direction.

Safety First

Never practice heading the ball without the help of a coach or other adult. Head injuries can occur if players head the ball incorrectly.

Use the Body

Most of the power of a well-struck header comes from the body. Snap the upper part of the body at the waist for power.

Make sure the neck remains stiff to prevent the head from snapping backward.
The forehead should be used whenever possible.
The arms should start out wide to maintain balance and then be brought in to help get higher into the air.

Air McBride

Brian McBride (20) has played in three World Cups for the United States. He currently plays with Fulham in the English Premier League. He is regarded as one of the best at playing balls in the air.

DEFENSE

Most of the attention in soccer goes to the person who scores the goals. However, a defender's role is crucial to a team's success. A team with poor defenders is a team that will struggle to win.

Defenders, sometimes called fullbacks, need to be fast in order to keep up with forwards and midfielders. They also need to be strong to keep opponents from taking the ball away from them. Balance and coordination by a defender will help with footwork. Quick feet will allow a defender to steal the ball from an opponent.

Defending a player who does not have the ball requires speed and stamina. Run with the offensive player so that he or she does not get open for a pass. Never let an offensive player get open for a good shot on goal.

Defenders also need to have good communication skills in order to know where to be on the field and who to defend. Another important skill is the ability to tackle, or take the ball away from an opponent.

Defenders have to be able to watch several things at one time. They have to know where the ball is and watch any opponents running near them.

Anticipation

One of the more important skills for a defender to have is the ability to anticipate what will happen on the field. Defenders can't simply react to what is already happening. Instead, a defender must have a good understanding of what will happen in order to gain better positioning on the field.

An important tool for the defense is to use the offside trap, which leaves an opposing player without the ball behind the defense. The ball is then given to the defending team.

JOCKEYING

A defender doesn't always have to knock the ball away from an opponent. A good defender can simply force an opponent to dribble to the sideline or toward more defenders, creating less room for the attacker to pass or dribble.

The ability to force players to go in a direction they don't want to go is called jockeying. It is a simple skill, but an important one, since jockeying slows the progress of the offensive player.

Apply pressure by staying within an arm's length of your opponent.

Containing an Opponent

Position a series of cones to create two parallel lines about fifteen yards apart. Player A should dribble the ball toward Player B. Player B should try to force Player A to dribble toward one line of cones.

DEFENSE

Make It Tough

Top defenders force offensive players to become uncomfortable while receiving a pass.

It is important to quickly get to an offensive player who has the ball. The less time an attacker has the ball, the harder it is to pass.

In most situations, a defender should try to guard a player at an angle and stay on the balls of the feet. If a defender squares up and stands flat-footed, it is easier for the offensive player to get around the defender.

TACKLING

Jockeying an opposing player is always the first option when playing defense. Sometimes, however, a defender needs to tackle, or knock the ball away from an attacker.

Attempt a tackle only when you are certain that it will knock the ball away from an opponent. A poor tackle will give the advantage to the offense and put pressure on the rest of the defenders.

Practice: Block Tackling

Player A dribbles toward Player B. As Player A approaches, Player B stands in front of Player A, plants his or her leg and attempts to take the ball away from Player A using the inside of the foot.

Top Notch Tackler

Pablo Mastroeni (below, left) is a longtime member of the United States national team and plays for the Colorado Rapids of Major League Soccer. He has played in two World Cups for the United States.

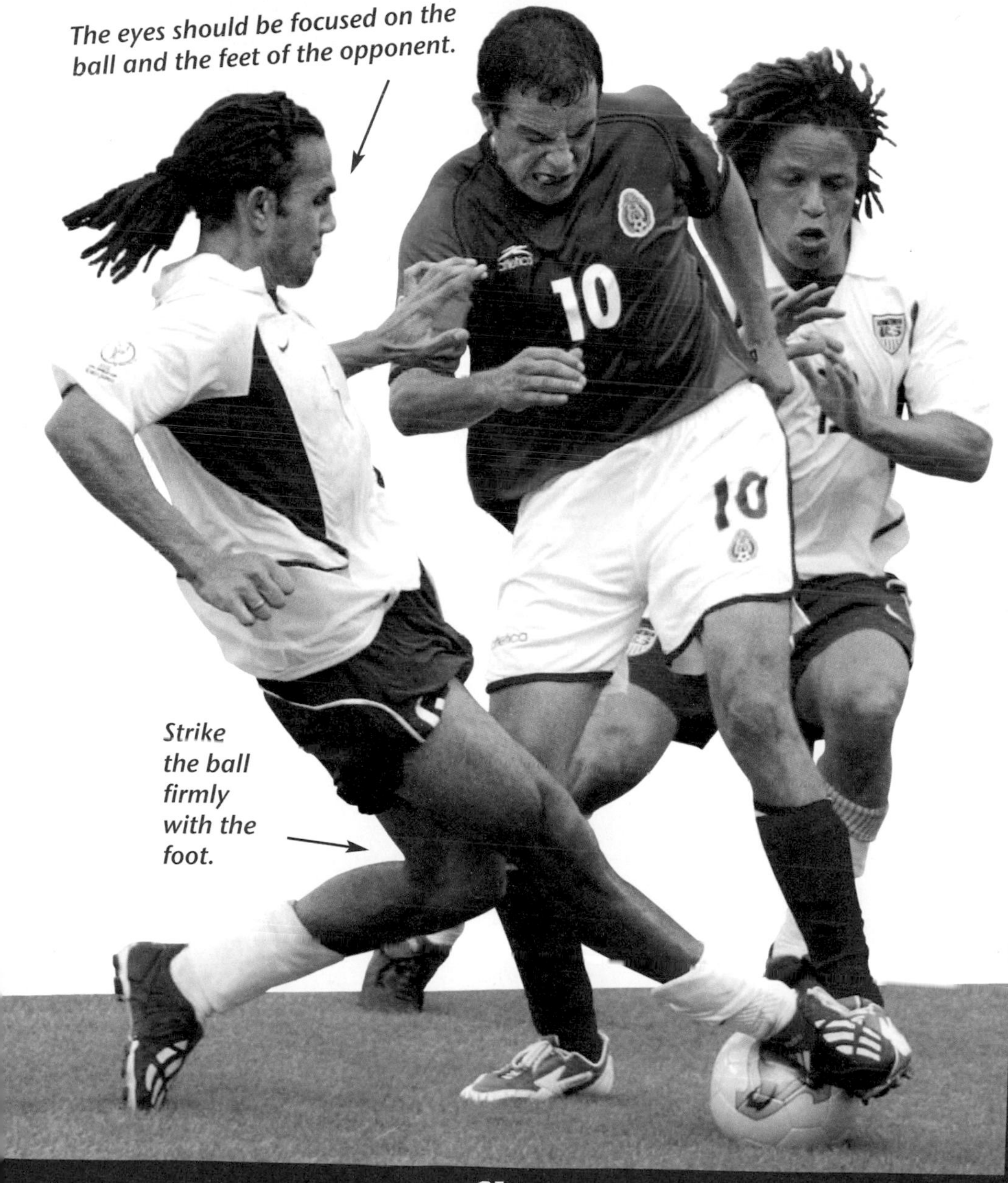

The eyes should be focused on the ball and the feet of the opponent.
Strike the ball firmly with the foot.

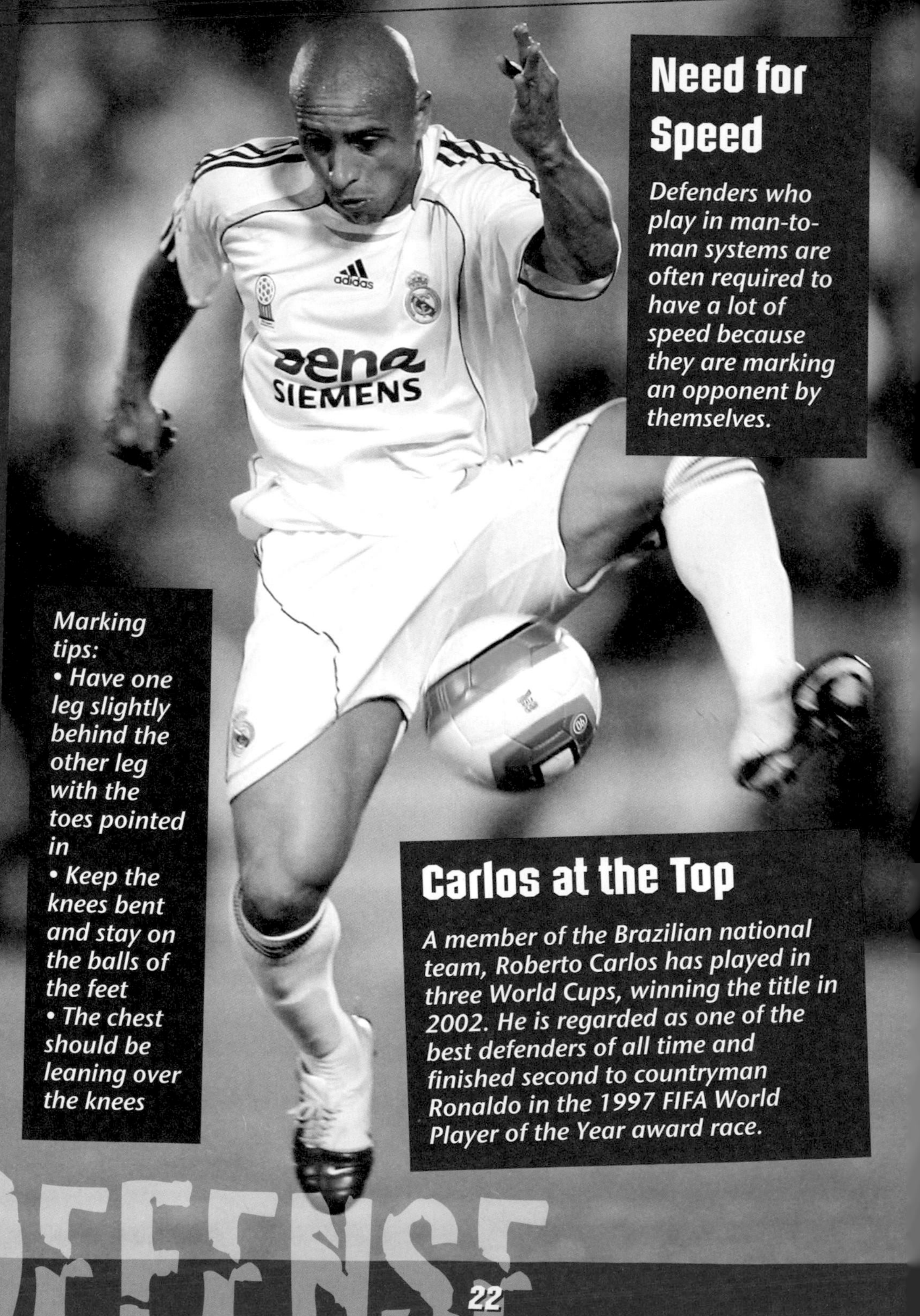

Need for Speed

Defenders who play in man-to-man systems are often required to have a lot of speed because they are marking an opponent by themselves.

Marking tips:

- *Have one leg slightly behind the other leg with the toes pointed in*
- *Keep the knees bent and stay on the balls of the feet*
- *The chest should be leaning over the knees*

Carlos at the Top

A member of the Brazilian national team, Roberto Carlos has played in three World Cups, winning the title in 2002. He is regarded as one of the best defenders of all time and finished second to countryman Ronaldo in the 1997 FIFA World Player of the Year award race.

DEFENSE

STYLES OF DEFENSE

When playing soccer, a zone or a man-to-man defense can be played.

A zone defense is based on defenders moving together, as if they are tied together by an invisible rope. A defender is responsible for guarding a specific area of the field. This style is an energy-efficient way to defend the ball for a player.

A man-to-man defense places more individual pressure on the defender. Each defender is assigned a specific opponent to mark, or guard. A coach may prefer this style because it allows defenders to match up with opponents of similar skill and size.

Both defenses require players to be able to guard players whether they have the ball or not.

Man-to-man Drills

In an area 20 yards by 20 yards, two teams of four players each attempt to kick the ball between two cones. The defenders try to cover the opposing player one-on-one. This is a great way to improve conditioning and skill.

OFFENSE

Once a team gains control of the ball, it is on offense, where the goal is to get the ball into the opposing team's net. While everyone gets involved on offense, the main offensive players are the forwards and the midfielders.

Midfielders, who line up in the middle of the field between the defenders and the forwards, are true transition players on the field. Not only do they help the defense, but midfielders are often responsible for starting any offensive attack. The ball is usually passed to a forward from a midfielder.

Forwards, or strikers, are usually the top scorers. They line up closest to the opposing goalkeeper.

The Need for Teamwork

Any time a player scores, he or she should be happy. However, it takes teamwork to score a goal.

Rarely does a player dribble down the field and score. Instead, it is passing that leads to scoring. So remember, good teamwork is the key to scoring.

An easy way to improve accuracy is by putting four targets on a wall or on the goal posts. Practice shooting at each target from five yards away and increase the distance in five-yard increments.

Speeding Down the Field

Many teams will have their fastest players at forward and in the midfield. This puts pressure on opposing teams, who may not have players fast enough to mark the faster forwards and midfielders.

Before retiring, Mia Hamm of the United States was one of the best players in the world.

As a member of the U.S. national team, she scored more international goals in her career—158—than any other player, male or female.

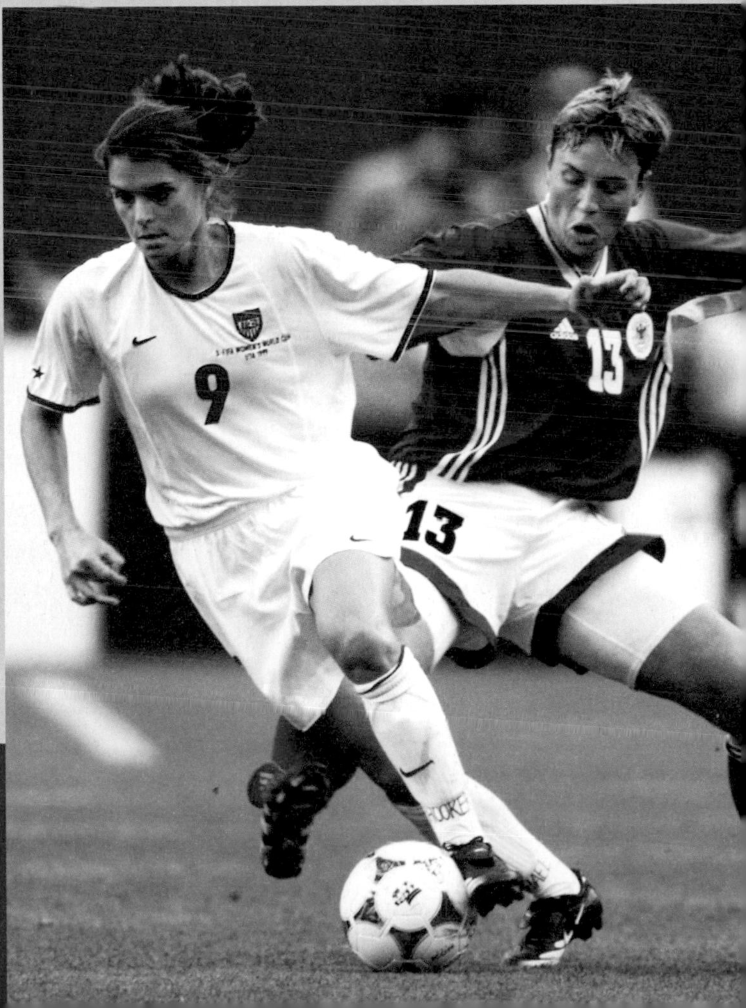

SHOOTING & STRIKING

A player can use the top of the foot as well as the inside or outside of the foot to kick, or strike, the ball.

No matter how one strikes the ball, however, the most important fundamental to remember is to keep the head down and over the ball. If the head does not stay down, the foot could miss the ball, or the ball could miss its target.

Keeping the head down and the body over the ball will keep the ball low and in the proper direction. If a striker leans back when shooting, the ball will often sail over the crossbar. Make sure to get the shot on target. Even if a goalkeeper stops the shot, there could be a rebound and another scoring chance.

Cristiano Ronaldo of Portugal (left) is one of the world's top scorers.

Practice

A striker may not have time to control a pass in the penalty box and then shoot. Sometimes a striker needs to one-time a ball, or kick a rolling ball while on the run. Have a teammate pass the ball, and without controlling the pass, strike it toward the goal.

Shooting with the top of the foot can create a powerful shot. However, a striker can also use the inside of the foot to shoot with effectiveness. The sidefoot shot requires more power than a pass.

The head should be looking down and over the ball.
The knee of the kicking leg should be above or a little in front of the ball the moment before making contact.
The non-kicking foot should be even with the ball and about six inches to the side with the foot pointing toward the goal.

Power or Accuracy?

When taking a shot, a player can shoot with power or accuracy. A shot with power is harder for a goalkeeper to defend but it isn't always accurate.

An accurate shot is usually more on target, but it has less power, which may make it easier for a goalie to stop. A striker has to determine if he or she needs to shoot with power or accuracy.

The Free Kick

David Beckham of the Los Angeles Galaxy and the English national team is considered the best free-kick specialist in the world. He can kick to the spot he is aiming for from 30 or 40 yards away.

The Penalty Kick

When taking a penalty kick, confidence is just as important as the ability to kick the ball. Also, accuracy is more important than power.

The Direct Kick

When taking a direct kick, the skills are similar to a corner kick. But, a player should try to raise the foot up when striking the ball to give it some top spin. This helps make the ball dip after rising up and over a wall of defenders.

CORNERS & DIRECT KICKS

While most goals come during the flow of play, many are scored on corner kicks or direct kicks, after a foul. These are called set plays because a team can set up players and try to run a certain play when the ball is kicked.

Corner kicks and direct kicks can be extremely effective if a team has players skilled in delivering the ball to a certain spot on the field from a distance. The main skill a good free-kick specialist has is the ability to curve the ball around or over defenders.

Teams can also run set plays off goal kicks. Even though goal kicks are taken from a team's own goal box, the powerful leg of a defender or keeper can help set up a play.

Aim for the Top

A shot into the top corner of the net is the toughest shot for a keeper to stop. Tie a target to the crossbar so it hangs just below the crossbar in the corner of each net. From a distance of 25 yards, curve a ball toward the targets.

GAINING POSITION

Soccer players are always on the move. On offense, players who do not have the ball move to open space to try to get a pass. The more the offensive team moves, the more scoring chances they will have. Players need to work together in order to make all of this movement work.

To get a short pass, you should move toward a space on the field where there are no defenders. This is called "running into space." It is also important to make sure the passer has a clear path to make the pass to you.

For longer passes toward the goal, you can "make a run." This means you will sprint up the field, trying to get behind the defense and receive a long pass. Be careful not to get behind the last defender until the ball is passed, however. If you do, the referee will call offsides, and the other team will get a free kick.

Practice

A simple game of "keep away" using three players helps with moving to open space. Two offensive players try to pass the ball back and forth without letting the one defender touch it.

Fleet-Footed

DeMarcus Beasley (left) plays for the United States national team and Rangers of the Scottish Premier League. Beasley, who has played in two World Cups, is good at making runs against opposing defenders to create scoring chances for himself and for his teammates.

Communication

Knowing what a teammate wants to do on offense is vital, but how can you communicate without a defender learning what the plan is? Eye contact is a great way to communicate.

Timing Counts

Speed and timing are useful to gain an advantage against a defender.

THROW-INS

When a ball goes out of bounds on the side of the field, a player must make a throw-in. This restarts the action. A good throw-in can also help a team score, or get the ball out of its defensive end of the field.

Throw-ins must be done in a special way. Both of the thrower's feet must be touching the ground when the ball is thrown. Also, one hand must be on each side of the ball. The ball must be thrown directly over the thrower's head, too. If any of these things are done wrong, the referee will give the ball to the other team.

To make your throw-ins fly farther, work on your upper-body strength.

Practice

Player A throws the ball to Player B standing 10 yards away. Player B then quickly passes back to Player A, who can then dribble the ball or pass.

This drill allows players to practice a variety of skills: the throw-in, receiving, and passing.

The hands should be in a "W" shape, with the thumbs touching and the fingers on the side of the ball.

The ball must be thrown over the head.

Bend the body slightly back and then straighten up, moving the shoulders and arms forward.

Both feet must be on the ground during a throw-in.

Top Thrower

John Terry of England is the captain of both the English national team and Chelsea of the English Premier League. A top-notch defender, he is also excellent at making long throw-ins.

Anyone Can Do It

Any player can throw the ball in. That is why it is important for all players to practice. Remember, the player making a throw-in can't touch the ball again until it is touched by another player.

Down the Line

If a team making a throw-in is deep in its own defensive territory, a safe way to get the ball out of danger is to throw the ball down the line.

Throw the ball as close to the sideline as possible away from the goal. Even if the team making the throw-in doesn't gain possession, the ball will be further away from the goal.

TRICKS

One of the best things about soccer is the creativity some players have with the ball. Acrobatic plays like jumps and flips make the crowd roar. Some of the best players even invent new moves.

One of the most spectacular plays a player can make is a bicycle kick. To achieve this trick, a player's back is facing the goal. While the ball is in the air, the player jumps up and kicks the ball over his body toward the goal.

Practice

The bicycle kick requires a player to land on his or her back. Make sure to practice this kick on a soft surface such as a mat or mattress, and make sure to have adult supervision. Brazilian legend Péle (below) made the bicycle kick his signature move.

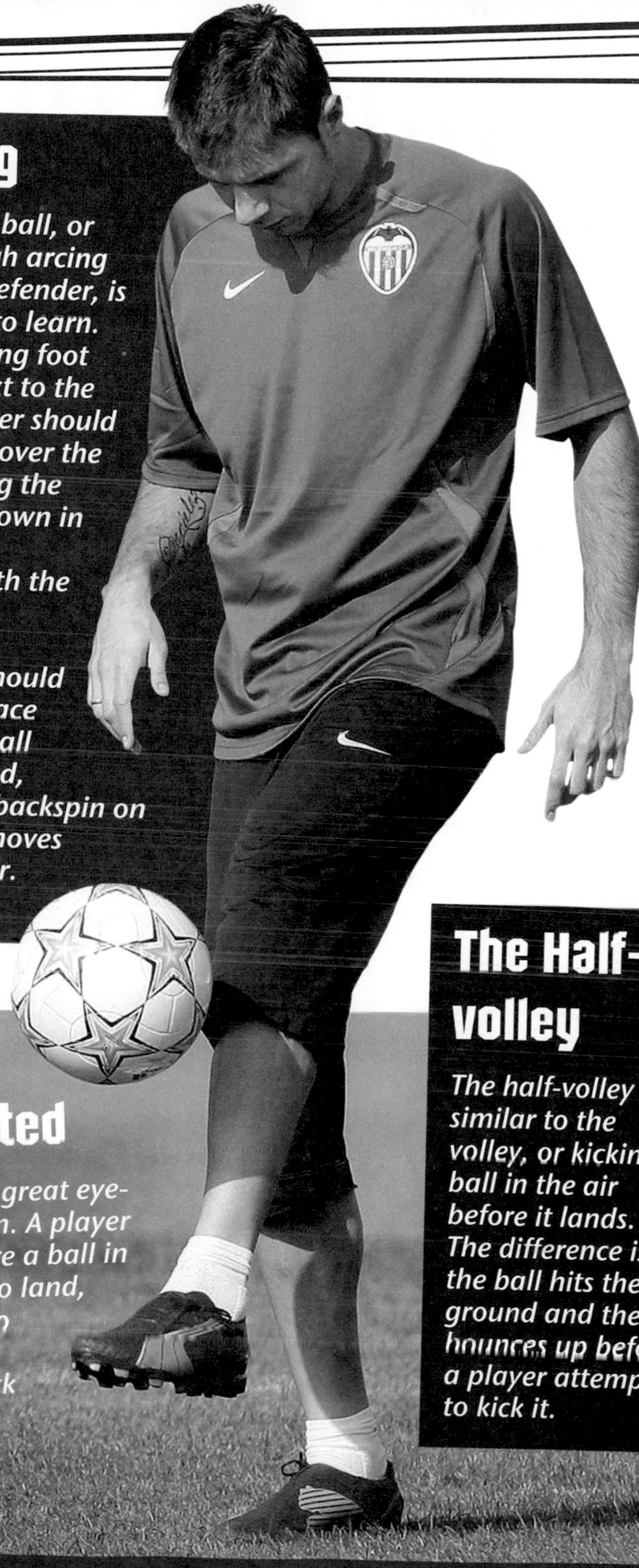

Chipping

Chipping the ball, or sending a high arcing pass over a defender, is a tough skill to learn. The non-kicking foot should be next to the ball. The player should almost stand over the ball and swing the kicking foot down in a short, sharp movement with the toes pointing down.

The foot should land in the space between the ball and the ground, putting some backspin on the ball as it moves through the air.

The Half-volley

The half-volley is similar to the volley, or kicking a ball in the air before it lands. The difference is the ball hits the ground and then bounces up before a player attempts to kick it.

Get It Started

A volley requires great eye-foot coordination. A player must judge where a ball in the air is going to land, and then get into position to kick. A volley is a quick way to start an offensive attack.

GOALKEEPING

A goalkeeper is always in the spotlight. It is the goalkeeper's job to keep the ball out of his or her team's goal. Everyone knows when a keeper doesn't perform well. A lot of pressure is placed on the person who plays that position.

Because the position is so demanding, it requires a different set of skills from the rest of the players on the field.

One of the top skills is the ability to communicate quickly and clearly. The goalie is in charge of lining up the defenders and letting them know where offensive players are.

Practice: Clearing a Backpass

Sometimes a keeper is not allowed to use the hands. This occurs when a teammate passes the ball back with his foot. A keeper must be able to clear the backpass away from the goal by kicking it, sometimes without stopping the ball first. During practice, Player A should kick a ball to a keeper, who then must kick the ball up the field.

Goalkeepers try to avoid diving for a ball unless absolutely necessary. Instead, they use footwork to get into position.

Know How to Fall

If a goalie has to dive to make a save, it is important to fall correctly. The whole body should fall as a unit. The body should follow the ball to the ground to help keep the ball from popping out of the grasp of the keeper. Use the ball as a way to break the fall if possible.

Goalkeeper Briana Scurry (below) helped the U.S. women's national team win the gold medal at the 1996 and 2004 Olympics, and the 1996 World Cup.

Standing Out in a Crowd

A goalie is easy to spot. He or she wears a different color shirt from the rest of the team. The shirts are often slightly padded for extra protection. Goalies also wear special padded gloves.

COMMUNICATION

Communication is important for all players, but especially for goalkeepers. The keeper is the only player always facing the whole field. He or she must act as a traffic cop and direct the defense. To do this, the keeper uses hand signals and voice commands.

The commands shouted out by a keeper must be clear and brief. Directions must also be shouted out quickly in order for defenders to avoid any confusion. Since communication is so important, a goalie must know when to talk and when not to. Hand signals are often used to position players on direct kicks.

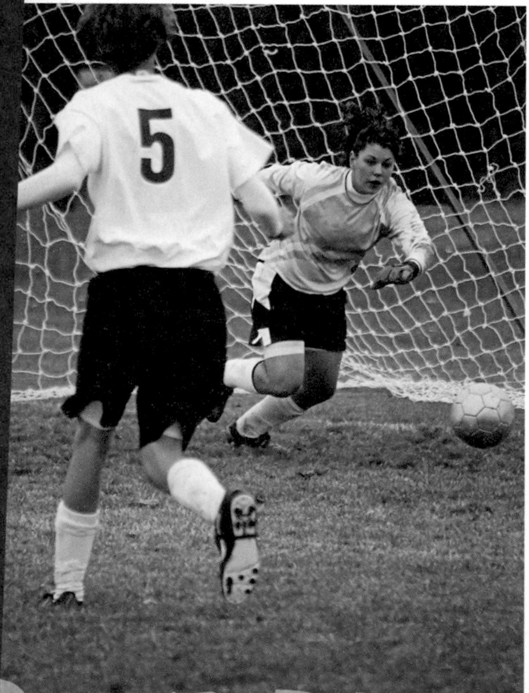

Practice

Get four players and a keeper in the goal box. Two players should be on offense, two on defense. A coach or another teammate should throw a ball into the air near the goal.

As players battle for position, the keeper yells "keeper" if he or she can get it, and "away" if not.

Keys to Remember

Communication skills a keeper should remember:

1) Be loud and repetitive
2) Be quick with commands
3) Be decisive
4) Get feedback from defenders so you know you are heard

A goalie should always project confidence when on the field. If a goalie is positive, the defenders will often remain positive.

Be Loud!

Tim Howard (above) is a keeper for the United States national team and plays for Everton of the English Premier League. Howard uses hand signals and verbal commands to communicate with his defenders during games.

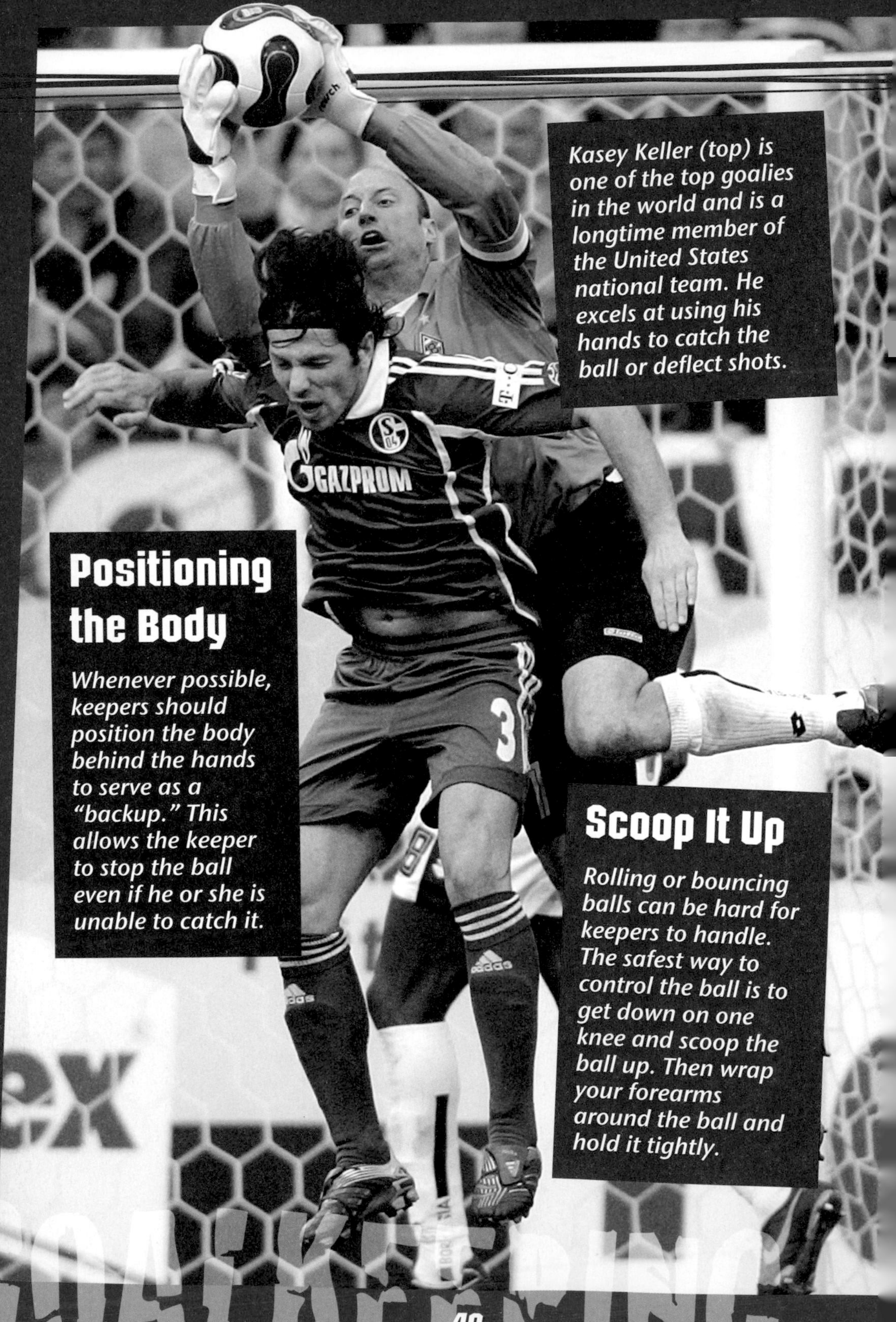

Kasey Keller (top) is one of the top goalies in the world and is a longtime member of the United States national team. He excels at using his hands to catch the ball or deflect shots.

Positioning the Body

Whenever possible, keepers should position the body behind the hands to serve as a "backup." This allows the keeper to stop the ball even if he or she is unable to catch it.

Scoop It Up

Rolling or bouncing balls can be hard for keepers to handle. The safest way to control the ball is to get down on one knee and scoop the ball up. Then wrap your forearms around the ball and hold it tightly.

HANDLING THE BALL

The ability to use the hands gives keepers an advantage over other players. So, the most important skill for goalkeepers to learn is how to catch the ball. This is a skill that should be practiced all the time.

Keepers can only use their hands inside of the penalty area. Keepers should always try to use their hands to save a shot. When catching a ball shot at chest level or higher, goalies use the "W" method to control the ball. The hands are behind the ball, close enough so that the thumbs can touch to form a "W" with the two index fingers.

If the shot is below chest level, the "W" gets turned upside down. The keeper should touch the pinkies together to catch the ball. The thumbs will then wrap around the sides of the ball. Whenever a keeper catches a ball, he or she should immediately pull it to the chest and wrap the arms around it.

Practice

From about ten yards away, Player A kicks the ball at the goalie. The keeper should catch each ball with the hands. Gradually, Player A should kick the ball harder and in different directions. This will force the keeper to move while still using the hands to catch the ball.

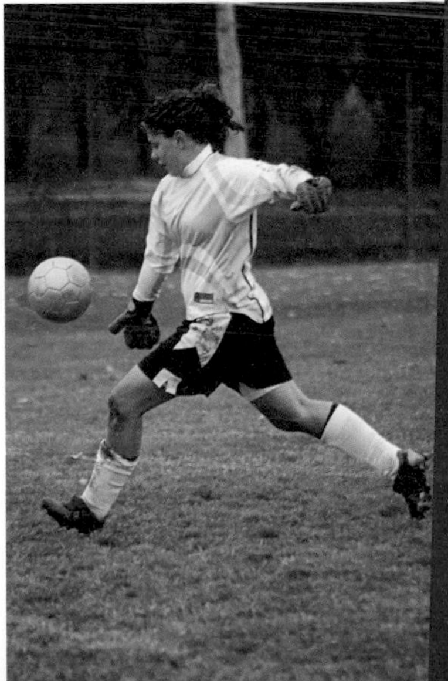

DEFENDING A SHOT

During a game, a goalie may be in a one-on-one situation against an opposing forward with the ball. The keeper should come off the goal line and move toward the striker. By moving toward the attacker, you create less goal space to aim for. But don't go too far away from the net. The attacker may be able to dribble around the goalie for an easy shot.

Practice

The keeper should stand with his or her back turned to Player A, who is standing 10 yards away. Player A kicks the ball, yelling "turn" during the kick. The keeper then turns to stop the ball.

Read & React

When defending a penalty kick, a goalie should try to read where the shooter will kick the ball. Look at his or her plant foot and torso just before the ball is kicked. They usually point where the shooter is aiming.

Always be aggressive when making a save.

Do not hesitate when going for the ball in the penalty box. It could be the difference between making a save or allowing a goal

Reflexes

Goalies do their best to get in the right position to make a save. Sometimes, though, they have to rely on their reflexes to stop a shot.

DEFENDING CROSSES

Long, high passes from the side of the field toward the goal are called crossing passes. Crossing passes become a larger part of the game as players become more skilled. Whether the pass is coming from a corner kick, free kick, or during the flow of play, a keeper must be aggressive.

On crosses near the goal, most goalies stand two to three yards away from the goal line. This makes the pass easier to catch or knock down.

Practice

With the goalie standing three yards off the goal line, Player A should lob crosses toward the goal. The keeper should race out and catch the ball at its highest point and secure the ball against the body.

Punching the Ball

It is not always possible to catch a cross. Sometimes, a keeper will punch the ball away from the goal instead.

The keeper should reach as high as possible in order to catch the ball at its highest point.

The keeper should always watch the flight of the ball and not the opposing players in the area.

Jumping with Both Legs

A keeper should be able to jump well off each leg. The ball will not always come into the goal area from the same direction.

Iker Casillas (left) is a top keeper in Europe who plays for the Spanish national team and for Real Madrid. Casillas is a quick goalie who defends crosses well with his ability to jump high and secure the ball.

GLOSSARY

★***cross***—A pass from one side of the field to either the center or the other side of the field.

★***defenders***—Players who play in front of the goal.

★***direct kick***—A free kick awarded when a player touches the ball with his or her hand or commits a foul against another player.

★***dribble***—Moving with the ball, either up the field or past defenders.

★***forward***—Players who play in the zone closest to the opposing goal. They are often responsible for most of the scoring.

★***foul***—Violation of the rules that leads to a free kick.

★***goal***—The moment when the ball crosses over the line between the goal posts. A goal is worth one point.

★***goalkeeper (keeper)***—The player who defends the goal and tries to keep the opposing team from scoring.

★***goal line***—The line running along the width of the field at each end.

★***marking***—Guarding an opponent.

★***midfielders***—The players who play between the forwards and defenders.

★***offside***—An infraction in which an offensive player is between the last defensive player and the goalkeeper before the ball is kicked to the offensive player.

★***passing***—Moving the ball from one player to another player on the same team.

★***penalty area***—The area in front of the goal where the goalkeeper is allowed to use his or her hands. The area measures 18 yards by 44 yards.

LEARN MORE

INTERNET ADDRESSES

★ ***Kids First Soccer***
http://www.kidsfirstsoccer.com

★ ***FUNdamental Soccer***
http://www.fundamentalsoccer.com

★ ***Soccer Training Info***
http://www.soccer-training-info.com

★ ***US Youth Soccer***
http://www.usyouthsoccer.org

BOOKS & VIDEOS

★ ***Soccer Fundamentals: A Better Way to Learn the Basics,*** by Danny Mielke. Champaign, IL: Human Kinetics, 2003.

★ ***Soccer for Dummies,*** by the United States Soccer Federation, Inc., Michael Lewis and Alexi Lalas. Hoboken, NJ: John Wiley & Sons, Inc. 2000.

★ ***The Complete Book of Soccer,*** by Chris Hunt. Richmond Hill, ON: Firefly Books, 2008.

★ ***The Fundamentals of Soccer with Stinky Shoe and Coach LaRoo [Video].*** 2002.

★ ***Little Leaguers: Learn to Play Soccer [DVD].*** Tulsa, OK: VCI Video, 2003.

INDEX

Business Plans Handbook

Business Plans Handbook

A COMPILATION OF ACTUAL BUSINESS PLANS DEVELOPED BY BUSINESSES THROUGHOUT NORTH AMERICA

VOLUME

13

Lynn M. Pearce,
Project Editor

THOMSON
GALE

Detroit • New York • San Francisco • New Haven, Conn. • Waterville, Maine • London

THOMSON
GALE

Business Plans Handbook, 13th Volume

Lynn M. Pearce

Project Editor
Lynn M. Pearce

Product Design
Jennifer Wahi

Composition and Electronic Capture
Evi Seoud

Manufacturing
Rita Wimberley

For more information, contact
The Gale Group, Inc.
27500 Drake Rd.
Farmington Hills, MI 48331-3535
Or you can visit our Internet site at
http://www.gale.com

LIBRARY OF CONGRESS CATALOGING-IN-PUBLICATION DATA

ISBN-13: 978-0-7876-6683-5
ISBN-10: 0-7876-6683-1
ISSN: 1084-4473

Printed in the United States of America
10 9 8 7 6 5 4 3 2 1

Contents

Highlights

Business Plans Handbook, Volume 13 (BPH-13) is a collection of actual business plans compiled by entrepreneurs seeking funding for small businesses throughout North America. For those looking for examples of how to approach, structure, and compose their own business plans, BPH-13 presents 20 sample plans, including plans for the following businesses:

- Advertising Brokerage Firm
- Barbecue Sauce Manufacturer
- Campus Apartment Complex
- Childrens' Indoor Recreation Center
- Corner Store
- Environmentally—Minded Residential Construction Company
- Ethnic Food Supplier
- Fitness Center
- Gift Store
- Home Renovation Contractor
- Landscaping Service
- Leather Accessory Manufacturer
- Meal Facilitation and Preparation Company
- Producer and Supplier of Plants and Flowers
- Restaurant
- Technology Solutions Provider
- Trademarked Resort Wear Distributor
- Veterinary Practice
- Wine Merchant and Storage Facility

FEATURES AND BENEFITS

BPH-13 offers many features not provided by other business planning references including:

- Twenty business plans, each of which represent an owner's successful attempt at clarifying (for themselves and others) the reasons that the business should exist or expand and why a lender should fund the enterprise.
- Two fictional plans that are used by business counselors at a prominent small business development organization as examples for their clients. (You will find these in the Business Plan Template Appendix.)
- A directory section that includes: listings for venture capital and finance companies, which specialize in funding start-up and second-stage small business ventures, and a comprehensive

listing of Service Corps of Retired Executives (SCORE) offices. In addition, the Appendix also contains updated listings of all Small Business Development Centers (SBDCs); associations of interest to entrepreneurs; Small Business Administration (SBA) Regional Offices; and consultants specializing in small business planning and advice. It is strongly advised that you consult supporting organizations while planning your business, as they can provide a wealth of useful information.

- A Small Business Term Glossary to help you decipher the sometimes confusing terminology used by lenders and others in the financial and small business communities.
- A cumulative index, outlining each plan profiled in the complete Business Plans Handbook series.
- A Business Plan Template which serves as a model to help you construct your own business plan. This generic outline lists all the essential elements of a complete business plan and their components, including the Summary, Business History and Industry Outlook, Market Examination, Competition, Marketing, Administration and Management, Financial Information, and other key sections. Use this guide as a starting point for compiling your plan.
- Extensive financial documentation required to solicit funding from small business lenders. You will find examples of: Cash Flows, Balance Sheets, Income Projections, and other financial information included with the textual portions of the plan.

Introduction

Perhaps the most important aspect of business planning is simply doing it. More and more business owners are beginning to compile business plans even if they don't need a bank loan. Others discover the value of planning when they must provide a business plan for the bank. The sheer act of putting thoughts on paper seems to clarify priorities and provide focus. Sometimes business owners completely change strategies when compiling their plan, deciding on a different product mix or advertising scheme after finding that their assumptions were incorrect. This kind of healthy thinking and re-thinking via business planning is becoming the norm. The editors of Business Plans Handbook, Volume 13 (BPH-13) sincerely hope that this latest addition to the series is a helpful tool in the successful completion of your business plan, no matter what the reason for creating it.

This thirteenth volume, like each volume in the series, offers genuine business plans used by real people. BPH-13 provides 20 business plans used by actual entrepreneurs to gain funding support for their new businesses. The business and personal names and addresses and general locations have been changed to protect the privacy of the plan authors.

NEW BUSINESS OPPORTUNITIES

As in other volumes in the series, BPH-13 finds entrepreneurs engaged in a wide variety of creative endeavors. Examples include a proposal for a fitness center, home builder, and two different restaurants. In addition, several other plans are provided, including an veterinary practice, a producer and supplier of plants and flowers, and a campus apartment complex.

Comprehensive financial documentation has become increasingly important as today's entrepreneurs compete for the finite resources of business lenders. Our plans illustrate the financial data generally required of loan applicants, including Income Statements, Financial Projections, Cash Flows, and Balance Sheets.

ENHANCED APPENDIXES

In an effort to provide the most relevant and valuable information for our readers, we have updated the coverage of small business resources. For instance, you will find: a directory section, which includes listings of all of the Service Corps of Retired Executives (SCORE) offices; an informative glossary, which includes small business terms; and a cumulative index, outlining each plan profiled in the complete Business Plans Handbook series. In addition we have updated the list of Small Business Development Centers (SBDCs); Small Business Administration Regional Offices; venture capital and finance companies, which specialize in funding start-up and second-stage small business enterprises; associations of interest to entrepreneurs; and consultants, specializing in small business advice and planning. For your reference, we have also reprinted the business plan template, which provides a comprehensive overview of the essential components of a business plan and two fictional plans used by small business counselors.

SERIES INFORMATION

If you already have the first twelve volumes of BPH, with this thirteenth volume, you will now have a collection of over 280 real business plans (not including the one updated plan in the second volume, whose original appeared in the first, or the two fictional plans in the Business Plan Template Appendix section of the second, third, fourth, fifth, sixth, and seventh volumes); contact information for hundreds of organizations and agencies offering business expertise; a helpful business plan template; a foreword providing advice and instruction to entrepreneurs on how to begin their research; more than 1,500 citations to valuable small business development material; and a comprehensive glossary of terms to help the business planner navigate the sometimes confusing language of entrepreneurship.

ACKNOWLEDGEMENTS

The Editors wish to sincerely thank the contributors to BPH-13, including:

- Gerald Rekve, Corporate Management Consultants
- Bo-Hung Ke, Robert Oesch and Jeriah Williams
- Paul Schieter, Eduardo Flores, and Alicia Beranek
- Tracey C. McCurrah and Elizabeth Timm
- Danielle Ferris
- Jay Fox, Brittani Lee, and Brian Wideman
- Greg Darnell, Kyle Jobe, Joe LaMonica, Audroy Speak and Dan Weller

The editors would also like to express their gratitude to Jerome Katz of the Cook School of Business at Saint Louis University. He has been instrumental in finding and securing high–quality, successful business plans for inclusion in this publication.

COMMENTS WELCOME

Your comments on Business Plans Handbook are appreciated. Please direct all correspondence, suggestions for future volumes of BPH, and other recommendations to the following:

Managing Editor, Business Product
Business Plans Handbook
The Gale Group
27500 Drake Rd.
Farmington Hills, MI 48331-3535

Phone: (248)699-4253
Fax: (248)699-8052
Toll-Free: 800-347-GALE
E-mail: BusinessProducts@gale.com

Advertising Brokerage Firm

Cover Art Advertising

12314 Stumpe St.
Regina, Saskatchewan S4X 1K7

Gerald Rekve

Cover Art Advertising will create a vinyl cover to fold over the Yellow Pages phone book's paper cover. This cover will provide advertisement opportunities for companies in the area. Cover Art Advertising will sell this advertisement space to companies on an annual basis.

BUSINESS OVERVIEW

We will be in the advertising business in the city of Regina, Saskatchewan. Our main focus will be to sell advertising space on phone book covers to local merchants. We will go out to the merchant's place of business and sell advertising space on the phone book covers. The phone book cover will be made out of vinyl and have twelve spots on the front and back and two spots on the spine. These spots will be posted for a period of twelve months.

Mission

Our mission will be to offer our advertisers a place to advertise on the phone book cover that gives the advertiser good value for the money spent. This cover also offers home owners a method to protect the book from becoming ripped and tattered. The phone book cover will be designed to look nice and all the ads on the phone book cover will be of a family nature.

Objectives

Our goal is to become a company that offers advertisers methods to increase their company's exposure by advertising on our phone book cover. Our main goal for the first year will be to have a sold out phone book cover in our local market, then based on these successes we will offer the phone book cover to other markets in the other cities in our province. These cities include Saskatoon, Prince Albert, Yorkton, Moosejaw and Swiftcurrent.

Market sizes:

Regina	195,000
Saskatoon	220,000
Prince Albert	95,000
Swift Current	22,000
Yorkton	17,000
Moose Jaw	25,000

In our first year we want to sell out the Regina phone book cover. In the long term we want grow our business to one profit market at a time.

BUSINESS STRATEGY

We will always focus on what's best for our business, our advertising clients and our home owners who will be using the phone book cover on a daily basis.

Our market will be the business advertisers in the phone book itself. This is a crazy concept because "Why would you spend money advertising on the cover of the book if you have an ad inside the phone book?" The answer is simple. The cover of the book is key because the advertisement will be at the top of the consumer's mind.

The business owners can be from all sectors except for the adult entertainment industries.

The phone book industry is considered mature with possible beginning market penetration lost to the internet phone books. As we look forward we project that the internet phone books will take a greater share of the phone number searches that take place. Having said this, we feel the phone book companies will take strategic positions to protect the mature phone book industry. We feel this will be one of our major advertising benefits, since the ad on the phone book's cover gives the advertiser "top of mind exposure".

MARKET ANALYSIS

Currently there are approximately 15,000 Regina–based businesses listed with the business licensing branch of the government. Of these 15,000 there is no way to know how many are in business until we start to call on them to sell advertising space.

There are a few major segments of these businesses that are broken down into categories such as:

- Home services
- Business services
- Auto services
- Food & restaurant services

We will take from these sectors the largest business advertisers in the yellow pages and make a short list of target customers to call on and make presentations too.

Customers

Biggest Advertisers
We broke down the phone book and separated the biggest advertisers. We did this because the advertising rates we will be charging the clients will be expensive. Knowing the biggest advertisers will allow us to sell only to clients who have the ability to pay our rates, and achieve our goal of being able to pay all our expenses with 55 percent of the book' cover sold. We want to be in a strong profit position to be able to expand into other markets.

Home Services
These services will include everything from home improvements and renovations to building. We will go through the phone book and select all the advertisers with advertisements larger than a half–page to start. Then we will make sales calls to each one of these businesses. We will make the sales call in person to limit the amount of gatekeeper turn away. A gatekeeper is someone in the business that limits access to decision makers, therefore limiting our ability to talk with the person that can say yes to our proposal. As well by making sales calls in person we can talk with staff and try to create a friendly relationship to start. Making sales calls over the phone for our product is harder and less successful on the first attempt.

Here is the list of advertisments with more than a half–page.

Cleanrite – 2 pages
Chem dry – 1 page
Dominion carpet – 1 pages
Cameo – 1/2 page
Steamatic – 1/2 page
Superior – 1/2 page
Dream carpets 1/2 page
Baynes carpet 1/2 pages
Flooring centre 1/2 page
End of role 1/2 page
Prestige interior 1/2 page
United carpet 1/2 page
Overhead doors 1/2 page
Regina window sales 1/2 page
Provincial window door 1/2 pages
Glacier glass
Friendly appliance 1 page
No 1 Appliance tech 1 page
Re- Appliable parts 1 page
Low Cost appliance 1/2 page
Ace repair 1/2 page
Econo maytag 1/2 page
Active appliance 1/2 page
His hers hair 1/2 page
Image 1 – 1/2 page
Aveda 1/2 page
International hair 1/2 page
Chatters 1/2 page
En vogue day spa 1/2

Auto services

Malibu chamois shine 1/2 page
Custom car care 1/2 page
Provincial auto body 2 pages
LK Auto body 2 pages
Western auto body 1 page
Bergens auto body 1 page
Advanced collision 1 page
Auto host 1 page
A B auto body 1/2 page
Matrix auto body 1/2 page
Carfax auto body 1/2 page
Macco auto body 1/2 page
Brady's autobody 1/2 page
Professional auto body 1/2 page
Regina auto body 1/2 page
Wascana auto body 1/2 page
Wilf's auto body 1/2 page
Cap city auto body 1/2 page
Dilawri auto body 1/2 page
General lube 1 page
Taylor auto sales 1 page
Bennett ford 1/2 page
Wheaton GM 1/2 page
Auto gallery 1/2 page
RMP GM auto sales 1/2 page
Auto parts plus 1/2 page
Canadian tire 1/2 page
Auto electric 1/2 page
Parts source 1/2 page
Budget car rental 1 page
Thrifty car rental 1 Page
Enterprise rent a car 2 page
Wheat Country Motors 1/2 page
Avis rental 1/2 page
National Car rental 1/2 page
Discount car rental 1/2 page
Auto host 1/2 page
Uhaul 1/2 page
Courtesy Auto rental 1/2 page
Plainsmen Auto 1 page
Autopro 1 page
General lube 1 page
Performace auto 1/2 page
JPL Auto 1/2 page
Taylor Auto body 1/2 page
Anderson collision 1/2 page
Image Auto body 1/2 page

The list provided above is just a small sample of how many advertisers are using the phone book. In our assessment there are at least 500 advertisers who ran an ad half–page or larger in the phone book. This represents at least $2,400,000 in annual revenue for the phone book for these half–page advertisers. On our phone book cover we will only have 67 spots to place advertising on and all of these spots are cover locations with high visibility. Based on our review of the market we are projecting to capture $140,000 in gross sales from the phone book cover in the Regina marketplace.

Customer Characteristics

All of our target clients will have already committed at least $9,500 annually to the phone book advertising. This means they know where they get the best bang for their advertising dollars. The addition of our phone book cover advertising expenses can be sold as an add–on. Since our lowest cost ad sells for $1,795 the advertiser can maintain the ad in the phone book and add the cover space as a bonus to their current advertising.

Our clients spend about 40 percent of their advertising budget in the phone book and will spend the rest in newspapers, flyers and radio, etc. This means our target clients spend about $28,000 annually on advertising. We are only asking for 5 percent of this to cover the cost of a 12 month ad on our phone book cover.

Customer Needs

All of clients will have one thing in common. They want to reach as many of their target clients as possible in order to maximize the efficiency of their advertising spending. Our clients want front page exposure at low input costs.

Customer Buying Decisions

Most of our clients are small locally owned businesses that can make buying decisions with local management and ownership. This will greatly increase our ability to sell to the right person in each company and make sure we will be able to influence the buying decision with our presentations.

COMPETITION

Radio stations

Frequency	Name	Format	Phone	Address
88.9	CKSB-1	CBC-French Music	306-347-9540	2440 Broad Street, Regina, SK S4P 0A5
90.9	CFVZ	Sports		Moose Jaw
91.3	CJTR	Community Radio	306-525-9741	1102 8th Avenue, Regina, SK, S4R 1C9
91.7	CBK-3 (Yorkton)	CBC Radio Two (talk/classical)	306-347-9540	2440 Broad Street, Regina, SK S4P 0A5
92.1	CHMX ("Lite 92")	adult contemporary	306-546-6200	2060 Halifax Street, Regina, SK, S4P 1T7
93.1	CFRY	Country	(204) 239-5111	350 River Road Portage la Prairie MB
94.1	CFGW "The Fox"	adult contemporary	306-782-9410	120 Smith Street East, YORKTON, SK S3N 3V3
94.1	CIMG "Eagle 94.1" (Swift Current)	classic rock	306-297-2671 Fax: 306-297-3051	410 Centre St, Shaunavon, SK S0N 2M0
94.5	Jack FM	Top 40	306-525-0000 Fax 306-347-8557	210-2401 Saskatchewan Drive Regina SK, S4P 4M8
95.7	CBK-4 (Swift Current)	CBC Radio 2	306-347-9540	2440 Broad Street Regina, SK S4P 0A5
96.3	CBK	CBC Radio 2	306-347-9540	2440 Broad Street Regina, SK S4P 0A5
97.1	CKFI "Magic 97.1"	adult contemporary		Swift Current
97.7	CBKF	CBC French	306-347-9540	2440 Broad Street Regina, SK S4P 0A5
98.9	CIZL "Z 99"	Adult contemporary	306 525-0000 Fax: 306 347-8557 Studio: 306 936-9999	210-2401 Saskatchewan Drive Regina, SK, S4P 4H8
99.1	CHRI - Z99	Regina Christian Radio		
100.7	CILG "Country 100"	Country	306-692-1007	1704 Main Street North MOOSE JAW, SK S6J 1L4
102.5	CBC1	Canadian Broadcasting Corporation	306-347-9540	2440 Broad Street, Regina, SK S4P 0A5
104.9	CFWF ("Wolf")	Rock	306-546-6200	2060 Halifax Street, REGINA, SK S4P 1T7

TV Stations

Global TV
CBC TV
CTV TV

Newspapers

LEADER POST – Daily newspaper
Regina Sun – Weekly newspaper
Prairie Dog – Bi weekly newspaper
Senior Today – Monthly newspaper
Auto Trader group of publications

Yellow Pages

Direct west yellow pages

Based on our market research, the yellow pages will be our greatest competitor and source of leads.

Risk Factors

There will always be risks going into business; however by knowing those risks from the outset we will greatly reduce our chances of failure based on our ability to plan for these risks.

The greatest risk would be another company to try to sell these types of phone book covers. These phone book covers are not in any of these markets based on our research to date. We would from the very beginning advertise the fact we are producing the phone book cover. This we are confidant would greatly reduce the risk of competitors starting to sell a similar product now that they know about us. Another risk is if the Yellow Pages company sells ads on the phone book cover itself or sells a vinyl cover like ours. We feel this will not happen for a number of reasons. First the phone book is owned by a government agency which also owns the phone company. This being said, they also risk alienating existing clients on the phone book inside because they would have the same limitations as we would in the number of advertisers they can put on the cover.

Another risk is if the phone book company in the second year that we produce the cover goes to our clients and offers them free ads in the phone book or reduced costs. This is most likely the greatest risk we face. Having said this we feel that this will only strengthen our sales pitch. Advertisers will not want to lose the front page exposure we are going to give them.

Finally the last risk is if clients do not accept our proposal and decline to advertise on the cover. We have mitigated this by reducing our risk by doing solid market research.

MARKETING & SALES

Strengths

Our key competitive strength will be the fact that there are only 64 places on the cover we produce to place an ad on. This greatly increases the value of the spots. This also gives our advertisers stronger market presence and exposure to the Regina market place.

We will be the only place in Regina where the consumer's ad will be in front of all the Regina marketplace for twelve months.

Weaknesses

Unfortunately, once the ads are placed, we will not be in the market for twelve months. The ads are all twelve–month ads. Also we can only sell ads to sixty–four advertisers.

Strategy

Our strategy is simple, place our phone book cover in every house and apartment in Regina. This allows us to give the advertisers maximum exposure. We will make sales calls to all our target clients.

We will hire two advertising sales staff to sell advertising to our targeted advertisers. Once we get set up, we will start selling advertising four months in advance of our deadline. This will give us the ability to make sure we call on every client. Once this market is completed we will go to the next market.

PRODUCTS & SERVICES

Product and Service Description

We will produce 9 x 7 inch phone book cover that wraps around the whole phone book. This cover will be printed on the outside with sixty-four ads and on the inside cover with eight ads.

Initially, we will offer this cover in eight markets within Saskatchewan.

Positioning of Products and Services

Our phone book cover will be strategically positioned as an ad on to our clients's existing advertising methods. We believe the client will see the benefit to take a small percentage of their advertising budget from radio, TV, newspaper and the phone book in order to get coverage on the cover we are selling.

Future Products and Services

Our main focus will be on phone book covers, and we will expand in areas that support these phone book covers. We will expand into other markets like Alberta and Manitoba in order to expand our business base. We will also keep in mind not to grow too fast that we lose sight of our main region. It will be nice to operate in every province in Canada. However we must be realistic also, and not expand too fast which could weaken our company.

Marketing Strategy

We will place strategic advertising in the local newspaper and send mailers via Canada post to target clients. The most important strategy will be to make sales calls on prospective advertisers. These in–person sales calls will be the best thing we can do in order to maximize sales and revenue.

Sales Tactics

Sales tactics will be managed the same way the big players like AT&T, IBM, and Xerox sell. We will have high-end presentations directly to the clients and decision makers. Our professional, well–researched sales presentations will win the hearts of our clients, allowing for our clients to have trust in our firm and our advertising products. At no point will we use negative sales tactics to sell our products. We always talk about our competitors as good companies and our products as a good fit to support present advertising methods.

Advertising

We will budget to advertise our services in the local newspaper and radio stations. We will use the internet to support the sales of our products to our clients.

We will also use our vehicles as a driving billboard, using signage on our minivans. We will also offer our clients a referral discount, if they recommend a friend who in turn runs an ad on our cover.

Promotions and Incentives

As part of our kick–off to get the public to use our phone book cover, each month we will have drawings for TVs, PlayStation 2s, software, etc. So every month the consumer simply needs to drop of their entry to any one of the businesses located on the cover of the phone book. This will insure the advertisers can see the actual draw of the cover to their business and they can track the results.

Once the phone book cover is done for Regina we will place ads on radio stations telling the public to watch for the cover and start playing the contest. We will also try to get as much free PR from the radio and TV stations as well as newspapers.

Trade Shows

We will book the annual chamber of commerce business trade show.

OPERATIONS

Jeffrey Withsot: VP of Operations

Matt Depareot: Advertising Sales Manager

Financials

Yellow page phone book cover

INCOME STATEMENT - For the year ending December 31, 2006

Month	Jan 1	Feb 2	Mar 3	Apr 4	May 5	June 6	July 7
Sales	**$30,000**	**$36,000**	**$42,000**	**$22,000**	**$27,500**	**$57,500**	**$60,500**
Net sales							
Cost of sales							
Opening inventory	—						
Phone book cover printing	13,000	12,000	15,000	15,000	19,000	19,000	19,000
	13,000	13,912	17,824	17,578	21,332	21,275	21,217
Gross profit as a %							
Expenses							
Salaries	7500	7500	7500		7500	7500	7500
Other wages	750	750	750	750	750	750	750
Benefits	204	204	204	204	204	204	204
Rent & equipment leases	1,800	1,800	1,800	1,800	1,800	1,800	1,800
Promotion	2,000	275	275	275	275	275	275
Maintenance	250	250	250	250	250	250	250
General and office expenses	300	300	300	300	300	300	300
Telephone and utilities	200	200	200	200	200	200	200
Insurance	166	166	166	166	166	166	166
Depreciation	750	750	750	750	750	750	750

Month	Aug 8	Sept 9	Oct 10	Nov 11	Dec 12	Total
Sales	**$28,500**	**$39,000**	**$32,000**	**$38,200**	**$12,500**	**$**
Net sales						
Cost of sales						
Opening inventory						—
Phone book cover printing	20,000	24,000	24,500	26,500	27,500	234,500
	22,160	26,409	26,654	28,899	29,719	234,500
Gross profit as a %						
Expenses						
Salaries	7500	7500	7500	7500	7500	
Other wages	750	750	750	750	750	9,000
Benefits	204	204	204	204	204	2,450
Rent & equipment leases	1,800	1,800	1,800	1,800	1,800	21,600
Promotion	270	270	270	270	270	5,000
Maintenance	250	250	250	250	250	3,000
General and office expenses	300	300	300	300	300	3,600
Telephone and utilities	200	200	200	200	200	2,400
Insurance	166	166	166	166	166	1,992
Depreciation	750	750	750	750	750	9,000

Yellow Page phone book cover

CASH FLOW STATEMENT - For the year ending December 31, 2006

	Jan	Feb	Mar	Apr	May	June	July
Month	1	2	3	4	5	6	7
Inflows							
Issuance of capital stock	100						
Collection of accounts receivable	30,000	20,000	15,000	15,000	24,000	24,000	25,000
Owner's initial investment	50,000	—	—	—	—	—	—
Outflows							
Incorporation costs	1,200						
Acquisition of fixed assets	5,000						
Repayment of shareholder loan			—	—	—	—	—
Payment of accounts payable	6,500	12,500	13,500	15,000	17,000	19,000	19,000

	Aug	Sept	Oct	Nov	Dec	Total
Month	8	9	10	11	12	
Inflows						
Issuance of capital stock						100
Collection of accounts receivable	26,000	27,000	22,000	24,000	27,000	
Owner's initial investment	—	—	—	—	—	50,000
Outflows						
Incorporation costs						1,200
Acquisition of fixed assets						5,000
Repayment of shareholder loan	5,000	5,000	5,000	5,000	5,000	13,000
Payment of accounts payable	19,500	22,000	24,250	25,500	27,000	220,750

Barbecue Sauce Manufacturer

FLAMETHROWER BARBECUE SAUCE

312 W. Ann St.
Ann Arbor, Michigan 48103

Bo-Hung Ke, Robert Oesch, and Jeriah Williams

FlameThrower barbecue sauce comes from a very unique and locally established restaurant, FlameThrower BBQ, located in Ann Arbor, Michigan. The restaurant has a well–established and local loyalty in the Detroit metropolitan area. Its delicious hickory–smoked meats basted in an incredible sweet vinegar–based sauce have a special quality unlike any other barbecue restaurant in the area. The current FlameThrower special barbecue sauce is the creation of its owner, Matteo Hill, and has developed a reputation of its own with customers. Based on customer feedback, we have a desire to mass produce and sell this sauce.

EXECUTIVE SUMMARY

FlameThrower barbecue sauce comes from a very unique and locally established restaurant, FlameThrower BBQ, located in Ann Arbor, Michigan. The restaurant has a well–established and local loyalty in the Detroit metropolitan area. Its delicious hickory–smoked meats basted in an incredible sweet vinegar–based sauce have a special quality unlike any other barbecue restaurant in the area. The current FlameThrower special barbecue sauce is the creation of its owner, Matteo Hill, and has developed a reputation of its own with customers. Other sauces have since been added to the FlameThrower menu, including a spicy sauce, wing sauce, and barbecue seasonings.

FlameThrower barbecue sauce is an excellent departure from the sauces currently on the market in the local region. Its robust flavor has a uniqueness that sets it aside from that of most nationally mass produced sauces. However, some of the limitations associated with the introduction of the sauce to the market pose potential threats, which include (a) limited regional and national exposure; (b) no national cook–off or convention entries; (c) resistance of sales in specialty boutiques due to loyalty to their own sauces and; (d) the limitations of the owner's resources and time to market and produce.

The current national bottled barbecue sauce industry has its high points. There is a growing trend for specialty sauces like FlameThrower and the overall market value is increasing. Locally, there are only a handful of barbecue sauce businesses that are in the metro area, which include Cayenne, Richard's BBQ, and Mesquite Tavern. There are about 13 different brands of barbecue sauces in local supermarkets that come in various sizes and flavors.

Due to the distinct differences in the selling process, customer requirements, and sales forecasts, the study was performed by dividing the introduction of the FlameThrower signature sauce into two main sales channels: Local Grocery Markets and Supermarket Chains. Neither venture is immediately feasible, as they cannot produce short–term financial profits and exhausts more of the owner's time than he has available. The majority of smaller local grocers sell their own bottled barbecue sauce, which causes them to limit the amount of other sauces they will carry. Pursuing the supermarket chain channel would require a very large initial investment, and the number of bottles that would have to be sold to break even is beyond reasonable investment and will not turn over foreseeable profit. We suggest reinvestigating the feasibility of this project in 3 years after pursuing a number of marketing activities. Some of those activities include: local events including the Catsup Bottle Festival and the International Horseradish Festival. Participation in such events is very inexpensive and will give FlameThrower an opportunity to provide a venue for new customers. Donations of the sauce to local schools for fundraisers and charities are also recommended. A "sauce swap" relationship in which Matteo displays other area sauces in the restaurant in exchange for them displaying his is another activity that could help build a mutually beneficial relationship with other stores while increasing brand recognition in the local area. We believe these kinds of activities will prove to further increase FlameThrower's brand equity.

PRODUCTS & SERVICES

Unique Benefits

The unique feature of this sauce is the original, well–balanced combination of ingredients that creates a truly unique and impressive barbecue sauce. The savor of the sauce makes it an excellent departure from the vinegary and/or overly smoky sauces that are available in the local region, while offering a more robust palette than that of nationally mass produced sauces. FlameThrower Barbecue Sauce is the signature sauce from the local well–regarded restaurant of the same name, which has been recently revived under new management. It is still known for its quality food, and most notably its sauce.

Risk Factors

The shortcomings of the product are: (a) FlameThrower brand image is strongest only in the Ann Arbor (Metro Detroit) area. There are some predicted challenges in selling the FlameThrower sauce outside of the area; (b) The sauce has not gained any exposure through any local, state, or national cook–offs or barbecue sauce conventions for potential first time buyers; (c) there are a limited number of boutique establishments where FlameThrower would be able to sell its product, and many of these places restrict their sales to their own specialty sauce; and (d) lastly, Matteo's time. The owner, Matteo Hill, is the sole owner and key manager for the already successful FlameThrower restaurant. His time and resources are limited and extremely valuable. He must be selective in making the best use of his time given his already successful but demanding restaurant activities.

ORGANIZATION

Stage of Development

The product has an existing, well–tested and received client base. The signature sauce is currently sold through the one location but there is currently no point–of–sale display. A well–designed and attractive bottle must still be selected and will be done so based upon (a) appeal to the consumer; (b) the optimum size(s) to be offered. To support short–term production forecasts, there will not be any additional production capacity required. However in the very long–term, there would be some further research and speculation in the increased capacity, only after short–term objectives are achieved. Even then, research and feasibility will have to be further investigated.

Legal Restrictions and Rights

The intellectual property in question, namely the FlameThrower sauce recipe, is known only by a handful of well–trusted employees. The ingredients, according to US FDA requirements, must be listed on the bottle, with the exception of flavorings and spices. Those ingredients can be listed on the packaging as "natural flavors, spices" and is where the true unique quality of the sauce lies. All OSHA, FDA, and health code standards are already met, and the internal bookkeeping can be handled by the same individual currently handling this function for the restaurant.

The logo that will adorn the bottle is already copyrighted, through Smith Graphics in 2004 and is owned wholly by Matteo Hill.

Insurance Requirements

There is no need for any additional insurance coverage. There are no initial plans to take on addition employees, but this may be considered if the additions of merchandisers and/or administrative personnel are required due to substantial growth as time progresses.

MARKET ANALYSIS

Specialty sauces and "home–grown recipes" have gained a strong niche market as many individuals are looking for increased diversity of flavors, while looking for a new "secret" brand. The growing interest in at home barbecuing and the introduction of a number of barbecue cooking shows has raised the quality of the food prepared, which for many justify (and even require) a quality local sauce.

National Barbecue Sauce Industry

According to industry research (2002–2005), US sauce, dressing and condiment revenues grew by 3.5 percent to just more than $14.4 billion. In real terms, overall value sales grew by 1.9 percent, compared to a relatively static performance in 2001. However, volume sales growth lagged behind value gains, increasing by only 1 percent to just more than 2,410,126 metric tons. This was speculated to be due, in a large part, to US consumers changing their product usage trends. Consumers have shifted to higher priced premium products with US consumer demand also demonstrating a growing trend towards higher unit priced specialty sauces. Logically, many manufactures have begun to produce more specialty ethnic sauces to jump on margin gains.

Local Barbecue Sauce Industry

According to industry research findings, there are four firms in the Detroit metro area barbecue sauce bottling business, of which all were able to survive during the 3 years (2002–2004) resulting in a failure rate of 0 percent. Due to the sales classification change of 1 company from $5 million to "unknown," the overall industry numbers are difficult to use for reliable analysis. However, since the annual revenues of this company are substantially larger than the other 3 companies (within the less than $200k sales class), their sales should not be included in this analysis.

The following illustrates the Detroit metro area market (these are averages over a three year period (2001–2004)):

Annual market volume ($)

	Year 1	Year 2	Year 3
Reported	6,000,000	6,600,000	7,500,001
Generated	3,582,138	3,456,810	4,523,484

Average annual sales ($)

	Firms	Small business	Startups
Yr1 Average Sales:	1,500,000	1,500,000	0
Yr2 Average Sales:	1,650,000	1,650,000	0
Yr3 Average Sales:	125,000	185,714	
Change Yr1 to Yr3	91.7%	87.6%	0.0%
Survivor Average Sales:	125,000	125,000	0
Survivor Change Yr1 to Yr3	91.7%	91.7%	0.0%

SOURCE: Bizminer.com release date May 2005

Industry Trends

To gain a perspective of how the sauce bottling and sale relates to the barbecue restaurant industry, we will present relevant industry trends. Barbecue sauce is usually the heart of a Barbecue restaurant, and almost every restaurant purports to have its own secret sauce recipe. The Local Marketing Research Profile provided by bizminer.com indicates that in the Detroit metro area there were 86 restaurants existing from July of 2002 to July of 2004.

The total number of restaurants combined comes to an annual market volume of $22.17 million in 2004. The average sales of small business barbecue restaurants is approximately $214,286 amongst 3–year surviving businesses, representing 3–year growth of 3.6 percent, which demonstrates that although average sales per small business is declining, it is declining at a much lower rate than that of the industry overall.

FlameThrower is in the small business segment classification. Industry figures indicate that the small business segment has a failure rate of 30 percent by year 3. As a very positive note, FlameThower restaurant far surpassed this possibility, as it has been an established restaurant for a number of years. The market share maintain by this small restaurant business segment of 3–year surviving firms is 13.53 percent, with the remainder being held by the larger, restaurant chain firms (bizminer.com).

COMPETITION

The primary restaurant competition includes Cayenne in Canton, Michigan, Richard's BBQ in Windsor, Canada, and Mesquite Tavern in East Lansing. Also, the bulk of the 86 metro area barbecue restaurants are within Detroit city limits, which are considered secondary competition due to having a different client base, based upon geographic proximity. Cayenne and Richard's BBQ are both of a similar size as FlameThrower, whereas Mesquite Tavern is in a different category since it is a restaurant chain, with 15 stores in Michigan, 3 in Illinois, 1 in Ohio, and 1 in Louisiana and has considerable more seating capacity.

CUSTOMERS

The customer base for FlameThrower is based in the Ann Arbor/Metro Detroit area; with the concentration of customer depleting as the distance range outside the Metro Detroit area is increased. FlameThrower's brand recognition almost completely dissipates once the entire Detroit metro area is viewed.

Due to the distinct differences in the selling process, customer requirements, and sales forecasts, we propose a split in the introduction of the FlameThrower signature sauce into two main sales channels: Local Grocery Markets and Supermarket Chains.

Local Grocery Markets

There are a number of local grocery vendors in the Detroit Metro East area. The search was focused on an area within a 15–mile range of FlameThrower Restaurant based upon the strength of the FlameThrower brand in this general area. Other criteria for identifying stores that are part of this sales channel were: (a) must be independently owned and operated; (b) must currently offer some kind of sauce (whether a full grocery store, meat market or butchers shop). Thirteen stores were identified as meeting all of these qualifications.

Competition

There are a number of competing brands that are available within all of the small grocer markets (including butcher shops) in the Detroit Metro East area; these brands are Spicy Sauce, Marc's

Marinade, and Chef LaPonde's BBQ Sauce. Spicy Sauce and Marc's Marinade are both local companies that internally handle the production and distribution of their own sauces. Both company have been in the bottled sauce business for a substantial number of years and produces a variety of sauces, but neither have any history within the restaurant business.

Another notable trend found across all of the butcher shops and meat markets was that most stores had their own brand of barbecue sauce. This represents 10 of the 13 qualifying stores and after discussion with the stores's owners would prove to be a major issue as they are not interested in carrying another local brand of barbecue unless a large number of customers begin to demand a particular sauce.

Customers

Since these stores purchase the sauce rather than holding inventory on consignment, the direct customers are the stores themselves. The end customers, if this sales channel were pursued, would be individuals who purchase ribs, brisket, chicken, and other items they intend to barbecue and would also be buying their sauce of choice from the meat market. The issue found with these direct customers (stores) is that only 3 of the 13 stores would even be interested in carrying FlameThrower signature sauce since they are interested in building demand for their own signature sauces.

Operating Expenses

The total cost to produce a pint of sauce for Matteo in–house is $0.76 and the cost of the actual bottle is $0.67, not including the $0.10 that each label will cost. Initial marketing for Matteo in–house production costs will include the $300 investment needed for label design, $8 an hour in wages to be paid to an employee to sample and sell the product in the individual stores for 10 hours per store and an average of 3 sample bottles per store. This would make annual operating expenses:

Revenue	$1,248.00
Variable costs	$477.36
Fixed costs	$553.77
Gross profit	$216.87
Taxes	$71.57
Net profit	**$145.30**

Initial startup costs

Production cost	$ 0.76
Bottle cost	$ 0.67
Label cost	$ 0.10
Initial case requirements	6
Bottles per case	12
Total bottles	72
Samples	$ 13.77
Sales wage	$240.00
Label design dost	$300.00
Initial production cost	$110.16
Total initial investment	**$663.93**

Profitability and Pricing

Based upon discussions with the management of the individual store locations, it can be expected that 312 pint bottles could be sold annually if local stores that claimed they would be interested were to sell the sauce. To be competitively priced in these stores, FlameThrower sauce would be sold for $4.00 per pint–size bottle.

Revenues	$1,248.00
COGS	$1,031.13
Taxes	$ 71.57
Net profit	**$ 145.30**

Mr. Hill currently sells his barbecue sauce at customer request within the restaurant. The prices currently being charged are: $21 for a gallon, $7 for a quart and $3.50 for a pint container. Due to pints being the most popular size within this sales channel, this would be the only size that would be sold. The price would have to be raised to establish it as a premium sauce and would be sold for $4 a pint–size bottle, as that is what the direct customers quoted as an average price they pay, as they mark up prices 33 percent.

Based on the Director of Sales at Food Stores R Us, a small manufacturer in Detroit, Michigan, an estimate of costs related to production is $20 dollars per case. Because Food Stores R Us is a small operation, they can produce at a base minimum of 100 cases (1200 bottles) for a single production line. The only fixed cost to consider in this operation is $300 for label design, since all other fixed cost are sunk costs. A break even analysis of this venue of sales is as follows:

Total bottles	1200
FC	
Label design	
TFC	$ 300
AFC	$ 300
	$ 0.25
VC	
Manufacturing cost	$2,000
TAC	$2,000
AVC	$ 1.92
TC	$2,300
ATC	**$ 1.92**

16 oz Barbecue bottles	
Initial order/bottles	1,200
Label design	$ 300
Manufacturing cost	$2,000
Sales price at local stores	$ 4.00
Supermarket's profit (markup)	30%
Price sold to local stores	$ 3.08
Production costs	$ 1.92
Profit per bottle sales	**$ 1.16**

Supermarket Chains

There are many large supermarket chain locations around the Ann Arbor area. The first step of getting sauce into the stores is to introduce the product to a supermarket distributor or buying manger. If at this stage the product is approved and received by the buyer, then a further discussion of the details of distribution is begun. At an estimate of $7,500 for an initial shipment of the product to the warehouse, an initial order requires at least 250 cases (approximately 3000 bottles/12 bottles per case). If the product cannot be sold out, Matteo will have to buy the product back from the supermarket at its retail price.

Competition

In brand analysis, we did a survey in several different supermarkets. There are basically 13 different brands of barbecue sauces with different sizes and flavors. Based on the information we collected from the manager of supermarket, the product that can be put on the fifth level shelf will have better sales because customers can see the product easily. Based on this logic, we can have two conclusions: (1) the first one is that we can pay extra money to put our product on the fifth level shelf. (2) The other conclusion is that Spicy Sauce, Marc's Marinade, and Chef LaPonde's BBQ Sauce have better sales than other brands.

Another important note is that products which are located on the fifth level of the shelf are there for two reasons, one is so that the product sells better than other similar products, another is the sauce producer invests more money to place their products in a more obvious location.

In flavor analysis, there basically 8 kinds of flavors, such as Hot, Smoked, Honey, Hickory, Original, Kansas City–Style, St. Louis–Style and Tennessee–Style.

Small brands and big brands prefer to produce their sauces into smaller bottles. These brands typically produce their sauce in 18oz bottles. One logical reason given by local managers for this is to encourage customers to try new products as customers don't have to buy much of the sauce to try a new one.

Customers

Since sales are done directly to stores, the stores' Purchasing Agents are the direct customer. The end customers are those individuals who shop in the local supermarket chain locations do so for convenience. They usually go to the store that has easy accessibility and within a 15–mile radius. It is important to understand that the motivations of a supermarket customer are usually low price and convenience. Customers of a local supermarket are usually local residents. The direct customer would be the supermarket Purchasing Agent, since the sale of the sauce will be directly to Food Stores R Us.

Pricing

The amount of initial order is 3000 bottles, and we also have to pay $7,500 to the supermarket in order to sell our product through their distribution. Based on Mr. Hill's suggestion, he preferred his product with middle price, after we research the market price; we suggested that he could sell his 18oz bottle as $1.15 and 28oz as $3.50. Based on the information of the supermarket's manager, supermarket will increase 30 percent of the buying price. For example, if the price were labeled as $1.15 dollar, the cost of buying the product would be $0.88 dollar. Based on this logic, we can assume that the price of 18 oz sauce that we sell to the supermarket would be $0.88, and the price of 28oz sauce that we sell to the supermarket would be $2.69 dollars.

Given an estimate of costs from local sauce manufacturers, a realistic estimate of costs is $20 dollars per case give or take depending on the sauce content and production process. From our research of supermarket requirements, we have to be able to ship 250 cases (12 bottles a case) to the warehouse, and expect a $7,500 cost for shelf space at a minimum, and $300 for label design. In our study, the initial order set up costs is $7,800. The major component of variable cost is the manufacturing cost, which is $5,000 for 250 cases. Based on the figures above, we determine that ATC (Average Total Costs) per 16oz bottle is $4.27.

We will have to sell our 16 ounces for $0.88 so that we can price the product competitively at $1.15 a bottle. This is how we will come to a typical supermarket mark up of 30 percent. So, if we sell one bottle per Food Stores R Us cost estimates, we have a cost $4.27 and will have to sell it to the supermarket at $0.88 per bottle. We would lose $3.39 when we sell each bottle.

Total bottles	3,000
FC	
Shelf cost	$ 7,500
Label design	$ 300
TFC	$ 7,800
AFC	$ 2.6
VC	
Manufacturing cost	$ 5,000
TAC	$ 5,000
AVC	$ 1.6
TC	$12,800
ATC	**$ 4.27**

16 oz barbecue bottles	16 oz
Shelf cost	$7,500
Initial order/bottles	3,000
Label design	$300
Manufacturing cost	$5,000
Sales price at supermarket	$1.15
Supermarket's profit (markup)	30%
Price sold to supermarket	$0.88
Production costs	$4.27
Profit (Loss) per bottle sales	($3.39)

In summary, if we acquire an outside manufacturer to produce and bottle the sauce and sell through supermarket chains, breakeven will never be reached. For every bottle sold, we lose $4.00, which is clearly not feasible.

FINANCIAL ANALYSIS

Custom Manufacturing Option

Since a profit cannot be earned through 16oz bottle sales of sauce that is produced internally, custom manufacturing becomes a strong possibility. Food Stores R Us, a local Detroit–based sauce manufacturer, handles sauce production for several barbecue sauce brands in the Metro Detroit Area. Establishing a relationship and manufacturing a sauce recipe is quite simple. The process involves (a) providing a sample of the product to the new product manager (of which they will sign a confidentiality statement); (b) they provide a test batch on the customer base; (c) there is further discussion of the size bottles and marketing issues; and (d) the new product manager and owner decide if a line or size change is necessary.

The initial cost of this endeavor is as follows:

Initial case requirement

400 cases
$20 per case
$8,000 initial production costs

At the current prices charged to the supermarkets, this method of production is unfeasible.

Initial supermarket expense	$ 7,500.00	$7,500.00
Production costs	$ 8,000.00	$8,000.00
Revenues	$ 4,224.00	$5,808.00
Gross profit	($11,276.00)	($9,692.00)

Sources of Start–up Capital

The money required to begin selling in the local grocery markets could be financed from internal cash. To venture into the Supermarket chains, additional funding could be acquired through a SBA 504 loan.

CONCLUSION

To pursue either of these sales channels at this stage of development is not feasible. Overall, such activities would require a great deal of time to pursue, which is something that Matteo does not have to spare. It is unfeasible to pursue the local grocery markets, since the majority of these stores sell their own bottled barbecue sauce limiting the amount of other sauces that they carry to those that receive a large number of customer requests. This results in too few stores shelving FlameThrower barbecue sauce to make this venture currently reasonable to pursue. Pursuing the supermarket chain channel would require a large initial investment and the number of bottles that would have to be sold to breakeven can not be realistically forecasted. We foresee the possibility of reinvestigating the feasibility of this project in 3 years after pursuing a number of suggested marketing activities.

We recommend that Matteo Hill use the money that would be invested into this project to further advertise the restaurant. The recommended marketing activities include becoming a vendor at local events including the Catsup Bottle Festival and the International Horseradish Festival. Participation in such events is very cheap and it will give FlameThrower barbecue sauce an opportunity to introduce people to their food and to display their bottled sauce for both new and existing companies, while proving their connection to the area. FlameThrower could also donate bottled sauce (using sauce that is leftover and not to be used for food) to local schools for their fundraisers to increase the presence of both their restaurant and sauce. A "sauce swap" where Matteo displays other area sauces in the restaurant (particularly those from the small grocery markets) in exchange for them displaying his, could help build a mutual beneficial relationship with the stores, opening the opportunity to do business with them in the future, while further increasing FlameThrower's brand equity.

If the activities are pursued and show signs of success, we foresee the possibility of selling in the local grocery markets 4–5 years from now, outsourcing production to a custom manufacturer such as Food Stores R Us in Detroit, Michigan and beginning to sell the sauce to chain grocery stores and through a website (Matteo already owns the rights to an appropriate domain name) in 8–10 years.

Campus Apartment Complex

FOURWINDS APARTMENTS

4123 Tuttle St.
Louisville, KY 40203

Fourwinds is an upscale apartment complex for students living near universities and colleges. We are proposing this new style of property for use around the thousands of college campuses throughout the country. This complex will also serve as an investment opportunity for the smaller real estate investor to have the opportunity to get into real estate by purchasing individual units within each apartment complex and then allowing our rental management company to lease them to students and staff on their behalf. The model is intended to be easily replicated across the country.

BUSINESS OVERVIEW

Fourwinds is an upscale apartment complex for students living near universities and colleges. We are proposing this new style of property for use around the thousands of college campuses throughout the country. This complex will also serve as an investment opportunity for the smaller real estate investor to have the opportunity to get into real estate by purchasing individual units within each apartment complex and then allowing our rental management company to lease them to students and staff on their behalf. The model is intended to be easily replicated across the country. Headache and maintenance can be avoided by both the tenant and investor with the on-site management that will be provided. The unique model of this business is displayed in the chart below:

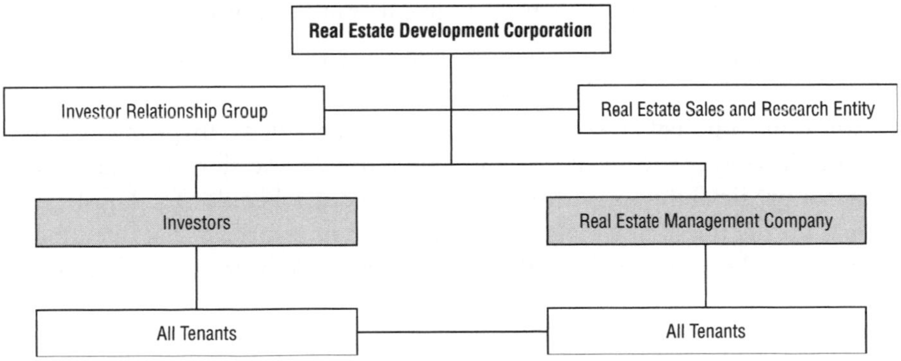

The business that Fourwinds is really in is providing peace of mind for tenants, the tenants' parents, and investors of the property. The largest aspect of our business is providing housing for students who need quality living space for a short time. Creating a sense of community among a group of similar tenants is a key goal of our model as well.

PRODUCTS & SERVICES

Our product has many unique features and benefits that would create a sustainable competitive advantage for Fourwinds. The most unique feature of our property is the ability to invest in a portion of an apartment complex. This spreads out the risk and financial strain to entice even the conservative investor. This feature also gets more members of the community involved and creates a more accommodating atmosphere to a project of this size in a town or city.

Multiple unit styles will be offered as a part of Fourwinds. We will have efficiencies and one bedroom offerings. There will also be "oversized" two–bedroom units capable of fitting 3–4 students. The most upscale apartments will be the penthouses. There will be from 2–5 penthouse units that will offer 3 bedrooms as well as special amenities and privileges. The upscale quality of Fourwinds controls the quality of the tenant. By charging higher rents, the "slum lord" mentality is avoided.

There are several amenities we will offer that will differentiate Fourwinds from the competition. At each tower a unique list of area businesses to visit will be distributed to each unit for the purpose of promoting local businesses and attracting tenants to the property. Lounge areas will be put throughout the buildings for studying, group work, or just a quiet space to get away from your roommate. This is a space that is often sorely lacking for students confined to a small area with several roommates. The most unique amenity that we will be offering will be limited furnishings for rooms. This saves parents who often have to travel long distances from having to rent trucks or spend thousands of dollars on new furniture. A restaurant space will be put on the ground floor that will deliver to the tenants within the building. Many of the units will include balconies. These are some of the more unique amenities we will include to differentiate ourselves from the competition. Some of the more standard amenities include:

- 24 hour security
- Closed–circuit surveillance system inside and out
- Internet access and cable television included in rent
- Recreational/Workout room
- Underground Parking
- Community building activities
- Knowledgeable full–time leasing office

These are some of the amenities that many complexes include to stay competitive in an already cut–throat market. We feel that blending the standard fare amenities with our unique concepts will create a rental development that students will not only want to live in, but pay a premium to live in.

Another unique feature of our product is the cycle in which we receive new tenants. It is inherently consistent. Most students will sign yearly leases beginning in the summer. This creates both a remarkable opportunity and a potential weakness for the development. Many people will be applying for moving in months in advance to secure a spot. The monthly addition of tenants will be at a minimum. This creates predictability in move–in and move–out schedules for logistical purposes. This also can cut costs during the summer when more units can be refurbished at one time instead of multiple times throughout the year. The benefits of this yearly cycle of tenants is the cost effectiveness, while the drawback is the cash flow issue if the building is not satisfactorily occupied by the fall semester.

Risk Factors

Many of our limitations are things that all rental properties must struggle with. Property must be available within walking distance to make the project be truly beneficial. If driving is involved, many students can not live in the Fourwinds and that would create more vacancies. The real estate development business is intense. Competing developers with more substantial cash flows could come in and spend us into the ground. The university that we are targeting could also create more on campus housing, hurting the number of students that move off campus. Many schools that would be candidates are in urban areas. This can often create the perception of a large apartment building being unsafe. This notion must be altered or at least soothed by offering things such as 24–hour security and cameras. The major flaw of Fourwinds is the reliance on the university. Institutions must keep their enrollment steady or rising, otherwise the tenant base will be greatly reduced. Restrictions from schools regarding scholarships and moving off campus must also be considered. Some universities tie academic scholarships to living on campus for some time, or for all four years. This could greatly affect the number of students who move to nearby apartments. These are the major limitations that could cause problems for Fourwinds.

BUSINESS STRATEGY

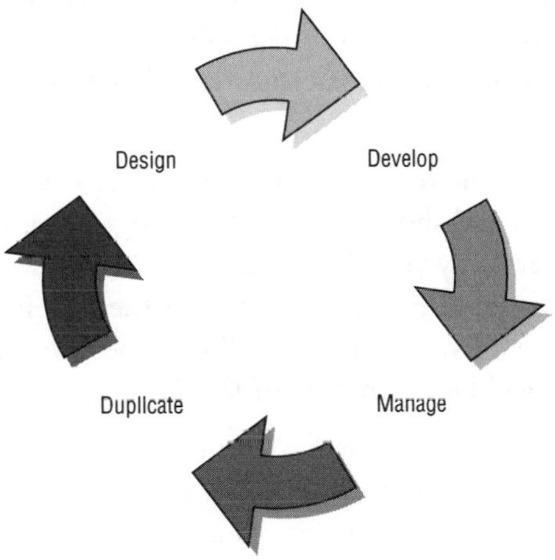

The process of building a project such as this involves four main stages: design, develop, manage, and duplicate. The design phase can be broken down into three main parts: finance, site selection, and blueprint. The financing stage will involve finding an investor or bank that will be willing to guarantee the necessary building funds if we can get 50 percent of the units sold before construction begins. This has successfully worked in many places with the condo–hotel industry and we believe it could work in the rental industry as well. Site selection is a key part of the process. Fourwinds has to be within walking distance, while still having enough space to build our project. The land must also be build worthy and at the right price. Finally, we will create the blueprint for the building. Each school will have to be slightly different to accommodate the size of the property and the unit needs for each individual school. These are the three key elements of the design phase.

The develop phase will be the most time and cost intensive. To begin development of the project, we will need to find a contractor. While searching out bids for the project, we will have to begin selling units. To further entice investors to purchase, a model unit will be built and fully furnished. Sales professionals will be hired to sell units on a commission basis to motivate them. When the contractor bids are in and we have sold half of the units, we will break ground. Throughout the building process, units will continue to be marketed and sold. A leasing office will be created when the project is nearly completed and a wait list will be started for tenants. When the building is completed, the development phase will end and the management phase will begin.

The management phase will be an ongoing effort. The leasing office will be moved inside the building and a full service staff will be installed. Marketing of the rental units will continue aggressively until capacity is reached. Unsold units will also continue to be listed by a realtor or sales staff in-house. Maintenance staff and amenities will be contracted out at this phase. Finishing the landscaping and other finishing touches will be completed early in this phase. The owner's association of Fourwinds will be formed. Quarterly owner meetings will be held, as well as a liaison for the owners in the leasing office. Day–to–day operations will be carried on here as part of the ongoing efforts. The last stage will be duplication. This stage will be discussed in greater detail in the Future Action Plan section.

CUSTOMERS

Fourwinds is a spin–off of the up and coming condominium–hotel trend toward real estate investing. A condominium–hotel operates like any typical luxury hotel, however each suite is privately owned, typically for investment purposes. In most typical condominium–hotels an individual will purchase a suite and an in-house rental management company set forth by the developer will manage the property, with a 50/50 revenue split. This concept has become very popular on the coast and has recently moved inward to Knoxville, Tennessee.

Complementing this trend toward fully managed investment real estate is a trend seen in American culture. Americans are undoubtedly living fast–paced lives and show no sign of slowing down. In fact, it appears as if Americans' daily lives are only moving faster every year. When time is of the essence, busy Americans may not have time in their day to manage a rental property on top of their daily routine. However, with an in–house rental management company busy Americans will only need to take their check to the bank each month, because everything else will be taken care of for them.

Changing lifestyles of today's youths reflect trends in student housing; from increased desires for privacy, to the respect for choice and flexibility, to the premium placed on aesthetics and design. "Students don't want their home to look like a prison," said Frankie Minor, housing director at Mizzou. UMSL's new $26 million, 430-bed Oak Hall, is far from a prison, featuring an outdoor heated pool, fitness room, barbecue pit, convenience store, sand volleyball court, and more (Post-Dispatch). Students today are more likely to have their own bedroom at home so they are demanding such privacy at school. U.S. Census figures from the last decade show the average family size has gotten smaller while the number of bedrooms in houses has increased. At Indiana State University's new residence hall, four suitemates share two bathrooms and a common living space. There is a pool table, a fitness room, flat–screen TVs, and sleek black couches on the first floor, which doubles as a student center. It is evident that today's youth are living large in housing that looks like anything but a dorm.

These students do not stop short at aesthetics. On a number of campuses students are able to hire personal maids to clean and do their laundry. They pay moving crews to pack and transport their stuff. They take advantage of grocery delivery services, and even arrive to school on the first day in limousines.

Students willing and able to pay $30,000–$40,000 per year tuition rates at private universities do not only desire such luxurious housing, they expect it. For example, at DePaul University, a private university in Chicago, students living in Loft–Right have all the amenities: expansive city views, granite countertops, modern designer furniture, and satellite TV. Students are willing to pay more than $1,000 a month for a private bedroom in a two or four–bedroom unit, with bathrooms shared by no more than two people.

Fourwinds will rival all other luxury housing for students on college campuses. We will offer every imaginable service and amenity, including modern designer furniture with a "turn–key" experience. Our units will be the talk of the town when students are living large and investors are reaping the

benefits of a captured audience demanding the best and willing to pay what it takes. This is a sound investment for anyone wanting to get involved in real estate or wanting to diversify their portfolio.

Another important trend related to our product is the enrollment and growth trends of the university that we locate near. University of Louisville recently released official censes figures which show the largest enrollment ever. A total of 11,145 students are participating in classes at the university. The previous record for overall University of Louisville enrollment was set in 2005 at 11,112 students. This year's freshman class made enrollment history. The University also received a record number of enrollment applications allowing them to be more selective.

Current University of Louisville housing arrangements can only house 3,437 students. This is merely 30 percent of the total university population. This is all the housing University of Louisville currently offers and as the trend continues to turn to off–campus housing we do not foresee any additional housing being added to the University's campus. In fact, several of the apartments will be torn down to make way for the new arena. This is further evidence as to why we foresee this project being a sound investment.

We have two separate sets of customers. One is our investment customer and the other is our residential tenant customer. Our investment customer is one who wants to purchase one of our apartment units as an investment. One customer segment would be parents of students because they have an understanding of university housing and are aware of the profits in off–campus student housing. A second customer segment would be real estate investors looking for rental property because our apartment units function similarly to other rental property except that they take advantage of being located near universities, which typically sustain high housing demands. These investors would be looking for hassle free investments which take little time involvement. Our investment customers would be described as middle to upper class with high disposable incomes. Many of them would be parents of at least one college–aged child. The parent segment would be located throughout the United States but would have a child attending the university were our development is located. The real estate investors looking for rental property would typically be located within driving distance of our development.

Our second set of customers is residential tenants. Our main customer segment here is students who attend the university by which we are located. Typically, they would range from undergraduate sophomores up to graduate students and already live on campus. These students would be looking for more space and more comfort. We would target both males and females. Another important aspect of this customer segment is the parents. In most cases, the parents will be the ones who actually pay the rent and give the finally authorization so we must not only attract students but must assure parents that their children will be safe and have a great place to live and learn. These parents will need to be open–minded to allowing their child to live off campus. A second customer segment for residential tenants will be employees of the university, such as professors or doctors and nurses of a university hospital. This segment will be characterized by people who want to have the convenience of living near their job. Due to the luxurious style and amenities of our buildings our tenants will be middle to upper class with high disposable incomes.

MARKET ANALYSIS

The United States real estate market has seen a decline in new housing construction in 2006. The Commerce Department said October housing starts came in at an annual pace of 1.486 million units, compared with a pace of 1.74 million units in September. Economists had forecasted October housing starts to fall to 1.690 million units from September's originally reported pace of 1.772 million. These statistics compared to October of 2005, 2.046 million units, show housing starts were down 27.4 percent. This slow down could be because new construction inventory homes has increased and that

they are not currently selling. We can speculate that with this slow down in new construction that it will help home builders sell some of their existing inventory.

The real estate market in Louisville around the campus and the Louisville metropolitan area has been on the decline for the past year. From November 17, 2004, through November 17, 2005, the sold properties in the residential area that consisted of a 1.5 mile radius around the campus had an average of 85 consecutive days on market with a median sale price of $303,583. Comparing this to the statistics from November 17, 2005, to November 17 2006, there was a slight rise to 106 consecutive days on market with a drop in the median sale price to $274,050.

These statistics show that homes are staying on the market a little bit longer and are not selling for as much as they were a year ago. This shows that there has been a change in what would be considered a sellers market last year to what is currently a buyers market. Home owners who are selling are lowering there prices in an attempt to attract more potential buyers and buyers are aware that they now have more negotiating power when they are writing an offer on a home. As a result the buyer will generally be able to purchase the home for a lower price than they would have been able to a year ago.

The chart below shows what the Louisville market looked like for the past year. The "other" section of the graph constitutes all the expired, withdrawn, and temporary off the market listings.

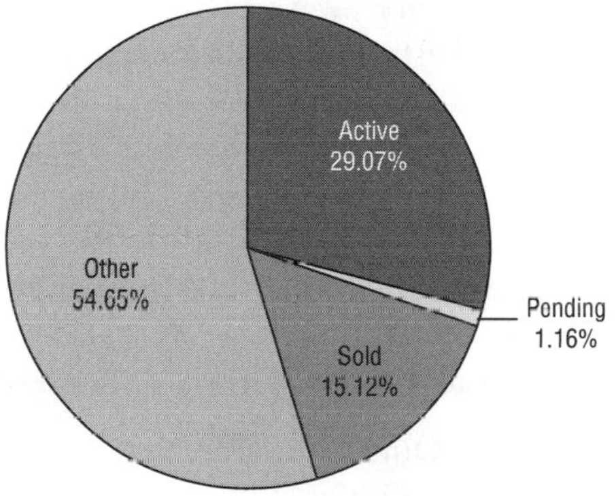

The property management and rental industry in the Louisville area is also slow. With the interest rates being at historic lows for the past few years, people who were not initially able to afford a home now were able. This has lead to less people renting, resulting in a large inventory of vacant homes waiting to be rented. Another factor that has lead to a higher inventory is that some of the people who have failed at their attempt to sell their house are putting there house up for rent. This has a negative effect on the market because landlords have to lower their price in order to attract more potential tenants.

In contrast to the greater Louisville area, the area directly surrounding University of Louisville has a very strong rental market. There are 11 main apartment complexes in the area that are composed of a little over 1,300 combined rental units. The majority of these complexes are completely rented out and some even have a waiting list for future occupancy. Due to the strong demand, these complexes are able to charge an inflated rental rate.

Growth Strategy

Despite all of the negatives in the housing and the property management markets, the specific areas on which we want to concentrate are around college campuses that have a housing shortage. University of

Louisville is one of these areas in which there is not enough housing to cover the demand and as a result students are paying a premium for rent.

Currently there are more than 7,000 undergraduates and 4,000 graduates attending school at University of Louisville, which is a record for the school. University of Louisville only has student housing that will cater to around 3,437 students which leaves over 7,000 students to fend for themselves. The area that directly surrounds the university only has about 1,300 units to cover the over flow.

Besides the shortage of housing for students around campus, the city of Louisville has identified a 246 acre biotech corridor that will be developing in the Midtown area. The majority of this corridor will be located directly west of the university and east of the hospital. There is also talk of a second biotech campus that will be 73 acres surrounding the University Medical Campus.

This new biotech campus has the capacity to change the Midtown market. Thomassman, who currently is one of the largest investors in the biotech corridor, is developing a $36 million dollar state–of–the–art biotech building right down the street from the university. With companies investing millions of dollars in this area there is definitely a chance that the Midtown market will improve in the future.

Currently in progress adjacent to University of Louisville's campus are two large developments, The Towers and Stonewall. The Towers, which is located on College Street, north of the main campus, is an older building that is going to be converted into condominiums. These condominiums will be starting at around $120,000 for a studio and will go up from there. The renovation has not begun but is expected to start in the spring of 2008. Stonewall, located off Appleby Street next to Emily's Diner, is going to be a 242 unit loft/apartment complex. This complex is still under construction and is planning to be finished prior to the fall 2007 school year. We believe that the building that we would develop and the differentiating features and benefits it would offer will directly cater to students' needs and would increase demand for our units to a higher point than our competitors' units.

Competition

Both the investment aspect and student housing aspect of our product will encounter competition. Competitors on the investment side include investing in stocks, bonds, mutual funds, CDs, and other real estate investments such as rental houses or condominium–hotels. Our product differentiates itself by offering a unique way of investing and another chance to diversify an existing portfolio. It takes advantage of the current trends in real estate investing and combines them with investing in apartment complexes that are near universities. This offers less risk because housing near universities is typically in high demand and will allow for a more predictable and stable level of return. In addition, investing in rental property such as ours provides certain tax advantages, such as deductions for mortgage interest. Also, our competition is unable to consciously compete with us. For example, stocks cannot knowingly increase their prices in order to give a higher rate of return and attract more investors.

Next, we look at competition in regards to the student housing aspect of our product. The first competitive force that we must consider is the university that we locate near because it has the ability to control the market due to its unique relationship to the students and parents and its large percentage of housing when compared to off–campus competitors.

At the University of Louisville market the university controls 53 percent of the units as shown in the graph below.

Percentage of units per competitor

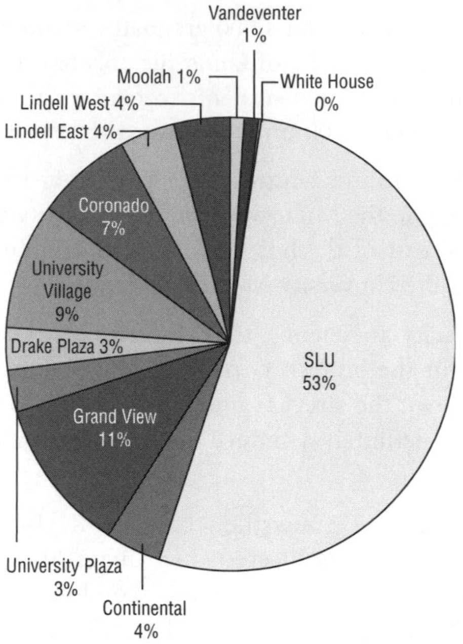

Even though the university is unable to house all of its students, it is still able to put competitive pressure on off–campus housing. For example, it has significant control over pricing. The off–campus competitors set their rent prices at a point where a tenant with roommates is able to pay about the same price to live off campus as it would take to live on campus. If the university changes its room rates then the off–campus competitors may need to change their rents to match. This actually occurred at University of Louisville. Students entering University of Louisville in the 2006–2007 school year would have $2,000 of their scholarship tied to room and board. If a student did not live on campus then $2,000 of their scholarship money would be taken away. This was done in response to the trend of students moving off–campus after freshman year. This was successful with some students whose parents would not allow them to move off campus due to the loss of scholarship money. However, the off–campus competitors showed no sign of concern and made no decreases in their pricing. In fact, rent increased at many of the off–campus competitors and wait lists continued to grow. This shows that there is still are a large portion of the market willing to pay a premium for more spacious and luxurious accommodations. Also, the university realized that their decision to subsidize living on campus through scholarship money could not be sustained because there is not enough campus housing to accommodate all students. This resulted in the repeal of the earlier decision to tie $2,000 of scholarship money to housing. For the 2007–2008 school year, no scholarship money will be directly tied to on–campus living. According to the current Student Government Association President Bob Tribek, the university does not view off–campus housing as a competitor but as a partner. University of Louisville recognizes the need of off–campus housing to accommodate its growing student body.

Next, we will look at the off–campus competitors around the university. They play a major role in our project because they dictate the kind of amenities that are required as a minimum for our building but also show us what amenities are lacking that we can provide as a means of differentiation. Their response to our entry into the market is limited because they will not easily be able to add the student–focused amenities that we will be offering, such as our lounge and breakout study rooms and the unique styling of our units. With the growing enrollment at University of Louisville and increasing demand for housing, it will be unlikely that a price war will initiate. With most buildings having wait lists, there is still enough room in the market for more housing. The following graph shows the percentage of units per building when we remove the university from the market.

Percentage of units per off-campus building

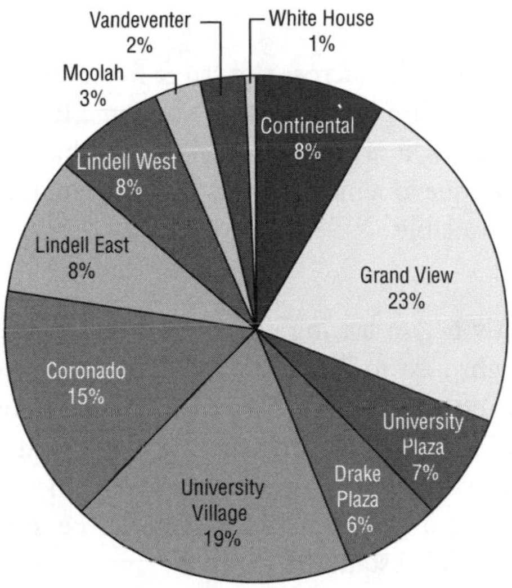

With the university removed from the market there is less concentration of units in one particular building. However, this means that differentiation becomes more important because we must compete with off–campus competitors by offering amenities that the students desire more and for which they are willing to pay more. The following is a discussion of off–campus apartment buildings that are considered the first alternatives to on–campus living at University of Louisville.

Stained Glass House:
The Stained Glass House is an art deco skyscraper located at the corner of Smith and Walnut, behind the hospital. It contains 107 units including efficiencies and one, two, and three bedroom apartments. This building welcomes student residents but limits them to the bottom eight floors of the building. Also, it is not directly across the street from the main campus. Students would have to walk about one block north to get there. Currently, there are four vacant units.

Gas is the only utility included with rent. Residents are responsible for a portion of electric, sewer, trash, and water. Cable television is supplied by Cook Communications and is paid by the resident. Internet and phone are available through the Stained Glass House's leasing office but for an extra fee. Some unique amenities available to residents are Bocce court, concierge, boardroom, party room, ice makers in refrigerators, and conditioned storage lockers for an extra charge.

Brown Tower:
Brown Tower is the newest apartment building to open around University of Louisville and is located on Greenfield Avenue behind Brad's Books. It contains 300 units including 320 square'foot studios and 520 square'foot one bedrooms. They are currently running a promotion of $100 dollars off each month's rent for the first three months. This building is not located in the most desirable place for students because it is located in an area with a stigma for crime and is a longer walk to classes than other available off–campus competitors. Also, its smaller units limit it to students who want to live by themselves rather than having roommates. However, all utilities are included in the rent. Some unique amenities available to residents are a 24–hour doorperson and a lounge/billiard room.

Brookside Village:
Brookside Village is located on the corner of Pine and Elm, behind the Medical Library. It contains 87 two bedroom apartments that range from 818 to 956 square feet with a 99 percent occupancy rate. This building is about a two block walk from campus, which is the farthest away, and many would not advise making this walk at night. Water, sewer, and trash are included in the rent. Cable television, telephone, and internet are paid by the resident. A unique amenity of this building is a jazz restaurant on the ground floor named Pianos at Brookside.

Country View Place:
Country View Place is located at the corner of Howard and Miller, across the street from the University of Louisville education building, which makes it a great location for education students. It contains 77 units including one and two bedroom apartments. Currently, it is completely filled and has a wait list. Water, sewer, and trash are included in the rent. Some unique amenities of this building are that it is all electric, has a swimming pool, and storage lockers are available.

Stonewall Apartments:
Stonewall is still under construction and has just recently begun leasing apartments. It is scheduled to open in January 2007. It is located on Appleby Street, right next to Emily's Diner. This is great location for students because it is across the street from campus and is located next to the university's two main bars, Emily's Diner and Whiskeytown Bar and Grill. The building contains 242 units and includes mainly one and two bedroom apartments and one four bedroom apartment. Internet, cable television, water, sewer, and trash will be included in the rent. Some unique amenities that will be available to residents are a swimming pool, game room, coffee shop, and restaurant.

Stonewall formed a partnership with the School of Economics. Forty–one of the units will be designated as housing for University of Louisville economics students. These apartments will be used to form a community for economics students who can share common meeting rooms, meditation areas, and kitchens.

Managed Properties:
The following properties are managed by Town Management, LLC. These properties are the most significant off–campus competitor because each property is located directly across the street from campus and they do the most to tailor to student tenants, such as security that understands and manages college parties and allowing deposits to be put down on apartments in order to hold them until the students can move off campus at the end of the school year.

Ashton Park:
Ashton Park is a 200 unit building located on Brownell across from the School of Business. It contains studios and one, two, and three bedroom apartments. However, the majority are two bedrooms. It is completely filled and has a wait list. The apartments in this building are very close together and some tenants complain of too much noise from neighboring units.

Utilities included in the rent are local telephone service, internet, recycling service, water, sewer, trash, gas, electric, and basic cable. Some unique amenities are an on–site ATM, bike racks, ballroom, arcade/game room, swimming pool, a restaurant, a bakery, and meeting center.

Holloway East:
Holloway East is located to the immediate west of the Ashton Park. This tower contains 110 apartments made up of one and three bedrooms. However, the majority are one bedroom apartments. The building is currently filled and has a wait list.

Utilities included in the rent are local telephone service, internet, recycling service, water, sewer, trash, gas, electric, and basic cable. Some unique amenities include bike racks and a swimming pool.

Holloway West:
Holloway West is located beside Holloway East. It contains 100 units including studios, one bedroom, and two bedroom apartments. Currently, it is fully occupied and has a wait list.

Utilities included in the rent are local telephone service, internet, recycling service, water, sewer, trash, gas, electric, and basic cable. Some unique amenities available to residents include a rooftop terrace, bike racks, and a swimming pool.

Freize Towers:
Frieze Towers is located on Haught, just west of Holloway Towers. It is home to the Frieze Theater and Lounge and the Frieze Lanes bowling alley. It contains forty units consisting of studios and one, two, and three bedroom apartments. However, the majority are three bedrooms. This building is known for its larger than average apartments. It is fully occupied and has a wait list.

Utilities included are internet, basic cable, local telephone, water, trash, sewer, and recycling services. Some unique amenities available to residents include a washer and dryer in each unit, bike racks, billiards and arcade, a swimming pool, and an on–site ATM.

Skyscape:
Skyscape is located on Campus Drive to the immediate east of Frieze Towers. It is designed for residents who want a quiet place to live and study. It is primarily occupied by graduate students. It contains twelve units including studios and one bedroom apartments and is fully occupied. Utilities included are gas, water, trash, sewer, basic cable, internet, and recycling services. Some unique amenities of this property include a swimming pool and a bike rack.

Brownstone Place:
Brownstone Place is located at the corner of Brownstone and Graham. It contains 30 units consisting of two and three bedroom apartments. It is viewed as the low cost option for off–campus housing. Currently, it is filled. Utilities included are water, sewer, and trash. A unique amenity that is included is a security system in each unit.

Additional Competition
One additional competitor to take into consideration is the idea of living at home or with relatives in the area. Students living at home represent potential for growth if we can attract them to living on their own and benefiting from the convenience of living next to campus in their own place.

GROWTH STRATEGY

Feasibility

We believe that this project is a GO. Based on the current housing demand near University of Louisville, the trends in campus living and real estate investing, the income bracket of many University of Louisville families, and the ability to duplicate this concept in other markets we feel that our idea is not only feasible but profitable.

Further Information Needed

We will need some more information to move forward. First, to proceed with the project in Louisville, we will have to know the exact price of the land. This initial purchase will be the first thing for which we need funding. Then we will have to find an architect to design the floor plans. With a specific floor plan drawn we can obtain exact bids on the cost of building.

As we work on the project in Louisville, the research process should continue in other cities. As stated earlier in our study, there are four phases to our project: design, develop, manage, and duplicate. In the duplicate phase we want to find new locations to expand into with a major university, steady growth in their incoming classes, on–campus housing that is at or near capacity, and available land that is large enough to accommodate our building and within walking distance of the campus. We would have to find a project supervisor for each city we expanded to or have one member of our team be project supervisor for each city (allowing us to work in up to five cities at once).

Additional Support

We will need a lot of additional support. We will need to find one main investor to be the initial investor. Once we have that investment to purchase the land and design the floor plan we will need to gain the support of a financial institution to gain a construction loan. The investor will need to continue to provide financial support and guidance.

A consideration for each new city we look into will be whether or not we can gain support from the university for which we are looking to provide housing. One of the first places we have discussed would be University of Kentucky, but if the administration of UK does not cooperate with us, we will never be able to move forward. We will have to be far enough into the plan at University of Louisville for the banks and construction companies in a new city to take us seriously and want to do the project in their city.

Also, the cost of living in one of our units will be higher than some of the other off–campus options. By charging higher rates, as stated earlier, the “slum lord” mentality can be avoided. Establishing a connection at each university where we are hoping to expand housing will be crucial. We will need to have someone within the university to find information about student and family demographics, housing needs, willingness to pay higher rents, and the general attitude of students.

Childrens' Indoor Recreation Center

INTERACTIVE GARDEN

6700 West Smithers Rd.
Portage, Indiana 46368

Gerald Rekve

A new business concept exists to service children aged 13 and under with a supervised indoor exercise and recreation facility. Market research shows that children often do not get the required amount of exercise to maintain a healthy lifestyle. Interactive Garden facilities provide an outlet for active children during poor weather or when the temperature is too hot or cold for outdoor play. Furthermore, parents want an environment for their children to play without harsh language and an arcade atmosphere.

BUSINESS OVERVIEW

Interactive Garden will provide a safe, clean, and stimulating environment for physically active children aged 13 and under to play in and explore. Interactive Garden's supervised, visually open play area will ensure children's safety, while challenging them to reach, think, interact, explore, and have fun. The store will require approximately 11,000 square feet, consisting of a giant 5,000 square foot play structure for children over the age of 4, a smaller play area for toddlers under the age of 4, an area with several interactive skill games, a snack bar with seating to accommodate 100 to 125 persons at a time, and a merchandise and souvenir stand. Both play areas have soft indoor play park equipment with extensive padding and no sharp edges. Furthermore, the game area will not offer video games, pinball–type games or games with a violent theme. For family celebrations, such as birthdays and special occasions, Interactive Garden will offer private party rooms hosted by trained staff to provide a child everything he/she would want in a birthday—several hours of supervised fun on the play structures, cake and ice cream, prizes, food and beverage, and game tokens. Interactive Garden desires playtime to be as rewarding for the parents as it is for the children, as they spend time together.

OPERATIONS

Location

Interactive Garden will be located in a recreation center on the west side of Portage, Indiana. Within a twenty–five mile drive from this location, there are at least 49,000 children at or under the age of 14, living in a household with average annual income exceeding $45,000. Furthermore, the Census Bureau expects the communities of Merrillville and Portage to be the fastest growing regions of Porter and Lake Counties over the next decade.

The nature and location of Interactive Garden's business will support both destination and walk–in shopping. Since the majority of birthday parties are pre–planned events, the exact location of Interactive Garden with respect to major shopping centers is not as critical as it is in other retail businesses. However, parents who are shopping with their children may desire an outlet for their children in the form of indoor exercise and recreation. Once customers are aware of Interactive Garden's location, they will return again and again. Figures from the corporate store indicate an average return rate of seven times per child per year. Our financial forecasts conservatively project 1/3 less. The awareness of our location will develop over several months due to advertising, word of mouth, and simple observation by shoppers in the area.

Interactive Garden will be located in Portage on West Smithers Road in the Copperwood Shopping Center. This shopping center consists of two separate buildings totaling 73,480 square feet of rental space and contains both destination and walk–by businesses. The center is primarily focused on providing family–related services to the local community. Within three miles of this location, census data indicates there are 9,854 children under the age of 14. Within five miles of this location, census data indicates there are 23,061 children under the age of 14. In addition, there are several elementary schools located in the proximity, a day care center directly behind the shopping center, and many other child–related businesses within a few blocks along West Smithers Rd. in either direction.

To better ensure Interactive Garden's success, the franchisor, Sweet Childhoods USA, must approve the final location and subject it to their proprietary location requirements.

Management Summary

The business will be operated on a full–time basis by a manager, Allison Schafer, who has had over five years of restaurant management experience. In addition, all member–managers will actively assist in the management of the business on a part–time basis.

FINANCIAL ANALYSIS

Start–Up Costs

The owners are requesting a loan to fund a portion of the start–up costs and inventory. They are also requesting a line of credit in the amount of $500,000. The owners are contributing $35,000 to the business venture and various investors are contributing another $40,000. The money will be needed in equal monthly installments commencing three months prior to opening and will be repaid in a steady manner from available operating cash flows. The loan will be entirely repaid within five years after opening with payments beginning three months after opening.

BUSINESS STRATEGY

Interactive Garden is a diversified destination family entertainment center combining recreation, entertainment, and restaurant facilities that creates substantial drawing power. Interactive Garden's basic focus is children's play and fitness for 1 to 13 year old children. At Interactive Garden, these activities have been packaged into a safe, clean, climate–controlled, supervised environment for children aged 13 and under to exercise and have fun while stimulating their imagination and challenging them physically. The indoor playpark is based on the premise that if you set a large number of children inside a safe, yet challenging, imaginative soft recreation facility area, they are going to have fun. They are also going to develop basic motor skills, social skills, muscle tone, and self–confidence. Furthermore, the parents can enjoy hours of close interaction with their children in a safe, secure, and stimulating environment.

Currently, there are no other indoor children playgrounds in the Western Indiana area. In addition, there are relatively few alternatives for children's birthday parties. Interactive Garden will be able to immediately fill this void in the market by providing extensive recreation, entertainment, and restaurant facilities for children to play in and explore. Within 1 year, Interactive Garden will be known as the primary recreation facility for children aged 1 to 13 and the destination of choice for children to enjoy birthday parties with friends. Interactive Garden's safe, secure, and clean environment will reassure parents while providing opportunities for their children to have fun in a stimulating environment.

Interactive Garden will base its appeal on providing a stimulating indoor environment for children to play in, while adhering to the strictest quality control standards emphasizing excellence in service, safety, security, food quality and value, sanitation, cleanliness, and creativity. Furthermore, Interactive Garden is dedicated to the continual development of creative themes and interactive designs that have entertainment and educational value that will ensure Interactive Garden's competitiveness and success in the family entertainment market years into the future.

MARKET ANALYSIS

Interactive Garden Indoor Recreation facilities serve an increasing need in our society. Studies show that American children are less active and less fit than they were even five years ago, probably due to increasing time in front of television sets and high–calorie/high–fat diets. Studies have also shown that less active children are more likely to be overweight, and overweight children have a greater propensity to become overweight adults. As people have become more aware of the healthy aspects of their lifestyles, enrollment in adult health clubs, aerobic exercise, recreational activities, and attention to nutrition has increased dramatically. This trend will continue as parents attempt to provide a healthier lifestyle for their children. Another area of parental concern is their children's safety. Nationally, as well as locally, concern for the physical well–being of children has created a further need for a safe play environment. This concern shows no sign of diminishing.

While it is difficult to determine the size of the Interactive Garden Indoor Recreation facility industry, there are currently about 49 million children 12 years old or younger in the United States and this figure is expected to rise to 51 million by the year 2000, according to the Bureau of Census. There are approximately 26 million households with children younger than 18 years of age, who spend about $1,800 per year on family entertainment or $46 billion annually. Per–capita expenditures on children's activities are likely to rise as families with children spend a larger percentage of their income on recreation. Children aged 4–12 spent, from their own income, $6 billion in 1989, up 41 percent from 1984. This increase in discretionary income is coming from several factors. First, the increase in dual income families has provided for more discretionary income to be spent on children. Second, women are having children later as evidenced by the rising birth rate among women in their thirties. Third, per–capita family income is increasing and families are choosing to take wealth increases in the form of leisure. Last, grandparents are living longer and spending more on their grandchildren. Based on these demographics, industry analysts believe that there is room for about 600 store locations in primary markets throughout the United States and an additional 200–300 in secondary markets.

Customers

With the recent concerns over child safety on outdoor recreation facility equipment, many schools have elected to remove their recreation facility equipment entirely. Parents are more aware than ever before over the safety and security of their children's play areas. Consequently, a safe, supervised indoor play area will enable parents to relax while their children enjoy playing in and exploring the soft indoor play park.

Interactive Garden will target children aged 13 and under within a 25–minute drive of Portage, comprising about 250,000 people of which at least 49,000 are under the age of 13. Within a five–mile radius of Portage, census information indicates there are approximately 23,000 children aged 13 and under, living in a household with an average annual income exceeding $55,000. These customers will form Interactive Garden's primary market base. Interactive Garden will also target children in the outlying regions of Porter County.

Unique Market Characteristics

Weekly Usage Patterns

With 60 to 65 percent of the costs fixed and only 35 to 40 percent variable, even small increases in capacity utilization can have a major impact on profitability. With a projected 60 percent of revenue coming from Friday through Sunday, it will be important to effectively utilize capacity on weekdays. Interactive Garden will provide the following services to increase customer usage during this period: group discounts to day care centers, churches, community groups, schools, etc., a frequent user card to encourage repeat customer visits, nutritious food to attract health–conscious families, and promoting birthday parties during the week.

Seasonality

The winter months are usually the strongest, and the beginning of spring and the beginning of the school year are usually the weakest periods. On a quarterly basis, Interactive Garden's best quarter should be the first, followed by the third, second, and fourth quarters. To manage this seasonal variation in customer demand, management will actively monitor weekly sales volume and maintain a flexible staffing arrangement.

Threat of a Fad Product

There is a risk that children may tire of the concept of indoor padded playgrounds. To keep the concept fresh, Interactive Garden will strive to introduce new play equipment, skill games, and/or new marketing concepts annually. In addition, the franchisor is committed to ongoing research and development in the area of child interaction and stimulation through consultation with staff child psychologists.

Safety/Liability Concerns

To reduce the potential for injuries and lawsuits, Interactive Garden will employ every means possible to protect children from hurting themselves on the play equipment. Interactive Garden will only utilize the softest and most extensively–padded equipment in the industry. Furthermore, Interactive Garden will employ trained staff to continuously monitor each play area and enforce the rules of the playpark. The playpark will be designed to provide parental viewing on all sides and at all times. Parents will also be encouraged to play in the equipment with their children (knee pads will be available for a nominal charge.) In addition, security wristbands will be issued to each person upon entering to ensure the child's safety and prohibit stranger abduction of children. Strict security measures will be observed at all times. Interactive Garden will carry a $1 million per occurrence liability insurance policy in the event of lawsuit.

PRODUCTS & SERVICES

Interactive Garden is geared for children 13 years old or younger who desire an imaginative, challenging, and fun environment in which to exercise, play, and explore. For safety, children must be accompanied by an adult in order to be admitted and adults are not permitted to enter without a child. Furthermore, each person admitted to the play park will receive a color–coded wristband identifying him/her with rest of the party. To further promote security, each person's wristband will only be removed when the entire party is present together at the exit desk. Trained staff will supervise the play areas at all times to ensure adherence to the play park rules while assisting the children to maximize their enjoyment of the facilities.

There will be several play areas within Interactive Garden; the largest, a 5,000 square foot structure targeting children aged 4 and over, will be comprised of a series of colorful tubes, slides, ball baths, climbing structures, air and water trampolines, obstacle courses, ramps, and stairs. A smaller play area will cater to toddlers and consist of cushions, ramps, a small ball bin, and toys. To encourage active participation by parents, all play areas will have a visually open design with comfortable rest areas in full view of the play structures.

Interactive Garden will also be equipped with a smaller area of interactive games designed to promote eye and hand coordination. This area will include the "Magic Keyboard", a unique piece of musical play equipment specifically designed for Interactive Garden parents. Children can also play several games of skill to win tickets redeemable for prizes. There will also be a snack bar with seating for 100 to 125 customers at a time. It will serve food and beverages that appeal to children and parents such as pizza, hot dogs, salads, sandwiches, popcorn, pop, fruit juice, cappuccino, cake, and ice cream. In addition, Interactive Garden will have a merchandise counter with small souvenirs emblazoned with the Interactive Garden logo such as T–shirts, sweaters, and hats.

Interactive Garden will have six private party rooms and will offer packages for birthdays and other special occasions hosted by staff members, significantly reducing the hassle and mess for parents. The design of the rooms will allow for groups as large as 30 children at a time. For family celebrations, Interactive Garden will offer three birthday packages for parties of 8 of more, consisting of a two hour limited time of play, birthday cake and ice cream, free game tokens, and, depending on the type of package, pizza or hot dogs, party favors for the guests, and a special gift for the birthday child.

Interactive Garden will strive to appeal to value–oriented customers who desire hours of entertainment for their children at reasonable prices. Interactive Garden will be competitively priced at $4.95 for unlimited play which is comparable to other forms of entertainment. However, the distinguishing feature of Interactive Garden will be its clean, safe, secure environment for children to play in while parents can either relax or participate in their child's activities.

MARKETING & SALES

Pricing & Profitability

Interactive Garden will derive its sales revenues from admissions, games of skill, restaurant/snack bar operations, birthday party packages, and gift shop and souvenir sales.

Admissions and Games

Admission fees will be $1.99 per child (ages 1–15) which includes unlimited play in all of the play areas. Adults will be admitted free of charge and encouraged to play in the play areas with their children. This price compares favorably to other forms of family entertainment such as movies where both adults and children must pay admission. The goal of Interactive Garden is for a visit to the play park to become a regular family event. Reflecting this goal, a frequent user card will enable a customer to receive discounts off future admissions to Interactive Garden after a specified number of paid admissions to the playpark. Statistics from the corporate location show the average child returning seven times per year. In addition, Interactive Garden will offer group discounts for groups of 12 or more at $3.35 per person to encourage day care centers, youth group activities, and summer camps to visit the playpark. For larger groups of 30 or more children, Interactive Garden offers a special package at $5.00 per child that includes unlimited play in the playpark, two game tokens per child, a slice of pizza or a hot dog, and a beverage.

Advertising

Interactive Garden will reach its target customers through such advertising media as local newspapers, local television, and direct mail campaigns. Local television advertising has been found to be very effective in reaching the target market segment of children 13 and under, so we will focus our efforts here. The advertising and promotion campaign will be funded through operating cash flows and will build upon the close proximity of the store to the corporate location. In addition, the franchisor will assist its franchisees through regional advertising programs to obtain synergy among all franchisees within the region. Interactive Garden will initially promote its concept through a Grand Opening advertisement campaign employing an invitation–only free evening for local business and government leaders and their children as well as local radio coverage. The franchisor will assist in the preparation of initial advertising and scheduling of promotions.

Competition

Competition in the children's recreation and entertainment industry consists of a highly diverse group of children's activities, including television, libraries, YMCAs, health clubs, parks and other recreation centers, movies, the zoo, and related activities. All of these activities provide for enjoyment by both the parents and the children. However, an Interactive Garden indoor recreation facility offers a safe, clean indoor environment for physical activity that is specifically designed for children. It provides children with the security and the skill development opportunities parents desire. Presently, there are no indoor children's playgrounds operating in the Portage area. Within a 25–minute drive from Portage are three primary competitors. After reviewing the characteristics and environment of each of these competitors, we believe that Interactive Garden offers several advantages over the existing competitors. First, Interactive Garden offers the lowest admission price, charging $4.95 per child, of any establishment dedicated to providing an extensive indoor recreation facility. Second, Interactive Garden encourages parents to participate in their children's recreational activities through a careful layout of the play park which ensures high–visibility of the play areas and close proximity for the parents. Third, Interactive Garden is the only indoor recreation facility that provides such unique play equipment as the Magic Keyboard, an air mattress, and games of skill that are specifically designed to promote child development. Fourth, Interactive Garden goes to extra lengths to ensure the safety and security of the environment by providing such extras as CPR certification for all employees of a certain level, video monitors of the entire play park, and strictly controlling the entrances and exits to Interactive Garden. Lastly, with the corporate Sweet Childhood USA location being so close to Chicago, name recognition should be high, as many of the potential customers have already been to the existing Interactive Garden location.

The other Interactive Garden's primary focus is on an extensive array of video games, mini–rides, interactive skill games, a puppet show, and food. Although it has a small play park area for toddlers, this location is primarily dedicated to food service and games. Consequently, it serves as a destination business for pre–planned visits, centered around its food service for family outings and birthday parties. It is an open layout with more windows than other children's entertainment centers and has the atmosphere of a large noisy cafeteria. It charges no entry fee, but maintains high prices for its pizza, ice cream, and beverages. Catering more to parents, it allows smoking and serves alcoholic beverages along with pizza, hot dogs, and nachos. It does not instill a sense of security for the parents, nor does it provide the challenging and stimulating environment that children desire.

Corner Store

MARTIN GENERAL STORE

20982 Onooto Rd.
Plymouth, Massachusetts 02360

Gerald Rekve

BUSINESS OVERVIEW

Business Description

Type of business: Grocery/Corner Store

Business Structure: Sole Proprietorship

Owner: Tom Martin

Products & Services

Martin General Store will be a full-time Corner Store operating 7 days a week, from 7:00 a.m.–12:00 p.m. selling pop/chips; toys; taxable cigarettes; and food products.

The store will offer friendly and personalized service, reasonably priced merchandise, tax exemption for status customers and a convenient location.

Mission

Martin General Store will strive to provide superior customer service and the highest quality groceries at an affordable price, while operating as a profit and growth oriented business.

Operations

The store will be located in a building that will be renovated and equipped with the necessary furnishings, shelving and plumbing. The approximate square footage of the unit is 1,400 square feet. The unit will have 3 rooms, consisting of an office, washroom and the retail store area.

Martin General Store is prepared to purchase the equipment and inventory necessary to begin operations immediately, upon approval of funding. Tom Martin recognized a need for a store in the area after a neighboring store closed. Tom Martin conducted a resident's survey asking about the need for a corner store and the community overwhelmingly supported the concept. There are no such stores within a 22–block radius, and the target market will include local residents.

The store will be situated in a 1,000 square foot building that is owned by the principal, it will be renovated with the appropriate shelving, refrigeration and cash counters required for operation. It is fully wired for electrical, security, and phones. The building will consist of 3 rooms–an office, a washroom and the main store area. The Principal, Tom Martin will, upon approval of funding, renovate the building, and purchase the necessary equipment and inventory. The Plymouth City Chief and Council have provided their full support and verbally agreed to support this venture.

Tom Martin seeks a $25,000.00 loan to establish a corner store. In addition Tom Martin will contribute $10,000.00 equity for a total project cost of $35,000.00, for which Tom Martin will renovate his building, install shelving, a cooler, air conditioner, cash counter, install signage and purchase inventory.

Production Process

Daily retail operations will consist of the following:

Business start up costs

1. Renovations	$ 120,000.00
2. Inventory	$ 15,000.00
3. Shelving	$ 4,500.00
4. Cooler lease deposit	$ 1,200.00
5. Air conditioner	$ 4,000.00
6. Signage	$ 6,000.00
7. Cash counter	$ 1,500.00
8. Operating capital	$ 500.00
Total	**$152,700.00**

Description of facility requirements

Electronic equipment:

Existing equipment	Value	Required equipment	Budget cost
Computer	$ 900.00	Air Conditioner	$500
Printer	$ 400.00		
Automobile	$2,000.00		
Software	$5,000.00		
Total:	**$8,300.00**	**Total:**	**$8,800.00**

Furniture/Fixtures:

Required furniture/fixtures	Budget cost
Shelving	$1,231.00
Signage	$ 500.00
Cash counter	$ 500.00
Total:	**$2,231.00**

- Open store, disarm alarm.
- Cash count, turn on necessary machinery, debit machine, etc.
- Do books from previous day, check inventory, order more stock if necessary.
- Handle sales.
- Close out cash and balance.
- Close store, arm alarm.

Business will commence operations based on the following work plan:

- Secure building, gut/renovate building.
- Installation of equipment necessary for business operations: Store shelving, cash counter, cash register, and debit machine.

Management Summary

Martin General Store will have 6 employees, one full–time and 5 part–time. Tom Martin will be the sole owner and primary operator for Martin General Store. Tom Martin has extensive retail experience in the retail grocery business as a supervisor for a local supermarket and has worked at a high volume hardware–store and also a government liquor store. He has identified four primary categories of product: pop/chips; toys; taxable cigarettes and food products.

Mrs. Smith will assist in daily operations of the store, and will handle bookkeeping and financial reporting. Within five years it is anticipated that the company would analyze the viability of hiring more part–time employees for 4 hours per day; however at this time there are no plans to hire any more employees within the first three years of business.

Management team background and experiences
Tom Martin has extensive retail experience that is crucial to the type of business he is opening. Mr. Martin's experience includes work at a retail grocery store, a high volume hardware store (sundry) sales, and liquor store sales. He has worked in retail sales for 12 years and is experienced with all aspects of daily operations including ordering, receiving, budgeting, merchandising, and daily banking. Tom Martin is particularly skilled in public relations, is very organized, is able to work independently, and is reliable, dependable and hardworking.

The experience that Tom Martin brings to the endeavor is invaluable, he has product knowledge, is familiar with large chain pricing and techniques, and their sales strategies. While working for the local grocery store Tom Martin established valuable wholesale contacts he will utilize in the new business.

MARKET ANALYSIS

Industry Sector: Retail

Over the last century, corner stores have provided a thriving service to local neighborhoods. Typically, corner stores are defined as neighborhood retail shops with a limited selection of merchandise, such as milk, bread and other household necessities. Corner stores are largely a cash–based business conveniently located for quick in and out shopping, and can be operated by two clerks. The consumer usually requires the services and products that the corner store offers on a daily, weekly or bi–weekly basis. Corner stores provide quick checkout times, extended hours of business and convenient locations. Considered a mature industry, corner stores are a powerful retailing group in the USA.

Within the industry U.S. Economic trends are similar to USA trends. A leading expert, Teri Richman, stated "That the Corner Store industry grew in 2000 in spite of high interest rates, a stagnant stock market, and a sign of an economic slowdown is a testament to the overall strength of the industry,". "It shows that the value that consumers place on the industry remains at an all–time high, and that the industry is delivering," Richman added. "No matter what the size of the Corner Store—whether it is a one–store operation or a company of several thousand, there is one consistent element: A Corner Store is an anchor business to the neighbourhoods of America," said Richman. "With approximately 120,000 Corner Store stores nationwide, people have convenient and immediate access to food products, beverages, cash, petroleum, and any necessity item. The Corner Store has become the gas station, quick–service restaurant, bank, and water cooler of a mobile, time–hungry society."

Customers

The customers that the store will target are the local residents. The area has no other such corner store in a 22 block radius, local resident's grocery needs being filled by Foods, Safeway, or PGA Food Market, all in the town of Plymouth. A small corner store, The Colonial Food Market, located six blocks away, did exist until six months ago, when it was forced to close due to the high rent/lease costs. This business had a proven market that Martin's General Sore will capitalize upon.

Tom Martin conducted a small survey within Plymouth (250 households) and the results indicated that there was overwhelming support for a small concept of having a corner store. The question asked was "Would you be in favor and buy products from a store located in the community?" The response was extremely favorable. This community support is crucial when the primary target customers are Plymouth residents. A copy of the survey is attached in the appendices of this business plan.

The business's secondary target client group is local residents within a 4 mile radius of Plymouth, or approximately 50,000 people.

Currently there are 35 households in this community, and an additional 250–300 households within a 12 block radius and approximately 40,000 households in the Plymouth District Municipality.

According to the Plymouth Community Profile 2001, Plymouth city residents spend $40.6 million dollars per year on grocery store and other food products. Based upon the number of households and the average spending, Plymouth city residents spend $8,000 per year on grocery store and other food products. Calculating the average spending based upon 300 homes in the local area at 7 percent of average spending, it is estimated that Martin General Store could conservatively gross $150,000.00 per year.

Martin's General Store has a potential target market, as follows:

- 800 local residents within the 10–block radius
- 108 community residents
- Plymouth Band Office, 15 employees, numerous visitors
- 250 students from Woodside Elementary School, parents & staff
- 430 students from Taylor Junior Secondary School, parents & staff
- 200 local Bingo players (Bingo games are held 4 times per week at the community hall next door)
- 30 Warehouse employees (1/2 block away)

Client demographics include local residents from all age groups and socioeconomic ranges, consisting primarily of families. A large secondary target group will be children and teens that regularly purchase candy, soft drinks and other fast–grab foods.

Success Factors

The business will succeed due to a variety of factors:

- There in no competition in the targeted neighborhood.
- Mr. Martin has a strong management work ethic; currently holds 2 jobs, and has excellent references from both.
- Mr. Martin's experience in retail grocery sales.
- Mr. Martin's wholesale contacts.
- There is a proven market.
- There is a local need.
- There is proven community support.

GROWTH STRATEGY

Advertising

Martin General Store anticipates growth to be based upon two primary client groups: Plymouth city residents and local in a 22 block radius. Local business will be generated through an aggressive marketing campaign to local residents, the band office, and the local bingo hall, and local preschools.

It is anticipated that the market penetration will increase over the next five years from 5 percent of local residents spending to 10 percent, and the client market area will increase to a 15–block radius.

The average customer that the business will target will be from all age groups, with an average household income of approximately $45,514 (2001-Statistics USA). Many households have both parents in the work force, 45.6 percent of USA women with children younger than six worked outside the home (Statistics USA, 2000).

According to the Plymouth Community Profile 2001, residents spend $44 million dollars per year on grocery store and other food products. Based upon the number of households and the average spending per person, Plymouth residents spend $6,800.00 per year on grocery store and other food products. Calculating the average spending based upon 235 homes in the local area at 5 percent of average spending it is estimated that Martin General Store could conservatively gross $100,000 per year.

Martin General Store will attract local clients and foster loyalty with competitive pricing, convenient location, and friendly service. In addition, the store will offer monthly specials, drawings, and promotions.

Tom Martin may join an industry association such Retail Council of USA (for a nominal annual fee), who provides the business with cost–saving services (such as low merchant rates on credit cards) and practical advice through newsletters and workshops.

Flyers will be distributed in the local area on a monthly basis advertising specials, draws and promotions. Tom Martin will display 2 sandwich boards, one for either store end.

COMPETITION

The direct competition for Martin General Store consists of one company:

7-Eleven

Address	1234 14th Avenue, Salt Lake City, Utah
Years in business	10 years
Market share	10%
Price/strategy	Same
Product/service	Same product, lower levels of client service.
Advantages	Longer hours, greater purchasing power, variety of products, gas-bar, lottery license.
Disadvantages	Distance

Martin General Store's indirect competition is 2 large grocery retailers, as listed below:

1. USA Safeway

Address	123 Street
Years in business	22 years
Market share	10%
Price/strategy	Same
Product/service	Greater buying power and variety of products
Advantages	Longer hours, more products, large promotional sales and industry name.
Disadvantage	Distance

2. Kroger Foods

Address	222 Street
2H7	
Years in business	24 years
Market share	12%
Price/strategy	Same
Product/service	Greater buying power and variety of products
Advantages	Longer hours, more products, large promotional sales and industry name.
Disadvantage	Distance

MARKETING & SALES

Pricing will be set at 30 percent–100 percent mark–up, dependant upon the following categories:

- Pop/ Chips: 50 percent mark up
- Toys: 100 percent mark up
- Cigarettes: 40 percent mark up
- Food Products: 45 percent mark up

No credit will be offered to customers. Sales will be cash, debit card or credit card. Suppliers will be on a C.O.D. basis, until 30 net terms can be established.

Expected sales from the first three years of operations:

Year 1	Year 2	Year 3
$150,000	$200,000	$290,000

BUSINESS FEASIBILITY

Strengths

The advantage that Martin General Store has is that there is no competition within a 22 block radius. The Colonial Food Market was located in the area until 6 months ago when it went out of business, due to high lease rates at that location. Tom Martin has the advantage of being a business based on community, where rent is not a factor in operations. In addition, Tom has a strong work ethic and an ability to deal with the public in a friendly and courteous manner.

Weaknesses

One weakness is the location. The business will be located on community; therefore suppliers may be hesitant to give terms.

Opportunities

There is the opportunity to expand the product line(s) that the store carries. Martin General Store anticipates that within the first two years of operation that it may qualify for a tax–exempt tobacco license and lottery goods. There is also the potential that the business may be able to employ local people part time.

Other services being considered are:

- ATM (Automated Teller Machine)
- Flower sales
- Local crafts
- Fresh coffee

Risk Factors

The major threat is the possibility that another corner store will open in the vicinity. Tom Martin will establish a loyal customer base to alleviate transfer of customers to another business.

Tom Martin will maintain one of his jobs to ensure financial obligations are met. He is considering giving terms to the band office and other organizations to ensure a positive cash flow.

BUSINESS STRATEGY

Martin General Store will succeed due to a variety of factors:

- Local Need: The customers that the store will target are the local residents. The area has no other corner store in a 22 block radius, with local residents' grocery needs being filled by Kroger Foods, Safeway, or 7-11.
- Proven Market: A small corner store did exist in the neighbourhood until 6 months ago, when it was forced to close due to the high rent/lease costs. This business had a proven market that Martin General Store will capitalize upon.
- Management Experience: The experience that Tom Martin brings to the endeavor is invaluable; he has product knowledge, is familiar with large chain pricing and techniques, and their sales strategies. While working for the local grocery and hardware store, Martin established valuable wholesale contacts that he will utilize in the new business.In addition, Tom Martin has an excellent work ethic, having held down two jobs that provide his excellent references. Finally, with regard to management experience, Tom Martin has an excellent relationship established with the necessary suppliers for this venture.
- Community Support: Tom Martin conducted a survey within the community and the results indicated that a small corner store had overwhelming support. A copy of the survey is attached in the appendices of this business plan.

Long–range plans include the acquisition of a tax–exempt cigarette license for the community, and a lottery license (keno) from the provincial government. These are time–consuming processes, but these product lines will be applied for in the first quarter.

Location

Strategically located near the geographic center of Plymouth is the major educational, transportation, distribution, industrial and commercial center for northern and central Massachusetts.

Population

The population of Plymouth is culturally diverse, with almost 50 different ethnic origins represented. Over 65 percent of people in Plymouth over the age of 15 have attained a high school diploma or a higher level of education. Based on 2000 estimates, the population of Plymouth is just over 290,000 with a population within a 30 minute commute of 90,000. The average annual growth rate is 1.1 percent (last five years).

Age distribution

Age and gender–2000 Census

	Salt Lake City		% Distribution	
	Male	Female	AG	Utah
All ages	37,980	37,170	100.0	100.0
0–14	9,295	8,735	24.0	19.7
15–24	5,965	5,850	15.7	13.0
25–44	12,970	13,095	34.7	32.7
45–64	7,655	7,035	19.5	21.8
65+	2,100	2,450	6.1	12.8

Level of education	Percentage of population
Some high school only	30
High school graduation only	15
Some college	40
Associate degrees	10
Bachelor degree or higher	5

Top ten employers

Employer	# of Employees
School district	240
USA forest products	2,400
Salt Lake City Regional Hospital	1,400
City of Salt Lake City	1,200
Ministry of State	1,200
College of Salt Lake City	700
Utah transportation	525
University of Northern Utah	400
Other	1,290
Private	230

Local Economy

The economy of Plymouth is in transition. The local economy has traditionally been supported primarily by forestry which is currently in decline. Because of the attraction of Massachusetts and the desire to stay in the area, people have taken lower level jobs those results in a high level of underemployment.

Labor Force

The total number in the labor force is 34,990. Labor force employed is 30,000 with a unemployed labor force of 4,990. The number of people not in the labor force is 18,900. The unemployment rate in Plymouth has averaged around 11 percent in the past year. Because of our excellent educational facilities, Plymouth has a highly skilled unemployed workforce.

Cost of labor

(Wages—average starting in USA dollars)

Occupation	Wage
Customer service representative	$11.00/hour
Clerical	$16.00/hour
Fast food worker	$8.00/hour
Retail sales clerk	$8.00/hour
Minimum wage	$7.60/hour

Environmentally–Minded Residential Construction Company

Green Earth Construction

721 Fossil Dr.
Abilene, Texas 79601

Gerald Rekve

Green Earth Construction is a residential construction business that focuses on building simple, quality homes using sustainable construction materials and renewable energy systems in the foothills and mountains surrounding Abilene.

EXECUTIVE SUMMARY

Green Earth Construction is a residential construction business that focuses on building simple, quality homes using sustainable construction materials and renewable energy systems in the foothills and mountains surrounding Abilene.

A typical Green Earth product will be a 1,600 to 1,900 square–foot, simple yet elegant Texas bi–level Baratch home constructed of alternative or "green" building materials (i.e. stone, recycled gyprock, fibrous cement, and/or earth). At a price of $150,000 to $190,000 with an average utility bill of $120 a month, this home costs less to build and operate than the typical single–family house, affording the owner more discretionary income for hobbies, sports, and vacations.

Marketing & Sales

Green Earth is targeting customers who make up an under–served niche market for environmentally sound homes. Our target customers can be defined as semi retired individuals who have as a significant concern in housing a desire to be surrounded by nature, respect the environment, and preserve for the future. Given their more limited purchasing power and more vocal concern for the environment, initially most of our buyers will fall into the Baby Boomer age and income category.

Our marketing strategy is to educate, focusing on customers who are sincerely interested in this type of housing and are seeking it out, rather than trying to convince people who are not motivated by a concern for the environment. Marketing tools will be low tech/high touch methods including word–of–mouth referrals and a website that will both promote Green Earth and provide a portal to sustainable building practices. Our identity will be one of integrity, honesty, standing by our product, and living by the principles on which the business is founded.

Growth Strategy

Green Earth is a developing business. The principal, Richard Brummer's goal for Green Earth Construction is to make this a lifestyle business for himself and one or two select craft workers who believe in living sustainable and optimizing the use of renewable energy sources and alternative building materials. Others will perform legal and accounting operations on contract. He will focus his efforts on project management and site/building/systems design; these are his best skills.

Brummer will buy land in the West Abilene or the surrounding area in the first half of 2005 and build a model home that will be his residence. Ground breaking is expected to begin this summer. The home will be a personal investment and achievement; financially separate from Green Earth Construction; this will also serve as a model project to verify construction costs and schedules. Promotion of Green Earth will begin while the home is under construction, with the first customer acquired by the time the model home is complete. The first sale home is expected to be complete by November 2007. Upon completion and verification of financial projections, Green Earth Construction will market their services to promote one or two additional project starts by the end of the year.

Operations strategy will minimize cost through simple, functional home design and maximize quality through passive solar design, maximized energy efficiency, and sound construction. To achieve this objective, Green Earth will utilize the design–build approach to construction. Design–build requires continual, open communication with the customer. Thus communication and trust is the basis for our operations.

Our business projections indicate that we will become profitable in our second year. We are starting the business with a reasonable cash cushion. Our cash position remains relatively stable for the first five years, and then grows substantially.

We project our net equity to be about $466,000 after year five. In that year, our return on equity will be nearly 14 percent, which compares to a typical ROE for the single family housing industry of 11 percent.

We plan to obtain funding through loans and family support.

Investment Opportunity

Because we are a lifestyle business, we do not plan to sell controlling interest in the company. We do believe that few great companies are built alone. We seek the support of lenders who will recognize a solid business plan, and who will understand the value that affordable Energy Saver homes will add to the community.

We have also signed agreements with potential investors for 40 percent of the company. Profit–sharing arrangements have been negotiated. Sharing in the accomplishment would be possible, too. Certainly, the investors would help us, and could have a huge impact on making a family's dreams come true.

Management Summary

Green Earth Construction is organized as an LLC and is designed to be a lifestyle business for the founder, Richard Brummer. A licensed Professional Accountant, Brummer has extensive construction project management experience, Accounting and a CMC in Construction Accounting and Management. He is also a Licensed Real Estate Broker Associate. Brummer has the vision and energy to devote to this business, combining quality construction, efficient management, and professionalism.

COMPANY HISTORY

Green Earth Construction is a forming residential construction business in Abilene. We will focus on building simple, quality homes using sustainable construction materials and renewable energy systems in the foothills and mountains surrounding Abilene. Green Earth will be organized as a limited liability corporation (LLC). Initially, Green Earth Construction will be a two–person team: a project manager/principal and a craftsperson/builder. The principal, Richard Brummer, will build a residence in 2005 that will serve as the model home to market the product and service. Our goal is to have two to three buyers under contract by the spring of 2007 and complete these by that year end. We intend to keep this a small, "lifestyle" business.

Mission

Protect the future through Energy Saver building, one house at a time.

PRODUCTS & SERVICES

Green Earth Construction plans to fill a void that falls between affordable manufactured housing, existing homes and custom top end homes that clutter mountain properties with their costly immensity. Our target market is the Baby Boomer age and income category, a group that values technology and the outdoors. While we cannot control rising land values, we want to provide affordable, natural solutions.

We plan to use a design–build approach, where we design a home to fit a customer's budget and then build it. As changes occur during construction (as they always do), we adjust the design, products, etc. as necessary to make sure the original budget is maintained. We will be "Energy Saver builders" in the type of products we use. We intend to use many non–traditional, environmentally–sound materials and methods. We will strive for the highest energy efficiency. Our systems approach to design will maximize energy efficiency and functionality.

Objectives

Green Earth Construction will start and remain a small, quality builder of Energy Saver homes. We will begin with minimal assets required for operations to make this a lifestyle business. We will take pride in the principles by which we run our business, build our homes, and live our lives. While we anticipate a growing demand for our product and services, we will maintain our mission to "protect the future and build green." A maximum production of ten homes a year is forecast for Green Earth. Formally speaking, there is no "exit strategy" for this business. Our investors are primarily ourselves and our customers. Typically construction companies are not sold because it is the people, their service and their skills, which sell the vision and the product. Should Brummer or other staff separate from the business, they would either be replaced or the volume of homes built would be reduced. Since the costs associated with home construction are typically covered by buyer financing, there are few assets to be lost (or sold) with the exception of the Green Earth manager or builder. Therefore, our job satisfaction is just as crucial as the quality of our product.

Products

Green Earth Construction is a contractor specializing in creating quality, comfortable, and affordable homes for the buyer concerned for our environment, the future, and simplifying the way we live. Green Earth Construction combines sustainable construction materials, methods and renewable energy sources to form a systems approach to home design in the Rocky Mountains and Farm Land of Abilene. Building an energy efficient solar home goes beyond providing additional layers of insulation and installing more windows facing south. It requires integrating all of the home systems that can benefit from solar energy without compromising aesthetics or construction quality.

A typical Green Earth product will be a 1,600 to 1,900 square–foot, simple yet elegant Texas bi–level Baratch home. Its massive walls made of straw, recycled gyprock, fibrous cement, and/or earth provide over twice the insulation and sound–proofing of a standard home. The earthen and tiled floor radiates the heat from the days' sun shining through large, double–pane windows along the south wall. It is bright and warm, even during the season's heaviest snowfall. It incurs marginal monthly utility bills by using innovative and efficient water and electrical systems, appliances, and fixtures. The structure blends with the lot on which it was placed; there is no need for "landscaping." Gardens and xeriscaping (low–water landscaping using native plantings) are irrigated from collected rainwater and filtered gray water.

It is a small house but hosts a great dinner party after a day in the backcountry. Plenty of space is provided to store the owner's outdoor gear collection. Living space is optimized by providing ample storage in partially conditioned space on the north side of the house. The earthen energy, warmth, and simplicity comfort its guests. It is a reminder to value the people and community it, versus the material clutter that fills most houses.

MARKET ANALYSIS

Green Earth Construction will be one of the growing subset of residential contractors building homes known as "Energy Saver builders." Energy Saver building encourages cost–effective and sustainable building methods, conservation of fossil fuels, water and other natural resources, recycling of construction materials, reducing solid waste, and improving indoor air quality.

The Home Builders Association of Abilene area, along with the Governments Office of Conservation, the Energuide Home Energy Rating Program, and Public Service Abilene created the Energy Saver Builder Program of Abilene (ESBP). There are currently 167 residential contractors who are enrolled with the ESBP as builders. About half of these builders are small, building an estimated one to 12 homes per year. Green Earth will qualify as an Energy Saver builder under ESBP and will compete for clients against these other smaller companies.

In order to enroll their product as a Built Energy Saver home, builders must meet a minimum criteria set by the program. While doing so does guarantee a certain level of environmental and health conscientiousness in home construction, it does not approach design and construction from a systems standpoint, using solar design, renewable energy sources, or less expensive, higher quality alternative materials.

In addition, the average price of a new home in the Abilene surrounding area in 2004 was $249,753. Including the average cost of one–half an acre of land of $120,000 and site improvements (well, septic, driveway, etc.) costing approximately $30,000, an Green Earth buyer can own a home in the Western Abilene Surrounding area for less than $200,000. These are the areas where Green Earth Construction will be distinguished from our competition.

The housing market nationwide and in the Farm Land is excellent. Although "Energy Saver building" is a small segment of the industry overall, national home building statistics indicate that it is growing rapidly.

On both a local and national level, the homebuilding market is strong. Nationwide, sales of new one–family houses in December 2004 were at a seasonally adjusted annual rate. Although this is 4 percent below the revised November rate of 13,000,000 it is 26 percent above the December 2000 rate of 9,000,000. Spending on new residential housing units during December 2004 was at a seasonally adjusted annual rate of $240 billion, 2 percent above the revised November estimate of $239 billion. Total starts of single–family homes are forecasted to reach 1,900,000 in 2005.

Locally, 201 single family houses were sold in 2004 in the Abilene area market, about a 17 percent increase over 2000. With a mean sale price of $180,000 the size of the local market is 3 billion. Energy Saver building comprises about 10 percent of the total local homebuilding market; thus the local market is about $300 million.

Market Trends

Quality of life and good employment opportunities are what draw people to Abilene. The 1990s has been a decade of remarkable growth in Abilene. Four million individuals call Abilene home, and state forecasters expect the population to surpass 5.5 million in the next 20 years.

The demand for environmentally sound housing is increasing steadily according to Association of Home Builder studies. About 35 percent of Americans describe themselves as environmentally active or sympathetic, while 56 percent think environmental protection and economic development go hand in hand.

Customers

New home buyers are motivated by the basic need for shelter. To make a difference in the existing home market, we must understand what motivates people to choose the houses they choose, and then we must provide something more desirable than the existing stock. The choice of housing within any given price bracket is influenced by:

- accommodation
- investment gain potential
- lifestyle desires
- community
- environmental considerations of building materials and utility costs

45 percent of respondents (regardless of age, income, or gender) to our marketing survey conducted in February, 2005 indicated that they were "somewhat" to "very" interested in Energy Saver homes.

Green Earth Construction will target customers who make up the under–served niche market of homebuyers who are very motivated by environmental issues. It is with this in mind that we will initially target the 45 to 67 year age group, often referred to as "Baby Boomers." Since our homes are designed to be "no frills" structures with prices between $140k and $180k, they will be fairly affordable to young people with limited disposable income. This is also the market segment with the greatest stake in preserving the environment since they will be concerned for the future of their own children. The potential market for these buyers is huge since young singles are the fastest growing household forming segment of the population.

Once Green Earth Construction is setup we can begin to target the other segments. Our primary focus will continue to be on environmentally–sound, affordable housing, but we will be open to adding the "frills" or conveniences that other buyers may be interested in, such as bamboo or cork flooring, tile, or other decorative touches.

Competition

The construction industry in Abilene is large and has attracted national companies. Green Earth Construction is prepared to meet them head–on by appealing to a distinct niche.

There are approximately 1,120 members of The Abilene Home Builders Association, and 490 belong to the Energy Saver Builder Program (ESBP). Additionally, there are many contractors and developers who do not belong to either organization. We will limit the discussion to those that market themselves through the professional organizations.

Competitors can respond quickly when it comes to the type of building we do, but we feel that most won't view us as competition. Since we are aiming at building five to ten homes per year, we fall outside the radar of the large companies. Their strategy is to provide something for everyone, not to target a specific type of buyer.

Direct competition is possible from Abilene–based Hardy Building Corp. This small Energy Saver builder has built 15 homes across Abilene, but would like to be more local to minimize the drive. Additionally, a new Energy Saver builder, Mitchell Products, is starting in Fort Worth, located about 160 miles from Abilene. However, even small builders who might view us as competition would have an entire methodology, not just a construction method to copy and provide the type of service Green Earth offers.

The purpose of Green Earth Construction is to design and build high–quality, environmentally–sound single family homes, one at a time. This will be achieved by positioning Green Earth Construction as a unique building company that creates quality, comfortable, and affordable homes for the buyer concerned for the environment. Our target market is different segments of the consumer market whose criteria for housing include affordability and the marketing tools to be utilized will be low tech/high touch methods including speakers's bureaus, word–of–mouth referrals, open houses, realtor/lender/ supplier referrals, conferences and seminars, and a website that will both promote Green Earth Construction and provide a portal to sustainable building practices. 2 percent of sales will be allocated to marketing.

We are targeting customers who make up an under–served niche market for environmentally sound homes. Our target customers can be defined as semi retired individuals who desire to be surrounded by nature, respect the environment, and preserve for the future. Customers will come from all age segments of the market—Baby Boomer, Empty Nesters, and Retirees. But given their more limited purchasing power and more vocal concern for the environment, most of our buyers initially will fall into the Baby Boomer age and income category. Our target market, therefore, is potentially very large.

Evidence that home buyers want Green Earth's product has been gathered in research conducted by the Abbie Marketing Group, Association of Home Builders, and our own market research. These data indicate that about half of those questioned expressed interest in sustainable building practices. Importantly, those who are interested in this type of home are not willing to pay a premium. Green Earth's systems and methodology will not require spending more for "being green."

Therefore, our marketing strategy is to "preach to the converted," focusing on customers who are sincerely interested in this type of housing and are seeking it out, rather than trying to convince people who are not motivated by a concern for the environment. Those who are deeply concerned about sustainability are likely to prefer dealing with a company that doesn't only "talk the talk." Since we will position ourselves as the only area builders that specialize in Energy Saver building, we believe we can capture most of the buyers who want a specialist. However, we do not intend to become a big builder using production building techniques; our goal is to build no more than 23 homes per year.

Green Earth Construction is a service–oriented company with a unique product designed for people who value simplicity and the natural environment. What differentiates our product in our target market is that we specialize in Energy Saving buildings, unlike our competitors who are able to provide Energy Saving design and construction, but don't specialize in it.

Our primary strength is our people. Our founder, Richard Brummer, has extensive construction project management experience, a CMC in Civil Accounting and a Construction Accounting and Management. He is also a Licensed Real Estate Broker Associate.

Our other strength is our integrity. We pride ourselves in our genuine commitment to the future of the earth, our respect for nature and her resources, and our desire to live in harmony with all things living. We design and build homes in tune with these values for people who share these values.

Our main weaknesses may be seen as an idealistic, healthy regard for the planet which may lead to a perception of our company as not serious about competing in a real–world environment. But Green Earth is serious about providing high–quality, environmentally–sound single family homes. Customers who are interested in this type of housing will select us because of the type of home we build and because of the professional, personalized service we offer.

Competitors can respond quickly when it comes to the type of building we do, but we feel that most won't view us as competition as we will only be building five to ten homes per year. Their strategy is to provide something for everyone, not to target a specific type of buyer. Additionally, even small builders who might view us as competition would have more than just a construction method to copy. We pride ourselves on a systems approach which needs the unique input of Green Earth's people and methodology. One aspect of what we do might be reproducible, but not the entire system.

Pricing Strategy

Using a target sales price of $150,000 to $190,000, Green Earth will use the design–build approach to pricing our natural homes. A budget is set from the very start of the project with the buyer and the home is designed and built around that budget. This is different from our competition:

- Production builders offer a small selection of specific homes with specific options at a set price.
- Other custom builders use design/build initially, but it is common for budgets to be exceeded because of design changes and inherent risks during construction (e.g. unfavorable site construction, weather delays). Many contractors make a large profit from these change orders, hence they welcome additions and modifications.

The design–build delivery method is very unique to residential construction but can be achieved with open communication and trust between Green Earth Construction and our clients. For example, if additional fill material is required because of poor soil conditions on which to place foundations, this is an added cost but a situation that was unforeseeable by Green Earth Construction prior to breaking ground (unless extensive geologic testing was performed). In our contract with the customer, this is an inherent risk in the process and must be addressed on a case–by–case basis. To maintain the original budget, modifications (e.g. reduction in size or type of materials) to the super–structure are evaluated to make up for the added cost for the foundation. This ultimately keeps our pricing down as we are not including these "factors of safety" into our costs (as most contractors would do).

This will be an attractive strategy for our customers. Not only does it designate a firm budget, it promotes continuous, open communication and trust between Green Earth and the buyer. This aspect of our business will sell itself as our production, hence our reputation, grows.

ADVERTISING

Green Earth Construction will employ a low tech/high touch strategy for advertising and promotion. Although some print advertising may be used, e.g., Yellow Pages ads and occasional newspaper advertising, we believe personal selling and publicity will be more effective ways to get our product before the eyes of consumers. Because it affords the greatest opportunity to focus on target markets and specific customers and to deliver a specific message, personal selling by the principal, Richard Brummer, will be the main form of promotion. Brummer will deliver talks to groups ranging from Chambers of Commerce to university groups and courses on environmentally–sound building. He will join speakers' bureaus and local planning boards to have access to other audiences and will participate in appropriate conferences and seminars. Additionally, his home will serve as a model home for tours so potential customers can see what their home will look like and talk personally with the builder. With his extensive relationships among local realtors and suppliers, Brummer will ask them to act as personal referrals, thus activating a word–of–mouth publicity network. As homes are built, customer word–of–mouth will grow this network.

Green Earth Construction will also have a web presence. The website will provide online advertising—vital to reach our technology–savvy target market. More importantly, the site will have a value–added function that provides a portal to sustainable building practices. Therefore, Green Earth will use the Internet to position itself as a company that not only builds Energy Saver homes but is a resource for "all things green."

Our annual budget of $20,000 for marketing and sales is low, but this is largely due to the fact that the business is small enough that it does not need a dedicated marketing/communications or sales staff, thus eliminating the need to allocate salaries for this function. The budget, therefore, comes entirely out of operating expenses. We anticipate the majority of our business will come through networking and reputation/word–of–mouth. We will maintain brochures, a web site, a Yellow Pages ad, and some small, periodical local advertising. Additionally, we will participate in one or two local trade shows annually.

A homebuyer's initial experience with Green Earth is spending a few hours "in the product". The model home—a simple, refined southwest Baratch home—has massive, light colored walls that reflect daylight throughout. The earthen and tiled floor radiates the heat from the days' sun shining through large windows along the south wall into the kitchen, dining nook, and living room. Guests are invited to go through the entire house, allowing us to describe the systems integrated within. We talk with the customer over lunch as we evaluate her budget and needs. We sketch some plans, conceptualize size and layout by comparing it with the model that surrounds us, and explain how we will design and construct the best home, by the same sustainability standards, for that amount of money.

OPERATIONS

Operations strategy will minimize cost through simple, functional home design and maximize quality through state–of–the art energy efficiency and sound construction. We anticipate longer project schedules than production–built homes because of permitting delays due to "nontraditional" systems and materials. We estimate approximately six months to design, permit, and construct each home. Finally, we will be flexible in our designs only to the extent that the customer is willing to pay for "extras" at a premium. Our mission is to provide a home that is easy to design, permit, construct, and maintain while being functional and appealing in its simplicity and durability.

Green Earth Construction will employ the design–build approach to residential construction, an increasingly popular delivery method in commercial and industrial construction. Design–build requires continual, open communication with the customer. The builder and manager must commit service and knowledge in return for the customer's trust and understanding, including any inherent risks or uncertainties that may arise during the course of the project.

Communication and trust is the basis for our operations. Green Earth will focus on core strengths of employees to maximize product quality, project efficiency, customer service, as well as our own job satisfaction.

We add value for our customers using the following philosophies:

- Design/build approach (maximize value for each customer);
- Systems approach (for sustainability, durability, comfort, and minimal life–cycle costs);
- Experienced, organized, resourceful, friendly project management;
- Live by the principles on which the business is founded.

During the first year of operations, Brummer will be responsible for the following tasks:

- Marketing
- Customer support
- Designs and budgets
- Obtaining architectural and accounting approvals and required permits/inspections
- Project management
- Back–office administrative support

As the business grows, accounting and billing will be outsourced. Once production reaches four homes or more, a new manager will be hired to assist with project coordination. Initially, a craftsperson will be responsible for all on–site activities, including:

- Carpentry and other trades
- Ordering materials and coordinating delivery
- Scheduling/coordination of all subcontractor work

One craftsperson can be expected to perform these activities to build three homes annually. Additional builders will be brought on as needed. Candidates will be experienced homebuilders who are professional, value their trade–skills, and live by the principles of Green Earth Construction. Our goal is to build a team where people do what they enjoy most.

Approximately half of the trades will be subcontracted. Our business with accountants, architects, subcontractors, and material suppliers will be performed using standard contract documents that will be reviewed by Green Earth's attorney. We will strive to work with only a few carefully selected designers and subcontractors on all of our projects to maintain a healthy working relationship. While we will work under a formal contract for all of our services, teamwork and negotiation will be emphasized to minimize disputes and maximize the project, the product, and our job satisfaction.

Green Earth Construction's operations will initially be home–based where Brummer will perform project management functions while the crafts worker will be on the job site. Brummer's home will also serve as the Green Earth Construction's model and will be located in the foothills or mountains west of Abliene. We anticipate a majority of building will be completed "in–season", or from April through November depending on the location of the home. While it is not uncommon to have mild winter weather to work, it is difficult to predict and maintain productivity. This winter "season" will be spent marketing and preparing designs/permits for upcoming projects and completing interior systems.

The company will own only office and communications equipment (computer, printer, copier, fax machine, telephones, and cellular phones). A truck and tools will be the property of the crafts worker to be deducted individually as business expenses. Specialty field equipment, such as survey instruments, scaffolding, etc. will be rented as necessary.

As Green Earth Construction grows beyond a production of five homes annually, we anticipate acquiring a small storage and office space in one of the surrounding towns. Storage will be used for excess building materials, tools, plumbing/electrical supplies, etc. The office space will be utilized for day–to–day project management operations for Brummer and the second manager.

FINANCIAL ANALYSIS

Operating Expenses

Cost of goods sold consists of the on–site labor, materials and rented equipment used by our craftspeople, subcontracted services, fees (architectural, accounting, permitting), and contingency (approximately 7 percent). It should be noted that site–specific fees subject to all new development (i.e., geologic testing, well or septic installation, water taps, utility tie–ins, drive ways) are NOT included in these costs. Installing a well, septic system and driveway on mountain properties can range from $16,000 to $39,000. Since these are unique and vary widely for each project, they will be addressed separately in our contract with the buyer.

Capital expenditures are minimal. Since we will be organized as an LLC, the project manager and crafts workers will be responsible for their own vehicles, tools, etc. that can be deducted as business expenses.

Larger equipment, tools, etc. will be rented. Green Earth Construction will own (or lease) telephones, computers, and associated office equipment only.

Development Strategy

The first priority of the principal is buying land and building a home that will both serve as a model home and residence. This home will serve as a feasibility study as to the pricing, process, and structural integrity for Green Earth Construction's marketable product. If it takes longer or costs more than anticipated, if permits and/or construction loans prove difficult to attain, or if building materials do not hold up as planned, these will all be valuable lessons to roll into our operational plans.

Plans for the model home have been selected. The factors that need to come together to make our concept work include securing land and a construction loan, hiring a crafts worker and getting bids for subcontractors, purchasing materials, breaking ground and getting to work. To this end we are actively looking for suitable lots in the mountains for construction, talking with qualified craftspeople and subcontractors, discussing permitting and zoning with city and surrounding area authorities, and investigating alternative building materials.

Marketing strategies will coincide with building. In addition, operational necessities including business phone lines, wireless phones and pagers must be procured.

Construction of the model home should be as straightforward as the construction of a customer's home. However, the same risks of any homebuilding endeavor apply: economic downturn, unforeseen environmental problems, natural disasters, and so on.

Development Timeline

A seven–month development timeline is attached. Development of Green Earth Construction will begin with the purchase of land on which to build the model home. Site selection is in progress and ground breaking is expected to begin this summer. Business promotion will begin while the home is under construction, with the first customer acquired by the time the model home is complete. The first sale home is expected to be complete by November 2007.

Development Expenses

Development expenses are minimal. Since Brummer will build the initial home as his residence and will pay for it with a conventional construction loan, the cost of building it is not considered in our financial analysis as a development expense. Additionally, for the first few years the model home will serve as the office, so no office lease expenses will accrue. Brummer and the crafts persons will use their own vehicles, so a company truck will not be needed, at least as the company gets started.

Our financial projections focus on building a profitable lifestyle business.

Financial Assumptions

Our business model makes the following significant financial assumptions:

- Before the business begins operation, Brummer will purchase land, design a house that demonstrates significant aspects of the Green Earth Construction philosophy, and build that house. The house will serve as his primary residence, as the place of business, and as a model of Green Earth work.
- Brummer will rely on savings and personal credit history to secure a construction loan and, subsequently, a long–term mortgage for that property. When he begins Green Earth's, Brummer will have a personal mortgage of about $140,000 and a strong credit history.
- Green Earth customers will purchase land themselves.

- Green Earth customers will secure their own construction financing, with Green Earth designated as their builder. Customers's lending institutions will arrange to make progress payments to Green Earth as the home is completed.

The assumptions imply that beginning the business will rely on finding customers who have better–than–average credit ratings or personal resources. We believe this is consistent with our initial target area.

We expect to lose about $15,000 in the first year, as we begin the business by completing a single home. Production ramps up to 3, 5, 7 and 8 homes in subsequent years. We expect to recover our initial losses after the second year, and proceed to build equity steadily, up to about $115,000 after year five. Our cash position should remain fairly steady for the first three years, and improve significantly in years four and five. In the fifth year, our return on equity is nearly 35 percent, which compares respectably with a typical value for the single family housing industry of 29 percent.

Capital Investment Requirements

As explained above, our capital investment is minimal. We will require enough working capital to provide for:

- Initial office equipment purchases (computers, fax, copier and software).
- Costs incurred before progress payments begin to arrive from the first project house.
- Ongoing operations, as expenses are incurred before progress payments are received.

An initial investment of $120,000 will be enough to meet our cash needs. With that much capital, projections indicate that cash reserves will drop to about $87,000 during the first year. Year–end reserves will fluctuate around $70,000 for the first three years.

We expect that funding will consist of:

- $66,000 of personal resources (personal savings, or investment from family members).
- A business loan of $ 120,000.

Beyond the funding needed for operations, we plan to seek an additional loan pre–approval of $150,000. We plan to use those funds to encourage our first customers and their lenders, to "buy in" to our business, by purchasing the building lot ourselves.

Risk Factors

We plan to aggressively ramp up home sales and production after the first year. If we sell or complete fewer homes than planned, our income projections will be delayed.

The risk of reduced sales is mitigated by the fact that we do not incur material, subcontractor or significant labor costs until a construction contract has been signed. Our plans to increase staff are conservative, and could be adjusted to cope with different levels of sales.

Construction delays are difficult to project, and have various possible causes—material shortages, weather, and design surprises. Because we expect to enter into contracts with a design–build philosophy, we plan to educate our customers and maintain very active communication right from the start. The design–build approach was developed to permit rapid, in–budget response to problems.

Our financial projections indicate that if we completed one less house per year than our baseline, our profits would be reduced, but we would still break even in the second year, make profit in the third, and keep our cash position positive.

Because we do not rely on selling homes to the upper end of the market (homes over $350,000), we believe a market downturn would not destroy us—it might even bring us a new segment of customers.

Exit Strategy

Formally speaking, there is no "exit strategy" for this business. Brummer expects to build an economically–sound lifestyle by building environmentally–sound homes. Should he or other staff members separate from the business, they would either be replaced or the volume of homes built would be reduced. Since the costs associated with home construction are typically covered by buyer financing, there are few assets to be lost (or sold) with the exception of the Green Earth manager or builder.

Funding Needs

We have baselined getting the bulk of our funds through loans. We believe this is compatible with a small, personal lifestyle business. Our business plan does permit some flexibility in this matter.

To meet our cash flow needs during the first five years of Green Earth Construction we will seek an operating loan in the amount of $30,000.

We would expect to pay a nominal premium above prime for this loan. Conservative cash flow projections indicate that 1/3 of the loan could be repaid after year three, with the balance to be repaid after year five.

We will look for an opportunity to take on an additional $150,000 of debt on reasonably favorable terms. This cash would be used for temporary purchase of buildable land, to be contractually agreed upon with a Green Earth Construction home buyer, to ease the buyer's financing situation.

We will seek a competitive rate for this loan, some nominal premium above prime. Cash flow projections indicate that interest on such a loan could be accommodated without significant impact. We would plan to repay the principal of the loan after year five, with a schedule to be negotiated with the lender.

We will seek a lender who has an interest in providing Green Earth with a significant competitive advantage early on. The land to be purchased could serve as collateral for this loan, and so we would consider a pre–qualified loan agreement which could take advantage of the collateral opportunity.

At the end of Year 5, our net equity is projected to be about $255,000.

Investment Opportunity

Because the success of Green Earth Construction will depend on the quality and speed of decisions by the founder, we are not prepared to offer controlling interest in the company.

However, we do believe that there are investors and organizations who are motivated by the same dreams we have. Sustainable housing is more than just an exploitable business niche. Therefore, we keep the option open to share the risks, the profits, and the accomplishment ofGreen Earth. We believe that, in the long term, we can offer a return on equity at least as large as the general home–building industry.

Our baseline plan is built on loans. We realize that not all lenders will choose to lend to a new home builder. However, we do believe that with growing demand for Energy Saver homes, growing government promotion of sustainable development, and the availability of support options such as SBA loan guarantees, we will be able to obtain the funds we need to make Green Earth a reality.

Investor funds would reduce our need for loans. We would not claim, however, to offer our investors extremely high rates of financial return. The proper role of an investor in Green Earth would have to be negotiated on an individual basis. Certainly, the right investor would help us, and could have a huge impact on making a family's dreams come true.

	Start-up analysis
Requirements	
Start-up expenses	
Legal/Incorporating	$ 3,600
Better business bureau fee	$ 299
Stationery etc.	$ 1,900
Brochures	$ 3,500
Mailings/Postal	$ 1,300
Advertising	$ 12,000
Company yard signs	$ 5,000
Insurance	$ 2,000
Answering service	$ 400
Website design	$ 2,800
Utilities start Up	$ 1,400
Rent	$ 3,600
Expensed equipment/Computer/Copier	$ 8,000
Office furnishings/Lease or used	$ 5,000
Office supplies	$ 1,900
Other/Miscellaneous	$ 2,000
Business software	$ 3,000
Total start-up expenses	$
Start-up assets needed	
Cash balance on starting date	$
Other current assets	$ 70,000
Total current assets	$
Long-term assets	$ 40,000
Total assets	$
Total requirements	
Funding	
Investment	
Investor 1	$200,000

Market analysis

Potentialcustomers	Growth	2003	2004	2005	2006	2007	CAGR
Home sellers	4%	180,000	208,000	224,000	245,000	247,000	3.00%
Home buyers	4%	146,000	152,000	159,000	167,000	169,000	3.00%
Property photography	4%	8,000	9,000	12,000	14,000	15,000	3.00%
Total	**4.00%**						

Ethnic Food Supplier

World Cuisine

341 Blanco Blvd.
Portland, OR 97201

Gerald Rekve

Worldwide Cuisine, located in Portland, Oregon, is a wholesaling company specializing in importing high–quality Indian, Chinese, Japanese, and Pakistani foods and repackaging them for sale to specialty food restaurants, retailers. The business was established to offer authentic Indian, Chinese, Japanese, and Pakistani foods to the growing immigrant population in the Portland area as well as an ever–increasing market of urban professionals who enjoy eating more adventurous specialty ethnic foods.

BUSINESS OVERVIEW

Research indicates that the International Foods industry in the United States has annual sales of $180 million and is growing at an average rate of 30 percent per year. The Portland market alone is estimated to be worth $25 million. In fact, the Indian, Chinese, Japanese, and Pakistani population in Portland—the end user of Worldwide Cuisine's products—is growing at 6 percent per year and an estimated 44 percent of this population purchase high–quality Indian, Chinese, Japanese, and Pakistani food products on a monthly basis. In the general population, 32 percent of people purchase specialty ethnic foods on a monthly basis. According to the Association of United States Food Distributors, ethnic food in general and Indian, Chinese, Japanese, and Pakistani food specifically are poised for substantial growth in Portland and a total of ten Indian, Chinese, Japanese, or Pakistani restaurants were opened in the greater Portland area in 2006–2007. We have reached revenues of $700,000 in our first year and project revenues of $1,500,000 in our second year in business.

Competition

There are a large number of competitors for our share of the market, some are small and others are large. Although all the ones we researched seem to be thriving, there are a number of categories on which we are competing. Price is the strongest factor: all large competitors sell their products at higher prices than Worldwide Cuisine. Our strong relationships with major Indian, Chinese, Japanese, and Pakistani exporters allow us to sell our products at a price comparable to or lower than the competition. In addition, the competitors have focused primarily on marketing to the Indian, Chinese, Japanese, and Pakistani buyer. Worldwide Cuisine fully exploits the potential market made up of non–Immigrant urban families that want to venture out and try something different. Young professionals would be another target market for us, achieved through attractive packaging and an extensive local brand awareness campaign.

Currently, we have very little direct competition as there are no other Indian, Chinese, Japanese, or Pakistani food wholesalers that sell exclusively to specialty restaurants and retailers. All of our competition is indirect in the form of wholesalers who sell predominantly to grocery store chains. They do not compete directly for business at the specialty stores but they do compete indirectly for the end Indian, Chinese, Japanese, or Pakistani food consumer. Market research shows that these generic brands currently account for 67 percent of the ethnic food market. There are 124 American companies that import food from Japan, however only 17 import so–called luxury items.

The largest roadblock facing potential competitors entering into our market is the difficulty and expense of establishing good relationships with suppliers in the Far East. My years of experience in the ethnic food market have enabled me to develop solid relationships built on trust and a 14–year track record. It would take years and many thousands of dollars in travel costs for a potential competitor of ours to match our network among Indian, Chinese, Japanese, or Pakistani suppliers.

We use a custom written software program in which we use four computer–based inventory control software systems designed for wholesalers. This software cost us close to $75,000 to write, but we needed it. We know our small competitors will never be able to afford to have this done. The software allows us to control the inventory from the time it leaves Asia to sitting on our warehouse shelf in Toronto. Because our entire product is food related, we have to insure quality of food and dispose of any outdated inventory. In fact we go one step further—if one of our clients buy a product and it does not sell, rather than the client having to leave the product on the store shelf, we will offer to buy the inventory back for 70 percent of what the client paid us for it. This also insures that we either stop selling or reduce inventory on product that does not sell. This will always insure the best in quality of food for our end users. We know our competitors do not offer this type of guarantee. We know it will cost us money, but in the long run feel it is best for our business's long term success and growth.

This is an advantage over a number of smaller food importers who continue to use more archaic and cumbersome hand–written inventory systems. By keeping track of inventory electronically, we are able to monitor when products were received as well as their "best before" dates. This results in a lower spoilage rate. In addition, this system allows us to track popular items, which are used in the development of additional product lines. The company also uses a fax machine as a rapid and efficient way of dispatching orders to overseas suppliers.

As part of the software we wrote, we also incorporate a security patch to USA's Homeland Security, allowing us as requested by police instant access to who bought our products, which ones they bought and the day the client took delivery of our products. This gives us instant ability to track shipments that may have been contaminated, contact the stores to pull off shelves, etc. We have already been approved for Homeland Security and the FDA for access to the USA Markets in the USA and Canada.

MANAGEMENT SUMMARY

Overview

As president and sole owner of Worldwide Cuisine, I own 100 percent of the company's shares. I bring my ten years experience working in my family's business in Japan to the company. I have forged long–term business relationships with three major Indian, Chinese, Japanese, and Pakistani food exporters, all of whom guarantee Worldwide Cuisine's excellent prices. In addition, I have been using the services of Makoto Nakano who is based in Japan and acts as a purchasing agent for the company. The company also uses the services of a sales agent, a part–time bookkeeper and a part–time delivery person.

Company Structure

Title: President

Name: Olivia Sheono

Qualifications: Business degree from the University of Tokyo; 7 years experience in sales and marketing at family business in Japan; excellent financial and management skills; strong understanding of ethnic cuisine.

As president, I am responsible for guiding the overall direction of the company, overseeing sales, marketing, human resource issues and accounting. I am also responsible for attending the International Food Show in November and will overseeing all marketing initiatives.

Title: Part–time Purchasing Agent

Name: Makoto Nakano

I have secured the services of Makoto Nakano who is based in Japan and acts as our part-time purchasing agent for the company, negotiating rates and managing relationships. He is uniquely responsible for quality control on–site in Asia, and inspects the products before they are shipped to Portland. His salary in $44,000. He is a resident of Japan and has 12 years experience in purchasing.

I have secured a sales agent who is paid 10 percent commission on gross sales. He has over five years experience in sales.

An accountant is responsible for processing customer orders, managing payables, receivables and generally overseeing the books.

I will hire three delivery staff with previous experience, a valid driver's license and a clean driving record. They will each be paid $23,000 per year, plus participate in a bonus system based on customer referrals, increase in sales and lack of complaints for late delivery, etc.

I hired temporary help for giving out free samples in booths in retail outlets. These positions are filled on an as needed basis and paid at minimum wage.

Compensation

Purchasing agent (Japan)	$44,000
Sales agent (Canada)	10% commission on sales
Bookkeeper part-time position	$27,000
Delivery person	$80,000

COMPANY HISTORY

Worldwide Cuisine was formed in Portland, Oregon. It is a wholesaling company specializing in importing high–quality Indian, Chinese, Japanese, or Pakistani foods and repackaging them for sale to specialty food restaurants and retailers. The business was established to offer authentic Indian, Chinese, Japanese, and Pakistani food to the growing Immigrant population in the Portland area as well as to an ever–increasing market of urban professionals who enjoy eating more adventurous specialty ethnic foods.

Business relationships with major Indian, Chinese, Japanese, or Pakistani food exporters have been established, and a purchasing agent, two sales staff members, an accountant and delivery staff have been hired. I have invested $78,000 to finance packaging, design, product and market research and $125,000 in working capital requirements.

MARKET ANALYSIS

The International Foods industry in Portland has annual sales of $450 million and is growing at an annual rate of approximately 12 percent. The gross profit margins in the food wholesale industry are typically between 27 and 36 percent.

Sectors within industry

- Manufacturers who sell to importers
- Distributors who sell products to wholesalers
- Wholesalers who sell to retailers
- Retailers who sell directly to the consumer restaurants who sell to the consumer

Seasonal Factors

Although certain sectors of the International Foods industry must contend with seasonal challenges, our company, Worldwide Cuisine, is relatively safe from such seasonal fluctuations in production since the majority of its products are rice and soy based. Rice and soy products can be grown throughout the year and are easy to acquire.

Growth Strategy

Consumer trends bode well for the international foods industry as Portland's population continues to become more ethnically diverse. In Portland, the Indian, Chinese, Japanese, and Pakistani population is growing at 13 percent per year and an estimated 22 percent of the local ethnic population purchase high–quality ethnic food products on a monthly basis. In the general population, 16 percent of people purchase specialty ethnic foods on a monthly basis. Recent market research indicates that ethnic food in general and Indian, Chinese, Japanese, and Pakistani food specifically are poised for substantial growth in Portland and a total of ten Indian, Chinese, Japanese, or Pakistani restaurants were opened in 2006–2007.

In addition, the early 2000s have seen a trend toward healthy, low–fat cooking with an emphasis on vegetarian cuisine.

Position in the Industry

Our company acts as a wholesaler, dedicated to importing high–quality Indian, Chinese, Japanese, and Pakistani delicacies, repackaging them for sale to specialty food restaurants and retailers. Unlike competition that sell mass market items to large grocery store chains, Worldwide Cuisine focuses on selling products to higher–end boutique food stores. Currently, of the 26 American companies that import food from Japan, only three import so–called luxury items. Of these companies, some are based in Portland; all the company's products are sold at a higher price point than our products, which gives us a significant niche in the retailing of high–quality yet reasonably priced food items. Also, since the direct competition is based primarily in Eastern Canada, we benefit from the lack of local competition as we grow the eastern Canada sector, we will look at western Canada and the USA markets.

Legal Issues

We have registered the Worldwide Cuisine name and intend to do the same for our best–selling product names.

MARKETING & SALES

Customers

Our target market is high–end specialty boutique food stores. Specialty retailers compete by selling unique products which are not available at large grocery chains. People choose to shop at specialty stores for a unique experience. Therefore our target market looks for suppliers, like Worldwide Cuisine who supply unique products that can't be found on the grocery store shelf.

The end–user of Worldwide Cuisine's products can be categorized into a few groups. The first is urban professionals between the ages of 22 and 60, living in the greater Portland area with a salary of greater than $44,000 per year who enjoy eating more adventurous ethnic foods and prefer to shop in gourmet or specialty food stores. The second is immigrants from Pacific Rim countries who are living in the Portland area and demand authentic, superior quality Indian, Chinese, Japanese, and Pakistani food products.

The Portland retail market for gourmet ethnic foods is estimated to be $53 million and sales have grown at an average annual rate of 3 percent over the last five years. This translates into more than three million units of product being sold per year in the greater Portland area.

Portland's population continues to become more and more ethnically diverse. With the recent events in the Middle East and Europe, there has been a large increase in immigrants to the United States. With an aging, baby boomer population with significant disposable income, projections for specialty food sales are positioned for continued growth. In addition, there has been a significant movement in the industry toward the production of low–fat and vegetarian foods that suit today's healthier eating habits.

Our strategy is to sell our authentic Indian, Chinese, Japanese, and Pakistani products to high–end specialty food retailers who cater to the tastes of upwardly mobile urban Portland residents. We have positioned ourselves as a specialty brand and not a generic or discount brand. We make our products available to high–end boutique food stores only. Considering the trend towards healthy, low–fat cooking in North American society, our gourmet products are marketed as low–fat healthy eating.

Sales/Distribution Plan

Worldwide Cuisine has contracts with one chain of health food stores and several specialty food shops. The company has purchased used trucks—at an estimated cost of $15,000—for deliveries. We have employed sales staff and delivery drivers.

Pricing Strategy

Due to our strong network of exporters in Japan, we are able to receive, and profitably sell, our products at a price comparable to wholesalers who supply the grocery chains's generic brands. Our prices are set in such a way that, in specialty and gourmet retail locations, Worldwide Cuisine's products are comparable to generic brands sold at large grocery stores.

After we do a credit check, customers will be given a payment term to be distributed evenly between 30, 60 and 90 days. Because of the nature of the product, there is no return policy. The client must pay for all their purchases for the first month, once the client has established a track record of writing good checks, we will review to offer the clients credit. We will also offer all our clients the ability to get discounts for payment when orders are delivered. This discount will range from 3–9 percent discount based on volume of previous month's purchases.

Advertising

In order to support our retail customers, Worldwide Cuisine products are advertised and promoted in a number of ways, including:

- Sponsorship of an ethnic cooking show on community access television: $3,000 annually
- Free sample booths in retail outlets ten times per year: $15,000 annually
- A company web site, which raises awareness of our products: $800 annually
- Printed coupons in community newspapers: $1,100 annually
- Distribution of flyers at gourmet stores: $500 for each product
- Media relations
- Mailers to retail and restaurants
- Sales person to call on target clients
- Alliance with local wine & beverage companies offering cross promotions

In addition, Worldwide Cuisine solicits press coverage from local newspapers. We write and distribute press releases to all local newspapers in the hope of being covered as a local news item. Many of the local newspapers do weekly features on Portland entrepreneurs and since there is intense local interest in entrepreneurs from Pacific Rim countries, Worldwide Cuisine makes a fitting profile. One of the company's advisory board members works with the local media and recommends our story regularly. Our advertising and promotional plan generated annual sales of $300,000 in our first year.

Given the success of this program, we will continue with a similar marketing strategy in the current year.

Worldwide Cuisine has produced business cards and glossy four color pamphlets outlining available products. The initial 1,000 copy print run cost $3,500 (including design). Based on initial response from retailers, we have not opted to print a second run but continue to distribute introductory flyers to launch new products.

In addition to having employed a sales representative, who is paid a 10 percent commission on gross sales, we will attend the Annual International Food Show in January as a way to expose our products to a broader potential market. The cost of exhibiting at the Food Show is estimated at $12,000.

OBJECTIVES

To date, I have invested $125,000 in packaging design, product, market research and other working capital requirements. The price commitments I have secured from three major Indian, Chinese, Japanese, and Pakistani exporters as well as contracts with one health food chain and several specialty foods shops continue to operate effectively.

In order to get our products to market, the following steps must take place:

- Place orders with exporters in Asia and Middle east
- Arrange for international payment for goods
- Coordinate delivery of products to Worldwide Cuisine warehouse facility
- Repackage products with Worldwide Cuisine's labels
- Negotiate sales orders with local retailers
- Process customer orders
- Deliver orders
- Invoice for orders
- Implement advertising and promotional plan
- Software for inventory beta–tested

RISK FACTORS

The following events could pose problems to the distribution of Worldwide Cuisine products:

- Change in government regulations around selling food products may force a change in package or product mix
- Trade war or restrictive duties on food imports from Asia could threaten supply

- Loss of key supplier, which would result in paying higher rates for products shipping problems, would cause significant delays in fulfilling orders
- Drop in the American Dollar will make buying Indian, Chinese, Japanese, and Pakistani products more expensive

To avoid these problems, we will use a bank loan to finance day to day operations and keep inventory sufficient to fulfill contracts and further develop our supplier network in Asia. We will also seek out back up suppliers in other markets.

In the event sales would become soft, we have put in place a contingency plan. We will introduce sake and other ethnic drinks which have proven to be popular during slumps in demand for our traditional, healthier product line. In addition, I am willing to lay off our delivery person and do deliveries myself, if required.

GROWTH STRATEGY

We have registered the Worldwide Cuisine name and continue to do the same for our best–selling products.

In an effort to network with other entrepreneurs, I am a member of:

- Oregon Entrepreneurs Association
- The Association of American Food Distributors
- U.S. Restaurant Food Association

Suppliers

We have established strong relationships with three Indian, Chinese, Japanese, and Pakistani exporters and combined with my experience in our family business, I have been doing business with them for 14 years.

- Pakistani Products
- Asian Foodstuffs
- Exotic Foods

All exporters have given us prices that are lower than those paid by other wholesalers. The terms for payment in full are 30 days plus a volume discount of 3 percent for orders in excess of $20,000.

OPERATIONS

Quality Control

We have a quality control manager on contract in Asia who inspects the products before they are shipped to Portland. In the event of a problem, the quality control manager notifies the exporting company and obtains an exchange or credit. Once inspected, the products are shipped to Portland.

Land & Equipment Requirements

Worldwide Cuisine leases a 3,000 square foot warehouse space for $30,000/annually (gross). The site is conveniently located near the airport to facilitate international shipments as well as visits from Indian, Chinese, Japanese, and Pakistani exporters. We also bought a fax machine, printer, copier and desktop computer for approximately $10,000.

Inventory Control

Worldwide Cuisine uses a computer–based software inventory control software system designed for wholesalers. The end result is a lower spoilage rate as well as the ability to track popular items. This is an advantage over a number of smaller food importers who continue to use more archaic and cumbersome hand–written inventory systems.

Time Frame for Production

It takes 3.5 weeks from the time our retail customers place an order, to the time the order is received. Factors that could negatively impact this time frame are supply shortages, trade embargoes, trade war or restrictive duties on food imports from Japan, loss of key suppliers, and shipping delays. To help offset these factors, Worldwide Cuisine warehouses quantities of popular products, which also allow us to accommodate rush orders.

FINANCIAL ANALYSIS

Income Statement

Operating expenses amount to $ 23,000 per month. Worldwide Cuisine will generate $700,000 in sales in its second year of operations. The gross profit is expected to remain at approximately 33 percent, yielding $120,000 to cover administrative expenses.

Cash Flow Statement

After the first year as a start–up operation, the company broke even, from a cash flow perspective. We are expecting our sales volume to increase by 35 percent in the second year. Our monthly purchases will increase to accommodate the growth in sales. We will need a line of credit to support working capital requirements in the months leading to and following the summer, which will be our peak season. During that time, we will be able to pay down the line as cash flows permit.

There is a difference between the terms we have from our suppliers and the terms we grant our customers, also necessitating use of the line of credit during our slower months. One of our goals will be to better match payment terms between our suppliers and customers.

Balance Sheet

At the balance sheet date, Worldwide Cuisine will be in a solid financial position.

CONCLUSION

In the next year, it is my goal to get 125 percent increase in our revenue as a wholesaling company specializing in importing high–quality Indian, Chinese, Japanese, and Pakistani food for sale to specialty retailers in North America. Since my business is based in Oregon I believe my chances for success are increased for a number of reasons:

- Statistics show that the international foods industry is growing at a rate of 23 percent per year.
- Although the growth of the Indian, Chinese, Japanese, and Pakistani population in Oregon could slow down, the 3 percent increase over the last four years indicates a robust market.
- There is little direct competition supplying Indian, Chinese, Japanese, and Pakistani food to specialty restaurants and retailers.

- As a result of my ten years working in the family's business in Asia, I have cultivated long term business relationships with three major ethnic food experts. Therefore, even if our preferred supplier is unable to meet our needs, we have a deep pool of contacts to turn to.
- Our supply of product is contingent on shipping over long distances. However, we have minimized this risk by starting to keep an inventory of our most popular products.

Our first year in business has proven to be successful. In order to continue realizing my business goals, I am asking for an operating line of $150,000 and I am willing to provide the assets of the business and a personal guarantee.

Appendix A

INCOME STATEMENT - For the year ending December 31, 2006

Month	Jan 1	Feb 2	Mar 3	Apr 4	May 5	June 6
Sales	**$35,000**	**$35,000**	**$39,000**	**$40,000**	**$45,000**	**$45,000**
Cost of sales						
Opening inventory	$20,000	$25,000	$30,000	$32,000	$36,000	$37,000
Purchases	20,000	20,000	20,000	25,000	25,000	21,000
	40,000	45,000	50,000	57,000	61,000	58,000
Ending inventory	(25,000)	(30,000)	(32,000)	(36,000)	(37,000)	(34,000)
	15,000	15,000	18,000	21,000	24,000	24,000
Gross profit	10,000	10,000	12,000	14,000	16,000	16,000
as a %	0.40	0.40	0.40	0.40	0.40	0.40
Expenses						
Salaries	15,000	15,000	15,000	15,000	15,000	15,000
Purchasing agent	1,250	1,250	1,250	1,250	1,250	1,250
Delivery wages	833	833	833	833	833	833
Sales commissions	2,500	2,500	3,000	3,500	4,000	4,000
Other wages	300	300	300	300	300	300
Benefits	267	267	267	267	267	267
Rent & equipment leases	1,500	1,500	1,500	1,500	1,500	1,500
Promotion	1,822	233	233	233	433	233
Delivery expenses	175	175	175	175	175	175
General and office expenses	150	150	150	150	150	150
Telephone and utilities	150	150	150	150	150	150
Insurance	150				150	150

Month	July 7	Aug 8	Sept 9	Oct 10	Nov 11	Dec 12
Sales	**$55,000**	**$60,000**	**$70,000**	**$80,000**	**$80,000**	**$70,000**
Cost of sales						
Opening inventory	$34,000	$28,000	$19,000	$13,000	$19,000	$25,000
Purchases	21,000	21,000	21,000	30,000	30,000	27,000
	55,000	49,000	40,000	43,000	49,000	52,000
Ending inventory	(28,000)	(19,000)	(13,000)	(19,000)	(25,000)	(31,000)
	27,000	30,000	27,000	24,000	24,000	21,000
Gross profit	18,000	20,000	18,000	16,000	16,000	14,000
as a %	0.40	0.40	0.40	0.40	0.40	0.40
Expenses						
Salaries	15,000	15,000	15000	15,000	15,000	15,000
Purchasing agent	1,250	1,250	1,250	1,250	1,250	1,250
Delivery wages	833	833	833	833	833	833
Sales commissions	4,500	5,000	4,500	4,000	4,000	3,500
Other wages	300	300	300	300	300	300
Benefits	267	267	267	267	267	267
Rent & equipment leases	1,500	1,500	1,500	1,500	1,500	1,500
Promotion	283	83	233	5,233	433	233
Delivery expenses	175	175	175	175	175	175
General and office expenses	150	150	150	150	150	150
Telephone and utilities	150	150	150	150	150	150
Insurance	150	150	150	150	150	

Appendix B

CASH FLOW - For the year ending December 31, 2006

	Jan 1	Feb 2	Mar 3	Apr 4	May 5	June 6
Inflows						
Collection of accounts receivable	28,255	22,555	26,455	29,755	24,655	27,955
Bank operating loan	25,555	22,555	6,555	7,555	4,555	—
	28,255	22,555	22,955	26,755	28,655	27,955
Outflows						
Repayment of bank loan	—	—	—	—	—	2,555
Payment of accounts payable	24,555	25,555	25,555	22,755	25,555	22,555
Monthly expenses (excl. dep'n)	22,522	22,922	22,422	22,922	22,622	22,422
	27,522	22,922	22,422	26,682	28,622	27,422
Increase (decrease) in cash	728	567	467	27	27	527
Cash, beginning	422	2,229	2,755	2,272	2,289	2,255
Cash, ending	**$2,229**	**$2,755**	**$2,272**	**$2,289**	**$2,255**	**$2,722**

	July 7	Aug 8	Sept 9	Oct 10	Nov 11	Dec 12	Total
Inflows							
Collection of accounts receivable	42,255	44,555	46,255	44,555	42,255	27,955	424,255
Bank operating loan	—	—	—	2,555	2,555	2,555	56,555
	42,255	44,555	46,255	46,555	44,255	45,955	485,255
Outflows							
Repayment of bank loan	5,555	8,555	22,555	—	—	—	26,555
Payment of accounts payable	22,555	22,555	22,555	27,755	25,555	27,755	282,255
Monthly expenses (excl. dep'n)	22,982	24,282	22,922	28,422	22,622	22,922	265,589
	29,982	42,782	45,922	46,282	42,622	45,682	474,829
Increase (decrease) in cash	2,267	767	267	(222)	627	267	—
Cash, beginning	2,722	2,989	4,755	5,522	4,889	5,555	5,772
Cash, ending	**$2,989**	**$4,755**	**$5,522**	**$4,889**	**$5,555**	**$5,772**	**$5,772**

Appendix C

Schedule detailing cash flow statement calculations

	Jan	Feb	Mar	Apr	May	June
Loan balance and interest chart	3	3	3	4	5	6
Opening balance	—	32,222	33,222	37,522	44,522	48,522
Advance	32,222	33,222	6,522	7,222	4,222	—
Repayment	—	—	—	—	—	(3,222)
Ending balance	32,222	33,222	37,522	44,522	48,522	46,522
Interest on average balance @ 5%	83	333	385	343	388	396
Accounts receivable						
Balance, beginning	35,222	33,752	35,352	38,852	34,352	39,522
Sales, net	35,222	35,222	32,222	35,222	42,222	42,222
Collections	(38,352)	(33,522)	(36,422)	(39,722)	(34,652)	(37,952)
Balance, ending	**$33,752**	**$35,352**	**$38,852**	**$34,352**	**$39,522**	**$43,552**
Collection of accounts receivable						
Assuming collection of net sales as follows						
	$35,222	$35,222	$32,222	$35,222	$42,222	$42,222
Collection 33% in 0–30 days	8,352	8,352	9,922	33,552	33,322	33,322
Collection 33% in 30–60 days	5,222	8,352	8,352	9,922	33,552	33,322
Collection 33% in 60–90 days	5,222	5,222	8,352	8,352	9,922	33,552
	$38,352	$33,522	$36,422	$39,722	$34,652	$37,952
Accounts payable						
Balance, beginning	$ 9,222	$ 5,222	$ 5,222	$ 5,222	$ 6,352	$ 6,352
Purchases	32,222	32,222	32,222	35,222	35,222	33,222
Payments	(34,222)	(32,222)	(32,222)	(33,752)	(35,222)	(33,222)
Balance, ending	**$5,222**	**$5,222**	**$5,222**	**$6,352**	**$6,352**	**$5,352**
Payment of expenses						
Purchases						
	32,222	32,222	32,222	35,222	35,222	33,222
Payment 75% in the month	35,222	35,222	35,222	38,752	38,752	35,752
Payment 35% in the following month	9,222	5,222	5,222	5,222	6,352	6,352
	$34,222	$32,222	$32,222	$33,752	$35,222	$33,222
Promotion/Marketing initiatives						
Sample booths						
	352	352	352	352	352	352
Ethnic cooking show	83	83	83	83	83	83
Printed flyers/website/opening ads	3,389	—	—	—	—	—
Coupons (quarterly)	322	—	—	—	322	—
International food show	—	—	—	—	—	—
	3,833	333	333	333	433	333

Appendix C [CONTINUED]

Schedule detailing cash flow statement calculations

	July	Aug	Sept	Oct	Nov	Dec	Total
Loan balance and interest chart	7	8	9	32	33	33	—
Opening balance	46,522	43,522	33,222	33,222	33,522	36,522	—
Advance	—	—	—	3,522	3,222	3,222	56,222
Repayment	(5,222)	(8,522)	(33,222)	—	—	—	(36,522)
Ending balance	43,522	33,222	33,222	33,522	36,522	39,522	$ 39,522
Interest on average balance @ 5%	367	332	339	392	328	333	—
Accounts receivable							
Balance, beginning	43,552	45,322	52,752	49,552	45,222	43,752	—
Sales, net	45,222	52,222	45,222	42,222	42,222	35,222	—
Collections	(43,352)	(44,552)	(46,322)	(44,552)	(43,352)	(37,952)	—
Balance, ending	**$45,322**	**$52,752**	**$ 49,552**	**$ 45,222**	**$ 43,752**	**$ 42,822**	—
Collection of accounts receivable							
Assuming collection of net sales as follows							
	$45,222	$52,222	$45,222	$42,222	$42,222	$35,222	—
Collection 33% in 0–30 days	34,852	36,522	34,852	33,322	33,322	33,552	—
Collection 33% in 30–60 days	33,322	34,852	36,522	34,852	33,322	33,322	—
Collection 33% in 60–90 days	33,322	33,322	34,852	36,522	34,852	33,322	—
	$43,352	$44,552	$46,322	$44,552	$43,352	$37,952	—
Accounts payable							
Balance, beginning	$ 5,352	$ 5,352	$ 5,352	$ 5,352	$ 7,522	$ 7,522	—
Purchases	33,222	33,222	33,222	32,222	32,222	37,222	—
Payments	(33,222)	(33,222)	(33,222)	(37,752)	(32,222)	(37,752)	—
Balance, ending	**$5,352**	**$5,352**	**$5,352**	**$7,522**	**$7,522**	**$6,752**	—
Payment of expenses							
Purchases							
	33,222	33,222	33,222	32,222	32,222	37,222	—
Payment 75% in the month	35,752	35,752	35,752	33,522	33,522	32,352	—
Payment 35% in the following month	5,352	5,352	5,352	5,352	7,522	7,522	—
	$33,222	$33,222	$33,222	$37,752	$32,222	$37,752	—
Promotion/Marketing initiatives							
Sample booths							
	—	—	352	352	352	352	3,522
Ethnic cooking show	83	83	83	83	83	83	3,222
Printed flyers/website/opening ads	—	—	—		—	—	—
Coupons (quarterly)	322	—	—	—	322	—	822
International food show	—	—	—	5,222	—	—	5,222
	383	83	333	5,333	433	333	8,322

FITNESS CENTER

Woodland Gym Ltd.

64 Palm Ave.
Beverly Hills, CA 90211

Gerald Rekve

Woodland Gym Ltd. is an established company in the fitness center industry in the affluent area of Beverly Hills, California. While the fitness market is ever changing, we feel based on our knowledge of the market we will be able to garner a large market share and profit from our targeted sector. The experience of our staff and management will put us in a winning position. Woodland Gym Ltd. was founded by one entrepreneur who has 18 years of fitness center business experience and has managed well–known fitness centers and fully understands the market potential and requirements for profitability.

BUSINESS OVERVIEW

Woodland Gym Ltd. fitness center is targeted towards men and women only, although children can join the family classes. Beverly Hills is an affluent area with many high–income housewives and mothers of school age children. There are also many professional men and women in Beverly Hills who need a more local fitness center to visit. There are over 860,000 people in the 5–mile radius of our store. The nearest competitor is two miles from Beverly Hills and does not offer the all the activities we propose.

Customers

Woodland Gym fitness center will be a premier, upmarket establishment. The main market sectors Woodland Gym will penetrate are:

- Housewives
- Men and professionals that require a work–out location convenient to their schedules
- Mothers of school age children
- Professional women

PRODUCTS & SERVICES

Core Product Offerings

- Aerobics instruction
- Strength training
- Endurance training

- Yoga
- Marathon training
- Cycling training
- Comprehensive gym facilities
- Beauty treatments
- General product/retail sales
- Vouchers
- Rekki

Gym Services

We will have three gymnasium areas that will house enough equipment to allow 55 people each to use the gym at once. The cost of the gym equipment and beauty room equipment is $40,000; all such equipment will be leased. Pricing will be $89 per month for unlimited use during peak times.

Organized Classes

We will have one main hall where all classes will take place. There will be three instructors to take these classes spanning peak times during the day (i.e. lunchtime) and evening and weekends. Classes to be offered will be for all levels of fitness from beginner to advanced, and these will be mixed during the week. Pricing will be $89 per month for unlimited classes.

Beauty Treatments

Body Therapy

- Tranquillity: This stress reducing massage helps improve sleep patterns by combining aromatherapy oils with deep relaxation movements and calming breathing techniques. (1 hour)
- Restorative: This tension reducing massage utilizes individually chosen aromatherapy oils combined with acupressure points to stimulate and release stress from the back, shoulders, neck, face and fee. This complete treatment can help to strengthen the nervous system and restore depleted energy. (30 minutes)
- Aromatherapy Massage: This highly personalized massage combines the actions of our highly therapeutic oils with the skills of the practitioner in order to relax and rebalance the recipient. Deep body techniques are complimented by a soothing scalp massage. (1 hour)
- Pre and Post Natal Massage: This treatment has been carefully designed for pregnancy and takes into account the special needs of mothers–to–be as well as those that are nursing. A specifically blended and safe essential oil has been created to take into account contraindications normally associated with pregnancy and breast–feeding. A well deserved relaxation hour. (1 hour)

Face Therapy

- Alliance Facial: Our use of botanical products is of the highest quality containing excellent nutrients including local flowers and herbs. The facial with its gentle lymph drainage of the face gives way to a deep exfoliating cleanse and tone, employing a face masque and scalp massage. Eye and lip balm complete the experience leaving you with a glowing sensation inside and out. (1 hour)
- Aromatherapy Facial: This beautifully tailored treatment with its replenishing and harmonising approach combines the exceptional attention to detail of the therapist with the exquisite array of natural products that are applied. From ingredients as luxurious as Egyptian rose and to green tea and honey, the synchronistic nature of the treatment culminates in a deeply relaxing scalp massage. (1 hour)

- Revitalizing Back, Face and Scalp Massage: This treatment commences with a deep cleanse of the back with our sea salt and essential oils which flows into a soothing back massage. A facial cleanse, massage and masque combining ingredients such as rose, green tea, honey is followed with a scalp massage. (1 hour)
- Replenishing and Nourishing Eye Treatment: Tired eyes will soon become soothed and refreshed as the therapist attends to this most sensitive of areas. This mini facial will awaken their hidden radiance beneath the surface. (25 minutes)

Nail Services

- Manicure: This holistic approach to the manicure includes a therapeutic hand massage with individually selected creams or oils. Cuticle push, file, colour, and shape aim to reveal the hands in all their glory. (1 hour)
- Pedicure: A wonderful massage with our trademarked foot paste product commences this therapeutic pedicure, which aims to soothe and relax the client as well as shaping, filing, polishing and painting the toenails. (1 hour)

Retail Products

The full range of skin and nail products we use will be offered for general sale to customers and passing trade.

MARKET ANALYSIS

The California economy has steady growth and the outlook is for this to continue. The fitness center business continues to be strong. In our area there is an untapped market with huge potential.

The current salon market in California comprises 12,370 outlets offering beauty treatments and is estimated to reach 14,425 by December 2005. Market turnover of salon–based outlets is expected to reach $1.15 billion by 2005 across 8,855 units, driven by strong consumer demand and increasingly busy lifestyles, greater affluence, and a growing focus on personal well–being and appearance. Greater media coverage of beauty and an ever–widening variety of beauty services available have also driven popularity and increased visits to fitness centers and spas over the past 2–3 years. These trends will continue to drive the market forward.

Key factors stimulating underlying growth have included increased public awareness of health and fitness issues, expansion in the private club sector, increased emphasis on niche market segments (such as females, the older generation, disabled users and the youth market), government schemes to encourage a health lifestyle and health service referrals.

The private sector accounts for around 78 percent of the total market in terms of value, with the public sector accounting for the balance.

The number of health and fitness facilities, including leisure centers, in the public sector is higher than in the private sector; however the nature of private clubs is that you generally pay higher prices, payment is in advance for membership (rather than paying for what you use), and the private facilities attract a larger number of paying members per establishment. In the private sector, one key recent trend has been the reduction in the share of revenue accounted for by joining fees, with clubs discounting on joining fees to attract established members, but attempting to balance this with increased membership charges. Some clubs do not charge joining fees. Ancillary revenue accounts for some 15 percent of all revenue, compared to around 40 percent in the US, suggesting that the California fitness centers will be seeking to generate additional ancillary revenue over the next few years.

The majority of consumers change beauty product brands "often" or "sometimes". "Value–for–money", "tailored to skin type" and "brand name" are key factors for selecting a given brand, while therapists and friends/family are the main purchase influencers.

Key opportunities and threats in the sector will include the corporate health and fitness sector, which has been one of the key growth areas in recent years, exemplified by the number of established specialist management companies entering the market and their increasing contract portfolios. Nevertheless it remains a key growth opportunity for future market growth, particularly as both the government and companies themselves see general well being and fitness as likely to reduce the amount of sick days taken over the year.

Consumers in California are also spending more on beauty products than in the past, while pharmacies and department stores remain the most popular places to purchase beauty product brands.

Key Market Statistics

Salon and Spa Visitors

- 46 percent of salon customers surveyed state they visit fitness centers more now than in the past, with 66 percent of customers visiting salons and spas for beauty and relaxation treatments at least once a month
- The main reasons for selecting a salon are convenience of location and the therapist, with 77 percent of customers indicating loyalty to their salon
- Salon customers' key health and beauty goals are "feel better", "pamper myself", and have "healthier skin"
- More than two–thirds of salon and spa customers believe themselves to be well–informed about the types of beauty products and services on the market
- "Value–for–money", "tailored to skin type", and "brand name" are key factors for selecting a given beauty product brand, while therapists and friends/family are the main purchase influencers
- The majority of customers change beauty product brands "often" or "sometimes" because they like to try established products, they noticed decreased effectiveness of their current products, or due to recommendations of their therapist, friends or family.
- While 45 percent of salon customers change brands often/sometimes to trial established products and gain more effective results, 35 percent remain highly loyal to their brands

Competition

There is one center that is 10 miles from Beverly Hills offering 60 percent of the range of products we will be offering. Our pricing will be on average 18 percent higher. We can charge a premium because we are local and the area is affluent. Our trainers will be qualified to the highest level and also offer personal training sessions. Our beauticians will be of a higher calibre than this competing salon to develop our presence.

Strengths

1. Fitness center professional with 18 years project management fitness center experience
2. High visibility premises in the downtown area

Risk Factors

1. Not currently offering some of the items offered at the competitors' locations
2. No credibility with target audience within the established competition's fitness center
3. Copycat fitness center companies
4. Economic downturn

There are no real outside threats to this business plan. It is driven by our own strengths in the market place.

Growth Strategy

1. The affluent customers in Beverly Hills make for an untapped market place
2. Potential customers within a 40-mile radius
3. Develop the growth of offering beauty treatments

OPERATIONS

The premises beside our current location are rented on a 5–year lease and are currently being used as offices. We have already registered the business with the local civic department.

We have developed the fitness center layout to include:

- Two halls for aerobic, kinetics and yoga classes
- An equipped gymnasium
- Five beauty rooms for treatments
- Reception area for booking in customers and selling products
- Waiting area for consultation, sales and rest area
- Shower and changing area for body treatments
- Administration office
- Computer system for bookings, stock control and accounting
- Color scheme is pastel
- Shop signage and A board included

The center will be open from 6am to 11pm Monday to Friday and 7am to 8pm on Saturdays and Sundays.

Management Summary

Woodland Gym limited is an established company set up and run by Julie Pineran, who has 18 years experience in the fitness center industry. The owner has start–up funds of $50,000 to fund the set–up costs and first four months cash flow. The expanded premises Woodland Gym needs have been secured and were previously used as offices.

We will have three beauticians and a receptionist. The owner will also be acting as manager for the salon. We will have five fitness coaches who will also offer personal training sessions and swap with the fitness studio lessons as well as look after people using the gym. We will recruit to have staff employed three weeks before opening so there is enough time for training everyone.

MARKETING & SALES

Grand Opening

The opening is all too important for every salon. We will have the launch event on January 1. We will invite local media for free memberships to the reporters for one year and run a competition in the local newspaper to win free treatments and classes for a month for 100 customers.

Marketing Plan

In addition to the opening, we need to ensure we build a presence fast. We will therefore put into place a comprehensive marketing plan to commence two weeks before launch. This will develop interest and communicate that we will be open for business:

- Local/free press—Teaser adverts two weeks before opening moving to stronger advertising closer to launch and including the newspaper competitions to be the first to use the center. There will be follow up flyers within the local papers for three months after the opening
- Website—We will develop a website and have it linked from fitness center directories and the local website
- Location—Large board advertising the impending opening
- Local magazines—There are three local glossy magazines we will take advertising and have the editor write a feature about the established center
- Word of mouth—The proprietor will visit each local shop and hand out a leaflet offering 50 percent discount in the first month. He will also visit local businesses offering the same discount
- Mailers—The post office will deliver special opening flyers into the doors of residents within 5 miles of the shop

We have allowed $2,500 for the opening, competitions and initial marketing plan.

FINANCIAL ANALYSIS

Revenues and profitability

Revenues forecasting for the first year of operation are exceptional. Net profits are forecast to be higher than average before tax and interest. In the following years the profit position will be dramatically improved due to our quality and service.

Investment

The investment to make the location ready for customers is $15,000. The cost of gym equipment and beauty room equipment is $20,000. This cost will be deferred because we will lease the equipment instead of purchasing it for our location. We are to purchase $5,000 of stock products to sell. We will also invest $1,100 in staff uniforms, robes, slippers and towels.

Gift Store

Little Treasures Gift Shop

5621 Leath St.
Fort Myers, Florida 33902

Gerald Rekve

EXECUTIVE SUMMARY

Business Overview

- Think through planned changes that will help grow our business and expand to a second location
- Confirm that we need a low–interest loan for $42,222 to increase our cash flow reserves

Company History

- Founded in 2007.
- Owned & operated by Marc Miskett.
- We sell a large variety of gift decor items like vases, pictures, nick nacks and unique furniture.
- Originally sold blinds and hardwood floorings.
- Consequently decided to phase out flooring because Home Depot opened a store in our city and the result, all our clients felt they were getting better pricing from Home Depot. We changed our products because we were losing too many sales.
- Moved to current location. Began offering e–gifts for both the home and the consumer. Business has really has taken off since. We were really impressed with how quickly our business started to grow.

Mission

We are committed to providing a unique assortment of gift and furnishings:

- In a way that promotes our belief in quality of service.
- So we can attract new customers and increase the variety of existing customers.
- As measured by an annual increase in sales of 18 percent.

OBJECTIVES

Personal Objectives

- Work less on weekends, spend more time doing hobbies.
- Start second location, which will result in more revenue and profit allowing me to work less, yet make more money.
- Earn enough to start taking winter vacations.
- In the long run, be in a great position to either sell or grow the business further.

Short–Term Objectives

- Hire two additional clerks in the next six months.
- Hire designer in the next twelve months.
- Identify markets that I can expand into.
- Keep eyes on product lines I can expand into.
- Watch competitors for trends.

Long–Term Objectives

- Grow sales by 45 percent within three years.
- Grow net profit before tax by 58 percent within two years.
- Expand to a second location to better serve our market and keep out direct competitors.
- Start increasing the staff so that we can spend more time on other family activities without working seven days a week.

COMPETITION

Wal–Mart:

- Large selection of low– and mid–priced designers, including glassware.
- Great location in downtown Fort Myers.
- Part of a national chain.
- Advertises every day in local newspaper.

Trinket Shoppe:

- Good selection of products.
- Around for over 18 years, so most residents know about it.
- Centrally located.

Peter's Gifts:

- Good location in the mall.
- Very popular for designers.
- Cramped store.
- High prices.

Fort Myers Tourist Trap:

- Located in the largest mall.
- Popular with young crowd.
- Carry a lot of tourist type gifts.

Competitive Advantages

- Our present store is located on the busiest shopping street in north–end Fort Myers.
- Well–known in the city.
- We have seen steady growth in the last four years.
- We project a 28 percent increase in sales in 2008.

PRODUCTS & SERVICES

- Franklin Mint
- Lamps
- Glass
- Imported items
- Ethnic items
- Native handmade items
- Picture frames, mirrors, kitchen accessories, theme and gift items currently account for 41percent of sales.
- Six percent discount on items purchased in volume (more than 52 items).
- Hand–carved pieces like mirror frames, frames, and rocking chairs currently account for 23 percent of sales.
- Coffee tables, bedside tables, and chests.
- Items for the bedroom and bathroom, including pillows, soap dishes, and toothbrush holders account for 14 percent of our sales.

MARKET ANALYSIS

Industry Factors and Trends

- Rising age of Fort Myers population means more people will be giving gifts.
- People choosing to stay and gift shop rather than travel.
- Increased media coverage and the 500 TV channel universe has allowed a number of TV Shows that cover every type of home decor and gift item. This has increased the public's desire to buy our products.
- Strong market for gift accessories.
- Not many stores offer merchandise that can't readily be found elsewhere.
- Some competitors' shops are cramped or impersonal.
- Opportunity for a gift decor store that offers unique items in a relaxing, attractive, personal atmosphere.

According to *Financial Post American Demographics*, $19 million was spent on furniture, appliances, home and furnishings in Greater Fort Myers in 2004. The 224,005 inhabitants spend more per capita on retail goods than any other product.

Economic Outlook

- Economic downturn causes many to put off buying big–ticket "luxury" items.
- Market for less expensive gifts strong.
- Local market for gift decor shows strong growth.
- Gift sales spike in the months leading up to a holiday, namely Christmas and Mother's Day.
- All of our product is purchased six months in advance, therefore tying up cash flow in mid–summer.

RISK FACTORS

Low– and mid–priced gift decor chains make it more difficult to compete on either price or selection.

We already have contingency plans in place:

- Personal wills.
- Money to invest.
- Personal life insurance.
- Commercial property insurance.
- General liability insurance.
- Workers' Compensation insurance intended for new employees.
- If something happens to one of us, the other one will continue running the store.
- If something happens to both of us, we will have the right to either continue to run business or sell it.
- Once our daughters come of age, they will be our replacements if they wish.
- If a major competitor moves onto our doorstep, we will launch a flyer campaign to existing customers with the slogan, "What makes your gift giving easy?"
- If one of our key suppliers ends our relationship, we will build alternate relationships with suppliers we identify.

CUSTOMERS

Our target market is made up of gift buyers, unique item collectors, and interior decorators. Specifically, gift buyers that buy 6–7 times per year) and people shopping for their own gifts that buy 4–7 times per year. They like to be the first person on the block with an unusual item. They appreciate fair value and clearly marked prices, and require the flexibility of a generous return policy. They also prefer personalized service. All of which we provide!

Customer Segment

- Gift buyers and established residents of Minot looking for reasonably priced, unique gift items.
- Our customers are mostly women between 24 and 55, either working or not.
- They spend on each average visit to our store $14.57.

- Our busiest days are Saturdays and Sundays along with Wednesday and Thursday evenings.
- Our customers are from all parts of the city we service. We are located in the north end of the city, yet we get a lot of clients from the south end of the city. This is the reason we want to put a location in the south end of the city.

MARKETING & SALES

We want our customers to feel:

- Excitement that goes with finding an unique item.
- Sense of calm that comes with shopping in a comfortable, quiet, and beautiful store.
- Feeling of confidence, as a result of our fairly extensive gift knowledge.

Pricing

We offer mid–range pricing on most items. With the exception of furniture, no item is priced higher than $188. Our picture frames are $23. We can't charge very low prices, since we must afford special suppliers and shipping costs that accumulate. We can't charge very high prices, because we want increase impulse buying by casual browsers.

Advertising

We have many advertising and promotional ideas.

- Our posters and some decor items displayed in the coffee shop next door.
- Sidewalk sign outside our store advertises sales.
- "28 percent off" coupons included in merchant flyer to area residents every 6 months.
- Advertisement in Saturday edition of Fort Myers newspaper.
- By end of year, we will launch a quarterly newsletter for existing customers that provides gift tips and updates on new merchandise.

Sales

- We are currently the only salespeople.
- Customers pay by VISA, MasterCard, American Express, debit card, cash, or check.
- Full refund with store receipt up to 62 days purchase after (5 percent of sales returned).
- Free delivery services (within the city limits) of large furniture items costing more than $120.00.

Alliances

We have a professional alliance with Grinders Coffee Shop (our next door neighbor and the most popular coffee shop in Fort Myers). We allow them to put two tables of outdoor seating outside our store. Advertisements for our store are featured in the coffee shop, and clearly–marked products from our store (e.g. framed pictures, flower vases) decorate the coffee shop.

MANAGEMENT SUMMARY

Marc Miskett:

- I keep the books and manage inventory.
- Previously worked as an office manager.

- We decide what merchandise to buy and how to display it in the store.
- Previously a store manager for Wal–Mart.

Julia Steiner:

- Store Assistant Manager
- Manages the store 20 hours/week. In the past, she only managed the store anytime we were away.

Hiring Plan

We plan to hire two full–time salesclerks within six months. They must have experience working in retail. They may be promoted to Store Manager within two years, which will give us more flexibility to spend time away from the store. The Store Manager's salary is $44,000 a year.

We will also hire more part–time salespeople within twelve months. This will accommodate increased store traffic. They will be paid $13 an hour.

We will post classified ads in the Fort Myers daily newspaper to find candidates. We will also find prospective high school student candidates through referrals

FINANCIAL ANALYSIS

Necessary Improvements

- $20,000 for leasehold improvements.
- Update fixtures to allow us to display gift and small accents.
- Install new lighting to spotlight key items.
- New shelving for stock room to allow greater small item inventory.
- $25,000 for one–time increase in gift inventory.
- $2,500 for another checkout, which will accommodate increased traffic and improve customer service.

TOTAL REQUIRED: $29,000; to be repaid from cash flow, with $4,000 annual repayments every March and annual interest at a rate of 8 percent.

Ratios

Ratio analysis	Industry profile
Sales growth	2.62%
Percent of total assets	
accounts receivable	17.07%
Inventory	35.01%
Other current assets	26.92%
Total current assets	79.00%
Long-term assets	21.00%
Total assets	100.00%
Current liabilities	35.69%
Long-term liabilities	14.48%
Total liabilities	50.17%
Net worth	49.83%
Percent of sales	
sales	100.00%
Gross margin	32.95%
Selling, general & administrative expenses	20.27%
Advertising expenses	1.64%
Profit before interest and taxes	1.81%
Main ratios	
current	1.95
Quick	0.81
Total debt to total assets	3.91%
Pre-tax return on net worth	54.85%
Pre-tax return on assets	8.66%
Business vitality profile	Industry

Ratio analysis	Industry profile
Sales per employee	$82,122
Survival rate	68.67%
Additional ratios	
Net profit margin	n.a
Return on equity	n.a
Activity ratios	
accounts receivable turnover	n.a
Collection days	n.a
Inventory turnover	n.a
Accounts payable turnover	n.a
Payment days	n.a
Total asset turnover	n.a
Debt ratios	
debt to net worth	n.a
Current liab. to liab.	n.a
Liquidity ratios	
net working capital	n.a
Interest coverage	n.a
Additional ratios	
assets to sales	n.a
Current debt/total assets	n.a
Acid test	n.a
Sales/net worth	n.a
Dividend payout	n.a

Class of worker

Unpaid family workers	27
Self employed workers in own not incorporated business	527
Government workers	1,530
Private wage and salary workers	12,808

Household income

Median household income

$200,000 or more	89
$150,000 to $199,999	103
$100,000 to $149,999	528
$75,000 to $99,999	871
$50,000 to $74,999	2,329
$35,000 to $49,999	2,230
$25,000 to $34,999	1,759
$15,000 to $24,999	1,865
$10,000 to $14,999	843
Less than $10,000	1,419

Poverty status – Below poverty level

Families	**975**
With related children under 18 years	841
Families with female householder, no husband present	**661**
With related children under 18 years	625

Median resident age: 33.7 years
Median household income: $35,714 (year 2000)
Median house value: $85,400 (year 2000)

Races in Fort Myers

- White non-hispanic (49.4%)
- Black (34.8%)
- Hispanic (10.5%)
- Other race (4.6%)
- Two or more races (3.1%)
- American Indian (0.9%)
- Vietnamese (0.8%)
- Asian Indian (0.7%)
- Chinese (0.6%)

(Total can be greater than 100% because Hispanics could be counted in other races)

Ancestries: Italian (16.6%), Irish (12.3%), German (9.8%), English (4.7%), Polish (3.3%), United States (2.2%).

Requirements

Start-up expenses	
Legal	$ 2,000
Publications/membership	$ 200
Office equipment	$ 2,000
Consultants	$ 5,000
Insurance	$ 1,200
Website development/hosting	$ 1,500
Website management	$ 1 00
Expensed equipment	$ 2,000
Other	$ 8,000
Total start-up expenses	
Start-up assets needed	
Cash balance on starting date	$10,000
Total requirements	
Funding	30,000
Investment	20,000

Sales forecast (planned)

Sales	2004	2005	2006	Direct cost of sales	2004	2005	2006
Gifts	$144,000	$168,000	$179,000	Gifts	$34,000	$46,000	$78,000
Seasonal items	$ 40,000	$ 60,000	$100,000	Seasonal items	$14,000	$19,000	$22,000
Total sales	**$184,000**	**$228,000**	**$279,000**	**Subtotal direct cost of sales**	**$48,000**	**$65,000**	**$100,000**

Home Renovation Contractor

STEPHENS CONTRACTING

1242 Rocky River Rd.
Baltimore, Maryland 21201

Gerald Rekve

Stephens Contracting does home renovations for all types of customers, ranging from refinishing basements to remodeling kitchens to building new additions. They administer the application process for all, choose permits and manage subcontractors, orders and stores building materials, and provide project management.

EXECUTIVE SUMMARY

Originally founded as a sole proprietorship in 1989 and incorporated in 2000, Stephens Contracting primarily does home renovation projects for customers in and around Baltimore, Maryland.

Residential construction is a $6 million market in Baltimore. In recent years, many general contractors have turned their attention to commercial building, and away from Baltimore area residents. Using a combined office and warehouse space and relying heavily on salvage materials, Stephens Contracting combines a long–standing reputation and reasonable pricing to target underserved, aging homeowners, with general contracting services that are marked by a commitment to minimal disruption of everyday life, fair cost, clear pricing, and excellent service.

In December 2006, Robert Richardson joined Stephens Contracting as a co–owner. This business plan establishes a blueprint for growing the business. It also documents the agreement between Matt Stephens and Robert Richardson about how the business will be run and how various contingencies will be handled.

BUSINESS OVERVIEW

Legal/name of business

Stephens Contracting

Business address

1242 Rocky River Rd., Baltimore MD 21201

Phone number

410-555-5555

Business Structure

Incorporated company.

Major shareholders	% Ownership
Matt Stephens	60%
Robert Richardson	40%

Date business established

April 2006; incorporated January 2007

Nature of business

General Contractor

Company History

Stephens Contracting was founded by Matt Stephens in 2006. Since then, the business has grown to over $600,000 in revenues. In winter of 2006, Matt Stephens invited Robert Richardson, a leading area subcontractor, to join Stephens Contracting as a co–owner.

ORGANIZATION

Business Strategy

Stephens Contracting is committed to being honest and upfront with customers, while minimizing the inconvenience that can accompany construction. The business aims for consistently strong financial performance, earned as by growth in referrals and the number of projects completed each year.

Objectives

Matt Stephens: Matt's motivation is the same as it was when he decided to start Stephens Contracting two years ago: make construction better for customers, and get paid well for it. In two years, he'd like Stephens Contracting to be able to operate without his everyday involvement, so he can take his company to the next step.

Robert Richardson: For Robert, joining Stephens Contracting is about seizing a new level of job security, and taking personal responsibility for his livelihood instead of being at the whim of general contractors and others.

Short–Term Objectives

1. Buy a pick–up truck by the end of January 2007
2. Complete 75 projects in 2007
3. Reach sales of $990,000 in 2007

Long–Term Objectives

1. Achieve increased profitability in 2007
2. Establish concrete succession plans within five years

PRODUCT OVERVIEW

Stephens Contracting does home renovations for all types of customers, ranging from refinishing basements to remodeling kitchens to building new additions. They administer the application process for all, choose permits and manage subcontractors, orders and stores building materials, and provide project management.

Competition

Stephens Contracting's competitive advantage combination is a result of its low overhead and great reputation since they buy the majority of building the materials at salvage yards or recycling depots, and the office and warehousing space is located on Matt's own premises, Stephens Contracting can get very competitive prices. Plus, its longstanding reputation for quality and integrity in the community makes a preferred it choice for home renovations.

Stephens Contracting's primary competition is as follows (listed in order of business size):

1. Group Contractors. With over 40 employees, Group Contractors does a wide range of projects, including residential, commercial, and institutional. It's known for its low prices. In Robert's experience, many local sub contractors complain about how hard it is to work with and get paid by the company.
2. Stone Builders. While its core business has always been resident at building and renovations, seems to be bidding on more and more commercial projects. It has a reputation for doing high quality work on time. The company's prices are high.
3. Elm Contracting. The core of Elm Contracting business is renovating old homes for new home-owners. With a slowdown in the housing market, it has been relatively hard hit in recent years. The business continues to have very good relationships with real agents in the area (the owner's wife is an agent), but now it's recently been seen around town doing more small commercial projects.
4. Handel Construction. Handel Construction focuses on building home additions and outdoor decks. While Handel has a long standing tradition for getting the job done at a reasonable price, a former customer complained that the company did not do a satisfactory job.
5. Wendell Contraction. Is a highly recommended for high–end bathroom and kitchen remodeling jobs. The quality of his work is *very* high.

Increasingly, many of Stephens Contracting's competitors are going after residential commercial and institutional projects. While those that continue to focus on home renovation are strong, and most have relatively narrow specialties. Also, Stephens Contracting sees room for improved customer service. That means an opportunity to provide both reasonable pricing and good service.

Because Baltimore is small, all of Stephens's competitors are well–known in the community. Consequently, reputation is *very* important. A key part of maintaining a strong reputation is strong relationships with reliable, high–quality subcontractors. This is one reason why Stephens Contracting decided to bring Robert—who brings great subcontracting experience and contacts—on board.

MARKET ANALYSIS

The percentage of the Baltimore population that are of the age 40 and up rose significantly between 1999 and 2007. Compared to other age groups, aging Baby Boomers tend to have more money to spend on services like general contracting.

Driven by the growth of home improvement chain stores, more and more home construction projects have been undertaken as do–it–yourself projects by homeowners themselves. That means less work for general contractors.

Housing construction usually dips before a recession hits and bounces back before the general economy does. While the number and dollar value of Baltimore residential building permits dropped steadily between 2000 and 2004, many think this trend is now reversing because of low interest rates and a strengthening local economy.

The do–it–yourself trend has been declining in the last few years mainly due to the concern home owners have for quality of work and environmental concerns such as global warming. The recent decline in residential building will lead many area general contractors concentrate more than ever on commercial and residential projects. At the same time, Stephens Contracting expects a strengthening economy and increased disposable income among Baby Boomers to cause the local market for residential contracting services—home and renovations in particular—to grow in the near future.

Regulatory factors and trends

A general contracting license is required for a project costing more than $500. To become licensed, one must pass a licensing exam after working for four years as a journeyman, foreman, contractor, or owner–builder. This means that Stephens's competitors all have a certain level of skill.

Environmental factors and trends

Increasingly homeowners prefer friendly contractors who care about the home needs and use building materials and techniques that meet the highest standards. As a result, general contractors will keep up with new "green" building practices products.

Customers

The average annual market for residential building was $47 million between and 2004 and 2007.

Customers for general contracting services can be broken into residential customers, commercial customers, and institutional customers. Residential customers can be divided into people building new homes and people making improvements to their homes, like additions or remodeling jobs.

Stephens Contracting targets people making improvements to their homes. In particular, the business goes after aging baby boomers, who have more disposable income and who are getting more reluctant to take on do–it–yourself jobs. In most cases these are working professionals who do not have the time to do any work themselves. These clients would rather hire contractors.

These customers place a premium on three things: competitive and fair project pricing, minimum disruption of their daily lives, and service that emphasizes trust and communication.

If they're not using Stephens Contracting these customers are either undertaking such projects themselves—which is becoming more difficult as they grow older—or they are employing other contractors. Existing customers say they choose Stephens Contracting because the company is easy to work with and delivers what it promises, at *very* good prices.

MARKETING & SALES

Stephens Contracting appeals to customers's desire for quality and competitive prices.

1. Ease–of–use, through "low–impact" construction methods and clear projects.
2. Reasonable costs, enabled by minimal overhead and material costs.
3. Confidence, via "fraud–proof" pricing and emphasis on communicating with customers.

Pricing

Stephens Contracting charges 20 percent of building costs as a general contracting fee. It caps its fee at a fixed price, specified in the project contract. This allows customers to clearly separate Stephens

Contracting's fee from building costs, while protecting them from unnecessary increases during the course of the project.

According to customers who have entertained bids from other contractors, competitor prices range from 16 percent to 22 percent of building costs. No other competitor is known to cap at a maximum fee. Stephens Contracting is able to charge such competitive prices because of its low office overhead and warehousing costs.

Advertising

Stephens Contracting already promotes its services through:

1. Printed business cards.
2. A Yellow Pages listing.
3. Signs with the business contact information on the lawn of any home currently being worked on.
4. Classified ad in local newspaper, weekly and daily newspaper.
5. Design website.
6. Post ads on local website classifieds owned by radio stations.

Services

1. When a prospective customer calls, Stephens Contracting's office manager, Matt sets up an appointment for a free consultation.
2. Matt Stephens or Robert conducts a free consultation at the prospective customer's home.
3. Matt Stephens and Robert work together complete to an estimate.
4. Once the customer has approved the estimate, a contract is drawn up for their signature.

OPERATIONS

Management Summary

- Matt Stephens, Owner/Operator. Prior to starting Stephens Contracting, Matt spent four years as contractor with Woodbend Contracting. Matt is responsible for pricing, supervision and client service.
- Robert Richardson, Owner/Operator. Robert has provided specialized services to fewer than 40 sub contractor's firms over the last 15 years. Robert is primarily responsible for managing the sub-contractors. This includes reviewing existing relationships on a regular basis, terms and recommending alternate subcontractors when necessary. He also shares project supervision client and service responsibilities with Robert.
- Cheryl Tomkin, Office Manager. Cheryl is responsible for most administrative duties, which includes keeping the company's books.

Matt and Robert will never take vacation at the same time to ensure there is always an administrator present to act on behalf of the company. In Robert's first few months with Stephens Consulting, he will accompany Matt on initial consultations and walk–through of projects whenever possible. After on the job, he will be allowed to conduct consultations and walk–throughs on his own.

Hiring Plans

On a day–to–day basis, Stephens' current staff of three should be sufficient for the several next years. After that, the business may hire another licensed general contractor at a salary that will probably exceed $66,000.

Suppliers

Materials Suppliers

Appleton Lumber Salvage. 60 day payment terms, 5 percent discount for payment in 40 days. Free weekly deliveries. Needed materials are sometimes unavailable. They will acquire them at the Home Depot Lumber Yard at average prices with a 40 day payment terms.

Labor Suppliers

Stephens Contracting has firmly established relationships with quality local subcontractors.

RISK FACTORS

Stephens Contracting holds both worker's compensation and general liability insurance. Matt and Robert both have life insurance, disability insurance and personal wills.

If one of the business owners is unable to work or dies, the other owner will continue running the business for at least five years. Stephens Contracting will work with law firm Watkins and Watkins to develop firm succession plans that provide for Matt's semi–retirement.

If a subcontractor delivers substandard work, Stephens Contracting will immediately replace this subcontractor with a qualified supplier from its pool of subcontractors. Stephens Contracting provides the affected customer with a 5 percent discount.

If subcontractors are unable to deliver for some circumstance like a union strike, Matt Stephens and Robert Richardson are prepared to complete the work themselves to the greatest extent possible. Between them, they have experience in nearly every trade required.

If sales fall more than 20 percent short of expectations in any year, both Matt and Robert have agreed to take a 20 percent salary cut.

FINANCIAL ANALYSIS

Stephens Contracting requires a $10,000 operating of credit to cover cash flow shortfalls.

Stephens Contracting is projected to do $990,000 in sales in 2007, with $248,800 in net profit.

Balance sheet

As of December 2005

Assets				*(Projected)*	*(Projected)*
Current Assets					
Cash	$ 5,699	$ 6,863	$ 51,955	$ 31,595	$ 39,953
Accounts receivable	51,775	57,516	58,356	51,598	58,111
Total current assets	**55,575**	**55,168**	**81,171**	**61,991**	**77,953**
Fixed assets (net of depreciation)					
Tools	5,856	5,585	5,171	3,599	3,199
Vehicles	11,959	8,565	5,855	31,599	15,119
Total net fixed assets	**15,785**	**11,751**	**8,935**	**35,198**	**17,318**
Other assets					
Long-term investments	11,111	31,111	55,100	55,111	51,001
Total other assets	**11,111**	**31,000**	**55,111**	**55,000**	**51,111**
Total assets	**$61,358**	**$75,918**	**$135,196**	**$131,189**	**$155,161**

Liabilities and equity					
Current liabilities					
Accounts payable	$55,863	$51,551	$55,787	$56,115	$59,761
Accrued liabilities	5,559	7,551	8,965	1,151	6,859
Total current liabilities			**53,753**	**57,365**	**56,611**
Total liabilities	**59,311**	**58,891**	**53,753**	**57,365**	**56,611**
Equity					
Equity contribute	1,111	1,111	36,111	36,111	36,111
Retained earnings	31,157	56,138	55,555	57,835	73,561
Total equity	**31,157**	**57,138**	**81,555**	**85,835**	**98,561**

Income statement

	2003	2004	2005	2006 (projected)	2007 (projected)	Assumptions
Sales	$713,615	$766,311	$831,651	$991,111	$1,189,111	11% increase
Cost of goods sold						
Direct costs	595,856	658,513	685,714	835,111	917,511	
Cost of goods sold	595,856	658,513	685,719	835,111	917,511	
Gross profit	118,769	137,713	156,953	165,111	181,511	
Expenses						
Owner's salaries	51,111	53,511	55,111	111,111	111,111	Flat salary while building business
Employee wages	53,111	55,111	55,111	55,111	56,111	per year raise
Accounting and legal	911	1,151	751	811	851	5% increase
Advertising and promotion	575	537	671	851	895	5% increase
Automobile and travel	3,965	5,811	5,666	5,611	5,781	5% increase
Bad debts						
Business taxes, fees,	3,111		1,611	—	—	5% increase
Licenses	911	1,153	1,153	1,111	1,151	5% increase
Rent	6,111	6,111	6,111	6,111	6,111	no change anticipated
Insurance	1,131	1,131	1,561	1,531	1,586	5% increase
Bank charges	187	316	361	376	391	5% increase
Maintenance and repairs		161	58	—	—	5% increase
Internet access/email			85	353	365	5% increase
Telephone	656	653	638	635	655	5% increase
Utilities	685	717	737	731	756	5% increase
Other office expenses	611	585	785	611	651	5% increase
Depreciation and amortization	5,655	3,711	3,161	11,537	7,581	51% declining balance
Expenses	113,359	115,181	3117			
Assumption total	118,661	161,569	159,935			
Net profit before income taxes	$16,551	$35,531	$38,381	$5,651	$31,575	
Income taxes						
Income tax rate	53.5%	53.1%	51.7%	51.7%	51.7%	
Income tax payable	5,559	7,551	8,965	1,151	6,859	
Net profit after income taxes	$11,191	$15,971	$19,516	$3,581	$15,756	

Expenses	113,359	115,181	3117		
Assumption total	118,661	161,569	159,935		
Net profit before income taxes	$16,551	$35,531	$38,381	$5,651	$31,575
Income taxes					
Income tax rate	53.5%	53.1%	51.7%	51.7%	51.7%
Income tax payable	5,559	7,551	8,965	1,151	6,859
Net profit after income taxes	$11,191	$15,971	$19,516	$3,581	$15,756

Business finances monthly cash flow

For the year ending December 31, 2005

	Jan	Feb	Mar	Apr	May	Jun	Jul	Aug	Sep	Oct	Nov
Cash Receipts											
Cash sales	31,111	31,111	31,111	35,111	51,111	55,111	55,111	55,111	55,111	51,111	35,111
Collection of accounts recieved	51,111	51,111	51,111	51,111	51,111	61,111	71,111	71,111	71,111	71,111	61,111
Total Cash Receipts	61,111	61,111	61,111	65,111	81,111	95,111	115,111	115,111	115,111	111,111	85,111
Cash Dispersements											
Direct Costs	51,111	51,111	51,111	51,111	63,511	75,111	87,511	87,511	87,511	87,511	75,111
Purchase of fixed assets	35,111				511						
Owner's salaries	8,555	8,555	8,555	8,555	8,555	8,555	8,555	8,555	8,555	8,555	8,555
Employee wages	3,917	3,917	3,917	3,917	3,917	3,917	3,917	3,917	3,917	3,917	3,917
Accounting and legal		811									
Advertising and promotion	191	61	61	61	61	61	61	61	61	61	61
Automobile and travel	511	511	511	511	511	511	511	511	511	511	511
Buisness taxes, fees, license	511						511				
Rent	511	511	511	511	511	511	511	511	511	511	511
Insurance	111	111	111	111	111	111	111	111	111	111	111
Bank charges	35	35	35	35	35	35	35	35	35	35	35
Internet access/email	31	31	31	31	31	31	31	31	31	31	31
Telephone	53	53	53	53	53	53	53	53	53	53	53
Utilities	71	71	71	61	61	61	51	51	51	61	61
Other office expenses	51	51	51	51	51	51	51	51	51	51	51
Total Cash Dispursements	88,166	65,356	63,556	63,536	75,536	87,536	111,516	99,916	99,916	99,936	87,536
Increase In Cash	(31,751)	(5,551)	(559)	319	766	579	1,151	1,655	3,316	3,779	5,551
Opening Cash Balance	18,111	(5,751)	(7,161)	(7,519)	(7,311)	(6,555)	(5,855)	(5,715)	(5,159)	(855)	1,957
Ending Cash Balance	(5,751)	(7,161)	(7,519)	(7,311)	(6,555)	(5,855)	(5,715)	(5,159)	(855)	1,957	5,378

Landscaping Service

Helping Hand, Inc.

47 Brookdale Ave.
Madison, Wisconsin 53704

Gerald Rekve

This business plan concentrates on the expansion of an existing landscaping business's scope. The goal is to make the landscaping business a year–round business, by adding handyman services.

EXECUTIVE SUMMARY

Helping Hand, Inc. has been in the landscaping business in Madison for the last six years. However, since the nature of the landscaping business is seasonal, we are interested in expanding our company into a handyman service and making it a year–round operation. Our goal is to offset the fixed costs our landscaping business incurs in the winter months thereby increasing the overall profitability of our company. With the addition of a handyman service, we project that our sales will increase by $190,000 for a combined total of $445,000. In order to achieve this goal, we are seeking a term loan of $100,000 to purchase the necessary handyman equipment.

We will offer our services to our existing residential and commercial client base. We have already secured commitments from existing clients as well as a local regional development sector which has been allocated for $15 million in renovation grants for low income families. In addition, the handyman business in Madison, Wisconsin is on the verge of substantial growth. The City of Madison has voted to contract out all handyman services which translate into an additional $25 million in potential new business. This brings the total market for private handyman services in Madison to $40 million. In light of this information, we hope to reach $500,000 in revenue from our handyman business within three years.

Business Strategy

Our strategy is to sell our services to both the residential and commercial sectors with two unique offers. We will guarantee service within twelve hours of the property damage. We will implement a flat monthly rate for handyman services based on the size of the property. Since an overly severe winter would negatively impact business sales and an overly mild winter would hamper residential sales, our policy is to keep an even split between residential and business customers, thereby minimizing undue risk.

Management Summary

Helping Hands, Inc. was formed in Madison, Wisconsin by Patrick and Jon O'Reilly. We own 100 percent of the company's shares.

All services will be provided by us—Patrick and Jon O'Reilly—with four maintenance people to be hired on a sub–contractor basis. As veteran small business owners, we have a good grasp of the fundamentals of running a handyman/landscaping company and have honed our sales and marketing skills.

We are confident that our business idea is a sound one and would be of use to our existing client base. Complete financial statements of our existing business are available upon request.

We have decided not to increase our salaries with the addition of the handyman business. This will keep

Title	Name	Job description	Qualifications
Co-owner	Patrick O'Reilly	Responsible for the overall running of the company, including the supervision of labor Responsible for building sales for the company and securing additional	Degree in landscape architecture from Calgary Polytechnic Institute 4 years experience in sales and operations in landscaping business Excellent management and negotiation skills
Co-owner	Jon O'Reilly	Responsible for all bookkeeping and marketing tasks for the company Responsible for all customer service	Graduate of 2 year business program at Medicine Hat College 3 years accounting experience for local trucking business
4 Handyman workers	TBA	Drive and operate vehicles	Minimum of 1 year experience in snow removal Valid drivers license with a clean driving record

Compensation

Position	Salary
Co-owners	$50,000 each/annual
4 Seasonal handyman	$37,000 each/annual
4 Occasional landscape staff	$12/hour

money in the business to ensure our success in the early years.

Professional Relationships

We have established good working relationships with a number of professionals as a result of operating our landscaping business.

Personnel Requirements

The four seasonal positions for maintenance worker will be made available to persons with a valid driver's license and a clean driving record. One year of handyman experience is required. Even though we currently have seasonal landscape employees, these positions have the potential to become year–round. Therefore landscaping skills will be considered a great asset. Handyman/maintenance worker will be paid based on an annual salary of $37,000. The occasional assistants, who will be under the seasonal driver's supervision, will be used on an as–needed basis and will be paid an hourly wage of $12.00.

PRODUCTS & SERVICES

Helping Hand, Inc. has been in the landscaping business in Madison for four years and has a history of profitability. However, since the nature of the landscaping business is seasonal, we are interested in expanding our company into handyman services and making it a year–round operation. We will offer our services to our existing residential and commercial clients.

We will offer a wide variety of handyman services which include the following:

- General repairs
- Home repairs
- Yard and fence repairs
- Deck building and repairs
- Roof repairs
- Carpet repairs
- Electrical repairs
- Small home appliance repairs
- Painting and staining
- Lawn care
- Landscaping
- Tree planting and removal
- Water fountain installation and repair
- Driveway brick landscaping
- Carpentry
- Woodworking
- Window repair
- Drywall and Gyp rock

MARKET ANALYSIS

As a northern state, Wisconsin has always had a need for handyman services during the winter. With the average person working longer hours and juggling more leisure activities than ever before, the need for professional handyman services have increased in the residential sector. Similarly, as the number of small businesses with limited staffs continues to increase, more professional handyman services are being used by these businesses as an alternative to bringing maintenance people in house. And, with new policies being implemented to fine people and businesses that fail to clear their property of public hazards by property or damaged fence hazards in the wintertime, market research indicates that handyman services will enjoy a growth rate of approximately 12 percent per year for the next five years due to Government grants now available.

On a local level, the city of Madison has recently voted to contract out $11.5 million in handyman services.

Industry Sectors

Residential sector: Private residences in the Madison area; primarily those mid–to–high income dwellings inhabited by busy professionals who don't have time to shovel.

Business sector: Primarily comprised of strip mall tenants and those operating from storefront locations in the greater Madison area. In addition, large institutions such as schools, hospitals and seniors' homes that, due to cutbacks, have decreased the number of maintenance workers employed, but still need to maintain a high level of winter safety.

Seasonal Factors

Helping Hand, Inc. is extremely sensitive to seasonal factors. A winter with a particularly heavy snowfall would result in an increase in demand for handyman services; conversely, a mild winter would be potentially be better to a handyman company depending on the way its contracts are priced, with more home owners getting outside work done. However, Madison weather patterns for the last ten years have been extremely stable and the average number of property damage from year to year doesn't vary more than 5 percent.

Growth Strategy

With the risk of a substantial fine from the municipal government for failure to remove public hazards caused by property damage or damaged fence within twelve hours of a incident , residential use of handyman services has increased by 12 percent over the last five years. Similarly, with lawsuits stemming from property negligence on the rise, local businesses are 44 percent more likely to contract out handyman services than ten years ago.

Position in the Industry

Having been in the landscaping business for six years, we have established a strong reputation for ourselves in the Madison community with both business and residential customers. We are known for offering friendly and competitively priced service and enjoy a high rate of referral business. Of our more than 300 customers, the vast majority have expressed a commitment to using our handyman services once they are fully functional.

Competition

There are currently a total of 140 handyman services in the Madison area. The two largest services—Craftsmen Company and Smith Brothers—currently control 20 percent of the local market. These companies are well established and have both been in business for more than 20 years. The remaining 80 percent is currently split between 138 smaller contractors. Although other contractors may try to cash in on the government's new government grant or the city's decision to contract landscaping or handyman services, Helping Hand, Inc. is in a practically favorable position. We have built up relationships with clients in both the residential and business sectors as well as the municipal government over the last four years. Therefore, we are in an excellent position not only to win contracts from the government, but also from private sectors and residential customers.

MARKETING & SALES

Use of Technology

We plan to make use of our computerized database, compiled during our four years in the landscape business, to market our handyman services to existing clients. This will be an advantage over a number of our competitors who do not use a database, since it will allow us to track services rendered for customers and to send out direct mail offers to them to solicit further business.

Although other contractors may try to cash in on the government's new government grants or city's decision to contract out contractors to remove public hazards caused by property damage, Helping Hand, Inc. is in a particularly favorable position. We have built up relationships with clients in both the residential and business sectors as well as the municipal government over the last four years.

Customers

The total market for handyman services is $4,000,000 which is comprised of the following markets:

Residential:

- comprised primarily of mid–to–upper income professional families in detached dwellings who are simply too busy to clear their own snow.
- The market is worth approximately $1.4 million.

Commercial: This market can be further broken down into three categories:

1. Small Business—consists largely of strip mall and store front locations in the downtown core. This Sector is worth approximately $2,454,000 in the Madison market.
2. Institutions—consists of schools, hospitals and other large public organizations, who have large budgets for maintenance and generally pay invoices within their 30 day terms. In total, the Madison market is worth approximately $3,454,000.
3. Municipal government contracts—In addition to the above–mentioned markets, a percentage of our business will be comprised of contracts from the city, who has decided to outsource all handymen in the Madison area. The contracts are estimated to be worth about $20 million.

Services

We will market ourselves as the year–round maintenance people who show individualized attention to our clients. Our larger competition is unable to offer this personalized service and—since they deal primarily with businesses and government contracts—they are more expensive. We will offer our clients reasonable prices and superior customer service. Through our handbills and direct marketing letters, we will position our services as an inexpensive and hassle–free way to maintain property. By using our services, residential customers will avoid paying fines.

Pricing Strategy

Commercial Customers: We will offer repairs for flat rate hourly fees based on the job that requires to be done.

Residential Customers: We estimate an average seasonal price range of $100–$900 depending upon the size of the job.

Credit Terms

Commercial customers: net 30 days on approved credit

Residential: 50 percent before we start the job and the balance when we are done.

We have made provisions for extended payment terms in our cash flow. We expect collections to be as follows: 75 percent to be collected in the first 30 days, 25 percent within 60 days. Special contracts would be negotiated for the significantly larger handyman work on the senior citizens' home, shopping mall and community college.

Sales and Distribution Plan

Through the operation of our landscaping business, we have established good working relationships with our existing client base. Our plan is to offer our handyman services to our existing landscaping client base in the residential and business sectors. We have already secured commitments from present clients as well as a local senior citizens' home, a shopping mall and a local community college. We intend to contact the remainder of our existing clients by mail and follow–up phone calls in order to introduce our new handyman service. We will do a limited amount of targeted advertising (see below) in order to generate sales leads. Sales leads will be closed by a phone call and an in–person sales call from one of the company's owners.

ADVERTISING

Our computerized database of landscaping clients will serve as a base from which to market our handyman services. It will allow us to track services rendered for customers and to send out direct mail offers to them to solicit further business.

Helping Hand, Inc.'s new services will be advertised and promoted in a number of ways:

- Produce and deliver 50,000 hand bills to be delivered door–to–door in November (estimated cost: $3,454)
- Advertise in the community newspaper on a weekly basis for November through March (estimated cost: $600 monthly)
- Post notices on bulletin boards in community centers, sports complexes, community colleges and shopping centers (estimated cost: $100)
- Send letters to our existing client base, advertising our services (estimated cost: $300)

We estimate the costs of promoting the new service will be $2,454 and will result in an additional $240,000 in gross annual sales.

OPERATIONS

We have already sourced a supplier of four–wheel–drive trucks, hauling trucks to transport any materials or debris found at the site, snow blowers and plow blades, and we have also located a storage area for this equipment. In addition, we have interviewed our existing landscaping client base and have gauged their level of interest in handyman services.

Helping Hand, Inc. will lease a 1,454 square foot storage space for our equipment at a rate of $600 per month. We plan on purchasing three trucks equipped with plow blades, snow blowers and three trailers. We will maintain our existing home office facility, which is already equipped with a fax machine, printer, copier and computer systems all of which we own outright.

Once our client commitments have been secured, winter weather is the only factor affecting the demand on service. In Madison we don't anticipate any drastic changes in weather conditions.

Our truck will do commercial properties in the early morning while parking lots are empty. Residential lots will be done late morning or early afternoon after people have left for work.

In order to be operational, the following steps must take place.

1. Obtain $159,000 of bank financing for additional equipment including:

- Three trucks equipped with plow blades
- Three snow blowers
- Three trailers

2. Secure a storage area for this equipment—budgeted cost $600 per month
3. Advertise our handyman services to our existing client base and the population of Madison at large
4. Negotiate with municipal government to obtain contracts for handyman and hire and train three laborers to help with operations.

Risk Factors

The following factors could pose problems to the business:

- Extremely severe winter conditions would render the commercial contracts uneconomical and could make guaranteed twelve–hour residential service unrealistic
- Extremely mild winter conditions would result in a decline in the number of residential jobs undertaken and negatively impact profits
- Damage to equipment would result in costly repair and replacement fees

Contingency Plan

In the last decade, Madison's winter weather patterns have been relatively stable with only a 15 percent variation in the number of the number of property damage from year to year. Therefore, it is unlikely that conditions will be drastically milder or more severe than usual. However, since an overly severe winter would negatively impact business sales and an overly mild winter would hamper residential sales, our policy is to keep an even split between residential and business customers, thereby minimizing undue risk. We will also purchase comprehensive insurance on all handyman equipment.

Alliances and Partnerships

In an effort to network with other entrepreneurs, we are members of the Madison Entrepreneurial Alliance Chamber of Commerce.

FINANCIAL ANALYSIS

Income Statement

An income statement showing incremental results of the handyman business has been prepared because the handyman "division" is intended to be an add–on service to our existing company. This existing company already has an administrative infrastructure set up that can accommodate the handyman business with negligible additional cost. The income statement indicates estimated gross sales of $240,000 for the first year with after–tax profit of approximately $24,000. Certain items included in the administrative expenses could be charged to the "division", however, that would not change the overall income or cash flow as these funds would be disbursed in the Landscape "division". Ongoing expenses relate to the operation of the vehicles and the salaries of handymen and workers. The equipment must be stored in the off season; insurance is still required and financing costs continue to be incurred during that period.

Cash Flow Statement

A term loan in the amount of $159,000 to finance the acquisition of handyman equipment is being sought. Since the division of our business is seasonal, cash generated is limited to the winter months, more specifically, November to April. The bulk of operating expenses also coincides with that period. However, certain fixed outflows would continue for the balance of the year including storage for the equipment, interest and insurance. The Cash Flow statement indicates that the division will generate a positive cash inflow of approximately $65,000.

Balance Sheet

The Balance Sheet demonstrates a strong financial position with $36,000 in cash, $37,000 of collectable accounts receivable and current liabilities of approximately $22,000. We will have capital assets in excess of $240,000 which will be the backbone of our future operation. As our business continues to grow, future capital additions may be required.

CONCLUSION

It is our goal to expand our existing landscaping business to include handyman services, making it a year–round operation. In order to achieve this goal, we are asking for a term loan of $159,000. Once we have secured this loan, and purchased the necessary equipment, we anticipate that our sales will increase by $240,000—approximately $24,000 of which we are projecting as net profit.

We have taken into consideration the fact that part–time drivers could present a risk by quitting or being laid off, and have agreed to do the driving if this should ever be the case until a replacement driver is hired. Although a year with light property damage or damaged/fallen fences would negatively affect our revenue from residential business, this will be offset by a reduction in part–time driver costs and will not affect the monthly billing of our corporate clients.

We are confident that our existing client base will use our services and we have secured commitments from a number of local businesses and institutions. Furthermore, since the City of Madison has voted to contract out all handyman services to private companies, now is the perfect time for Helping Hand, Inc. to expand.

Income statement

For the year ending October 31, 2005

Month	Nov 1	Dec 2	Jan 3	Feb 4	Mar 5	Apr 6
Sales	**$—**	**$—**	**$—**	**$—**	**$—**	**$25,000**
Expenses						
Salaries						23,222
Other wages						16,000
Benefits						2,750
Equipment storage	600	600	600	600	600	600
Promotion	500	500	500	500	500	500
Truck operating/maintenance costs	500	500	500	500	500	500
General and office expenses	300	300	300	300	300	300
Rent and occupancy costs	1,454	1,454	1,454	1,454	1,454	1,454
Insurance	600	600	600	600	600	600
Depreciation	1,454	1,454	1,454	1,454	1,454	1,454
Interest	—	—	—	—	—	—
Income before income taxes						
Income taxes						
Net income						

Month	May 7	June 8	July 9	Aug 10	Sept 11	Oct 12
Sales	**$40,000**	**$50,000**	**$60,000**	**$65,000**	**$60,000**	**$45,000**
Expenses						
Salaries	23,222	23,222	23,222	23,222	23,222	23,222
Other wages	22,000	24,000	24,000	25,000	26,000	24,000
Benefits	3,205	3,432	4,114	4,114	4,114	3,659
Equipment storage	600	600	600	600	600	600
Promotion	500	500	500	500	500	500
Truck operating/maintenance costs	500	500	500	500	500	500
General and office expenses	300	300	300	300	300	300
Rent and occupancy costs	1,454	1,454	1,454	1,454	1,454	1,454
Insurance	600	600	600	600	600	600
Depreciation	1,454	1,454	1,454	1,454	1,454	1,454
Interest	—	—	—	—	—	—
Income before income taxes						
Income taxes						
Net income						

Income statement

For the year ending October 31, 2006

Month	Nov 1	Dec 2	Jan 3	Feb 4	Mar 5	Apr 6	May 7
Sales	**$30,000**	**$38,000**	**$42,000**	**$45,000**	**$45,000**	**$25,000**	**$40,000**
Expenses							
Salaries	$23,222	$23,222	$23,222	$23,222	$23,222	$23,222	$23,222
Other wages	9,660	9,660	9,660	9,660	9,660	15,000	19,547
Benefits	1,551	1,551	1,551	1,551	1,551	2,750	3,205
Equipment storage	1,200	1,200	1,200	1,200	1,200	1,200	1,200
Promotion	2,270	370	370	370	370	250	250
Truck Operating/Maintenance costs	1,000	1,000	1,000	1,000	1,000	500	500
General and office expenses	450	450	450	450	450	300	300
Rent and occupancy costs	1,454	1,454	1,454	1,454	1,454	1,454	1,454
Insurance	1,200	1,200	1,200	1,200	1,200	1,200	1,200
Depreciation	4,625	4,625	4,625	4,625	4,625	4,625	4,625
Interest	—	1,042	1,028	1,015	1,001	987	973
	35,956	34,056	34,056	34,056	34,056	39,825	44,826
Net income (loss) before income taxes							
Income taxes							
Net Income (loss)							

Month	June 8	July 9	Aug 10	Sept 11	Oct 12	Total
Sales	**$50,000**	**$60,000**	**$65,000**	**$60,000**	**$45,000**	**$545,000**
Expenses						
Salaries	$23,222	$23,222	$23,222	$23,222	$23,222	$150,000
Other wages	21,820	28,640	28,640	28,640	24,093	214,678
Benefits	3,432	4,114	4,114	4,114	3,659	33,144
Equipment storage	1,200	1,200	1,200	1,200	1,200	14,400
Promotion	250	250	250	250	250	5,454
Truck operating/Maintenance costs	500	500	500	500	500	8,454
General and office expenses	300	300	300	300	300	4,350
Rent and occupancy costs	1,454	1,454	1,454	1,454	1,454	18,000
Insurance	1,200	1,200	1,200	1,200	1,200	14,400
Depreciation	4,625	4,625	4,625	4,625	4,625	55,454
Interest	959	945	931	916	902	10,700
	47,327	54,828	54,828	54,828	49,827	518,472
Net income (loss) before income taxes						
Income taxes						
Net Income (loss)						

CASH FLOW - For the year ending October 31, 2006

	Nov 1	Dec 2	Jan 3	Feb 4	March 5	Apr 6	May 7
Inflows							
Collection of accounts receivable	$60,000	$35,000	$34,000	$44,750	$46,250	$43,000	$43,750
Bank term loan	100,000	—	—	—	—	—	—
	$155,000	$32,000	$37,000	$41,750	$44,250	$40,000	$33,750
Outflows							
Acquisition of fixed assets	$159,000						
Repayment of bank loan	—	1,700	1,800	1,800	1,700	1,800	1,800
Payment income tax installments	500	500	500	500	500	500	500
Monthly expenses (excl. dep'n)	31,400	29,800	29,000	29,600	29,799	35,400	40,454
Increase (Decrease) in cash	(1,831)	455	5,441	10,178	12,664	2,631	(8,634)

	June 8	July 9	Aug 10	Sept 11	Oct 12
Inflows					
Collection of accounts receivable	$38,750	$50,000	$58,750	$62,454	$57,454
Bank term loan	—	—	—	—	—
	$38,750	$50,000	$58,750	$62,454	$57,454
Outflows					
Acquisition of fixed assets					
Repayment of bank loan	1,697	1,711	1,725	1,739	1,754
Payment income tax installments	500	500	500	500	500
Monthly expenses (excl. dep'n)	42,400	50,200	50,400	50,700	45,700
Increase (Decrease) in cash	(6,148)	(2,414)	6,322	10,057	10,044

Leather Accessory Manufacturer

SAFARI LEATHERWORKS

56 Cooke Rd.
Butte, Montana 59707

Paul Scheiter, Eduardo Flores, and Alicia Beranek

We manufacture high performance cases for professional grade knives. Our company focuses on creating the sheaths to be paired with high end knives, usually those costing more than two hundred US dollars. The products are a welcomed upgrade from the standard plastic versions which are notorious throughout the industry for being noisy, cracking easily, and melting in hot weather. We seek your counsel in helping us to determine a realistic course of action. For the purposes of this business plan, we have devised a strategy that will accelerate the company assuming a business loan of $100K.

EXECUTIVE SUMMARY

From its beginning in a one hundred square foot college dorm room, Safari Leatherworks has grown into an internationally recognized business that specializes in manufacturing high performance cases for professional grade knives. The cases (more commonly called sheaths), are constructed from the finest leather available and designed to provide unequaled function, durability, and aesthetic appeal. Our company focuses on creating the sheaths to be paired with high end knives, usually those costing more than two hundred US dollars. The products are a welcomed upgrade from the standard plastic versions that are notorious throughout the industry for being noisy, cracking easily, and melting in hot weather.

The niche market for these leather sheaths draws a variety of outdoor enthusiasts, collectors, hunters, campers, and active duty soldiers. Sales are direct retail and sold to the end user via the internet, where they can purchase our products using a credit card. Internet marketing has proven to be a successful strategy and will continue to be the most emphasized method as Safari Leatherworks grows to the next level.

As the business expands, Safari Leatherworks has taken steps to protect intellectual property, thereby maintaining a competitive advantage in the market place, and differentiating our goods. Currently we have a patent pending for a highly unique and functional apparatus that can be used on nearly all knife sheath closure straps. Future inventions of equal or similar potential will also be protected through the registration of patents.

At this time, business operations are focusing heavily on building production capacity through the investment in state of the art tools and machinery. The handcrafted element of the products makes it challenging to mass produce, yet this characteristic allows us to achieve maximum quality. This translates into a high average retail price, usually above one hundred dollars. This high price point also succeeds in making the Safari Leatherworks brand illusive and desirable.

Our long term goal is to maintain a business–to–consumer model and grow into a company that offers hundreds of different products for purchase on our internet store: www.safarileatherworks.com We recognize that our core strength is the ability to inspire a feeling of adventure in our customers and build strong brand loyalty. This will effectively create our own tribe of brand loyal customers. We intend to achieve by using several unique marketing strategies that will be elaborated later in this document. We believe that a slow-medium paced growth strategy will be the most healthy and effective way to prepare this company for long run success. Additionally, this will allow us to hone our business skills and industry expertise in a way that will make the company a more stable entity when it reaches a mature stage.

Immediate operational objectives are focused heavily on transferring production of the goods to a domestic manufacturing facility. The major hurdle for this business is to boost production as quickly and efficiently as possible while maintaining the "USA Handmade" image that our customers have come to respect and appreciate. We believe that production outsourced to facilities on the Pacific Rim, or any low cost country would cause a deterioration of the Safari Leatherworks brand image, and we are therefore committed to producing these goods within the United States. It is worth mentioning that as managers of the business, we are not entirely opposed to such a scenario, but are certain that it would require a separate brand that would appeal to a different market. Maintaining a separate brand for lower priced items would also prevent dilution of the Safari Leatherworks image. Finally, we are passionate about serving our patriotic customers that tend to be heavily concentrated within this niche industry. Maintaining production in the United States also allows us to advertise this admirable quality while feeling positive about the jobs we will create.

GROWTH STRATEGY

Given the fact that Safari Leatherworks started as a student business, and has grown entirely organically, we are now facing a crossroads whereby we must decide to continue expanding the business with company earnings, or seek investment capital to accelerate it more rapidly. We feel compelled to mention our reluctance to rush the process too quickly as our success to this point has been the result of developing and applying business skills as they are learned. Premature expansion of the company could result in an unnecessary failure. At the same time, there is a risk of thinking too small and passing up a critical opportunity for growth. We seek your counsel in helping us to determine a realistic course of action. For the purposes of this business plan, we have devised a strategy that will accelerate the company assuming a business loan of $100K.

BUSINESS STRATEGY

Mission

We awaken people to the adventures of the outdoors by supplying them with professional grade leather sheaths. On the surface we are a manufacturing company, but the products are actually a method to unlock the adventurous personality of their owners. Our business and customers are best described as "Safari Bwanas". Members are loyal to the brand and share *our* values. As leaders, it is our responsibility to grow the tribe through clarity of purpose, discipline of methods, and consistency of products.

Company Values

- **Adventure:** It's not for everyone. Some people prefer activities that are safe, secure, and away from the peril of the wilderness. We live for the excitement of the unknown, especially if it involves being outside. Safari Leatherworks products are a physical tool that enables people to pursue their own adventures in the outdoors.

- **Communication:** By committing to an open dialogue, we prevent problematic situations. This ideal extends beyond personal relationships within the business; we also hold ourselves accountable for maintaining communication with our customers. We respond quickly to emails and inquiries, while kindly handling all customer interactions. At the same time, we are clear about the nature of our products and policies thereby minimizing the potential for confusion.
- **Generosity:** The health of the tribe depends on each member contributing to the vision while knowing that the success of group determines the success of the individual. As we progress toward our many goals, we keep the well being of customers and employees at the forefront of our actions. Those who identify with our vision are able to grow within the company and develop as a person. By giving them the opportunity to grow, they happily devote themselves to the cause.

MANAGEMENT SUMMARY

- **Matthew McNamara:** Currently a student at University of Montana, Matthew is graduating in May of 2008 with a Bachelor's degree in entrepreneurship. He has been the sole owner of Safari Leatherworks LLC since August of 2006, when he started the business in his college dorm room. Over the course of nearly two years, Matthew has built the business into a sustainable entity. He has learned the value of thinking creatively and developing strong relationships both personally and professionally. Upon graduation, he intends to run the company full time while continuing to grow as an entrepreneur and strengthen his business skills.
- **Jane Schmidt:** Jane is a University of Montana student majoring in entrepreneurship with an additional concentration in economics. Her entrepreneurial interests lie in fundraising and venture capitalism, as well as community non–profits. Jane's broad range of professional interests have been strengthened through several diverse internships, including an accounting internship with a local marketing firm.
- **Patrick Keberg:** Currently a University of Montana student, majoring in Business Administration with a double concentration in Marketing and Management. Patrick's business skills have been developed over the course of several internships including a position in 2006 with Block Advertising Agency. Within this company he worked on a special project with the company's Smith Flavored Tea account that involved event marketing and sponsorship. His primary job tasks included marketing research and Spanish–English translation for the company's customers and clients. 2004 was highlighted by his internship with the Spanish Soaps and Detergents, LLC marketing department in Madrid. This internship required his involvement with accounts control, specializing in budgets and database marketing. Patrick's extracurricular activities included having active membership in student organizations like the International Student Federation and The Spanish Student Association.

From the beginning of the business to present day, the company has been run almost exclusively by Matthew McNamara, while utilizing the resources of outside contractors on a limited basis. Future plans will consist of two primary strategies that will be simultaneously implemented. The existing workshop where all of the current production takes place will become the prototyping facility. At the same time, production for the line items will be outsourced to a domestic manufacturing plant. The prototyping facility will be used for the development of new products and as a back up for supply shortages and small production runs.

The daily operations of the company will be handled by a qualified business manager that will be hired at the beginning of 2008. The core responsibilities of this position are processing web site orders, ordering inventory, and handling customer inquiries. In 2009, a fulltime position will be created that will be dedicated specifically to customer relationship management.

COMPANY HISTORY

Unlike most businesses, Safari Leatherworks did not begin with the intention to create a profitable brand, but rather it grew from Matthew McNamara's existing passion for being a craftsman and his constant desire to spend time outside. Matthew first came up with the business concept while attending a week long wilderness survival class. During this class, the necessity to use a knife was present in nearly every skill taught. Almost everyone in the class had a professional grade wilderness survival knife that cost several hundred dollars, and not one of them had a leather case that matched the quality of the knife. Most of the sheaths were constructed of a material called kydex which is a type of thermoformed plastic. A kydex sheath, like many plastics, is prone to a variety of problems. It is loud, cracks easily, and will even melt like a tape cassette if left in a hot car. After having owned several of these plastic sheaths, Matthew was as dissatisfied as the other students until he set out to make his own leather version. After seeking the tutelage of a master leathersmith, he began selling products on the internet and gradually applied the skills learned in school, effectively building the business piece by piece.

Matthew recently won second place in the 2006 Student Business Leadership Awards, an international business competition for full time undergraduates that run a successful company when not in class. For 2006 there were over three hundred competitors from different ten regions around the globe. After regional eliminations, the final ten competitors flew in from around the world to compete in Chicago. Upon wining the second place position, Matthew was featured in several publications including Montana Journal, Butte Times, Entrepreneur Magazine, and Business Times. Additionally, the business has been recognized on a variety of entrepreneurial websites.

The focus of the business for the last several months has been to invest in equipment that will maximize production efficiency before hiring the first employee. Currently, the manufacturing is done almost exclusively by Matthew, with some limited assistance from outside contractors.

MARKET ANALYSIS

Tactical and Survival Knife Industry

Safari Leatherworks is best classified as a company that serves the outdoor and tactical knife industry. In this context, the word tactical knife implies a capability of being used for military applications. Tactical knives are characterized by being larger than normal: usually between four and nine inches in blade length, and are engineered to be ergonomic for the user. Additionally they are often dark in color so as to minimize their visibility in a combat environment. After 9/11, the growing interest in personal security has been a boost for this segment of the knife industry, particularly amongst active duty soldiers in Iraq and Afghanistan (The Shooting Industry, VOL 51 155.6). However, the market for US manufacturers of knives is shrinking due to the increasing quality of imports from the orient. Specifying an exact market size is difficult because almost all of the companies in this industry are privately owned and do not openly share sales information. Having said that, we believe there is room in the industry for a profitable business because of our track record of success and fact that there are virtually no direct competitors at this time.

Leather Industry

Safari Leatherworks is classified under SIC code 3199: Leather Goods Not Elsewhere Classified. The industry is characterized by equestrian goods such as crops, saddles, stirrups and other industrial products like machinery aprons and welding gear. According to statistics from 2000 there were roughly four hundred small leather businesses of this type, most of them employing less than twenty people at an average wage of $8.46 per hour. These companies are geographically concentrated in Texas, California, and Ohio (www.allbusiness.com).

Trade Shows

The leading industry trade show for our sector is called the "SHOT Show" which stands for Shooting, Hunting, and Outdoor Trade. This trade show is held annually in differing locations across the United States. It gathers manufacturers, retailers, and supporting businesses of all types from the industry. We believe that attending the SHOT show will be a critical step forward for learning more detailed information about our industry and finding potential opportunities. As of yet, we have been unable to attend due to schedule conflicts with classes.

CUSTOMERS

People that buy Safari Leatherworks products fall into several broad categories: outdoor enthusiasts, collectors, and active duty soldiers (usually deployed in Iraq or Afghanistan). Customers tend to be patriotic and place high value on the US handmade characteristic of the products. They are avid outdoorsmen and tend to use tools like knives and sheaths on a daily basis as determined by their lifestyle: either in combat or recreation. Other types of buyers are usually collectors who buy the products out of admiration for the quality and craftsmanship. In many cases, a high price point creates a large degree of value from the consumer's perspective and entices them to buy. We maintain focus on the segment of customers that have high–end tastes. This allows us to achieve necessary profit margins and keeps our revenue streams coming from individuals that have expendable income. In many cases, if it's not expensive they won't buy it.

PRODUCTS & SERVICES

Quality

Safari Leatherworks is a company that focuses on developing and manufacturing high performance leather cases for professional grade knives. Knife cases, commonly referred to as sheaths, are attached to a person's belt and allow the user to carry the blade in a way that is easy to access while simultaneously protecting it and its user from harm. Sheaths are accessories to knives but are equally important considering the extreme environments where these tools are used: mostly remote wilderness areas and combat operations.

We compete to have the best leather sheath on the market by delivering a product that is functional, reliable, and artistic. More importantly, the selling process conveys our personal commitment to this ideal throughout the customer experience. We are not a low cost competitor; we compete to have the most expensive product of its kind on the market.

USA Hand Made

Every stitch, fold, and rivet is carefully constructed and monitored by Montana area craftsmen. The human attention necessary to create our products allows us to deliver passion and artistic creativity along with the functionality that characterizes our leather sheaths. Future mass production operations will be conducted domestically in a facility that is capable of meeting our quality standards.

Finest Materials

All leather is heavy grade vegetable tanned cowhide, weighing ten ounces per square foot. Materials are purchased from the Kentsey Leather Company of Butte, one of the most reputable suppliers of its kind in the world. Kentsey hides are known for consistency, suppleness, and strength. From the consumer's perspective, plastic sheaths are anything but desirable and are an ongoing annoyance for serious outdoorsmen and military operatives. The benefits of kydex are almost exclusively advantageous to the companies selling the sheaths, because they are inexpensive and easy to manufacture in large quantities. Consequently, there has been a gap in quality that the knife industry has been unable to bridge. Some of the more quality oriented knife manufacturers do not include sheaths with their knives for the reason that they do not want a substandard sheath associated with their high quality knives. As a result, buyers are left to find their own sheath maker of which there are dozens in operation on a small scale, few of them larger than a two person business. Needless to say, there are limited options available when knife owners seek to purchase a quality sheath, and wait times are often weeks or months because of the limited production capacity of the small shops that can make them.

Safari Leatherworks solves these problems by offering a product that is unparalleled in quality and is immediately available to the customer. We focus on creating sheaths that are designed for specific popular knives on the market, and are constantly improving our products based on the needs of our customers. We pride ourselves on quality control, durability, and having outstanding customer relations. Safari sheaths are sold mostly within the U.S., but have also been shipped to numerous countries abroad, primarily active duty soldiers in Iraq and Afghanistan. One soldier even reported that he was able to rescue an injured comrade from a damaged humvee using the knife he was carrying in a Safari sheath.

GROWTH STRATEGY

As the company continues to grow, it will rely heavily on product line expansion and internet marketing to drive sales. We have proven a successful sales model in the making of sheaths for existing knife companies within the industry. Essentially our accessory products piggyback on the existing credibility of some of the high end manufacturers within the industry. Customers tend to find us accidentally while they are in search of a knife, and then decide to purchase the sheath that goes with it. There are many areas of growth to be explored, especially considering that Safari has offered little more than three products during its entire life as a business. With literally hundreds of popular knives on the market, there are many directions for expansion.

With hundreds of popular high–end knives on the market, there are many different types of sheaths that could be manufactured while maintaining direct retail over the website. The first stage of expansion would aim to increase the product line from the three sheaths we currently offer, to ten or more. This alone could increase revenue by a factor of ten. There are a variety of knife designs that would warrant a sheath in our price range: between one hundred and three hundred dollars. Some of these designs are made by companies like AdamArsenal, who do not even provide a basic sheath for their knives. The notable brands include:

- Rodney Rodder: One of the leading suppliers of quality tactical knives, Rodney Rodder is known for their unique designs that use high performance steel available in 154 CM and S30V.
- Sandstorm: Well known for their partnerships with high profile wilderness professionals, combat operatives, and martial artists. Sandstorm has a broad range of knife designs that appeal to unique niche markets within the industry, and are well known to be a preferred choice among active duty soldiers.
- Adam Knives: Specializing in unique semi–production grade knives with multiple custom options available to the user. Employs the use of cutting edge manufacturing technology, and uses proprietary steel called "silversteel".

Universal Sheath Line

Often customers request sheaths to be made for knife models that are rare, unusual, or require a considerable degree of time to build a custom sheath. The universal sheath line will be a common design that comes in a multitude of different sizes, such that we will be able to sell an appropriate sheath to someone regardless of the knife's dimensions. Shoppers will even be able to print a PDF file off of the website that has a line drawing of the exact size and shape of the sheath. This way they can simply hold their knife up to the paper to see if it will fit inside the sheath. A printing set up like this will reduce the number of returns and engage the customer with an interactive process. From a production standpoint, this arrangement will be vastly more efficient than creating a new sheath pattern every time a customer would like a special order.

Customization

One of the most alluring qualities of a leather product is the ability to personalize it through custom colors, accessories, and especially engraving. This is particularly desirable for the military units where a small group of soldiers will often use the same equipment, and take pride in displaying their unit crest. Safari Leatherworks can easily outsource this step to a laser engraving company that can quickly imprint logos, names, phrases, and even photographic pictures onto the leather.

OPERATIONS

Product Design & Development

Essential Elements

The process for constructing any Safari Leatherworks sheath must include four core elements: high quality materials, handcraftsmanship, durability, and aesthetic appeal. These are the essential ingredients that make the finished product desirable to our customers, differentiate us from substitute goods, and allow us to achieve a high price point: usually above one hundred dollars. Our customers have come to especially appreciate the domestic hand crafted nature of these products, and it seems that they are a welcomed respite in a world where most production goods are outsourced to overseas manufacturers on the Pacific Rim.

Materials

The raw leather material is vegetable tanned cowhide, which is purchased from Kentsey Leather Company, one of the most reputable tanneries in the world. Each hide goes through a stringent process of quality control that assesses key factors like thickness, scarring, and pliability. Hardware components such as rivets, studs, and snaps are sourced from a variety of vendors, and are usually purchased in quantity to achieve wholesale discounts.

Processes

The Safari production facility itself is currently home based, but employs some of the best equipment in the industry for sheath production. Highlights include the Barney Stamper, which can stamp out any leather pattern in less than ten seconds, as well as the Ultima Pro sewing machine that is renowned for its ability to sew elegantly without leaving presser foot marks on the leather. Some sheath designs are even press molded to fit the exact dimensions of its counterpart knife. In these situations, 1:1 scale model plastic castings are used in lieu of the actual metal knife. This allows for rapid manufacturing without sacrificing expensive knives to the production process. Before completion, every sheath is embossed with the Safari Leatherworks logo. It is also worth mentioning that every exposed leather surface receives a coating of waterproofing finish for extended durability in wet weather.

Production

These types of leather products are unique in that they cannot be produced in an automated assembly line. As one can understand from the mentioned processes, equipment and logistical planning can speed manufacturing greatly, however there will always be the necessity for human involvement in each of the steps required to make a sheath. Initially, this could appear as a sever limitation to growth, however it is remarkably easy to break down each step and systemize it so as to train production workers. Given the relatively low cost of materials coupled with the high price point, making and selling these sheaths is economically feasible. Take for example the current best seller, which is priced at $109.00. This sheath uses roughly eight dollars in materials and can be constructed from start to finish with an average time of just thirty–five minutes. The manufacturing of most sheaths requires the following processes:

1. Cut out patterns from raw materials
2. Dye leather to desired color
3. Glue into perform assembly
4. Press mold the leather around knife casting
5. Sand and buff edges
6. Sew
7. Apply waterproofing agent
8. Attach straps
9. Final sanding and buffing
10. Attach closure mechanism

OSHA Compliance

While most of the production is outsourced, the prototyping facility will still require adherence to government regulations regarding the use potentially dangerous chemicals and machines. Safety requirements will be implemented by the company so that our processes are OSHA compliant. Some of these precautions will require that the worker(s):

- Wear respirators when handling chemicals and dyes, as well as for activities that generate dust such as sanding and grinding
- Use gloves when handling certain chemicals and dyes, or when using specific hand tools like shears or cutting blades
- Wear ear protection for loud activities like the operating of the leather cutter which uses an air compressor.
- Wear eye protection when necessary for things like drilling, grinding, and buffing.
- Wear steel toed boots in the workshop

Obtaining OSHA certification will not be a difficult process because the Safari Leatherworks workshop will not have any lethal hazards to employees. Additionally, OSHA offers a free consulting service to help businesses become compliant with their standards.

Equipment

Safari Leatherworks uses industrial machinery and hand tools for the most efficient construction of sheaths. Some of the current and future equipment includes:

- Ultima Pro Sewing Machine: The leather industry's leading heavy duty sewing machine that will sew multiple layers of leather up to one inch thick. The introduction of the sewing machine has decreased production time by thirteen minutes per unit on average, as compared with sewing by hand.

- Barney Stamper: Generates thirty thousand pounds of pressure onto cutting dyes that will stamp out any necessary pattern of leather in less than ten seconds. Using this tool is five to ten times faster than cutting out leather with a pair of scissors.
- Embossing Press: Used to imprint the Safari Logo or any type of artwork onto a leather sheath. This machine employs the use of magnesium stamps that can be produced from any black and white image.
- Spindle Sander: Puts an exact ninety degree angle on the edge of a leather sheath, which makes the product symmetrical and keeps stitches in consistent orientation.
- Buffing wheel: Used to add finishing touches to the edges of a sheath when used in conjunction with a special compound.
- Molding Blanks: Duplicate plastic castings of the exact knife which for which sheaths are made. The molding blanks are for a process called wet forming which allows the leather to be conformed around the knife for a perfect fit.
- Snap Setter: Allows for the rapid installation of durable snaps, eyelets, and rivets.

Quality Assurance

Specific and measurable standards of quality will be assessed for every sheath before it is packaged and sent to the warehouse. The criteria for each model will differ slightly, but will be designed to determine the grade of leather, quality of finished edges, stitch length, and symmetry. Acceptable products will fall within a certain range that will be scored on a point basis. Products that do not meet the minimum standards will be discarded, saved for training purposes, or sold as cosmetic seconds. Maintaining consistent quality will be one of the major challenges of outsourcing production. Before moving forward with this strategy, we intend to create a contractual obligation that will hold the manufacturer responsible for consistent production.

Multiple Suppliers

As a measure to defend against potentially crippling supply shortages we intend to divide production for different sheath lines between two manufactures. This will allow us to maintain a source of production in the even of a catastrophic event such as a fire. Similarly, it gives us alternative options if production at one facility is delayed.

Logistics

After products leave the manufacturing facility, they are sent to a warehousing company in Illinois. When customers order from the website, packages are shipped to them directly from Illinois, thereby eliminating the need for additional labor to maintain our next business day shipping policy. In addition to reducing costs, the warehousing company will be able to handle any amount of daily orders that Safari Leather-works could generate. This system also allows us to offer a full range of shipping services including UPS, USPS, FedEx, and DHL. International and military orders require no additional attention from the Safari staff because the warehousing service will also complete any necessary formalities with customs.

Returns are processed at the manufacturing facility in order to check for damaged products, and to repackage the goods for sale to the next customer. All internet customers are notified immediately by email, and are then notified again with tracking number upon the shipment of their goods.

MARKETING & SALES

Internet Marketing

Safari Leatherworks has driven sales almost exclusively through internet marketing. Internet sales have proven successful largely because of the nature of the products: they are accessories for existing knives on the market. Therefore, in order to market the leather sheaths we focus on attracting internet shoppers that are in search of specific knives. When they find our site, they are not initially intending to purchase a leather sheath but end up doing so because it is a unique product that no one else offers, and it differentiates our website from the hundreds of others that sell knives.

Internet marketing in itself can be broken down into two broad categories: "Pay–per–click" (PPC), and "search engine optimization" (SEO). PPC is an immediately effective strategy in which advertisers bid for key words that potential customers may be using in the search engines. When the potential customer types in those words, they will see the normal search results, but will also be shown a variety of ads from the marketer. In this scenario, we are only charged if an internet searcher clicks on one of those ads. Safari Leatherworks currently uses PPC to drive 50 percent of all visitors to the website.

The other method, SEO is a slower but ultimately more powerful method of internet marketing. SEO relies on designing and structuring a website to be "search engine friendly" such that it achieves high rankings for specific key words. There are hundreds of different variables that can affect the rank of a website in the search engine, so much so that it has become a completely new science of its own. We use a software program called web–position that scans the code of the website and returns instructions for more efficient optimization of key words. By employing this program alone, Safari Leatherworks has climbed rapidly through the search engines, having our most important keywords on the first page of Google with some of them shifting in out of the second and third ranking. In time they will likely elevate to first place. As an example try a Google search of different brands of quality knives. You will notice our ads as well as a relatively high position ranking in the center content area.

Future Marketing

The Safari Bwanas

Future marketing operations will be geared toward inspiring our values throughout the customer's experience. Our intention is to create an adventurous feeling through the branding of our products, leaving the owner with a sense of belonging to "The Safari Bwanas". We intend to accomplish this through a highly interactive website, contests, promotional DVDs, endorsements, email newsletters, and product packaging.

- Interactive website: Visitors will be able to vote on their preference for upcoming products, discuss their experiences in an online forum, and submit their own pictures of Safari products being used in the field. Additionally, the website will have a variety of articles and streaming videos relating to wilderness survival and the practical application of our products. Similarly, there will be an archive of stories and testimonials that are submitted by product owners.
- Contests: To inspire people to use our products we will regularly hold prize contests for the best pictures of our sheaths in action. This creates a fun reason for people to get some experience with our goods, and will increase the overall buzz of the Safari Leatherworks brand.
- Promotional DVDs: These will be promotional tools available to anyone for free upon request. The content of the DVD will give an overview of the design, development, production, and use of Safari Leatherworks products.
- Product packaging: Sheaths will come with a certificate of authenticity, letter from the sheath maker, an instructional DVD and packaged in an environmentally sustainable, yet clever manner. The signed letter from the sheath maker accentuates the quality people most appreciate about Safari Leatherworks products: the handcraftsmanship. The outermost packaging will resemble a cigar box, with a hinged lid and snap closure. The wooden box would be unfinished except for the Safari logo on the top. The sheath would be nested in shredded plant polymers, available from most packaging suppliers in bulk. This material is similar to the potato polymer bags used in grocery stores, which is biodegradable and environmentally friendly. The certificate of authenticity, signed letter from the

sheath maker and DVD would all rest on top of the sheath. The letter and certificate of authenticity all reinforce the handmade and exclusive aspect of Safari products.

- Endorsements: We intend to seek the recommendation and endorsement from well known and respected people within the industry such as wilderness survival instructors.
- Email newsletters: Every week we will send out an email newsletter that will encourage customers to visit the website. The contents of this email will include featured customer stories, how–to articles, upcoming products, and interviews (customers, Safari staff, or survival instructors).
- Magazines: Although the primary marketing focus will concentrate on the internet, we eventually plan to advertise in several specialty magazines that relate to knives, knife making, hunting, shooting, and other outdoor sports. Magazine advertising may be an effective way to increase sales, but only when we believe the internet marketing opportunities have been maximized. It is more difficult and expensive to gain recognition through the magazine ads, while it is cheap and immediately effective to pursue internet marketing. Additionally it is an area that is largely untapped for competing search engine rankings.
- Word of Mouth: Safari Leatherworks continually focuses on delivering a quality product and outstanding service to every customer; we simply do not give them a reason to complain. This simple ideal has been the driving force of our positive reputation and is extremely important given the "start up" status of the company. Regardless of what strategies we employ to reach new customers, there will always be a heavy focus on maintaining communication with our existing buyers, and ensuring they are happy with their purchases. We give them the best products available, deliver them quickly, and resolve any conflicts immediately. In our opinion this personalized service is a marketing strategy itself. It keeps people spreading good remarks, and creates evangelists who go out of *their* way to tell others about Safari Leatherworks.

Sales

As production capacity increases, we have identified several areas in which to generate further sales beyond our current focus. As it stands, Safari Leatherworks has generated sales almost exclusively from the sale of the three different knives and the accompanying leather sheaths.

Public Relations

The winning of the SBLA competition helped establish Safari Leatherworks as a reputable entity from a business standpoint, but further action will need to be taken on a consistent basis to maintain the company image in the eyes of our consumers. Several potential PR strategies include:

- Press Releases: Knife publications are continually looking for unique stories and innovative products to write about. Safari Leatherworks can make a standard practice of issuing press releases every time a new product is introduced or a significant advance is made, such as with a new partnership or contract.
- Customer Database: Collecting and maintaining expansive details about our customers will help us to better accommodate their needs and to plan for future business decisions. Data can be collected during the checkout process on the website, or by interviewing customers over the phone. An example of pertinent information will include: the reason for their purchase, other types of products collected, and the means by which they found our company. This will also help us to determine the purchasing history of any given customer and to isolate key factors for their demographic.
- Testimonials: An expansive list of positive testimonials has already been compiled, and continues to grow every week. Most comments focus on the good service or outstanding products. One letter from a soldier detailed the use of his sheath while rescuing a fallen soldier from a humvee

in Iraq. These types of statements make a profound impact on new buyers, while serving as a good measure to let us know we are achieving our goals. We can produce copies of these letters upon request.

COMPETITION

Now and throughout history, leather crafting has been a skill of the artisans. It requires attention to detail, a sense of creativity, and the desire to work using the hands. For this reason, it has largely remained a trade that is most often confined by the production abilities of a single person or a small group. In many ways, the word "leather worker" is synonymous with the word "artist". The artistic nature of the work is quite evident when looking at the existing competition for Safari Leatherworks. The vast majority of competitors are single person operations or small husband–and–wife businesses. These competitors are heavily motivated by working within their trade and involving themselves on a personal level with the production of their wears. They are not engaged in a growth mindset, and are not focused on accelerating their businesses beyond the restraints of their own elbow grease.

Small Competitors

There are many smalltime leatherworkers who are direct competition to Safari; however we speculate that they will prove to be the least significant threats in the long run because of the weakness of their business structures. A mere handful of these businesses are:

- Tough Leatherworks
- Robert's Leathercraft
- Pine Forest Custom Knives
- Leather by Brett

Potential Major Competitors

There are several significant long term threats to Hedgehog that could come from external competition. Perhaps the most likely source would be an existing holster company such as Wayne Holsters, Harley's Leather Accessories, or Wilderness Equipment. All of these companies have a strong reputable businesses and outstanding products within the firearms industry. It would not be a far leap for them to cross over into the knife sheath sector using their existing equipment and facilities. The most we can do from a defensive standpoint is to continually differentiate our products and develop Safari into an extremely reputable brand. This will set us up to compete on the same level if one of these companies should decide to expand into the sheath business.

Another source of competition could stem from an existing knife company that decides to assemble a leather sheath division within their current operations. This could diminish Safari's sheath sales because some customers would certainly be compelled to purchase a sheath that is the same brand as the knife. On the other hand, this situation represents more of an opportunity by partnering with one of these knife companies on a contract basis.

The threat of competition from imported goods, from Asia for example, is a rather insignificant threat because the U.S. made nature of these products is a heavy definer of the target market. Almost all the knives that Safari makes sheaths for are manufactured in the U.S., and it is mostly the lower end market that produces knives in Asian countries. Safari Leatherworks is a price competitor, but not in the traditional sense. Rather than compete to have the lowest prices, our goal is to have the most expensive sheath on the market. We would be far more concerned with the entry of a similar company that values a high price point and seeks to capture part of the exclusive market.

Intellectual Property

Safari Leatherworks designed and developed a unique invention that can be used on the closure strap of nearly any knife. Normally, when leather is in a fixed position for an extended period of time, its molecular structure changes such that it maintains that shape. This is the usual situation when the closure strap of a sheath has been fastened around the handle of a knife. When the user goes to release the strap, it tends to stay in the same place and interfere with the extraction of the blade from the sheath. This can result in accidental cutting of the strap or the knife becoming entangled. In an emergency situation, a small hang up like this could be very dangerous by delaying or preventing the knife from being used at that time. Matthew McNamara invented a very simple application of an elastic cord that when attached to a closure strap will eliminate this problem. As soon as the user unfastens the strap, the cord will pull it away and out of the cutting path of the knife, thereby eliminating the possibility of damaging the strap.

RISK FACTORS

Internal Risks

- Inability to meet demand: occurs if Safari Leatherworks does not effectively use its resources to supply existing markets with the products they desire. This is perhaps the most serious risk because the handcrafted nature of the products requires a trained and reliable staff to keep the company running.
- Inventory surplus
- Unused capacity
- Fire, flood, theft, or other property damage
- Product defect causes lawsuit or recall of a large number of goods

External Risks

- Bans or restrictions on the sale, ownership, or ability to use and carry knives.
- Price increases for raw materials including leather and steel
- Changes or restrictions to national parks, hunting grounds and other locations where tactical knives are used
- Status of international conflicts and wars
- Entry of new competitors
- Failure of partnered businesses such as knife companies or discontinuation of similar contractual relationships

FINANCIAL ANALYSIS

Financial Timeline

Quarter Two of 2007

- Sales: $30,000
- Income: $(3,673)
- Units sold: 75
- Enhance website
- Production outsourced entirely

Quarter Three of 2007

- Sales: $51,000
- Income: $21,787
- Units sold: 227

Quarter Four of 2007

- Sales: $102,000
- Income: $47,878
- Units sold: 453

Quarter One of 2008

- Sales: $156,000
- Income: $52,705
- Units sold: 693
- Hire first employee
- Increase marketing operations: launch professional endorsements and instructional DVD.

Quarter Two of 2008

- Sales: $214,000
- Income: $76,577
- Units sold: 951

Quarter Three of 2008

- Sales: $246,000
- Income: $89,749
- Units sold: 1,093

Quarter Four of 2008

- Sales: $255,000
- Income: $93,653
- Units sold: 1,133

Quarter One of 2009

- Sales: $264,000
- Income: $81,497
- Units sold: 1,174
- Hire second employee
- Begin magazine marketing campaign

Quarter Two of 2009

- Sales: $273,000
- Income: $85,614
- Units sold: 1,213

Quarter Three of 2009

- Sales: $282,000
- Income: $88,906
- Units sold: 1,253

Quarter Four of 2009

- Sales: $291,000
- Income: $92,611
- Units sold: 1,294

Financial Assumptions

- Employees paid hourly at $15 with a 5 percent increase per calendar year
- 1st employee hired in Jan 2008
- 2nd employee hired in Jan 2009
- Unit sold per month is based on average selling price of $225 per unit
- COGS is 40 percent of sales revenue and is based on average unit cost of $90
- 10 percent of COGS is for materials and 90 percent is for assembly
- Merchandise sales are 94 percent of revenue
- Shipping sales are 6 percent of revenue
- Shipping expense is 69 percent of shipping revenue
- Credit card processing is 2.7 percent of sales revenue
- Shipping and credit card processing are expensed before calculating gross margin
- PPC marketing is 2 percent of sales
- "Other Marketing" is 10 percent of sales
- Magazine marketing is fixed at $2700 per month based on 1/3 page ads in 3 magazines
- E-Commerce expense (web hosting and related fees) is fixed at $125 per month
- Product liability insurance assumes $1,000,000 coverage at $1000 per month

Meal Facilitation and Preparation Company

Kitchen Helper, LLC

3141 Traunter St.
Effingham, IL 62401

Tracey C. McCurrach and Elizabeth Timm

Kitchen Helper, LLC was formed as a Limited Liability Corporation in the State of Illinois in May of 2005. The company is a new entrant into an emerging segment of the restaurant industry called Meal Facilitation and Preparation (MFP). Meal prep businesses represent a high growth market segment that offers a new choice to consumers. In a society where people value healthy, delicious meals yet feel constantly pressed for time, meal prep businesses offer a positive alternative.

BUSINESS OVERVIEW

The process of meal prep begins when a customer signs up to attend a session at a MFP store. The customer selects menu items to make from a list of recipes that are offered that month. Generally, 12 menu selections, each serving four to six people, can be prepared during a 2–hour session. When the customer arrives at the store, all of the preparation for the dishes has already been done. Stations are set up with the equipment, ingredients and step–by–step instructions for making each recipe. The customer moves from station to station, assembling the recipes. All recipes are put in a Ziploc bag or an aluminum pan, which the customer takes home and freezes. Thawing and cooking instructions are affixed to each dish.

The two primary business models for MFP businesses are franchise operations and independent stores. Currently, 156 MFP companies with 372 store locations are in operation. The largest players are franchises, specifically Cooking with Friends with 76 stores and Minute Meals with 68 locations. Several other companies have a handful of stores clustered in certain geographic areas. The remainder of the locations are independent businesses. In Illinois, Minute Meals currently has locations in metro Chicago, Springfield, and Bloomington. Cooking with Friends is located in Chicago and is expected to open in Arlington Heights. Spices and Stuff opened in July, 2005 in Evanston. Jane and Mitzy is open in Decatur and just announced their first franchise expansion in the same area.

The key to success for Kitchen Helper is to differentiate itself from the competition through product and service offerings, while delivering on its promise of providing delicious, nutritious meals quickly and easily. The company's strategy is to focus on the customer experience. This premise drives every decision. Kitchen Helper is positioned as a high quality, cost–effective and fun solution for family meals. The benefits to the consumer include saving time and money, healthier meals, delicious recipes, nutritional information, simple preparation, and putting fun back into meal preparation.

The primary target market for Kitchen Helper consists of families, with the female head of household as the primary purchaser. Demographically, these families are represented by adults between the ages of 35 and 54 with children in the home. The household income of the target market is in excess of $30,000 or more. This target customer values convenience, and is more and more "time–challenged". She is also aware of the importance of good nutrition for herself and her family but finds providing those meals increasingly difficult.

Kitchen Helper primary product/service is a solution to the customer's dilemma of preparing high–quality, nutritious, and cost–effective meals with a minimum of time and expense. Our primary service is giving our customers the ability to come to our store and quickly assemble a variety of delicious menu selections. This service results in a physical product for the customer. In addition, the company offers meal assembly, delivery, packaged meals, private parties, and gift certificates.

Operationally, the company website is one of the key elements to success. It is designed to be very simple to understand and easy to navigate. Kitchen Helper is also purchasing a web-based software package for handling the back–end processes specific to a MFP business. The system will manage order processing, purchasing and inventory control functions. Since inventory is purchased to order, very little waste is anticipated.

Kitchen Helper is currently negotiating for space for an anchor store in the Effingham area. Estimates of local market size total 1450 consumers in the immediate area and approximately 5200 in the larger demographic area. Our growth strategy calls for opening additional stores. The following areas are targeted for expansion in the next 2 to 5 years: Chicago, Carbondale, Cicero, and Naperville.

Conservative estimates and assumptions have been used in the preparation of projected start–up and 2nd and 3rd year financials for the company. These projections indicate that the company will approach break–even near the end of the first year of operation. We anticipate investing again in the company by opening a second location early in 2007. Careful attention to actual operating results will influence the company's ability to expand quicker or more slowly than anticipated.

Kitchen Helper is owned by Anne Relitz and Susan Stiliz. Ms. Relitz is the company's Chief Management Officer, while Ms. Stiliz is the company's Chief Operating Officer. Ms. Relitz has worked with numerous small businesses in the areas of strategic and marketing planning. Ms. Stiliz has a systems background and is adept at designing and implementing processes. Both women have extensive experiences in a wide range of businesses. Their skills, however, are varied and complementary. The company is currently funded by equal participation of the two partners, with $50,000 on deposit with Stone Bank. We are seeking a loan of $75,000 to finance the purchase of equipment and supplies and to provide working capital. At present, these are the only sources of funds being considered.

OBJECTIVES

Mission

Kitchen Helper, LLC is in the business of providing high quality, cost–effective meal solutions for families and organizations. We provide a combined product and service that enables time–challenged families to create their own nutritious and delicious meals.

Our philosophy of business:

- Kitchen Helper operates with the highest level of integrity and business ethics.
- We establish relationships with our customers, suppliers, employees and other professionals without regard to an individual's race, religion, sex or personal choices.
- Our customers are the reason that we are in business.
- Kitchen Helper conducts all of its business activities in anticipation of mutual benefit.

- Our stores offer a safe, comfortable and supportive atmosphere where customers and employees truly benefit from and enjoy the time they spend with us.
- Kitchen Helper is a responsible, environmentally sensitive corporate citizen and an active member of its local communities.

Goals for the first year

- Launch the Kitchen Helper concept in the Effingham area in 2005.
- Educate the local marketplace about the concept of meal assembly.
- Provide high quality, effective meal solutions that provide a genuine alternative to today's food choices and a positive experience for our customers.
- Achieve breakeven, profitability and other financial milestones as outlined in the financial projections of this business plan.

Growth Strategy

- Expand the Kitchen Helper concept within the state of Illinois by opening five to eight additional stores and satellite operations over the next three to five years.
- Be recognized as having a positive presence in our local business communities.
- Assume an active leadership role in the industry association.
- Establish the Kitchen Helper brand as the leader in meal assembly businesses in this region.

Measures of Success

First Year of Operations

- Secure additional funding of $75,000 via bank loan
- Complete operational training of partners
- Launch company website, including corporate identity, concept, initial calendar and recipes
- Complete store design
- Open anchor store
- Initiate word of mouth and concept understanding in local area
- Fill customer sessions as scheduled in financial projections; operate at capacity by month 3
- Reach operating break–even within first 6 months
- Introduce assembly, delivery, and special package products; develop and introduce signature dessert
- Implement customer satisfaction surveys and referral tracking; generate positive customer satisfaction as measured by survey results, referrals, orders and testimonials
- Receive positive review(s) in local media
- Attract, hire and train two store managers and six session assistants
- Manage cost and revenue projections according to financial plan
- Add limited retail items to store
- Conduct a local fund-raiser and/or community sponsorship
- Participate in inaugural industry association meeting (Fall, 2005)
- Invite advisory board members
- Review and update business plan by yearend

Second Year of Operations

- Expand computer capabilities to handle multiple locations
- Expand recipe catalog to 100+ selections
- Hire and train an additional store manager and three session assistants
- Evaluate location demographics and competitors for second location
- Open second store
- Prototype university-demographic store
- Introduce thematic private parties
- Evaluate and expand retail product selections
- Conduct two fund-raisers and/or community sponsorships
- Actively participate in expansion and promotion of industry association
- Manage cost and revenue projections according to financial plan
- Update competitive analysis with focus on northeast Illinois businesses
- Review and update business plan by year–end

Third—Fifth Year of Operations

- Evaluate location demographics and competitors for additional locations
- Hire and retain three additional store managers and nine session assistants
- Expand recipe selections to 150+
- Open locations three, four and five
- Conduct two fund–raisers and/or community sponsorships per store
- Manage cost and revenue projections according to financial plan
- Review and update business plan by year end

COMPANY HISTORY

Kitchen Helper, LLC, is a new entrant into an emerging segment of the restaurant industry called Meal Facilitation and Preparation (MFP). Meal preparation or meal assembly businesses represent a high growth market segment that offers new choices to consumers. In a society where people feel constantly pressed for time, yet value healthy, delicious meals and family meal times, meal prep businesses offer a new alternative.

Under this concept, the customer selects, via a calendar posted on the company's website, a session scheduled at the meal prep store. The customer also selects from a limited number of dishes that are offered by the company that month. Generally, 12 menu selections can be prepared during a two–hour session. When the customer arrives at the store, all of the preparation for the dishes has already been done. For the customer, this eliminates recipe development and selection, grocery shopping, and preparing any of the ingredients. In the store, stations are set up with all of the equipment and ingredients needed to make each recipe. In addition, step–by–step assembly instructions are posted at the station.

The customer is given brief instructions if they are new to the store and provided with a printed list of the items they have selected. They then move from station to station, assembling the recipes they have selected. During this step, the customer is able to adapt the recipe to the needs and tastes of her family. For example, if her children do not like onions, she can leave them out; if she loves spicy food, she can double the amount of pepper. All recipes end up in either a Ziploc bag or an aluminum pan, which the customer takes home and freezes. Thawing and cooking instructions are affixed to each dish; therefore, all the customer needs to do is reach into their freezer and pull out their selection for their next meal. And another prime benefit—the cleanup is done by the store staff!

Through this concept, the customer is given the tools necessary to create delicious, high–quality, nutritious meals customized to their particular tastes, at a fraction of the time and hassle of homemade meals. And, at a per–serving cost of $3.00 or less, meal assembly is also a very cost–effective solution for the customer.

INDUSTRY ANALYSIS

The overall restaurant industry is forecasted to produce $476 billion dollars in direct sales, or roughly 4 percent of the U.S. gross domestic product, by the close of 2005. With 12.2 million employees, the industry is the largest private–sector employer. Over 900,000 locations serve more than 70 billion meal and snack occasions nationwide per year. Although new, the Meal Facilitation and Preparation segment of the industry is expected to grow exponentially in coming years.

In the state of Illinois, restaurants will add $14 billion in sales to the economy this year. The industry will employee an estimated 543,000 residents of Illinois, a figure that is projected to top 600,000 by 2015. Restaurant and foodservice employment today represents 10 percent of the total employment in Illinois and is expected to continue to add a total of almost 60,000 new jobs by 2015.

The Meal Facilitation and Preparation (MFP) market is no more that 3 years old. Services that offered convenience and assistance in preparing meals started as home–based businesses in the 1980s. But it was not until the publication of an article by Working Mother magazine in February of 2003 that the industry began to see formal and explosive growth. In fact, data on this segment is limited, and the numbers that are available are very fluid. Most tracking considers MFP as a sub segment of the personal chef market, which is itself a segment of the restaurant industry. According to the United States Professional Chef Association (USPCA), this industry now includes about 6,000 personal–chef service businesses. Estimated at about $100 million, this segment is expected to grow to $2 to $3 million in the next 5 years.

MFPs are a result of a further refinement of the personal chef market. Consumers continue to demand convenience, but they also want meals that are both tasty and nutritious. Moreover, the marketplace is now demanding an affordable alternative to hiring a personal chef. MFPs responded to this demand by enabling customers to prepare meals themselves, with none of the hassles of developing recipes, grocery shopping, or even chopping their own vegetables. The meals are made according to the customers's tastes, and then taken home to be stored in the freezer, ready when needed. This allows customers to control their meals while at the same time saving time and money.

As an emerging market, MFPs today are located in over 40 states and Canada. The concept has caught on quickly in the regions where entrepreneurs have capitalized on the demand and launched stores. As of July, 2005, the Easy Meal Preparation Association (EMPA) had identified 156 MRP companies with 372 store locations. The largest players are Cooking with Friends out of Saginaw, Michigan with 76 stores and Minute Meals of San Diego, California with 68 locations. More information on these companies is included in the Competitive Analysis.

Industry Statistics

- According to the U.S. Personal Chef Association, more than 60 percent of Americans don't think about what's for dinner until after 4 p.m.
- The typical American household spent an average of $2,276 on food away from home in 2002, and 90 percent of all take–home meals came from a fast–food restaurant.
- One out of three consumers has used curbside takeout at a table service restaurant.
- Households in metropolitan areas tend to spend more on food away from home than non–metropolitan households.
- Household spending on food away from home is heavily influenced by household income, with expenditures rising dramatically for households with income of $30,000 or more.
- Families, represented by households with adults between the ages of 35 and 44 and an average size of 3.2 spent the largest total amount on food away from home. (2002)
- Households headed by 35–44 year olds allocated the greatest amount—an average of $2,712—to food away from home, followed by households headed by persons between the ages of 45 and 54.
- Total spending on food away from home posted by households composed of a husband, wife and children was 43 percent higher than the national average at $3,257.
- Americans are cooking less often at home. Data from the Department of Energy's Residential Energy Consumption Survey (RECS), which collect data on household characteristics as well as energy consumption, indicates that Americans are cooking less at home (2003) than previously (1993). The percentage of households cooking, on average, "two or more times a day" as well as "once a day" declined for all sizes of households.
- The trend toward less and less preparation of food while still eating at home continues to drive the development of new products and services.
- Convenience continues to be a primary factor in consumer purchase decisions.

MANAGEMENT SUMMARY

Kitchen Helper, LLC was formed as a Limited Liability Corporation in the State of Illinois in May of 2005. The company is owned entirely by Anne Relitz and Susan Stiliz as equal partners. We believe this is the appropriate structure for maximum flexibility and lowest cost during the start–up of the business. We are currently in the process of approving an operating agreement between the partners that clarifies the agreement between the parties and provides for the continuation of the business.

Anne Relitz is the company's Chief Management Officer, while Susan Stiliz is the company's Chief Operating Officer. Under these designations, Anne is primarily responsible for the overall strategy and business management of Kitchen Helper, including business planning, marketing and public relations, financing, and human resources. Susan's priorities focus on the operations of the business, including physical space and equipment, recipe development and evaluation, technology acquisition and maintenance, and regulatory compliance.

Strengths of the Management Team

Anne Relitz's credentials include a Bachelor's degree in Business Administration from Indiana University, as well as a Masters in Business Administration in Marketing and Organizational Behavior from the J.L. Kellogg Graduate School of Management at Northwestern University. Her work experience includes software consulting, marketing at General Electric, managing an interdisciplinary educational research institute at Northwestern University, and teaching at a variety of colleges and universities. She owned her own consulting firm, specializing in business and market planning and execution for start–up and high–growth organizations and was a counselor for the Small Business Administration.

Susan Stiliz graduated from Depauw University with a degree in Psychology and completed Penn State's Computer Career program. She has been employed at several firms, where her emphasis was on systems consulting, design and implementation. Susan is also an active church member, PTA vice–president and Scout leader. Susan's background in systems analysis and computer technology give her a strong expertise in understanding the operational flow of the operation and systemic requirements of the business. She is also adept at handling the technologies involved in Kitchen Helper, particularly the management of the website and back end systems. More complete resumes of the partners are included in Appendices B and C.

Both partners have accumulated decades of experience working in a variety of businesses. Our experiences cover all of the major functional areas of business; however, each brings different talents and strengths to bear on the challenges of this business. Anne's strength is in strategy, planning, marketing and creativity. Susan has a solid reputation for getting things done, and blends her systems thinking with a keen attention to detail. Together, they recognize what they bring to the table, and where they need help. Both are willing to commit their personal, professional, and financial resources to creating and building Kitchen Helper. An added benefit is that the partners are also members of the primary demographic group that Kitchen Helper is targeting—busy women with families who value their time and seek cost–effective solutions to the issues they face in managing their homes and families.

Weaknesses of the Management Team

The owners recognize that the partnership is lacking in expertise in some of the primary functional areas required by this business. The most critical weakness—and a key to the success of this business—is the lack of hands–on operating experience. While both partners have worked in restaurants and food service, the operating needs of the meal assembly business are unique. Particularly since this is an evolving business, we need to acquire this operating knowledge as efficiently and quickly as possible.

To address one major weakness in the food operations area, both Susan and Anne passed the ServeSafe course on safe food handling offered by the National Restaurant Association Educational Foundation. This enables them both to manage a food operation as certified by the State of Illinois Department of Health.

Additionally, Kitchen Helper has entered into an agreement with Smith and Thompson LLC of Chicago, Illinois. Kitchen Helper has agreed to purchase the operations manual and training package offered by this company. Smith and Thompson operates the Cooking with Friends MFP business, a company that is one of the most successful operations to emerge. The Kitchen Helper partners are scheduled to attend training onsite at a Cooking with Friends facility on August 12 and 13, 2005. As a result of this training, we expect our understanding of the operations of the business to be greatly enhanced.

The partners also recognize the value of retaining experts in certain areas that are critical to the success of the company. While we possess a general understanding of law, accounting and finance, graphic and store design, computer and web support and human resources, we have retained firms with specialized expertise in these areas. Additionally, as members of the recently organized Easy Meal Prep Association (EMPA), the company taps into the many resources provided by this industry group.

Human Resources and Advisory Board

Kitchen Helper will be staffed with primarily the two partners, supported by permanent part–time employees and consulting professionals in the specialties mentioned earlier. The partners do not intend to take any compensation for the first year of the business. After that, the possibility of compensation will be evaluated in light of opportunities to expand the business.

Primary hires over the first year of operation include two store managers and six service personnel. These people will be trained in the business, as well as ServeSafe safe food handling, and will gain experience at the anchor store. Hiring will continue as each new store location is opened. Prior to moving ahead with a new store, one new store manager and three service reps must be hired and trained.

Kitchen Helper anticipates hiring from the local employment pool, which includes a diverse group of people who prefer part–time employment. These include a large number of stay–at–home parents, as well as students and recent graduates. Our wage rate for service reps will be approximately 50 percent above the minimum wage rate. Store managers will be offered opportunities for advancement and compensation aligned with the skills and experiences they bring to the company. In addition, employees will be offered meals at discounted rates. It is anticipated that we will be able to satisfy our personnel requirements.

Kitchen Helper is in the process of inviting a number of individuals to join our effort in an advisory role. We intend to fashion an advisory board of about 7 individuals who will offer both insight and tough questions for our business. As of this writing, we do not have firm commitments from any individuals and therefore do not feel we can publish any names. As an example of the type of advisor we are seeking, we are inviting a local specialty food and wine entrepreneur, a representative from a major retail kitchen business, and a retired executive from a major international bank.

Records Management, Reporting, and Management Controls

Data collection and reporting for Kitchen Helper will cover three main areas: management control, financial systems, and regulatory compliance. The software management system that is being purchased by the business provides much of the necessary data capture and reporting capabilities for management control. Financial data will be relayed into the QuickBooks system, which is also utilized by our accounting firm. Regulatory reporting as required by the Health Department requires the retention of numerous forms. Most of this information is captured manually on specific forms and filed for the requisite time period. These information reporting requirements are spelled out in the Kitchen Helper Operating Manual.

Legal

The business is currently in the process of putting into place several legal documents. Primary among these is the Kitchen Helper Operating Agreement between the partners, which describes the business relationship. This document also considers appropriate contingencies in the event of different scenarios that may affect one or both partners and provides for the continuation of the business. Secondly, Kitchen Helper is entering into a Software License Agreement with Smith and Thompson, LLC, to purchase their back–end software system, designed specifically for MFP, and a protected territory. The operations training that is being provided by Cooking with Friends also necessitates an agreement between the two companies. It is anticipated that these agreements, and the company's real estate obligations, will be the bulk of the early legal expenses for the business.

PRODUCTS & SERVICES

In keeping with our strategic focus on the customer, Kitchen Helper views its primary product/service as providing a solution to the customer's dilemma of providing tasty, nutritious meals with a minimum of time and expense. Our primary service is giving our customers the ability to come to our store and quickly assemble a variety of proven menu selections. This service results in a physical product for the customer of up to 12 dishes of 4 to 6 servings each. These meals are taken home and frozen, then prepared according to the provided instructions when the customer chooses. Kitchen Helper also offers meal assembly, delivery within a limited area, packaged meals for new mothers, private parties, and gift certificates. In the future, we plan to offer limited kitchen and cooking items for sale.

The key to Kitchen Helper's long–term success is to differentiate itself from the competition while delivering on its promise to the consumer of providing delicious, nutritious meals quickly and easily. While the needs of the customer drive our service, the resulting food products are driven by our recipes. All of our recipes are developed by professional chefs and family tested specifically for this type of preparation and storage. The end result is nutritious and tasty foods that are enjoyed by both adults and children.

Kitchen Helper uses superior ingredients, such as restaurant–quality meats, poultry and seafood, which are a grade above that which the customers can buy in the grocery store. We use real flavorings, juices, and extracts, and often choose fresh herbs over dried. Fresh fruits and vegetables are utilized whenever possible, and we add no preservatives during meal assembly. This results in food products that are superior in taste and more nutritionally balanced than those offered by many of our competitors. Nutritional information for each recipe is available on our website.

The Kitchen Helper calendar offers seasonal menus with wide appeal, with at least 14 different choices per month. The company also monitors consumer response to our recipes, and will continue to develop and test new offerings. Popular recipes will be repeated based on customer demand.

Another aspect of the Kitchen Helper experience is the social opportunity for people to gather together. Kitchen Helper does not promote this aspect as the primary benefit like some competitors do, but we intend to make the customer's time in our stores a fun and productive experience. Kitchen Helper sessions are an opportunity for customers to meet with new and old friends, to share their cooking experience, and simply enjoy time with others. In many ways, this aspect of the experience harkens back in time, particularly for women, where it was common to gather together to complete household and family duties.

MARKET ANALYSIS

Target Market

The primary target market for Kitchen Helper consists of families, with the female head of household as the primary purchaser. Demographically, these families are represented by adults between the ages of 35 and 54 with children in the home. The household income of the target market is in excess of $30,000 or more.

This target customer values convenience, yet finds herself more and more "time–challenged". She is also aware of the importance of good nutrition for herself and her family, but finds providing those meals increasingly difficult. Also, parents know that time spent together as a family can have a significant positive impact on themselves and their children. Yet these shared times, particularly meal times, are falling victim to numerous activities and conflicting schedules. Many parents opt for the convenience of fast food or restaurant take–out at the expense of proper nutrition and family time, with a significant impact on the family budget.

These consumers have the financial means to try new products and will spend on services that they feel will simplify their life or benefit themselves or their families in some way. Once convinced of the value of a product, these consumers tend to be brand–loyal. Women tend to rely on word–of–mouth and the opinions of their friends, co–workers and neighbors, especially with regard to family issues.

Kitchen Helper's anchor store is located in the Effingham area in Effingham County, Illinois. The 2000 census estimated the population of Effingham at 13,641, while statistics on the City of Teutopolis indicated a population of 7,307 people living in 2,986 households. Of these households, 66 percent are families, and nearly one third have children under the age of 18 living with them. The average family size is 2.85. The median income for Teutopolis households is $62,180, with families earning $78,947. The racial makeup of the city is primarily white (88 percent), with the next largest group being African–American.

Effingham encompasses an area of over nine miles and houses the major shopping areas in Effingham County. The population of this area adds an additional 5,261 individuals, with a median household income of $98,186. Seventy percent of the residents are married, and 90 percent have attained a high school education or better. The population is relatively even with respect to gender. Estimates of local market size total 1,450 consumers in the immediate area and approximately 5,200 in the larger demographic area of Teutopolis.

The facility under consideration for Kitchen Helper's anchor store is centrally located among these communities. It is along one of the busiest commercial and retail thoroughfares, Main Street. This high–traffic area is easily accessible for customers, employees, and visitors. 7,051 people of an average age of 46 live within 1 mile of this location, and almost 40,000 individuals (median age 42) are within three miles. The median household income within this radius approaches $ 70,000. The proximity and customer profile of the residents of this area provide a rich market opportunity for Kitchen Helper.

Competition

In a broad sense, Kitchen Helper and other MFP businesses compete with all of the other options that a consumer has for meals. These options range from traditional home meal preparation to formal table service restaurants and everything in between. Due to the emphasis with MFP companies on the convenience of this option, competition comes mainly from fast–food companies and take–out service to full service restaurants, as well as prepared foods that can be purchased in local grocers.

For the MFP market specifically, the two primary business models are franchise operations and independent stores. As of July, 2005, the Easy Meal Preparation Association (EMPA) has identified 156 MRP companies with 372 store locations. The largest players in the franchise group are Cooking with Friends out of Madison, Wisconsin with 76 stores and Minute Meals of Seattle, Washington with 68 locations. Several other companies, including Spices and Stuff (IL) and Jane and Mitzy (IL) have five to 10 stores clustered in a specific geographic area. Several of these companies are now offering franchises in an effort to expand. The rest of the locations are comprised of independent businesses operating generally a single location.

In Illinois, the Minute Meals franchise currently has locations in Bloomington, Chicago, and Springfield. Cooking with Friends is located in Chicago and is expected to open this year in Arlington Heights. Spices and Stuff (eight locations nationwide) opened in July, 2005 in Evanston. An independent business, Jane and Mitzy, is open in Decatur and just announced their first franchise expansion in the same area.

In order to get a true understanding of some of these competitors, we have "mystery shopped" four different locations, including Cooking with Friends (Chicago), Minute Meals (Springfield, IL), Spices and Stuff (Evanston), and Jane and Mitzy (Decatur, IL). We also visited most of the available websites, gathered information from industry association members, and conducted phone interviews. We have evaluated each of the major franchise operations. In fact, several of the franchises are aggressively seeking buyers in this area. Our analysis shows that, in the long run, each of the franchises is vulnerable in a significant way. For example, Jane and Mitzy is built on a retro, "party girl" type of atmosphere, and the food products are mediocre. Minute Meals has been dubbed "the future McDonald's of the industry" by one association member, reflecting their strategy of high volume without much service or product quality. (Their operations use processed canned and prepared foods in very basic recipes).

Cooking with Friends has built its reputation on its association with the Culinary School of Chicago, but is lacking in clear marketing and branding.

We believe that an independent business provides the best model for long–term success, particularly in light of the expense of acquiring and maintaining a franchise. Being independent, coupled with Kitchen Helper's differentiation and positioning in the local market, will allow us to adapt to the changing business environment as the market grows and eventually matures. We do expect this to be a highly competitive business, however, and we are prepared to respond to various competitors as necessary. Due to the early stage of development of this market, we believe there is room and time to establish our concept and brand before head–to–head competition becomes a major issue.

As an independent business, Kitchen Helper also benefits from its membership in the EMPA. This association allows us to collaborate with a wide variety of similar businesses across the country. In this way, Kitchen Helper can assess the best practices of these companies and implement them, if appropriate, in our area. The communication afforded through this organization has already been extremely beneficial to our research, understanding, and business plan development.

Risk Factors

Barriers to entry in this market are fairly low, although a capital contribution of approximately $100,000 is required to launch a store operation. General operating knowledge of restaurants or food service is beneficial. However, the operations of MFPs are relatively straight forward and do not require any particular technical expertise. Compliance issues, particularly health, safety and zoning issues, must be addressed. Technologies, including website and software support, are central to the business, but there are no proprietary or complex technological requirements.

Due to the attractiveness of this market segment and the limited barriers to entry, we believe that a proliferation of companies will enter this new market niche. Our focus is on not only launching Kitchen Helper successfully, but providing the necessary foundation to carry the company through the competitive years ahead.

MARKETING & SALES

At Kitchen Helper, our customers are the reason we are in business. This premise drives everything about the business and is the foundation of our strategy. Analysis of the competition indicates that most MFP companies are employing a narrowly defined strategy that focuses on the physical product (entrees, dinners, suppers) or facilities (kitchen). Kitchen Helper focuses on the customer *experience.* This customer–centered strategy will allow us greater flexibility and broader appeal as the Kitchen Helper concept and the overall market develop.

In order to succeed, Kitchen Helper must effectively position its product/service and clearly differentiate this brand from the competition. Then, Kitchen Helper must deliver on the customer promise of providing delicious, nutritious meals quickly and easily. That customer promise is a potent value proposition: *Kitchen Helper provides high quality, cost–effective, nutritious and delicious meal solutions.* For the customer, this means less time, less work, no waste, no cleanup, and at a price that beats other alternatives. And, we accomplish all this in a supportive, comfortable, and fun environment.

Kitchen Helper is positioned as a high quality, cost–effective solution for family meals. The benefits to the consumer are numerous. They include: less time spent on finding recipes and preparing menus, grocery shopping, preparation and cooking; less money (consumers are challenged to add their grocery, fast food and take–out costs and compare to Kitchen Helper); healthier meals made with high quality ingredients; delicious, seasonal, proven recipes, reduced stress on the cook and the family; nutritional information available for each menu item; great taste and broad appeal of recipes; ability to bring meal time back for the family; selections can be frozen for up to six months; simple preparation, since dishes can be cooked in 30 minutes or less; good leftovers; putting fun back into meal preparation; a comfortable, inviting yet highly functional environment. This positioning, and the benefits it offers, links back to the fundamental strategy of keeping the customer at the center of our business.

Kitchen Helper has implemented this focus on the customer from the very beginning, starting with the selection of the company name. Instead of following the lead of competitors such as Minute Meals, Spices and Stuff, Jane and Mitzy, the Kitchen Helper name combines a customer focus with a sense of excitement and anticipation. The "Kitchen" links the name to cooking, yet at the same time is not explicit in its promise. It creates interest and draws the customer in. This name also allows the flexibility to offer expanded product and services in the future.

In a similar fashion, we believe that attention to detail, from the customer's perspective, will enhance our in–store experience. For example, many local ordinances require people with long hair who handle food to pull their hair back. The solution offered by some competitors has been to advise clients to pull their hair back before attending a session, or providing them with a bandana when they arrive. Most women would agree that tying a bandana on their head is cumbersome at best, and not something they would like to "be seen" in. Kitchen Helper is fashioning a custom, color–coordinated bandana–band, which is a bandana in front and an elastic headband in the back. This headgear holds the hair back effectively, yet is comfortable and easy to wear. (We have even been complimented on the look of this piece of equipment!)

Kitchen Helper is also implementing a number of programs that will support communication with the customer. On our website, we invite customers to contact us with their questions, comments, and suggestions. Following attendance at any session, customers will be invited to provide feedback on their experience as well as the recipes. Our customer database also includes opportunities for special reminders, such as birthdays, and incentives such as private parties and referral recognition.

Pricing

In keeping with an image that connotes higher quality and better taste, Kitchen Helper is adopting a pricing policy that positions the company slightly above, but competitive with, similar offerings. In this way, we have greater flexibility to offer alternative and short–term pricing actions, such as offering coupons or specials, on a controlled basis. This will allow us to implement specific programs in response to competitive situations as well.

Current prices for competitors have hovered just under $200 for 12 menu selections. In northeast Illinois, current competitors are priced at $189 for Cooking with Friends and $197 for Minute Meals. A current industry benchmark is to keep costs at or below 50 percent of the retail food cost. We will hold our price per serving for the customer under $3.00 and have set our cost per dish at $7.50, including packaging. Pricing for ancillary products and services will be slightly above similar offerings by our competitors. For the first store, our pricing will be set at $197 for 12 selections and $149 for eight:

Retail price (12)	Price per dish	Price per serving (6)	@ 7.50 Cost %
$199	$16.58	$2.76	45%
$197	$16.42	$2.74	46%
$195	$16.25	$2.71	46%
$189	$15.75	$2.63	48%
$185	$15.42	$2.57	49%

OPERATIONS

Location

In any retail business, particularly food related, location is a key factor in success. Meal assembly businesses are somewhat more of a "drive to" location than many restaurants or retail operations; however, it is still important to be located in a well–traveled commercial area. Kitchen Helper is currently negotiating for space in the Main Street area of Effingham, Illinois. This location will be our anchor store.

Our growth strategy for Kitchen Helper centers around this initial location and adds to the company's capacity by opening several 'satellite' locations. These locations will have about the same customer space and function as the anchor store, but will be more limited in back–end kitchen capabilities. Special preparation requiring a full kitchen will be done at the central location. Utilizing this type of "hub and spoke" system will enable the company to more rapidly expand the Kitchen Helper brand. This strategy will also reduce the expensive overhead of kitchen facilities in each store.

Given the first location in the Effingham area, the following areas are targeted for expansion in the next two to five years: Chicago, Carbondale, Cicero, and Naperville. Each of these areas is demographically attractive. The order of store openings has not been finalized and will be determined in part by demand and the availability of space.

Following the expansion of the initial area through the addition of five to seven satellite locations, Kitchen Helper will consider the possibility of repeating this growth pattern in another area. Detailed plans for this growth stage have not been included in this plan, since we envision that opportunity to be at least five years in the future.

Store Design

The interior of the store is critical to the customer experience. Many of our competitors' stores look and feel similar to a commercial kitchen. Again, our goal is to focus on the customer and make her feel welcome and comfortable. The interior design and furnishings will need to be highly functional and practical, but the same time, we want the customer to feel 'at home' in our location. Therefore, our interior design is focused on making the store environment more similar to an upscale home kitchen than the industrial kitchens of some of our competitors. Elements such as lighting, music, and a 'gathering area' are all being taken into account in order to make the customer feel welcome. This will again help to differentiate us from the competition and strengthen our customer relationship. An interior designer has been retained to implement our design ideas.

Promotion

As a young business, Kitchen Helper relies on word–of–mouth and referrals to build its customer base. Programs are being planned to capture attention and target specific consumer groups. We will also reward customers for referrals and provide an incentive for people who organize groups for a private party.

Several pre–opening sessions are planned for invited opinion leaders in our community. We are adopting a 'secretive' theme for these sessions and are asking customers to help us fine–tune our concept as well as try out some recipes. Press releases announcing the business will be sent to local business, community, and cooking–related media. The initial release will be followed with additional news releases on at least a quarterly basis. The company website will also be used to promote our services.

Highly target direct mail will be used to introduce Kitchen Helper to households in the immediate area. In addition, Kitchen Helper will promote its business through the local school system by conducting a fund–raiser and supporting school activities. Family–oriented organizations, including local churches, synagogues, and community organizations, will receive our news and be invited to attend appropriate events.

The location of our anchor store also provides opportunities for cross–marketing with other tenants. Several of these businesses cater to the same demographic group that we are trying to reach. Creative, cost–effective promotions will be developed with a few of these organizations.

Marketing Timeline and Budget

The focus of Kitchen Helper marketing activities in the first six months of operation will be to introduce the Kitchen Helper concept to the local community through word–of–mouth and public relations activities. These include the pre–parties, announcements and press activities mentioned earlier. A Grand Opening celebration is also scheduled for Month three of operation. In the second six months of the first year, limited direct mail, cross–marketing promotions with local vendors, and school promotions will be key. These activities will be supported by repeat announcements to local media.

In the second year of operation, marketing activities will be expanded to include additional direct mail, limited print advertising, additional community/school activities, and media activities surrounding the opening of a second location. In addition, both partner will be active in association, commerce, and women's business organizations and will be available to speak about the company and related topics.

The marketing budget is initially very limited in the first year of operation, with the initial $1,500 being dedicated to the design of the company's logo and colors, print production of business cards, stationary, and initial brochures, and website design and implementation. Thereafter, $250 per month is allocated to cover the scheduled activities, with an additional $250 for extra expenses associated with the grand opening. In the second year, this figure is increased, with extra resources surrounding the grand opening of a second location. This level stays constant for the third year of operation, although marketing is one of the top priorities for additional funding if finances allow.

Services

As a meal facilitation and preparation facility, Kitchen Helper enables the customer to prepare a large number of dishes quickly and easily, while enjoying the comfortable, fun environment at the store. In order to begin the process, customers may be directed to our website, or they can call the store to initiate their order. The customer order and fulfillment process includes the following steps:

1. Customers register online via our secure website, in person at the store or via phone for a session date and time. Sessions are generally scheduled in 2–hour blocks and the calendar is posted by month. A customer can assemble up to 12 meals per 2–hour session, or may choose to bring a friend and split the meals with that person. Kitchen Helper also offers an 8–recipe option.

2. Recipes are selected by the customer from our monthly menu. The customer chooses 12 out of approximately 14 options. She may choose to make double quantities of the same recipe if desired. Menu selections change monthly and are seasonally appropriate.

3. Sessions are booked using a credit card, but the customer is given the option to pay by cash or check once they have arrived at the store. New customers also sign an agreement outlining their responsibilities and the company's limits of liability. If a customer signs up for a session, but is unable to attend, Kitchen Helper offers to assemble the meals for pick up at the store or delivery. (These services incur extra charges). No–shows are charged 60 percent of their session fee, unless they can be rescheduled within a reasonable time period. Any excess inventory or extra meals are assembled by the Kitchen Helper staff, frozen, and placed in our cooler. These meals are then made available for purchase by session or walk–in customers.

4. The website provides a wealth of information for the customer, including information on how the Kitchen Helper concept works, a map to the store and answers to common questions. Customers

can also contact the store for help. When the customer attends a session, she is asked to bring a cooler or basket with her in order to carry the finished meals home.

5. When the customer arrives at the store, she is greeted and given brief instructions on the Kitchen Helper process if this is her first visit. She then grabs her apron, pulls back her hair, washes her hands, and receives a printed list of the recipes she has selected.
6. The customer begins to assemble the meals on her list by moving to a workstation that has been set up specifically for one of the recipes she has selected. Each station is equipped and stocked with all the necessary ingredients, as well as step–by–step instructions for making that recipe. Appropriate measuring spoons, cups, and mixing tools are also right at the station. The customer simply measures out the proper amount of each ingredient and mixes according to directions. At this point, she also has the option to vary the recipe according to her tastes. For example, if her family does not like onions, she merely leaves that out of her dish. If she loves hot pepper, she can simply add more.
7. All assembled meals are packaged in either a Ziploc freezer bag or an aluminum pan with a lid. Thawing and cooking instructions are affixed to each dish. When the customer finishes making the dish, she places it in her designated holding area and moves on to the next station. Customers are asked to wash their hands or replace their gloves before moving to the next station.
8. This process continues until the customer finishes her whole order, at which time she takes her cooler full of meals home to be frozen for up to six months. From that point, all the customer needs to do is reach into her freezer and pull out her choice for her next meal. She simply follows the defrosting and cooking instructions on the label.
9. Work surfaces are wiped after each customer use, and the Kitchen Helper staff insures that everything the next customer needs is available and all utensils are clean. Workstations are restocked and cleaned between each session.

Website and Back–End Processes

The Kitchen Helper website is the portal into the company for our customers. It is designed to be very simple to understand and easy to navigate. In developing the website, particular attention is being paid to its impact on the consumer, including ease of use, attractiveness, presentation of the corporate identity, and accuracy and completeness of information. The website provides the customer with value–added services, including an interactive session calendar, a customer shopping cart, secure log–in with password encryption, and integrated credit card processing.

Kitchen Helper is also purchasing a web–based software package which provides the back–office processes necessary to run our MFP operation. We selected this vendor due to the experience of the firm and the design of the software, which is specific to an MFP business and stems from the firm's own MFP operation. The back–end software hooks to and shares information with the company's website. The website captures information for back–office management. Both the website and back–end systems will be hosted 24 hours a day, seven days per week.

Purchasing and inventory control are directly related to the number of customers scheduled for each session and the recipes they choose to make. This information drives the ordering of grocery items, ingredients, and package materials. The orders flow through the company's back–end system, where they are combined with vendor information, inventory control, and costing data. Once a customer order is submitted, the recipe selections are processed in the order tracking software. The system breaks down the individual ingredients and amounts needed for those recipes and combines it with other orders. A product purchasing list is generated. Non–perishable foods (canned goods, spices, etc) are entered into the inventory control sheet and automatically reduced when orders are placed. The software tracks when 'on hand' ingredients are low and adds them to the weekly purchasing list. The system also creates prep instructions, customer lists, and the required assembly and cooking instructions. Since inventory is purchased to order, very little waste is anticipated and inventory losses are minimal.

Reporting and Management
In addition to the functions necessary for operations, the software system also provides reporting and management tools for the business. Some of the functions included are:

- Control Panel and Summary—displays current activity on revenue, payments, session counts, service counts and individual customer orders
- Grocery Report—evaluates current ingredient order needs by timeframe
- Entree Count Report—prepares for sessions by retrieving specific entree counts within a specific timeframe
- Sales Tax Report—generates sales data for any timeframe and distinguishes between taxable and non–taxable sales for tax reporting purposes
- Custom Reports on Order History/Trends
- Calendar Manager—adds and updates calendar events and session schedules
- Order Manager—interactively adds and updates orders as needed
- Customer Manager—manages customer information (name, address, phone, etc)
- Recipe Catalog Manager—creates, adds and maintains recipes (integrates with Ingredient Manager)
- Menu Manager—manages monthly menu offerings, which allows selections from the Recipe Catalog to build menus
- Ingredient Manager—adds, updates and manages ingredients, including packaging

Food Handling and Safety

A major component of the operations of this business involve safe food handling and preparation. This is an area that is generally taken for granted by the consuming public, but which has a tremendous downside to any establishment that does not plan and manage food processes appropriately. Realizing that this was a critical gap in knowledge, both Susan and Anne have taken and passed the ServeSafe class, which certifies them in food handling and safety. It is the company's policy that all employees receive appropriate food safety training.

Business Rollout

To roll out the Kitchen Helper concept, the management team has developed a plan that will allow us to test our business model and still be aggressive with plans to open our stores and stay ahead of the competition. Several private parties with invited guests are intended to test the products and procedures that are in place. Customers will be given the opportunity to experience the Kitchen Helper concept firsthand in exchange for their feedback, comments and suggestions. Secondly, temporary space in a local church is being secured, so that the company can begin operations on a limited basis while the build–out of the retail space is completed. The lease and build–out of approximately 2000 square feet of retail space is in the early stages of development.

Exit Strategies

At this point in time, the partners do not anticipate exiting the company until at least five years, and more likely a decade, of business experience has been acquired. However, at any time, we recognize that an exit might be offered or become necessary. The operating agreement between the partners addresses the potential of one partner buying out the business and continuing to operate. In the event that an outside offer for purchase is received, the partners will give careful consideration to the offer at that time.

At some point between the company's fifth and tenth year of operation, it is likely that the partners will pursue the sale of the company. It is highly unlikely, unless the economic environment changes significantly, that an Initial Public Offering (IPO) would be feasible. It is more likely that the owners would pursue the private sale of Kitchen Helper, either to an individual, a group of investors, or another company seeking to enter the industry.

Business Ethics and Standards

Kitchen Helper operates, at all times, with the highest sense of business and ethical standards. It is the company's policy to be honest and forthright in all of its business practices and to treat customers, suppliers and employees with respect and fairness without regard to race, religion, sex, age, or personal lifestyle choices. The company's Operations and Training Manuals reflect this policy, and the management team leads by example. Additionally, under the guidance of a professional accounting firm, Kitchen Helper adheres to standard accounting and financial practices. We do not tolerate false or misleading advertising or any use of our company name, image, or operations in a way that compromises the integrity of the firm.

FINANCIAL ANALYSIS

The financial information included here is the management team's best estimate of first year start–up and ongoing costs for Kitchen Helper. The projections for the first year have been shared with the financial consultant for the industry association and have passed the 'test of reasonableness' for this industry. With the implementation of the QuickBooks accounting system, as well as the back–end software system described earlier, the assumptions and projections will be constantly scrutinized and updated as actual data becomes available.

Kitchen Helper is currently funded by equal participation on the part of the two partners. The company has deposited $50,000 with Stone Bank to fund the business start–up. The company is seeking a loan of $75,000 to fund the purchase of equipment and supplies, and to provide working capital. At present, these are the only sources of funds being considered. As the business reaches break–even and begins to be profitable, the owners expect to use the proceeds to pay off the loan and to subsidize future growth.

In light of the emerging nature of this industry, several keys to the financial success of the company are evident. These include: cost containment, especially on food costs; minimizing preparation and cleanup time, thereby making efficient use of direct labor; careful management of the business's cash flow; committing to as minimal amount of overhead as possible without sacrificing the business concept; and negotiating favorable terms on all agreements.

Assumptions

The following assumptions have been utilized in constructing the estimates of the first year start–up and operating costs:

- The first year begins in July, 2005 and continues through June of 2006.
- Pre–operating expenses include primarily marketing (company identity design and implementation), legal (partner agreement, software license agreement, operations training purchase agreement, real estate lease, and construction agreement), and website and software purchase and development.
- Limited operations begin in temporary facility in October 2005.

- One focus group per month in September and October 2005.
- Retail space is leased and expenses occurred beginning in November 2005. Rent is estimated at $20 per square foot (triple net) for 1,800 square feet of space ($3,000 per month).
- Improvements required for retail space total $12,000 spread over four months.
- Number of sessions per month builds slowly during the first few months of operation and reaches a maximum of 12 after six months.
- Average number of customers per session is conservatively estimated at eight, while our goal is 12 and the maximum allowed is 14.
- Number of dishes per session is estimated at 10 to account for customers who may order only eight selections instead of the traditional 12.
- Revenue per customer is estimated at $175, which assumes two-thirds of the customers buy 12 selections and one-three buy eight selections.
- Bank charges are estimated at two percent.
- Cost per selection is held at $7.50 including packaging.
- Grand opening is held in January, 2006.
- Computer expenses include purchase of the software back–end as well as website design plus ongoing support and hosting fees. Where possible, installment payment options are taken. The 'lite' version of the software system reaches capacity as 12 sessions per month for the first location. An upgrade is planned in the second year.
- Direct labor is estimated at two people earning $10 per hour for three hours per session. The partners take no salary during this period.
- Equipment purchase is estimated at $25,500 and is spread out over 10 months.
- Training and Development includes the initial operations training for the partners and ongoing food safety courses for employees.

These assumptions were used to construct the second and third year quarterly projections:

- Software upgraded for more capacity and multiple locations—final quarter of 2006
- Retail location requires less improvement
- Second location is opened in January, 2007
- Retail kitchen products contribute to revenue
- Two store managers are in place in addition to session assistants
- Owners continue to defer salary in lieu of new store
- Professional services are increased with second store
- Other revenue and cost assumptions remain basically unchanged

These financial projections indicate that the company will operate at a slight loss at the conclusion of the first year of operation. In year two, we continue to invest by opening a second location and show a profit by year end. Year three projections indicate the company will generate a net income of over $100,000.

Break-even analysis

The following is the revenue required in Year 1 to breakeven at net income before taxes, including all start-up expenses:

Breakeven revenue required	$166,744	
Cost of goods sold	$66,364	(39.8%)
Gross margin	$100,380	(60.2%)
Operating expenses	$100,380	
Net income (EBITDA)	-0-	

Balance sheet

As of August 1, 2005	
Assets	
Current assets:	
Cash	$48,600
A/R	0
Inventories	0
Total current assets	$48,600
Fixed Assets:	
Equipment	
Office equipment	
Less depreciation	
Total fixed assets	0
Intangibles:	
Goodwill, etc.	
Total intangible assets	0
Total Assets	$48,600
Liabilities	
Current Liabilities:	
A/P	0
Expenses payable	$ 7,700
Total current liabilities	$ 7,700
Long-term liabilities:	
Notes payable	
Total long-term liabilities	0
Total liabilities	$ 7,700
Stockholder's equity	
Owner's equity	$40,900
Total stockholder's equity	$40,900
Total liabilities & Stockholders equity	**$48,600**

Producer and Supplier of Plants and Flowers

BOUNTYFULL FARMS

41451 Wood Field Run
Armada, Michigan 48005

Danielle Ferris

Bountyfull Farms will produce quality cut flowers and foliage to be sold to florists and wholesalers. We will fill the needs of a niche market and will keep focused on what products to offer our clients. Local production, large diversity of material, and quality fresh products will be our trademarks.

BUSINESS OVERVIEW

Company History

Bountyfull Farms is located on ten fertile acres east of Armada, Michigan. Although ground was planted first in 2006, Bountyfull Farms has been the dream of owner/grower Rebecca Samuelson for seven years. With a background in horticulture and a creative streak, a fresh flower farm is the perfect outlet for Rebecca's talents. With a large variety of annuals planted fresh each year as well as many perennials to return every year, Bountyfull Farms offers locally grown fresh cut flowers—the best that Michigan can grow!

Bountyfull Farms will produce quality cut flowers and foliage to be sold to florists and wholesalers. We will fill the needs of a niche market and will keep focused on what products to offer our clients. Local production, large diversity of material, and quality fresh products will be our trademarks. It is our goal to be fully self-supporting within three years.

Management Summary

Rebecca Samuelson, Owner—Ms. Samuelson possesses the skills necessary for such an undertaking. She has earned both an associates degree and a bachelor's degree in horticulture. In addition to this education, she has seven years of experience at a botanic garden and one year of experience at a landscaping firm. Her strengths include quality production and maintenance of plants with a positive interaction with clients and the general public.

Marketing & Sales

The first year we will grow a majority of annuals with a few perennials started. As revenue is produced, we plan to add perennials to production each year.

The primary market for Bountyfull Farms will be the greater Armada, Michigan area. The area is experiencing phenomenal growth and I hope to tap into that market. The number of markets is growing in the Armada metro area as the area develops and grows. Armada is called a "Rising Smart Growth Star" by the Smart Growth Network.

Armada is the second largest city in Michigan with a population of about 200,000. There are roughly 1.3 million people within the greater Armada metropolitan area, making it the second largest metropolis in the state as well.

In November 1998, Armada was named by Fortune magazine as one of the Top 10 Best Cities for Business in the U.S.

According to Armada/Macomb County Convention & Visitors Bureau, Armada has $500 million in new attractions, meeting facilities and recreational venues.

Median age	30.6
Completed at least some college (% of residents)	52.6%
Married	39.7%
Divorced	10.9%
Amount spent on vacations (domestic and foreign, household average per year)	$6,041

Median family income (per year)	$49,677
Family purchasing power (annual, cost-of-living adjusted)	$55,817
Sales tax	6.00%
State income tax rate (highest bracket)	3.90%
State income tax rate (lowest bracket)	3.90%
Auto insurance premiums (average for the state)	$ 2,575
Job growth % (2000–2005)	0.55%

We will spend time this winter approaching local florist shops, acquainting them with our business and products, and then returning later when we have product to sell. We will also approach local floral wholesalers and possibly grocery stores.

Price will be determined by individual varieties of the plants. Price guidelines, such as those from the USDA, will form the basis for the prices charged, but local demand will determine the final cost.

PRODUCTS & SERVICES

Bouquet Subscription

Bountyfull Farms is pleased to offer a weekly bouquet subscription service. Subscriptions can be purchased ahead of time and, when the flowers begin to bloom, a fresh bouquet can be delivered locally to a location of your choice. Bouquets will reflect what is blooming in the garden that week.

A bouquet subscription is the perfect way to bring the outdoors in! A bouquet subscription can be a wonderful gift for Christmas, Mother's Day, and birthdays (and just because!). Bring a smile week after week to your spouse, your mother, your assistant, someone in extended care, a best friend. Flowers are the perfect way to brighten a home, an office, and a day.

Flowers add a perfect welcoming touch to waiting rooms and offices, as well as foyers and dinner tables. A bouquet subscription can say "Happy Birthday," "Thank You," "Get Well," "Thinking of You," and "I Love You."

How it works

Once the flowers begin to bloom, an arrangement will be delivered to you every week. The vases are recycled—so when a new arrangement is delivered, the old vase is picked up. And you will have weeks of beautiful flowers to enjoy!

The subscription service can be purchased in different weekly increments.

- 4 weeks–$90
- 6 weeks–$130
- 8 weeks–$175

For deliveries outside a 15 mile radius from the farm, a $5.00 charge will be added to each delivery.

Flowers by the Bucket

A bucket of fresh flowers to use as you wish—if you would prefer to make your own arrangements, a bucket of fresh flowers can be delivered to you to use as you wish!

Special Events

Bountyfull Farms would be pleased to supply the flowers for your special events, such as birthday parties or special get–togethers. Please contact us to see how we can meet your needs.

FINANCIAL ANALYSIS

We currently have $2,000 in start–up capital for the business. We plan to research possible grants this winter. The owner will keep her regular job until the business is able to support her— hopefully no longer than 2 or 3 years.

We anticipate the needs for the first year to include the following purchases:

- Seeds
- Electric fence supplies
- Hoses and watering supplies
- Fertilizer
- Support netting
- Stem cutter
- Seeder
- Support netting
- Possible cooler unit
- Miscellaneous (buckets/labels/etc.)

The first year will be a mixed year as we will still be working and doing the farming on the side. However, we hope to generate $5000 net profit next year.

The day–to–day accountant will be Ms. Samuelson. For more in–depth work, we will defer to the accountant, Hugo Stocks. He will be more knowledgeable about farming and what particulars pertain to our situation.

OPERATIONS

Evenings will be spent harvesting and maintaining the farm. One day a week will focus on delivery and selling what we have harvested. In addition, Saturdays will be devoted to working on the farm with tasks requiring more time that just a few hours here and there.

We do not intend to hire any additional labor. Friends and relatives may be utilized as necessary for small tasks such as bookkeeping and deliveries.

The owner will be living and working out of the farm, so all expenses will be covered at least for the first year. The only additional cost is the necessary insurance for the business. To cover these costs, the owner will maintain regular employment in addition to the farm so that some steady income will be coming in.

The full list of necessary equipment will be researched and purchased this winter. Appropriate purchases will be discussed with some mentor friends who are already in the business.

Professional Affiliations

Bountyfull Farms is a member of the Association of Specialty Cut Flower Growers. The Association was formed in 1988 to unite and inform growers in the production and marketing of field and greenhouse cut flowers. It provides information on growing techniques, marketing strategies, and new developments in the industry that you won't find anywhere else.

CONCLUSION

It is our goal to be farming full–time by 2007 or 2008. The more time we can devote to developing the business, the more money we will be able to generate. We are also willing to look into other avenues to make the farm more productive year–round, such as growing/selling cool season vegetables and possibly growing plants to sell. Nevertheless, the primary goal is to introduce many new possibilities for cut flower or well–grown locally produced cut flowers into the local cut flower market.

Restaurant

CAFE FRESCO

31 Culver Ave.
Windsor, ON N9B 3P4

Gerald Rekve

This business plan is for an old style Italian cafe that's concept will be based on traditional cooking methods. Our goal is to have a high standard of food for the restaurant. We will meet this goal while trying to provide menu items incorporating our imported ingredients, and being mindful of the well being of our customers (and our staff).

EXECUTIVE SUMMARY

Business Overview

Cafe Fresco Inc. is a Windsor–based company that will operate Cafe Fresco, a single unit, medium–size restaurant serving healthy, Italian style food. The restaurant will be located at 31 Culver Ave., Windsor, Canada.

The company will operate as a corporation and will be owned and operated in Windsor by the partners.

The company was incorporated in September of 2006 and elected sub–chapter S.

The founders are Gino Scarpilli and Vincent Hanna. Gino is the President and Vincent is the Vice President. There are a total of 25,000 shares of common stock issued. Gino and Vincent each own 12,000 and the remainder are retained by the company for future distribution. In addition they have loaned the company $8,000 of their own money for research and start–up costs.

A suitable site for the first restaurant was found last month and lease negotiations are in the final stages. The location will be on Culver Ave., just outside Main and First Streets and close to a dense population of the target market. When the lease is signed there will be two months of free rent for construction and in that time, the balance of the start–up funds must be raised. With that phase completed, Cafe Fresco can then open and the operations phase of the project can begin.

The location is that of an old paint and wallpaper store, with lots of parking in the back as well free street parking after 5:00pm. The renovation of the location will be done by the partners to save money and will be built with the help of contractors that will help in the areas of electrical and plumbing.

Mission

The company's goal is that of an old style Italian cafe based on traditional cooking methods. Our goal is to have a high standard of food for the restaurant. We will meet this goal while trying to provide menu items incorporating our imported ingredients, and being mindful of the well being of our customers (and our staff), as well as the high quality of attitude, generosity between management, customers, and vendors.

With the high turnover of help for cafes, we will rely on family to fill in where required until we are off the ground and making a profit. Awareness of all these factors will give our efforts lasting effects for our basic financial goals.

Business Strategy

If the business is meeting its projections by end of year one, we will start scouting for a second location and develop plans for the next unit. Our five year goal is to have two restaurants in the Windsor area with a combined annual profit of between $50,000 and $100,000. We will look for more locations that will meet our needs to expand in a slow and orderly fashion. The goal is to keep the business small and easy to manage.

Market Analysis

Although the restaurant industry is very competitive, the lifestyle changes created by modern living continue to fuel its steady growth. More and more people have less time, resources, and ability to cook for themselves. Trends are very important and Cafe Fresco is well positioned for the current interest in lighter, healthier foods at moderate to low prices.

Household spending on foodservice jumps 8.7%

(Jan. 16, 2006) The average Canadian household spent $1,931 on food and alcohol from restaurants and licensed establishments in 2005 – an increase of $154 or 8.7% over 2004 – according to a new report from Statistics Canada.

This increase in foodservice spending by households is the largest since 1998 and follows several years of sluggish growth. Household spending at grocery and liquor stores grew only 1.0% to $5,944 in 2005, but accounts for more than 75% of the total household food dollar.

Growth in Ontario – which accounts for nearly 40% of Canadian foodservice sales – combined with robust gains in Western Canada were largely responsible for the gains in foodservice expenditures. Household spending in Ontario bounced back in 2005 with a 9.1% increase – the result of pent-up demand following several years of sluggish growth. Similarly, rising incomes and booming economies in the western provinces fuelled spending throughout the region.

Households in British Columbia retained top spot in 2005, spending an average of $2,293 at restaurants and bars – $362 more than the national average. At 16.6%, Alberta posted the fastest growth in 2005, but ranks second with average household spending on foodservice of $2,252. A healthy provincial economy boosted household spending on foodservice in Saskatchewan 9.9%, to $1,380.

Average household spending in Quebec ranked below Manitoba and Prince Edward Island in 2005 even though Quebec boasts a higher per capita disposable income.

With the lowest disposable income, households in the Atlantic region spend less at restaurants and bars than the rest of Canada. Below-average disposable income restrained household spending on foodservice in Nova Scotia and New Brunswick to $1,504 and $1,486 in 2005. Although Newfoundland and Labrador's average household spending at grocery and liquor stores is the fifth highest in the country, spending on foodservice fell 1.4% to $1,096 in 2005.

Overall foodservice sales growth in 2005 did not keep pace with the 8.7% gain in household spending. Commercial foodservice sales were limited to 3.5%, due to lower tourism levels. It also must be noted that Statistics Canada uses different survey methodologies to calculate household spending and foodservice revenues, and there is a margin of error around both data sets.

Average annual household spending on foodservice

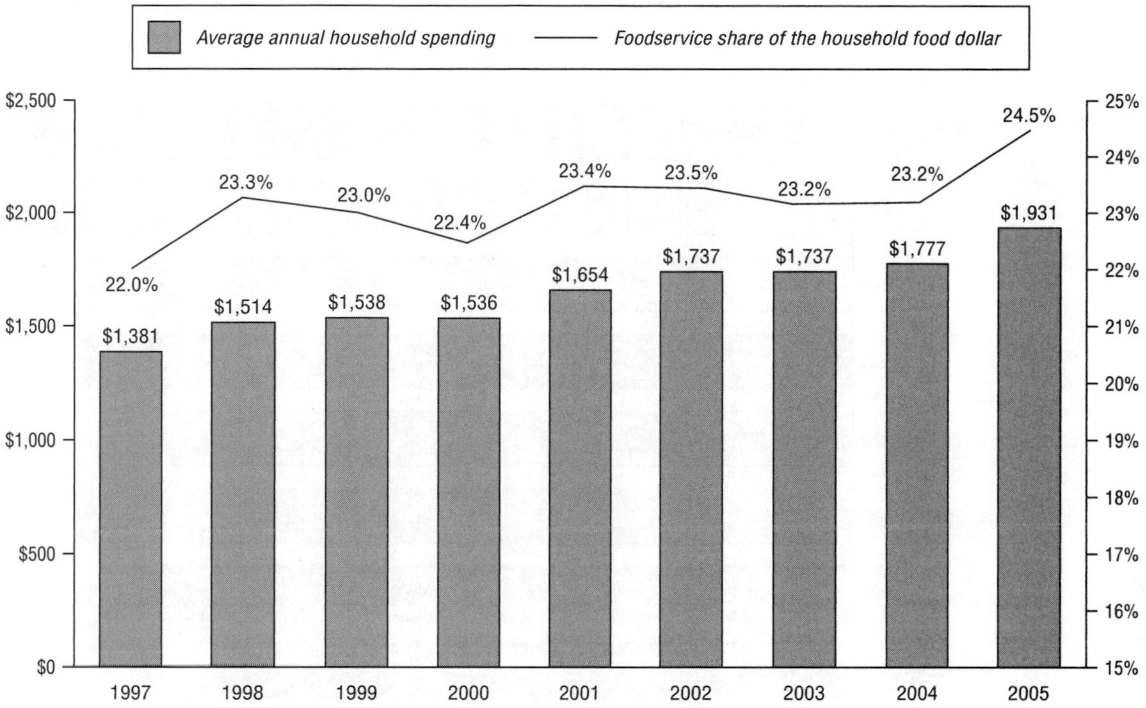

SOURCE: Survey of Household Spending, Statistics Canada

Average household spending on food and alcohol—2005

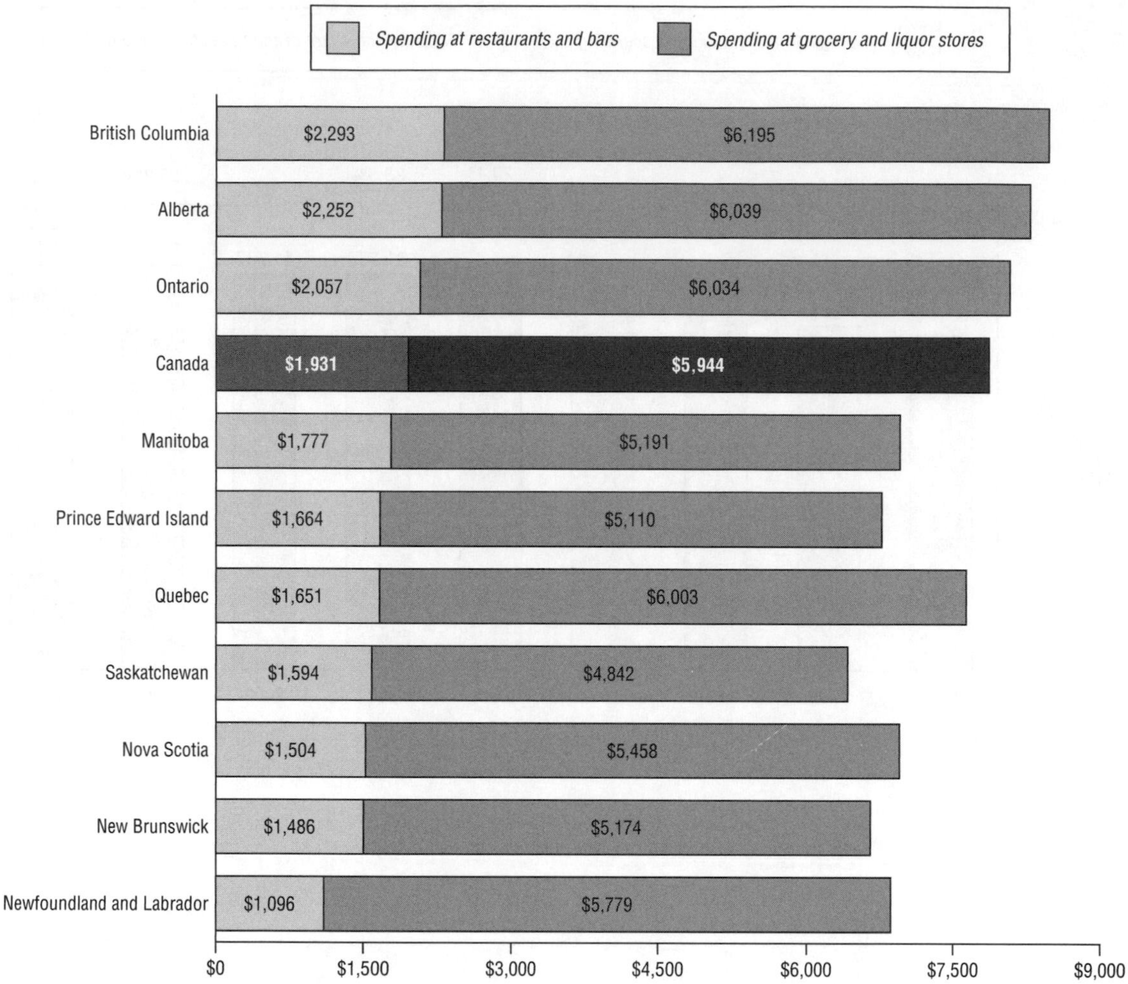

SOURCE: 2005 Survey of Household Spending, Statistics Canada

Year-over-year change in household spending at restaurants and bars

(2005 over 2004)

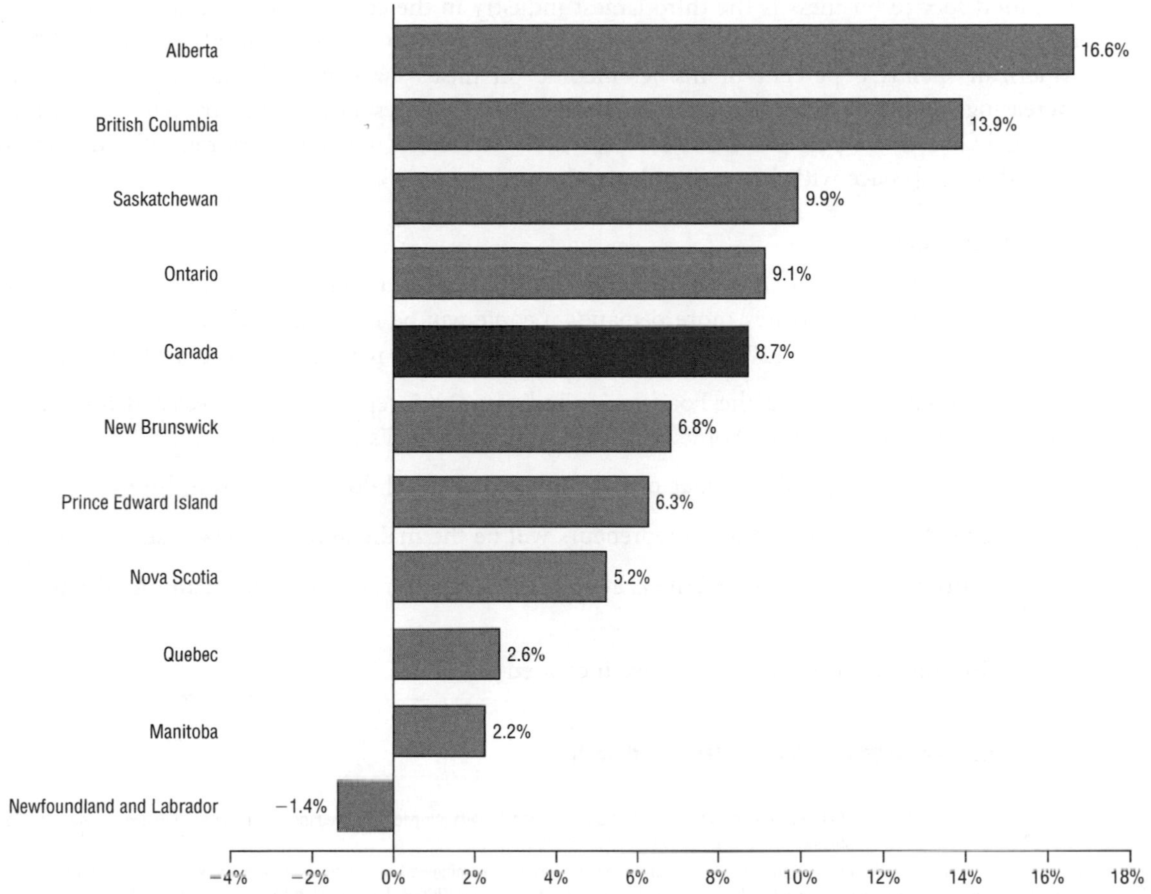

SOURCE: 2005 Survey of Household Spending, Statistic Canada

Consumer Spending

- The average Canadian household visits a restaurant for a meal or snack 526 times per year. Meals and snacks sourced from restaurants account for 1 in 10 meal occasions. Source: CREST/NPD Group; NPD Group Eating Patterns in Canada Report, October 2005 release.
- The average Canadian household spends 22.1 percent of its total food dollar on foodservice, compared to 41.4 percent for U.S. households Source: CRFA's, and the Bureau of Labour Statistics
- The most popular food and beverage ordered at Canadian restaurants are French fries and regular coffee. Source: CREST/NPD Group and CRFA's
- The average check size at a restaurant is $6.36 including taxes, but excluding tips. Source: CREST/NPD Group and CRFA's
- The average household sources a meal or snack from a restaurant 11.4 times over a two-week period. Source: CREST/NPD Group and CRFA's

- The percentage of restaurant meals and snacks eaten off-premise has increased from 53 percent in 1994 to 60.4 percent in 2005 due to the increased popularity of drive-through service. Source: CREST/NPD Group and CRFA's

The food service business is the third largest industry in the country. It accounts for over $199 billion annually in sales. The independent restaurant accounts for 19 percent of that total. The average American spends 8 percent of his/her income on meals away from home. This number has been increasing for the past few years. In the past ten years the restaurant industry has out–performed the national GNP by 32 percent. There are 1100 new restaurants opening every month and over 300 more needed to keep pace with increasing demand.

Growth Strategy

The predicated growth trend is very positive both in short and long–term projections. CRFA cites again that as modern living creates more demands, people will be compelled to eat more meals away from home. The CRFA Report (2006) estimates this as high as 23 percent over the next five years.

In 1998 the CRFA released the Foodservice Industry 2005 report which forecasted how the industry might look in the year 2005. Some highlights from the panel's findings:

- Consumers will spend a greater proportion of their food dollar away from home.
- Independent operators and entrepreneurs will be the main source of new restaurant concepts.
- Nutritional concerns will be critical at all types of foodservice operations, and food flavours will be important.
- Environmental concerns will receive increased attention.

Western Canada leads with 8.4% sales growth in June

(September 14, 2006) Revenues at restaurants, caterers and bars in Western Canada jumped 8.4% in June according to Statistics Canada, thanks to robust economic activity and explosive job growth throughout the region.

Saskatchewan and Alberta benefited from healthy demand at limited-service restaurants and bars, realizing year-over-year commercial foodservice sales growth of 10.6% and 9.9% respectively. Foodservice sales in British Columbia grew 7.5% in June, a notable improvement from modest growth in May. In Manitoba, foodservice sales rose 6.1% – a welcome change from a 6.8% decline a year earlier.

The picture for foodservice demand in the rest of Canada was less rosy, however. Despite a strong start to the year, foodservice sales in Central Canada decelerated to 3.4% growth in June. A high Canadian dollar led to significant job losses in the manufacturing sector and reduced the number of international travellers to the region. Full-service restaurant sales in Ontario slipped for the third straight month due to lacklustre demand and a decline in the number of establishments.

In Atlantic Canada, high gasoline prices and a drop in the number of tourists restrained foodservice sales growth to an anaemic 0.8% in June. While sales in Nova Scotia advanced 3.3%, this was in comparison to a 5.3% drop a year earlier. Weak demand in Newfoundland and Labrador and declines in Prince Edward Island and New Brunswick contributed to the region's weak June sales.

Overall, foodservice sales in Canada grew 4.8% in June 2006 compared to June 2005. Caterers led all segments with year-over-year growth of 12.2% in June, followed by limited-service restaurants at 8.9%. Full-service restaurant sales grew a tepid 1.3% in June with weak demand across most of Canada, while bar sales slipped 0.8%, the segment's tenth consecutive monthly decline in sales.

Commercial foodservice sales growth by region

(June 2006 over June 2005)

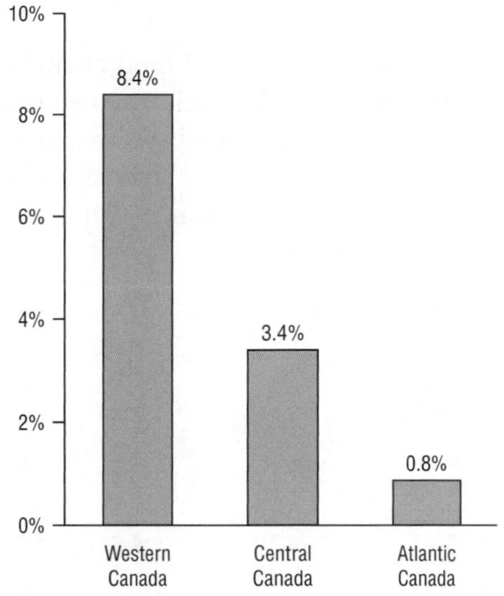

Note: Data are unadjusted for menu inflation

SOURCE: Statistics Canada

Saskatchewan's foodservice industry at a glance

Industry sales in 2005:	$1.2 billion
Share of provincial GDP:	2.9%
Number of employees:	29,900
Foodservice share of provincial workforce:	6.2%
Foodservice employees under the age of 25:	15,800
Number of restaurants, bars and caterers:	1,793
Independently owned and operated:	59.3%
Average annual profit before tax:	$30,261

The population and demographics of First and Main Streets have remained steady for the last five years. Tourism has increased 13 percent over the last six years and is predicted to keep growing. Local businesses are increasing at a rate of 5 percent yearly.

The idea of a imported food consciousness through nutritional awareness and dietary change has been slowly building for the last two years. The extensive government studies and new Food Guide Pyramid have given everyone a new definition of a balanced, healthy diet. This is not a fad but a true dietary trend where people are going to restaurants and want the food that has been organically grown and cooked based on old traditions. Italian food is just that.

This idea is backed by the scientific and medical community, the media, and the government, and also endorsed by the big food manufacturers. As stated in the Foodservice 2000 report, this trend will be even more important by the turn of the century.

A few years back the Rolling Stones played a concert in Windsor to a sold out audience. After that event you could not find an empty restaurant seat in the city, and ever since the restaurant business has noticed that their daily client count has averaged above what it was prior to the concert. The owners of the restaurant cannot put their finger on why this is, but feel there was definitely a momentum shift for the better. Talking with the owners of the restaurants, they tell us that this trend is continuing.

Competition

There are over two dozen restaurants in the Main and First Street area that sell food at similar prices. Although this presents an obvious challenge in terms of market share, it also indicates the presence of a large, strong potential. The newest competitors have made their successful entry based on an innovative concept or novelty. Cafe Fresco will offer an innovative product in a familiar style at a competitive price. Our aggressive plans of take–out and delivery will also give us an advantage to create a good market share before the competition can adjust or similar concepts appear.

Competing with Cafe Fresco for the target market are these food providers:

Harwood's	24 Fairford Street East	306-693-7778
Hopkins Dining Parlour & Curiosity Shoppe	65 Athabasca Street West	306-692-5995
Juliana Pizza & Restaurant (1978) Ltd	5064 4th Avenue	306-543-1221
Kelsey's Restaurant	2665 Gordon Road	306-585-8883
Kelsey's Restaurant	1875 Victoria Avenue East	306-761-9000
Little Caesar's Pizza	220 Broadway Street East	306-783-2266
Luiggi's Pasta House	2625 29th Avenue	306-949-7427
Memories Fine Dining	1717 Victoria Ave	306-522-1999
Montana's Cookhouse Saloon	2655 Gordon Road	306-569-1557
Moxie's Classic Grill	2037 Park Street	306-781-5655
Moxie's Restaurant	2037 Park Street	306-781-5655

Independent operators include Moxie's, Pizza Hut, Montana's, Iruna, and The Border Cafe. Most are ethnic based and will carry at least two similar menu items. Moxie's and Memories are long-standing businesses while the others are fairly new. They all are doing very well.

The major chain restaurants are House of Blues, Romano's Pizza and Pasta Restaurant and Little Caesars Pizza and Pasta Restaurant. All are relatively new but well established and profitable. They have big resources of marketing and/or a specialty product or attraction (Luigi's Pasta House is also a live music club). Gebs Pasta Restaurant Supplies Ltd Foods and Cysco both service 24,000 Main and First Street students but their product is not appealing enough to prevent students from eating out five to seven meals a week. In addition there are two local catering companies that deliver prepared meals daily to offices.

Competitive Strategy

There are three major ways in which we will create an advantage over our competitors:

- Product identity, quality, and novelty
- High employee motivation and good sales attitude
- Innovative and aggressive service options.

Cafe Fresco will be the only restaurant among all of the competition which focuses the entire menu on healthy, low–fat cooking. Each of the competitors offers at least one "healthy" selection on their menu. Moxie's Den even has an entire section called "On the Lighter Side" but in all cases they are always seen as alternatives to the main style being offered. The target market will perceive Cafe Fresco as the destination location for healthy, low–fat cooking.

Once they have tried the restaurant, their experience will be reinforced by friendly, efficient, knowledgeable service. Return and repeat business will be facilitated by accessible take–out and delivery options. At the time of this writing all of the competitors offered take–out but only two (Little Tony's Pizza and Pasta Restaurant and Raymond's Pizza and Pasta Restaurant).

MARKETING & SALES

Market Penetration

Entry into the market should not be a problem. The store has high visibility with heavy foot traffic all day long. The local residents and students always support new restaurants and the tourists do not have fixed preferences. In addition, $2,000 has been budgeted for a pre–opening advertising with a local radio station and public relations campaign. Due to the weak newspaper readership we will not budget any money for the daily newspaper. We will advertise in a weekly newspaper that will help us build our clients. The newspaper only has 20,000 circulation but has a strong readership base.

Advertising

Focusing on the unique aspect of the product theme (healthy, tasty foods) a mix of marketing vehicles will be created to convey our presence, our image, and our message.

- Print media—local weekly newspapers, magazines and student publications
- Broadcast media—local programming and special interest shows
- Radio stations—CDASH FM, CBAK FM, CADC AM
- Hotel guides, concierge relations, Chamber of Commerce brochures
- Direct mail—subscriber lists, offices for delivery
- Miscellaneous—yellow pages, charity events

A public relations firm has been retained to create special events and solicit print and broadcast coverage, especially at the start–up.

The marketing effort will be split into three phases:

1. Opening—An advanced notice (press packet) sent out by the PR firm to all media and printed announcement ads in key places. Budget–$ 29,000
2. Ongoing—A flexible campaign (using the above media), assessed regularly for effectiveness. Budget– $3,000
3. Future plans and Strategic Opportunities—Catering to offices (even outside of our local area) may become a large part of gross sales. At that point a sales agent would be hired to directly market our products for daily delivery or catered functions.

PRODUCTS & SERVICES

Products

Cafe Fresco will be offering a menu of food and beverages with a distinctive image. There will be three ways to purchase these products; table service at the restaurant, take–out from the restaurant, and delivery to home or office.

The Menu

The Cafe Fresco menu is moderate sized, and moderately–low priced offering a collection of ethnic and American items with a common theme—healthy (low–fat, low cholesterol, natural ingredients), flavorful, and familiar. Our goal is to create the image of light, satisfying, and still nutritious food. All menu items will be cooked from scratch in the kitchen, like it was 100 years ago in Italy.

Food production and assembly will take place in the kitchen of the restaurant. Fresh vegetables, meat and dairy products will be used to crate most of the dishes from scratch. The chef will exercise strict standards of sanitation, quality production, and presentation or packaging over the kitchen and service staff.

Services

There will be three ways a customer can purchase food.

- They may sit down at one of the 67 seats in the dining room and get full service from a waiter.
- A separate take–out counter will service those who wish to pick up their food. Most take–out food will be prepared to order with orders coming from either the telephone or fax.
- Delivery (an indirect form of take–out) will be available at certain times and to a limited area.

The Cafe Fresco Catering service will be offered in year two of the business once the cliental has grown to a level that is easy to manage.

Potential Services

There is a market segment that prefers to eat this type of cooking at home although they do not have the time to cook. There are already caterers and even mail order companies that provide individuals and families with up to a month's supply of pre–prepared meals.

This opportunity will be researched and developed on a trial basis. If successful, it could become a major new source of income without creating the need for additional staff or production space. At this point the owners have no desire to franchise the concept; they want to keep it small and easy to manage. They just want to cook good food.

CUSTOMERS

The market for Cafe Fresco products covers a large area of diverse and densely populated groups. Although it will be located in a downtown urban setting, it is an area where people travel to eat out and one that is also frequented by tourists. It is also an area known for and catering to the demographic group we are targeting.

The First and Main Street area is one of the most desirable retail locations in Windsor. The Windsor Chamber of Commerce rates it as the third best retail market in the city. There are more than 400 businesses in a two square mile area with average sales of $187 per square foot.

The customer base will come from 3 major segments:

- Local population—The city of Windsor with a year–round population of 199,000 is centrally located in the Windsor area and is within 15 minutes drive of 8 major suburbs.
- Colleges and Universities—First and Main Streets alone have two different schools within walking distance of Culver Ave.
- Tourism—Between hotels, motels, bed & breakfast rooms and inns, there are over 1,500 rooms available. Last year they were at a 81 percent occupancy rate.
- Local businesses—The Windsor Chamber of Commerce lists over three hundred businesses with an average of three employees in the First and Main Street square area.

The food concept and product image of Cafe Fresco will attract three different customer profiles:

- The 23–55 age bracket—This includes anyone on a restricted or prescribed diet, or those who have committed to a healthy diet but want authentic Italian food served in a real Italian Restaurant.
- The large population of Italians in the city—Imported foods from Italy allow for the real feel restaurant experience.

- Other market segments—"if you try it, you will like it." Through marketing, publicity, and word–of–mouth, people will seek out a new experience and learn that nutritious food can be tasty, fun, convenient, and inexpensive.

OPERATIONS

Facilities & Offices

The restaurant is at 31 Culver Ave. and is a 2,400 square foot space. The licenses and codes' issues are all in order. New equipment and dining room furnishings will be purchased and installed by the general contractor. Offices of the corporation are presently at Gino Scarpilli's home but will be moved to the restaurant after opening.

Hours of Operation

The restaurant will be open for lunch and dinner six days a week. Service will begin at 10:00 AM and end at 12:00 AM. The restaurant will be open Christmas and Thanksgiving.

Employee Training & Education

Employees will be trained not only in their specific operational duties but in the philosophy and applications of our concept. They will receive extensive information from the chef and be kept informed of the latest information on healthy eating.

Systems & Controls

A big emphasis is being placed on extensive research into the quality and integrity of our products. They will constantly be tested for our own high standards of freshness and purity. Food costs and inventory control will be handled by our computer system and checked daily by management.

Food Production

All of the food will be prepared on the premises. The kitchen will be designed for high standards of sanitary efficiency and cleaned daily. Food will be made mostly to order and stored in large coolers in the basement. We have hired a local well known contractor to design and build a kitchen that meet the highest in food quality standards, surpassing the requirements set by the government regulating this area.

Delivery & Catering

Food for delivery may be similar to take–out (prepared to order) or it may be prepared earlier and stocked. Catering will be treated as deliveries.

We will lease a fleet of white mini vans that will have our logo and advertising on them. The purpose for this will be to give solid exposure to the world and when people think of our restaurant they will have a good impression. The vans will be cargo vans with specially designed heated cupboards inside, keeping the food fresh and warm.

The vans will always be clean and washed. We will have a total of four vans. All of the drivers will wear chef uniforms to portray a professional image.

Management Summary

Gino Scarpilli, President. Gino Scarpilli is also the owner and manager of a local weekly newspaper. In 1995, a local weekly newspaper became so popular and profitable, he decided to buy into the newspaper concept.

Gino brings with him a track record of success in the natural foods industry. His management style is innovative and in keeping with the corporate style outlined in the mission statement.

Board of Directors

An impressive board of directors has been assembled that represents some top professionals from the area. They will be a great asset to the development of the company.

Consultants & Professional Support Resources

At the present, no outside consults have been retained, excepting the design department at MarketingDesigners Inc. A business plan was written by www.corporatemanagementconsultants.com.

Management to be Added

We are presently searching for a General Manager and Executive Chef. These key employees will be well chosen and given incentives for performance and growth.

Management Structure & Style

Gino Scarpilli will be the President and Chief Operating Officer. The General Manager and Chef will report to him. The Assistant Manager and Sous–Chef will report to their respective managers, and all other employees will be subordinate to them.

Ownership

Gino Scarpilli and Vincent Hanna—the stockholders—will retain ownership with the possibility of offering stock to key employees if deemed appropriate.

Compensation & Incentives

Cafe Fresco will offer competitive wages and salaries to all employees with benefit packages available to key personnel only.

OBJECTIVES

Cafe Fresco is an innovative concept that targets a new, growing market. We assume that the market will respond, and grow quickly in the next five years. Our goals are to create a reputation of quality, consistency and security (safety of food) that will make us the leader of a new style of dining. Our marketing efforts will be concentrated on take–out and delivery—the areas of most promising growth. As the market changes, new products may be added to maintain sales. After the restaurant opens, we will keep a close eye on sales and profit. If we are on target at the end of Year 1, we will look to expand to a second unit.

RISK FACTORS

With any new venture, there is risk involved. The success of our project hinges on the strength and acceptance of a fairly new market. After Year 1, we expect some copycat competition in the form of other independent units. Chain competition will be much later. Meanwhile, Gino will continue to work at the local daily newspaper as an advertising sales representative.

CONCLUSION

Ideally, Cafe Fresco will become profitable, and in the long run be a place to go to.

APPENDIX

	M-T-D	%	Y-T-D	%	M-T-D	%	Y-T-D	%
Occupancy expenses								
Rent	19,000	4.98%	165,000	5.53%	13,500	4.93%	148,500	5.32%
Insurance	3,500	1.16%	38,500	1.29%	3,150	1.15%	34,650	1.24%
Utilities	7,700	1.99%	71,400	2.39%	5,400	1.97%	64,260	2.30%
Total occupancy		**8.13%**	**274,900**	**9.22%**	**22,050**	**8.06%**	**247,410**	**8.86%**
General & administrative								
Contributions	320	0.08%	3,000	0.10%	225	0.08%	2,700	0.10%
Office supplies	2,100	1.16%	38,500	1.29%	3,150	1.15%	34,650	1.24%
Dues & subscriptions	200	0.03%	1,100	0.04%	90	0.03%	990	0.04%
Education		0.00%	1,750	0.06%	0	0.00%	1,575	0.06%
Bank charges	700	0.07%	2,200	0.07%	180	0.07%	1,980	0.07%
Professional	8,000	0.33%	11,000	0.37%	900	0.33%	9,900	0.35%
Payroll processing	1565	0.21%	6,875	0.23%	563	0.21%	6,188	0.22%
Telephone	1,900	0.37%	12,100	0.41%	990	0.36%	10,890	0.39%
Sundry	1200	0.17%	5,500	0.18%	450	0.16%	4,950	0.18%
Licenses & permits	600	0.03%	1,500	0.05%	90	0.03%	1,350	0.05%
Total general & administrative		**2.45%**	**83,525**	**2.80%**	**6,638**	**2.43%**	**75,173**	**2.69%**
Ebitda		6.83%	375,910	12.61%	33,902	12.39%	394,629	14.13%
Other items								
Depreciation	7700	1.49%	49,500	16.43%	4,050	1.48%	44,550	1.60%
Interest expenses		1.58%	55,575	1.86%	5,225	1.91%	61,133	2.19%
Total depreciation & interest		3.07%	105,075	3.52%	9,275	3.39%	105,683	3.78%
Net profit/(loss) before taxes		3.76%	270,835	9.08%	24,627	9.00%	288,946	10.35%
Income taxes		0.15%	10,833	0.36%	985	0.36%	11,558	0.41%
Net income	10,865	3.61%	260,002	8.72%	23,642	8.64%	277,389	

Assets

Current assets	
Cash checking	$662
Cash payroll	2,300
Cash money marketing	4,000
Total cash	
Amex rec.	21,222
Visa/MC rec.	3,233
House accounts	11,000
Prepaid expenses	12,000
Inventory	
Food	30,000
Wine	12,000
Liquor	13,000
Beer	4,000
Other bev	2,000
Total inventory	
Total current assets	340,902
Fixed assets	
Furniture & equipment	215,000
Leasehold improvements	230,000
Accumulated depreciation	
Net fixed assets	
Other assets	
Security deposits	2,000
Liquor license	3,400
Artwork	2,000
Total other assets	7,400
Total assets	793,302

Liabilities & stockholders' equity

Current liabilities	
Current portion st debt	$3,000
Accounts payable	6,000
Accrued wages	6,000
Accrued income taxes	12,000
Accrued payroll taxes	19,000
Gift certificates payable	1,000
Total current liabilities	47,000
Total liabilities	
Stockholders' equity	
Capital stock	1,000
Paid in capital	1,000
Retained earnings	7,000
Total stockholders' equity	9,000
Total liabilities & stockholders' equity	56,000

Restaurant

Tokyo Sun

917 Lawson St.
Ann Arbor, MI 48107

Gerald Rekve

EXECUTIVE SUMMARY

Tokyo Sun is an eating establishment focusing on healthy, nutritious food, to the local downtown area.

Tokyo Sun will be an upscale service specializing in a combination of salads plus high–end menu items from specific recipes focusing on the seafood cuisine.

Based on this distinct menu, Tokyo Sun will follow a differentiation strategy that will provide unique, or hard to find choices for patrons.

The keys to success for Tokyo Sun will be repeat business, an excellent location convenient to downtown businesses, and its unique Pacific cuisine.

The company will be a sole proprietorship owned by Martha Rood. Martha Rood will be providing $29,000 capital investment and there will be an additional $60,000 raised in short term loan.

Entering into this market will not be easy; the industry is highly competitive, with periodic overcapacity, low margins, and low entry/exit barriers. In addition, there are a large number of substitutes, and the suppliers to this market have a great deal of power.

The company has acquired an excellent site in the downtown area and intends to provide a upscale environment to draw in the company's main target market segment, the business professionals. The company will seek to provide these customers with the maximum number of services to create the greatest sales volume during the company's peak hours of operation.

The company will have a comprehensive marketing, advertising, and promotion campaign that will maximize word–of–mouth marketing and will consist of newspaper radio, printed material, billboards and discounts.

The company has planned to offer its products at a slightly higher price than that of its competitors. This is to provide credibility to its clients as an upscale establishment that provides a unique menu. This will also provide the funds to cover the higher than expected operating costs due to the differentiated and expanded menu.

It is estimated that the company will earn revenues of approximately $130,000 by year three, and maintain a solid cash flow.

Objectives

Tokyo Sun seeks to achieve the following goals:

- Profit by the end of the first year.
- Repay debt from original financing by the end of the second year.
- Provide an income for founder–owner with income growth possibilities.
- Sales of $500,000 in the first year.
- Sales of more than $800,000 by the fourth year.

Mission

Tokyo Sun will be an upscale deli specializing in a combination of fast hot or cold sandwiches and salads plus specific recipes focusing on Pacific cuisine.

Based on this distinct menu, Tokyo Sun will follow a differentiation strategy that will provide unique or hard to find choices to deli patrons. This will provide Martha Rood with the ability to charge slightly more for its food services than most competitors and return a significant profit.

BUSINESS STRATEGY

Keys to Success

- Repeat business. Every customer who comes in once should want to return, and recommend us. Word–of–mouth marketing is a powerful ally.
- Hire top notch chefs and offer training to keep the chef top of his/her game, and pay the chef top wages to ensure they stay with us.
- Location. Convenience is essential to us; we need to be close to our market because we are not trying to get people to travel to reach us.
- The right food, variety with a Pacific Rim theme, with a price high enough to establish credibility, but not so high as to limit customers.

Company Ownership

At its initial stages, Tokyo Sun is a sole proprietorship owned by Martha Rood, founder and president. It will be registered with the country as a fictitious business name. We will move up to incorporate as recommended by our attorney later, based on growth of the business and conditions as they arise.

Start–up Summary

Start–up costs and initial financing are listed here. Martha Rood will be investing $29,000 of savings and guaranteeing a loan for another $60,000 with personal assets.

Start-up analysis	
Requirements	200,000
Start-up expenses	75,000
Legal	2,500
Stationery etc.	1,200
Rent	5,600
Expensed equipment	12,000
Other	5,000
Total start-up expense	
Start-up assets needed	
Cash balance on starting date	89,000
Start-up inventory	15,000
Other short-term assets	
Total short-term assets	
Long-term assets	
Total assets	
Total requirements	
Funding	60,000
Investment	
Owner/founder	29,000
Other	
Total investment	
Short-term liabilities	
Accounts payable	1,200
Current borrowing	50,000
Other short-term liabilities	
Subtotal short-term liabilities	
Long-term liabilities	60,000
Total liabilities	
Loss at start-up	
Total capital	
Total capital and liabilities	

Company Locations and Facilities

Tokyo Sun will be located in Ann Arbor, Michigan on the corner of State Street and Zion Ave. The facilities will include an 89 person capacity eating area, counter front area, and backroom area where refrigerators, commercial stoves and ovens are located.

PRODUCTS & SERVICES

Tokyo Sun offers a dinner and lunch menu, fresh cold cuts, drinks, and take–out prepared dishes. Our menu will include:

Sushi

(One serving consists of two pieces)

Alaska king crab
Amaebi (sweet shrimp)
Blue fin tuna
Ebi (boiled shrimp)
Escolar (seared fatty white tuna)
Hamachi (yellowtail)
Hirame (fluke)
Hokkigai (surf clam)
Hotategai (scallop)
Ika (squid)
Ikura (salmon roe)
Kanikama (crab stick)
Masago (crab roe)
Quail eggs
Saba (spanish mackeral)
Shake-fresh salmon
Shake-smoked salmon
Spicy scallop (original or jalapeno)
Spicy tuna (original or jalapeno)
Suzuki (bass)
Tako (boiled octopus)
Tamago (layered chicken eggs)
Tarako (cod roe)
Unagi (bbq fresh water eel)
Uni (sea urchin)

Maki Sushi

(One serving consists of 6 pieces unless noted)

Alaska roll (smoked salmon, cream cheese & masago)
Crab salad roll
Gobo maki (pickled burdock)
Kampo maki (oriental squash)
Mexican roll (boiled shrimp & avocado)
Natto maki (fermented soybeans)
Sake kawa maki (smoked salmon skin & cucumber)
Spicy scallop maki (original or jalapeno)
Spider maki (soft shell crab roll & masago) 4pcs
Tekka maki (tuna roll)
California roll (crab stick & cucumber)
Futomaki (crab stick, shrimp, tamago, pickle & cucumber) 4 pcs
Ikura maki (salmon roe)
Kappa maki
Negi hamachi maki (yellowtail & scallions)
Philadelphia roll (smoked salmon, cream cheese & masago)
Shrimp tempura maki (shrimp tempura, cucumber & crab roe) 4pcs
Spicy tekka maki (spicy tuna original or jalapeno)
Takuwan maki (pickled radish)
Unagi maki (bbq fresh water eel)
Ume maki (plum paste & oba leaf)

Specialty rolls

Black & White	white fish tempura, scallions, black sesame seeds & seaweed
Buddy Buddy	tuna, hamachi & wasabi tobiko topped with fresh salmon & ikura
Grand Canyon	unagi, avocado & cucumber topped with broiled white tuna, masago & silver sauce
Green Dragon	Alaska king crab, unagi & tempura crunch with avocado
Hawaiianspicy	salmon, tempura crunch & cucumber topped with avocado & tuna
Jumbocrab	stick, cucumber, hamachi, unagi & masago
Fire Island	California roll & tempura crunch topped with spicy tuna & scallions
Fuji Volcano	shrimp tempura topped with unagi & spicy masago sauce
Matsu	unagi, avocado, crabstick, tamago & masago
Rainbow	California roll topped with tuna, white fish, smoked salmon, shrimp & hamachi
Snow Mountain	shrimp tempura & cucumber topped with Alaska king crab & masago
Tekka Tuna	spicy tuna, tempura crunch topped with tuna sashimi

Appetizers

Roll appetizer

(3pcs California roll, 3pcs crab salad roll, 3pcs takka maki, 3pcs negi hamachi)

Sashimi appetizer combo

(tuna, white fish & octopus)
Sushi appetizer combo (nigiri: tuna, white fish, shrimp, 2 pcs tekka maki)crabstick &

Avocado salad

Spicy tako salad

Spicy shralmp salad
Ika sansai
Seaweed salad
Sunomono choice of: crab, octopus or shrimp

Sushi Combinations
(served with Miso soup & salad)

Chirashi
Assorted Sashimi on a bed of sushi rice

Cooked Sushi Combo
Pieces of nigiri to include : shrimp, octopus, crab stick, tamago, smoked salmon & acrab salad roll

Deluxe Sashimi
3pcs blue fin, fresh salmon, hamachi, white fish, tako & 2pcs kani & tamago

Hand Roll Special
3 handrolls: one tuna, one yellowtail & one crab salad roll

Matsu Sushi Dinner
California roll, spicy tekka maki, 5pcs nigiri sushi consisting of: tuna, shrimp, white fish, tamago and smoked salmon

Omakase
Chef's choice of Sashimi

Rolls Rolls Rolls
Three pices of each: tekka maki, negi hamachi maki, California roll, Mexican roll, Alaska roll, Philadelphia roll and 4 pieces of futomaki

Traditional Sushi Dinner
Nigiri sushi consisting of: tuna, white fish, mackeral, smoked salmon, yellowtail, shrimp, octopus, crab stick, tamago, crab roe & tekkamaki

Traditional Sushi & Sashimi Dinner
Traditional Sushi Dinner plus sashimi appetizer

Future Products & Services

Martha Rood is planning on introducing new menu items as time and profitability permit. Furthermore as a recognized local authority on Ann Arbor's cooking board, Martha Rood plans to offer her soon–to–be–published cookbook on the restaurant's premises.

MARKET ANALYSIS

We have three main markets:

- People who work in the downtown area during the day, who will be looking for high–end food and convenience for meals and lunch.
- Surrounding businesses looking for business meeting/dining rooms that offer high–end menu items.
- Workers looking for take–out food to take to meetings or at the end of the workday.

Each of these market segments consists of people who either work in the downtown area or flow through this area during the normal work week. As such, there will be an undetermined percentage of each market that will be seeking an eating establishment that will meet the requirements of healthy food and a pleasant atmosphere. Furthermore, Tokyo Sun will cater to the growing trend of middle–class professionals who seek a different cuisine than that of the established food chains.

As stated before, customers desire fast, healthy food that will appeal to their aesthetic tastes and is provided in a comfortable atmosphere. In addition, they desire a memorable dining experience that provides them with the chance to relax in the middle of the day. All of this needs to be delivered to the customer with the least amount of hassle. Furthermore, customers will also need a facility that can provide them with delicious, convenient take–home meals when there is no opportunity to cook at home.

Market Segmentation

The total potential market in units is shown in the following table and chart, by type of market point.

Market analysis

Market analysis potential customers	Growth	2006	2007	%
Local businesses	0%	500	500	0.00%
Local workers	2%	21,224	21,648	2.00%
Other downtown traffic	1%	15,455	15,610	1.00%
Total	**1.55%**	**37,179**	**37,758**	**1.55%**

For the business market we need to focus on specific companies with specific opportunities. For individuals we need to lever off word–of–mouth recommendations, probably depending on business customers.

The business market has the potential of providing large volume sales to the company during the peak hours of 11:00 AM–2:00 PM, 5:00 PM–9:00 PM both through small groups of business people visiting Tokyo Sun and delivery orders. Satisfaction of this group will provide a vital long–term revenue stream. For the business market, the company plans to do specific target marketing through flyers, business discounts, billboards, and creating a record of fast delivery.

For the individual groups seeking meals or lunch downtown, or take–home meals, it is necessary for the company to build an effective word–of–mouth marketing strategy. The company will do this slowly, realizing that much of this will grow from its business market. The company is also planning on doing a number of joint marketing efforts with other local companies such as the production and distribution of a referral book to be given to various individuals. This in turn would help to drive our word–of–mouth marketing efforts.

Market Trends

One of the most important recent trends in eating is the rise of interest in consuming healthier foods. The best known example of this is the move toward organic foodstuffs. Martha Rood realizes that there is a significant percentage of the population in Southeast Michigan that is demanding more and more naturally grown, organic meats and vegetables and the company is well positioned to take advantage of this change. Martha Rood has already concluded preliminary deals with organic growers and suppliers that will allow the company to take advantage of this new market need.

Market Growth

We have no indication of market growth in this pulverized and diffused market. No statistics are available for the local food industry in Ann Arbor. What we do know is that there is growth potential, and plenty of potential market for the right combination of service, quality and choice.

Risk Factors

The restaurant industry is highly fragmented and competitive. Each company within this field has low capital costs and low margins, which create this high intensity of competition.

Suppliers have a great deal of power in setting and negotiating the prices of their products and services to the smaller eating establishments. This is due to the fact that the suppliers who absorb the greatest amounts of cash from "mom and pop" outfits are large food distribution companies such as General Foods. These companies are more consolidated than the restaurant industry, have deeper pockets, an almost limitless number of substitute customers, and finally they are the single most important supplier to Tokyo Sun's industry. Therefore, these companies can set whatever price they wish to. Furthermore, labor is a supplier in this industry as well, and salaries for such individuals are well known and not very flexible.

There also exists a very high degree of rivalry among firms due to the perceived overcapacity in this field. The larger companies often have cost advantages due to economies of scale that allow them to out compete with smaller rivals.

The barriers to entry and exit are very low in this industry. Switching costs are virtually nonexistent and the costs to entry and exit the market are low. The large number of competitors in this field including substitutes such as McDonald's, Subway Sandwiches, and Coco's mean that the pricing for such services are very competitive. The only way to have an advantage in this industry is either a low cost leadership principal applied aggressively to all aspects of the business or to differentiate the entire eating experience through better and more unique food and to build up customer relations to a point where the switching costs are raised.

COMPETITION

Business Participants

The restaurant industry is "pulverized" in other words, it consists of an almost infinite number of companies from the small "mom and pop" style to the national chains.

Competition and Buying Patterns

- Location is critical to success. Proximity to workers is very important, so is convenient parking for the end–of–workday traffic stopping to pick up takeout dishes.
- Price is not very sensitive as long as we are not too high. Low price or lowest price is not essential. Many target customers mistrust low prices in a deli.
- Quality of food matters. If the price isn't too high and the food is good, we'll have growth through repeat business.
- Focus is an advantage; focusing on Pacific Rim food will draw customers from the competition, which will provide particularly deep pockets that provide for growth.

Competitive Comparison

The competition facing Tokyo Sun is vast. This includes every eating establishment in the Ann Arbor area. Major competitors include all high–end restaurants and many other "mom and pop" style organizations too numerous to list. Furthermore, there are a large number of substitute suppliers from grocery stores that offer prepackaged meals to upscale sit down restaurants such as Dante's. Drawing any sort of general conclusions from such a vast array of competitors is difficult, but you can say that just about every conceivable product or service idea, and just about every taste is encompassed within this group.

Smaller restaurants, due to lack of money or sales are only able to carry out the most basic of marketing strategies. Tokyo Sun intends to have an advantage by creating higher profits that will in turn grow marketing efforts. However, the larger firms have comprehensive national marketing strategies that draw in hundreds of customers per week. Tokyo Sun's answer to this is to promote its local flavor and cuisine and draw in those individuals who see fast food as unhealthy and of low quality. Therefore the owner of Tokyo Sun believes that there is significant opportunity to gain local market share.

GROWTH STRATEGY

Advertising

Our marketing strategy focuses mainly on making our existence known to the people working close to our location. It also depends on making our Pacific theme known to those same people.

We can focus on local marketing: our signage, a grand opening party, and flyers to local offices. Our main sales literature will consist of flyers sent though the mail, and promotional advertisements offered to local businesses. Relevant information such as a comprehensive menu, costs, description of some of Tokyo Sun's more distinct items, and address and delivery number will be included.

The company plans to use local radio as one of the means for promotion. Martha Rood is currently making arrangements to have a grand opening party that will include having a local radio station participate and air it over the radio. In addition the company is planning to use flyers to local businesses, direct mailers, billboards, etc. Billboards and radio will be used for the first six months to establish customer awareness and product attractiveness. Mailers and flyers will then be used to advertise sales promotions that will help bring in customers. One fortunate aspect of the restaurant business is that once a potential customer steps into the establishment, the chances of purchase are very high. So the promotional plan will be to draw people in to the deli and then seek to provide them with a superior eating experience. We need to offer fast service at peak times. The key is a good crowd balance, so that we never look empty but we are never so full that we turn people away. Lines have to move fast. We need a good selection of convenient foods.

Our most important sales strategy is develop repeat business. Every customer who comes in has to want to return. To that end, we will offer some of the more established sales strategies such as discount cards, special menu days, and a regularly changing menu. Tokyo Sun intends to keep accurate track of what types of sandwiches and other foods sell well and to create a program of customer feedback through surveys. With this information we will be able to streamline our food line to match the local tastes and encourage more people to eat at Tokyo Sun.

Finally we will design a home/business delivery system that will allow for the dropping off of food within 1/2 hour after the order is made to ensure the best possible eating experience and customer return rate.

OPERATIONS

Strategy and Implementation Summary

The main thrust of strategy is to lever our ideal location and specialized cuisine into higher profits through sales volume and higher prices. We understand the underlying needs and give the customer what they really need.

Pricing

Our pricing strategy will focus on providing high quality, healthy food that is quick and has a unique flair. Because of this, we expect to be able to charge somewhat more for our products than other stores, as long as the customers agree that the food is better than average.

Strategic Alliances

The company is currently seeking strategic alliances in two sectors. First, to work with other suppliers that will allow us to expand the company's menu line into coffee products and desserts. The second type of alliance the company is seeking is with local businesses that could be used to promote customer awareness and preference. A deal with a local radio station where a contest could win free lunch for an entire office is being explored.

With our unique menu we want to ensure that we are the only business that sets up alliances with only the best companies in their sectors.

Management Summary

This is a small company with our employee categories including counter clerks, kitchen help, and busboys. We assume 14 employees total, the owner–founder plus four counter clerks, two in the kitchen, and two busboys.

The owner–founder will be in attendance during normal business hours, 7 a.m. to 6 p.m. seven days per week. In addition, specific other employees will have supervisory roles.

The operation of the business allows for us to manage our employee's with flexibility in mind. We will give our staff the ability to take time off when needed or work extra hours to help them make more money. We feel by offering this, service we will be in a position to maintain good relationships with the staff and grow our business.

The management will consist of Ms. Martha Rood. Ms. Rood has been involved in the cooking profession all her life and has acquired a local reputation for creating inventive and tasty recipes focusing on Ann Arbor's cuisine. For the past seven years she has run a cooking class business out of her home and will have her first cookbook published next year. Desiring to have an independent business that would provide more income, Martha Rood attended Jeffers Community College where she obtained a BS in business in preparation for starting her own deli.

We will out source the marketing manager who will work part–time for us on a need basis and an accountant.

FINANCIAL ANALYSIS

The benchmarks chart shows changes in sales, operating expenses, gross margin, and collection days. We think the chart speaks for itself, and what it says is that the numbers and assumptions are reasonable.

Projected Profit and Loss

We assume a slightly higher gross margin than industry standards for eating places, because we don't have the full slate of meals or servers. Also, kitchen and busboy employees are not included in cost of sales, for simplicity.

Because we're new to this business, we've adjusted the profitability into normal range by adding a relatively large amount of additional expenses. That gives us a buffer for the additional unforeseen expenses that we expect will come up. If they don't, then we'll be more profitable than normal for the deli business.

Profit and loss (planned)

Pro forma profit and loss	2007
Sales	340,000
Direct cost of sales	240,000
Other kitchen expenses	20,000
Total cost of sales	**260,000**
Gross margin	
Gross margin %	
Operating expenses:	
Advertising/Promotion	20,000
Rent	15,000
Payroll expense	120,000
Payroll burden	20,000
Depreciation	
Utilities	12,000
Insurance	1,200
All other	2,700

With the financing plan as projected, the business remains cash positive throughout the first three years. During year two and three, it is expected that a significant amount of cash will be used to upgrade facilities and purchase new equipment.

Business Ratios

Standard business ratios are for the eating establishment industry as a whole. Because of the vast number of firms in this industry and the incredible variety that exists between firms, there is variance between the industry standard and a specific company like Sushi Restaurant. However, the ratios do show a healthy company that has appropriate costs plus asset and liability allocation.

Ratios (Planned)

	Industry
Sales growth	7.60%
Percent of total assets	
Accounts receivable	4.50%
Inventory	3.60%
Other short-term assets	35.60%
Total short-term assets	43.70%
Long-term assets	56.30%
Total assets	100.00%
Other short-term liabilities	**32.70%**
Subtotal short-term liabilities	23.10%
Long-term liabilities	28.50%
Total liabilities	51.60%
Net worth	48.40%
Percent of sales	
Sales	100.00%
Gross margin	60.50%
Selling, general & Administrative expenses	39.80%
Advertising expenses	3.20%
Profit before interest and taxes	0.70%
Main ratios	
Current	0.98
Quick	0.65
Total debt to total assets	61.20%
Pre-tax return on net worth	1.70%
Pre-tax return on assets	4.30%

Technology Solutions Provider

Exceed Expectations

274 Windsor Ave.
Bismarck, North Dakota 58501

Jay Fox, Brittani Lee, and Brian Wideman

Exceed Expectations is a full service information technology integrator that offers small to mid–sized companies technological business solutions. The company concentrates their efforts towards the accounting, industrial, legal, medical, and distribution industries, and provide business process reengineering, custom software application development, network support, and hosting solutions.

EXECUTIVE SUMMARY

Exceed Expectations was founded in 2000 as a Sub–Chapter S Corporation located in Bismark, North Dakota. It is a full service information technology integrator that offers small to mid–sized companies technological business solutions. We concentrate our efforts towards the accounting, industrial, legal, medical, and distribution industries. We currently service 104 companies in the Bismark area. Exceed Expectations currently has four owners with a total of nine full–time staff members.

Exceed Expectations' four services are Business Process Reengineering, Custom Software Application Development, Network Support, and Hosting Solutions. Through these areas of expertise we strive to foster and maintain solid relationships with our clients, fine tune our four services, and continue to develop innovative software applications that will redefine the way our clients do business. We plan to maintain our current 24–hour support service and service our clients whenever it is convenient to them.

It is crucial to our success that we understand our competition by developing our knowledge of their products, services, strengths, and weaknesses. We want to offer a higher quality service than our competitors and keep our prices competitive. Our main competitors are T&T Technology, Portals R Us, and William Tracy Software Developers. We differentiate ourselves from our competitors by establishing positive, trusted relationships. Our good relations with our clients are a reflection of our proven services, our 24 hour support, and the fact that we do not require binding contractual agreements for support.

Our marketing plan consists of two prongs that target three different groups of current clients. Our objective is to up–sell our services to the top 24 revenue generating clients. First, we want to target our top four clients (group 1). We plan to up–sell one of our four services to two of these clients. We also want to establish a referral base with these top four clients based on the fact that they do a lot of business with us and are happy with the services we provide them. Our second group is made up of the next 6 clients. We hope to up–sell to these clients as well, in hopes of "bumping them up" to group 1. This will expand our top tier of clients (clients that account for over $20,000). The third group consists of the remaining 14 clients. There is substantial room for growth in this group, and we hope to up–sell services to six of these clients, "bumping them up" into group 2. Achieving the goals established for each of the three client groups will increase annual revenue by roughly $150,000.

The purpose of this plan is to create a strategy for Exceed Expectations that will increase its revenues by targeting its top 24 current clients. After performing a revenue stream analysis, and constructing a promotion/up–selling strategy, we feel that Exceed Expectations can substantially increase its revenues and use the plan over and over to build a larger top tier of clients (those which generate revenues of $20,000 or more). Overall, this business plan will give the reader an in–depth understanding of the company, along with a plan for growth in the future.

BUSINESS OVERVIEW

Mission

Exceed Expectations strives to achieve consistent growth both internally and externally, foster and maintain positive relationships with each and every client, and offer cutting edge software and services at the speed of technology.

Exceed Expectations helps small to medium sized companies increase revenues, retain customers, and reduce direct and indirect costs, by pinpointing and redesigning value chain systems and processes by providing full information technology solutions.

Company History

Tim Hoogert and Mike Wilson worked for a software development company called Software Writers, Inc. The tech bubble burst and Software Writers, Inc. began downsizing. Mike and Tim took what they learned at Software Writers, Inc. and figured they could make some changes and formed their own software/tech company that would offer businesses more complete products and services. They combined their skills and experience that they received from Software Writers, Inc. to form Exceed Expectations in the year 2000. Their goal was to bring highly demanded technology solutions to small and mid–sized businesses in the Bismark area. From day one Exceed Expectations continually worked to improve its own operations, and has been profitable since its first year.

Despite consistent profitability in the first four years of existence, Software Writers, Inc. was not where Tim and Mike wanted it to be. A stronger management background was needed for the company to expand and increase revenues. To bring aboard some management expertise, Exceed Expectations merged with ComputerSavvy in January, 2005. Aaron Wilham, the Chief Executive Officer of ComputerSavvy, would now serve as the CEO of Exceed Expectations. He brought with him the management background and decision making abilities Tim and Mike were seeking. Following the merger in 2005, revenues approached $1 million in fiscal year 2005, and revenues for fiscal year 2006 are expected to break the $1 million mark (revenues for 2006 are estimated to be $1.12 million based upon first quarter data). Exceed Expectations has provided IT solutions for over 100 businesses in the greater Bismark area since the merger in January, 2005.

Exceed Expectations helps businesses become more efficient and increase revenues by re–designing business processes and by providing software and services that cut costs. Our Microsoft certified team members each have different areas of expertise specializing in one area of our services in order to bring customers the most complete business solution possible. Through ongoing network support, in–depth analysis, business process reengineering, software application development, and hosting solutions, we can provide businesses with the equipment and services required in the technology driven environment of today.

ORGANIZATION

Current Market Position

At this time, we are a profitable business with annual sales of $1 million that seeks expansion. Over the past five years Exceed Expectations has provided IT solutions to a wide variety of companies, including a billion dollar medical firm, and a multi–million dollar accounting firm. We currently have 104 clients in the Bismark area, and are continually offering our services to new businesses in this area, while attempting to up–sell services to current clients. We will continue to provide our current clients with hosting support, network support, and business process analysis while striving to develop new software applications that will enhance their efficiency. In March of 2006, Exceed Expectations obtained a Microsoft license that allows us to offer our clients a wide variety of Microsoft software applications. This software will help us redefine the way our clients do business, making them more proficient and ultimately more profitable.

Management Summary

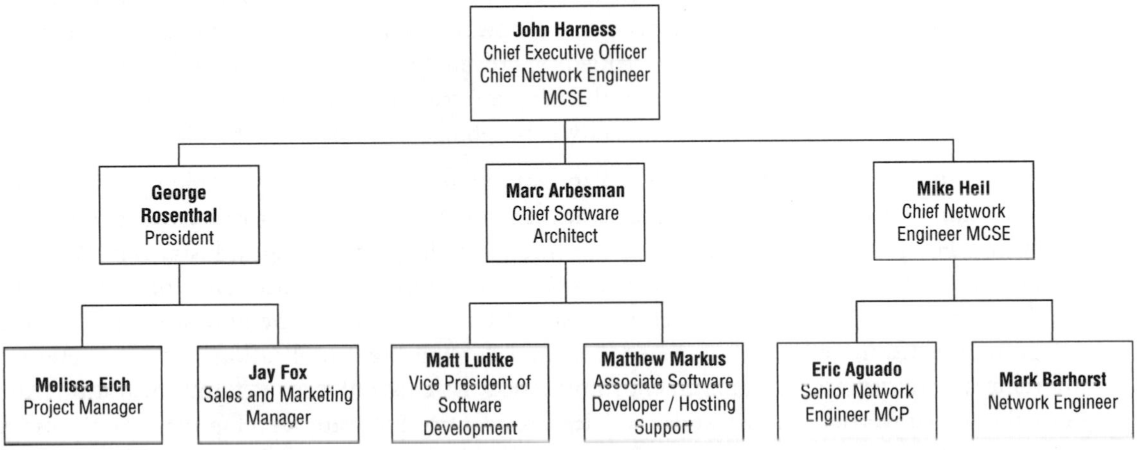

Exceed Expectations is registered as a Subchapter S–Corporation.

Exceed Expectations currently has four major divisions: Business Process Reengineering, Software Application Development, Hosting, and Network Support. Each of the four owners heads one division, but contributes their knowledge and skills to each of the four divisions. Tim Hoogert heads the Business Process Reengineering division. The Software Application Development division is run by Mike Wilson. Hosting is CEO Aaron Wilham's division, and Jeff Booth controls the Network Support division. The four owners' complimenting skills give Exceed Expectations a diverse management team. The six other full time employees round out the Exceed Expectations team and help support the four owners. A brief biography of each of the four owners, along with a summary of the positions and certifications of the supporting six employees, is provided below.

- Aaron Wilham: Part owner and Chief Executive Officer Aaron Wilham serves as Exceed Expectations' visionary. He makes the decisions and creates the plans for action. He also overlooks company financials and heads the company's Network Support Department. Aaron earned a BA degree in Marketing and Communications from Carleton College in Northfield, Minnesota. He has nine years of experience in the technology consulting industry as a Network Engineer and five years of experience as the CEO of ComputerSavvy. Aaron is a Microsoft Certified Systems Engineer and brings documented managerial experience and success to the Exceed Expectations team.

- Tim Hoogart: Exceed Expectation's second part owner, Tim Hoogart, serves as the company's Chief Operating Officer. He is the Chief Software Architect and also heads the company's customer support department. Tim graduated from the University of Notre Dame with a Bachelor of Science degree in Computer Science. He had his first programming job as a sophomore at Notre Dame's Computer Science department. He has also interned as a network and systems administrator at IBM. Tim has five years of experience in the technology consulting industry along with a complete technical understanding of Exceed Expectation's four services. His ability to communicate with clients in a non–technical manner is his greatest strength. This ability helps foster the positive relationships with clients that set Exceed Expectations apart from its competitors.
- Mike Wilson: Mike Wilson is the president of Exceed Expectations and is also the designer of our Business Process Reengineering system. Mike graduated from Western Michigan University with a degree in Sales. He has eight years of technology consulting experience not only in sales, but also in software development. He is also 6 Sigma certified, meaning he has received extensive training in business process improvement.
- Jeff Booth: Jeff Booth serves as Exceed Expectations's Chief Network Engineer. Jeff received an Associates degree in Computer Science from University of North Dakota, Bismarck. He has had prior work experience managing corporate networks at TRECK Corp. and is also knowledgeable in help desk solutions. Jeff is a Certified Microsoft Systems Engineer and brings seven years of technology consulting experience to the Exceed Expectations team. He has obtained A+ Technician Certification and claims his best quality is his ability to implement the plans Aaron creates.

The six other members of the Exceed Expectations team include Mike Amerson, Ian Wood, Peter Richardson, Hal Ricke, Karen Sal, and Pedro Amero. Mike Amerson serves as an additional network engineer. He has five years of experience in the technology consulting industry. Ian Wood is Exceed Expectation's Sales and Marketing Manager. He also manages client accounts, provides analysis work, and contributes to the firm's marketing efforts. Peter Richardson is the newest member of the Exceed Expectations team, provides hosting support and develops new application software. Peter is a junior developer with degrees in Management Information Systems and Business Administration from Southern Illinois University. Hal Ricke is the Vice President of Software Development. He is also a project manager, database administrator, and software developer. Karen Sal is Exceed Expectation's project manager. She has a BA degree in Mass Communications with emphasis in print and broadcast journalism. She has eight years of experience as a marketing manager and has overseen daily operations for a wide array of small to mid–sized businesses in the travel and real–estate industries. Rounding out the Exceed Expectations team is Pedro Amero, Exceed Expectation's Senior Network Technician. He has six years of experience in the technology consulting industry, working for a wide array of companies such as the U.S. Army, Best Buy, and Deloitte & Touche. He has many certifications: wifi certification (TEC), MCP, A+, Networking +, and MCSE.

Two employees were recently laid off. One was young, inexperienced, and lacked the diverse skill set that Exceed Expectations requires. The other was a software developer that did not meet expectations.

Each member of the Exceed Expectations team brings a wide array of skills and expertise to the team. The four owners combine for 29 years of experience in the technology consulting industry, and the six other supporting employees add an additional 17 years of experience. Our experienced and certified staff work together to provide your business with complete IT solutions.

PRODUCTS & SERVICES

From ongoing network support to documenting and improving the way you do business, Exceed Expectations has the certified & experienced staff to deliver the services and equipment you need to run a business in today's increasingly technology driven environment. Our staff has a combined forty–six years of experience in the technology consulting industry. All of Exceed Expectations's services are designed to help our clients increase the production of their workforce, eliminate unnecessary costs, increase revenues and maximize profits.

The following sections outline and describe the four services (Business Process Reengineering, Software Application Development, Network Support, and Hosting) that Exceed Expectations offers. Business Process Reengineering and Software Application Development are listed next to one another because they are tied closely together. Network Support and Hosting Solutions are not listed in any particular order.

Business Process Reengineering and Software Application Development are two services that Exceed Expectations groups together because the services compliment one another. Once a client decides to use Exceed Expectations for Business Process Reengineering, there is a 35 percent chance that they will use Exceed Expectation's software development service to build a custom application.

Business Process Reengineering

Exceed Expectations's Business Process Reengineering (BPR) capability examines the efficiency and effectiveness of a company's current processes and practices. It ensures that they deliver the highest quality goods and services, in the most productive way, at the most competitive prices. BPR help companies to beat their competition, and become more innovative. Companies can apply BPR to all aspects of their business. Our consultants have a combined 12 years of business process consulting experience.

Exceed Expectations has helped their clients to improve execution and meet the needs of customers better through BPR. But its real advantages are reduced cycle times in information processing, increased quality and customer satisfaction. We examine our client's business process and remove unnecessary steps that may contain high risk for human error or tends to drive up costs.

Exceed Expectations works with each client to assess its operating practices, costs incurred, and effectiveness. We understand the demands of high growth businesses and the advantages of scale and scope. We extend the current value within your company by eliminating inefficiencies from processes. Productivity is enhanced by employing IT solutions and streamlining data flow.

Exceed Expectations's BPR prices their analysis and consulting work depending on the scale of the project. In the past, Exceed Expectations's BPR division has priced projects starting at $6,000 to $20,000. Once a client decides to use Exceed Expectations for Business Process Reengineering, there is a 35 percent chance that they will use Exceed Expectations's software development service to build a custom application.

This portion of Exceed Expectations's business has been successful by bringing in six of our top ten revenue generating clients. We need to start tracking the amount of hours put into each analysis project so we can fully understand our project quoting process and so we can figure out our profit margins per project.

Software Application Development

Exceed Expectations's software application development service is based around the same principals as our business process reengineering service. They both strive to enhance our client's work environment. Computer software allows companies to leverage their resources by employing systems to manage every aspect of their business and increase overall profitability of their organization. The key to increasing operating profits is improving the efficiency in which steps are conducted to complete a single job. Exceed Expectations excels at automating tasks that previously required manual intervention. Within any industry each company has specific methods to completing day–to–day tasks. These methods are what separate and give an advantage among the competition. Exceed Expectations ensures that your competitive advantage stays intact while tailoring the business rules to reflect a more consistent and well defined process.

By implementing management systems tailored to these processes, we ensure consistency throughout the organization. This allows managers to use the tools necessary to take the "pulse" of their company at any given time.

Our software application developers have created an engineering environment that focuses on collaboration, interaction, and content management technologies. When we develop an application, we take into consideration that our customer's business will expand so the application is scalable and adaptable to that measure of change. We provide the customer with the proper tools to make changes on crucial parts of their software package's functionality (i.e.: add more users, change permission settings, modify a statistical report, or even temporarily remove a feature if desired).

As important as implementation is, post–implementation support continues for the life of the software. As a local company, Exceed Expectations's developers, network engineers, and product managers are nearby and available on short notice to address changing industry requirements or simply offer on–site support.

Exceed Expectations designs system architecture to operate in a true client/server environment easing technical administration by offering automated deployment of our software and low hardware and network requirements. Any future modifications to Exceed Expectations software can be completed from the server, and do not require a visit to each individual desktop.

The pricing for software depends on the scale of the application. In this situation, we would estimate a price and offer a quote to the customer because each software application can contain various features. For example, an e–store would have many different features than a full scale order processing/ distribution system. Exceed Expectations is in the process of developing two different software applications that will have a set price at the base level. One of these programs is a lead management system and the other is a sales training system. These packages will have a set price to begin with unless the customer desires more features and/or more functionality.

Exceed Expectations does not currently offer boxed software applications because we have taken a customer focused approach when developing an application. Our software development staff needs to start tracking how many hours they spend on developing each application in order to determine our profitability margins.

Network Support Solutions

Exceed Expectations employs a dedicated team of Microsoft Certified consultants with a combined twenty–seven years of professional business network consulting experience. Supporting well over 100 networks in the Bismarck area for a wide variety of businesses and organizations, you can trust that Exceed Expectations has the experience and knowledge to expertly handle your IT infrastructure needs.

Our company is a Microsoft Certified Partner, Microsoft Certified Business Solutions Partner, and Dell Authorized Partner and Reseller. In addition, our consultants have many certifications from many other vendors specializing in security and data backup/recovery.

Exceed Expectations's Network Support Services are priced as follows:

- $110/hr is the flat rate
- There are no extra fees for travel time
- One hour on–site minimum
- The flat rate does not increase because of emergencies

Exceed Expectations's Network Support provides our clients with a certified expert with a cell phone who is on call anytime you need them. Our Network Support staff offer a wide variety of solutions.

Hosting Solutions

Exceed Expectations implemented hosting services in February of 2005. Exceed Expectations does not provide hosting solutions to make a large profit, but instead it is viewed more as an accessory service that can be offered with our network support or software application development. Exceed Expectations has made minimal profit margins (1 percent–2 percent), if any at all by providing hosting solutions.

It is important for our customers to know that all of our hosting facilities are located in downtown Bismarck at a secure data center called Wisteria, and another data center in Fargo called Host Answers. Exceed Expectations has chosen these facilities because we trust their technical expertise and their reliable data center infrastructure which regulates temperature and protects against disasters.

Hosting consists of Exceed Expectations providing various web–based applications, served through a sophisticated environment and infrastructure. Our customers are able to utilize the same unified environment via the internet. We make sure that our customer's data is secured through firewalls and maintained by a local team of network engineers. Exceed Expectation's hosted solutions include:

- Microsoft Exchange, including Outlook 2003 & Blackberry Enterprise Server
- Web Access to email, Calendar, Tasks & Contacts
- Calendar Sharing/Collaboration
- Advanced Spam Filtering & Anti–Virus
- 100 percent Blackberry Wireless Handheld Synchronization
- Daily Data Backup & Advanced Environment Security
- 250MB Storage per Mailbox & 24/7 Tech Support

We also provide other hosted solutions such as Microsoft Sharepoint which is a document management system that can be set up for more than 100 users. We also provide domain hosting which is when we host your website or software application. We own dedicated servers which mean we can host a company's database and make sure their data stays secure.

Exceed Expectations's Hosting Division has is in the process of implementing a new service called Microsoft ASP. This service will allow companies to subscribe to Microsoft software packages without them actually having to buy the package itself. This is new service is a more affordable solution because they will be able to subscribe and only have to pay a monthly fee opposed to buying the normal package at bulk price. The Microsoft ASP products and pricing schemes are located in the back of the Products and Services section.

The hosting services and prices are located in Appendix A.

COMPETITION

Exceed Expectations takes two different approaches to evaluating our competition. We evaluate our competition based on companies that serve similar IT solutions to the same portion of the Bismarck Market, and those companies that we have directly competed with for specific clients.

Understanding our competitors and their strengths and weaknesses is an advantage for our company to gain critical information about our customers. As a result, our goal was to find out exactly who we considered to be our competitors and then analyze them according to what information we felt was important. Consequently, the following analysis portion of this paper focuses mainly on competitors in the greater Bismarck area.

Exceed Expectations understands that there are other firms that offer business process reengineering, but this is not a service that we advertise even though it does generate a substantial amount of annual revenue. We will be up–selling this service to our current clients in our effort to generate more revenue from our current accounts. We feel the same way about hosting solutions because there are literally thousands of other companies that offer hosting solutions, but it is not one of our top revenue generating services, so we are not threatened by other companies that offer this service. Exceed Expectations is concerned with other companies that offer software application development and network support solutions. Software application development generates nearly 25 percent of our operating revenue, while network support generates nearly 50 percent of our operating revenue.

The lack of this information is a problem for Exceed Expectations and this knowledge is vital for a company's success. We collected and analyzed the following companies in the greater Bismarck area that directly compete with and provide similar services to Exceed Expectations.

Software Application Development Competition

The Westin Group
43 Block Dr.

Grand Forks

T: 701–321–4352

F: 701–321–4123

The Westin Group is a technology firm owned by Ken Westin and is located in Bismarck County. They currently have twelve employees and they generate $1,000,000 to $2,500,000 in annual sales revenue. Many of the services they offer are things like: web design, search engine optimization, shopping cart software, and a variety of other tools to allow you to sell online. The table below shows which services The Westin Group offers that are similar to Exceed Expectations.

Business process reengineering	Software development	Network support	Hosting solutions
—	X	X	Will offer in future

The Westin Group focuses on the client. They position themselves as a partner in the customers's operations. Their main focus is creating strong client partnerships and delivering a highly personalized level of service. They do this by improving and automating their client's processes, creating new productivity tools, B2B sites, B2C sites, shopping cart capabilities, eCommerce, online marketing, and increased market awareness through enticing websites. Essentially, they look to help their clients get a better return through technology. From looking at the language on their website and through research, we believe that this company attempts to offer a similar customer driven business model that closely matches Exceed Expectation's customer dedication.

The Westin Group does not concentrate on selling prepackaged software applications. The reason for this is because they position themselves as a company that offers highly personalized service. They look to provide unique solutions that focus on the individual client. However, they do offer a four page website template for $599. One of their main points is that they will focus on the client's use of technology to provide a better return in the company. This means that each company is going to require a unique solution according to specific needs.

Network Support Competition

Information Superhighway Portal, Inc.
981 Treetops Blvd.

Tioga, ND

T: 701–664–1231

F: 701–664–1802

Information Superhighway Portal, Inc. is a technology firm that is located in Bismarck County and is owned by their parent company Superhighway, LLC. Information on Superhighway, LLC is located in the last paragraph about Information Superhighway Portal, Inc. They currently have five to nine employees and generate around $1,000,000.00 to $2,500,000.00 in annual sales revenue. It was also noted that they have a satisfactory credit rating. The table below shows which services Information Superhighway Portal, Inc. offers that are similar to Exceed Expectations.

Business process reengineering	Software development	Network support	Hosting solutions
—	—	X	X

Information Superhighway Portal, Inc. offers a different range of solutions. Their main focus is being your full service provider for all of your networking, internet, and computer hardware and software needs. Again they also strive to ensure that customer satisfaction is their highest priority. They look to be a company's "comprehensive service provider" by offering fast internet connectivity, reliable web hosting, state–of–the–art server hosting and managed network services. Essentially, Information Superhighway Portal, Inc. wants to be your company's "one contact, one bill, one solution." Their primary focus is to provide a company with all of the tools and technology that they need to effectively run their business and manage it for them as well.

Since the majority of the services they offer deal with software, hardware, and network systems, many of their services would technically be "boxed products." This is true simply because of the nature of the services they offer, however, that does not mean that Information Superhighway Portal, Inc. is not capable of customizing their solutions to make them unique for each of their clients. They do not necessarily offer a blanket solution for all of their clients. They have varying levels of solutions to appeal to every size client.

Superhighway, LLC
Information Superhighway Portal, Inc. is a subsidiary of a much larger company called Superhighway, LLC. This is important information because this provides them with substantial financial stability. They currently generate $10,000,000.00 to $20,000,000.00 in annual sales revenue. It was also noted that they have a very good credit rating. They currently have fifty local employees. Superhighway, LLC sells DVDs and prepackaged computer software. They have a retail outlet on Brown Ave. in Bismarck County that generates around $1,000,000.00 to $2,500,000 in annual sales revenue. Here is a list of the Superhighway, LLC executives:

- Larry Abuot, President
- Jeri Abuot, Controller
- Adam Wixom, VP Data Processing
- Gail Brown, VP Human Resources
- Gail Brown, VP Marketing

- Chris Thompson, VP Sales
- Kathy Poorse, Purchasing Agent

Direct Network Support Competition

Destin Network Support
California Headquarters

1325 Stone School Dr.

San Diego, CA 92101

United States

T: 619–213–5000

Toll Free: (866) 213–1133

Fax: 619–213–5001

Peoria Branch

425 Ravine Rd.

Peoria, IL

61601

Direct Network Support (DNS) is a privately held company network support company that is headquartered in San Diego, California that has twenty–three branch offices in sixteen states across the country. The company has a total of 350 employees with an average of fifteen employees at each branch office. Each of the location averages around $500,000.00 to $2,500,000.00 in annual sales revenue depending on how many employees. The average sales revenue generated per sales representative is $148,600.00 per year. It is estimated that they have around $52,000,000.00 in sales revenue per year. It was also noted that Direct Network Support has a satisfactory credit rating. The table below shows which services DNS offers that are similar to Exceed Expectations.

Business process reengineering	Software development	Network support	Hosting solutions
—	—	—	—

The DNS branch office in Peoria has not been performing well for the past six months. Exceed Expectations received news that they were having a difficult time covering their monthly overhead costs. It was understood that they were paying their employees an inflated salary for the Peoria job market. They were paying their network technicians 35 percent more than the industry average. Most network technicians earn $50K to $55K per year while the network technicians were averaging $75K. They were forced to relieve some of their technicians from their duties, but they still had to service all of their clients with a reduced staff. Exceed Expectations took advantage of DNS's problem and gained two new networking clients. Exceed Expectations is still trying to take advantage of this situation.

MARKETING & SALES

Exceed Expectations's marketing objective is based on growth promotion strategy of our services to current clients. We have decided which clients to target after performing a revenue stream analysis. From this analysis, we have concluded that 83 percent of our revenue comes from 24 clients. This strategy involves a "two prong" approach. This approach is a combination of up–selling and cross–selling to penetrate a concentrated group of customers.

Customers

After performing the revenue analysis we have come to the conclusion that 83 percent of Exceed Expectation's revenue comes from 24 existing clients. We have segmented these top 24 clients into three different groups based upon the amount of revenue they generate.

Group 1 ($20K+):

The first group consists of our top six current clients and they generate 54 percent of our total revenue. We found that three of six currently use business process reengineering, three of six use software application development, three of six use network support, and three of six use hosting services. Despite the fact that this group is our largest revenue provider, there is still plenty of room for growth. For each of our four services there are three clients to target. Our goal for this group is to up–sell business process reengineering and software application development to two of the four clients in this group. Based upon the relationship Exceed Expectations has developed with this client group we will also attempt to use them as a referral base in order to acquire new business in the future.

Group 2 ($10K - $20K):

The second group consists of four clients (#7-#10) that generate 10 percent of our total revenue. We found that two of four currently use business process reengineering, one of four use software application development, three of four use network support, and one of four use hosting services. Our goal for this group is to increase their spending to $20K+. We plan to do this by up–selling software application development to the two clients that are currently not using this service.

Group 3 ($5K - $10K):

The third group consists of fourteen clients (#10-#24) that generate 19 percent of our total revenue. We found that three of fourteen currently use business process reengineering, two out fourteen use software application development, eleven of fourteen use network support, and eleven of fourteen use hosting services. Our goal for this group is to increase their spending to $10K+ over the course of two years. We plan to do this by up–selling software application development to the twelve clients that are currently not using this service. We also plan to up–sell business process reengineering to the eleven current clients that are not using this service. There is considerable room for growth in this group. Since software application development generates a considerable amount of revenue we hope to up–sell six out of the possible twelve clients. Business process reengineering also generates a substantial amount of revenue, and we hope to get six out of the eleven possible clients to use this service. If we can accomplish this moderate success rate of roughly 50 percent we can add six clients to the $10K to $20K group. On average this would increase revenue by $7K to $8K per client.

We hope to achieve the following results for each of the groups. Group 1 will generate an additional $80K to $100K in revenue, Group 2 will generate an additional $30K in revenue, and Group 3 will generate an additional $40K in revenue.

Business Strategy

We plan to accomplish our up–selling goals by delegating this responsibility to the sales team. Our Sales team is comprised of Mike Amerson, Ian Wood, Peter Richardson. The majority of this responsibility will be given to Peter Richardson. It is safe to assume that Peter will have 250 days to sell out of the year. In order for these goals to be accomplished, Peter would have to sell $800 per day. Last year, Peter personally sold $470,000 worth of services which averages out to $1,880 per day. These statistics show that our goals set are indeed realistic. This also leaves time for Peter to finalize sales with new clients even further, increasing our total revenues.

Exceed Expectations's promotion strategy will take place with the efforts of the sales team, coupled with the efforts of the network technicians. These two groups are constantly at our client's offices, so they are capable of discovering whether or not our competitors are supplying the same services to the client. Our network technicians will work to find out which services the client needs or which are not being met by our competition. This will allow our sales team to customize their sales pitch depending on the client's needs and wants.

Market Analysis

Exceed Expectations's competitive edge is our established relationships with our top revenue generating clients. These outstanding relationships have developed for a number of reasons. Our clients rely on us for our expertise and technical abilities. They can contact us twenty–four hours a day whenever they may need assistance. We do not hold our clients under binding contractual agreements because we want to keep our clients based upon the exceptional work we provide for them. The technologies we develop and deploy specifically for our clients allow them to realize gains and efficiencies which lead to higher profits. We take pride in our customer retention rate because it is a reflection of the good relationship with our customers. For the past five years (even before the merger) our top five revenue generating clients have been the using our services. Building and maintaining these relationships is the quality that sets us apart from our competitors.

Marketing Strategy Summary

Exceed Expectations's Marketing Strategy is based upon a revenue stream analysis. The results from this analysis showed us that our top twenty–four revenue generating clients account for 83 percent of our total revenue. We also discovered which clients are using what services we provide. This information showed us which clients we are going to up–sell to and what we need to offer them. We are going to take a two prong approach to increase the revenue from these specific clients. First, we will attempt to up–sell business process reengineering and software application development to the top six clients. Second, we will target the remaining eighteen clients in hopes of moving them into the $20K+ tier along with the top six clients. Peter's efforts will be a key component in achieving our two goals. Based upon his past success rate, we are confident in his abilities to sell the additional $150,000 worth of services. The sales network technicians will compliment Peter's efforts by finding out which services our clients need. This will result in more focused sales efforts and an enhanced success rate. While implementing this strategy we will strive to build and maintain the positive relationships that set us apart from our competition.

GROWTH STRATEGY

Income Statement

1. Revenue will increase by $30,000 in 2006 as a result of up–selling to our six current customers (Tier 1, Appendix B) with gross sales of $20,000 or more.
2. Revenue will increase by $40,000 in 2007 as a result of up–selling to our ten current customers (Tier 1 & 2, Appendix B) with gross sales of $10,000 or more.
3. Revenue will increase by $40,000 in 2008 as a result of up–selling to our twenty–four current customers (Tier 1, 2 & 3, Appendix B) with gross sales of $5,000 or more.
4. Cost of Goods Sold is 56 percent of revenue in the 2nd quarter of 2006 and will remain consistent as revenue increases due to historical quarterly financials.

APPENDIX

Appendix A

	Standard	Advanced
Setup fee	Never - order now	Never - order now
Monthly recurring	$20	$30
Main features		
Disk space	500MB	1000MB
Bandwidth	25GB	50GB
FTP accounts	5	Unlimited
Security usernames	10	10
Daily backups	Yes	Yes
Control panel	Yes	Yes
Security monitoring	Yes	Yes
Daily security sweep	Yes	Yes
Triple-redundant 10Mb connection	Yes	Yes
Site statistic features		
Search engine data	Yes	Yes
Full visitor details	Yes	Yes
70+ standard reports	Yes	Yes
Download raw logs	Yes	Yes
E-mail features		
E-mail accounts	50	250
POP3/IMAP	Yes	Yes
Spam filtering	Yes	Yes
Virus scanning	Yes	Yes
Content filtering	Yes	Yes
Advanced web mail	Yes	Yes
Alias accounts	Unlimited	Unlimited
Auto responders	Yes	Yes
SMTP authentication	Yes	Yes
Alternative SMTP port	Yes (TCP 587)	Yes (TCP 587)
Mailing lists	Yes	Yes
Database features		
Datasources/DSNs	Unlimited	Unlimited
MySQL disk space	25MB	100MB
Microsoft SQL disk space	25MB	100MB
Microsoft access	Yes	Yes
Supported scripting		
ASP.NET	Yes	Yes
PHP	Yes	Yes
Active state perl	Yes	Yes
Server side XML	Yes	Yes
WinCGI	Yes	Yes
Unique CGI-BIN	Yes	Yes
Extra features		
Shared SSL	Yes	Yes
24/7 Support	Yes	Yes
ASP/.NET components	Yes	Yes
Microsoft index server	Yes	Yes
Supported applications		
Microsoft frontpage	Yes	Yes
Visual studio	Yes	Yes
Macromedia dreamweaver	Yes	Yes
Adobe GoLive	Yes	Yes
Macromedia Flash	Yes	Yes
Windows Media	Yes	Yes
Real Audio/Video	Yes	Yes

	E-mail
Setup Fee	Never
Monthly Recurring	$10
Main features	
Disk space	250MB
Daily backups	Yes
Control panel	Yes
Security monitoring	Yes
Daily security sweep	Yes
Triple-redundant 10Mb connection	Yes
E-mail features	
E-mail accounts	250
POP3/IMAP	Yes
Spam filtering	Yes
Virus scanning	Yes
Content filtering	Yes
Advanced web mail	Yes
Alias accounts	Unlimited
Auto responders	Yes
SMTP Authentication	Yes
Alternative SMTP port	TCP 587
List server	Yes

	SharePoint
Setup fee	Never
Monthly recurring	$50
Main features	
Disk space	5000MB
Bandwidth	25GB
Sharepoint usernames	100
Daily backups	Yes
Control panel	Yes
Security monitoring	Yes
Daily security sweep	Yes
Triple-redundant connection	Yes
Extra features	
Virus scanning	Yes
24/7 Emergency support	Yes

	Exchange	+Blackberry
Setup fee	Never	Never
Monthly recurring	$10	$10
Main features		
Disk space	250MB	250MB
Bandwidth	Unlimited	Unlimited
Security monitoring	Yes	Yes
Real-time security	Yes	Yes
High speed	Yes	Yes
Security features		
SPAM filtering	Yes	Yes
Content filtering	Yes	Yes
Virus scanning	Yes	Yes
Daily backups	Yes	Yes
Outlook features		
Outlook web access	Yes	Yes
Public folders	5/Domain	5/Domain
VPN access	Yes	Yes
RPC over HTTP	Yes	Yes
Attachment limit	25MB	25MB
Server location		
Physical security	Triple layers	Triple layers
Power protection	Full	Full
Tier 1 connections	3	3
24/7 Monitoring	Onsite	Onsite

	Co-Located (Your server/Our rack)	Standard* (Our Server/Our rack)	Advanced* (Our Server/Our rack)
Setup fee	Never - Order Now	$199 - Order now	$299 - Order now
Monthly recurring	$99	$199	$299
Main features			
Bandwidth	100GB	100GB	100GB
Rack space	4U	4U	4U
Security monitoring	Yes	Yes	Yes
Daily security sweep	Yes	Yes	Yes
Gigabit backbone	Yes	Yes	Yes
10Mb Ethernet connection	Yes	Yes	N/A
100Mb Ethernet connection	Optional	Optional	Yes
Server Features			
Brand	N/A	Dell PowerEdge	Dell PowerEdge
Processor	N/A	Single P4 2.8GHz	Dual Xeon 2.8GHz
RAM (expandable)	N/A	1024MB	2GB
Hard disk (mirrored)	N/A	Minimum 74GB	Minimum 146GB
Operating system	N/A	Customer choice	Customer choice
Hardware warranty	N/A	8x5xNBD	24x7x4-Hour
Extra features			
Gateway virus/Spyware filter	Yes	Yes	Yes
24/7 Monitoring	Yes	Yes	Yes
Support from MCSE	Yes	Yes	Yes
Online disk-based backup	5GB (Expandable)	10GB (Expandable)	20GB (Expandable)

	Exchange	+Blackberry
Setup fee	Never	Never
Monthly recurring	$10	$25
Main features		
Disk space	250MB	250MB
Bandwidth	Unlimited	Unlimited
Security monitoring	Yes	Yes
Real-time security	Yes	Yes
High speed	Yes	Yes
Security features		
SPAM filtering	Yes	Yes
Content filtering	Yes	Yes
Virus scanning	Yes	Yes
Daily backups	Yes	Yes
Outlook features		
Outlook web access	Yes	Yes
Public folders	5/Domain	5/Domain
VPN access	Yes	Yes
RPC over HTTP	Yes	Yes
Attachment limit	25MB	25MB
Server location		
Physical security	Triple layers	Triple layers
Power protection	Full	Full
Tier 1 connections	3	3
24/7 Monitoring	Onsite	Onsite

	Shared	Dedicated
Setup fee	Never	Call
Monthly recurring	$50	Varies
Main features		
Disk space	10GB	Varies
Bandwidth	N/A	Starts@100GB
Security monitoring	Yes	Yes
Real-time security	Yes	Yes
High Speed	10 Mbps	10–100 Mbps
Security features		
Virus scanning	Yes	Yes
Daily backups	Yes	Yes
Outlook features		
Enterprise manager access	Yes	Yes
Scheduled tasks	Yes	Yes
VPN access	Yes	Yes
RPC over HTTP	N/A	Yes
Server location		
Physical security	Triple layers	Triple layers
Power protection	Full	Full
Tier 1 connections	3	3
24/7 monitoring	Onsite	Onsite

	Filtering
Setup fee	Never
Monthly fee (10/25/50 Users)	$10/$35/$50
Main features	
Bandwidth	Unlimited
Security monitoring	Yes
Real-time security	Yes
High speed	Yes
Security features	
SPAM filtering	Yes
Virus scanning	Yes
Features	
Search inside compressed files?	Yes
Dual MX records for redundancy?	Yes
Attachment limit	25MB
Server location	
Physical security	Triple layers
Power protection	Full
Tier 1 connections	3
24/7 monitoring	Onsite

	Filtering
Setup fee	Never
Monthly fee (10/25/50 Users)	$10/$35/$50
Main features	
Bandwidth	Unlimited
Security monitoring	Yes
Real-time security	Yes
High speed	Yes
Security features	
SPAM filtering	Yes
Virus scanning	Yes
Features	
Search inside compressed files?	Yes
Dual MX records for redundancy?	Yes
Attachment limit	25MB
Server location	
Physical security	Triple layers
Power protection	Full
Tier 1 connections	3
24/7 monitoring	Onsite

Appendix B—Financial Charts

Client Revenue Tier Chart

Client revenue tier chart

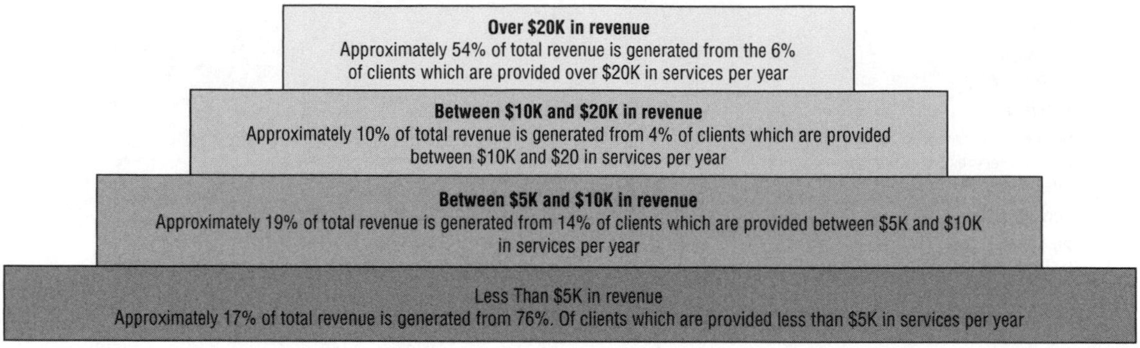

Over $20K in revenue
Approximately 54% of total revenue is generated from the 6% of clients which are provided over $20K in services per year
Between $10K and $20K in revenue
Approximately 10% of total revenue is generated from 4% of clients which are provided between $10K and $20 in services per year
Between $5K and $10K in revenue
Approximately 19% of total revenue is generated from 14% of clients which are provided between $5K and $10K in services per year
Less Than $5K in revenue
Approximately 17% of total revenue is generated from 76%. Of clients which are provided less than $5K in services per year

Revenue Stream Analysis

				Revenue					Services						
ThrottleNet clients (104)	# of Serv.	Income	Industry	Greater than $20,000	Between $20,000 & $10,000	Between $10,000 & $5,000	Less than $5,000	Total	Net.	Host	BPR	Soft	One Service	Two Services	Three Services
Client 1	1	$79,309.00	Distribution	1				1			1		1		
Client 2	3	$77,111.03	Medical	1				1	1	1		1			1
Client 3	2	$56,730.27	Marketing	1				1		1	1			1	
Client 4	1	$29,002.34	Accounting	1				1	1				1		
Client 5	2	$28,000.00	Distribution	1				1			1	1		1	
Client 6	2	$24,556.83	Medical	1				1	1	1				1	
Client 7	2	$19,144.83	Industrial		1			1	1	1				1	
Client 8	2	$14,486.16	Financial		1			1	1		1			1	
Client 9	2	$10,545.00	Accounting		1			1			1	1		1	
Client 10	1	$10,390.17	Realty		1			1	1				1		
Client 11	2	$10,000.00	Legal					1			1	1		1	
Client 12	2	$ 9,825.99	Distribution			1		1	1	1				1	
Client 13	2	$ 9,227.00	Marketing			1		1	1	1				1	
Client 14	2	$ 8,220.50	Distribution			1		1	1	1				1	
Client 15	2	$ 7,217.17	Industrial			1		1	1	1				1	
Client 16	1	$ 7,003.17	Industrial			1		1		1			1		
Client 17	1	$ 6,576.67	Industrial			1		1	1				1		
Client 18	2	$ 6,504.00	Distribution			1		1	1	1				1	
Client 19	2	$ 6,022.00	Industrial			1		1	1	1				1	
Client 20	2	$ 5,912.33	Recreation			1		1	1	1				1	
Client 21	2	$ 5,732.17	Medical			1		1	1	1				1	
Client 22	1	$ 5,717.33	Industrial			1		1			1		1		
Client 23	2	$ 5,693.33	Legal			1		1	1	1				1	
Client 24	2	$ 5,312.50	non-profit			1		1			1	1		1	
Client 25	2	$ 5,256.99	Legal			1		1	1	1				1	
Client 26	2	$ 4,799.50	Distribution			1	1	1	1	1				1	
Client 27	1	$ 4,780.50	Industrial				1	1		1			1		
Client 28	2	$ 4,582.00	Industrial				1	1	1	1				1	
Client 29	2	$ 4,405.00	Legal				1	1	1	1				1	
Client 30	1	$ 4,324.12	Financial				1	1	1				1		
Client 31	2	$ 3,927.50	Accounting				1	1	1	1				1	
Client 32	1	$ 3,791.00	Medical				1	1	1				1		
Client 33	1	$ 3,576.51	Retail				1	1	1				1		
Client 34	1	$ 3,275.83	Legal				1	1	1				1		
Client 35	2	$ 2,847.00	Industrial				1	1	1	1				1	
Client 36	1	$ 2,819.70	Retail				1	1	1				1		
Client 37	2	$ 2,725.00	Distribution				1	1	1	1				1	
Client 38	2	$ 2,644.50	Industrial				1	1	1			1		1	
Client 39	2	$ 2,499.00	Distribution				1	1		1		1		1	
Client 40	2	$ 2,458.00	Medical				1	1	1	1				1	
Client 41	1	$ 2,439.50	Legal				1	1	1				1		
Client 42	2	$ 2,336.33	Realty				1	1	1	1				1	
Client 43	1	$ 2,335.00	Legal				1	1	1				1		
Client 44	1	$ 2,328.00	Industrial				1	1	1				1		
Client 45	1	$ 2,214.83	Industrial				1	1	1				1		
Client 46	2	$ 2,164.00	Legal				1	1	1	1				1	
Client 47	1	$ 2,142.33	Medical				1	1	1				1		
Client 48	2	$ 2,118.67	Technology				1	1	1	1				1	
Client 49	1	$ 1,800.00	Recruiting Firm				1	1		1			1		
Client 50	1	$ 1,567.00	Financial				1	1	1				1		
Client 51	1	$ 1,164.84	Insurance				1	1	1				1		
Client 52	1	$ 907.50	Industrial				1	1	1				1		
Client 53	2	$ 870.00	Legal				1	1	1	1				1	
Client 54	1	$ 848.34	Marketing				1	1		1			1		
Client 55	1	$ 829.00	Industrial				1	1				1	1		
Client 56	2	$ 825.00	Distribution				1	1		1		1		1	
Client 57	1	$ 817.33	Realty				1	1	1				1		
Client 58	1	$ 810.00	Commercial				1	1				1	1		
Client 59	1	$ 797.50	Retail				1	1	1				1		
Client 60	1	$ 672.50	Realty				1	1		1			1		
Client 61	1	$ 660.00	Industrial				1	1	1				1		
Client 62	1	$ 650.83	Financial				1	1	1				1		
Client 63	1	$ 634.96	Industrial				1	1	1				1		
Client 64	1	$ 630.00	Medical				1	1		1			1		
Client 65	1	$ 625.00	Industrial				1	1			1		1		
Client 66	1	$ 607.33	Accounting				1	1		1			1		
Client 67	1	$ 605.00	Accounting				1	1		1			1		

Revenue Stream Analysis [CONTINUED]

ThrottleNet clients (104)	# of Serv.	Income	Industry	Revenue: Greater than $20,000	Revenue: Between $20,000 & $10,000	Revenue: Between $10,000 & $5,000	Revenue: Less than $5,000	Revenue: Total	Services: Net.	Services: Host	Services: BPR	Services: Soft	Services: One Service	Services: Two Services	Services: Three Services
Client 68	1	$ 550.00	Distribution				1	1		1			1		
Client 69	1	$ 467.50	Medical				1	1		1			1		
Client 70	1	$ 462.72	Financial				1	1			1		1		
Client 71	1	$ 395.00	non-profit				1	1		1			1		
Client 72	1	$ 394.17	Industrial				1	1		1			1		
Client 73	1	$ 385.00	Industrial				1	1		1			1		
Client 74	2	$ 385.00	Legal				1	1	1	1				1	
Client 75	2	$ 385.00	Medical				1	1	1	1				1	
Client 76	1	$ 367.50	Industrial				1	1		1			1		
Client 77	1	$ 340.00	Distribution				1	1				1	1		
Client 78	1	$ 321.67	Retail				1	1		1			1		
Client 79	1	$ 315.00	Technology				1	1		1			1		
Client 80	1	$ 300.00	Medical				1	1		1			1		
Client 81	1	$ 275.00	Industrial				1	1		1			1		
Client 82	1	$ 260.00	Recreation				1	1		1			1		
Client 83	1	$ 240.00	Distribution				1	1		1			1		
Client 84	1	$ 220.00	Medical				1	1	1				1		
Client 85	1	$ 155.00	Realty				1	1		1			1		
Client 86	1	$ 150.00	Retail				1	1		1			1		
Client 87	1	$ 120.00	Distribution				1	1		1			1		
Client 88	1	$ 120.00	Marketing				1	1		1			1		
Client 89	1	$ 120.00	Marketing				1	1		1			1		
Client 90	1	$ 120.00	non-profit				1	1		1			1		
Client 91	1	$ 120.00	non-profit				1	1		1			1		
Client 92	1	$ 120.00	Retail				1	1		1			1		
Client 93	1	$ 110.00	Distribution				1	1	1				1		
Client 94	1	$ 110.00	Financial				1	1	1				1		
Client 95	1	$ 110.00	Industrial				1	1	1				1		
Client 96	1	$ 110.00	Realty				1	1	1				1		
Client 97	1	$ 110.00	Retail				1	1	1				1		
Client 98	1	$ 80.00	Consulting				1	1		1			1		
Client 99	1	$ 60.00	Industrial				1	1		1			1		
Client 100	1	$ 60.00	Medical				1	1		1			1		
Client 101	1	$ 60.00	Photography				1	1		1			1		
Client 102	1	$ 40.00	Insurance				1	1		1			1		
Client 103	1	$ 20.00	Medical				1	1		1			1		
Client 104	1	–$ 607.00	Accounting				1	1	1				1		
Total		**$548,704.29**		**6**	**4**	**15**	**79**	**104**	**56**	**63**	**10**	**11**	**69**	**34**	**1**

INCOME STATEMENT

Income Statement

	2005				2006	
	Q'1*	Q'2*	Q'3*	Q'4*	Q'1*	Q'2
Revenue*	$193,000	$244,000	$244,000	$299,000	$288,000	$303,000
Cost of Goods Sold	$128,000	$190,000	$156,000	$151,000	$161,000	$170,000
Gross Profit	**$ 65,000**	**$ 54,000**	**$ 88,000**	**$148,000**	**$127,000**	**$133,000**
Gross Profit Margin	**33.7%**	**22.1%**	**36.1%**	**49.5%**	**44.1%**	**43.9%**
Automobile Expense	$ 1,000	$ 2,000	$ 3,000	$ 3,000	$ 3,000	$ 3,000
Bank Service Charges	$ 1,000	$ 1,000	$ 1,000	$ 1,000	$ 1,000	$ 1,000
Building Expense	$ 6,000	$ 3,000	$ 6,000	$ 6,000	$ 6,000	$ 6,000
Equipment Rental	$ 1,000	$ 2,000	$ 4,000	$ 6,000	$ 6,000	$ 6,000
Hosting-Expense	$ 1,000	$ 3,000	$ 11,000	$ 5,000	$ 12,000	$ 18,000
Insurance	$ 3,000	$ 2,000	$ 3,000	$ 1,000	$ 3,000	$ 3,000
Advertising/Marketing	$ 20,000	$ 14,000	$ 3,000	$ 1,000	$ 2,000	$ 2,000
Administrative Expenses	$ 24,000	$ 22,000	$ 20,000	$ 12,000	$ 12,000	$ 11,000
Outside Services	$ —	$ 1,000	$ 2,000	$ —	$ —	$ —
Professional Expenses	$ 12,000	$ 13,000	$ 8,000	$ 11,000	$ 11,000	$ 11,000
Taxes	$ 4,000	$ —	$ 1,000	$ 3,000	$ 4,000	$ 4,000
Meals, Entertainment & Travel	$ 1,000	$ 1,000	$ —	$ 2,000	$ 1,000	$ 1,000
Employee gifts	$ —	$ 1,000	$ —	$ 2,000	$ —	$ —
Total Expenses	$ 74,000	$ 65,000	$ 62,000	$ 53,000	$ 61,000	$ 66,000
Net Income	**$ (9,000)**	**$(11,000)**	**$ 26,000**	**$ 95,000**	**$ 66,000**	**$ 67,000**
YTD Net Income	**$ (9,000)**	**$(20,000)**	**$ 6,000**	**$101,000**	**$ 66,000**	**$133,000**
Net Income %	**−5%**	**−5%**	**11%**	**32%**	**23%**	**22%**

	2006		2007				2008
	Q'3*	Q'4	Q'1	Q'2	Q'3	Q'4	FY
Revenue*	$318,000	$338,000	$333,000	$343,000	$353,000	$368,000	$1,512,000
Cost of Goods Sold	$179,000	$190,000	$187,000	$193,000	$198,000	$207,000	$ 847,000
Gross Profit	**$139,000**	**$148,000**	**$146,000**	**$150,000**	**$155,000**	**$161,000**	**$ 665,000**
Gross Profit Margin	**43.7%**	**43.8%**	**43.8%**	**43.7%**	**43.9%**	**43.8%**	**44.0%**
Automobile Expense	$ 3,000	$ 4,000	$ 4,000	$ 4,000	$ 4,000	$ 5,000	$ 19,000
Bank Service Charges	$ 1,000	$ 1,000	$ 1,000	$ 1,000	$ 1,000	$ 1,000	$ 4,000
Building Expense	$ 6,000	$ 6,000	$ 6,000	$ 6,000	$ 6,000	$ 6,000	$ 22,000
Equipment Rental	$ 6,000	$ 6,000	$ 6,000	$ 6,000	$ 6,000	$ 6,000	$ 22,000
Hosting-Expense	$ 18,000	$ 18,000	$ 20,000	$ 20,000	$ 20,000	$ 20,000	$ 82,000
Insurance	$ 3,000	$ 3,000	$ 3,000	$ 3,000	$ 3,000	$ 3,000	$ 3,000
Advertising/Marketing	$ 2,000	$ 2,000	$ 3,000	$ 3,000	$ 3,000	$ 3,000	$ 14,000
Administrative Expenses	$ 13,000	$ 14,000	$ 15,000	$ 15,000	$ 15,000	$ 15,000	$ 72,000
Outside Services	$ —	$ —	$ —	$ —	$ —	$ —	$ —
Professional Expenses	$ 11,000	$ 12,000	$ 12,000	$ 12,000	$ 12,000	$ 12,000	$ 12,000
Taxes	$ 4,000	$ 4,000	$ 4,000	$ 4,000	$ 4,000	$ 4,000	$ 17,000
Meals, Entertainment & Travel	$ 1,000	$ 1,000	$ 1,000	$ 1,000	$ 1,000	$ 1,000	$ 4,000
Employee gifts	$ —	$ 2,000	$ —	$ —	$ —	$ 2,000	$ 1,500
Total Expenses	$ 68,000	$ 73,000	$ 75,000	$ 75,000	$ 75,000	$ 78,000	$ 272,500
Net Income	**$ 71,000**	**$ 75,000**	**$ 71,000**	**$ 75,000**	**$ 80,000**	**$ 83,000**	**$ 392,500**
YTD Net Income	**$204,000**	**$279,000**	**$ 71,000**	**$146,000**	**$226,000**	**$309,000**	**$ 392,500**
Net Income %	**22%**	**22%**	**21%**	**22%**	**23%**	**23%**	**26%**

*Historical Financial Data
**A break-down of revenue by services was unavailable

BALANCE SHEET

Balance Sheet

	2005				2006	
	Q'1*	Q'2*	Q'3*	Q'4*	Q'1*	Q'2
Assets						
Cash	$(16,000)	$(27,000)	$(14,000)	$ 56,000	$134,000	$208,000
Accounts Receivable	$ 39,000	$ 49,000	$ 49,000	$ 78,000	$ 79,000	$ 79,000
Shareholder Loan	$ —	$ —	$ 10,000	$ 10,000	$ 10,000	$ 10,000
Total Current Assets	**$ 23,000**	**$ 22,000**	**$ 45,000**	**$144,000**	**$223,000**	**$297,000**
Fixed Assets						
Computer Hardware	$ 8,000	$ 8,000	$ 8,000	$ 8,000	$ 8,000	$ 8,000
Office Furniture	$ 4,000	$ 4,000	$ 4,000	$ 4,000	$ 4,000	$ 4,000
Accumulated Depreciation	$(12,000)	$(12,000)	$(12,000)	$(12,000)	$(12,000)	$(12,000)
Total Fixed Assets	**$ —**	**$ —**	**$ —**	**$ —**	**$ —**	**$ —**
Total Assets	**$ 23,000**	**$ 22,000**	**$ 45,000**	**$144,000**	**$223,000**	**$297,000**
Liabilities						
Current Liabilities						
Accounts Payable	$ 20,000	$ 25,000	$ 25,000	$ 30,000	$ 43,000	$ 46,000
Other Current Liabilities						
Taxes payable	$ 9,000	$ 14,000	$ 11,000	$ 10,000	$ 10,000	$ 14,000
Total Current Liabilities	**$ 29,000**	**$ 39,000**	**$ 36,000**	**$ 40,000**	**$ 53,000**	**$ 60,000**
Total Liabilities	**$ 29,000**	**$ 39,000**	**$ 36,000**	**$ 40,000**	**$ 53,000**	**$ 60,000**
Equity						
Capital Stock	$ 3,000	$ 3,000	$ 3,000	$ 3,000	$ 3,000	$ 3,000
Retained Earnings	$ (9,000)	$(20,000)	$ 6,000	$101,000	$167,000	$234,000
Total Equity	**$ (6,000)**	**$(17,000)**	**$ 9,000**	**$104,000**	**$170,000**	**$237,000**
Total Liabilities & Equity	**$ 23,000**	**$ 22,000**	**$ 45,000**	**$144,000**	**$223,000**	**$297,000**

	2006		2007				2008
	Q'3*	Q'4	Q'1	Q'2	Q'3	Q'4	FY
Assets							
Cash	$280,000	$356,000	$428,000	$505,000	$586,000	$669,000	$ 955,000
Accounts Receivable	$ 83,000	$ 88,000	$ 87,000	$ 90,000	$ 92,000	$ 96,000	$ 217,000
Shareholder Loan	$ 8,000	$ 6,000	$ 4,000	$ 2,000	$ —	$ —	$ —
Total Current Assets	**$371,000**	**$450,000**	**$519,000**	**$597,000**	**$678,000**	**$765,000**	**$1,172,000**
Fixed Assets							
Computer Hardware	$ 8,000	$ 8,000	$ 8,000	$ 8,000	$ 8,000	$ 8,000	$ 8,000
Office Furniture	$ 4,000	$ 4,000	$ 4,000	$ 4,000	$ 4,000	$ 4,000	$ 4,000
Accumulated Depreciation	$(12,000)	$(12,000)	$(12,000)	$(12,000)	$(12,000)	$(12,000)	$ (12,000)
Total Fixed Assets	**$ —**	**$ —**	**$ —**	**$ —**	**$ —**	**$ —**	**$ —**
Total Assets	**$371,000**	**$450,000**	**$519,000**	**$597,000**	**$678,000**	**$765,000**	**$1,172,000**
Liabilities							
Current Liabilities							
Accounts Payable	$ 48,000	$ 51,000	$ 50,000	$ 52,000	$ 53,000	$ 56,000	$ 61,000
Other Current Liabilities							
Taxes payable	$ 15,000	$ 16,000	$ 15,000	$ 16,000	$ 16,000	$ 17,000	$ 26,000
Total Current Liabilities	**$ 63,000**	**$ 67,000**	**$ 65,000**	**$ 68,000**	**$ 69,000**	**$ 73,000**	**$ 87,000**
Total Liabilities	**$ 63,000**	**$ 67,000**	**$ 65,000**	**$ 68,000**	**$ 69,000**	**$ 73,000**	**$ 87,000**
Equity							
Capital Stock	$ 3,000	$ 3,000	$ 3,000	$ 3,000	$ 3,000	$ 3,000	$ 3,000
Retained Earnings	$305,000	$380,000	$451,000	$526,000	$606,000	$689,000	$1,082,000
Total Equity	**$308,000**	**$383,000**	**$454,000**	**$529,000**	**$609,000**	**$692,000**	**$1,085,000**
Total Liabilities & Equity	**$371,000**	**$450,000**	**$519,000**	**$597,000**	**$678,000**	**$765,000**	**$1,172,000**

*Historical Financial Data

CASH FLOW

Cash Flow Statement

	2005				2006	
	Q'1*	Q'2*	Q'3*	Q'4*	Q'1*	Q'2
Operating activities						
Net Income	$ (9,000)	$(11,000)	$ 26,000	$ 95,000	$ 66,000	$ 67,000
Adjustment to reconcile net income to net cash provided by operations:						
Operating activities						
Accounts Receivable	$(12,000)	$(10,000)	$ —	$(29,000)	$ (1,000)	$ —
Shareholder Loan	$ —	$ —	$(10,000)	$ —	$ —	$ —
Accounts Payable	$ 5,000	$ 5,000	$ —	$ 5,000	$ 13,000	$ 3,000
Taxes	$ 5,000	$ 5,000	$ (3,000)	$ (1,000)	$ —	$ 4,000
Net cash provided by operating activities	$(11,000)	$(11,000)	$ 13,000	$ 70,000	$ 78,000	$ 74,000
Financing activities						
Capital Stock	$ —	$ —	$ —	$ —	$ —	$ —
Net cash provided by financing activities	$ —	$ —	$ —	$ —	$ —	$ —
Net cash increase for period	**$(11,000)**	**$(11,000)**	**$ 13,000**	**$ 70,000**	**$ 78,000**	**$ 74,000**
Cash at beginning of period	$ (5,000)	$(16,000)	$(27,000)	$(14,000)	$ 56,000	$ 134,000
Cash at end of period	**$(16,000)**	**$(27,000)**	**$(14,000)**	**$ 56,000**	**$134,000**	**$ 208,000**

*Historical Financial Data

	2006		2007				2008
	Q'3*	Q'4	Q'1	Q'2	Q'3	Q'4	FY
Operating activities							
Net Income	$ 71,000	$ 75,000	$71,000	$ 75,000	$ 80,000	$ 83,000	$ 393,000
Adjustment to reconcile net income to net cash provided by operations:							
Operating activities							
Accounts Receivable	$ (4,000)	$ (5,000)	$ 1,000	$ (3,000)	$ (2,000)	$ (4,000)	$(121,000)
Shareholder Loan	$ 2,000	$ 2,000	$ 2,000	$ 2,000	$ 2,000	$ —	$ —
Accounts Payable	$ 2,000	$ 3,000	$ (1,000)	$ 2,000	$ 1,000	$ 3,000	$ 5,000
Taxes	$ 1,000	$ 1,000	$ (1,000)	$ 1,000	$	$ 1,000	$ 26,000
Net cash provided by operating activities	$ 72,000	$ 76,000	$ 72,000	$ 77,000	$ 81,000	$ 83,000	$ 303,000
Financing activities							
Capital Stock	$ —	$ —	$ —	$ —	$ —	$ —	$ —
Net cash provided by financing activities	$ —	$ —	$ —	$ —	$ —	$ —	$ —
Net cash increase for period	**$ 72,000**	**$ 76,000**	**$ 72,000**	**$ 77,000**	**$ 81,000**	**$ 83,000**	**$ 303,000**
Cash at beginning of period	$208,000	$280,000	$356,000	$428,000	$505,000	$586,000	$ 669,000
Cash at end of period	**$280,000**	**$356,000**	**$428,000**	**$505,000**	**$586,000**	**$669,000**	**$ 972,000**

*Historical Financial Data

Trademarked Resort Wear Distributor

MUSKRAT BLUFFS APPAREL

45 Resort Way
South Lake Tahoe, California 96150

Muskrat Bluffs Apparel is a brand of resort wear and casual lifestyle clothing that is about enjoying the good life and expressing it. Our inspiration comes from the Muskrat Bluffs Resort and Entertainment Complex, a locale where many are enjoying the good life.

EXECUTIVE SUMMARY

As I sit in my office wading through the mounds of work and encounter one frustration after another, I close my eyes and imagine myself at Muskrat Bluffs. A place where I can sip my favorite drink, watch the sunset over the beautiful lake, and enjoy the company of good friends. I can see myself kicking back and saying, "Ahhh—this is the good life." The tension leaves me and I am left to relax.

There is nothing better than the good life. Every person's idea of the good life is a little different than the next. The one common theme is that the good life is about doing what you love to do. It is about enjoying life and living your dream. It can be about relaxing on the shoreline in seclusion or enjoying a lively time with friends. It is what you want to make it. What's the good life to you?

Muskrat Bluffs Apparel is a brand of resort wear and casual lifestyle clothing that is about enjoying the good life and expressing it. Our inspiration comes from the Muskrat Bluffs Resort and Entertainment Complex, a locale where many are enjoying the good life. It is a place where one can get away from the office and remember what it feels like to kick back and say, "Ahhh—this is the good life."

Muskrat Bluffs Apparel will enter the market by establishing a location in the Resort and Yacht Club at Muskrat Bluffs, which is connected to the Entertainment Complex on beautiful Lake Tahoe. This resort destination will welcome over 250,000 visitors each year and has plans to add an additional four resorts over the next ten years throughout the United States and Mexico. Muskrat Bluffs Apparel will be the exclusive resort wear and casual lifestyle clothing in the Resort and Yacht Club at Muskrat Bluffs.

Most of the visitors to the resort are baby boomers and empty nesters with high discretionary incomes, a zest for enjoying life, and a desire for high quality clothing. In addition, the complex attracts people of all ages who are yearning to enjoy the good life and find ways to express it. The customers of the Resort and Yacht Club at Muskrat Bluffs and the Entertainment Complex are Muskrat Bluffs' target customers. As we grow at the Resort and Yacht Club at Muskrat Bluffs, we will begin to spread the good life at trade shows so that other customers around the country can enjoy the pleasures of Muskrat Bluffs.

With our location at the Resort and Yacht Club at Muskrat Bluffs, we can bring our brand to life. Customers can experience what it feels like to enjoy the good life. Muskrat Bluffs Apparel will be there to facilitate the customers' enjoyment of the good life and to express it in a line of clothing that will remind them of what it feels like to kick back and say, "Ahhh—this is the good life."

The passion behind Muskrat Bluffs Apparel and the reason for its efforts is to express the good life. Muskrat Bluffs is a company that is about doing what you love to do, enjoying life, and living your dream. Our dream at Muskrat Bluffs is for people to relax how they see fit and to have a great time doing it. Nothing makes us happier than when we are doing what we love to do. Providing great apparel in a great atmosphere while making some new friends is what we love to do. We are committed to our customers and we are committed to high quality in our products, our service, and in our lives.

When you are enjoying what you do, you can do amazing things as our financial statements reflect. As you read through our business plan, please enjoy and take a little time to think about what the good life is to you.

OBJECTIVES

The objectives of Muskrat Bluffs are:

1. To provide the customers of the Resort and Yacht Club at Muskrat Bluffs and the Entertainment Complex with high quality resort wear and casual lifestyle clothing.
2. To focus on the customer and make them part of the Muskrat Bluffs experience.
3. To sell Muskrat Bluffs Apparel in new locales by the end of our third year of business.
4. To promote the Muskrat Bluffs lifestyle and resorts.

MISSION

To be an expression of the good life. Muskrat Bluffs Apparel is inspired to express life's dreams in style. We believe living your dream is what life is all about and behind every decision made by Muskrat Bluffs. Muskrat Bluffs Apparel consists of only the highest quality materials and is available at lifestyle destinations. We are dedicated to doing the right thing in our office, in our professional relationships, and in our community.

Enjoy our destination, enjoy our brand.

Keys to Success

A few of Muskrat Bluffs Apparel's keys to success are:

1. Offering high quality, desirable resort wear and casual lifestyle clothing in a location that brings our brand and image alive.
2. Converting customers from "just looking" to buying.
3. Generating word–of–mouth marketing.
4. Creating repeat business.

BUSINESS OVERVIEW

Muskrat Bluffs Apparel is a line of resort wear and casual lifestyle clothing inspired by the Muskrat Bluffs Entertainment Complex, which is a four–story 30,000 sq. ft. waterfront mega entertainment complex. The top floor is the Muskrat Bluffs restaurant, which offers gourmet dining in a fun, relaxed atmosphere. Muskrat Love Nightclub entertains guests on the middle two floors. The lowest level includes the Mega Muskrat sports bar and grill, a tiki bar, concert stage, the Muskrat Mini Mart, and Wet Rat Shop, which is a convenience store and seller of Muskrat Bluffs souvenirs. Muskrat Bluffs Apparel will establish its first retail location in the lobby of the Resort and Yacht Club at Muskrat Bluffs, which will be physically connected to the entertainment complex. The Resort and Yacht Club at Muskrat Bluffs will boast 116 luxury rooms, a 100 slip yacht club, a salon and spa (located across from the Muskrat Bluffs Apparel Shop), indoor/outdoor swimming pool with swim–up bar, handball/racquetball courts, indoor/outdoor sand volleyball court, workout facility, a one screen movie theater, and a 10,000 sq. ft. convention center.

The focus of Muskrat Bluffs Apparel is marketing and selling its resort wear and casual lifestyle clothing to customers of the Muskrat Bluffs restaurant and the Resort and Yacht Club at Muskrat Bluffs. An outside fashion consultant and a private label clothing contractor will assist Muskrat Bluffs in designing and producing our clothing. In the third year of operation we will begin marketing and selling at trade shows throughout the United States. We will continue to establish our own boutiques in new Muskrat Bluffs locations and Resort and Yacht Club at Muskrat Bluffs complexes. Currently, four additional Muskrat Bluffs Resort and Yacht Club complexes are to be added over the next ten years throughout the United States and Mexico.

PRODUCTS

Muskrat Bluffs Apparel offers a line of resort wear and casual lifestyle clothing for men and women age 21 to 65. Muskrat Bluffs products are inspired by the Muskrat Bluffs. The product line and pricing is based on observational research of the Muskrat Bluffs clientele and expert interviews conducted with key Muskrat Bluffs Inc. employees and fashion consultants. The following table contains the list of products and prices available from Muskrat Bluffs Apparel.

	Production cost	Wholesale markup	Wholesale price	Retail markup	Retail price
Men's clothing					
Polo shirt	$16.50	50%	$ 33.00	56%	$ 75
Camp shirt	$24.20	50%	$ 48.40	56%	$110
Button collar short	$17.60	50%	$ 35.20	56%	$ 80
Button collar long	$19.80	50%	$ 39.60	56%	$ 90
Pocket-T	$ 7.70	50%	$ 15.40	56%	$ 35
Band collar	$17.60	50%	$ 35.20	56%	$ 80
Shorts	$12.10	50%	$ 24.20	56%	$ 55
Slacks	$16.50	50%	$ 33.00	56%	$ 75
Board shorts	$12.10	50%	$ 24.20	56%	$ 55
Swimsuits	$11.00	50%	$ 22.00	56%	$ 50
Women's clothing					
Polo shirt	$16.50	50%	$ 33.00	56%	$ 75
Fitted T-Shirt	$14.30	50%	$ 28.60	56%	$ 65
Tank	$13.20	50%	$ 26.40	56%	$ 60
Summer dresses	$27.50	50%	$ 55.00	56%	$125
Shorts	$12.10	50%	$ 24.20	56%	$ 55
Jogging suit	$24.20	50%	$ 48.40	56%	$110
Capri pants	$13.20	50%	$ 26.40	56%	$ 60
Slacks	$13.20	50%	$ 26.40	56%	$ 60
Cover-ups	$15.40	50%	$ 30.80	56%	$ 70
Swimsuits			$ 52.80	56%	$120
Misc. items					
Towels	$ 6.60	50%	$ 13.20	56%	$ 30
Robes	$18.70	50%	$ 37.40	56%	$ 85
Beach bags	$16.50	50%	$ 33.00	56%	$ 75
Belts	$11.00	50%	$ 22.00	56%	$ 50
Sandals			$ 13.20	56%	$ 30
Maui Jim sunglasses			$110.00	56%	$250

The quality of fabric is a distinguishing characteristic of clothing, so Muskrat Bluffs will use the highest quality fabrics with bright, fun colors and designs to reflect the customers' demands for high quality and unique resort wear and casual lifestyle clothing. Every article of clothing will display the Muskrat Bluffs logo which serves as a reminder of guests' experiences at the Resort and Yacht Club at Muskrat Bluffs and the Muskrat Bluffs, as well as an expression of high quality casual wear that reflects enjoying the good life.

The following product descriptions and pictures display the basic design concepts and styles behind the products that Muskrat Bluffs Apparel will produce and market under its brand. Women's swim suits and sandals for men and women will not be designed or produced by Muskrat Bluffs Apparel but will be purchased for resale. Muskrat Bluffs Apparel will also retail Maui Jim sunglasses.

Men's Clothing

Short–sleeved polo shirt

1. Pique knit
2. Two–button placket
3. Ribbed polo collar
4. Open hem
5. Muskrat Bluffs logo accents the chest
6. Machine washable
7. Cotton/polyester

Camp Shirt

1. Short–sleeved
2. Pajama collar
3. Button–front
4. Straight hem with side slits
5. Muskrat Bluffs logo accents the chest
6. Machine washable
7. Silk/cotton

Button–front short–sleeved shirt with collar

1. Button–down collar
2. Chest pocket with Muskrat Bluffs logo
3. Double back pleats
4. Slightly curved shirttails
5. Machine washable
6. Cotton/linen

Button–front long–sleeved shirt with collar

1. Chest pocket with Muskrat Bluffs logo
2. Point collar
3. Adjustable barrel cuffs
4. Double back pleats

5. Slightly curved shirttails
6. Machine washable
7. Cotton/linen

Pocket T–shirt

1. Crewneck
2. Chest pocket with Muskrat Bluffs logo
3. Machine washable
4. Cotton

Band collar shirt

1. Short–sleeved
2. Button–front
3. Chest pocket with Muskrat Bluffs logo
4. Double back pleats
5. Slightly curved shirttails
6. Machine washable
7. Cotton/silk

Shorts

1. Zip fly with button closure
2. Front slant pockets; back button pockets
3. Flat front
4. Belt loops
5. Approximate inseam: 9″
6. Machine washable
7. Cotton/silk

Slacks

1. Zip fly with button closure
2. Front slant pockets; back button pockets
3. Flat front
4. Belt loops
5. Machine washable
6. Cotton/silk

Board shorts

1. Velcro fly
2. Side pockets; single back patch pocket with Velcro flap
3. Drawstring and elastic waist

4. Machine washable
5. Cotton/polyester/nylon

Swim suits

1. Drawstring and elastic waist
2. Side pockets; single back patch pocket with Velcro flap
3. Mesh lining
4. Machine washable
5. Cotton/polyester/nylon

Women's Clothing

Short–sleeved polo shirt

1. Breathable stretch cotton mesh, mercerized for added luster
2. Two–button placket
3. Ribbed polo collar and armbands
4. Even–vented hem with inner grosgrain taping
5. Muskrat Bluffs logo accents the chest
6. Machine washable
7. Cotton/elastane

Fitted T–shirt

1. Crewneck
2. Muskrat Bluffs logo accents the chest
3. Machine washable
4. Cotton

Tank

1. Scooped neckline
2. Muskrat Bluffs logo accents the chest
3. Machine washable
4. Cotton/spandex

Summer dresses

1. Slips on over the head
2. Form–fitting at bust; easy–fitting at hip
3. Machine washable
4. Cotton

Shorts

1. Sailor short style
2. Zip fly with hook–and–bar closure
3. Front slant pockets; back besom pockets

4. Belt loops
5. Approximate inseam: 7″
6. Machine washable
7. Cotton/spandex

Jogging suit

1. Soft hoody jacket with full zip front and drawstring hood
2. Soft, stretchy pants with drawstring waist and straight legs
3. Muskrat Bluffs logo accents the chest of jacket
4. Machine washable
5. Cotton/nylon/spandex

Capri pants

1. Zip fly with button closure
2. Front slant pockets; back besom pockets
3. Belt loops
4. Machine washable
5. Cotton/spandex

Slacks

1. Zip fly with hook–and–eye closure
2. Flat–front style
3. Front slant pockets; back besom pockets
4. Belt loops
5. Machine washable
6. Cotton/spandex

Cover–ups

1. Sleeveless dress
2. Two–way zipper in front
3. Slit pockets
4. Slits at hem
5. Muskrat Bluffs logo accents the chest
6. Machine washable
7. Cotton

Miscellaneous Items

Towels

1. 6.5′ by 3′
2. Displays Muskrat Bluffs logo
3. Machine washable
4. Cotton

Robes

1. Kimono style robe
2. Unisex
3. Two large pockets at hip
4. Muskrat Bluffs logo accents the chest
5. Machine washable
6. Cotton

Beach bags

1. Solid–colored webbed straps
2. Striped terry toweling
3. Muskrat Bluffs logo
4. Snap tab closure
5. Interior zip and wall pockets
6. Cotton/terylene

Belts

1. Casual style
2. Men's and women's
3. Black and brown
4. Nickel buckle
5. Leather

OPERATIONS

Muskrat Bluffs Apparel will utilize an outside fashion consultant who is familiar with the Muskrat Bluffs style and brand to assist in product development and to monitor fashion trends. After an extensive search, Muskrat Bluff Apparel's products will be designed and manufactured by Toggles, which is a private label clothing manufacturer located in Racine, Wisconsin. Toggles will design the pattern for each article of clothing, assist in procuring the fabric, manufacture the clothing, place the Muskrat Bluff logo and tag on each piece, and ship them to Muskrat Bluffs. Please, refer to the appendix for a list of selection criteria and other private label contractors that were considered.

Using Toggles will allow Muskrat Bluffs Apparel to take advantage of the experience and production capabilities of an established clothing manufacturer without the large initial investment and overhead expenses. This enables Muskrat Bluffs Apparel to focus its experience and resources on marketing and sales.

The minimum run for each clothing design is 300 pieces. This includes three different fabric choices and four different sizes for each run (S, M, L, XL).

Muskrat Bluffs management and its outside fashion consultant will be traveling to Toggles in the fall of 2007 for a four hour consultation to have a template made for each design of clothing and to choose the fabrics. With the advice and expertise of Toggles and the Muskrat Bluffs consultant, we will determine all of the final specifications for each product. Then Toggles can begin production and ship the clothes to Muskrat Bluffs in Lake Tahoe by March of 2008.

According to Toggles, the costs involved with Muskrat Bluffs Apparel's products include fabric, labor, trim, labels, and shipping. Please refer to the appropriate table for unit costs of each product.

Based on industry norms and analysis, Muskrat Bluffs Apparel charges a wholesale price that provides the company with a 50 percent markup on all items. The retail price for Muskrat Bluffs Apparel allows retailers to achieve a markup of 56 percent on all items. Muskrat Bluffs' prices are competitive, yet reflective of its quality. This pricing strategy enables the company to differentiate itself from its direct competitors. For a list of prices for each item, refer to the appropriate table.

MARKET ANALYSIS

Lake Tahoe is comprised of a four–county area including Placer County, Nevada County, El Dorado County, and Douglas County. Total population of the four–county area is 163,259. Total apparel store sales in Lake Tahoe for 2005 was $159,659,000 and total apparel store sales in all of California for 2005 was $2,898,417,000. Total disposable income in California for 2005 was $114,511,668,000.

The following table contains pertinent demographic information about the four counties that make up Lake Tahoe.

	Camden County	Miller County	Pulaski County	Morgan County	Laclede County
Population	39,432	24,712	44,187	20,436	34,492
Persons age 18–64	61.6%	61.4%	66.9%	57.7%	61%
Households	15,779	9,284	13,433	7,850	12,760
Median household income	$36,802	$31,293	$37,681	$31,084	$31,488

SOURCE: U.S. Census Bureau

According to the Lake Tahoe Convention and Visitors Bureau, Lake Tahoe attracts 5 million visitors per year with a majority visiting between Memorial Day and Labor Day. The majority of visitors travel from Nevada, Oregon, and Washington.

	Missouri	Illinois	Kansas	USA
Population	5,800,310	12,763,371	2,744,687	301,595,197
Persons age 18–64	62.9%	62.6%	62.4%	62.8%
Females/Males	51.1%/48.9%	50.9%/49.1%	50.3%/49.7%	50.7%/49.3%
Households	2,194,594	4,591,779	1,037,891	105,480,101
Median household income	$40,870	$47,367	$43,113	$43,318

SOURCE: U.S. Census Bureau

Customers

At the Resort and Yacht Club at Muskrat Bluffs, Muskrat Bluffs Apparel will segment its customers into three groups: Resort Guests, Muskrat Bluffs Patrons, and Yacht Club Guests.The following table and chart covers the number of potential customers from the Resort and Yacht Club at Muskrat Bluffs and the Muskrat Bluffs Entertainment Complex.

Potential customers	Growth	Year 1	Year 2	Year 3	Year 4	Year 5	CAGR
Resort guests	10%	55,042	60,546	66,601	73,261	144,298	27.25%
Horny Toad patrons	10%	180,000	198,000	217,800	239,580	360,000	18.92%
Yacht Club guests	10%	20,000	22,000	24,200	26,620	40,000	18.92%
Total		**255,042**	**280,546**	**308,601**	**339,461**	**544,298**	**20.87%**

Target customers at Toad Cove

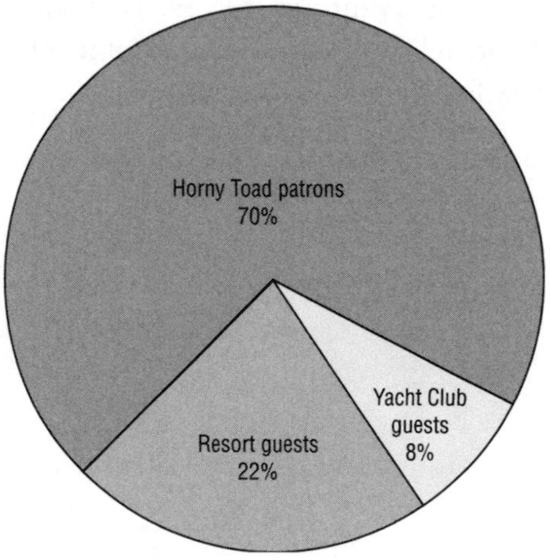

Resort Guests

Muskrat Bluffs Apparel's primary target customers are the guests of the Resort at Muskrat Bluffs because the Muskrat Bluffs Apparel Shop will be located in the resort's lobby.

Muskrat Bluffs Apparel will target Resort at Muskrat Bluffs guests because the room prices are on the high–end of resorts in Lake Tahoe. These high room prices (average is $250/night) are an indicator of customers with high discretionary incomes who are willing and able to purchase high quality clothing at premium prices.

Resort at Muskrat Bluffs guests are not only willing and able to purchase high quality clothing, but they desire it because it is an expression of themselves. Most of the guests will be from Nevada, Washington, and Oregon. The average age range will be between 35 to 65 with a college education.

Muskrat Bluffs Entertainment Complex Patrons

Muskrat Bluffs Apparel will also target Entertainment Complex patrons. Entertainment Complex patrons can be divided into three groups based on what level of the Complex they choose to frequent: Stage Level, Nightclub Level, and Restaurant Level.

Stage Level patrons can be described as baby boomers and empty nesters with high discretionary incomes and a fun–loving attitude. These baby boomers and empty nesters are the primary clientele at the Complex.

Nightclub Level patrons are typically customers between the ages of 21–34 with a fun–loving attitude and a willingness to spoil themselves while enjoying the Entertainment Complex.

Restaurant Level patrons are a combination of the Stage and Nightclub Level patrons. Customers are of all ages and may included families. Once again, the baby boomers and empty nesters are the primary clientele at the Entertainment Complex.

The Muskrat Bluffs Apparel Shop will be located next to the entrance of the Muskrat Bluffs on the Restaurant Level. Customers typically experience dinner waits during the summer season which causes them to explore the entire Muskrat Bluffs facility because many of the patrons are not necessarily guests of the adjacent Resort and Yacht Club at Muskrat Bluffs. This is an optimal time to entice these customers to shop at Muskrat Bluffs. Many of these customers have high discretionary incomes, a willingness to spend money because they are on vacation, and a desire to purchase a high quality piece that reminds them of their experiences at the Muskrat Bluffs.

Yacht Club Guests

Yacht Club at Muskrat Bluffs guests are the third target customer group because these guests will be staying on the docks located in Muskrat Bluffs.

The Yacht Club guests are similar to the Resort at Muskrat Bluffs guests in that they have high discretionary incomes, a willingness to spend money while on vacation, and a desire for high quality clothing. The age range for these customers is 40–65. Many will be baby boomers and empty nesters. These customers spend a large amount of time on their boats, but they will frequently be visiting the Resort at Muskrat Bluffs and the Muskrat Bluffs Entertainment Complex for meals and entertainment.

BUSINESS STRATEGY

As previously stated in the Market and Demographic Analysis, total apparel store sales in Lake Tahoe for 2005 was $159,659,000 and total apparel store sales in all of California for 2005 was $2,898,417,000. Total disposable income in California for 2005 was $114,511,668,000. Lake Tahoe is predominantly a tourist location, which welcomes 5 million visitors per year. Most visitors vacation to Lake Tahoe between Memorial Day and Labor Day.

The apparel industry consists of three core sectors: designers or jobbers, manufacturers, and retailers. Designers or jobbers develop apparel items by purchasing materials, designing concepts, developing prototypes, and hiring manufacturers. Manufacturers mass produce the apparel items based on the samples created by the designers. Retailers market the clothing to the public.

A variety of relationships and arrangements may exist between these three sectors. For example, a designer may produce only clothing concepts and prototypes and then contract manufacturers to mass produce them. The designer might sell its products directly to a number of retailers. On the other hand, a designer might not only produce concepts and prototypes but also operate a retail or direct marketing business and therefore outsource only the manufacturing. Muskrat Bluffs Apparel resembles a combination of designer and retailer. Toggles, Muskrat Bluffs' private label contractor, is considered a manufacturer. Large companies may include divisions corresponding to all three of these sectors.

Muskrat Bluffs Apparel is sensitive to foreign production's effect on manufacturing costs. However, at this time it is too risky for the company to begin producing abroad because it is a highly complex environment that offers little recourse if the company is wronged. Muskrat Bluffs Apparel would prefer a manufacturer located in the United States.

However, it is important to note that the apparel industry is becoming increasingly global with many United States companies outsourcing manufacturing to low–cost countries such as China, Mexico, India, Vietnam, Turkey, and Singapore. Globalization will continue as trade barriers continue to be reduced and eliminated. Some analysts predict China to become the largest exporter of clothing to the United States. However, others believe that Central and South American countries will outpace China due to their close proximity to the United States. Fred Abernathy and David Weil wrote in the *Washington Post*, "Costs remain a driving factor, but the proximity advantage will grow even greater in a post–quota world as retailers raise the bar ever higher on the responsiveness and flexibility required of their suppliers."

Another major trend in the apparel industry is a recent change in consumer preferences in developed countries such as the United States. In the past, consumers purchased apparel based on the lowest price or a particular brand. Recently, consumers are demanding value and quality instead. Muskrat Bluffs Apparel's pricing strategy and emphasis on quality reflects this change in customer preferences.

Specific information on the resort wear and casual lifestyle markets is limited. However, resort wear and causal lifestyle clothing has become a year–round fashion style and competes in the menswear and womenswear markets. Thus, it is important to examine the size, growth, and leading revenue sources of the United States menswear and womenswear markets.

Menswear

By 2009, the menswear market is forecasted to reach a value of $112 billion. The compounded annual growth rate is 2.6 percent during the 2004–2009 period. Below are the forecasted values for the United States menswear market from the Business and Company Resource Center database:

Year	Value	Growth
2007	$105.8 billion	2.50%
2008	$108.8 billion	2.80%
2009	$112 billion	2.90%

In the United States, trousers are the leading revenue source and are followed by shirts. The following chart is a break–down of the United States menswear market:

United States menswear market

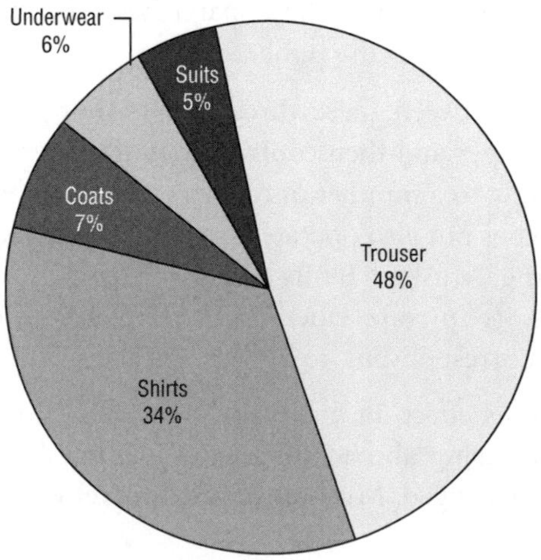

Womenswear

The womenswear market is forecasted to reach a value of $191.6 billion by 2010 with a compounded annual growth rate of 2.6 percent for the 2005–2010 period. The following table contains the forecasted values for the United States womenswear market:

Year	Value	Growth
2007	$176.3 billion	2.40%
2008	$181.2 billion	2.70%
2009	$186.2 billion	2.80%
2010	$191.6 billion	2.90%

The dress, skirt, and trouser category comprises the largest revenue generating source followed by the blouse and top category. The following is a break–down of the United States womenswear market:

United States womenswear market

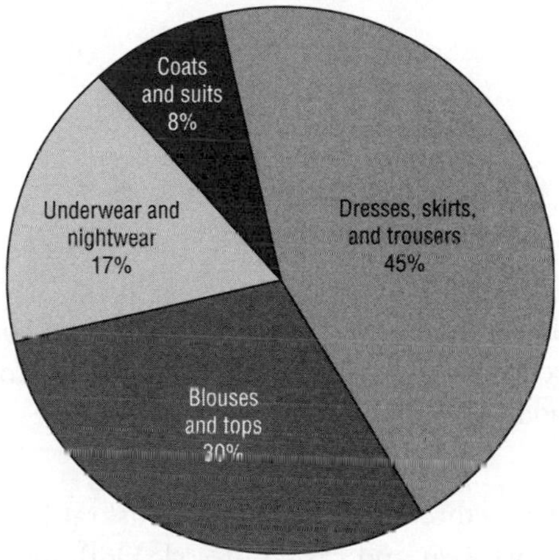

COMPETITION

The apparel business is a highly competitive industry, which contains a mix of global and regional competitors. Muskrat Bluffs Apparel's competition can be divided into two main categories: Direct Competitors and Indirect Competitors.

Direct Competitors

ResortWear Originals started in 2000 with the goal to create a brand that celebrates the American experience. ResortWear Originals specializes in resort wear and casual lifestyle clothing for the stylish male who wants his clothing to tell his story. The collections include camp shirts, polo shirts, T–shirts, sweaters, khakis, jeans, jackets, sport coats, dress shirts, belts, and swim suits. The centerpiece of the collections is ResortWear's signature line of limited edition embroidered shirts.

Some basic ResortWear pricing:

- Signature shirts = $150 to $175
- Camp shirts = $95 to $150

- Polo shirts = $75 to $105
- T–shirts = $60
- Shorts = $80 to $90

ResortWear Originals is currently sold at the BeachCove Resort in Lake Tahoe, where Muskrat Bluffs Apparel is starting. Also, boutiques, online retailers, and large brick–and–mortar retailers such as Nordstrom and Saks Fifth Avenue carry Muskrat Bluffs in the United States and the Caribbean.

Natty Gentleman began in 1996 when a group of college students wanted to express their love for the beach through a line of resort wear. At first, they experienced trouble finding retailers to sell their clothes so they started their own restaurant. The Natty Gentleman's Cafe served as an outlet to sell directly to customers and as a marketing tool to assist in selling to clothing stores.

Natty Gentleman's brand is built around a life of relaxation and long weekends. Every decision is approached with the question of "What would a nattily dressed gentleman do?" and the company prides itself on using only the finest materials and having unique fabric designs. Natty Gentleman is the premier name in resort wear.

Some basic Natty Gentleman pricing:

Men's clothing	Women's clothing
Camp shirt = $90 to $140	Dresses = $98 to $178
T-shirt = $32 to $40	Tank = $48 to $64
Polo shirt = $72 to $125	Polo shirt = $68 to $88
Shorts = $72 to $85	Shorts = $78 to $98
Pants = $90 to $125	Pants = $89 to $145

Natty Gentleman also sells a line of accessories including watches, ties, belts, footwear, and cologne as well as a line of furniture. The company's products are available at boutiques, department stores, and online retailers throughout the United States, Canada, and Dubai. In the Lake Tahoe area, the BeachCove Resort sells Natty Gentleman products.

ResortWear Originals and Natty Gentleman are not the only direct competitors of Muskrat Bluffs. They are simply the most pertinent because they both sell resort wear and casual lifestyle clothing and both have a presence in Lake Tahoe, which is where Muskrat Bluffs Apparel is starting. Other direct competitors include:

- ShipShore Apparel—Located in Maine, ShipShore Apparel specializes in men's resort wear and categorizes its clothing as Dock–to–Dine Apparel. It is made for going from a day of fishing in New England to enjoying an upscale dinner without having to change. The company has been in operation for almost two years and has only local distribution. The company claims that the hardest part of selling clothing and building a brand is having a highly–trafficked and unique place to begin selling. Muskrat Bluffs Apparel has such a location.
- Coastline Clothes—Located in New Orleans, Coastline Clothes produces casual wear for men, women, and children. The company started in 1995 by selling ties inspired by the French Quarter. Currently, the company offers a full range of clothing and accessories that express the inspiration of the Bayou. Coastline Clothes sells through four company–owned stores located in Louisiana and its website.

Indirect Competitors

Muskrat Bluffs Apparel will compete with a diverse group of companies. The first type of indirect competitors are the more general clothing companies such as Levi Strauss & Co., VF Corporation, Ralph Lauren, and J. Crew to name a few. These industry leaders have grown over the years and are now well–established. They have production and distribution throughout the world and own some of the largest brands in clothing.

Our indirect competitors also include the stores in Lake Tahoe because Lake Tahoe is the site of Muskrat Bluffs Apparel's first shop. The area is home to a 110–store outlet mall, which includes outlet stores of the above mentioned large general clothing companies. In addition to the outlet mall there are a handful of T–shirt shops that sell low–priced Lake Tahoe souvenir shirts.

Muskrat Bluffs Apparel's competition comes in many shapes and sizes. It includes direct competitors in the resort wear and casual lifestyle market, indirect competitors such as large global clothing brands, and mom–and–pop souvenir T–shirt shops.

The competitors mentioned in this analysis are by no means an exhaustive list. They simply serve as a glimpse of Muskrat Bluffs' competitive environment and prove the viability of the market. Researching the competition will be an ongoing process for Muskrat Bluffs Apparel because the company has the opportunity to learn from what other designers are showing and because new competitors may enter at any time. The importance of tracking the competition will grow in the future as Muskrat Bluffs products are made available outside of the Lake Tahoe area.

ORGANIZATION

Strengths

- Location to sell in high–traffic area of a high–end resort destination
- Captured audience from the Resort and Yacht Club at Muskrat Bluffs and the Muskrat Bluffs Entertainment Complex
- Experience in marketing to clientele of the Lake Tahoe area
- Experience in retail
- Recognizable brand in the Lake Tahoe and throughout Nevada, California, Washington, Oregon
- Connections to celebrities from Lake Tahoe area

Risk Factors

- Lack of experience in fashion design and clothing manufacturing
- Little brand recognition outside of the Lake Tahoe area
- Low sales volume in Lake Tahoe outside of summer season
- Numerous competitors ranging from multinational corporations to local start–ups
- Retailers not willing to sell Muskrat Bluffs Apparel
- Changes in fashion and consumer preferences and failure to adapt

Growth Strategy

- Expansion plan of Muskrat Bluffs Entertainment Complex and Resort and Yacht Club at Muskrat Bluffs to five locations in resort destinations throughout the United States and Mexico in the next ten years
- Growing popularity of resort wear and casual lifestyle clothing
- Potential to grow beyond regional resort wear and casual lifestyle company to a national company

- Occasions to place Muskrat Bluffs Apparel in the hands of national touring bands that are brought to the Muskrat Bluffs Entertainment Complex for the "Outdoor Concerts at Muskrat Bluffs"

MARKETING & SALES

Exposure

One of the hardest parts of selling clothing and building a brand is having a highly–trafficked and unique place to begin selling. Muskrat Bluffs Apparel has this problem solved through its location inside the Resort and Yacht Club at Muskrat Bluffs, which is the company's main competitive edge because it provides an initial selling point with high foot traffic, affluent customers, and events such as concerts that attract celebrities and publicity. We have the opportunity to bring our brand and image to life. Customers can feel what Muskrat Bluffs Apparel expresses through their experiences at the resort. Since this location is in a resort, we can invite boutique owners and buyers to stay at the resort as our guests and use the location as a live sales tool for the purpose of selling to outside retailers. This is similar to the strategy that was employed by ResortWear Originals.

The Resort and Yacht Club at Muskrat Bluffs and the Muskrat Bluffs Entertainment Complex will be expanding throughout the United States and Mexico and Muskrat Bluffs Apparel has the opportunity to be the exclusive resort wear and casual lifestyle clothing in all future locations. This competitive edge provides Muskrat Bluffs with new locations to sell its products and the ability to gain exposure in new markets and find additional retailers to supply.

Muskrat Bluffs Apparel will establish its retail locations in the high–traffic area of the Resort and Yacht Club at Muskrat Bluffs and the Muskrat Bluffs Entertainment Complex, which welcomes around 250,000 customers per year. The marketing strategy will focus on the customers inside this resort because these customers are a captured audience who are on vacation and willing to indulge themselves. Also, it will begin to build awareness of Muskrat Bluffs Apparel outside Lake Tahoe. The goal of the marketing strategy is to build an image of enjoying the good life and to entice customers to visit the Muskrat Bluffs Apparel Shop. The marketing strategy will be accomplished through the following methods:

1. **Grand Opening.** Muskrat Bluffs Apparel will host a grand opening celebration in conjunction with the opening of the Resort and Yacht Club at Muskrat Bluffs. First adopters, high–profile executives, and sports stars from Nevada and California will be in attendance. The grand opening is an occasion for publicity throughout California and the bordering states. Muskrat Bluffs Apparel will build its image of enjoying the good life by having the opportunity to debut its line and put it in the hands of the influencers of fashion in Lake Tahoe, Nevada, and California.
2. **"Outdoor Concerts at Muskrat Bluffs".** Muskrat Bluffs Apparel will benefit from the "Outdoor Concerts at Muskrat Bluffs" held at the Muskrat Bluffs Entertainment Complex, which has hosted such national entertainers as Neil Diamond, Johnny Cash, and Rush. The concerts provide an influx of customers and many explore the complex while enjoying the entertainment. The events help Muskrat Bluffs Apparel build awareness with its target customer groups and from geographic locations outside the Lake Tahoe area. We can express our image of enjoying the good life through associating ourselves with the customers' concert experiences. We will promote the resort wear and casual lifestyle clothing on stage throughout the concerts and will provide pieces of Muskrat Bluffs Apparel to the entertainers in order to put the clothing in the hands of highly–visible individuals who perform throughout the country. Providing our products to national performers assists us in marketing to resort and Muskrat Bluffs guests as well as to new potential customers outside of Lake Tahoe.

3. **Banners and Signs.** Muskrat Bluffs Apparel banners and signs will be prominently displayed throughout the Resort and Yacht Club at Muskrat Bluffs and the Entertainment Complex. The goal of these banners and signs is to build the Muskrat Bluffs Apparel image of enjoying the good life, keep this image and the Muskrat Bluffs name in front of customers, build a connection between Muskrat Bluffs Apparel and the customers' experiences at the Resort and Yacht Club at Muskrat Bluffs and the Muskrat Bluffs, and direct customers to our retail location. Based on Muskrat Bluffs' target customer groups, the banners and signs will be tailored to their audience based on where they are located in the complex: Stage Level, Nightclub Level, or Restaurant Level.

4. **Menu Inserts.** The menu of the Muskrat Bluffs restaurant contains the story of the owner and provides information on other properties that he is developing. Customers are frequently seen reading the story and information during their waits for tables and once they are seated. Muskrat Bluffs Apparel will place an insert in the Muskrat Bluffs menus because this provides exposure to both resort guests and those just visiting the Muskrat Bluffs property. The menu inserts have the same goals as the signs and banners: to build the Muskrat Bluffs Apparel image of enjoying the good life, to keep this image and the Muskrat Bluffs name in front of customers, to build a connection between Muskrat Bluffs Apparel and the customers' experiences at the Resort and Yacht Club at Muskrat Bluffs and the Entertainment Complex, and direct customers to our retail location.

5. **Retail Location and Experience.** Muskrat Bluffs' retail location will enable it to be viewed by the thousands of visitors to the Resort and Yacht Club at Muskrat Bluffs and the Entertainment Complex, so it is vital that the store front is eye–catching and is in line with our vision of being an expression of the good life. The customers' experience inside the Muskrat Bluffs Apparel Shop is our number one priority because this is an opportunity to build our image as well as convert our large captured audience into customers. The store and staff's actions will express the vision, mission, quality, and uniqueness of Muskrat Bluffs Apparel.

6. **Word–of–Mouth.** Word–of–mouth marketing is one of the most effective marketing strategies for a company because it is customers sharing their experiences with Muskrat Bluffs Apparel to other customers. The grand opening, the "Outdoor Concerts at Muskrat Bluffs" and the retail location and experience will establish a solid foundation for positive word–of–mouth, which will carry Muskrat Bluffs Apparel's marketing messages beyond the Lake Tahoe area because guests visit the resort from throughout the United States.

7. **Bluffs Magazine.** *Bluffs Magazine* is a publication about enjoying the good life while at Lake Tahoe. It is freely distributed throughout Lake Tahoe and at boat shows throughout the United States. The free distribution serves as another marketing medium to guests of the resort and exposes Muskrat Bluffs Apparel to potential customers outside of Lake Tahoe because guests come from outside the area and the boat shows are located throughout the United States. 30,000 copies are distributed annually and Muskrat Bluffs Apparel will have a variety of ads.

Sales Strategy

Muskrat Bluffs Apparel's primary sales strategy is selling directly to customers in the Muskrat Bluffs Apparel Shop. Retail sales enable Muskrat Bluffs Apparel to interact with the customers and provide a memorable experience that will excite customers to tell others about the apparel.

The sales associates will be educated in the latest resort wear and casual lifestyle clothing trends and will provide fashion advice in a professional and courteous manner. The customers' experience is Muskrat Bluffs Apparel's number one priority because it affects our image, our word–of–mouth marketing, and is an expression of our vision and mission. Commissions for sales associates in Muskrat Bluffs Apparel Shops could lead to pushy salespeople that drive customers away, so the sales associates will not be paid on commission because Muskrat Bluffs' goal is not to force customers into buying products but to assist customers in their purchases and add to their overall experiences with Muskrat Bluffs Apparel.

Each sale is an opportunity to learn more about our customers, so we will begin to build a database of customers' home addresses and email addresses. We will keep customers' information private and will use it to learn where customers live and what the demographics of their hometowns are. Also, we will begin a direct marketing campaign by sending periodic e–newsletters with updates on Muskrat Bluffs Apparel and Lake Tahoe. As the Muskrat Bluffs collection grows we will begin to publish a catalog that will be mailed and e–mailed to customers.

Another aspect of Muskrat Bluffs Apparel's sales strategy is to sell clothing to special events, such as charitable golf outings and corporate retreats. These events typically provide event–goers with high quality, brand name shirts with the name of the event embroidered on them. Special events are an effective way to sell large quantities of clothing, purge extra inventory, and generate sales in the off season from October to April. At the same time, selling Muskrat Bluffs Apparel to these events provides exposure to new customers who are from outside the Lake Tahoe area. We will personally sell to special events occurring at Lake Tahoe and beyond.

In the third year of operation, Muskrat Bluffs Apparel will begin selling at clothing trade shows. Trade shows are an effective way to present Muskrat Bluffs products to a large number of interested buyers from a wide range of retail operations. Many buyers attend these trade shows in order to discover new products and brands and to stock their stores. Muskrat Bluffs also benefits from the opportunities to build relationships with future retailers, gather sales leads, and to begin selling outside Lake Tahoe. Trade show sales will augment the direct sales from the Lake Tahoe Apparel Shops.

Timeline

The following table and chart display the major milestones for Muskrat Bluffs Apparel:

Milestones	Start Date	End Date
Design products	9/1/2007	12/31/2007
Manufacture products	1/1/2008	3/1/2008
Set up store and marketing materials	1/1/2008	3/31/2008
Grand opening	4/1/2008	5/1/2008
Begin selling at trade shows	4/1/2010	3/31/2011
Open second Toad Cove apparel shop	4/1/2012	3/31/2013

Milestones

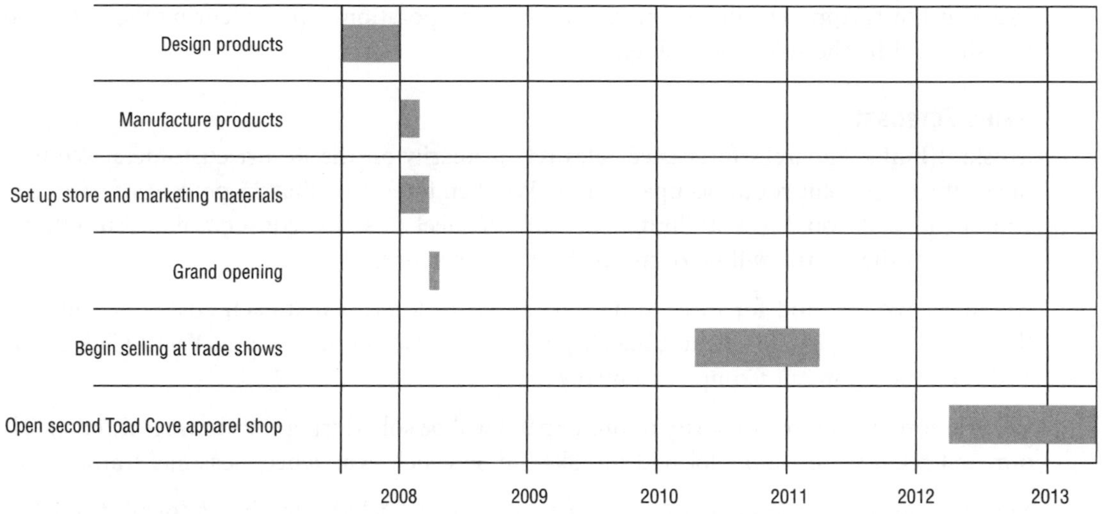

MANAGEMENT SUMMARY

Muskrat Bluffs Apparel will have one full–time general manager and one full–time assistant manager for each Muskrat Bluffs Apparel Shop. The managers will be responsible for handling the day–to–day operations, working in the Muskrat Bluffs Apparel Shop, and hiring and managing the seasonal help.

Four seasonal employees will be hired for twelve weeks between Memorial Day and Labor Day and will work part–time at a rate of $8 per hour. The seasonal employees will serve as sales associates in the Muskrat Bluffs Apparel Shop to assist with the large influx of customers in the summer season.

The executive management team of Muskrat Bluffs Apparel will include Louis Graham, Cheryl Stegman, and Steven Jones. The team will be responsible for:

- The strategic direction of Muskrat Bluffs Apparel.
- Working with outside fashion consultants to track trends and develop products.
- Managing the finances.
- Marketing.
- Attending trade shows.
- Selling to special events and outside retailers.
- Hiring and managing the general manager and assistant manager.

FINANCIAL ANALYSIS

Muskrat Bluffs Apparel is looking for an investor to secure a $500,000 line of credit for the company. At this time selection is limited to the owner of the Muskrat Bluffs Entertainment Complex.

$250,000 will be used to purchase initial inventory, supplies, and establish a cash balance for initial operating expenses. The remaining $250,000 will be available in the unforeseen event that Muskrat

Bluffs Apparel has no sales in Year 1. Based on current financial projections, the entire $250,000 utilized will be paid back by the end of Year 3.

Muskrat Bluffs Apparel will be a privately–held S corporation. Upon securing the line of credit the said investor will be the sole stockholder.

Sales Forecast

Muskrat Bluffs Apparel's forecasted sales rely primarily on the Resort customers. We forecasted these sales off a 65 percent room occupancy rate. We then forecasted that 25 percent of every room occupied will spend $100 on Muskrat Bluffs Apparel. We feel this is a conservative assumption because the majority of the rooms will be occupied by 1 to 4 persons.

An alternative method for forecasting our sales is to forecast that each customer will spend $100 and then capture 2.8 percent of the 250,000 people who visit the Resort and Yacht Club at Muskrat Bluffs and the Entertainment Complex annually.

We also foresee that the majority of our apparel will be sold during the summer months. This is because our first retail store will be located in Lake Tahoe which experiences seasonal traffic.

You will also find an appendix to our financials which includes the breakdown of our forecasted sales for each individual item we will be selling.

Muskrat Bluffs Apparel Shop's sales increase 7 percent each year, consisting of 3 percent inflation and 4 percent due to the effects of marketing and increased awareness.

In Year 3, we will expand from the Resort and Yacht Club at Muskrat Bluffs and the Entertainment Complex and start selling our products at trade shows. We will attend one trade show in Dallas, TX and one in Las Vegas, NV. The cost of reserving a booth at one of these trade shows is about $10,000. The expenses incurred at trade shows will be covered by our advertising and travel budgets. We are forecasting that we will be able to sell 50 percent of our Toad Muskrat Bluffs Apparel Shop sales.

In Year 4, we will continue to sell our products at trade shows and forecast matching our Muskrat Bluffs Apparel Shop sales.

In Year 5, we will be opening a second Muskrat Bluffs Apparel Shop which will double Muskrat Bluffs Apparel Shop sales. We will also continue selling at trade shows and forecast our sales to be one and a half times our Muskrat Bluffs Apparel Shop sales.

Inventory

We have set up our inventory system in a way in which we will make one order per year, unless we are running low on a specific item. The order will be made in late January/early February to ensure it will be ready for the summer. We have included enough extra inventory to ensure our store will be fully stocked through the winter and until we can receive our next year's order. The year end inventory may seem low because this represents the last day of the year. On the first day of the year you will notice a dramatic increase in inventory and it will continue to decrease until the first of the next year.

Rent Expense

Our rent expense includes all lease hold improvements for Muskrat Bluffs Apparel Shop and the initial cost of setting up a POS system. The store is 1,800 sq. ft. with an additional 300 sq. ft. store room. Additional storage is available if needed at no additional cost.

Miscellaneous Financial Information

- All sales, including credit card sales, are treated as cash sales and are the reason why there are no account receivables. We will use a cash basis except for inventory. At a later date we will switch to an accrual basis.

- Currently income at the end of each year is reinvested back into Muskrat Bluffs Apparel Inc.
- Income is currently assumed to be taxed at the rate of 40 percent.
- Our expenses will increase by 3 percent in Years 2–5 due to inflation and double in Year 5 due to the second store opening.
- Debt Service Coverage Ratio is figured with the following formula: (Revenue + Debt + Interest) / (Debt + Interest)

Line of Credit

- $500,000 revolving line of credit, 9 percent interest only, to be renewed every 12 months.
- $250,000 will be utilized.
- In the 1st Quarter of Year 2, $50,000 will be paid back.
- In the 4th Quarter of Year 2, $100,000 will be paid back.
- In the 3rd Quarter of Year 3, the remaining $100,000 will be paid back.

Veterinary Practice

FOUR LEGGED FRIENDS CLINIC

900 Timkin Rd.
Arlington Heights, IL 60005

Gerald Rekve

EXECUTIVE SUMMARY

Four Legged Friends Clinic (FLFC) is a new veterinary practice, in Arlington Heights, Illinois. FLFC will be distinguished from other veterinary practices by its focus on farm animals and house pet issues as well as expertise in alternative treatments.

It aims to be the first choice for farm animals and house pet owners in Arlington Heights that want the best for their farm animal or pet.

Veterinary care in the greater Chicago area is a $2,000,000 sized market and it's growing. Positioned as a good choice for Arlington Heights farm animals and pet owners, FLFC will offer owners care of older farm animals and house pets. These customers are likely to visit veterinarian more than once a year and make veterinary care decisions based on quality rather price. We will have promotional efforts set up to attract customers.

Company History

Born and raised in Arlington Heights, I studied veterinary at Northwestern University. After my education I worked for the college for two years, and then went off to work at a large local veterinarian in Chicago. Since this I noticed a need for more veterinary clinics in Arlington Heights. There were a couple of reasons. Over the past five years, there has been about a 36 percent increase in the number of farm animals in a 60 mile radius of Arlington Heights. In addition to this increase, the population of Arlington Heights has increased by 22 percent, therefore increasing the amount of potential pet owners. The final reason is that the existing vet clinics cannot keep up with the business.

Growth Strategy

Four Legged Friends Clinic will be profitable by the end first of its year. By the end of its third year, it will likely grow to include another veterinarian. I am currently investing $45,000 in start–up funding to supplement my father's $18,000 investment in the business. These additional funds will primarily be used to buy veterinary equipment.

Management Summary

Patricia Pugh: After working with a successful veterinary practice in Chicago, I decided to return to my hometown of Arlington Heights to establish a veterinary practice to serve the region's farm animals and house pet owners especially.

OBJECTIVES

Personal Objectives

- Re–establish myself in my hometown of Arlington Heights.
- Undertake the challenge of creating a profitable and respected practice.
- Achieve balance between my work and personal life, as I plan to have children in the next few years.
- Earn sufficient income to pay off my personal debt within two years.

Company's Short–Term Objectives

- Secure office and kennel space by September 2006.
- Obtain start–up financing of $100,000 by July 2006.
- Open for business by October 2006.
- Hire a technician and an assistant by October 2006.
- Have 200 active patients by the end of the first year.
- Volunteer with the local Zoo, in order to make contacts.
- Talk with the local newspaper, to see if they would print a weekly pets column that I write.
- Offer a pets tips series for the local radio station to play.
- Be profitable by the end of the first year.

Company's Long–Term Objectives

- Have 500 active patients by the end of the second year.
- Have 700 active patients by the end of the third year.
- Hire another veterinarian by the end of the fourth year.

Mission

Offer best service as well as conventional and non–traditional veterinary services in a way that stresses compassion, and quality–of–life for pets and owners.

SERVICES

General treatment for pets and farm animals, preventative vaccination, diagnosis, treatment, surgery and kennel facilities for domestic pets. The kennel portion of our business will be larger than traditional veterinarian offices. We will have a year round service open 7 days a week. This will allow for clients to drop off their pets for either a day or a week. We feel this kennel will add extra revenue to our office and allow for clients to become comfortable with us, while we build long term clients.

By focusing on farm animals and house pets, The Four Legged Friends Clinic will offer a variety of expertise, experience, and high–quality operation unmatched by other traditional veterinary clinics located in Arlington Heights. Also, no other area veterinarian has the well rounded training that we will offer to our clients.

MARKET ANALYSIS

Demographic Factors and Trends

- Dog pet population is in a slow down over the past few years, this however is being offset by higher growth in the number of farm animals & other household pets.
- Baby Boomers are getting older and tend to have more disposable income to spend on their pets, therefore we will see more visits by boomer clients with the money to spend.
- According to the Arlington Heights Economic Department, Arlington Heights has been the third fastest growing city in Illinois since 2005 and Arlington Heights has now over 125,000 residents.

Social Factors and Trends

- Pet owners are embracing veterinary service like preventative dental care.
- The city also now passed a bylaw stating all cats must be neutered and licensed. This has greatly increased the amount of cat neutering that is required.

Such products and services will probably be offered more if interest continues to increase.

Economic Factors and Trends

- The current economic hot market has positively affected market the for essential veterinary services
- The market for "non–traditional" veterinary product and services may grow even more quickly as the economy continues to grow.
- The Arlington Heights economy continues to grow while it shifts more toward oil and gas business.

Technological Factors and Trends

- New veterinary technologies are constantly emerging. Forinstance, using laser therapy to treat tissue disorders in small animals is gaining acceptance. As technologies continue to be designed, I anticipate upgrading my practice's equipment and skills.
- Many veterinarians are using practice management software to help run their businesses. We will want to invest in this specialized software.

Regulatory Factors and Trends

- Veterinarians in Canada must study for at least two years at a university, and then graduate from a 4–year program at an accredited college of veterinary medicine. To qualify for a provincial license, veterinarians must pass the North American Veterinary Licensing Exam.
- According to the American Veterinary Medical Association, American veterinary colleges only graduate 400 new veterinarians each year.

Environmental Factors and Trends

- Veterinary medicine involves handling chemicals that could potentially harm humans. Special steps must be taken in the administration, storage, and disposal of medicines, vaccine needles, and blood samples, resulting in additional costs.
- With the spread of West Nile and similar viruses, veterinarians today must adhere to strict guidelines for reporting any infection that is listed in the federal government database. These controls are in place for the betterment of humans as well as protection for the animals.

The Arlington Heights population and the Baby Boomers' disposable income are causing an increase in the amount of money spent on pet care in Arlington Heights that will probably continue to increase in the coming years. At this time, the number of veterinarians remains restricted by the number of veterinary colleges. As a result, the demand may exceed the supply, and practicing veterinarians will likely enjoy a steady rise in business. Specialty treatments like preventative dental care will become more popular and will represent significant sources of income for veterinarians.

Arlington Heights, Illinois demographic profile 2002

(Primary trade area)

July 1, 2002 Population (Primary): 62,129
% change 1996 > 2002: +7.07%
Average annual growth rate: 1.15%
Average household income: $51,133
Retail sales: 42% above national avg.
Average family income: $55,527.00
Per capita income: $20,497.00
Private households: 24,905
Family size: 3.0
Housing starts (2000): 413

Market Size

According to Research Inc., 24 percent of American households have at least one pet. Based on the most recent American census data, this suggests that about 45,000 pet owners live in the greater Arlington Heights area. The average pet owner spends about $230 per year on pet health care. As a result, the market for veterinary services in the Arlington Heights area is estimated to be over $5 million.

Competition

Goodland Animal Clinic:

- Strengths: Large staff (at least 12 full–time veterinarians); strong relationships with area kennels
- Weaknesses: Aging equipment and higher than average pricing

Arlington Heights Pet Palace:

- Strength: Reasonable prices
- Weaknesses: Young staff; small, crowded kennel facility

Lakefront Vet Clinic:

- Strength: In business in Arlington Heights since 1947
- Weaknesses: Limited parking; expensive vaccines

Windy City Clinic:

- Strengths: Excellent reputation for dog–specific care; services include preventative dental care; also sells dog food and other products
- Weaknesses: Higher than average pricing

CUSTOMERS

At FLFC, my primary target customers are farm animals and house pet owners, specifically owners of older farm animals and house pets. Owners of older farm animals and house pets tend to:

- Visit the veterinarian more than once a year, due to the age of their pet.
- Make veterinary care decisions based on quality of care, rather than on price.
- Encounter more pet health problems that can be treated using alternative methods, in conjunction with conventional treatment.

These customers will choose FLFC because as their farm animals and house pet's age, my clinic can offer an unparalleled range of animal–focused expertise in treating both the common and rare ailments that afflict farm animals and house pets.

Sales & Mark Position

FLFC Client Benefits

- The sense of community and the comfort that comes with using a veterinarian that specializes in treating the species they love.
- The exclusivity that comes with knowing that their pet is being cared for by the only veterinarian in the area with alternative pet care expertise.
- The security that comes with knowing that everything is being done to prolong and improve the quality of their pets' lives.

BUSINESS STRATEGY

Customers will be required to pay immediately by cash, check, debit card, VISA or MasterCard.

Except in the case of checkups, farm animals & house pet owners will receive follow–up calls from my assistant within 24 hours after their appointment, to check on their pet's well–being. Premises permitting, kennel facilities will also be offered. Existing customers will be able to leave healthy pets in the overnight facility for a small fee.

As the Veterinarian and owner of FLFC, I will be responsible for running the business and providing veterinary care to customers' pets.

Advertising

Planned promotional efforts are in keeping with the American Veterinary Medical Association Advertising Guidelines.

- A free workshop for farm animals and house pets owners in "Feline Health and Happiness" to be conducted at a busy local bookstore, Professor's Books, several weeks before the opening of the practice. Attendees' names will be collected, and I will send them an announcement of the practice's opening.
- A listing in the Yellow Pages.
- Meetings with area veterinarians, to build relationships and channels for referrals.
- An article about the practice in the Lifestyles section of Arlington Heights' local newspaper.
- Birthday cards sent to customers' pets.

New clients will either be referred by other veterinarians and pet businesses, or they will choose my practice based on promotional efforts. All services will be rendered in FLFC offices.

Alliances

Our business and strategic alliances include:

- Grooming Gods is a high–end grooming company
- Arlington Animal Hospital, which has agreed to help offer me 2–hour on–call veterinary service clinic, will be the only "Approved Referral"

When I'm away from my practice for short periods of time, Dr. Alfred Benito at the Arlington Animal Hospital has agreed to care for my patients.

Operations

1. Premises: I am buying a free–standing building close to major streets, in residential neighborhoods that are appropriately zoned and can be easily converted into a veterinary practice and kennel space. To maximize exposure to the under–served community, I am specifically looking in neighborhoods. Cost: $1,500–$ 2,500 per month, paid for initially from the $30,000 equity investment I've made from the business.
2. Renovation of space: I expect I will have to convert the premises into a more suitable veterinary practice. Cost: Approximately $15,000, including furniture
3. Veterinary start–up package: I will order this package from Animal Supplies Inc. It includes digital walk–on scale, treatment tub, hydraulic table, machine, feline spay pack, x–ray machine, film and supplies, a blood chemistry unit, used kennel cages, and other equipment. Cost: Approximately $ 48,000, financing required.
4. Computer hardware and software: To manage the practice's front office, I intend to buy a computer from Computer Associates and management software from Veterinary PDM Inc.

I am seeking $65,000 in bank loans to finance the purchase of veterinary equipment.

Risk Factors

I already have life and disability insurance and need to obtain critical illness insurance. My employees will be covered by workers' compensation insurance.

I have a will. While I don't have anybody in mind to take over my practice if I become unable to work, I have given my parents' contact information for competitors who would be potential buyers if something should happen to me.

If my supplier fails to deliver a shipment, suddenly raises its prices, or goes for business out of town, I have established a relationship with a back–up supplier of animal and house pets equipment in Chicago.

If I am unable to find a full–time assistant with practice experience, I will consider part–timers with only administrative experience.

If I need legal advice, I will retain the services of Robert Smith, a partner at the law firm of Smith and Smith Law Firm and one of the leading law firms in Arlington Heights. I will arrange a small line of credit or overdraft protection to cover any unforeseen expenses or to accommodate slow payment by a client.

Management Summary

Advisors

- Fred Brown, a chartered accountant
- Cindy Blum, Manager of a consulting firm

Administrative Assistant

- Responsibilities: Making appointments, ordering supplies, managing files, processing bills and payment, other clerical duties
- Required experience: At least three years of employment at another veterinarian clinic or health care practice.
- Salary: $21,000
- Start date: February 2007

Veterinary Technician

- Responsibilities: Assisting with physical examinations, surgery, immunizations, extracting teeth, and caring for in the farm animals and house pets' kennels
- Required experience: A Veterinary Technician or Health Technician diploma from a nationally–recognized college, plus at least four years working with companion animals (preferably farm animals and house pets) at another veterinarian practice
- Start date: February 2007

Through referrals, I already have leads on a number of qualified candidates for both positions.

I will also use the following methods to acquire potential employees:

- Place want ads in the Arlington Heights shopper
- Post listings at online job sites
- Contact employment agencies.

Staff training will be ongoing.

By the end of my third year of operation, I expect to hire a second veterinarian to grow the clinic and give me more flexibility to be away from the clinic when necessary. The new hire's areas of expertise will depend upon the needs of the practice at that time, but I expect to pay them around $55,000 per year.

PRODUCTS & SERVICES

Services

In general, FLFC's prices for conventional diagnostics and treatment will be relatively high, in line with its exclusive positioning. Here are the clinic's intended prices for representative veterinary services.

For non–traditional treatments like acupuncture, FLFC will charge $57 per forty–minute session. Kennel services will cost $19 per night.

We will offer the following services in our clinic:

- Walk–in service
- Overnight care
- Seven days a week, 24 hours a day, call–in service
- Off–site service (the Vet will go to your farm)
- Routine animal care services
- Surgeries
- Neutering
- GPS Tagging for tracking animals

Veterinary On–Call Services

A veterinarian is on call 24 hours a day, 365 days a year (366 in a leap year) to provide veterinary services to animals involved in research projects. During working hours, a veterinarian may be contacted by the university telephone system or by cell phone. After hours and on holidays the cell phone number should be used. Veterinary Services is committed to responding to emergency calls within ten minutes. Telephone numbers are available from facility managers and should be posted in a prominent location. If you use the cell phone system and your call is not immediately answered, please leave a message including your telephone number and remain by the phone. If your call is not answered within 10 minutes please call again. We also request that you notify the department of any call which is not answered in a timely fashion.

Drugs and Supplies

The Department of Animal Care and Veterinary Services maintains and keeps inventory of commonly used veterinary drugs and supplies. Drugs are only sold in accordance with an approved "Application to Use Animals in Teaching and Testing". Restricted drugs are only dispensed in small amounts. Accurate record keeping and suitable storage facilities are prerequisites. Buprenorphine is a commonly used analgesic that is available from ACVS.

Items are sold on a cost plus basis and are charged directly to the investigators account number. Items may be ordered specifically for an investigator. There is no additional charge for this service unless immediate delivery is required. In such instances, shipping and handling will also be applied.

Veterinary Consultation

Veterinarians are available to discuss such topics as anaesthetic and analgesic regimes, animal models, surgical methods etc. There is no charge for this service.

It is recommended that investigators, technicians and other research staff take advantage of this service prior to the submission of invasive animal use protocols. The veterinarian will attempt to identify problems which may arise during the review process. This may expedite the review process.

In addition, information is available on animal handling equipment, zoonotic diseases, specialized surgical instrumentation and other topics related to animals in research.

Consultations may be made over the telephone, or in person, either in the animal laboratory or in the offices of Animal Care and Veterinary Services.

Rent–Vet Services

A full-time licensed Veterinary Technician is available to perform animal procedures based on an hourly rate. Time should be booked as soon in advance as possible. Examples of techniques commonly performed include:

- antibody raising procedures
- blood collection
- anaesthesia
- post–operative care and monitoring
- surgical assistance
- haematology
- biochemistry

Licensed veterinarians are also available to perform surgical or other experimental procedures.

Veterinary Rounds and Veterinary Health Checks

University veterinarians make routine visits to all holding facilities. This provides research staff with the opportunity to discuss problems with animal care or research methods. The veterinarian discusses the visit with the facility manager and research staff and prepares a brief report, which is sent to the facility manager and members of the Animal Use Subcommittee. In addition, on a less frequent basis, visits are made to research laboratories.

In addition to the above visits, arrangements can be made to have a veterinarian observe procedures, examine animals or perform post–mortem procedures. You may contact the department directly, or have the facility manager make the necessary arrangements.

Loans and Rentals

The Department of Animal Care and Veterinary Services makes a number of items available to investigators. There is usually a daily stipend applied. The income from this charge is used to maintain the various items. A partial list of some of the items is included below. If you are interested in obtaining additional information, please have the facility manager make the necessary arrangements.

- rodent induction chambers
- circulating water heating pads
- glass bead instrument sterilizers
- ultrasonic instrument cleaner
- surgical instruments
- restraints
- mice
- rabbits
- gas anaesthetic machines
- heat lamps
- surgical drape packs
- surgical greens

Reference Library and Handouts

The Department of Animal Care and Veterinary Services maintains a departmental library. The library is available for 'in–house' use. Subjects covered include Anaesthesia and Analgesia, Medicine, Surgery, Animal Models and Animal Husbandry. In addition to texts there are also instructional and informative video and audiotape presentations which may be viewed in the library. Journals specifically related to Laboratory Animal Medicine are also available for use within the library.

In addition to the above, handouts on animal diseases and procedures are available. Some of these are available on the website.

Pathology Services

A clinical veterinarian is available to perform post–mortem evaluation of animals where the cause of the animal's demise is unknown. There is no charge for this service. Additional testing such as histology or bacteriology is charged out on a cost plus basis. In addition the veterinarian performs routine necropsies as part of facility health surveillance. There is no charge to the investigator for any costs involved in these procedures.

A veterinarian is available to perform necropsies as part of a research protocol, however in this case the procedure would be charged out as a rent–a–vet service.

FINANCIAL ANALYSIS

Throughout the first twelve months of business, FLFC will have a steady cash flow.

In its first year of business, FLFC is projected to do $347,000 in sales, with $44,000 profit.

Start-up requirements

Start-up expenses	
Legal	$ 2,900
Stationery, etc.	$ 1,800
Brochures	$ 4,500
Consultants	$ 5,000
Insurance	$ 4,000
Rent	$ 2,500
Equipment	$ 57,000
Other	$ 23,000
Total start-up expenses	$100,700
Start-up assets needed	
Cash balance on starting date	$ 67,000
Other current assets	$ 0
Total current assets	$ 67,000
Funding	
Investment	
Current liabilities	
Accounts payable	$ 0
Current borrowing	$ 0
Other current liabilities	$ 0
Current liabilities	$ 0
Long-term liabilities	$ 65,000
Total liabilities	$ 65,000

Market analysis

Potential customers	Growth	2003	2004	2005	2006	2007	CAGR
Commercial	5%	12,000	14,500	15,000	17,000	19,005	5.00%
Residential	5%	160,000	170,500	180,000	190,000	199,500	5.00%

Wine Merchant and Storage Facility

Wine Seller Cellar

5123 Walnut St.
Baltimore, Maryland 21201

Greg Darnell, Kyle Jobe, Joe LaMonica, Audrey Speak, and Dan Weller

The Wine Seller Cellar is a dream come true for people living in crowded cities, small apartments, or anyone with a large wine collection and no place to store it. The Wine Seller Cellar is a full service wine merchant and storage facility that offers the perfect environment to store your wine. Whether you don't have the space, proper storage conditions in your home, or you're simply clueless as to what conditions will provide for optimal aging, Wine Seller Cellar is the place for you. Not only does the facility offer perfect and safe storage for your wine, but we also offer a fine selection of wines and champagnes that can be enjoyed right there at our wine bar.

BUSINESS OVERVIEW

The Wine Seller Cellar will provide people with a place to store their wine in the proper storing conditions. Our storage will also save space in people's apartments, houses, etc. Another unique advantage is that the facility has 24 hour access.

The facility will also have a wine bar. People will have a place to enjoy their wine with friends and other wine connoisseurs. This will help create a great customer experience. This will also give people the opportunity to try other wines. If we are successful, there could be an opportunity to create a wine of our own.

This is an opportunity to become a trend setter in Baltimore. A great way to start this trend would be by word–of–mouth, which could make storing wine and enjoying it at our facility the "thing to do". This trend setting will allow us to capitalize on being a first mover in the Baltimore area. If successful, we could branch out to other east–coast cities.

PRODUCTS & SERVICES

The business that we are in is the sale and storage of alcoholic beverages. We will compete with other bars, yet differ from them in the sense that the bar section of the facility is strictly a wine bar. The facility is also a place for people to store any amount of wine and have the freedom to access it at any time.

Unique Features and Benefits

As many already know, most wine gets better with age. But in order to achieve the exact "matured" taste, wine needs to be stored in a proper and extremely particular environment. Our facility offers a state–of–the–art storage locker that provides the perfect environment for your wine collection. Many factors go into the growth and maturity of wine. These include: ideal temperature, ideal humidity, the right amount of light, the right amount of air flow and insulation, and a storage place that is vibration free. The Wine Seller Cellar was created to provide all of these features to insure optimal growth and maturity.

The storage cellars are protected by 24 hour security cameras. An access code is needed in order to enter the storage cellar. This not only provides the security of your wine, but the security of those who wish to access the cellar after hours since the storage section of the facility is conveniently accessible 24 hours a day.

There is a wine bar located at the storage facility for everyone to enjoy, whether they store wine with us or simply want to stop in to enjoy a glass of wine in our comfortable, unique atmosphere. People can even drop in to enjoy a bottle of their own wine that they have stored in our facility.

The facility is convenient to all customers in numerous ways. First, if they choose to store wine with us, they have the freedom to access their collection at any time of the day, on any day of the week. Next, the facility gives wine lovers the chance to either start a collection, or to continue their existing collection without the worry of crowding their homes or storing their wine improperly. This is especially convenient for those who live in apartments or condos and have no extra room for a desired wine collection.

These specific features meet the needs or preferences of the customer because it is a great way to build, or continue to build a wine collection. With plenty of storage space available at our facility, there is no need to limit your wine collection. And this even applies to people who *do* have the room in their homes to store wine, yet do not have the knowledge or time to create the perfect wine–storing environment. Why invest in fine wines if they cannot be properly stored and matured?

Currently in the Baltimore area there are no facilities like this that exist. The Red Carpet Room at the Inn at the Park does have a similar service though. There is a Wine Room with a dine–in wine cellar. This is primarily used for large parties, business meetings, or events, whereas our facility can be used for many other occasions.

The benefit of our service compared to the competition is that it applies to a broader market. Anyone who wishes to store wine, any amount, is welcome to utilize the facility. They are able to stop by at any time to pick up their wine, not just during business hours. The facility is also available to other customers who simply want to stop in for a glass or two of wine.

Risk Factors

There are few limitations to our service since wine drinking has increased greatly over the years and is predicted to continue growing. Yet there are some matters to take into consideration. First, the insurance cost to protect the facility and to serve alcohol is very high. There is a large liability placed on the facility since the storage lockers will contain a vast amount of others' "property". Another slighter limitation to our service is introducing it to the market. Since there are basically no other facilities similar to ours that exist in the area, it could be difficult convincing people to try new ideas, such as ours.

MARKET ANALYSIS

Our service has surpassed the idea stage since there are currently facilities very similar to ours in existence in other states. Researching these existing facilities has proved that the idea is quite plausible and successful; leading us to believe that it will flourish in the Baltimore area. Since very few are located in the area, the competition is scarce, allowing for a perfect market niche. To help matters along, the consumption of wine in the United States has greatly increased recently and is only expected to continue increasing.

Industry Trends

There are very few wine storage facilities on the East Coast. Wine storage locations are becoming popular on the east coast. The closest wine storage facility that operates strictly as a wine storage location is in Bangor. A wine storage location in Baltimore would offer a unique service and accommodate a growing market trend. A wine storage facility could offer its services to wineries, shop owners, distributors, importers, exporters, restaurants, wine clubs, schools, or any other kind of institution. Baltimore contains 147,000 housing units and 78,000 rent occupied units. The city is experiencing new growth and expansion and more people will be living in apartments and lofts with limited storage space. Root Avenue in downtown Baltimore is an area that is experiencing much revitalization that could accommodate such a business. A factor to be considered while starting a wine storage business would be that 98 percent of all wine sold in retail stores is drunk within 24 hours. A wine storage facility would be marketed to people who have wine collections or people that save their wine for occasions and aging considerations. Establishing a perceived benefit for the proper storage of wine will be crucial to the success of a wine storage business. As people drink wine for their beverage of choice their knowledge of the product will increase also. If people understand that the taste of wine is affected by how it is stored then they will see the need to keep it in an ideal condition.

More people are choosing to drink wine but many wine drinkers are unaware of the proper storage techniques needed to keep wine in its ideal state. Many people store wine because of its investment value. During the last few years, the value of wine purchased young and properly stored has increased many times over. With the increasing popularity of wine, this trend is expected to continue to grow. Many people work on a rotation system, storing wine for their own consumption in future years. The best system is to buy fine wines upon release and properly store them until they mature. For any wine lover, storing wine well is very important. There are a few simple principles that need to be understood in order to select proper wine storage conditions. Ideal wine conditions are difficult to establish in a home or loft. A good storage location for wine is generally dark, is free of vibration, has high humidity and has a low stable temperature. Generally accepted 'ideal' conditions are 50 to 55 degrees and 70 percent humidity or higher. The high humidity is important because it keeps the corks from drying and minimizes evaporation. The only problem with even higher levels of humidity is that it brings on growth of mold on the labels or the loosening of labels that have water soluble glue.

There are many studies that show how wine consumption is increasing. Adults now prefer to drink wine over beer. Wine is aligned with cultural trends in America, including a focus on family and tradition. For the first time since Gallup began measuring Americans' drinking preferences in 1992, wine passed beer in 2005 as the alcoholic beverage adult drinkers consume most often. Gallup's Consumption Habits poll found that 39 percent of American drinkers consume wine most often, and 36 percent consume beer most often. That data followed research conducted on behalf of Wine Market Council that also showed the "Millennial" generation (consumers between 21 and 30 years old) taking a strong liking to wine. Currently the U.S. is the fourth largest producer of wine in the world yet only accounts for approximately 4.2 percent of the total wine export market based on volume. One reason for this disparity can be attributed to the low level of strategic importance placed on exporting by most U.S. wineries.

By 2008, U.S. consumers will account for 25 percent of all the wine drunk in the world, up from 19 percent, according to a new study conducted for the Bordeaux–based trade group, VinExpo. This would make the United States top spot for World Wine consumption. Wine consumption is increasing everywhere; there is a predicted 14.7 percent worldwide increase in total wine industry revenues by 2008. U.S. wine consumption growth began a steady climb in 1991 after the CBS "60 Minutes" French Paradox broadcast and hundreds of other news media reported on the favorable health effects of moderate wine consumption. Wine sales in the U.S. have undergone constant growth since 1975. California wine sales in the U.S. reached another record high of 441 million gallons in 2005 with a retail value of $16.5 billion, according to wine industry consultant Jon Fredrikson of Woodside and publisher of the Gomberg-Fredrikson Report. Total California winery shipments to all markets both in the U.S. and abroad reached 532 million gallons (223.9 nine–liter cases) last year. The strong performance reflects the overall growth trend of wine demand in the U.S. and can be attributed to several developments. Wine has enjoyed the most positive image it has had in years from consumers, the media and government. The May 2005 U.S. Supreme Court decision on direct–to–consumer sales not only benefited U.S. wineries, but had a favorable impact on public opinion and awareness of wine. Shortly after the ruling, a Gallup poll named wine as America's most preferred alcohol beverage citing growth trends from several different demographic groups.

The popularity of the hit movie "Sideways" continued to lift the public's interest in wine, particularly in Pinot Noir from California. U.S. supermarket sales also reflected the growth of upscale wines, with wines priced $6 and above showing double–digit increases by volume, according to ACNielsen, which tracks laser–scanning data from 3000 supermarkets across the country. For the second year in recent history, red wine edged out white as the top seller by volume in food stores, holding a 41.7 percent market share. White accounted for an estimated 41.0 percent share, while blush represented 17.4 percent share of volume. Still benefiting from the "Sideways" effect, Pinot Noir shipments experienced a dramatic 70 percent jump in food stores, compared to the previous year, though from a small base of two percent share by volume. Chardonnay remained the top–selling wine, followed by Merlot, White Zinfandel and Cabernet Sauvignon. Together, these top four varietals totaled 53 percent of all table wine volume in food stores.

The U.S. wine market, with the adult population, aged 21 to 65, has grown by 10.4 million since 2000. "Echo Boomers," the adult children of the "Baby Boomer" generation that adopted wine in the 1960s and 1970s, are increasingly making wine more a part of their lifestyle. The leading edge of the Echo Boomer generation, the 70 million Americans who will be between the ages of 11 and 28 in 2005, began to reach the legal drinking age of 21 in 1998. The Millennial generation is providing the wine industry with extreme growth potential according to the Wine Market Council. Baby Boomers, who currently make up the largest segment of the U.S. population, also favor wine.

Several industries play an integral role in the idea. The wine industry is important, because without a demand for wine then there will be no need for a place to store wine. The idea also encompasses the service industry in the sense that the portable wine storage is providing a service for customers. If demand for services such as storing wine tapers off, then there is no need to offer a wine storage service.

The probable industry for the idea would be drinking places for alcoholic beverages. This industry has a SIC code of 5813. This industry deals mainly with the wholesale of alcoholic beverages. Although the idea primarily deals with wine storage, there will still be a wine bar (which was given as an example) with some sales. Either way, the wine self–storage facility will allow people to consume wine inside the premises which would make it a drinking place for alcoholic beverages.

There is very good market potential for this industry. "By the mid–2000s the U.S. wine industry was picking up. California wineries shipped a record amount of products, with approximately 428 million gallons shipped domestically, from a total 522 million gallons shipped worldwide. While so–called "extreme value" varieties continued to sell well, the expensive premium wines also were seeing increases, accounting for 64 percent of industry revenues (Business & Company Resource Center)."

"By the decade's end, the Australian Wine Bureau reported that more than 4 million cases of Australian wine would be shipped to the United States by 2001, and by 2026 shipments should total more than 10 million cases with an estimated value of $440 million (Business & Company Resource Center)."

These quotes show that the demand for U.S. wine and foreign wines from places like Australia is on the rise. Therefore, this industry is in a period of growth due to the increasing wine sales. Demand for wine has been rising, and thus the demand for a place to store it should also increase over the next couple of years. The graph below shows that there has been an upward trend in wine sales since 1999, and this trend is projected to continue into the year 2009.

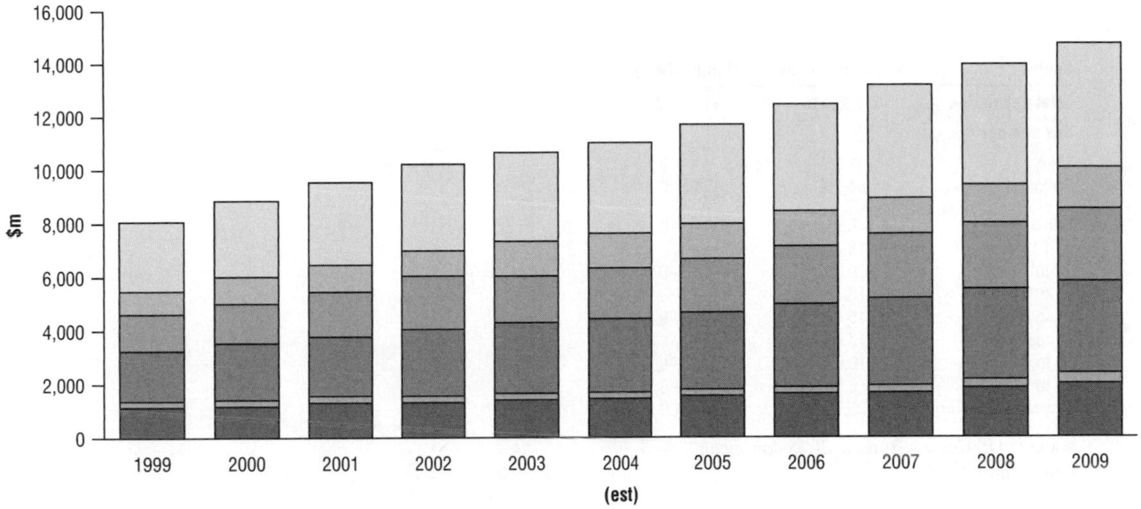

Technology should only help the industry, because people will be able to look at the different wines available in the world to purchase. The internet will also allow the wine storage facility to have a website that would allow potential customers to find out about the location, prices, etc. The wine storage will also have state of the art technology in order to make sure that it offers the mot ideal place to store wine. Other technological devices like security cameras and alarms that will ensure that the customers have the best experience in storing their wine and enjoying it too.

COMPETITION

There is no direct competition in Baltimore for a wine storage facility. Our service will be very unique to the city of Baltimore. This uniqueness will help us to have a first mover advantage in the city of Baltimore. However, direct competition for a wine self-storage does exist outside of Baltimore. Some of the cities where this idea is already in place are in cities like Bangor, Maine, and Madison, Wisconsin.

There is competition within Baltimore for our business. Regarding wine storage, we will be competing with companies that offer wine storage in people's homes. This is a big reason why the suburbs will not be the ideal location for our service. People in the suburbs have more room to create a place to store their own wine. However, we will have a lot of competition in Baltimore along the lines of a place for drinking alcoholic beverages. We will be competing with the various bars and clubs throughout the city. We will want to attract people to come to our place to drink wine rather than go to another bar to drink wine. The biggest threat in the city will be wine bars.

CUSTOMERS

The two largest segments of the U.S. population are the echo boomer generation and the baby boomer generation. Both of these demographics enjoy wine. The table below displays the age breakdown for the Baltimore area in the year 2005. This table shows that the nation wide age phenomenon applies to the city of Baltimore too. Just like throughout the country, the baby boomers (41–59 years) represent a large percentage of people in Baltimore. The echo boomer generation (11–28 years) also represents a large percentage of the population. The baby boomers are the current target audience, and this is the largest audience in Baltimore. The echo boomers represent a chance for growth into the future. And this growth is present in the city of Baltimore.

Subject	Total population	Margin of error
Total population	**2,725,336**	**+/−4,235**
Sex and age		
Male	48.3%	+/−0.1
Female	51.7%	+/−0.1
Under 5 years	6.6%	+/−0.1
5 to 17 years	18.1%	+/−0.1
18 to 24 years	9.2%	+/−0.1
25 to 34 years	12.7%	+/−0.1
35 to 44 years	15.1%	+/−0.1
45 to 54 years	15.4%	+/−0.1
55 to 64 years	10.6%	+/−0.1
65 to 74 years	6.5%	+/−0.1
75 years and over	5.7%	+/−0.1

SOURCE: US Census Bureau, 2005 American Community Survey

The echo boomer (Millennial) generation represent people aged 12–29 in 2006. "The Millennial generation is providing the wine industry with the 'kind of growth potential not seen in more than 30 years,' according to the Wine Market Council (Mintel Reports)." This growth potential will create the customer base needed for the wine business to continue growing into the future. When looking at starting a business, it is very important to make sure that there will be a demand, and this quote reaffirms the fact that there will be a demand for years to come. It is up to us to recognize this demand and provide the proper supply to meet this demand.

Scarborough Research also revealed that consumers aged 21–35 are 84 percent more likely to spend more than $20 for a bottle of premium wine than those aged 35–54. This indicates that the increased wine consumption of this generation will also be more profitable for winemakers (Mintel Reports)."

The need for wine storage will be even more important if these echo boomers are purchasing more expensive wine, because they will want some place to store this wine. This quote once again provides positive reinforcement for the service that we will offer. Most people will not want to spend money to store cheap wine, but people will definitely want a place to store more expensive wine. The bottom line is that if someone is going to go out of there way to spend the money on good wine, then they will want to spend the money on a place to store their wine at the proper conditions so that they may have the best experience when it comes to enjoying their wine.

The baby boomer generation is the main target demographic. This demographic is also the largest generation. They also have the most disposable income. The best thing is that this generation enjoys drinking wine. All of these facts are very positive for the industry and specifically our service. We could not ask for anything better, because our target audience is the largest audience, and this audience has the most money to spend on our service. Therefore, our customer base is the ideal base that every business would want to possess.

"Wine industry researcher MFK Research reported that, in the year 2000, consumers in their forties and fifties (which covers Baby Boomers) drank an average of 14 bottles and 16 bottles of wine, respectively. This is in comparison to an average of 15 bottles consumed by individuals in their sixties, and ten bottles consumed by individuals in their thirties (Mintel Reports)."

This quote reaffirms the fact that the baby boomers are wine drinkers. Once the baby boomers start to retire, they can store wine in our wine storage. They can also enjoy their wine at the wine bar provided with friends and family as a means of recreation. Our service will provide the baby boomers with more than a place to store and drink wine. We will provide an experience that the boomers will not be able to find anywhere else in the city of Baltimore, Maryland. This unique service should do very well.

According to the Fall 2004 Simmons NCS (Mintel Reports): 37 percent of adult respondents over age 21 drink wine, 35 percent of male respondents drink wine 39 percent of female respondents drink wine, older respondents drink more than younger respondents, more educated people tend to be more inclined to drink wine. These facts are also favorable for the industry. Women make up the largest percentage of people in Baltimore. This is good, because women are more inclined to drink wine. Another thing from above is that older people drink more wine than younger people which coincides with our research that the baby boomers enjoy their wine. Another positive trend is that more educated people tend to drink wine. This will provide favorable demographic for us in the future. The city of Baltimore has many local universities and college enrollment has been on the rise too. This will create more educated people in the city for years to come who will enjoy drinking wine.

ADVERTISING

We will reach target consumers by picking a location where the target consumers live and go out. The best location would be downtown. More people are starting to move back to the downtown area which will be beneficial to us if we do indeed choose a downtown location. Our service will also provide people a place to go before and after downtown attractions such as concerts, games, etc. Most of the entertainment in Baltimore occurs in the downtown area. We can capitalize on this fact. People often want to go somewhere before and after an event. Our wine storage service will provide people with an opportunity to socialize with friends and families by enjoying their wine before and after these events. Our service will also help with the revitalization of downtown Baltimore. Our place will bring more people and business into the downtown area. Therefore, we think that downtown will be the ideal location. This will be especially true if the baby boomers start to move out of the suburbs and back downtown. This trend could easily start to happen. As the boomers kids move out of their houses, they will be looking to downsize. Therefore, the apartments and lofts that exist downtown could be an ideal place for the baby boomers.

Another option for our service would be Boston. There are several advantages of choosing Boston. There are a lot of businesses in Boston. This would be beneficial, because people can enjoy their wines stored in the wine storage while entertaining clients. It will also provide people with a place to go after work hours for a happy hour type of environment. Another big advantage about Boston is that there is a lot of money in Boston. A great way for our service to make money is to attract some of the wealthy residents and workers in Boston. Following the money will be a good way to make money. However, there are already a lot of nice restaurants and bars in the area. I think the downtown Baltimore area has the most potential for growth. Therefore, Boston would be a good location, but downtown Baltimore is still the ideal location for our service.

Yet another option to locate our service is the suburbs. There are a lot of baby boomers in the suburbs. However, these baby boomers might not want to stay there once their kids move out of the house. These boomers will no longer need the space that the suburbs offer them. Another reason why the suburbs will not be the best location is that these people will already have a lot of space to store their wine. While they will not have the optimal storing conditions that we will offer, they will still have a cheaper substitute that will be good enough for them. Also, it would be more beneficial for these people to have a place downtown to enjoy their wine, because it will give them a place to go when they do indeed go downtown for events. Therefore, we do not think that the suburbs will be the best location for our service.

Advertising will be important in order to spread the word about our unique service to the city of Baltimore. A great way to advertise is by creating a website. People will be able to see what we are all about by simply visiting our website. We will provide things such as: services offered, directions, contact information, etc. Another way we will advertise is by making newspaper and magazine ads. Another way we will advertise is by doing so at the stores where the wine is actually purchased. This should be very beneficial, because when people actually go to purchase their wine they will see our advertisement which will provide them a place to store and enjoy their newly bough wine. The best part is that everyone who purchases wine is someone we want to target, because we want to target all wine drinkers. Word–of–mouth will also help in the advancement of the business. Happy customers will tell their friends and family which should create more business. People are more likely to listen to someone they know then some random person on a commercial. Therefore, a big way we will penetrate our market is by advertising, especially by word–of–mouth.

GROWTH STRATEGY

There is a huge market for this industry, especially in the downtown Baltimore area. This offers our everyday wine connoisseur a way to properly store their wine while having the option to come and use our elegant lounge area to indulge in their wine while meeting new and exciting people within their community. After we open our first location and market our industry we could expand and open up locations around the area and possibly offer our own brand of wine. The service we wish to create is past the idea stage and already in existence in a few other states. From researching these existing successful facilities and their locations, a wine storage facility in the Baltimore area seems very feasible.

Next Steps

One thing we will definitely need to inquire about is the start–up capital. We will need money in order to buy property, build a storage facility, hire people, and various other marketing expenses. Some of the sources for start–up capital would include: wealthy owners who have the funds to invest into the business, family and friends, and loans. We will need to get a bank loan. We will want to try and obtain a favorable rate. We also need to open a business bank account.

We will also want to talk to people who have been successful with this idea in other cities. We would want to find out things like: how long it would take to get the business operational, how long it will take for construction if built from scratch, how long to hire and train employees, and would there be opportunities to expand business into other markets. Specifically we would want to know if we could expand into other market in the Midwest, and even in other areas of the United States.

Management Summary

- Mentor: Peter Raset
- Idea Originator: Tiffany O'Conner
- Attorney: TBD. Will establish the type of business organization (i.e. LLC, Partnership, Sole Proprietorship, etc.) and acquire a permit to sell alcohol on the premises.
- Accountant: TBD. Will keep the books.
- Contractor: TBD. Will help us with finding and building the wine storage facility.
- Website Designer: TBD. Will create a unique and informative website to attract customers.

Business Plan Template

USING THIS TEMPLATE

A business plan carefully spells out a company's projected course of action over a period of time, usually the first two to three years after the start-up. In addition, banks, lenders, and other investors examine the information and financial documentation before deciding whether or not to finance a new business venture. Therefore, a business plan is an essential tool in obtaining financing and should describe the business itself in detail as well as all important factors influencing the company, including the market, industry, competition, operations and management policies, problem solving strategies, financial resources and needs, and other vital information. The plan enables the business owner to anticipate costs, plan for difficulties, and take advantage of opportunities, as well as design and implement strategies that keep the company running as smoothly as possible.

This template has been provided as a model to help you construct your own business plan. Please keep in mind that there is no single acceptable format for a business plan, and that this template is in no way comprehensive, but serves as an example.

The business plans provided in this section are fictional and have been used by small business agencies as models for clients to use in compiling their own business plans.

GENERIC BUSINESS PLAN

Main headings included below are topics that should be covered in a comprehensive business plan. They include:

Business Summary

Purpose
Provides a brief overview of your business, succinctly highlighting the main ideas of your plan.

Includes

- Name and Type of Business
- Description of Product/Service
- Business History and Development
- Location
- Market
- Competition
- Management
- Financial Information
- Business Strengths and Weaknesses
- Business Growth

Table of Contents

Purpose
Organized in an Outline Format, the Table of Contents illustrates the selection and arrangement of information contained in your plan.

Includes

- Topic Headings and Subheadings
- Page Number References

Business History and Industry Outlook

Purpose

Examines the conception and subsequent development of your business within an industry specific context.

Includes

- Start-up Information
- Owner/Key Personnel Experience
- Location
- Development Problems and Solutions
- Investment/Funding Information
- Future Plans and Goals
- Market Trends and Statistics
- Major Competitors
- Product/Service Advantages
- National, Regional, and Local Economic Impact

Product/Service

Purpose

Introduces, defines, and details the product and/or service that inspired the information of your business.

Includes

- Unique Features
- Niche Served
- Market Comparison
- Stage of Product/Service Development
- Production
- Facilities, Equipment, and Labor
- Financial Requirements
- Product/Service Life Cycle
- Future Growth

Market Examination

Purpose

Assessment of product/service applications in relation to consumer buying cycles.

Includes

- Target Market
- Consumer Buying Habits
- Product/Service Applications
- Consumer Reactions
- Market Factors and Trends
- Penetration of the Market
- Market Share
- Research and Studies
- Cost
- Sales Volume and Goals

Competition

Purpose

Analysis of Competitors in the Marketplace.

Includes

- Competitor Information
- Product/Service Comparison
- Market Niche
- Product/Service Strengths and Weaknesses
- Future Product/Service Development

Marketing

Purpose
Identifies promotion and sales strategies for your product/service.

Includes

- Product/Service Sales Appeal
- Special and Unique Features
- Identification of Customers
- Sales and Marketing Staff
- Sales Cycles
- Type of Advertising/Promotion
- Pricing
- Competition
- Customer Services

Operations

Purpose
Traces product/service development from production/inception to the market environment.

Includes

- Cost Effective Production Methods
- Facility
- Location
- Equipment
- Labor
- Future Expansion

Administration and Management

Purpose
Offers a statement of your management philosophy with an in-depth focus on processes and procedures.

Includes

- Management Philosophy
- Structure of Organization
- Reporting System
- Methods of Communication
- Employee Skills and Training
- Employee Needs and Compensation
- Work Environment
- Management Policies and Procedures
- Roles and Responsibilities

Key Personnel

Purpose
Describes the unique backgrounds of principle employees involved in business.

Includes

- Owner(s)/Employee Education and Experience
- Positions and Roles
- Benefits and Salary
- Duties and Responsibilities
- Objectives and Goals

Potential Problems and Solutions

Purpose
Discussion of problem solving strategies that change issues into opportunities.

Includes

- Risks
- Litigation
- Future Competition
- Economic Impact
- Problem Solving Skills

Financial Information

Purpose

Secures needed funding and assistance through worksheets and projections detailing financial plans, methods of repayment, and future growth opportunities.

Includes

- Financial Statements
- Bank Loans
- Methods of Repayment
- Tax Returns
- Start-up Costs
- Projected Income (3 years)
- Projected Cash Flow (3 years)
- Projected Balance Statements (3 years)

Appendices

Purpose

Supporting documents used to enhance your business proposal.

Includes

- Photographs of product, equipment, facilities, etc.
- Copyright/Trademark Documents
- Legal Agreements
- Marketing Materials
- Research and or Studies
- Operation Schedules
- Organizational Charts
- Job Descriptions
- Resumes
- Additional Financial Documentation

Fictional Food Distributor

Commercial Foods, Inc.

3003 Avondale Ave.
Knoxville, TN 37920

This plan demonstrates how a partnership can have a positive impact on a new business. It demonstrates how two individuals can carve a niche in the specialty foods market by offering gourmet foods to upscale restaurants and fine hotels. This plan is fictional and has not been used to gain funding from a bank or other lending institution.

STATEMENT OF PURPOSE

Commercial Foods, Inc. seeks a loan of $75,000 to establish a new business. This sum, together with $5,000 equity investment by the principals, will be used as follows:

- Merchandise inventory $25,000
- Office fixture/equipment $12,000
- Warehouse equipment $14,000
- One delivery truck $10,000
- Working capital $39,000
- Total $100,000

DESCRIPTION OF THE BUSINESS

Commercial Foods, Inc. will be a distributor of specialty food service products to hotels and upscale restaurants in the geographical area of a 50 mile radius of Knoxville. Richard Roberts will direct the sales effort and John Williams will manage the warehouse operation and the office. One delivery truck will be used initially with a second truck added in the third year. We expect to begin operation of the business within 30 days after securing the requested financing.

MANAGEMENT

A. Richard Roberts is a native of Memphis, Tennessee. He is a graduate of Memphis State University with a Bachelor's degree from the School of Business. After graduation, he worked for a major manufacturer of specialty food service products as a detail sales person for five years, and, for the past three years, he has served as a product sales manager for this firm.

B. John Williams is a native of Nashville, Tennessee. He holds a B.S. Degree in Food Technology from the University of Tennessee. His career includes five years as a product development chemist in gourmet food products and five years as operations manager for a food service distributor.

Both men are healthy and energetic. Their backgrounds complement each other, which will ensure the success of Commercial Foods, Inc. They will set policies together and personnel decisions will be made jointly. Initial salaries for the owners will be $1,000 per month for the first few years. The spouses of both principals are successful in the business world and earn enough to support the families.

They have engaged the services of Foster Jones, CPA, and William Hale, Attorney, to assist them in an advisory capacity.

PERSONNEL

The firm will employ one delivery truck driver at a wage of $8.00 per hour. One office worker will be employed at $7.50 per hour. One part-time employee will be used in the office at $5.00 per hour. The driver will load and unload his own trucks. Mr. Williams will assist in the warehouse operation as needed to assist one stock person at $7.00 per hour. An additional delivery truck and driver will be added the third year.

LOCATION

The firm will lease a 20,000 square foot building at 3003 Avondale Ave., in Knoxville, which contains warehouse and office areas equipped with two-door truck docks. The annual rental is $9,000. The building was previously used as a food service warehouse and very little modification to the building will be required.

PRODUCTS AND SERVICES

The firm will offer specialty food service products such as soup bases, dessert mixes, sauce bases, pastry mixes, spices, and flavors, normally used by upscale restaurants and nice hotels. We are going after a niche in the market with high quality gourmet products. There is much less competition in this market than in standard run of the mill food service products. Through their work experiences, the principals have contacts with supply sources and with local chefs.

THE MARKET

We know from our market survey that there are over 200 hotels and upscale restaurants in the area we plan to serve. Customers will be attracted by a direct sales approach. We will offer samples of our products and product application data on use of our products in the finished prepared foods. We will cultivate the chefs in these establishments. The technical background of John Williams will be especially useful here.

COMPETITION

We find that we will be only distributor in the area offering a full line of gourmet food service products. Other foodservice distributors offer only a few such items in conjunction with their standard product line. Our survey shows that many of the chefs are ordering products from Atlanta and Memphis because of a lack of adequate local supply.

SUMMARY

Commercial Foods, Inc. will be established as a foodservice distributor of specialty food in Knoxville. The principals, with excellent experience in the industry, are seeking a $75,000 loan to establish the business. The principals are investing $25,000 as equity capital.

The business will be set up as an S Corporation with each principal owning 50% of the common stock in the corporation.

Fictional Hardware Store

Oshkosh Hardware, Inc.

123 Main St.
Oshkosh, WI 54901

The following plan outlines how a small hardware store can survive competition from large discount chains by offering products and providing expert advice in the use of any product it sells. This plan is fictional and has not been used to gain funding from a bank or other lending institution.

EXECUTIVE SUMMARY

Oshkosh Hardware, Inc. is a new corporation that is going to establish a retail hardware store in a strip mall in Oshkosh, Wisconsin. The store will sell hardware of all kinds, quality tools, paint, and housewares. The business will make revenue and a profit by servicing its customers not only with needed hardware but also with expert advice in the use of any product it sells.

Oshkosh Hardware, Inc. will be operated by its sole shareholder, James Smith. The company will have a total of four employees. It will sell its products in the local market. Customers will buy our products because we will provide free advice on the use of all of our products and will also furnish a full refund warranty.

Oshkosh Hardware, Inc. will sell its products in the Oshkosh store staffed by three sales representatives. No additional employees will be needed to achieve its short and long range goals. The primary short range goal is to open the store by October 1, 1994. In order to achieve this goal a lease must be signed by July 1, 1994 and the complete inventory ordered by August 1, 1994.

Mr. James Smith will invest $30,000 in the business. In addition, the company will have to borrow $150,000 during the first year to cover the investment in inventory, accounts receivable, and furniture and equipment. The company will be profitable after six months of operation and should be able to start repayment of the loan in the second year.

THE BUSINESS

The business will sell hardware of all kinds, quality tools, paint, and housewares. We will purchase our products from three large wholesale buying groups.

In general our customers are homeowners who do their own repair and maintenance, hobbyists, and housewives. Our business is unique in that we will have a complete line of all hardware items and will be able to get special orders by overnight delivery. The business makes revenue and profits by servicing our customers not only with needed hardware but also with expert advice in the use of any product we sell. Our major costs for bringing our products to market are cost of merchandise of 36%, salaries of $45,000, and occupancy costs of $60,000.

Oshkosh Hardware, Inc.'s retail outlet will be located at 1524 Frontage Road, which is in a newly developed retail center of Oshkosh. Our location helps facilitate accessibility from all parts of town and reduces our delivery costs. The store will occupy 7500 square feet of space. The major equipment involved in our business is counters and shelving, a computer, a paint mixing machine, and a truck.

THE MARKET

Oshkosh Hardware, Inc. will operate in the local market. There are 15,000 potential customers in this market area. We have three competitors who control approximately 98% of the market at present. We feel we can capture 25% of the market within the next four years. Our major reason for believing this is that our staff is technically competent to advise our customers in the correct use of all products we sell.

After a careful market analysis, we have determined that approximately 60% of our customers are men and 40% are women. The percentage of customers that fall into the following age categories are:

Under 16: 0%

17–21: 5%

22–30: 30%

31–40: 30%

41–50: 20%

51–60: 10%

61–70: 5%

Over 70: 0%

The reasons our customers prefer our products is our complete knowledge of their use and our full refund warranty.

We get our information about what products our customers want by talking to existing customers. There seems to be an increasing demand for our product. The demand for our product is increasing in size based on the change in population characteristics.

SALES

At Oshkosh Hardware, Inc. we will employ three sales people and will not need any additional personnel to achieve our sales goals. These salespeople will need several years experience in home repair and power tool usage. We expect to attract 30% of our customers from newspaper ads, 5% of our customers from local directories, 5% of our customers from the yellow pages, 10% of our customers from family and friends, and 50% of our customers from current customers. The most cost effect source will be current customers. In general our industry is growing.

MANAGEMENT

We would evaluate the quality of our management staff as being excellent. Our manager is experienced and very motivated to achieve the various sales and quality assurance objectives we have set. We will use a management information system that produces key inventory, quality assurance, and sales data on a weekly basis. All data is compared to previously established goals for that week, and deviations are the primary focus of the management staff.

GOALS IMPLEMENTATION

The short term goals of our business are:

1. Open the store by October 1, 1994
2. Reach our breakeven point in two months
3. Have sales of $100,000 in the first six months

In order to achieve our first short term goal we must:

1. Sign the lease by July 1, 1994
2. Order a complete inventory by August 1, 1994

In order to achieve our second short term goal we must:

1. Advertise extensively in Sept. and Oct.
2. Keep expenses to a minimum

In order to achieve our third short term goal we must:

1. Promote power tool sales for the Christmas season
2. Keep good customer traffic in Jan. and Feb.

The long term goals for our business are:

1. Obtain sales volume of $600,000 in three years
2. Become the largest hardware dealer in the city
3. Open a second store in Fond du Lac

The most important thing we must do in order to achieve the long term goals for our business is to develop a highly profitable business with excellent cash flow.

FINANCE

Oshkosh Hardware, Inc. Faces some potential threats or risks to our business. They are discount house competition. We believe we can avoid or compensate for this by providing quality products complimented by quality advice on the use of every product we sell. The financial projections we have prepared are located at the end of this document.

JOB DESCRIPTION-GENERAL MANAGER

The General Manager of the business of the corporation will be the president of the corporation. He will be responsible for the complete operation of the retail hardware store which is owned by the corporation. A detailed description of his duties and responsibilities is as follows.

Sales

Train and supervise the three sales people. Develop programs to motivate and compensate these employees. Coordinate advertising and sales promotion effects to achieve sales totals as outlined in budget. Oversee purchasing function and inventory control procedures to insure adequate merchandise at all times at a reasonable cost.

Finance

Prepare monthly and annual budgets. Secure adequate line of credit from local banks. Supervise office personnel to insure timely preparation of records, statements, all government reports, control of receivables and payables, and monthly financial statements.

Administration

Perform duties as required in the areas of personnel, building leasing and maintenance, licenses and permits, and public relations.

Organizations, Agencies, & Consultants

A listing of Associations and Consultants of interest to entrepreneurs, followed by the ten Small Business Administration Regional Offices, Small Business Development Centers, Service Corps of Retired Executives offices, and Venture Capital and Finance Companies.

Associations

This section contains a listing of associations and other agencies of interest to the small business owner. Entries are listed alphabetically by organization name.

American Business Women's Association
9100 Ward Pkwy.
PO Box 8728
Kansas City, MO 64114-0728
(800)228-0007
E-mail: abwa@abwa.org
Website: http://www.abwa.org
Jeanne Banks, National President

American Franchisee Association
53 W Jackson Blvd., Ste. 1157
Chicago, IL 60604
(312)431-0545
E-mail: info@franchisee.org
Website: http://www.franchisee.org
Susan P. Kezios, President

American Independent Business Alliance
222 S Black Ave.
Bozeman, MT 59715
(406)582-1255
E-mail: info@amiba.net
Website: http://www.amiba.net
Jennifer Rockne, Director

American Small Businesses Association
206 E College St., Ste. 201
Grapevine, TX 76051
800-942-2722
E-mail: info@asbaonline.org
Website: http://www.asbaonline.org/

American Women's Economic Development Corporation
216 East 45th St., 10th Floor
New York, NY 10017
(917)368-6100
Fax: (212)986-7114
E-mail: info@awed.org
Website: http://www.awed.org
Roseanne Antonucci, Exec. Dir.

Association for Enterprise Opportunity
1601 N Kent St., Ste. 1101
Arlington, VA 22209
(703)841-7760
Fax: (703)841-7748
E-mail: aeo@assoceo.org
Website: http://
www.microenterpriseworks.org
Bill Edwards, Exec.Dir.

Association of Small Business Development Centers
c/o Don Wilson
8990 Burke Lake Rd.
Burke, VA 22015
(703)764-9850
Fax: (703)764-1234
E-mail: info@asbdc-us.org
Website: http://www.asbdc-us.org
Don Wilson, Pres./CEO

BEST Employers Association
2505 McCabe Way
Irvine, CA 92614
(949)253-4080
800-433-0088
Fax: (714)553-0883
E-mail: info@bestlife.com
Website: http://www.bestlife.com
Donald R. Lawrenz, CEO

Center for Family Business
PO Box 24219
Cleveland, OH 44124
(440)460-5409
E-mail: grummi@aol.com
Dr. Leon A. Danco, Chm.

Coalition for Government Procurement
1990 M St. NW, Ste. 400
Washington, DC 20036
(202)331-0975
E-mail: info@thecgp.org
Website: http://www.coalgovpro.org
Paul Caggiano, Pres.

Employers of America
PO Box 1874
Mason City, IA 50402-1874
(641)424-3187
800-728-3187
Fax: (641)424-1673
E-mail: employer@employerhelp.org
Website: http://www.employerhelp.org
Jim Collison, Pres.

Family Firm Institute
200 Lincoln St., Ste. 201
Boston, MA 02111
(617)482-3045
Fax: (617)482-3049
E-mail: ffi@ffi.org
Website: http://www.ffi.org
Judy L. Green, Ph.D., Exec.Dir.

Independent Visually Impaired Enterprisers
500 S 3rd St., Apt. H
Burbank, CA 91502
(818)238-9321
E-mail:
abazyn@bazyncommunications.com
http://www.acb.org/affiliates
Adris Bazyn, Pres.

International Association for Business Organizations
3 Woodthorn Ct., Ste. 12
Owings Mills, MD 21117
(410)581-1373
E-mail: nahbb@msn.com
Rudolph Lewis, Exec. Officer

International Council for Small Business
The George Washington University
School of Business and Public Management
2115 G St. NW, Ste. 403
Washington, DC 20052
(202)994-0704
Fax: (202)994-4930
E-mail: icsb@gwu.edu
Website: http://www.icsb.org
Susan G. Duffy. Admin.

International Small Business Consortium
3309 Windjammer St.
Norman, OK 73072
E-mail: sb@isbc.com
Website: http://www.isbc.com

Kauffman Center for Entrepreneurial Leadership
4801 Rockhill Rd.
Kansas City, MO 64110-2046
(816)932-1000
E-mail: info@kauffman.org
Website: http://www.entreworld.org

National Alliance for Fair Competition
3 Bethesda Metro Center, Ste. 1100
Bethesda, MD 20814
(410)235-7116
Fax: (410)235-7116
E-mail: ampesq@aol.com
Tony Ponticelli, Exec.Dir.

National Association for the Self-Employed
PO Box 612067
DFW Airport
Dallas, TX 75261-2067
(800)232-6273
E-mail: mpetron@nase.org
Website: http://www.nase.org
Robert Hughes, Pres.

National Association of Business Leaders
4132 Shoreline Dr., Ste. J & H
Earth City, MO 63045
Fax: (314)298-9110
E-mail: nabl@nabl.com
Website: http://www.nabl.com/
Gene Blumenthal, Contact

National Association of Private Enterprise
PO Box 15550
Long Beach, CA 90815
888-224-0953
Fax: (714)844-4942
Website: http://www.napeonline.net
Laura Squiers, Exec.Dir.

National Association of Small Business Investment Companies
666 11th St. NW, Ste. 750
Washington, DC 20001
(202)628-5055
Fax: (202)628-5080
E-mail: nasbic@nasbic.org
Website: http://www.nasbic.org
Lee W. Mercer, Pres.

National Business Association
PO Box 700728
5151 Beltline Rd., Ste. 1150
Dallas, TX 75370
(972)458-0900
800-456-0440
Fax: (972)960-9149
E-mail: info@nationalbusiness.org
Website: http://
www.nationalbusiness.org
Raj Nisankarao, Pres.

National Business Owners Association
PO Box 111
Stuart, VA 24171
(276)251-7500
(866)251-7505
Fax: (276)251-2217
E-mail: membershipservices@nboa.org
Website: http://www.rvmdb.com.nboa
Paul LaBarr, Pres.

National Center for Fair Competition
PO Box 220
Annandale, VA 22003
(703)280-4622
Fax: (703)280-0942
E-mail: kentonp1@aol.com
Kenton Pattie, Pres.

National Family Business Council
1640 W. Kennedy Rd.
Lake Forest, IL 60045
(847)295-1040
Fax: (847)295-1898
E-mail: lmsnfbc@email.msn.com
Jogn E. Messervey, Pres.

National Federation of Independent Business
53 Century Blvd., Ste. 250
Nashville, TN 37214
(615)872-5800
800-NFIBNOW
Fax: (615)872-5353
Website: http://www.nfib.org
Jack Faris, Pres. and CEO

National Small Business Association
1156 15th St. NW, Ste. 1100
Washington, DC 20005
(202)293-8830
800-345-6728
Fax: (202)872-8543
E-mail: press@nsba.biz
Website: http://www.nsba.biz
Rob Yunich, Dir. of Communications

PUSH Commercial Division
930 E 50th St.
Chicago, IL 60615-2702
(773)373-3366
Fax: (773)373-3571
E-mail: info@rainbowpush.org
Website: http://www.rainbowpush.org
Rev. Willie T. Barrow, Co-Chm.

Research Institute for Small and Emerging Business
722 12th St. NW
Washington, DC 20005
(202)628-8382
Fax: (202)628-8392
E-mail: info@riseb.org
Website: http://www.riseb.org
Allan Neece, Jr., Chm.

Sales Professionals USA
PO Box 149
Arvada, CO 80001
(303)534-4937
888-736-7767
E-mail: salespro@salesprofessionals-usa.com
Website: http://www.salesprofessionals-usa.com
Sharon Herbert, Natl. Pres.

Score Association - Service Corps of Retired Executives
409 3rd St. SW, 6th Fl.
Washington, DC 20024
(202)205-6762
800-634-0245
Fax: (202)205-7636
E-mail: media@score.org
Website: http://www.score.org
W. Kenneth Yancey, Jr., CEO

Small Business and Entrepreneurship Council
1920 L St. NW, Ste. 200
Washington, DC 20036
(202)785-0238
Fax: (202)822-8118
E-mail: membership@sbec.org
Website: http://www.sbecouncil.org
Karen Kerrigan, Pres./CEO

Small Business in Telecommunications
1331 H St. NW, Ste. 500
Washington, DC 20005
(202)347-4511
Fax: (202)347-8607
E-mail: sbt@sbthome.org
Website: http://www.sbthome.org
Lonnie Danchik, Chm.

Small Business Legislative Council
1010 Massachusetts Ave. NW, Ste. 540
Washington, DC 20005
(202)639-8500
Fax: (202)296-5333
E-mail: email@sblc.org
Website: http://www.sblc.org
John Satagaj, Pres.

Small Business Service Bureau
554 Main St.
PO Box 15014
Worcester, MA 01615-0014
(508)756-3513
800-343-0939
Fax: (508)770-0528
E-mail: membership@sbsb.com
Website: http://www.sbsb.com
Francis R. Carroll, Pres.

Small Publishers Association of North America
1618 W COlorado Ave.
Colorado Springs, CO 80904
(719)475-1726
Fax: (719)471-2182
E-mail: span@spannet.org
Website: http://www.spannet.org
Scott Flora, Exec. Dir.

SOHO America
PO Box 941
Hurst, TX 76053-0941
800-495-SOHO
E-mail: soho@1sas.com
Website: http://www.soho.org

Structured Employment Economic Development Corporation
915 Broadway, 17th Fl.
New York, NY 10010
(212)473-0255
Fax: (212)473-0357
E-mail: info@seedco.org
Website: http://www.seedco.org
William Grinker, CEO

Support Services Alliance
107 Prospect St.
Schoharie, NY 12157
800-836-4772
E-mail: info@ssamembers.com
Website: http://www.ssainfo.com
Steve COle, Pres.

United States Association for Small Business and Entrepreneurship
975 University Ave., No. 3260
Madison, WI 53706
(608)262-9982
Fax: (608)263-0818
E-mail: jgillman@wisc.edu
Website: http://www.ususbe.org
Joan Gillman, Exec. Dir.

Consultants

This section contains a listing of consultants specializing in small business development. It is arranged alphabetically by country, then by state or province, then by city, then by firm name.

Canada

Alberta

Common Sense Solutions
3405 16A Ave.
Edmonton, AB, Canada
(403)465-7330
Fax: (403)465-7380
E-mail: gcoulson@comsensesolutions.com
Website: http://
www.comsensesolutions.com

Varsity Consulting Group
School of Business
University of Alberta
Edmonton, AB, Canada T6G 2R6
(780)492-2994
Fax: (780)492-5400
Website: http://www.bus.ualberta.ca/vcg

Viro Hospital Consulting
42 Commonwealth Bldg., 9912 - 106 St. NW
Edmonton, AB, Canada T5K 1C5
(403)425-3871
Fax: (403)425-3871
E-mail: rpb@freenet.edmonton.ab.ca

British Columbia

SRI Strategic Resources Inc.
4330 Kingsway, Ste. 1600
Burnaby, BC, Canada V5H 4G7
(604)435-0627
Fax: (604)435-2782
E-mail: inquiry@sri.bc.ca
Website: http://www.sri.com

Andrew R. De Boda Consulting
1523 Milford Ave.
Coquitlam, BC, Canada V3J 2V9
(604)936-4527
Fax: (604)936-4527
E-mail: deboda@intergate.bc.ca
Website: http://
www.ourworld.compuserve.com/
homepages/deboda

The Sage Group Ltd.
980 - 355 Burrard St.
744 W Haistings, Ste. 410
Vancouver, BC, Canada V6C 1A5
(604)669-9269
Fax: (604)669-6622

Tikkanen-Bradley
1345 Nelson St., Ste. 202
Vancouver, BC, Canada V6E 1J8
(604)669-0583
E-mail:
webmaster@tikkanenbradley.com
Website: http://
www.tikkanenbradley.com

Ontario

The Cynton Co.
17 Massey St.
Brampton, ON, Canada L6S 2V6
(905)792-7769
Fax: (905)792-8116
E-mail: cynton@home.com
Website: http://www.cynton.com

Begley & Associates
RR 6
Cambridge, ON, Canada N1R 5S7
(519)740-3629
Fax: (519)740-3629
E-mail: begley@in.on.ca
Website: http://www.in.on.ca/~begley/
index.htm

CRO Engineering Ltd.
1895 William Hodgins Ln.
Carp, ON, Canada K0A 1L0
(613)839-1108
Fax: (613)839-1406
E-mail: J.Grefford@ieee.ca
Website: http://www.geocities.com/
WallStreet/District/7401/

Task Enterprises
Box 69, RR 2 Hamilton
Flamborough, ON, Canada L8N 2Z7
(905)659-0153
Fax: (905)659-0861

HST Group Ltd.
430 Gilmour St.
Ottawa, ON, Canada K2P 0R8
(613)236-7303
Fax: (613)236-9893

Harrison Associates
BCE Pl.
181 Bay St., Ste. 3740
PO Box 798
Toronto, ON, Canada M5J 2T3
(416)364-5441
Fax: (416)364-2875

TCI Convergence Ltd. Management Consultants
99 Crown's Ln.
Toronto, ON, Canada M5R 3P4
(416)515-4146
Fax: (416)515-2097
E-mail: tci@inforamp.net
Website: http://tciconverge.com/index.1.html

Ken Wyman & Associates Inc.
64B Shuter St., Ste. 200
Toronto, ON, Canada M5B 1B1
(416)362-2926
Fax: (416)362-3039
E-mail: kenwyman@compuserve.com

JPL Business Consultants
82705 Metter Rd.
Wellandport, ON, Canada L0R 2J0
(905)386-7450
Fax: (905)386-7450
E-mail: plamarch@freenet.npiec.on.ca

Quebec

The Zimmar Consulting Partnership Inc.
Westmount
PO Box 98
Montreal, QC, Canada H3Z 2T1
(514)484-1459
Fax: (514)484-3063

Saskatchewan

Trimension Group
No. 104-110 Research Dr.
Innovation Place, SK, Canada S7N 3R3
(306)668-2560
Fax: (306)975-1156
E-mail: trimension@trimension.ca
Website: http://www.trimension.ca

Corporate Management Consultants
PO Box 7570 Station Main
Saskatoon, SK, Canada, S7K 4L4
(306)343-8415
Fax: (650)618-2742
E-mail:
cmccorporatemanagement@shaw.ca
Website:
http://www.Corporatemanagementconsultants.com
Gerald Rekve

United states

Alabama

Business Planning Inc.
300 Office Park Dr.
Birmingham, AL 35223-2474
(205)870-7090
Fax: (205)870-7103

Tradebank of Eastern Alabama
546 Broad St., Ste. 3
Gadsden, AL 35901
(205)547-8700
Fax: (205)547-8718
E-mail: mansion@webex.com
Website: http://www.webex.com/~tea

Alaska

AK Business Development Center
3335 Arctic Blvd., Ste. 203
Anchorage, AK 99503
(907)562-0335
Free: 800-478-3474
Fax: (907)562-6988
E-mail: abdc@gci.net
Website: http://www.abdc.org

Business Matters
PO Box 287
Fairbanks, AK 99707
(907)452-5650

Arizona

Carefree Direct Marketing Corp.
8001 E Serene St.
PO Box 3737
Carefree, AZ 85377-3737
(480)488-4227
Fax: (480)488-2841

Trans Energy Corp.
1739 W 7th Ave.
Mesa, AZ 85202
(480)827-7915
Fax: (480)967-6601
E-mail: aha@clean-air.org
Website: http://www.clean-air.org

CMAS
5125 N 16th St.
Phoenix, AZ 85016
(602)395-1001
Fax: (602)604-8180

Comgate Telemanagement Ltd.
706 E Bell Rd., Ste. 105
Phoenix, AZ 85022
(602)485-5708
Fax: (602)485-5709
E-mail: comgate@netzone.com
Website: http://www.comgate.com

Moneysoft Inc.
1 E Camelback Rd. #550
Phoenix, AZ 85012
Free: 800-966-7797
E-mail: mbray@moneysoft.com

Harvey C. Skoog
PO Box 26439
Prescott Valley, AZ 86312
(520)772-1714
Fax: (520)772-2814

LMC Services
8711 E Pinnacle Peak Rd., No. 340
Scottsdale, AZ 85255-3555
(602)585-7177
Fax: (602)585-5880
E-mail: louws@earthlink.com

Sauerbrun Technology Group Ltd.
7979 E Princess Dr., Ste. 5
Scottsdale, AZ 85255-5878
(602)502-4950
Fax: (602)502-4292
E-mail: info@sauerbrun.com
Website: http://www.sauerbrun.com

Gary L. McLeod
PO Box 230
Sonoita, AZ 85637
Fax: (602)455-5661

Van Cleve Associates
6932 E 2nd St.
Tucson, AZ 85710
(520)296-2587
Fax: (520)296-3358

California

Acumen Group Inc.
(650)949-9349
Fax: (650)949-4845
E-mail: acumen-g@ix.netcom.com
Website: http://pw2.netcom.com/~janed/acumen.html

On-line Career and Management Consulting
420 Central Ave., No. 314
Alameda, CA 94501
(510)864-0336
Fax: (510)864-0336
E-mail: career@dnai.com
Website: http://www.dnai.com/~career

Career Paths-Thomas E. Church & Associates Inc.
PO Box 2439
Aptos, CA 95001
(408)662-7950
Fax: (408)662-7955
E-mail: church@ix.netcom.com
Website: http://www.careerpaths-tom.com

Keck & Co. Business Consultants
410 Walsh Rd.
Atherton, CA 94027
(650)854-9588
Fax: (650)854-7240
E-mail: info@keckco.com
Website: http://www.keckco.com

Ben W. Laverty III, PhD, REA, CEI
4909 Stockdale Hwy., Ste. 132
Bakersfield, CA 93309
(661)283-8300
Free: 800-833-0373
Fax: (661)283-8313
E-mail: cstc@cstcsafety.com
Website: http://www.cstcsafety.com/cstc

Lindquist Consultants-Venture Planning
225 Arlington Ave.
Berkeley, CA 94707
(510)524-6685
Fax: (510)527-6604

Larson Associates
PO Box 9005
Brea, CA 92822
(714)529-4121
Fax: (714)572-3606
E-mail: ray@consultlarson.com
Website: http://www.consultlarson.com

Kremer Management Consulting
PO Box 500
Carmel, CA 93921
(408)626-8311
Fax: (408)624-2663
E-mail: ddkremer@aol.com

W and J PARTNERSHIP
PO Box 2499
18876 Edwin Markham Dr.
Castro Valley, CA 94546
(510)583-7751
Fax: (510)583-7645
E-mail: wamorgan@wjpartnership.com
Website: http://www.wjpartnership.com

JB Associates
21118 Gardena Dr.
Cupertino, CA 95014
(408)257-0214
Fax: (408)257-0216
E-mail: semarang@sirius.com

House Agricultural Consultants
PO Box 1615
Davis, CA 95617-1615
(916)753-3361
Fax: (916)753-0464
E-mail: infoag@houseag.com
Website: http://www.houseag.com/

3C Systems Co.
16161 Ventura Blvd., Ste. 815
Encino, CA 91436
(818)907-1302
Fax: (818)907-1357
E-mail: mark@3CSysCo.com
Website: http://www.3CSysCo.com

Technical Management Consultants
3624 Westfall Dr.
Encino, CA 91436-4154
(818)784-0626
Fax: (818)501-5575
E-mail: tmcrs@aol.com

RAINWATER-GISH & Associates, Business Finance & Development
317 3rd St., Ste. 3
Eureka, CA 95501
(707)443-0030
Fax: (707)443-5683

Global Tradelinks
451 Pebble Beach Pl.
Fullerton, CA 92835
(714)441-2280
Fax: (714)441-2281
E-mail: info@globaltradelinks.com
Website: http://www.globaltradelinks.com

Strategic Business Group
800 Cienaga Dr.
Fullerton, CA 92835-1248
(714)449-1040
Fax: (714)525-1631

Burnes Consulting
20537 Wolf Creek Rd.
Grass Valley, CA 95949
(530)346-8188
Free: 800-949-9021
Fax: (530)346-7704
E-mail: kent@burnesconsulting.com
Website: http://www.burnesconsulting.com

Pioneer Business Consultants
9042 Garfield Ave., Ste. 312
Huntington Beach, CA 92646
(714)964-7600

Beblie, Brandt & Jacobs Inc.
16 Technology, Ste. 164
Irvine, CA 92618
(714)450-8790
Fax: (714)450-8799
E-mail: darcy@bbjinc.com
Website: http://198.147.90.26

Fluor Daniel Inc.
3353 Michelson Dr.
Irvine, CA 92612-0650
(949)975-2000
Fax: (949)975-5271
E-mail: sales.consulting@fluordaniel.com
Website: http://www.fluordanielconsulting.com

MCS Associates
18300 Von Karman, Ste. 710
Irvine, CA 92612
(949)263-8700
Fax: (949)263-0770
E-mail: info@mcsassociates.com
Website: http://www.mcsassociates.com

Inspired Arts Inc.
4225 Executive Sq., Ste. 1160
La Jolla, CA 92037
(619)623-3525
Free: 800-851-4394
Fax: (619)623-3534
E-mail: info@inspiredarts.com
Website: http://www.inspiredarts.com

The Laresis Companies
PO Box 3284
La Jolla, CA 92038
(619)452-2720
Fax: (619)452-8744

RCL & Co.
PO Box 1143
737 Pearl St., Ste. 201
La Jolla, CA 92038
(619)454-8883
Fax: (619)454-8880

Comprehensive Business Services
3201 Lucas Cir.
Lafayette, CA 94549
(925)283-8272
Fax: (925)283-8272

The Ribble Group
27601 Forbes Rd., Ste. 52
Laguna Niguel, CA 92677
(714)582-1085
Fax: (714)582-6420
E-mail: ribble@deltanet.com

Norris Bernstein, CMC
9309 Marina Pacifica Dr. N
Long Beach, CA 90803
(562)493-5458
Fax: (562)493-5459
E-mail: norris@ctecomputer.com
Website: http://foodconsultants.com/bernstein/

Horizon Consulting Services
1315 Garthwick Dr.
Los Altos, CA 94024
(415)967-0906
Fax: (415)967-0906

Brincko Associates Inc.
1801 Avenue of the Stars, Ste. 1054
Los Angeles, CA 90067
(310)553-4523
Fax: (310)553-6782

Rubenstein/Justman Management Consultants
2049 Century Park E, 24th Fl.
Los Angeles, CA 90067
(310)282-0800
Fax: (310)282-0400
E-mail: info@rjmc.net
Website: http://www.rjmc.net

F.J. Schroeder & Associates
1926 Westholme Ave.
Los Angeles, CA 90025
(310)470-2655
Fax: (310)470-6378
E-mail: fjsacons@aol.com
Website: http://www.mcninet.com/GlobalLook/Fjschroe.html

Western Management Associates
5959 W Century Blvd., Ste. 565
Los Angeles, CA 90045-6506
(310)645-1091
Free: (888)788-6534
Fax: (310)645-1092
E-mail: gene@cfoforrent.com
Website: http://www.cfoforrent.com

Darrell Sell and Associates
Los Gatos, CA 95030
(408)354-7794
E-mail: darrell@netcom.com

Leslie J. Zambo
3355 Michael Dr.
Marina, CA 93933
(408)384-7086
Fax: (408)647-4199
E-mail: 104776.1552@compuserve.com

Marketing Services Management
PO Box 1377
Martinez, CA 94553
(510)370-8527
Fax: (510)370-8527
E-mail: markserve@biotechnet.com

William M. Shine Consulting Service
PO Box 127
Moraga, CA 94556-0127
(510)376-6516

Palo Alto Management Group Inc.
2672 Bayshore Pky., Ste. 701
Mountain View, CA 94043
(415)968-4374
Fax: (415)968-4245
E-mail: mburwen@pamg.com

BizplanSource
1048 Irvine Ave., Ste. 621
Newport Beach, CA 92660
Free: 888-253-0974
Fax: 800-859-8254
E-mail: info@bizplansource.com
Website: http://www.bizplansource.com
Adam Greengrass, President

The Market Connection
4020 Birch St., Ste. 203
Newport Beach, CA 92660
(714)731-6273
Fax: (714)833-0253

Muller Associates
PO Box 7264
Newport Beach, CA 92658
(714)646-1169
Fax: (714)646-1169

International Health Resources
PO Box 329
North San Juan, CA 95960-0329
(530)292-1266
Fax: (530)292-1243
Website: http://www.futureofhealthcare.com

NEXUS - Consultants to Management
PO Box 1531
Novato, CA 94948
(415)897-4400
Fax: (415)898-2252
E-mail: jimnexus@aol.com

Aerospcace.Org
PO Box 28831
Oakland, CA 94604-8831
(510)530-9169
Fax: (510)530-3411
Website: http://www.aerospace.org

Intelequest Corp.
722 Gailen Ave.
Palo Alto, CA 94303
(415)968-3443
Fax: (415)493-6954
E-mail: frits@iqix.com

McLaughlin & Associates
66 San Marino Cir.
Rancho Mirage, CA 92270
(760)321-2932
Fax: (760)328-2474
E-mail: jackmcla@msn.com

Carrera Consulting Group, a division of Maximus
2110 21st St., Ste. 400
Sacramento, CA 95818
(916)456-3300
Fax: (916)456-3306
E-mail: central@carreraconsulting.com
Website: http://www.carreraconsulting.com

Bay Area Tax Consultants and Bayhill Financial Consultants
1150 Bayhill Dr., Ste. 1150
San Bruno, CA 94066-3004
(415)952-8786
Fax: (415)588-4524
E-mail: baytax@compuserve.com
Website: http://www.baytax.com/

AdCon Services, LLC
8871 Hillery Dr.
Dan Diego, CA 92126
(858)433-1411
E-mail: adam@adconservices.com
Website: http://www.adconservices.com
Adam Greengrass

California Business Incubation Network
101 W Broadway, No. 480
San Diego, CA 92101
(619)237-0559
Fax: (619)237-0521

G.R. Gordetsky Consultants Inc.
11414 Windy Summit Pl.
San Diego, CA 92127
(619)487-4939
Fax: (619)487-5587
E-mail: gordet@pacbell.net

Freeman, Sullivan & Co.
131 Steuart St., Ste. 500
San Francisco, CA 94105
(415)777-0707
Free: 800-777-0737
Fax: (415)777-2420
Website: http://www.fsc-research.com

Ideas Unlimited
2151 California St., Ste. 7
San Francisco, CA 94115
(415)931-0641
Fax: (415)931-0880

Russell Miller Inc.
300 Montgomery St., Ste. 900
San Francisco, CA 94104
(415)956-7474
Fax: (415)398-0620
E-mail: rmi@pacbell.net
Website: http://www.rmisf.com

PKF Consulting
425 California St., Ste. 1650
San Francisco, CA 94104
(415)421-5378
Fax: (415)956-7708
E-mail: callahan@pkfc.com
Website: http://www.pkfonline.com

Welling & Woodard Inc.
1067 Broadway
San Francisco, CA 94133
(415)776-4500
Fax: (415)776-5067

Highland Associates
16174 Highland Dr.
San Jose, CA 95127
(408)272-7008
Fax: (408)272-4040

ORDIS Inc.
6815 Trinidad Dr.
San Jose, CA 95120-2056
(408)268-3321
Free: 800-446-7347
Fax: (408)268-3582
E-mail: ordis@ordis.com
Website: http://www.ordis.com

Stanford Resources Inc.
20 Great Oaks Blvd., Ste. 200
San Jose, CA 95119
(408)360-8400
Fax: (408)360-8410
E-mail: sales@stanfordsources.com
Website: http://
www.stanfordresources.com

Technology Properties Ltd. Inc.
PO Box 20250
San Jose, CA 95160
(408)243-9898
Fax: (408)296-6637
E-mail: sanjose@tplnet.com

Helfert Associates
1777 Borel Pl., Ste. 508
San Mateo, CA 94402-3514
(650)377-0540
Fax: (650)377-0472

Mykytyn Consulting Group Inc.
185 N Redwood Dr., Ste. 200
San Rafael, CA 94903
(415)491-1770
Fax: (415)491-1251
E-mail: info@mcgi.com
Website: http://www.mcgi.com

Omega Management Systems Inc.
3 Mount Darwin Ct.
San Rafael, CA 94903-1109
(415)499-1300
Fax: (415)492-9490
E-mail: omegamgt@ix.netcom.com

The Information Group Inc.
4675 Stevens Creek Blvd., Ste. 100
Santa Clara, CA 95051
(408)985-7877
Fax: (408)985-2945
E-mail: dvincent@tig-usa.com
Website: http://www.tig-usa.com

Cast Management Consultants
1620 26th St., Ste. 2040N
Santa Monica, CA 90404
(310)828-7511
Fax: (310)453-6831

Cuma Consulting Management
Box 724
Santa Rosa, CA 95402
(707)785-2477
Fax: (707)785-2478

The E-Myth Academy
131B Stony Cir., Ste. 2000
Santa Rosa, CA 95401
(707)569-5600
Free: 800-221-0266
Fax: (707)569-5700
E-mail: info@e-myth.com
Website: http://www.e-myth.com

Reilly, Connors & Ray
1743 Canyon Rd.
Spring Valley, CA 91977
(619)698-4808
Fax: (619)460-3892
E-mail: davidray@adnc.com

Management Consultants
Sunnyvale, CA 94087-4700
(408)773-0321

RJR Associates
1639 Lewiston Dr.
Sunnyvale, CA 94087
(408)737-7720
E-mail: bobroy@rjrassoc.com
Website: http://www.rjrassoc.com

Schwafel Associates
333 Cobalt Way, Ste. 21
Sunnyvale, CA 94085
(408)720-0649
Fax: (408)720-1796
E-mail: schwafel@ricochet.net
Website: http://www.patca.org

Staubs Business Services
23320 S Vermont Ave.
Torrance, CA 90502-2940
(310)830-9128
Fax: (310)830-9128
E-mail: Harry_L_Staubs@Lamg.com

Out of Your Mind ... and Into the Marketplace
13381 White Sands Dr.
Tustin, CA 92780-4565
(714)544-0248
Free: 800-419-1513
Fax: (714)730-1414
E-mail: lpinson@aol.com
Website: http://www.business-plan.com

Independent Research Services
PO Box 2426
Van Nuys, CA 91404-2426
(818)993-3622

Ingman Company Inc.
7949 Woodley Ave., Ste. 120
Van Nuys, CA 91406-1232
(818)375-5027
Fax: (818)894-5001

Innovative Technology Associates
3639 E Harbor Blvd., Ste. 203E
Ventura, CA 93001
(805)650-9353

Grid Technology Associates
20404 Tufts Cir.
Walnut, CA 91789
(909)444-0922
Fax: (909)444-0922
E-mail: grid_technology@msn.com

Ridge Consultants Inc.
100 Pringle Ave., Ste. 580
Walnut Creek, CA 94596
(925)274-1990
Fax: (510)274-1956
E-mail: info@ridgecon.com
Website: http://www.ridgecon.com

Bell Springs Publishing
PO Box 1240
Willits, CA 95490
(707)459-6372
E-mail: bellsprings@sabernet
Website: http://www.bellsprings.com

Hutchinson Consulting and Appraisal
23245 Sylvan St., Ste. 103
Woodland Hills, CA 91367
(818)888-8175
Free: 800-977-7548
Fax: (818)888-8220
E-mail: r.f.hutchinson-cpa@worldnet.att.net

Colorado

Sam Boyer & Associates
4255 S Buckley Rd., No. 136
Aurora, CO 80013
Free: 800-785-0485
Fax: (303)766-8740
E-mail: samboyer@samboyer.com
Website: http://www.samboyer.com/

Ameriwest Business Consultants Inc.
PO Box 26266
Colorado Springs, CO 80936
(719)380-7096
Fax: (719)380-7096
E-mail: email@abchelp.com
Website: http://www.abchelp.com

GVNW Consulting Inc.
2270 La Montana Way
Colorado Springs, CO 80936
(719)594-5800
Fax: (719)594-5803
Website: http://www.gvnw.com

M-Squared Inc.
755 San Gabriel Pl.
Colorado Springs, CO 80906
(719)576-2554
Fax: (719)576-2554

Thornton Financial FNIC
1024 Centre Ave., Bldg. E
Fort Collins, CO 80526-1849
(970)221-2089
Fax: (970)484-5206

TenEyck Associates
1760 Cherryville Rd.
Greenwood Village, CO 80121-1503
(303)758-6129
Fax: (303)761-8286

Associated Enterprises Ltd.
13050 W Ceder Dr., Unit 11
Lakewood, CO 80228
(303)988-6695
Fax: (303)988-6739
E-mail: ael1@classic.msn.com

The Vincent Company Inc.
200 Union Blvd., Ste. 210
Lakewood, CO 80228
(303)989-7271
Free: 800-274-0733
Fax: (303)989-7570
E-mail: vincent@vincentco.com
Website: http://www.vincentco.com

Johnson & West Management Consultants Inc.
7612 S Logan Dr.
Littleton, CO 80122
(303)730-2810
Fax: (303)730-3219

Western Capital Holdings Inc.
10050 E Applwood Dr.
Parker, CO 80138
(303)841-1022
Fax: (303)770-1945

Connecticut

Stratman Group Inc.
40 Tower Ln.
Avon, CT 06001-4222
(860)677-2898
Free: 800-551-0499
Fax: (860)677-8210

Cowherd Consulting Group Inc.
106 Stephen Mather Rd.
Darien, CT 06820
(203)655-2150
Fax: (203)655-6427

Greenwich Associates
8 Greenwich Office Park
Greenwich, CT 06831-5149
(203)629-1200
Fax: (203)629-1229
E-mail: lisa@greenwich.com
Website: http://www.greenwich.com

Follow-up News
185 Pine St., Ste. 818
Manchester, CT 06040
(860)647-7542
Free: 800-708-0696
Fax: (860)646-6544
E-mail: Followupnews@aol.com

Lovins & Associates Consulting
309 Edwards St.
New Haven, CT 06511
(203)787-3367
Fax: (203)624-7599
E-mail: Alovinsphd@aol.com
Website: http://www.lovinsgroup.com

JC Ventures Inc.
4 Arnold St.
Old Greenwich, CT 06870-1203
(203)698-1990
Free: 800-698-1997
Fax: (203)698-2638

Charles L. Hornung Associates
52 Ned's Mountain Rd.
Ridgefield, CT 06877
(203)431-0297

Manus
100 Prospect St., S Tower
Stamford, CT 06901
(203)326-3880
Free: 800-445-0942
Fax: (203)326-3890
E-mail: manus1@aol.com
Website: http://www.RightManus.com

RealBusinessPlans.com
156 Westport Rd.
Wilton, CT 06897
(914)837-2886
E-mail: ct@realbusinessplans.com
Website: http://www.RealBusinessPlans.com
Tony Tecce

Delaware

Focus Marketing
61-7 Habor Dr.
Claymont, DE 19703
(302)793-3064

Daedalus Ventures Ltd.
PO Box 1474
Hockessin, DE 19707
(302)239-6758
Fax: (302)239-9991
E-mail: daedalus@mail.del.net

The Formula Group
PO Box 866
Hockessin, DE 19707
(302)456-0952
Fax: (302)456-1354
E-mail: formula@netaxs.com

Selden Enterprises Inc.
2502 Silverside Rd., Ste. 1
Wilmington, DE 19810-3740
(302)529-7113
Fax: (302)529-7442
E-mail: selden2@bellatlantic.net
Website: http://
www.seldenenterprises.com

District of Columbia

Bruce W. McGee and Associates
7826 Eastern Ave. NW, Ste. 30
Washington, DC 20012
(202)726-7272
Fax: (202)726-2946

McManis Associates Inc.
1900 K St. NW, Ste. 700
Washington, DC 20006
(202)466-7680
Fax: (202)872-1898
Website: http://www.mcmanis-mmi.com

Smith, Dawson & Andrews Inc.
1000 Connecticut Ave., Ste. 302
Washington, DC 20036
(202)835-0740
Fax: (202)775-8526
E-mail: webmaster@sda-inc.com
Website: http://www.sda-inc.com

Florida

BackBone, Inc.
20404 Hacienda Court
Boca Raton, FL 33498
(561)470-0965
Fax: 516-908-4038
E-mail: BPlans@backboneinc.com
Website: http://www.backboneinc.com
Charles Epstein, President

Whalen & Associates Inc.
4255 Northwest 26 Ct.
Boca Raton, FL 33434
(561)241-5950
Fax: (561)241-7414
E-mail: drwhalen@ix.netcom.com

E.N. Rysso & Associates
180 Bermuda Petrel Ct.
Daytona Beach, FL 32119
(386)760-3028
E-mail: erysso@aol.com

Virtual Technocrats LLC
560 Lavers Circle, #146
Delray Beach, FL 33444
(561)265-3509
E-mail: josh@virtualtechnocrats.com;
info@virtualtechnocrats.com
Website: http://
www.virtualtechnocrats.com
Josh Eikov, Managing Director

Eric Sands Consulting Services
6193 Rock Island Rd., Ste. 412
Fort Lauderdale, FL 33319
(954)721-4767
Fax: (954)720-2815
E-mail: easands@aol.com
Website: http://
www.ericsandsconsultig.com

Professional Planning Associates, Inc.
1975 E. Sunrise Blvd. Suite 607
Fort Lauderdale, FL 33304
(954)764-5204
Fax: 954-463-4172
E-mail: Mgoldstein@proplana.com
Website: http://proplana.com
Michael Goldstein, President

Host Media Corp.
3948 S 3rd St., Ste. 191
Jacksonville Beach, FL 32250
(904)285-3239
Fax: (904)285-5618
E-mail: msconsulting@compuserve.com
Website: http://
www.mediaservicesgroup.com

William V. Hall
1925 Brickell, Ste. D-701
Miami, FL 33129
(305)856-9622
Fax: (305)856-4113
E-mail: williamvhall@compuserve.com

F.A. McGee Inc.
800 Claughton Island Dr., Ste. 401
Miami, FL 33131
(305)377-9123

Taxplan Inc.
Mirasol International Ctr.
2699 Collins Ave.
Miami Beach, FL 33140
(305)538-3303

T.C. Brown & Associates
8415 Excalibur Cir., Apt. B1
Naples, FL 34108
(941)594-1949
Fax: (941)594-0611
E-mail: tcater@naples.net.com

RLA International Consulting
713 Lagoon Dr.
North Palm Beach, FL 33408
(407)626-4258
Fax: (407)626-5772

Comprehensive Franchising Inc.
2465 Ridgecrest Ave.
Orange Park, FL 32065
(904)272-6567
Free: 800-321-6567
Fax: (904)272-6750
E-mail: theimp@cris.com
Website: http://www.franchise411.com

Hunter G. Jackson Jr. - Consulting Environmental Physicist
PO Box 618272
Orlando, FL 32861-8272
(407)295-4188
E-mail: hunterjackson@juno.com

F. Newton Parks
210 El Brillo Way
Palm Beach, FL 33480
(561)833-1727
Fax: (561)833-4541

Avery Business Development Services
2506 St. Michel Ct.
Ponte Vedra Beach, FL 32082
(904)285-6033
Fax: (904)285-6033

Strategic Business Planning Co.
PO Box 821006
South Florida, FL 33082-1006
(954)704-9100
Fax: (954)438-7333
E-mail: info@bizplan.com
Website: http://www.bizplan.com

Dufresne Consulting Group Inc.
10014 N Dale Mabry, Ste. 101
Tampa, FL 33618-4426
(813)264-4775
Fax: (813)264-9300
Website: http://www.dcgconsult.com

Agrippa Enterprises Inc.
PO Box 175
Venice, FL 34284-0175
(941)355-7876
E-mail: webservices@agrippa.com
Website: http://www.agrippa.com

Center for Simplified Strategic Planning Inc.
PO Box 3324
Vero Beach, FL 32964-3324
(561)231-3636
Fax: (561)231-1099
Website: http://www.cssp.com

Georgia

Marketing Spectrum Inc.
115 Perimeter Pl., Ste. 440
Atlanta, GA 30346
(770)395-7244
Fax: (770)393-4071

Business Ventures Corp.
1650 Oakbrook Dr., Ste. 405
Norcross, GA 30093
(770)729-8000
Fax: (770)729-8028

Informed Decisions Inc.
100 Falling Cheek
Sautee Nacoochee, GA 30571
(706)878-1905
Fax: (706)878-1802
E-mail: skylake@compuserve.com

Tom C. Davis & Associates, P.C.
3189 Perimeter Rd.
Valdosta, GA 31602
(912)247-9801
Fax: (912)244-7704
E-mail: mail@tcdcpa.com
Website: http://www.tcdcpa.com/

Illinois

TWD and Associates
431 S Patton
Arlington Heights, IL 60005
(847)398-6410
Fax: (847)255-5095
E-mail: tdoo@aol.com

Management Planning Associates Inc.
2275 Half Day Rd., Ste. 350
Bannockburn, IL 60015-1277
(847)945-2421
Fax: (847)945-2425

Phil Faris Associates
86 Old Mill Ct.
Barrington, IL 60010
(847)382-4888
Fax: (847)382-4890
E-mail: pfaris@meginsnet.net

Seven Continents Technology
787 Stonebridge
Buffalo Grove, IL 60089
(708)577-9653
Fax: (708)870-1220

Grubb & Blue Inc.
2404 Windsor Pl.
Champaign, IL 61820
(217)366-0052
Fax: (217)356-0117

ACE Accounting Service Inc.
3128 N Bernard St.
Chicago, IL 60618
(773)463-7854
Fax: (773)463-7854

AON Consulting Worldwide
200 E Randolph St., 10th Fl.
Chicago, IL 60601
(312)381-4800
Free: 800-438-6487
Fax: (312)381-0240
Website: http://www.aon.com

FMS Consultants
5801 N Sheridan Rd., Ste. 3D
Chicago, IL 60660
(773)561-7362
Fax: (773)561-6274

Grant Thornton
800 1 Prudential Plz.
130 E Randolph St.
Chicago, IL 60601
(312)856-0001
Fax: (312)861-1340
E-mail: gtinfo@gt.com
Website: http://www.grantthornton.com

Kingsbury International Ltd.
5341 N Glenwood Ave.
Chicago, IL 60640
(773)271-3030
Fax: (773)728-7080
E-mail: jetlag@mcs.com
Website: http://www.kingbiz.com

MacDougall & Blake Inc.
1414 N Wells St., Ste. 311
Chicago, IL 60610-1306
(312)587-3330
Fax: (312)587-3699
E-mail: jblake@compuserve.com

James C. Osburn Ltd.
6445 N. Western Ave., Ste. 304
Chicago, IL 60645
(773)262-4428
Fax: (773)262-6755
E-mail: osburnltd@aol.com

Tarifero & Tazewell Inc.
211 S Clark
Chicago, IL 60690
(312)665-9714
Fax: (312)665-9716

Human Energy Design Systems
620 Roosevelt Dr.
Edwardsville, IL 62025
(618)692-0258
Fax: (618)692-0819

China Business Consultants Group
931 Dakota Cir.
Naperville, IL 60563
(630)778-7992
Fax: (630)778-7915
E-mail: cbcq@aol.com

Center for Workforce Effectiveness
500 Skokie Blvd., Ste. 222
Northbrook, IL 60062
(847)559-8777
Fax: (847)559-8778
E-mail: office@cwelink.com
Website: http://www.cwelink.com

Smith Associates
1320 White Mountain Dr.
Northbrook, IL 60062
(847)480-7200
Fax: (847)480-9828

Francorp Inc.
20200 Governors Dr.
Olympia Fields, IL 60461
(708)481-2900
Free: 800-372-6244
Fax: (708)481-5885
E-mail: francorp@aol.com
Website: http://www.francorpinc.com

Camber Business Strategy Consultants
1010 S Plum Tree Ct
Palatine, IL 60078-0986
(847)202-0101
Fax: (847)705-7510
E-mail: camber@ameritech.net

Partec Enterprise Group
5202 Keith Dr.
Richton Park, IL 60471
(708)503-4047
Fax: (708)503-9468

Rockford Consulting Group Ltd.
Century Plz., Ste. 206
7210 E State St.
Rockford, IL 61108
(815)229-2900
Free: 800-667-7495
Fax: (815)229-2612
E-mail: rligus@RockfordConsulting.com
Website: http://
www.RockfordConsulting.com

RSM McGladrey Inc.
1699 E Woodfield Rd., Ste. 300
Schaumburg, IL 60173-4969
(847)413-6900
Fax: (847)517-7067
Website: http://www.rsmmcgladrey.com

A.D. Star Consulting
320 Euclid
Winnetka, IL 60093
(847)446-7827
Fax: (847)446-7827
E-mail: startwo@worldnet.att.net

Indiana

Modular Consultants Inc.
3109 Crabtree Ln.
Elkhart, IN 46514
(219)264-5761
Fax: (219)264-5761
E-mail: sasabo5313@aol.com

Midwest Marketing Research
PO Box 1077
Goshen, IN 46527
(219)533-0548
Fax: (219)533-0540
E-mail: 103365.654@compuserve

Ketchum Consulting Group
8021 Knue Rd., Ste. 112
Indianapolis, IN 46250
(317)845-5411
Fax: (317)842-9941

MDI Management Consulting
1519 Park Dr.
Munster, IN 46321
(219)838-7909
Fax: (219)838-7909

Iowa

McCord Consulting Group Inc.
4533 Pine View Dr. NE
PO Box 11024
Cedar Rapids, IA 52410
(319)378-0077
Fax: (319)378-1577
E-mail: smmccord@hom.com
Website: http://www.mccordgroup.com

Management Solutions L.C.
3815 Lincoln Pl. Dr.
Des Moines, IA 50312
(515)277-6408
Fax: (515)277-3506
E-mail: wasunimers@uswest.net

Grandview Marketing
15 Red Bridge Dr.
Sioux City, IA 51104
(712)239-3122
Fax: (712)258-7578
E-mail: eandrews@pionet.net

Kansas

Assessments in Action
513A N Mur-Len
Olathe, KS 66062
(913)764-6270
Free: (888)548-1504
Fax: (913)764-6495
E-mail: lowdene@qni.com
Website: http://www.assessments-in-action.com

Maine

Edgemont Enterprises
PO Box 8354
Portland, ME 04104
(207)871-8964
Fax: (207)871-8964

Pan Atlantic Consultants
5 Milk St.
Portland, ME 04101
(207)871-8622
Fax: (207)772-4842
E-mail: pmurphy@maine.rr.com
Website: http://www.panatlantic.net

Maryland

Clemons & Associates Inc.
5024-R Campbell Blvd.
Baltimore, MD 21236
(410)931-8100
Fax: (410)931-8111
E-mail: info@clemonsmgmt.com
Website: http://www.clemonsmgmt.com

Imperial Group Ltd.
305 Washington Ave., Ste. 204
Baltimore, MD 21204-6009
(410)337-8500
Fax: (410)337-7641

Leadership Institute
3831 Yolando Rd.
Baltimore, MD 21218
(410)366-9111
Fax: (410)243-8478
E-mail: behconsult@aol.com

Burdeshaw Associates Ltd.
4701 Sangamore Rd.
Bethesda, MD 20816-2508
(301)229-5800
Fax: (301)229-5045
E-mail: jstacy@burdeshaw.com
Website: http://www.burdeshaw.com

Michael E. Cohen
5225 Pooks Hill Rd., Ste. 1119 S
Bethesda, MD 20814
(301)530-5738
Fax: (301)530-2988
E-mail: mecohen@crosslink.net

World Development Group Inc.
5272 River Rd., Ste. 650
Bethesda, MD 20816-1405
(301)652-1818
Fax: (301)652-1250
E-mail: wdg@has.com
Website: http://www.worlddg.com

Swartz Consulting
PO Box 4301
Crofton, MD 21114-4301
(301)262-6728

Software Solutions International Inc.
9633 Duffer Way
Gaithersburg, MD 20886
(301)330-4136
Fax: (301)330-4136

Strategies Inc.
8 Park Center Ct., Ste. 200
Owings Mills, MD 21117
(410)363-6669
Fax: (410)363-1231
E-mail: strategies@strat1.com
Website: http://www.strat1.com

Hammer Marketing Resources
179 Inverness Rd.
Severna Park, MD 21146
(410)544-9191
Fax: (305)675-3277
E-mail: info@gohammer.com
Website: http://www.gohammer.com

Andrew Sussman & Associates
13731 Kretsinger
Smithsburg, MD 21783
(301)824-2943
Fax: (301)824-2943

Massachusetts

Geibel Marketing and Public Relations
PO Box 611
Belmont, MA 02478-0005
(617)484-8285
Fax: (617)489-3567
E-mail: jgeibel@geibelpr.com
Website: http://www.geibelpr.com

Bain & Co.
2 Copley Pl.
Boston, MA 02116
(617)572-2000
Fax: (617)572-2427
E-mail: corporate.inquiries@bain.com
Website: http://www.bain.com

Mehr & Co.
62 Kinnaird St.
Cambridge, MA 02139
(617)876-3311
Fax: (617)876-3023
E-mail: mehrco@aol.com

Monitor Company Inc.
2 Canal Park
Cambridge, MA 02141
(617)252-2000
Fax: (617)252-2100
Website: http://www.monitor.com

Information & Research Associates
PO Box 3121
Framingham, MA 01701
(508)788-0784

Walden Consultants Ltd.
252 Pond St.
Hopkinton, MA 01748
(508)435-4882
Fax: (508)435-3971
Website: http://
www.waldenconsultants.com

Jeffrey D. Marshall
102 Mitchell Rd.
Ipswich, MA 01938-1219
(508)356-1113
Fax: (508)356-2989

Consulting Resources Corp.
6 Northbrook Park
Lexington, MA 02420
(781)863-1222
Fax: (781)863-1441
E-mail: res@consultingresources.net
Website: http://
www.consultingresources.net

Planning Technologies Group L.L.C.
92 Hayden Ave.
Lexington, MA 02421
(781)778-4678
Fax: (781)861-1099
E-mail: ptg@plantech.com
Website: http://www.plantech.com

Kalba International Inc.
23 Sandy Pond Rd.
Lincoln, MA 01773
(781)259-9589
Fax: (781)259-1460
E-mail: info@kalbainternational.com
Website: http://
www.kalbainternational.com

VMB Associates Inc.
115 Ashland St.
Melrose, MA 02176
(781)665-0623
Fax: (425)732-7142
E-mail: vmbinc@aol.com

The Company Doctor
14 Pudding Stone Ln.
Mendon, MA 01756
(508)478-1747
Fax: (508)478-0520

Data and Strategies Group Inc.
190 N Main St.
Natick, MA 01760
(508)653-9990
Fax: (508)653-7799
E-mail: dsginc@dsggroup.com
Website: http://www.dsggroup.com

The Enterprise Group
73 Parker Rd.
Needham, MA 02494
(617)444-6631
Fax: (617)433-9991
E-mail: lsacco@world.std.com
Website: http://www.enterprise-
group.com

PSMJ Resources Inc.
10 Midland Ave.
Newton, MA 02458
(617)965-0055
Free: 800-537-7765
Fax: (617)965-5152
E-mail: psmj@tiac.net
Website: http://www.psmj.com

Scheur Management Group Inc.
255 Washington St., Ste. 100
Newton, MA 02458-1611
(617)969-7500
Fax: (617)969-7508
E-mail: smgnow@scheur.com
Website: http://www.scheur.com

I.E.E.E., Boston Section
240 Bear Hill Rd., 202B
Waltham, MA 02451-1017
(781)890-5294
Fax: (781)890-5290

Business Planning and Consulting Services
20 Beechwood Ter.
Wellesley, MA 02482
(617)237-9151
Fax: (617)237-9151

Michigan

Walter Frederick Consulting
1719 South Blvd.
Ann Arbor, MI 48104
(313)662-4336
Fax: (313)769-7505

Fox Enterprises
6220 W Freeland Rd.
Freeland, MI 48623
(517)695-9170
Fax: (517)695-9174
E-mail: foxjw@concentric.net
Website: http://www.cris.com/~foxjw

G.G.W. and Associates
1213 Hampton
Jackson, MI 49203
(517)782-2255
Fax: (517)782-2255

Altamar Group Ltd.
6810 S Cedar, Ste. 2-B
Lansing, MI 48911
(517)694-0910
Free: 800-443-2627
Fax: (517)694-1377

Sheffieck Consultants Inc.
23610 Greening Dr.
Novi, MI 48375-3130
(248)347-3545
Fax: (248)347-3530
E-mail: cfsheff@concentric.net

Rehmann, Robson PC
5800 Gratiot
Saginaw, MI 48605
(517)799-9580
Fax: (517)799-0227
Website: http://www.rrpc.com

Francis & Co.
17200 W 10 Mile Rd., Ste. 207
Southfield, MI 48075
(248)559-7600
Fax: (248)559-5249

Private Ventures Inc.
16000 W 9 Mile Rd., Ste. 504
Southfield, MI 48075
(248)569-1977
Free: 800-448-7614
Fax: (248)569-1838
E-mail: pventuresi@aol.com

JGK Associates
14464 Kerner Dr.
Sterling Heights, MI 48313
(810)247-9055
Fax: (248)822-4977
E-mail: kozlowski@home.com

Minnesota

Health Fitness Corp.
3500 W 80th St., Ste. 130
Bloomington, MN 55431
(612)831-6830
Fax: (612)831-7264

Consatech Inc.
PO Box 1047
Burnsville, MN 55337
(612)953-1088
Fax: (612)435-2966

Robert F. Knotek
14960 Ironwood Ct.
Eden Prairie, MN 55346
(612)949-2875

DRI Consulting
7715 Stonewood Ct.
Edina, MN 55439
(612)941-9656
Fax: (612)941-2693
E-mail: dric@dric.com
Website: http://www.dric.com

Markin Consulting
12072 87th Pl. N
Maple Grove, MN 55369
(612)493-3568
Fax: (612)493-5744
E-mail: markin@markinconsulting.com
Website: http://
www.markinconsulting.com

Minnesota Cooperation Office for Small Business & Job Creation Inc.
5001 W 80th St., Ste. 825
Minneapolis, MN 55437
(612)830-1230
Fax: (612)830-1232
E-mail: mncoop@msn.com
Website: http://www.mnco.org

Enterprise Consulting Inc.
PO Box 1111
Minnetonka, MN 55345
(612)949-5909
Fax: (612)906-3965

Amdahl International
724 1st Ave. SW
Rochester, MN 55902
(507)252-0402
Fax: (507)252-0402
E-mail: amdahl@best-service.com
Website: http://www.wp.com/
amdahl_int

Power Systems Research
1365 Corporate Center Curve, 2nd Fl.
St. Paul, MN 55121
(612)905-8400
Free: (888)625-8612
Fax: (612)454-0760
E-mail: Barb@Powersys.com
Website: http://www.powersys.com

Missouri

Business Planning and Development Corp.
4030 Charlotte St.
Kansas City, MO 64110
(816)753-0495
E-mail: humph@bpdev.demon.co.uk
Website: http://www.bpdev.demon.co.uk

CFO Service
10336 Donoho
St. Louis, MO 63131
(314)750-2940
E-mail: jskae@cfoservice.com
Website: http://www.cfoservice.com

Nebraska

International Management Consulting Group Inc.
1309 Harlan Dr., Ste. 205
Bellevue, NE 68005
(402)291-4545
Free: 800-665-IMCG
Fax: (402)291-4343
E-mail: imcg@neonramp.com
Website: http://www.mgtconsulting.com

Heartland Management Consulting Group
1904 Barrington Pky.
Papillion, NE 68046
(402)339-2387
Fax: (402)339-1319

Nevada

The DuBois Group
865 Tahoe Blvd., Ste. 108
Incline Village, NV 89451
(775)832-0550
Free: 800-375-2935
Fax: (775)832-0556
E-mail: DuBoisGrp@aol.com

New Hampshire

Wolff Consultants
10 Buck Rd.
Hanover, NH 03755
(603)643-6015

BPT Consulting Associates Ltd.
12 Parmenter Rd., Ste. B-6
Londonderry, NH 03053
(603)437-8484
Free: (888)278-0030
Fax: (603)434-5388
E-mail: bptcons@tiac.net
Website: http://www.bptconsulting.com

New Jersey

Bedminster Group Inc.
1170 Rte. 22 E
Bridgewater, NJ 08807
(908)500-4155
Fax: (908)766-0780
E-mail: info@bedminstergroup.com
Website: http://
www.bedminstergroup.com
Fax: (202)806-1777
Terry Strong, Acting Regional Dir.

Delta Planning Inc.
PO Box 425
Denville, NJ 07834
(913)625-1742
Free: 800-672-0762
Fax: (973)625-3531
E-mail: DeltaP@worldnet.att.net
Website: http://deltaplanning.com

Kumar Associates Inc.
1004 Cumbermeade Rd.
Fort Lee, NJ 07024
(201)224-9480
Fax: (201)585-2343
E-mail: mail@kumarassociates.com
Website: http://kumarassociates.com

John Hall & Company Inc.
PO Box 187
Glen Ridge, NJ 07028
(973)680-4449
Fax: (973)680-4581
E-mail: jhcompany@aol.com

Market Focus
PO Box 402
Maplewood, NJ 07040
(973)378-2470
Fax: (973)378-2470
E-mail: mcss66@marketfocus.com

Vanguard Communications Corp.
100 American Rd.
Morris Plains, NJ 07950
(973)605-8000
Fax: (973)605-8329
Website: http://www.vanguard.net/

ConMar International Ltd.
1901 US Hwy. 130
North Brunswick, NJ 08902
(732)940-8347
Fax: (732)274-1199

KLW New Products
156 Cedar Dr.
Old Tappan, NJ 07675
(201)358-1300
Fax: (201)664-2594
E-mail: lrlarsen@usa.net
Website: http://
www.klwnewproducts.com

PA Consulting Group
315A Enterprise Dr.
Plainsboro, NJ 08536
(609)936-8300
Fax: (609)936-8811
E-mail: info@paconsulting.com
Website: http://www.pa-consulting.com

Aurora Marketing Management Inc.
66 Witherspoon St., Ste. 600
Princeton, NJ 08542
(908)904-1125
Fax: (908)359-1108
E-mail: aurora2@voicenet.com
Website: http://
www.auroramarketing.net

Smart Business Supersite
88 Orchard Rd., CN-5219
Princeton, NJ 08543
(908)321-1924
Fax: (908)321-5156
E-mail: irv@smartbiz.com
Website: http://www.smartbiz.com

Tracelin Associates
1171 Main St., Ste. 6K
Rahway, NJ 07065
(732)381-3288

Schkeeper Inc.
130-6 Bodman Pl.
Red Bank, NJ 07701
(732)219-1965
Fax: (732)530-3703

Henry Branch Associates
2502 Harmon Cove Twr.
Secaucus, NJ 07094
(201)866-2008
Fax: (201)601-0101
E-mail: hbranch161@home.com

Robert Gibbons & Company Inc.
46 Knoll Rd.
Tenafly, NJ 07670-1050
(201)871-3933
Fax: (201)871-2173
E-mail: crisisbob@aol.com

PMC Management Consultants Inc.
6 Thistle Ln.
Three Bridges, NJ 08887-0332
(908)788-1014
Free: 800-PMC-0250
Fax: (908)806-7287
E-mail: int@pmc-management.com
Website: http://www.pmc-
management.com

R.W. Bankart & Associates
20 Valley Ave., Ste. D-2
Westwood, NJ 07675-3607
(201)664-7672

New Mexico

Vondle & Associates Inc.
4926 Calle de Tierra, NE
Albuquerque, NM 87111
(505)292-8961
Fax: (505)296-2790
E-mail: vondle@aol.com

InfoNewMexico
2207 Black Hills Rd., NE
Rio Rancho, NM 87124
(505)891-2462
Fax: (505)896-8971

New York

Powers Research and Training Institute
PO Box 78
Bayville, NY 11709
(516)628-2250
Fax: (516)628-2252
E-mail: powercocch@compuserve.com
Website: http://www.nancypowers.com

Consortium House
296 Wittenberg Rd.
Bearsville, NY 12409
(845)679-8867
Fax: (845)679-9248
E-mail: eugenegs@aol.com
Website: http://www.chpub.com

Progressive Finance Corp.
3549 Tiemann Ave.
Bronx, NY 10469
(718)405-9029
Free: 800-225-8381
Fax: (718)405-1170

Wave Hill Associates Inc.
2621 Palisade Ave., Ste. 15-C
Bronx, NY 10463
(718)549-7368
Fax: (718)601-9670
E-mail: pepper@compuserve.com

Management Insight
96 Arlington Rd.
Buffalo, NY 14221
(716)631-3319
Fax: (716)631-0203
E-mail:
michalski@foodserviceinsight.com
Website: http://
www.foodserviceinsight.com

Samani International Enterprises, Marions Panyaught Consultancy
2028 Parsons
Flushing, NY 11357-3436
(917)287-8087
Fax: 800-873-8939
E-mail: vjp2@biostrategist.com
Website: http://www.biostrategist.com

Marketing Resources Group
71-58 Austin St.
Forest Hills, NY 11375
(718)261-8882

Mangabay Business Plans & Development
Subsidiary of Innis Asset Allocation
125-10 Queens Blvd., Ste. 2202
Kew Gardens, NY 11415
(905)527-1947
Fax: 509-472-1935
E-mail: mangabay@mangabay.com
Website: http://www.mangabay.com
Lee Toh, Managing Partner

ComputerEase Co.
1301 Monmouth Ave.
Lakewood, NY 08701
(212)406-9464
Fax: (914)277-5317
E-mail: crawfordc@juno.com

Boice Dunham Group
30 W 13th St.
New York, NY 10011
(212)924-2200
Fax: (212)924-1108

Elizabeth Capen
27 E 95th St.
New York, NY 10128
(212)427-7654
Fax: (212)876-3190

Haver Analytics
60 E 42nd St., Ste. 2424
New York, NY 10017

(212)986-9300
Fax: (212)986-5857
E-mail: data@haver.com
Website: http://www.haver.com

The Jordan, Edmiston Group Inc.
150 E 52nd Ave., 18th Fl.
New York, NY 10022
(212)754-0710
Fax: (212)754-0337

KPMG International
345 Park Ave.
New York, NY 10154-0102
(212)758-9700
Fax: (212)758-9819
Website: http://www.kpmg.com

Mahoney Cohen Consulting Corp.
111 W 40th St., 12th Fl.
New York, NY 10018
(212)490-8000
Fax: (212)790-5913

Management Practice Inc.
342 Madison Ave.
New York, NY 10173-1230
(212)867-7948
Fax: (212)972-5188
Website: http://www.mpiweb.com

Moseley Associates Inc.
342 Madison Ave., Ste. 1414
New York, NY 10016
(212)213-6673
Fax: (212)687-1520

Practice Development Counsel
60 Sutton Pl. S
New York, NY 10022
(212)593-1549
Fax: (212)980-7940
E-mail: pwhaserot@pdcounsel.com
Website: http://www.pdcounsel.com

Unique Value International Inc.
575 Madison Ave., 10th Fl.
New York, NY 10022-1304
(212)605-0590
Fax: (212)605-0589

The Van Tulleken Co.
126 E 56th St.
New York, NY 10022
(212)355-1390
Fax: (212)755-3061
E-mail: newyork@vantulleken.com

Vencon Management Inc.
301 W 53rd St.
New York, NY 10019
(212)581-8787
Fax: (212)397-4126
Website: http://www.venconinc.com

Werner International Inc.
55 E 52nd, 29th Fl.
New York, NY 10055
(212)909-1260
Fax: (212)909-1273
E-mail: richard.downing@rgh.com
Website: http://www.wernertex.com

Zimmerman Business Consulting Inc.
44 E 92nd St., Ste. 5-B
New York, NY 10128
(212)860-3107
Fax: (212)860-7730
E-mail: ljzzbci@aol.com
Website: http://www.zbcinc.com

Overton Financial
7 Allen Rd.
Peekskill, NY 10566
(914)737-4649
Fax: (914)737-4696

Stromberg Consulting
2500 Westchester Ave.
Purchase, NY 10577
(914)251-1515
Fax: (914)251-1562
E-mail:
strategy@stromberg_consulting.com
Website: http://
www.stromberg_consulting.com

Innovation Management Consulting Inc.
209 Dewitt Rd.
Syracuse, NY 13214-2006
(315)425-5144
Fax: (315)445-8989
E-mail: missonneb@axess.net

M. Clifford Agress
891 Fulton St.
Valley Stream, NY 11580
(516)825-8955
Fax: (516)825-8955

Destiny Kinal Marketing Consultancy
105 Chemung St.
Waverly, NY 14892
(607)565-8317
Fax: (607)565-4083

Valutis Consulting Inc.
5350 Main St., Ste. 7
Williamsville, NY 14221-5338
(716)634-2553
Fax: (716)634-2554
E-mail: valutis@localnet.com
Website: http://
www.valutisconsulting.com

North Carolina

Best Practices L.L.C.
6320 Quadrangle Dr., Ste. 200
Chapel Hill, NC 27514
(919)403-0251
Fax: (919)403-0144
E-mail: best@best:in/class
Website: http://www.best-in-class.com

Norelli & Co.
Bank of America Corporate Ctr.
100 N Tyron St., Ste. 5160
Charlotte, NC 28202-4000
(704)376-5484
Fax: (704)376-5485
E-mail: consult@norelli.com
Website: http://www.norelli.com

North Dakota

Center for Innovation
4300 Dartmouth Dr.
PO Box 8372
Grand Forks, ND 58202
(701)777-3132
Fax: (701)777-2339
E-mail: bruce@innovators.net
Website: http://www.innovators.net

Ohio

Transportation Technology Services
208 Harmon Rd.
Aurora, OH 44202
(330)562-3596

Empro Systems Inc.
4777 Red Bank Expy., Ste. 1
Cincinnati, OH 45227-1542
(513)271-2042
Fax: (513)271-2042

Alliance Management International Ltd.
1440 Windrow Ln.
Cleveland, OH 44147-3200
(440)838-1922
Fax: (440)838-0979
E-mail: bgruss@amiltd.com
Website: http://www.amiltd.com

Bozell Kamstra Public Relations
1301 E 9th St., Ste. 3400
Cleveland, OH 44114
(216)623-1511
Fax: (216)623-1501

E-mail: jfeniger@cleveland.bozellkamstra.com
Website: http://www.bozellkamstra.com

Cory Dillon Associates
111 Schreyer Pl. E
Columbus, OH 43214
(614)262-8211
Fax: (614)262-3806

Holcomb Gallagher Adams
300 Marconi, Ste. 303
Columbus, OH 43215
(614)221-3343
Fax: (614)221-3367
E-mail: riadams@acme.freenet.oh.us

Young & Associates
PO Box 711
Kent, OH 44240
(330)678-0524
Free: 800-525-9775
Fax: (330)678-6219
E-mail: online@younginc.com
Website: http://www.younginc.com

Robert A. Westman & Associates
8981 Inversary Dr. SE
Warren, OH 44484-2551
(330)856-4149
Fax: (330)856-2564

Oklahoma

Innovative Partners L.L.C.
4900 Richmond Sq., Ste. 100
Oklahoma City, OK 73118
(405)840-0033
Fax: (405)843-8359
E-mail: ipartners@juno.com

Oregon

INTERCON - The International Converting Institute
5200 Badger Rd.
Crooked River Ranch, OR 97760
(541)548-1447
Fax: (541)548-1618
E-mail: johnbowler@crookedriverranch.com

Talbott ARM
HC 60, Box 5620
Lakeview, OR 97630
(541)635-8587
Fax: (503)947-3482

Management Technology Associates Ltd.
2768 SW Sherwood Dr, Ste. 105
Portland, OR 97201-2251
(503)224-5220
Fax: (503)224-5334
E-mail: lcuster@mta-ltd.com
Website: http://www.mgmt-tech.com

Pennsylvania

Healthscope Inc.
400 Lancaster Ave.
Devon, PA 19333
(610)687-6199
Fax: (610)687-6376
E-mail: health@voicenet.com
Website: http://www.healthscope.net/

Elayne Howard & Associates Inc.
3501 Masons Mill Rd., Ste. 501
Huntingdon Valley, PA 19006-3509
(215)657-9550

GRA Inc.
115 West Ave., Ste. 201
Jenkintown, PA 19046
(215)884-7500
Fax: (215)884-1385
E-mail: gramail@gra-inc.com
Website: http://www.gra-inc.com

Mifflin County Industrial Development Corp.
Mifflin County Industrial Plz.
6395 SR 103 N
Bldg. 50
Lewistown, PA 17044
(717)242-0393
Fax: (717)242-1842
E-mail: mcide@acsworld.net

Autech Products
1289 Revere Rd.
Morrisville, PA 19067
(215)493-3759
Fax: (215)493-9791
E-mail: autech4@yahoo.com

Advantage Associates
434 Avon Dr.
Pittsburgh, PA 15228
(412)343-1558
Fax: (412)362-1684
E-mail: ecocba1@aol.com

Regis J. Sheehan & Associates
Pittsburgh, PA 15220
(412)279-1207

James W. Davidson Company Inc.
23 Forest View Rd.
Wallingford, PA 19086
(610)566-1462

Puerto Rico

Diego Chevere & Co.
Metro Parque 7, Ste. 204
Metro Office
Caparra Heights, PR 00920
(787)774-9595
Fax: (787)774-9566
E-mail: dcco@coqui.net

Manuel L. Porrata and Associates
898 Munoz Rivera Ave., Ste. 201
San Juan, PR 00927
(787)765-2140
Fax: (787)754-3285
E-mail: m_porrata@manuelporrata.com
Website: http://manualporrata.com

South Carolina

Aquafood Business Associates
PO Box 13267
Charleston, SC 29422
(843)795-9506
Fax: (843)795-9477
E-mail: rraba@aol.com

Profit Associates Inc.
PO Box 38026
Charleston, SC 29414
(803)763-5718
Fax: (803)763-5719
E-mail: bobrog@awod.com
Website: http://www.awod.com/gallery/business/proasc

Strategic Innovations International
12 Executive Ct.
Lake Wylie, SC 29710
(803)831-1225
Fax: (803)831-1177
E-mail: stratinnov@aol.com
Website: http://www.strategicinnovations.com

Minus Stage
Box 4436
Rock Hill, SC 29731
(803)328-0705
Fax: (803)329-9948

Tennessee

Daniel Petchers & Associates
8820 Fernwood CV
Germantown, TN 38138
(901)755-9896

Business Choices
1114 Forest Harbor, Ste. 300
Hendersonville, TN 37075-9646

(615)822-8692
Free: 800-737-8382
Fax: (615)822-8692
E-mail: bz-ch@juno.com

RCFA Healthcare Management Services L.L.C.
9648 Kingston Pke., Ste. 8
Knoxville, TN 37922
(865)531-0176
Free: 800-635-4040
Fax: (865)531-0722
E-mail: info@rcfa.com
Website: http://www.rcfa.com

Growth Consultants of America
3917 Trimble Rd.
Nashville, TN 37215
(615)383-0550
Fax: (615)269-8940
E-mail: 70244.451@compuserve.com

Texas

Integrated Cost Management Systems Inc.
2261 Brookhollow Plz. Dr., Ste. 104
Arlington, TX 76006
(817)633-2873
Fax: (817)633-3781
E-mail: abm@icms.net
Website: http://www.icms.net

Lori Williams
1000 Leslie Ct.
Arlington, TX 76012
(817)459-3934
Fax: (817)459-3934

Business Resource Software Inc.
2013 Wells Branch Pky., Ste. 305
Austin, TX 78728
Free: 800-423-1228
Fax: (512)251-4401
E-mail: info@brs-inc.com
Website: http://www.brs-inc.com

Erisa Adminstrative Services Inc.
12325 Hymeadow Dr., Bldg. 4
Austin, TX 78750-1847
(512)250-9020
Fax: (512)250-9487
Website: http://www.cserisa.com

R. Miller Hicks & Co.
1011 W 11th St.
Austin, TX 78703
(512)477-7000
Fax: (512)477-9697
E-mail: millerhicks@rmhicks.com
Website: http://www.rmhicks.com

Pragmatic Tactics Inc.
3303 Westchester Ave.
College Station, TX 77845
(409)696-5294
Free: 800-570-5294
Fax: (409)696-4994
E-mail: ptactics@aol.com
Website: http://www.ptatics.com

Perot Systems
12404 Park Central Dr.
Dallas, TX 75251
(972)340-5000
Free: 800-688-4333
Fax: (972)455-4100
E-mail: corp.comm@ps.net
Website: http://www.perotsystems.com

ReGENERATION Partners
3838 Oak Lawn Ave.
Dallas, TX 75219
(214)559-3999
Free: 800-406-1112
E-mail: info@regeneration-partner.com
Website: http://www.regeneration-partners.com

High Technology Associates - Division of Global Technologies Inc.
1775 St. James Pl., Ste. 105
Houston, TX 77056
(713)963-9300
Fax: (713)963-8341
E-mail: hta@infohwy.com

MasterCOM
103 Thunder Rd.
Kerrville, TX 78028
(830)895-7990
Fax: (830)443-3428
E-mail: jmstubblefield@mastertraining.com
Website: http://www.mastertraining.com

PROTEC
4607 Linden Pl.
Pearland, TX 77584
(281)997-9872
Fax: (281)997-9895
E-mail: p.oman@ix.netcom.com

Alpha Quadrant Inc.
10618 Auldine
San Antonio, TX 78230
(210)344-3330
Fax: (210)344-8151
E-mail: mbussone@sbcglobal.net
Website:http://www.a-quadrant.com
Michele Bussone

Bastian Public Relations
614 San Dizier
San Antonio, TX 78232
(210)404-1839
E-mail: lisa@bastianpr.com
Website: http://www.bastianpr.com
Lisa Bastian CBC

Business Strategy Development Consultants
PO Box 690365
San Antonio, TX 78269
(210)696-8000
Free: 800-927-BSDC
Fax: (210)696-8000

Tom Welch, CPC
6900 San Pedro Ave., Ste. 147
San Antonio, TX 78216-6207
(210)737-7022
Fax: (210)737-7022
E-mail: bplan@iamerica.net
Website: http://www.moneywords.com

Utah

Business Management Resource
PO Box 521125
Salt Lake City, UT 84152-1125
(801)272-4668
Fax: (801)277-3290
E-mail: pingfong@worldnet.att.net

Virginia

Tindell Associates
209 Oxford Ave.
Alexandria, VA 22301
(703)683-0109
Fax: 703-783-0219
E-mail: scott@tindell.net
Website: http://www.tindell.net
Scott Lockett, President

Elliott B. Jaffa
2530-B S Walter Reed Dr.
Arlington, VA 22206
(703)931-0040
E-mail: thetrainingdoctor@excite.com
Website: http://www.tregistry.com/jaffa.htm

Koach Enterprises - USA
5529 N 18th St.
Arlington, VA 22205
(703)241-8361
Fax: (703)241-8623

Federal Market Development
5650 Chapel Run Ct.
Centreville, VA 20120-3601

(703)502-8930
Free: 800-821-5003
Fax: (703)502-8929

Huff, Stuart & Carlton
2107 Graves Mills Rd., Ste. C
Forest, VA 24551
(804)316-9356
Free: (888)316-9356
Fax: (804)316-9357
Website: http://www.wealthmgt.net

AMX International Inc.
1420 Spring Hill Rd. , Ste. 600
McLean, VA 22102-3006
(703)690-4100
Fax: (703)643-1279
E-mail: amxmail@amxi.com
Website: http://www.amxi.com

Charles Scott Pugh (Investor)
4101 Pittaway Dr.
Richmond, VA 23235-1022
(804)560-0979
Fax: (804)560-4670

John C. Randall and Associates Inc.
PO Box 15127
Richmond, VA 23227
(804)746-4450
Fax: (804)730-8933
E-mail: randalljcx@aol.com
Website: http://www.johncrandall.com

McLeod & Co.
410 1st St.
Roanoke, VA 24011
(540)342-6911
Fax: (540)344-6367
Website: http://www.mcleodco.com/

Salzinger & Company Inc.
8000 Towers Crescent Dr., Ste. 1350
Vienna, VA 22182
(703)442-5200
Fax: (703)442-5205
E-mail: info@salzinger.com
Website: http://www.salzinger.com

The Small Business Counselor
12423 Hedges Run Dr., Ste. 153
Woodbridge, VA 22192
(703)490-6755
Fax: (703)490-1356

Washington

Burlington Consultants
10900 NE 8th St., Ste. 900
Bellevue, WA 98004
(425)688-3060
Fax: (425)454-4383
E-mail:
partners@burlingtonconsultants.com
Website: http://
www.burlingtonconsultants.com

Perry L. Smith Consulting
800 Bellevue Way NE, Ste. 400
Bellevue, WA 98004-4208
(425)462-2072
Fax: (425)462-5638

St. Charles Consulting Group
1420 NW Gilman Blvd.
Issaquah, WA 98027
(425)557-8708
Fax: (425)557-8731
E-mail: info@stcharlesconsulting.com
Website: http://
www.stcharlesconsulting.com

Independent Automotive Training Services
PO Box 334
Kirkland, WA 98083
(425)822-5715
E-mail: ltunney@autosvccon.com
Website: http://www.autosvccon.com

Kahle Associate Inc.
6203 204th Dr. NE
Redmond, WA 98053
(425)836-8763
Fax: (425)868-3770
E-mail: randykahle@kahleassociates.com
Website: http://www.kahleassociates.com

Dan Collin
3419 Wallingord Ave N, No. 2
Seattle, WA 98103
(206)634-9469
E-mail: dc@dancollin.com
Website: http://members.home.net/dcollin/

ECG Management Consultants Inc.
1111 3rd Ave., Ste. 2700
Seattle, WA 98101-3201
(206)689-2200
Fax: (206)689-2209
E-mail: ecg@ecgmc.com
Website: http://www.ecgmc.com

Northwest Trade Adjustment Assistance Center
900 4th Ave., Ste. 2430
Seattle, WA 98164-1001
(206)622-2730
Free: 800-667-8087
Fax: (206)622-1105
E-mail: matchingfunds@nwtaac.org
Website: http://www.taacenters.org

Business Planning Consultants
S 3510 Ridgeview Dr.
Spokane, WA 99206
(509)928-0332
Fax: (509)921-0842
E-mail: bpci@nextdim.com

West Virginia

Stanley & Associates Inc./ BusinessandMarketingPlans.com
1687 Robert C. Byrd Dr.
Beckley, WV 25801
(304)252-0324
Free: 888-752-6720
Fax: (304)252-0470
E-mail: cclay@charterinternet.com
Website: http://
www.BusinessandMarketingPlans.com
Christopher Clay

Wisconsin

White & Associates Inc.
5349 Somerset Ln. S
Greenfield, WI 53221
(414)281-7373
Fax: (414)281-7006
E-mail: wnaconsult@aol.com

Small business administration regional offices

This section contains a listing of Small Business Administration offices arranged numerically by region. Service areas are provided. Contact the appropriate office for a referral to the nearest field office, or visit the Small Business Administration online at www.sba.gov.

Region 1

U.S. Small Business Administration
Region I Office
10 Causeway St., Ste. 812
Boston, MA 02222-1093
Phone: (617)565-8415
Fax: (617)565-8420
Serves Connecticut, Maine, Massachusetts, New Hampshire, Rhode Island, and Vermont.

Region 2

U.S. Small Business Administration
Region II Office
26 Federal Plaza, Ste. 3108
New York, NY 10278

Phone: (212)264-1450
Fax: (212)264-0038
Serves New Jersey, New York, Puerto Rico, and the Virgin Islands.

Region 3

U.S. Small Business Administration
Region III Office
Robert N C Nix Sr. Federal Building
900 Market St., 5th Fl.
Philadelphia, PA 19107
(215)580-2807
Serves Delaware, the District of Columbia, Maryland, Pennsylvania, Virginia, and West Virginia.

Region 4

U.S. Small Business Administration
Region IV Office
233 Peachtree St. NE
Harris Tower 1800
Atlanta, GA 30303
Phone: (404)331-4999
Fax: (404)331-2354
Serves Alabama, Florida, Georgia, Kentucky, Mississippi, North Carolina, South Carolina, and Tennessee.

Region 5

U.S. Small Business Administration
Region V Office
500 W. Madison St.
Citicorp Center, Ste. 1240
Chicago, IL 60661-2511
Phone: (312)353-0357
Fax: (312)353-3426
Serves Illinois, Indiana, Michigan, Minnesota, Ohio, and Wisconsin.

Region 6

U.S. Small Business Administration
Region VI Office
4300 Amon Carter Blvd., Ste. 108
Fort Worth, TX 76155
Phone: (817)684-5581
Fax: (817)684-5588
Serves Arkansas, Louisiana, New Mexico, Oklahoma, and Texas.

Region 7

U.S. Small Business Administration
Region VII Office
323 W. 8th St., Ste. 307
Kansas City, MO 64105-1500
Phone: (816)374-6380
Fax: (816)374-6339
Serves Iowa, Kansas, Missouri, and Nebraska.

Region 8

U.S. Small Business Administration
Region VIII Office
721 19th St., Ste. 400
Denver, CO 80202
Phone: (303)844-0500
Fax: (303)844-0506
Serves Colorado, Montana, North Dakota, South Dakota, Utah, and Wyoming.

Region 9

U.S. Small Business Administration
Region IX Office
330 N Brand Blvd., Ste. 1270
Glendale, CA 91203-2304
Phone: (818)552-3434
Fax: (818)552-3440
Serves American Samoa, Arizona, California, Guam, Hawaii, Nevada, and the Trust Territory of the Pacific Islands.

Region 10

U.S. Small Business Administration
Region X Office
2401 Fourth Ave., Ste. 400
Seattle, WA 98121
Phone: (206)553-5676
Fax: (206)553-4155
Serves Alaska, Idaho, Oregon, and Washington.

Small business development centers

This section contains a listing of all Small Business Development Centers, organized alphabetically by state/U.S. territory, then by city, then by agency name.

Alabama

Alabama SBDC
UNIVERSITY OF ALABAMA
2800 Milan Court Suite 124
Birmingham, AL 35211-6908
Phone: 205-943-6750
Fax: 205-943-6752
E-Mail: wcampbell@provost.uab.edu
Website: http://www.asbdc.org
Mr. William Campbell Jr, State Director

Alaska

Alaska SBDC
UNIVERSITY OF ALASKA - ANCHORAGE
430 West Seventh Avenue, Suite 110
Anchorage, AK 99501
Phone: 907-274 -7232
Fax: 907-274-9524
E-Mail: anerw@uaa.alaska.edu
Website: http://www.aksbdc.org
Ms. Jean R. Wall, State Director

American Samoa

American Samoa SBDC
AMERICAN SAMOA COMMUNITY COLLEGE
P.O. Box 2609
Pago Pago, American Samoa 96799
Phone: 011-684-699-4830
Fax: 011-684-699-6132
E-Mail: htalex@att.net
Mr. Herbert Thweatt, Director

Arizona

Arizona SBDC
MARICOPA COUNTY COMMUNITY COLLEGE
2411 West 14th Street, Suite 132
Tempe, AZ 85281
Phone: 480-731-8720
Fax: 480-731-8729
E-Mail: mike.york@domail.maricopa.edu
Website: http://www.dist.maricopa.edu.sbdc
Mr. Michael York, State Director

Arkansas

Arkansas SBDC
UNIVERSITY OF ARKANSAS
2801 South University Avenue
Little Rock, AR 72204
Phone: 501-324-9043
Fax: 501-324-9049
E-Mail: jmroderick@ualr.edu
Website: http://asbdc.ualr.edu
Ms. Janet M. Roderick, State Director

California

California - San Francisco SBDC
Northern California SBDC Lead Center
HUMBOLDT STATE UNIVERSITY
Office of Economic Development
1 Harpst Street 2006A, Siemens Hall
Arcata, CA, 95521

Phone: 707-826-3922
Fax: 707-826-3206
E-Mail: gainer@humboldt.edu
Ms. Margaret A. Gainer, Regional Director

California - Sacramento SBDC
CALIFORNIA STATE UNIVERSITY - CHICO
Chico, CA 95929-0765
Phone: 530-898-4598
Fax: 530-898-4734
E-Mail: dripke@csuchico.edu
Website: http://gsbdc.csuchico.edu
Mr. Dan Ripke, Interim Regional Director

California - San Diego SBDC
SOUTHWESTERN COMMUNITY COLLEGE DISTRICT
900 Otey Lakes Road
Chula Vista, CA 91910
Phone: 619-482-6388
Fax: 619-482-6402
E-Mail: dtrujillo@swc.cc.ca.us
Website: http://www.sbditc.org
Ms. Debbie P. Trujillo, Regional Director

California - Fresno SBDC
UC Merced Lead Center
UNIVERSITY OF CALIFORNIA - MERCED
550 East Shaw, Suite 105A
Fresno, CA 93710
Phone: 559-241-6590
Fax: 559-241-7422
E-Mail: crosander@ucmerced.edu
Website: http://sbdc.ucmerced.edu
Mr. Chris Rosander, State Director

California - Santa Ana SBDC
Tri-County Lead SBDC
CALIFORNIA STATE UNIVERSITY - FULLERTON
800 North State College Boulevard, LH640
Fullerton, CA 92834
Phone: 714-278-2719
Fax: 714-278-7858
E-Mail: vpham@fullerton.edu
Website: http://www.leadsbdc.org
Ms. Vi Pham, Lead Center Director

California - Los Angeles Region SBDC
LONG BEACH COMMUNITY COLLEGE DISTRICT
3950 Paramount Boulevard, Ste 101
Lakewood, CA 90712
Phone: 562-938-5004
Fax: 562-938-5030
E-Mail: ssloan@lbcc.edu
Ms. Sheneui Sloan, Interim Lead Center Director

Colorado

Colorado SBDC
OFFICE OF ECONOMIC DEVELOPMENT
1625 Broadway, Suite 170
Denver, CO 80202
Phone: 303-892-3864
Fax: 303-892-3848
E-Mail: Kelly.Manning@state.co.us
Website: http://www.state.co.us/oed/sbdc
Ms. Kelly Manning, State Director

Connecticut

Connecticut SBDC
UNIVERSITY OF CONNECTICUT
1376 Storrs Road, Unit 4094
Storrs, CT 06269-1094
Phone: 860-870-6370
Fax: 860-870-6374
E-Mail: richard.cheney@uconn.edu
Website: http://www.sbdc.uconn.edu
Mr. Richard Cheney, Interim State Director

Delaware

Delaware SBDC
DELAWARE TECHNOLOGY PARK
1 Innovation Way, Suite 301
Newark, DE 19711
Phone: 302-831-2747
Fax: 302-831-1423
E-Mail: Clinton.tymes@mvs.udel.edu
Website: http://www.delawaresbdc.org
Mr. Clinton Tymes, State Director

District of Columbia

District of Columbia SBDC
HOWARD UNIVERSITY
2600 6th Street, NW Room 128
Washington, DC 20059
Phone: 202-806-1550
Fax: 202-806-1777
E-Mail: hturner@howard.edu
Website: http://www.dcsbdc.com/
Mr. Henry Turner, Executive Director

Florida

Florida SBDC
UNIVERSITY OF WEST FLORIDA
401 East Chase Street, Suite 100
Pensacola, FL 32502
Phone: 850-473-7800
Fax: 850-473-7813
E-Mail: jcartwri@uwf.edu
Website: http://www.floridasbdc.com
Mr. Jerry Cartwright, State Director

Georgia

Georgia SBDC
UNIVERSITY OF GEORGIA
1180 East Broad Street
Athens, GA 30602
Phone: 706-542-6762
Fax: 706-542-6776
E-mail: aadams@sbdc.uga.edu
Website: http://www.sbdc.uga.edu
Mr. Allan Adams, Interim State Director

Guam

Guam Small Business Development Center
UNIVERSITY OF GUAM
Pacific Islands SBDC
P.O. Box 5014 - U.O.G. Station
Mangilao, GU 96923
Phone: 671-735-2590
Fax: 671-734-2002
E-mail: casey@pacificsbdc.com
Website: http://www.uog.edu/sbdc
Mr. Casey Jeszenka, Director

Hawaii

Hawaii SBDC
UNIVERSITY OF HAWAII - HILO
308 Kamehameha Avenue, Suite 201
Hilo, HI 96720
Phone: 808-974-7515
Fax: 808-974-7683
E-Mail: darrylm@interpac.net
Website: http://www.hawaii-sbdc.org
Mr. Darryl Mleynek, State Director

Idaho

Idaho SBDC
BOISE STATE UNIVERSITY
1910 University Drive
Boise, ID 83725
Phone: 208-426-3799
Fax: 208-426-3877
E-mail: jhogge@boisestate.edu
Website: http://www.idahosbdc.org
Mr. Jim Hogge, State Director

Illinois

Illinois SBDC
DEPARTMENT OF COMMERCE AND ECONOMIC OPPORTUNITY
620 E. Adams, S-4
Springfield, IL 62701
Phone: 217-524-5700
Fax: 217-524-0171
E-mail: mpatrilli@ildceo.net

Website: http://www.ilsbdc.biz
Mr. Mark Petrilli, State Director

Indiana

Indiana SBDC
INDIANA ECONOMIC DEVELOPMENT CORPORATION
One North Capitol, Suite 900
Indianapolis, IN 46204
Phone: 317-234-8872
Fax: 317-232-8874
E-mail: dtrocha@isbdc.org
Website: http://www.isbdc.org
Ms. Debbie Bishop Trocha, State Director

Iowa

Iowa SBDC
IOWA STATE UNIVERSITY
340 Gerdin Business Bldg.
Ames, IA 50011-1350
Phone: 515-294-2037
Fax: 515-294-6522
E-mail: jonryan@iastate.edu
Website: http://www.iabusnet.org
Mr. Jon Ryan, State Director

Kansas

Kansas SBDC
FORT HAYS STATE UNIVERSITY
214 SW Sixth Street, Suite 301
Topeka, KS 66603
Phone: 785-296-6514
Fax: 785-291-3261
E-mail: ksbdc.wkearns@fhsu.edu
Website: http://www.fhsu.edu/ksbdc
Mr. Wally Kearns, State Director

Kentucky

Kentucky SBDC
UNIVERSITY OF KENTUCKY
225 Gatton College of Business Economics Building
Lexington, KY 40506-0034
Phone: 859-257-7668
Fax: 859-323-1907
E-mail: lrnaug0@pop.uky.edu
Website: http://www.ksbdc.org
Ms. Becky Naugle, State Director

Louisiana

Louisiana SBDC
UNIVERSITY OF LOUISIANA - MONROE
College of Business Administration
700 University Avenue
Monroe, LA 71209
Phone: 318-342-5506
Fax: 318-342-5510
E-mail: wilkerson@ulm.edu
Website: http://www.lsbdc.org
Ms. Mary Lynn Wilkerson, State Director

Maine

Maine SBDC
UNIVERSITY OF SOUTHERN MAINE
96 Falmouth Street P.O. Box 9300
Portland, ME 04103
Phone: 207-780-4420
Fax: 207-780-4810
E-mail: jrmassaua@maine.edu
Website: http://www.mainesbdc.org
Mr. John Massaua, State Director

Maryland

Maryland SBDC
UNIVERSITY OF MARYLAND
7100 Baltimore Avenue, Suite 401
College Park, MD 20742
Phone: 301-403-8300
Fax: 301-403-8303
E-mail: rsprow@mdsbdc.umd.edu
Website: http://www.mdsbdc.umd.edu
Ms. Renee Sprow, State Director

Massachusetts

Massachusetts SBDC
UNIVERSITY OF MASSACHUSETTS
School of Management, Room 205
Amherst, MA 01003-4935
Phone: 413-545-6301
Fax: 413-545-1273
E-mail: gep@msbdc.umass.edu
Website: http://msbdc.som.umass.edu
Ms. Georgianna Parkin, State Director

Michigan

Michigan SBTDC
GRAND VALLEY STATE UNIVERSITY
510 West Fulton Avenue
Grand Rapids, MI 49504
Phone: 616-331-7485
Fax: 616-331-7389
E-mail: lopuckic@gvsu.edu
Website: http://www.misbtdc.org
Ms. Carol Lopucki, State Director

Minnesota

Minnesota SBDC
MINNESOTA SMALL BUSINESS DEVELOPMENT CENTER
1st National Bank Building
332 Minnesota Street, Suite E200
St. Paul, MN 55101-1351
Phone: 651-297-5773
Fax: 651-296-5287
E-mail: michael.myhre@state.mn.us
Website: http://www.mnsbdc.com
Mr. Michael Myhre, State Director

Mississippi

Mississippi SBDC
UNIVERSITY OF MISSISSIPPI
B-19 Jeanette Phillips Drive
P.O. Box 1848
University, MS 38677
Phone: 662-915-5001
Fax: 662-915-5650
E-mail: wgurley@olemiss.edu
Website: http://www.olemiss.edu/depts/mssbdc
Mr. Doug Gurley, Jr., State Director

Missouri

Missouri SBDC
UNIVERSITY OF MISSOURI
1205 University Avenue, Suite 300
Columbia, MO 65211
Phone: 573-882-1348
Fax: 573-884-4297
E-mail: summersm@missouri.edu
Website: http://www.mo-sbdc.org/index.shtml
Mr. Max Summers, State Director

Montana

Montana SBDC
DEPARTMENT OF COMMERCE
301 South Park Avenue, Room 114 / P.O. Box 200505
Helena, MT 59620
Phone: 406-841-2746
Fax: 406-444-1872
E-mail: adesch@state.mt.us
Website: http://commerce.state.mt.us/brd/BRD_SBDC.html
Ms. Ann Desch, State Director

Nebraska

Nebraska SBDC
UNIVERSITY OF NEBRASKA - OMAHA
60th & Dodge Street, CBA Room 407
Omaha, NE 68182
Phone: 402-554-2521
Fax: 402-554-3473
E-mail: rbernier@unomaha.edu
Website: http://nbdc.unomaha.edu
Mr. Robert Bernier, State Director

Nevada

Nevada SBDC
UNIVERSITY OF NEVADA - RENO
Reno College of Business
Administration, Room 411
Reno, NV 89557-0100
Phone: 775-784-1717
Fax: 775-784-4337
E-mail: males@unr.edu
Website: http://www.nsbdc.org
Mr. Sam Males, State Director

New Hampshire

New Hampshire SBDC
UNIVERSITY OF NEW HAMPSHIRE
108 McConnell Hall
Durham, NH 03824-3593
Phone: 603-862-4879
Fax: 603-862-4876
E-mail: Mary.Collins@unh.edu
Website: http://www.nhsbdc.org
Ms. Mary Collins, State Director

New Jersey

New Jersey SBDC
RUTGERS UNIVERSITY
49 Bleeker Street
Newark, NJ 07102-1993
Phone: 973-353-5950
Fax: 973-353-1110
E-mail: bhopper@njsbdc.com
Website: http://www.njsbdc.com/home
Ms. Brenda Hopper, State Director

New Mexico

New Mexico SBDC
SANTA FE COMMUNITY COLLEGE
6401 Richards Avenue
Santa Fe, NM 87505
Phone: 505-428-1362
Fax: 505-471-9469
E-mail: rmiller@santa-fe.cc.nm.us
Website: http://www.nmsbdc.org
Mr. Roy Miller, State Director

New York

New York SBDC
STATE UNIVERSITY OF NEW YORK
SUNY Plaza, S-523
Albany, NY 12246
Phone: 518-443-5398
Fax: 518-443-5275
E-mail: j.king@nyssbdc.org
Website: http://www.nyssbdc.org
Mr. Jim King, State Director

North Carolina

North Carolina SBDTC
UNIVERSITY OF NORTH CAROLINA
5 West Hargett Street, Suite 600
Raleigh, NC 27601
Phone: 919-715-7272
Fax: 919-715-7777
E-mail: sdaugherty@sbtdc.org
Website: http://www.sbtdc.org
Mr. Scott Daugherty, State Director

North Dakota

North Dakota SBDC
UNIVERSITY OF NORTH DAKOTA
1600 E. Century Avenue, Suite 2
Bismarck, ND 58503
Phone: 701-328-5375
Fax: 701-328-5320
E-mail:
christine.martin@und.nodak.edu
Website: http://www.ndsbdc.org
Ms. Christine Martin-Goldman, State Director

Ohio

Ohio SBDC
OHIO DEPARTMENT OF DEVELOPMENT
77 South High Street
Columbus, OH 43216
Phone: 614-466-5102
Fax: 614-466-0829
E-mail: mabraham@odod.state.oh.us
Website: http://www.ohiosbdc.org
Ms. Michele Abraham, State Director

Oklahoma

Oklahoma SBDC
SOUTHEAST OKLAHOMA STATE UNIVERSITY
517 University, Box 2584, Station A
Durant, OK 74701
Phone: 580-745-7577
Fax: 580-745-7471
E-mail: gpennington@sosu.edu
Website: http://www.osbdc.org
Mr. Grady Pennington, State Director

Oregon

Oregon SBDC
LANE COMMUNITY COLLEGE
99 West Tenth Avenue, Suite 390
Eugene, OR 97401-3021
Phone: 541-463-5250
Fax: 541-345-6006
E-mail: carterb@lanecc.edu
Website: http://www.bizcenter.org
Mr. William Carter, State Director

Pennsylvania

Pennsylvania SBDC
UNIVERSITY OF PENNSYLVANIA
The Wharton School
3733 Spruce Street
Philadelphia, PA 19104-6374
Phone: 215-898-1219
Fax: 215-573-2135
E-mail: ghiggins@wharton.upenn.edu
Website: http://pasbdc.org
Mr. Gregory Higgins, State Director

Puerto Rico

Puerto Rico SBDC
INTER-AMERICAN UNIVERSITY OF PUERTO RICO
416 Ponce de Leon Avenue, Union Plaza, Seventh Floor
Hato Rey, PR 00918
Phone: 787-763-6811
Fax: 787-763-4629
E-mail: cmarti@prsbdc.org
Website: http://www.prsbdc.org
Ms. Carmen Marti, Executive Director

Rhode Island

Rhode Island SBDC
BRYANT UNIVERSITY
1150 Douglas Pike
Smithfield, RI 02917
Phone: 401-232-6923
Fax: 401-232-6933
E-mail: adawson@bryant.edu
Website: http://www.risbdc.org
Ms. Diane Fournaris, Interim State Director

South Carolina

South Carolina SBDC
UNIVERSITY OF SOUTH CAROLINA
College of Business Administration
1710 College Street
Columbia, SC 29208
Phone: 803-777-4907
Fax: 803-777-4403
E-mail: lenti@moore.sc.edu
Website: http://scsbdc.moore.sc.edu
Mr. John Lenti, State Director

South Dakota

South Dakota SBDC
UNIVERSITY OF SOUTH DAKOTA
414 East Clark Street, Patterson Hall
Vermillion, SD 57069
Phone: 605-677-6256
Fax: 605-677-5427
E-mail: jshemmin@usd.edu
Website: http://www.sdsbdc.org
Mr. John S. Hemmingstad, State Director

Tennessee

Tennessee SBDC
TENNESSEE BOARD OF REGENTS
1415 Murfressboro Road, Suite 540
Nashville, TN 37217-2833
Phone: 615-898-2745
Fax: 615-893-7089
E-mail: pgeho@mail.tsbdc.org
Website: http://www.tsbdc.org
Mr. Patrick Geho, State Director

Texas

Texas-North SBDC
DALLAS COUNTY COMMUNITY COLLEGE
1402 Corinth Street
Dallas, TX 75215
Phone: 214-860-5835
Fax: 214-860-5813
E-mail: emk9402@dcccd.edu
Website: http://www.ntsbdc.org
Ms. Liz Klimback, Region Director

Texas-Houston SBDC
UNIVERSITY OF HOUSTON
2302 Fannin, Suite 200
Houston, TX 77002
Phone: 713-752-8425
Fax: 713-756-1500
E-mail: fyoung@uh.edu
Website: http://sbdcnetwork.uh.edu
Mr. Mike Young, Executive Director

Texas-NW SBDC
TEXAS TECH UNIVERSITY
2579 South Loop 289, Suite 114
Lubbock, TX 79423
Phone: 806-745-3973
Fax: 806-745-6207
E-mail: c.bean@nwtsbdc.org
Website: http://www.nwtsbdc.org
Mr. Craig Bean, Executive Director

Texas-South-West Texas Border Region SBDC
UNIVERSITY OF TEXAS - SAN ANTONIO
501 West Durango Boulevard
San Antonio, TX 78207-4415
Phone: 210-458-2742
Fax: 210-458-2464
E-mail: albert.salgado@utsa.edu
Website: http://www.iedtexas.org
Mr. Alberto Salgado, Region Director

Utah

Utah SBDC
SALT LAKE COMMUNITY COLLEGE
9750 South 300 West
Sandy, UT 84070
Phone: 801-957-3493
Fax: 801-957-3488
E-mail: Greg.Panichello@slcc.edu
Website:http://www.slcc.edu/sbdc
Mr. Greg Panichello, State Director

Vermont

Vermont SBDC
VERMONT TECHNICAL COLLEGE
PO Box 188, 1 Main Street
Randolph Center, VT 05061-0188
Phone: 802-728-9101
Fax: 802-728-3026
E-mail: lquillen@vtc.edu
Website: http://www.vtsbdc.org
Ms. Lenae Quillen-Blume, State Director

Virgin Islands

Virgin Islands SBDC
UNIVERSITY OF THE VIRGIN ISLANDS
8000 Nisky Center, Suite 720
St. Thomas, VI 00802-5804
Phone: 340-776-3206
Fax: 340-775-3756
E-mail: wbush@webmail.uvi.edu
Website: http://rps.uvi.edu/SBDC
Mr. Warren Bush, State Director

Virginia

Virginia SBDC
GEORGE MASON UNIVERSITY
4031 University Drive, Suite 200
Fairfax, VA 22030-3409
Phone: 703-277-7727
Fax: 703-352-8515
E-mail: jkeenan@gmu.edu
Website: http://www.virginiasbdc.org
Ms. Jody Keenan, Director

Washington

Washington SBDC
WASHINGTON STATE UNIVERSITY
534 E. Trent Avenue
P.O. Box 1495
Spokane, WA 99210-1495
Phone: 509-358-7765
Fax: 509-358-7764
E-mail: barogers@wsu.edu
Website: http://www.wsbdc.org
Mr. Brett Rogers, State Director

West Virginia

West Virginia SBDC
WEST VIRGINIA DEVELOPMENT OFFICE
Capital Complex, Building 6, Room 652
Charleston, WV 25301
Phone: 304-558-2960
Fax: 304-558-0127
E-mail: csalyer@wvsbdc.org
Website: http://www.wvsbdc.org
Mr. Conley Salyor, State Director

Wisconsin

Wisconsin SBDC
UNIVERSITY OF WISCONSIN
432 North Lake Street, Room 423
Madison, WI 53706
Phone: 608-263-7794
Fax: 608-263-7830
E-mail: erica.kauten@uwex.edu
Website: http://www.wisconsinsbdc.org
Ms. Erica Kauten, State Director

Wyoming

Wyoming SBDC
UNIVERSITY OF WYOMING
P.O. Box 3922
Laramie, WY 82071-3922
Phone: 307-766-3505
Fax: 307-766-3406
E-mail: DDW@uwyo.edu
Website: http://www.uwyo.edu/sbdc
Ms. Debbie Popp, Acting State Director

Service corps of retired executives (score) offices

This section contains a listing of all SCORE offices organized alphabetically by state/U.S. territory, then by city, then by agency name.

Alabama

SCORE Office (Northeast Alabama)
1330 Quintard Ave.
Anniston, AL 36202
(256)237-3536

SCORE Office (North Alabama)
901 South 15th St, Rm. 201
Birmingham, AL 35294-2060
(205)934-6868
Fax: (205)934-0538

SCORE Office (Baldwin County)
29750 Larry Dee Cawyer Dr.
Daphne, AL 36526
(334)928-5838

SCORE Office (Shoals)
612 S. COurt
Florence, AL 35630
(256)764-4661
Fax: (256)766-9017
E-mail: shoals@shoalschamber.com

SCORE Office (Mobile)
600 S Court St.
Mobile, AL 36104
(334)240-6868
Fax: (334)240-6869

SCORE Office (Alabama Capitol City)
600 S. Court St.
Montgomery, AL 36104
(334)240-6868
Fax: (334)240-6869

SCORE Office (East Alabama)
601 Ave. A
Opelika, AL 36801
(334)745-4861
E-mail: score636@hotmail.com
Website: http://www.angelfire.com/sc/score636/

SCORE Office (Tuscaloosa)
2200 University Blvd.
Tuscaloosa, AL 35402
(205)758-7588

Alaska

SCORE Office (Anchorage)
510 L St., Ste. 310
Anchorage, AK 99501
(907)271-4022
Fax: (907)271-4545

Arizona

SCORE Office (Lake Havasu)
10 S. Acoma Blvd.
Lake Havasu City, AZ 86403
(520)453-5951
E-mail: SCORE@ctaz.com
Website: http://www.scorearizona.org/lake_havasu/

SCORE Office (East Valley)
Federal Bldg., Rm. 104
26 N. MacDonald St.
Mesa, AZ 85201
(602)379-3100
Fax: (602)379-3143
E-mail: 402@aol.com
Website: http://www.scorearizona.org/mesa/

SCORE Office (Phoenix)
2828 N. Central Ave., Ste. 800
Central & One Thomas
Phoenix, AZ 85004
(602)640-2329
Fax: (602)640-2360
E-mail: e-mail@SCORE-phoenix.org
Website: http://www.score-phoenix.org/

SCORE Office (Prescott Arizona)
1228 Willow Creek Rd., Ste. 2
Prescott, AZ 86301
(520)778-7438
Fax: (520)778-0812
E-mail: score@northlink.com
Website: http://www.scorearizona.org/prescott/

SCORE Office (Tucson)
110 E. Pennington St.
Tucson, AZ 85702
(520)670-5008
Fax: (520)670-5011
E-mail: score@azstarnet.com
Website: http://www.scorearizona.org/tucson/

SCORE Office (Yuma)
281 W. 24th St., Ste. 116
Yuma, AZ 85364
(520)314-0480
E-mail: score@C2i2.com
Website: http://www.scorearizona.org/yuma

Arkansas

SCORE Office (South Central)
201 N. Jackson Ave.
El Dorado, AR 71730-5803
(870)863-6113
Fax: (870)863-6115

SCORE Office (Ozark)
Fayetteville, AR 72701
(501)442-7619

SCORE Office (Northwest Arkansas)
Glenn Haven Dr., No. 4
Ft. Smith, AR 72901
(501)783-3556

SCORE Office (Garland County)
Grand & Ouachita
PO Box 6012
Hot Springs Village, AR 71902
(501)321-1700

SCORE Office (Little Rock)
2120 Riverfront Dr., Rm. 100
Little Rock, AR 72202-1747
(501)324-5893
Fax: (501)324-5199

SCORE Office (Southeast Arkansas)
121 W. 6th
Pine Bluff, AR 71601
(870)535-7189
Fax: (870)535-1643

California

SCORE Office (Golden Empire)
1706 Chester Ave., No. 200
Bakersfield, CA 93301
(805)322-5881
Fax: (805)322-5663

SCORE Office (Greater Chico Area)
1324 Mangrove St., Ste. 114
Chico, CA 95926
(916)342-8932
Fax: (916)342-8932

SCORE Office (Concord)
2151-A Salvio St., Ste. B
Concord, CA 94520
(510)685-1181
Fax: (510)685-5623

SCORE Office (Covina)
935 W. Badillo St.
Covina, CA 91723
(818)967-4191
Fax: (818)966-9660

SCORE Office (Rancho Cucamonga)
8280 Utica, Ste. 160
Cucamonga, CA 91730
(909)987-1012
Fax: (909)987-5917

SCORE Office (Culver City)
PO Box 707
Culver City, CA 90232-0707
(310)287-3850
Fax: (310)287-1350

SCORE Office (Danville)
380 Diablo Rd., Ste. 103
Danville, CA 94526
(510)837-4400

SCORE Office (Downey)
11131 Brookshire Ave.
Downey, CA 90241
(310)923-2191
Fax: (310)864-0461

SCORE Office (El Cajon)
109 Rea Ave.
El Cajon, CA 92020
(619)444-1327
Fax: (619)440-6164

SCORE Office (El Centro)
1100 Main St.
El Centro, CA 92243
(619)352-3681
Fax: (619)352-3246

SCORE Office (Escondido)
720 N. Broadway
Escondido, CA 92025
(619)745-2125
Fax: (619)745-1183

SCORE Office (Fairfield)
1111 Webster St.
Fairfield, CA 94533
(707)425-4625
Fax: (707)425-0826

SCORE Office (Fontana)
17009 Valley Blvd., Ste. B
Fontana, CA 92335
(909)822-4433
Fax: (909)822-6238

SCORE Office (Foster City)
1125 E. Hillsdale Blvd.
Foster City, CA 94404
(415)573-7600
Fax: (415)573-5201

SCORE Office (Fremont)
2201 Walnut Ave., Ste. 110
Fremont, CA 94538
(510)795-2244
Fax: (510)795-2240

SCORE Office (Central California)
2719 N. Air Fresno Dr., Ste. 200
Fresno, CA 93727-1547
(559)487-5605
Fax: (559)487-5636

SCORE Office (Gardena)
1204 W. Gardena Blvd.
Gardena, CA 90247
(310)532-9905
Fax: (310)515-4893

SCORE Office (Lompoc)
330 N. Brand Blvd., Ste. 190
Glendale, CA 91203-2304
(818)552-3206
Fax: (818)552-3323

SCORE Office (Los Angeles)
330 N. Brand Blvd., Ste. 190
Glendale, CA 91203-2304
(818)552-3206
Fax: (818)552-3323

SCORE Office (Glendora)
131 E. Foothill Blvd.
Glendora, CA 91740
(818)963-4128
Fax: (818)914-4822

SCORE Office (Grover Beach)
177 S. 8th St.
Grover Beach, CA 93433
(805)489-9091
Fax: (805)489-9091

SCORE Office (Hawthorne)
12477 Hawthorne Blvd.
Hawthorne, CA 90250
(310)676-1163
Fax: (310)676-7661

SCORE Office (Hayward)
22300 Foothill Blvd., Ste. 303
Hayward, CA 94541
(510)537-2424

SCORE Office (Hemet)
1700 E. Florida Ave.
Hemet, CA 92544-4679
(909)652-4390
Fax: (909)929-8543

SCORE Office (Hesperia)
16367 Main St.
PO Box 403656
Hesperia, CA 92340
(619)244-2135

SCORE Office (Holloster)
321 San Felipe Rd., No. 11
Hollister, CA 95023

SCORE Office (Hollywood)
7018 Hollywood Blvd.
Hollywood, CA 90028
(213)469-8311
Fax: (213)469-2805

SCORE Office (Indio)
82503 Hwy. 111
PO Drawer TTT
Indio, CA 92202
(619)347-0676

SCORE Office (Inglewood)
330 Queen St.
Inglewood, CA 90301
(818)552-3206

SCORE Office (La Puente)
218 N. Grendanda St. D.
La Puente, CA 91744
(818)330-3216
Fax: (818)330-9524

SCORE Office (La Verne)
2078 Bonita Ave.
La Verne, CA 91750
(909)593-5265
Fax: (714)929-8475

SCORE Office (Lake Elsinore)
132 W. Graham Ave.
Lake Elsinore, CA 92530
(909)674-2577

SCORE Office (Lakeport)
PO Box 295
Lakeport, CA 95453
(707)263-5092

SCORE Office (Lakewood)
5445 E. Del Amo Blvd., Ste. 2
Lakewood, CA 90714
(213)920-7737

SCORE Office (Long Beach)
1 World Trade Center
Long Beach, CA 90831

SCORE Office (Los Alamitos)
901 W. Civic Center Dr., Ste. 160
Los Alamitos, CA 90720

SCORE Office (Los Altos)
321 University Ave.
Los Altos, CA 94022
(415)948-1455

SCORE Office (Manhattan Beach)
PO Box 3007
Manhattan Beach, CA 90266
(310)545-5313
Fax: (310)545-7203

SCORE Office (Merced)
1632 N. St.
Merced, CA 95340
(209)725-3800
Fax: (209)383-4959

SCORE Office (Milpitas)
75 S. Milpitas Blvd., Ste. 205
Milpitas, CA 95035

(408)262-2613
Fax: (408)262-2823

SCORE Office (Yosemite)
1012 11th St., Ste. 300
Modesto, CA 95354
(209)521-9333

SCORE Office (Montclair)
5220 Benito Ave.
Montclair, CA 91763

SCORE Office (Monterey Bay)
380 Alvarado St.
PO Box 1770
Monterey, CA 93940-1770
(408)649-1770

SCORE Office (Moreno Valley)
25480 Alessandro
Moreno Valley, CA 92553

SCORE Office (Morgan Hill)
25 W. 1st St.
PO Box 786
Morgan Hill, CA 95038
(408)779-9444
Fax: (408)778-1786

SCORE Office (Morro Bay)
880 Main St.
Morro Bay, CA 93442
(805)772-4467

SCORE Office (Mountain View)
580 Castro St.
Mountain View, CA 94041
(415)968-8378
Fax: (415)968-5668

SCORE Office (Napa)
1556 1st St.
Napa, CA 94559
(707)226-7455
Fax: (707)226-1171

SCORE Office (North Hollywood)
5019 Lankershim Blvd.
North Hollywood, CA 91601
(818)552-3206

SCORE Office (Northridge)
8801 Reseda Blvd.
Northridge, CA 91324
(818)349-5676

SCORE Office (Novato)
807 De Long Ave.
Novato, CA 94945
(415)897-1164
Fax: (415)898-9097

SCORE Office (East Bay)
519 17th St.
Oakland, CA 94612
(510)273-6611
Fax: (510)273-6015
E-mail: webmaster@eastbayscore.org
Website: http://www.eastbayscore.org

SCORE Office (Oceanside)
928 N. Coast Hwy.
Oceanside, CA 92054
(619)722-1534

SCORE Office (Ontario)
121 West B. St.
Ontario, CA 91762
Fax: (714)984-6439

SCORE Office (Oxnard)
PO Box 867
Oxnard, CA 93032
(805)385-8860
Fax: (805)487-1763

SCORE Office (Pacifica)
450 Dundee Way, Ste. 2
Pacifica, CA 94044
(415)355-4122

SCORE Office (Palm Desert)
72990 Hwy. 111
Palm Desert, CA 92260
(619)346-6111
Fax: (619)346-3463

SCORE Office (Palm Springs)
650 E. Tahquitz Canyon Way Ste. D
Palm Springs, CA 92262-6706
(760)320-6682
Fax: (760)323-9426

SCORE Office (Lakeside)
2150 Low Tree
Palmdale, CA 93551
(805)948-4518
Fax: (805)949-1212

SCORE Office (Palo Alto)
325 Forest Ave.
Palo Alto, CA 94301
(415)324-3121
Fax: (415)324-1215

SCORE Office (Pasadena)
117 E. Colorado Blvd., Ste. 100
Pasadena, CA 91105
(818)795-3355
Fax: (818)795-5663

SCORE Office (Paso Robles)
1225 Park St.
Paso Robles, CA 93446-2234
(805)238-0506
Fax: (805)238-0527

SCORE Office (Petaluma)
799 Baywood Dr., Ste. 3
Petaluma, CA 94954
(707)762-2785
Fax: (707)762-4721

SCORE Office (Pico Rivera)
9122 E. Washington Blvd.
Pico Rivera, CA 90660

SCORE Office (Pittsburg)
2700 E. Leland Rd.
Pittsburg, CA 94565
(510)439-2181
Fax: (510)427-1599

SCORE Office (Pleasanton)
777 Peters Ave.
Pleasanton, CA 94566
(510)846-9697

SCORE Office (Monterey Park)
485 N. Garey
Pomona, CA 91769

SCORE Office (Pomona)
485 N. Garey Ave.
Pomona, CA 91766
(909)622-1256

SCORE Office (Antelope Valley)
4511 West Ave. M-4
Quartz Hill, CA 93536
(805)272-0087
E-mail: avscore@ptw.com
Website: http://www.score.av.org/

SCORE Office (Shasta)
737 Auditorium Dr.
Redding, CA 96099
(916)225-2770

SCORE Office (Redwood City)
1675 Broadway
Redwood City, CA 94063
(415)364-1722
Fax: (415)364-1729

SCORE Office (Richmond)
3925 MacDonald Ave.
Richmond, CA 94805

SCORE Office (Ridgecrest)
PO Box 771
Ridgecrest, CA 93555
(619)375-8331
Fax: (619)375-0365

SCORE Office (Riverside)
3685 Main St., Ste. 350
Riverside, CA 92501
(909)683-7100

SCORE Office (Sacramento)
9845 Horn Rd., 260-B
Sacramento, CA 95827
(916)361-2322
Fax: (916)361-2164
E-mail: sacchapter@directcon.net

SCORE Office (Salinas)
PO Box 1170
Salinas, CA 93902
(408)424-7611
Fax: (408)424-8639

SCORE Office (Inland Empire)
777 E. Rialto Ave.
Purchasing
San Bernardino, CA 92415-0760
(909)386-8278

SCORE Office (San Carlos)
San Carlos Chamber of Commerce
PO Box 1086
San Carlos, CA 94070
(415)593-1068
Fax: (415)593-9108

SCORE Office (Encinitas)
550 W. C St., Ste. 550
San Diego, CA 92101-3540
(619)557-7272
Fax: (619)557-5894

SCORE Office (San Diego)
550 West C. St., Ste. 550
San Diego, CA 92101-3540
(619)557-7272
Fax: (619)557-5894
Website: http://www.score-sandiego.org

SCORE Office (Menlo Park)
1100 Merrill St.
San Francisco, CA 94105
(415)325-2818
Fax: (415)325-0920

SCORE Office (San Francisco)
455 Market St., 6th Fl.
San Francisco, CA 94105
(415)744-6827
Fax: (415)744-6750
E-mail: sfscore@sfscore.
Website: http://www.sfscore.com

SCORE Office (San Gabriel)
401 W. Las Tunas Dr.
San Gabriel, CA 91776
(818)576-2525
Fax: (818)289-2901

SCORE Office (San Jose)
Deanza College
208 S. 1st. St., Ste. 137
San Jose, CA 95113
(408)288-8479
Fax: (408)535-5541

SCORE Office (Silicon Valley)
84 W. Santa Clara St., Ste. 100
San Jose, CA 95113
(408)288-8479
Fax: (408)535-5541
E-mail: info@svscore.org
Website: http://www.svscore.org

SCORE Office (San Luis Obispo)
3566 S. Hiquera, No. 104
San Luis Obispo, CA 93401
(805)547-0779

SCORE Office (San Mateo)
1021 S. El Camino, 2nd Fl.
San Mateo, CA 94402
(415)341-5679

SCORE Office (San Pedro)
390 W. 7th St.
San Pedro, CA 90731
(310)832-7272

SCORE Office (Orange County)
200 W. Santa Anna Blvd., Ste. 700
Santa Ana, CA 92701
(714)550-7369
Fax: (714)550-0191
Website: http://www.score114.org

SCORE Office (Santa Barbara)
3227 State St.
Santa Barbara, CA 93130
(805)563-0084

SCORE Office (Central Coast)
509 W. Morrison Ave.
Santa Maria, CA 93454
(805)347-7755

SCORE Office (Santa Maria)
614 S. Broadway
Santa Maria, CA 93454-5111
(805)925-2403
Fax: (805)928-7559

SCORE Office (Santa Monica)
501 Colorado, Ste. 150
Santa Monica, CA 90401
(310)393-9825
Fax: (310)394-1868

SCORE Office (Santa Rosa)
777 Sonoma Ave., Rm. 115E
Santa Rosa, CA 95404
(707)571-8342
Fax: (707)541-0331
Website: http://www.pressdemo.com/community/score/score.html

SCORE Office (Scotts Valley)
4 Camp Evers Ln.
Scotts Valley, CA 95066
(408)438-1010
Fax: (408)438-6544

SCORE Office (Simi Valley)
40 W. Cochran St., Ste. 100
Simi Valley, CA 93065
(805)526-3900
Fax: (805)526-6234

SCORE Office (Sonoma)
453 1st St. E
Sonoma, CA 95476
(707)996-1033

SCORE Office (Los Banos)
222 S. Shepard St.
Sonora, CA 95370
(209)532-4212

SCORE Office (Tuolumne County)
39 North Washington St.
Sonora, CA 95370
(209)588-0128
E-mail: score@mlode.com

SCORE Office (South San Francisco)
445 Market St., Ste. 6th Fl.
South San Francisco, CA 94105
(415)744-6827
Fax: (415)744-6812

SCORE Office (Stockton)
401 N. San Joaquin St., Rm. 215
Stockton, CA 95202
(209)946-6293

SCORE Office (Taft)
314 4th St.
Taft, CA 93268
(805)765-2165
Fax: (805)765-6639

SCORE Office (Conejo Valley)
625 W. Hillcrest Dr.
Thousand Oaks, CA 91360
(805)499-1993
Fax: (805)498-7264

SCORE Office (Torrance)
3400 Torrance Blvd., Ste. 100
Torrance, CA 90503

(310)540-5858
Fax: (310)540-7662

SCORE Office (Truckee)
PO Box 2757
Truckee, CA 96160
(916)587-2757
Fax: (916)587-2439

SCORE Office (Visalia)
113 S. M St,
Tulare, CA 93274
(209)627-0766
Fax: (209)627-8149

SCORE Office (Upland)
433 N. 2nd Ave.
Upland, CA 91786
(909)931-4108

SCORE Office (Vallejo)
2 Florida St.
Vallejo, CA 94590
(707)644-5551
Fax: (707)644-5590

SCORE Office (Van Nuys)
14540 Victory Blvd.
Van Nuys, CA 91411
(818)989-0300
Fax: (818)989-3836

SCORE Office (Ventura)
5700 Ralston St., Ste. 310
Ventura, CA 93001
(805)658-2688
Fax: (805)658-2252
E-mail: scoreven@jps.net
Website: http://www.jps.net/scoreven

SCORE Office (Vista)
201 E. Washington St.
Vista, CA 92084
(619)726-1122
Fax: (619)226-8654

SCORE Office (Watsonville)
PO Box 1748
Watsonville, CA 95077
(408)724-3849
Fax: (408)728-5300

SCORE Office (West Covina)
811 S. Sunset Ave.
West Covina, CA 91790
(818)338-8496
Fax: (818)960-0511

SCORE Office (Westlake)
30893 Thousand Oaks Blvd.
Westlake Village, CA 91362
(805)496-5630
Fax: (818)991-1754

Colorado

SCORE Office (Colorado Springs)
2 N. Cascade Ave., Ste. 110
Colorado Springs, CO 80903
(719)636-3074
Website: http://www.cscc.org/score02/index.html

SCORE Office (Denver)
US Custom's House, 4th Fl.
721 19th St.
Denver, CO 80201-0660
(303)844-3985
Fax: (303)844-6490
E-mail: score62@csn.net
Website: http://www.sni.net/score62

SCORE Office (Tri-River)
1102 Grand Ave.
Glenwood Springs, CO 81601
(970)945-6589

SCORE Office (Grand Junction)
2591 B & 3/4 Rd.
Grand Junction, CO 81503
(970)243-5242

SCORE Office (Gunnison)
608 N. 11th
Gunnison, CO 81230
(303)641-4422

SCORE Office (Montrose)
1214 Peppertree Dr.
Montrose, CO 81401
(970)249-6080

SCORE Office (Pagosa Springs)
PO Box 4381
Pagosa Springs, CO 81157
(970)731-4890

SCORE Office (Rifle)
0854 W. Battlement Pky., Apt. C106
Parachute, CO 81635
(970)285-9390

SCORE Office (Pueblo)
302 N. Santa Fe
Pueblo, CO 81003
(719)542-1704
Fax: (719)542-1624
E-mail: mackey@iex.net
Website: http://www.pueblo.org/score

SCORE Office (Ridgway)
143 Poplar Pl.
Ridgway, CO 81432

SCORE Office (Silverton)
PO Box 480
Silverton, CO 81433
(303)387-5430

SCORE Office (Minturn)
PO Box 2066
Vail, CO 81658
(970)476-1224

Connecticut

SCORE Office (Greater Bridgeport)
230 Park Ave.
Bridgeport, CT 06601-0999
(203)576-4369
Fax: (203)576-4388

SCORE Office (Bristol)
10 Main St. 1st. Fl.
Bristol, CT 06010
(203)584-4718
Fax: (203)584-4722

SCORE office (Greater Danbury)
246 Federal Rd.
Unit LL2, Ste. 7
Brookfield, CT 06804
(203)775-1151

SCORE Office (Greater Danbury)
246 Federal Rd., Unit LL2, Ste. 7
Brookfield, CT 06804
(203)775-1151

SCORE Office (Eastern Connecticut)
Administration Bldg., Rm. 313
PO 625
61 Main St. (Chapter 579)
Groton, CT 06475
(203)388-9508

SCORE Office (Greater Hartford County)
330 Main St.
Hartford, CT 06106
(860)548-1749
Fax: (860)240-4659
Website: http://www.score56.org

SCORE Office (Manchester)
20 Hartford Rd.
Manchester, CT 06040
(203)646-2223
Fax: (203)646-5871

SCORE Office (New Britain)
185 Main St., Ste. 431
New Britain, CT 06051
(203)827-4492
Fax: (203)827-4480

SCORE Office (New Haven)
25 Science Pk., Bldg. 25, Rm. 366
New Haven, CT 06511
(203)865-7645

SCORE Office (Fairfield County)
24 Beldon Ave., 5th Fl.
Norwalk, CT 06850
(203)847-7348
Fax: (203)849-9308

SCORE Office (Old Saybrook)
146 Main St.
Old Saybrook, CT 06475
(860)388-9508

SCORE Office (Simsbury)
Box 244
Simsbury, CT 06070
(203)651-7307
Fax: (203)651-1933

SCORE Office (Torrington)
23 North Rd.
Torrington, CT 06791
(203)482-6586

Delaware

SCORE Office (Dover)
Treadway Towers
PO Box 576
Dover, DE 19903
(302)678-0892
Fax: (302)678-0189

SCORE Office (Lewes)
PO Box 1
Lewes, DE 19958
(302)645-8073
Fax: (302)645-8412

SCORE Office (Milford)
204 NE Front St.
Milford, DE 19963
(302)422-3301

SCORE Office (Wilmington)
824 Market St., Ste. 610
Wilmington, DE 19801
(302)573-6652
Fax: (302)573-6092
Website: http://www.scoredelaware.com

District of Columbia

SCORE Office (George Mason University)
409 3rd St. SW, 4th Fl.
Washington, DC 20024
800-634-0245

SCORE Office (Washington DC)
1110 Vermont Ave. NW, 9th Fl.
Washington, DC 20043
(202)606-4000
Fax: (202)606-4225
E-mail: dcscore@hotmail.com
Website: http://www.scoredc.org/

Florida

SCORE Office (Desota County Chamber of Commerce)
16 South Velucia Ave.
Arcadia, FL 34266
(941)494-4033

SCORE Office (Suncoast/Pinellas)
Airport Business Ctr.
4707 - 140th Ave. N, No. 311
Clearwater, FL 33755
(813)532-6800
Fax: (813)532-6800

SCORE Office (DeLand)
336 N. Woodland Blvd.
DeLand, FL 32720
(904)734-4331
Fax: (904)734-4333

SCORE Office (South Palm Beach)
1050 S. Federal Hwy., Ste. 132
Delray Beach, FL 33483
(561)278-7752
Fax: (561)278-0288

SCORE Office (Ft. Lauderdale)
Federal Bldg., Ste. 123
299 E. Broward Blvd.
Ft. Lauderdale, FL 33301
(954)356-7263
Fax: (954)356-7145

SCORE Office (Southwest Florida)
The Renaissance
8695 College Pky., Ste. 345 & 346
Ft. Myers, FL 33919
(941)489-2935
Fax: (941)489-1170

SCORE Office (Treasure Coast)
Professional Center, Ste. 2
3220 S. US, No. 1
Ft. Pierce, FL 34982
(561)489-0548

SCORE Office (Gainesville)
101 SE 2nd Pl., Ste. 104
Gainesville, FL 32601
(904)375-8278

SCORE Office (Hialeah Dade Chamber)
59 W. 5th St.
Hialeah, FL 33010
(305)887-1515
Fax: (305)887-2453

SCORE Office (Daytona Beach)
921 Nova Rd., Ste. A
Holly Hills, FL 32117
(904)255-6889
Fax: (904)255-0229
E-mail: score87@dbeach.com

SCORE Office (South Broward)
3475 Sheridian St., Ste. 203
Hollywood, FL 33021
(305)966-8415

SCORE Office (Citrus County)
5 Poplar Ct.
Homosassa, FL 34446
(352)382-1037

SCORE Office (Jacksonville)
7825 Baymeadows Way, Ste. 100-B
Jacksonville, FL 32256
(904)443-1911
Fax: (904)443-1980
E-mail: scorejax@juno.com
Website: http://www.scorejax.org/

SCORE Office (Jacksonville Satellite)
3 Independent Dr.
Jacksonville, FL 32256
(904)366-6600
Fax: (904)632-0617

SCORE Office (Central Florida)
5410 S. Florida Ave., No. 3
Lakeland, FL 33801
(941)687-5783
Fax: (941)687-6225

SCORE Office (Lakeland)
100 Lake Morton Dr.
Lakeland, FL 33801
(941)686-2168

SCORE Office (St. Petersburg)
800 W. Bay Dr., Ste. 505
Largo, FL 33712
(813)585-4571

SCORE Office (Leesburg)
9501 US Hwy. 441
Leesburg, FL 34788-8751
(352)365-3556
Fax: (352)365-3501

SCORE Office (Cocoa)
1600 Farno Rd., Unit 205
Melbourne, FL 32935
(407)254-2288

SCORE Office (Melbourne)
Melbourne Professional Complex
1600 Sarno, Ste. 205

Melbourne, FL 32935
(407)254-2288
Fax: (407)245-2288

SCORE Office (Merritt Island)
1600 Sarno Rd., Ste. 205
Melbourne, FL 32935
(407)254-2288
Fax: (407)254-2288

SCORE Office (Space Coast)
Melbourn Professional Complex
1600 Sarno, Ste. 205
Melbourne, FL 32935
(407)254-2288
Fax: (407)254-2288

SCORE Office (Dade)
49 NW 5th St.
Miami, FL 33128
(305)371-6889
Fax: (305)374-1882
E-mail: score@netrox.net
Website: http://www.netrox.net/~score/

SCORE Office (Naples of Collier)
International College
2654 Tamiami Trl. E
Naples, FL 34112
(941)417-1280
Fax: (941)417-1281
E-mail: score@naples.net
Website: http://www.naples.net/clubs/score/index.htm

SCORE Office (Pasco County)
6014 US Hwy. 19, Ste. 302
New Port Richey, FL 34652
(813)842-4638

SCORE Office (Southeast Volusia)
115 Canal St.
New Smyrna Beach, FL 32168
(904)428-2449
Fax: (904)423-3512

SCORE Office (Ocala)
110 E. Silver Springs Blvd.
Ocala, FL 34470
(352)629-5959

Clay County SCORE Office
Clay County Chamber of Commerce
1734 Kingsdey Ave.
PO Box 1441
Orange Park, FL 32073
(904)264-2651
Fax: (904)269-0363

SCORE Office (Orlando)
80 N. Hughey Ave.
Rm. 445 Federal Bldg.
Orlando, FL 32801
(407)648-6476
Fax: (407)648-6425

SCORE Office (Emerald Coast)
19 W. Garden St., No. 325
Pensacola, FL 32501
(904)444-2060
Fax: (904)444-2070

SCORE Office (Charlotte County)
201 W. Marion Ave., Ste. 211
Punta Gorda, FL 33950
(941)575-1818
E-mail: score@gls3c.com
Website: http://www.charlotte-florida.com/business/scorepg01.htm

SCORE Office (St. Augustine)
1 Riberia St.
St. Augustine, FL 32084
(904)829-5681
Fax: (904)829-6477

SCORE Office (Bradenton)
2801 Fruitville, Ste. 280
Sarasota, FL 34237
(813)955-1029

SCORE Office (Manasota)
2801 Fruitville Rd., Ste. 280
Sarasota, FL 34237
(941)955-1029
Fax: (941)955-5581
E-mail: score116@gte.net
Website: http://www.score-suncoast.org/

SCORE Office (Tallahassee)
200 W. Park Ave.
Tallahassee, FL 32302
(850)487-2665

SCORE Office (Hillsborough)
4732 Dale Mabry Hwy. N, Ste. 400
Tampa, FL 33614-6509
(813)870-0125

SCORE Office (Lake Sumter)
122 E. Main St.
Tavares, FL 32778-3810
(352)365-3556

SCORE Office (Titusville)
2000 S. Washington Ave.
Titusville, FL 32780
(407)267-3036
Fax: (407)264-0127

SCORE Office (Venice)
257 N. Tamiami Trl.
Venice, FL 34285
(941)488-2236
Fax: (941)484-5903

SCORE Office (Palm Beach)
500 Australian Ave. S, Ste. 100
West Palm Beach, FL 33401
(561)833-1672
Fax: (561)833-1712

SCORE Office (Wildwood)
103 N. Webster St.
Wildwood, FL 34785

Georgia

SCORE Office (Atlanta)
Harris Tower, Suite 1900
233 Peachtree Rd., NE
Atlanta, GA 30309
(404)347-2442
Fax: (404)347-1227

SCORE Office (Augusta)
3126 Oxford Rd.
Augusta, GA 30909
(706)869-9100

SCORE Office (Columbus)
School Bldg.
PO Box 40
Columbus, GA 31901
(706)327-3654

SCORE Office (Dalton-Whitfield)
305 S. Thorton Ave.
Dalton, GA 30720
(706)279-3383

SCORE Office (Gainesville)
PO Box 374
Gainesville, GA 30503
(770)532-6206
Fax: (770)535-8419

SCORE Office (Macon)
711 Grand Bldg.
Macon, GA 31201
(912)751-6160

SCORE Office (Brunswick)
4 Glen Ave.
St. Simons Island, GA 31520
(912)265-0620
Fax: (912)265-0629

SCORE Office (Savannah)
111 E. Liberty St., Ste. 103
Savannah, GA 31401
(912)652-4335
Fax: (912)652-4184
E-mail: info@scoresav.org
Website: http://www.coastalempire.com/score/index.htm

(708)709-3750
Fax: (708)503-9322

SCORE Office (Mattoon)
1701 Wabash Ave.
Mattoon, IL 61938
(217)235-5661
Fax: (217)234-6544

SCORE Office (Quad Cities)
622 19th St.
Moline, IL 61265
(309)797-0082
Fax: (309)757-5435
E-mail: score@qconline.com
Website: http://www.qconline.com/business/score/

SCORE Office (Naperville)
131 W. Jefferson Ave.
Naperville, IL 60540
(708)355-4141
Fax: (708)355-8355

SCORE Office (Northbrook)
2002 Walters Ave.
Northbrook, IL 60062
(847)498-5555
Fax: (847)498-5510

SCORE Office (Palos Hills)
10900 S. 88th Ave.
Palos Hills, IL 60465
(847)974-5468
Fax: (847)974-0078

SCORE Office (Peoria)
124 SW Adams, Ste. 300
Peoria, IL 61602
(309)676-0755
Fax: (309)676-7534

SCORE Office (Prospect Heights)
1375 Wolf Rd.
Prospect Heights, IL 60070
(847)537-8660
Fax: (847)537-7138

SCORE Office (Quincy Tri-State)
300 Civic Center Plz., Ste. 245
Quincy, IL 62301
(217)222-8093
Fax: (217)222-3033

SCORE Office (River Grove)
2000 5th Ave.
River Grove, IL 60171
(708)456-0300
Fax: (708)583-3121

SCORE Office (Northern Illinois)
515 N. Court St.
Rockford, IL 61103
(815)962-0122
Fax: (815)962-0122

SCORE Office (St. Charles)
103 N. 1st Ave.
St. Charles, IL 60174-1982
(847)584-8384
Fax: (847)584-6065

SCORE Office (Springfield)
511 W. Capitol Ave., Ste. 302
Springfield, IL 62704
(217)492-4416
Fax: (217)492-4867

SCORE Office (Sycamore)
112 Somunak St.
Sycamore, IL 60178
(815)895-3456
Fax: (815)895-0125

SCORE Office (University)
Hwy. 50 & Stuenkel Rd. Ste. C3305
University Park, IL 60466
(708)534-5000
Fax: (708)534-8457

Indiana

SCORE Office (Anderson)
205 W. 11th St.
Anderson, IN 46015
(317)642-0264

SCORE Office (Bloomington)
Star Center
216 W. Allen
Bloomington, IN 47403
(812)335-7334
E-mail: wtfische@indiana.edu
Website: http://www.brainfreezemedia.com/score527/

SCORE Office (South East Indiana)
500 Franklin St.
Box 29
Columbus, IN 47201
(812)379-4457

SCORE Office (Corydon)
310 N. Elm St.
Corydon, IN 47112
(812)738-2137
Fax: (812)738-6438

SCORE Office (Crown Point)
Old Courthouse Sq. Ste. 206
PO Box 43
Crown Point, IN 46307
(219)663-1800

SCORE Office (Elkhart)
418 S. Main St.
Elkhart, IN 46515
(219)293-1531
Fax: (219)294-1859

SCORE Office (Evansville)
1100 W. Lloyd Expy., Ste. 105
Evansville, IN 47708
(812)426-6144

SCORE Office (Fort Wayne)
1300 S. Harrison St.
Ft. Wayne, IN 46802
(219)422-2601
Fax: (219)422-2601

SCORE Office (Gary)
973 W. 6th Ave., Rm. 326
Gary, IN 46402
(219)882-3918

SCORE Office (Hammond)
7034 Indianapolis Blvd.
Hammond, IN 46324
(219)931-1000
Fax: (219)845-9548

SCORE Office (Indianapolis)
429 N. Pennsylvania St., Ste. 100
Indianapolis, IN 46204-1873
(317)226-7264
Fax: (317)226-7259
E-mail: inscore@indy.net
Website: http://www.score-indianapolis.org/

SCORE Office (Jasper)
PO Box 307
Jasper, IN 47547-0307
(812)482-6866

SCORE Office (Kokomo/Howard Counties)
106 N. Washington St.
Kokomo, IN 46901
(765)457-5301
Fax: (765)452-4564

SCORE Office (Logansport)
300 E. Broadway, Ste. 103
Logansport, IN 46947
(219)753-6388

SCORE Office (Madison)
301 E. Main St.
Madison, IN 47250
(812)265-3135
Fax: (812)265-2923

SCORE Office (Marengo)
Rt. 1 Box 224D
Marengo, IN 47140
Fax: (812)365-2793

Guam

SCORE Office (Guam)
Pacific News Bldg., Rm. 103
238 Archbishop Flores St.
Agana, GU 96910-5100
(671)472-7308

Hawaii

SCORE Office (Hawaii, Inc.)
1111 Bishop St., Ste. 204
PO Box 50207
Honolulu, HI 96813
(808)522-8132
Fax: (808)522-8135
E-mail: hnlscore@juno.com

SCORE Office (Kahului)
250 Alamaha, Unit N16A
Kahului, HI 96732
(808)871-7711

SCORE Office (Maui, Inc.)
590 E. Lipoa Pkwy., Ste. 227
Kihei, HI 96753
(808)875-2380

Idaho

SCORE Office (Treasure Valley)
1020 Main St., No. 290
Boise, ID 83702
(208)334-1696
Fax: (208)334-9353

SCORE Office (Eastern Idaho)
2300 N. Yellowstone, Ste. 119
Idaho Falls, ID 83401
(208)523-1022
Fax: (208)528-7127

Illinois

SCORE Office (Fox Valley)
40 W. Downer Pl.
PO Box 277
Aurora, IL 60506
(630)897-9214
Fax: (630)897-7002

SCORE Office (Greater Belvidere)
419 S. State St.
Belvidere, IL 61008
(815)544-4357
Fax: (815)547-7654

SCORE Office (Bensenville)
1050 Busse Hwy. Suite 100
Bensenville, IL 60106
(708)350-2944
Fax: (708)350-2979

SCORE Office (Central Illinois)
402 N. Hershey Rd.
Bloomington, IL 61704
(309)644-0549
Fax: (309)663-8270
E-mail: webmaster@central-illinois-score.org
Website: http://www.central-illinois-score.org/

SCORE Office (Southern Illinois)
150 E. Pleasant Hill Rd.
Box 1
Carbondale, IL 62901
(618)453-6654
Fax: (618)453-5040

SCORE Office (Chicago)
Northwest Atrium Ctr.
500 W. Madison St., No. 1250
Chicago, IL 60661
(312)353-7724
Fax: (312)886-5688
Website: http://www.mcs.net/~bic/

SCORE Office (Chicago–Oliver Harvey College)
Pullman Bldg.
1000 E. 11th St., 7th Fl.
Chicago, IL 60628
Fax: (312)468-8086

SCORE Office (Danville)
28 W. N. Street
Danville, IL 61832
(217)442-7232
Fax: (217)442-6228

SCORE Office (Decatur)
Milliken University
1184 W. Main St.
Decatur, IL 62522
(217)424-6297
Fax: (217)424-3993
E-mail: charding@mail.millikin.edu
Website: http://www.millikin.edu/academics/Tabor/score.html

SCORE Office (Downers Grove)
925 Curtis
Downers Grove, IL 60515
(708)968-4050
Fax: (708)968-8368

SCORE Office (Elgin)
24 E. Chicago, 3rd Fl.
PO Box 648
Elgin, IL 60120
(847)741-5660
Fax: (847)741-5677

SCORE Office (Freeport Area)
26 S. Galena Ave.
Freeport, IL 61032
(815)233-1350
Fax: (815)235-4038

SCORE Office (Galesburg)
292 E. Simmons St.
PO Box 749
Galesburg, IL 61401
(309)343-1194
Fax: (309)343-1195

SCORE Office (Glen Ellyn)
500 Pennsylvania
Glen Ellyn, IL 60137
(708)469-0907
Fax: (708)469-0426

SCORE Office (Greater Alton)
Alden Hall
5800 Godfrey Rd.
Godfrey, IL 62035-2466
(618)467-2280
Fax: (618)466-8289
Website: http://www.altonweb.com/score/

SCORE Office (Grayslake)
19351 W. Washington St.
Grayslake, IL 60030
(708)223-3633
Fax: (708)223-9371

SCORE Office (Harrisburg)
303 S. Commercial
Harrisburg, IL 62946-1528
(618)252-8528
Fax: (618)252-0210

SCORE Office (Joliet)
100 N. Chicago
Joliet, IL 60432
(815)727-5371
Fax: (815)727-5374

SCORE Office (Kankakee)
101 S. Schuyler Ave.
Kankakee, IL 60901
(815)933-0376
Fax: (815)933-0380

SCORE Office (Macomb)
216 Seal Hall, Rm. 214
Macomb, IL 61455
(309)298-1128
Fax: (309)298-2520

SCORE Office (Matteson)
210 Lincoln Mall
Matteson, IL 60443

SCORE Office (Marion/Grant Counties)
215 S. Adams
Marion, IN 46952
(765)664-5107

SCORE Office (Merrillville)
255 W. 80th Pl.
Merrillville, IN 46410
(219)769-8180
Fax: (219)736-6223

SCORE Office (Michigan City)
200 E. Michigan Blvd.
Michigan City, IN 46360
(219)874-6221
Fax: (219)873-1204

SCORE Office (South Central Indiana)
4100 Charleston Rd.
New Albany, IN 47150-9538
(812)945-0066

SCORE Office (Rensselaer)
104 W. Washington
Rensselaer, IN 47978

SCORE Office (Salem)
210 N. Main St.
Salem, IN 47167
(812)883-4303
Fax: (812)883-1467

SCORE Office (South Bend)
300 N. Michigan St.
South Bend, IN 46601
(219)282-4350
E-mail: chair@southbend-score.org
Website: http://www.southbend-score.org/

SCORE Office (Valparaiso)
150 Lincolnway
Valparaiso, IN 46383
(219)462-1105
Fax: (219)469-5710

SCORE Office (Vincennes)
27 N. 3rd
PO Box 553
Vincennes, IN 47591
(812)882-6440
Fax: (812)882-6441

SCORE Office (Wabash)
PO Box 371
Wabash, IN 46992
(219)563-1160
Fax: (219)563-6920

Iowa

SCORE Office (Burlington)
Federal Bldg.
300 N. Main St.
Burlington, IA 52601
(319)752-2967

SCORE Office (Cedar Rapids)
2750 1st Ave. NE, Ste 350
Cedar Rapids, IA 52401-1806
(319)362-6405
Fax: (319)362-7861
E:mail: score@scorecr.org
Website: http://www.scorecr.org

SCORE Office (Illowa)
333 4th Ave. S
Clinton, IA 52732
(319)242-5702

SCORE Office (Council Bluffs)
7 N. 6th St.
Council Bluffs, IA 51502
(712)325-1000

SCORE Office (Northeast Iowa)
3404 285th St.
Cresco, IA 52136
(319)547-3377

SCORE Office (Des Moines)
Federal Bldg., Rm. 749
210 Walnut St.
Des Moines, IA 50309-2186
(515)284-4760

SCORE Office (Ft. Dodge)
Federal Bldg., Rm. 436
205 S. 8th St.
Ft. Dodge, IA 50501
(515)955-2622

SCORE Office (Independence)
110 1st. St. east
Independence, IA 50644
(319)334-7178
Fax: (319)334-7179

SCORE Office (Iowa City)
210 Federal Bldg.
PO Box 1853
Iowa City, IA 52240-1853
(319)338-1662

SCORE Office (Keokuk)
401 Main St.
Pierce Bldg., No. 1
Keokuk, IA 52632
(319)524-5055

SCORE Office (Central Iowa)
Fisher Community College
709 S. Center
Marshalltown, IA 50158
(515)753-6645

SCORE Office (River City)
15 West State St.
Mason City, IA 50401
(515)423-5724

SCORE Office (South Central)
SBDC, Indian Hills Community College
525 Grandview Ave.
Ottumwa, IA 52501
(515)683-5127
Fax: (515)683-5263

SCORE Office (Dubuque)
10250 Sundown Rd.
Peosta, IA 52068
(319)556-5110

SCORE Office (Southwest Iowa)
614 W. Sheridan
Shenandoah, IA 51601
(712)246-3260

SCORE Office (Sioux City)
Federal Bldg.
320 6th St.
Sioux City, IA 51101
(712)277-2324
Fax: (712)277-2325

SCORE Office (Iowa Lakes)
122 W. 5th St.
Spencer, IA 51301
(712)262-3059

SCORE Office (Vista)
119 W. 6th St.
Storm Lake, IA 50588
(712)732-3780

SCORE Office (Waterloo)
215 E. 4th
Waterloo, IA 50703
(319)233-8431

Kansas

SCORE Office (Southwest Kansas)
501 W. Spruce
Dodge City, KS 67801
(316)227-3119

SCORE Office (Emporia)
811 Homewood
Emporia, KS 66801
(316)342-1600

SCORE Office (Golden Belt)
1307 Williams
Great Bend, KS 67530
(316)792-2401

SCORE Office (Hays)
PO Box 400
Hays, KS 67601
(913)625-6595

SCORE Office (Hutchinson)
1 E. 9th St.
Hutchinson, KS 67501
(316)665-8468
Fax: (316)665-7619

SCORE Office (Southeast Kansas)
404 Westminster Pl.
PO Box 886
Independence, KS 67301
(316)331-4741

SCORE Office (McPherson)
306 N. Main
PO Box 616
McPherson, KS 67460
(316)241-3303

SCORE Office (Salina)
120 Ash St.
Salina, KS 67401
(785)243-4290
Fax: (785)243-1833

SCORE Office (Topeka)
1700 College
Topeka, KS 66621
(785)231-1010

SCORE Office (Wichita)
100 E. English, Ste. 510
Wichita, KS 67202
(316)269-6273
Fax: (316)269-6499

SCORE Office (Ark Valley)
205 E. 9th St.
Winfield, KS 67156
(316)221-1617

Kentucky

SCORE Office (Ashland)
PO Box 830
Ashland, KY 41105
(606)329-8011
Fax: (606)325-4607

SCORE Office (Bowling Green)
812 State St.
PO Box 51
Bowling Green, KY 42101
(502)781-3200
Fax: (502)843-0458

SCORE Office (Tri-Lakes)
508 Barbee Way
Danville, KY 40422-1548
(606)231-9902

SCORE Office (Glasgow)
301 W. Main St.
Glasgow, KY 42141
(502)651-3161
Fax: (502)651-3122

SCORE Office (Hazard)
B & I Technical Center
100 Airport Gardens Rd.
Hazard, KY 41701
(606)439-5856
Fax: (606)439-1808

SCORE Office (Lexington)
410 W. Vine St., Ste. 290, Civic C
Lexington, KY 40507
(606)231-9902
Fax: (606)253-3190
E-mail: scorelex@uky.campus.mci.net

SCORE Office (Louisville)
188 Federal Office Bldg.
600 Dr. Martin L. King Jr. Pl.
Louisville, KY 40202
(502)582-5976

SCORE Office (Madisonville)
257 N. Main
Madisonville, KY 42431
(502)825-1399
Fax: (502)825-1396

SCORE Office (Paducah)
Federal Office Bldg.
501 Broadway, Rm. B-36
Paducah, KY 42001
(502)442-5685

Louisiana

SCORE Office (Central Louisiana)
802 3rd St.
Alexandria, LA 71309
(318)442-6671

SCORE Office (Baton Rouge)
564 Laurel St.
PO Box 3217
Baton Rouge, LA 70801
(504)381-7130
Fax: (504)336-4306

SCORE Office (North Shore)
2 W. Thomas
Hammond, LA 70401
(504)345-4457
Fax: (504)345-4749

SCORE Office (Lafayette)
804 St. Mary Blvd.
Lafayette, LA 70505-1307
(318)233-2705
Fax: (318)234-8671
E-mail: score302@aol.com

SCORE Office (Lake Charles)
120 W. Pujo St.
Lake Charles, LA 70601
(318)433-3632

SCORE Office (New Orleans)
365 Canal St., Ste. 3100
New Orleans, LA 70130
(504)589-2356
Fax: (504)589-2339

SCORE Office (Shreveport)
400 Edwards St.
Shreveport, LA 71101
(318)677-2536
Fax: (318)677-2541

Maine

SCORE Office (Augusta)
40 Western Ave.
Augusta, ME 04330
(207)622-8509

SCORE Office (Bangor)
Peabody Hall, Rm. 229
One College Cir.
Bangor, ME 04401
(207)941-9707

SCORE Office (Central & Northern Arroostock)
111 High St.
Caribou, ME 04736
(207)492-8010
Fax: (207)492-8010

SCORE Office (Penquis)
South St.
Dover Foxcroft, ME 04426
(207)564-7021

SCORE Office (Maine Coastal)
Mill Mall
Box 1105
Ellsworth, ME 04605-1105
(207)667-5800
E-mail: score@arcadia.net

SCORE Office (Lewiston-Auburn)
BIC of Maine-Bates Mill Complex
35 Canal St.
Lewiston, ME 04240-7764
(207)782-3708
Fax: (207)783-7745

SCORE Office (Portland)
66 Pearl St., Rm. 210
Portland, ME 04101
(207)772-1147
Fax: (207)772-5581
E-mail: Score53@score.maine.org
Website: http://www.score.maine.org/chapter53/

SCORE Office (Western Mountains)
255 River St.
PO Box 252
Rumford, ME 04257-0252
(207)369-9976

SCORE Office (Oxford Hills)
166 Main St.
South Paris, ME 04281
(207)743-0499

Maryland

SCORE Office (Southern Maryland)
2525 Riva Rd., Ste. 110
Annapolis, MD 21401
(410)266-9553
Fax: (410)573-0981
E-mail: score390@aol.com
Website: http://members.aol.com/score390/index.htm

SCORE Office (Baltimore)
The City Crescent Bldg., 6th Fl.
10 S. Howard St.
Baltimore, MD 21201
(410)962-2233
Fax: (410)962-1805

SCORE Office (Bel Air)
108 S. Bond St.
Bel Air, MD 21014
(410)838-2020
Fax: (410)893-4715

SCORE Office (Bethesda)
7910 Woodmont Ave., Ste. 1204
Bethesda, MD 20814
(301)652-4900
Fax: (301)657-1973

SCORE Office (Bowie)
6670 Race Track Rd.
Bowie, MD 20715
(301)262-0920
Fax: (301)262-0921

SCORE Office (Dorchester County)
203 Sunburst Hwy.
Cambridge, MD 21613
(410)228-3575

SCORE Office (Upper Shore)
210 Marlboro Ave.
Easton, MD 21601
(410)822-4606
Fax: (410)822-7922

SCORE Office (Frederick County)
43A S. Market St.
Frederick, MD 21701
(301)662-8723
Fax: (301)846-4427

SCORE Office (Gaithersburg)
9 Park Ave.
Gaithersburg, MD 20877
(301)840-1400
Fax: (301)963-3918

SCORE Office (Glen Burnie)
103 Crain Hwy. SE
Glen Burnie, MD 21061
(410)766-8282
Fax: (410)766-9722

SCORE Office (Hagerstown)
111 W. Washington St.
Hagerstown, MD 21740
(301)739-2015
Fax: (301)739-1278

SCORE Office (Laurel)
7901 Sandy Spring Rd. Ste. 501
Laurel, MD 20707
(301)725-4000
Fax: (301)725-0776

SCORE Office (Salisbury)
300 E. Main St.
Salisbury, MD 21801
(410)749-0185
Fax: (410)860-9925

Massachusetts

SCORE Office (NE Massachusetts)
100 Cummings Ctr., Ste. 101 K
Beverly, MA 01923
(978)922-9441
Website: http://www1.shore.net/~score/

SCORE Office (Boston)
10 Causeway St., Rm. 265
Boston, MA 02222-1093
(617)565-5591
Fax: (617)565-5598
E-mail: boston-score-20@worldnet.att.net
Website: http://www.scoreboston.org/

SCORE office (Bristol/Plymouth County)
53 N. 6th St., Federal Bldg.
Bristol, MA 02740
(508)994-5093

SCORE Office (SE Massachusetts)
60 School St.
Brockton, MA 02401
(508)587-2673
Fax: (508)587-1340
Website: http://www.metrosouthchamber.com/score.html

SCORE Office (North Adams)
820 N. State Rd.
Cheshire, MA 01225
(413)743-5100

SCORE Office (Clinton Satellite)
1 Green St.
Clinton, MA 01510
Fax: (508)368-7689

SCORE Office (Greenfield)
PO Box 898
Greenfield, MA 01302
(413)773-5463
Fax: (413)773-7008

SCORE Office (Haverhill)
87 Winter St.
Haverhill, MA 01830
(508)373-5663
Fax: (508)373-8060

SCORE Office (Hudson Satellite)
PO Box 578
Hudson, MA 01749
(508)568-0360
Fax: (508)568-0360

SCORE Office (Cape Cod)
Independence Pk., Ste. 5B
270 Communications Way
Hyannis, MA 02601
(508)775-4884
Fax: (508)790-2540

SCORE Office (Lawrence)
264 Essex St.
Lawrence, MA 01840
(508)686-0900
Fax: (508)794-9953

SCORE Office (Leominster Satellite)
110 Erdman Way
Leominster, MA 01453
(508)840-4300
Fax: (508)840-4896

SCORE Office (Bristol/Plymouth Counties)
53 N. 6th St., Federal Bldg.
New Bedford, MA 02740
(508)994-5093

SCORE Office (Newburyport)
29 State St.
Newburyport, MA 01950
(617)462-6680

SCORE Office (Pittsfield)
66 West St.
Pittsfield, MA 01201
(413)499-2485

SCORE Office (Haverhill-Salem)
32 Derby Sq.
Salem, MA 01970
(508)745-0330
Fax: (508)745-3855

SCORE Office (Springfield)
1350 Main St.
Federal Bldg.
Springfield, MA 01103
(413)785-0314

SCORE Office (Carver)
12 Taunton Green, Ste. 201
Taunton, MA 02780
(508)824-4068
Fax: (508)824-4069

SCORE Office (Worcester)
33 Waldo St.
Worcester, MA 01608
(508)753-2929
Fax: (508)754-8560

Michigan

SCORE Office (Allegan)
PO Box 338
Allegan, MI 49010
(616)673-2479

SCORE Office (Ann Arbor)
425 S. Main St., Ste. 103
Ann Arbor, MI 48104
(313)665-4433

SCORE Office (Battle Creek)
34 W. Jackson Ste. 4A
Battle Creek, MI 49017-3505
(616)962-4076
Fax: (616)962-6309

SCORE Office (Cadillac)
222 Lake St.
Cadillac, MI 49601
(616)775-9776
Fax: (616)768-4255

SCORE Office (Detroit)
477 Michigan Ave., Rm. 515
Detroit, MI 48226
(313)226-7947
Fax: (313)226-3448

SCORE Office (Flint)
708 Root Rd., Rm. 308
Flint, MI 48503
(810)233-6846

SCORE Office (Grand Rapids)
111 Pearl St. NW
Grand Rapids, MI 49503-2831
(616)771-0305
Fax: (616)771-0328
E-mail: scoreone@iserv.net
Website: http://www.iserv.net/~scoreone/

SCORE Office (Holland)
480 State St.
Holland, MI 49423
(616)396-9472

SCORE Office (Jackson)
209 East Washington
PO Box 80
Jackson, MI 49204
(517)782-8221
Fax: (517)782-0061

SCORE Office (Kalamazoo)
345 W. Michigan Ave.
Kalamazoo, MI 49007
(616)381-5382
Fax: (616)384-0096
E-mail: score@nucleus.net

SCORE Office (Lansing)
117 E. Allegan
PO Box 14030
Lansing, MI 48901
(517)487-6340
Fax: (517)484-6910

SCORE Office (Livonia)
15401 Farmington Rd.
Livonia, MI 48154
(313)427-2122
Fax: (313)427-6055

SCORE Office (Madison Heights)
26345 John R
Madison Heights, MI 48071
(810)542-5010
Fax: (810)542-6821

SCORE Office (Monroe)
111 E. 1st
Monroe, MI 48161
(313)242-3366
Fax: (313)242-7253

SCORE Office (Mt. Clemens)
58 S/B Gratiot
Mt. Clemens, MI 48043
(810)463-1528
Fax: (810)463-6541

SCORE Office (Muskegon)
PO Box 1087
230 Terrace Plz.
Muskegon, MI 49443
(616)722-3751
Fax: (616)728-7251

SCORE Office (Petoskey)
401 E. Mitchell St.
Petoskey, MI 49770
(616)347-4150

SCORE Office (Pontiac)
Executive Office Bldg.
1200 N. Telegraph Rd.
Pontiac, MI 48341
(810)975-9555

SCORE Office (Pontiac)
PO Box 430025
Pontiac, MI 48343
(810)335-9600

SCORE Office (Port Huron)
920 Pinegrove Ave.
Port Huron, MI 48060
(810)985-7101

SCORE Office (Rochester)
71 Walnut Ste. 110
Rochester, MI 48307
(810)651-6700
Fax: (810)651-5270

SCORE Office (Saginaw)
901 S. Washington Ave.
Saginaw, MI 48601
(517)752-7161
Fax: (517)752-9055

SCORE Office (Upper Peninsula)
2581 I-75 Business Spur
Sault Ste. Marie, MI 49783
(906)632-3301

SCORE Office (Southfield)
21000 W. 10 Mile Rd.
Southfield, MI 48075
(810)204-3050
Fax: (810)204-3099

SCORE Office (Traverse City)
202 E. Grandview Pkwy.
PO Box 387
Traverse City, MI 49685
(616)947-5075
Fax: (616)946-2565

SCORE Office (Warren)
30500 Van Dyke, Ste. 118
Warren, MI 48093
(810)751-3939

Minnesota

SCORE Office (Aitkin)
Aitkin, MN 56431
(218)741-3906

SCORE Office (Albert Lea)
202 N. Broadway Ave.
Albert Lea, MN 56007
(507)373-7487

SCORE Office (Austin)
PO Box 864
Austin, MN 55912
(507)437-4561
Fax: (507)437-4869

SCORE Office (South Metro)
Ames Business Ctr.
2500 W. County Rd., No. 42
Burnsville, MN 55337
(612)898-5645
Fax: (612)435-6972
E-mail: southmetro@scoreminn.org
Website: http://www.scoreminn.org/southmetro/

SCORE Office (Duluth)
1717 Minnesota Ave.
Duluth, MN 55802
(218)727-8286
Fax: (218)727-3113
E-mail: duluth@scoreminn.org
Website: http://www.scoreminn.org

SCORE Office (Fairmont)
PO Box 826
Fairmont, MN 56031
(507)235-5547
Fax: (507)235-8411

SCORE Office (Southwest Minnesota)
112 Riverfront St.
Box 999
Mankato, MN 56001
(507)345-4519
Fax: (507)345-4451
Website: http://www.scoreminn.org/

SCORE Office (Minneapolis)
North Plaza Bldg., Ste. 51
5217 Wayzata Blvd.
Minneapolis, MN 55416
(612)591-0539
Fax: (612)544-0436
Website: http://www.scoreminn.org/

SCORE Office (Owatonna)
PO Box 331
Owatonna, MN 55060
(507)451-7970
Fax: (507)451-7972

SCORE Office (Red Wing)
2000 W. Main St., Ste. 324
Red Wing, MN 55066
(612)388-4079

SCORE Office (Southeastern Minnesota)
220 S. Broadway, Ste. 100
Rochester, MN 55901
(507)288-1122
Fax: (507)282-8960
Website: http://www.scoreminn.org/

SCORE Office (Brainerd)
St. Cloud, MN 56301

SCORE Office (Central Area)
1527 Northway Dr.
St. Cloud, MN 56301
(320)240-1332
Fax: (320)255-9050
Website: http://www.scoreminn.org/

SCORE Office (St. Paul)
350 St. Peter St., No. 295
Lowry Professional Bldg.
St. Paul, MN 55102
(651)223-5010
Fax: (651)223-5048
Website: http://www.scoreminn.org/

SCORE Office (Winona)
Box 870
Winona, MN 55987
(507)452-2272
Fax: (507)454-8814

SCORE Office (Worthington)
1121 3rd Ave.
Worthington, MN 56187
(507)372-2919
Fax: (507)372-2827

Mississippi

SCORE Office (Delta)
915 Washington Ave.
PO Box 933
Greenville, MS 38701
(601)378-3141

SCORE Office (Gulfcoast)
1 Government Plaza
2909 13th St., Ste. 203
Gulfport, MS 39501
(228)863-0054

SCORE Office (Jackson)
1st Jackson Center, Ste. 400
101 W. Capitol St.
Jackson, MS 39201
(601)965-5533

SCORE Office (Meridian)
5220 16th Ave.
Meridian, MS 39305
(601)482-4412

Missouri

SCORE Office (Lake of the Ozark)
University Extension
113 Kansas St.
PO Box 1405
Camdenton, MO 65020
(573)346-2644
Fax: (573)346-2694
E-mail: score@cdoc.net
Website: http://sites.cdoc.net/score/

Chamber of Commerce (Cape Girardeau)
PO Box 98
Cape Girardeau, MO 63702-0098
(314)335-3312

SCORE Office (Mid-Missouri)
1705 Halstead Ct.
Columbia, MO 65203
(573)874-1132

SCORE Office (Ozark-Gateway)
1486 Glassy Rd.
Cuba, MO 65453-1640
(573)885-4954

SCORE Office (Kansas City)
323 W. 8th St., Ste. 104
Kansas City, MO 64105
(816)374-6675
Fax: (816)374-6692
E-mail: SCOREBIC@AOL.COM
Website: http://www.crn.org/score/

SCORE Office (Sedalia)
Lucas Place
323 W. 8th St., Ste.104
Kansas City, MO 64105
(816)374-6675

SCORE office (Tri-Lakes)
PO Box 1148
Kimberling, MO 65686
(417)739-3041

SCORE Office (Tri-Lakes)
HCRI Box 85
Lampe, MO 65681
(417)858-6798

SCORE Office (Mexico)
111 N. Washington St.
Mexico, MO 65265
(314)581-2765

SCORE Office (Southeast Missouri)
Rte. 1, Box 280
Neelyville, MO 63954
(573)989-3577

SCORE office (Poplar Bluff Area)
806 Emma St.
Poplar Bluff, MO 63901
(573)686-8892

SCORE Office (St. Joseph)
3003 Frederick Ave.
St. Joseph, MO 64506
(816)232-4461

SCORE Office (St. Louis)
815 Olive St., Rm. 242
St. Louis, MO 63101-1569
(314)539-6970
Fax: (314)539-3785
E-mail: info@stlscore.org
Website: http://www.stlscore.org/

SCORE Office (Lewis & Clark)
425 Spencer Rd.
St. Peters, MO 63376
(314)928-2900
Fax: (314)928-2900
E-mail: score01@mail.win.org

SCORE Office (Springfield)
620 S. Glenstone, Ste. 110
Springfield, MO 65802-3200
(417)864-7670
Fax: (417)864-4108

SCORE office (Southeast Kansas)
1206 W. First St.
Webb City, MO 64870
(417)673-3984

Montana

SCORE Office (Billings)
815 S. 27th St.
Billings, MT 59101
(406)245-4111

SCORE Office (Bozeman)
1205 E. Main St.
Bozeman, MT 59715
(406)586-5421

SCORE Office (Butte)
1000 George St.
Butte, MT 59701
(406)723-3177

SCORE Office (Great Falls)
710 First Ave. N
Great Falls, MT 59401
(406)761-4434
E-mail: scoregtf@in.tch.com

SCORE Office (Havre, Montana)
518 First St.
Havre, MT 59501
(406)265-4383

SCORE Office (Helena)
Federal Bldg.
301 S. Park
Helena, MT 59626-0054
(406)441-1081

SCORE Office (Kalispell)
2 Main St.
Kalispell, MT 59901
(406)756-5271
Fax: (406)752-6665

SCORE Office (Missoula)
723 Ronan
Missoula, MT 59806
(406)327-8806
E-mail: score@safeshop.com
Website: http://missoula.bigsky.net/score/

Nebraska

SCORE Office (Columbus)
Columbus, NE 68601
(402)564-2769

SCORE Office (Fremont)
92 W. 5th St.
Fremont, NE 68025
(402)721-2641

SCORE Office (Hastings)
Hastings, NE 68901
(402)463-3447

SCORE Office (Lincoln)
8800 O St.
Lincoln, NE 68520
(402)437-2409

SCORE Office (Panhandle)
150549 CR 30
Minatare, NE 69356
(308)632-2133
Website: http://www.tandt.com/SCORE

SCORE Office (Norfolk)
3209 S. 48th Ave.
Norfolk, NE 68106
(402)564-2769

SCORE Office (North Platte)
3301 W. 2nd St.
North Platte, NE 69101
(308)532-4466

SCORE Office (Omaha)
11145 Mill Valley Rd.
Omaha, NE 68154
(402)221-3606
Fax: (402)221-3680
E-mail: infoctr@ne.uswest.net
Website: http://www.tandt.com/score/

Nevada

SCORE Office (Incline Village)
969 Tahoe Blvd.
Incline Village, NV 89451
(702)831-7327
Fax: (702)832-1605

SCORE Office (Carson City)
301 E. Stewart
PO Box 7527
Las Vegas, NV 89125
(702)388-6104

SCORE Office (Las Vegas)
300 Las Vegas Blvd. S, Ste. 1100
Las Vegas, NV 89101
(702)388-6104

SCORE Office (Northern Nevada)
SBDC, College of Business Administration
Univ. of Nevada
Reno, NV 89557-0100
(702)784-4436
Fax: (702)784-4337

New Hampshire

SCORE Office (North Country)
PO Box 34
Berlin, NH 03570
(603)752-1090

SCORE Office (Concord)
143 N. Main St., Rm. 202A
PO Box 1258
Concord, NH 03301
(603)225-1400
Fax: (603)225-1409

SCORE Office (Dover)
299 Central Ave.
Dover, NH 03820
(603)742-2218
Fax: (603)749-6317

SCORE Office (Monadnock)
34 Mechanic St.
Keene, NH 03431-3421
(603)352-0320

SCORE Office (Lakes Region)
67 Water St., Ste. 105
Laconia, NH 03246
(603)524-9168

SCORE Office (Upper Valley)
Citizens Bank Bldg., Rm. 310
20 W. Park St.
Lebanon, NH 03766
(603)448-3491
Fax: (603)448-1908
E-mail: billt@valley.net
Website: http://www.valley.net/~score/

SCORE Office (Merrimack Valley)
275 Chestnut St., Rm. 618
Manchester, NH 03103
(603)666-7561
Fax: (603)666-7925

SCORE Office (Mt. Washington Valley)
PO Box 1066
North Conway, NH 03818
(603)383-0800

SCORE Office (Seacoast)
195 Commerce Way, Unit-A
Portsmouth, NH 03801-3251
(603)433-0575

New Jersey

SCORE Office (Somerset)
Paritan Valley Community College, Rte. 28
Branchburg, NJ 08807
(908)218-8874
E-mail: nj-score@grizbiz.com.
Website: http://www.nj-score.org/

SCORE Office (Chester)
5 Old Mill Rd.
Chester, NJ 07930
(908)879-7080

SCORE Office (Greater Princeton)
4 A George Washington Dr.
Cranbury, NJ 08512
(609)520-1776

SCORE Office (Freehold)
36 W. Main St.
Freehold, NJ 07728
(908)462-3030
Fax: (908)462-2123

SCORE Office (North West)
Picantinny Innovation Ctr.
3159 Schrader Rd.
Hamburg, NJ 07419
(973)209-8525
Fax: (973)209-7252
E-mail: nj-score@grizbiz.com
Website: http://www.nj-score.org/

SCORE Office (Monmouth)
765 Newman Springs Rd.
Lincroft, NJ 07738
(908)224-2573
E-mail: nj-score@grizbiz.com
Website: http://www.nj-score.org/

SCORE Office (Manalapan)
125 Symmes Dr.
Manalapan, NJ 07726
(908)431-7220

SCORE Office (Jersey City)
2 Gateway Ctr., 4th Fl.
Newark, NJ 07102
(973)645-3982
Fax: (973)645-2375

SCORE Office (Newark)
2 Gateway Center, 15th Fl.
Newark, NJ 07102-5553
(973)645-3982
Fax: (973)645-2375
E-mail: nj-score@grizbiz.com
Website: http://www.nj-score.org

SCORE Office (Bergen County)
327 E. Ridgewood Ave.
Paramus, NJ 07652
(201)599-6090
E-mail: nj-score@grizbiz.com
Website: http://www.nj-score.org/

SCORE Office (Pennsauken)
4900 Rte. 70
Pennsauken, NJ 08109
(609)486-3421

SCORE Office (Southern New Jersey)
4900 Rte. 70
Pennsauken, NJ 08109
(609)486-3421
E-mail: nj-score@grizbiz.com
Website: http://www.nj-score.org/

SCORE Office (Greater Princeton)
216 Rockingham Row
Princeton Forrestal Village
Princeton, NJ 08540
(609)520-1776
Fax: (609)520-9107
E-mail: nj-score@grizbiz.com
Website: http://www.nj-score.org/

SCORE Office (Shrewsbury)
Hwy. 35
Shrewsbury, NJ 07702
(908)842-5995
Fax: (908)219-6140

SCORE Office (Ocean County)
33 Washington St.
Toms River, NJ 08754
(732)505-6033
E-mail: nj-score@grizbiz.com
Website: http://www.nj-score.org/

SCORE Office (Wall)
2700 Allaire Rd.
Wall, NJ 07719
(908)449-8877

SCORE Office (Wayne)
2055 Hamburg Tpke.
Wayne, NJ 07470
(201)831-7788
Fax: (201)831-9112

New Mexico

SCORE Office (Albuquerque)
525 Buena Vista, SE
Albuquerque, NM 87106
(505)272-7999
Fax: (505)272-7963

SCORE Office (Las Cruces)
Loretto Towne Center
505 S. Main St., Ste. 125
Las Cruces, NM 88001
(505)523-5627
Fax: (505)524-2101
E-mail: score.397@zianet.com

SCORE Office (Roswell)
Federal Bldg., Rm. 237
Roswell, NM 88201
(505)625-2112
Fax: (505)623-2545

SCORE Office (Santa Fe)
Montoya Federal Bldg.
120 Federal Place, Rm. 307
Santa Fe, NM 87501
(505)988-6302
Fax: (505)988-6300

New York

SCORE Office (Northeast)
1 Computer Dr. S
Albany, NY 12205
(518)446-1118
Fax: (518)446-1228

SCORE Office (Auburn)
30 South St.
PO Box 675
Auburn, NY 13021
(315)252-7291

SCORE Office (South Tier Binghamton)
Metro Center, 2nd Fl.
49 Court St.
PO Box 995
Binghamton, NY 13902
(607)772-8860

SCORE Office (Queens County City)
12055 Queens Blvd., Rm. 333
Borough Hall, NY 11424
(718)263-8961

SCORE Office (Buffalo)
Federal Bldg., Rm. 1311
111 W. Huron St.
Buffalo, NY 14202
(716)551-4301
Website: http://www2.pcom.net/score/buf45.html

SCORE Office (Canandaigua)
Chamber of Commerce Bldg.
113 S. Main St.
Canandaigua, NY 14424
(716)394-4400
Fax: (716)394-4546

SCORE Office (Chemung)
333 E. Water St., 4th Fl.
Elmira, NY 14901
(607)734-3358

SCORE Office (Geneva)
Chamber of Commerce Bldg.
PO Box 587
Geneva, NY 14456
(315)789-1776
Fax: (315)789-3993

SCORE Office (Glens Falls)
84 Broad St.
Glens Falls, NY 12801
(518)798-8463
Fax: (518)745-1433

SCORE Office (Orange County)
40 Matthews St.
Goshen, NY 10924
(914)294-8080
Fax: (914)294-6121

SCORE Office (Huntington Area)
151 W. Carver St.
Huntington, NY 11743
(516)423-6100

SCORE Office (Tompkins County)
904 E. Shore Dr.
Ithaca, NY 14850
(607)273-7080

SCORE Office (Long Island City)
120-55 Queens Blvd.
Jamaica, NY 11424
(718)263-8961
Fax: (718)263-9032

SCORE Office (Chatauqua)
101 W. 5th St.
Jamestown, NY 14701
(716)484-1103

SCORE Office (Westchester)
2 Caradon Ln.
Katonah, NY 10536
(914)948-3907
Fax: (914)948-4645
E-mail: score@w-w-w.com
Website: http://w-w-w.com/score/

SCORE Office (Queens County)
Queens Borough Hall
120-55 Queens Blvd. Rm. 333
Kew Gardens, NY 11424
(718)263-8961
Fax: (718)263-9032

SCORE Office (Brookhaven)
3233 Rte. 112
Medford, NY 11763
(516)451-6563
Fax: (516)451-6925

SCORE Office (Melville)
35 Pinelawn Rd., Rm. 207-W
Melville, NY 11747
(516)454-0771

SCORE Office (Nassau County)
400 County Seat Dr., No. 140
Mineola, NY 11501
(516)571-3303
E-mail: Counse1998@aol.com
Website: http://members.aol.com/Counse1998/Default.htm

SCORE Office (Mt. Vernon)
4 N. 7th Ave.
Mt. Vernon, NY 10550
(914)667-7500

SCORE Office (New York)
26 Federal Plz., Rm. 3100
New York, NY 10278
(212)264-4507
Fax: (212)264-4963
E-mail: score1000@erols.com
Website: http://users.erols.com/score-nyc/

SCORE Office (Newburgh)
47 Grand St.
Newburgh, NY 12550
(914)562-5100

SCORE Office (Owego)
188 Front St.
Owego, NY 13827
(607)687-2020

SCORE Office (Peekskill)
1 S. Division St.
Peekskill, NY 10566
(914)737-3600
Fax: (914)737-0541

SCORE Office (Penn Yan)
2375 Rte. 14A
Penn Yan, NY 14527
(315)536-3111

SCORE Office (Dutchess)
110 Main St.
Poughkeepsie, NY 12601
(914)454-1700

SCORE Office (Rochester)
601 Keating Federal Bldg., Rm. 410
100 State St.
Rochester, NY 14614
(716)263-6473
Fax: (716)263-3146
Website: http://www.ggw.org/score/

SCORE Office (Saranac Lake)
30 Main St.
Saranac Lake, NY 12983
(315)448-0415

SCORE Office (Suffolk)
286 Main St.
Setauket, NY 11733
(516)751-3886

SCORE Office (Staten Island)
130 Bay St.
Staten Island, NY 10301
(718)727-1221

SCORE Office (Ulster)
Clinton Bldg., Rm. 107
Stone Ridge, NY 12484
(914)687-5035
Fax: (914)687-5015
Website: http://www.scoreulster.org/

SCORE Office (Syracuse)
401 S. Salina, 5th Fl.
Syracuse, NY 13202
(315)471-9393

SCORE Office (Utica)
SUNY Institute of Technology, Route 12
Utica, NY 13504-3050
(315)792-7553

SCORE Office (Watertown)
518 Davidson St.
Watertown, NY 13601
(315)788-1200
Fax: (315)788-8251

North Carolina

SCORE office (Asheboro)
317 E. Dixie Dr.
Asheboro, NC 27203
(336)626-2626
Fax: (336)626-7077

SCORE Office (Asheville)
Federal Bldg., Rm. 259
151 Patton
Asheville, NC 28801-5770
(828)271-4786
Fax: (828)271-4009

SCORE Office (Chapel Hill)
104 S. Estes Dr.
PO Box 2897
Chapel Hill, NC 27514
(919)967-7075

SCORE Office (Coastal Plains)
PO Box 2897
Chapel Hill, NC 27515
(919)967-7075
Fax: (919)968-6874

SCORE Office (Charlotte)
200 N. College St., Ste. A-2015
Charlotte, NC 28202
(704)344-6576
Fax: (704)344-6769
E-mail: CharlotteSCORE47@AOL.com
Website: http://www.charweb.org/business/score/

SCORE Office (Durham)
411 W. Chapel Hill St.
Durham, NC 27707
(919)541-2171

SCORE Office (Gastonia)
PO Box 2168
Gastonia, NC 28053
(704)864-2621
Fax: (704)854-8723

SCORE Office (Greensboro)
400 W. Market St., Ste. 103
Greensboro, NC 27401-2241
(910)333-5399

SCORE Office (Henderson)
PO Box 917
Henderson, NC 27536
(919)492-2061
Fax: (919)430-0460

SCORE Office (Hendersonville)
Federal Bldg., Rm. 108
W. 4th Ave. & Church St.
Hendersonville, NC 28792
(828)693-8702
E-mail: score@circle.net
Website: http://www.wncguide.com/score/Welcome.html

SCORE Office (Unifour)
PO Box 1828
Hickory, NC 28603
(704)328-6111

SCORE Office (High Point)
1101 N. Main St.
High Point, NC 27262
(336)882-8625
Fax: (336)889-9499

SCORE Office (Outer Banks)
Collington Rd. and Mustain
Kill Devil Hills, NC 27948
(252)441-8144

SCORE Office (Down East)
312 S. Front St., Ste. 6
New Bern, NC 28560
(252)633-6688
Fax: (252)633-9608

SCORE Office (Kinston)
PO Box 95
New Bern, NC 28561
(919)633-6688

SCORE Office (Raleigh)
Century Post Office Bldg., Ste. 306
300 Federal St. Mall
Raleigh, NC 27601
(919)856-4739
E-mail: jendres@ibm.net
Website: http://www.intrex.net/score96/score96.htm

SCORE Office (Sanford)
1801 Nash St.
Sanford, NC 27330
(919)774-6442
Fax: (919)776-8739

SCORE Office (Sandhills Area)
1480 Hwy. 15-501
PO Box 458
Southern Pines, NC 28387
(910)692-3926

SCORE Office (Wilmington)
Corps of Engineers Bldg.
96 Darlington Ave., Ste. 207
Wilmington, NC 28403
(910)815-4576
Fax: (910)815-4658

North Dakota

SCORE Office (Bismarck-Mandan)
700 E. Main Ave., 2nd Fl.
PO Box 5509
Bismarck, ND 58506-5509
(701)250-4303

SCORE Office (Fargo)
657 2nd Ave., Rm. 225
Fargo, ND 58108-3083
(701)239-5677

SCORE Office (Upper Red River)
4275 Technology Dr., Rm. 156
Grand Forks, ND 58202-8372
(701)777-3051

SCORE Office (Minot)
100 1st St. SW
Minot, ND 58701-3846
(701)852-6883
Fax: (701)852-6905

Ohio

SCORE Office (Akron)
1 Cascade Plz., 7th Fl.
Akron, OH 44308
(330)379-3163
Fax: (330)379-3164

SCORE Office (Ashland)
Gill Center
47 W. Main St.
Ashland, OH 44805
(419)281-4584

SCORE Office (Canton)
116 Cleveland Ave. NW, Ste. 601
Canton, OH 44702-1720
(330)453-6047

SCORE Office (Chillicothe)
165 S. Paint St.
Chillicothe, OH 45601
(614)772-4530

SCORE Office (Cincinnati)
Ameritrust Bldg., Rm. 850
525 Vine St.
Cincinnati, OH 45202
(513)684-2812
Fax: (513)684-3251
Website: http://www.score.chapter34.org/

SCORE Office (Cleveland)
Eaton Center, Ste. 620
1100 Superior Ave.
Cleveland, OH 44114-2507
(216)522-4194
Fax: (216)522-4844

SCORE Office (Columbus)
2 Nationwide Plz., Ste. 1400
Columbus, OH 43215-2542
(614)469-2357
Fax: (614)469-2391
E-mail: info@scorecolumbus.org
Website: http://www.scorecolumbus.org/

SCORE Office (Dayton)
Dayton Federal Bldg., Rm. 505
200 W. Second St.
Dayton, OH 45402-1430
(513)225-2887
Fax: (513)225-7667

SCORE Office (Defiance)
615 W. 3rd St.
PO Box 130
Defiance, OH 43512
(419)782-7946

SCORE Office (Findlay)
123 E. Main Cross St.
PO Box 923
Findlay, OH 45840
(419)422-3314

SCORE Office (Lima)
147 N. Main St.
Lima, OH 45801
(419)222-6045
Fax: (419)229-0266

SCORE Office (Mansfield)
55 N. Mulberry St.
Mansfield, OH 44902
(419)522-3211

SCORE Office (Marietta)
Thomas Hall
Marietta, OH 45750
(614)373-0268

SCORE Office (Medina)
County Administrative Bldg.
144 N. Broadway
Medina, OH 44256
(216)764-8650

SCORE Office (Licking County)
50 W. Locust St.
Newark, OH 43055
(614)345-7458

SCORE Office (Salem)
2491 State Rte. 45 S
Salem, OH 44460
(216)332-0361

SCORE Office (Tiffin)
62 S. Washington St.
Tiffin, OH 44883
(419)447-4141
Fax: (419)447-5141

SCORE Office (Toledo)
608 Madison Ave, Ste. 910
Toledo, OH 43624
(419)259-7598
Fax: (419)259-6460

SCORE Office (Heart of Ohio)
377 W. Liberty St.
Wooster, OH 44691
(330)262-5735
Fax: (330)262-5745

SCORE Office (Youngstown)
306 Williamson Hall
Youngstown, OH 44555
(330)746-2687

Oklahoma

SCORE Office (Anadarko)
PO Box 366
Anadarko, OK 73005
(405)247-6651

SCORE Office (Ardmore)
410 W. Main
Ardmore, OK 73401
(580)226-2620

SCORE Office (Northeast Oklahoma)
210 S. Main
Grove, OK 74344
(918)787-2796
Fax: (918)787-2796
E-mail: Score595@greencis.net

SCORE Office (Lawton)
4500 W. Lee Blvd., Bldg. 100, Ste. 107
Lawton, OK 73505
(580)353-8727
Fax: (580)250-5677

SCORE Office (Oklahoma City)
210 Park Ave., No. 1300
Oklahoma City, OK 73102
(405)231-5163
Fax: (405)231-4876
E-mail: score212@usa.net

SCORE Office (Stillwater)
439 S. Main
Stillwater, OK 74074
(405)372-5573
Fax: (405)372-4316

SCORE Office (Tulsa)
616 S. Boston, Ste. 406
Tulsa, OK 74119
(918)581-7462
Fax: (918)581-6908
Website: http://www.ionet.net/~tulscore/

Oregon

SCORE Office (Bend)
63085 N. Hwy. 97
Bend, OR 97701
(541)923-2849
Fax: (541)330-6900

SCORE Office (Willamette)
1401 Willamette St.
PO Box 1107
Eugene, OR 97401-4003
(541)465-6600
Fax: (541)484-4942

SCORE Office (Florence)
3149 Oak St.
Florence, OR 97439
(503)997-8444
Fax: (503)997-8448

SCORE Office (Southern Oregon)
33 N. Central Ave., Ste. 216
Medford, OR 97501
(541)776-4220
E-mail: pgr134f@prodigy.com

SCORE Office (Portland)
1515 SW 5th Ave., Ste. 1050
Portland, OR 97201
(503)326-3441
Fax: (503)326-2808
E-mail: gr134@prodigy.com

SCORE Office (Salem)
416 State St. (corner of Liberty)
Salem, OR 97301
(503)370-2896

Pennsylvania

SCORE Office (Altoona-Blair)
1212 12th Ave.
Altoona, PA 16601-3493
(814)943-8151

SCORE Office (Lehigh Valley)
Rauch Bldg. 37
Lehigh University
621 Taylor St.
Bethlehem, PA 18015

(610)758-4496
Fax: (610)758-5205

SCORE Office (Butler County)
100 N. Main St.
PO Box 1082
Butler, PA 16003
(412)283-2222
Fax: (412)283-0224

SCORE Office (Harrisburg)
4211 Trindle Rd.
Camp Hill, PA 17011
(717)761-4304
Fax: (717)761-4315

SCORE Office (Cumberland Valley)
75 S. 2nd St.
Chambersburg, PA 17201
(717)264-2935

SCORE Office (Monroe County-Stroudsburg)
556 Main St.
East Stroudsburg, PA 18301
(717)421-4433

SCORE Office (Erie)
120 W. 9th St.
Erie, PA 16501
(814)871-5650
Fax: (814)871-7530

SCORE Office (Bucks County)
409 Hood Blvd.
Fairless Hills, PA 19030
(215)943-8850
Fax: (215)943-7404

SCORE Office (Hanover)
146 Broadway
Hanover, PA 17331
(717)637-6130
Fax: (717)637-9127

SCORE Office (Harrisburg)
100 Chestnut, Ste. 309
Harrisburg, PA 17101
(717)782-3874

SCORE Office (East Montgomery County)
Baederwood Shopping Center
1653 The Fairways, Ste. 204
Jenkintown, PA 19046
(215)885-3027

SCORE Office (Kittanning)
2 Butler Rd.
Kittanning, PA 16201
(412)543-1305
Fax: (412)543-6206

SCORE Office (Lancaster)
118 W. Chestnut St.
Lancaster, PA 17603
(717)397-3092

SCORE Office (Westmoreland County)
300 Fraser Purchase Rd.
Latrobe, PA 15650-2690
(412)539-7505
Fax: (412)539-1850

SCORE Office (Lebanon)
252 N. 8th St.
PO Box 899
Lebanon, PA 17042-0899
(717)273-3727
Fax: (717)273-7940

SCORE Office (Lewistown)
3 W. Monument Sq., Ste. 204
Lewistown, PA 17044
(717)248-6713
Fax: (717)248-6714

SCORE Office (Delaware County)
602 E. Baltimore Pike
Media, PA 19063
(610)565-3677
Fax: (610)565-1606

SCORE Office (Milton Area)
112 S. Front St.
Milton, PA 17847
(717)742-7341
Fax: (717)792-2008

SCORE Office (Mon-Valley)
435 Donner Ave.
Monessen, PA 15062
(412)684-4277
Fax: (412)684-7688

SCORE Office (Monroeville)
William Penn Plaza
2790 Mosside Blvd., Ste. 295
Monroeville, PA 15146
(412)856-0622
Fax: (412)856-1030

SCORE Office (Airport Area)
986 Brodhead Rd.
Moon Township, PA 15108-2398
(412)264-6270
Fax: (412)264-1575

SCORE Office (Northeast)
8601 E. Roosevelt Blvd.
Philadelphia, PA 19152
(215)332-3400
Fax: (215)332-6050

SCORE Office (Philadelphia)
1315 Walnut St., Ste. 500
Philadelphia, PA 19107
(215)790-5050
Fax: (215)790-5057
E-mail: score46@bellatlantic.net
Website: http://www.pgweb.net/score46/

SCORE Office (Pittsburgh)
1000 Liberty Ave., Rm. 1122
Pittsburgh, PA 15222
(412)395-6560
Fax: (412)395-6562

SCORE Office (Tri-County)
801 N. Charlotte St.
Pottstown, PA 19464
(610)327-2673

SCORE Office (Reading)
601 Penn St.
Reading, PA 19601
(610)376-3497

SCORE Office (Scranton)
Oppenheim Bldg.
116 N. Washington Ave., Ste. 650
Scranton, PA 18503
(717)347-4611
Fax: (717)347-4611

SCORE Office (Central Pennsylvania)
200 Innovation Blvd., Ste. 242-B
State College, PA 16803
(814)234-9415
Fax: (814)238-9686
Website: http://countrystore.org/business/score.htm

SCORE Office (Monroe-Stroudsburg)
556 Main St.
Stroudsburg, PA 18360
(717)421-4433

SCORE Office (Uniontown)
Federal Bldg.
Pittsburg St.
PO Box 2065 DTS
Uniontown, PA 15401
(412)437-4222
E-mail: uniontownscore@lcsys.net

SCORE Office (Warren County)
315 2nd Ave.
Warren, PA 16365
(814)723-9017

SCORE Office (Waynesboro)
323 E. Main St.
Waynesboro, PA 17268
(717)762-7123
Fax: (717)962-7124

SCORE Office (Chester County)
Government Service Center, Ste. 281
601 Westtown Rd.
West Chester, PA 19382-4538
(610)344-6910
Fax: (610)344-6919
E-mail: score@locke.ccil.org

SCORE Office (Wilkes-Barre)
7 N. Wilkes-Barre Blvd.
Wilkes Barre, PA 18702-5241
(717)826-6502
Fax: (717)826-6287

SCORE Office (North Central Pennsylvania)
240 W. 3rd St., Rm. 227
PO Box 725
Williamsport, PA 17703
(717)322-3720
Fax: (717)322-1607
E-mail: score234@mail.csrlink.net
Website: http://www.lycoming.org/score/

SCORE Office (York)
Cyber Center
2101 Pennsylvania Ave.
York, PA 17404
(717)845-8830
Fax: (717)854-9333

Puerto Rico

SCORE Office (Puerto Rico & Virgin Islands)
PO Box 12383-96
San Juan, PR 00914-0383
(787)726-8040
Fax: (787)726-8135

Rhode Island

SCORE Office (Barrington)
281 County Rd.
Barrington, RI 02806
(401)247-1920
Fax: (401)247-3763

SCORE Office (Woonsocket)
640 Washington Hwy.
Lincoln, RI 02865
(401)334-1000
Fax: (401)334-1009

SCORE Office (Wickford)
8045 Post Rd.
North Kingstown, RI 02852
(401)295-5566
Fax: (401)295-8987

SCORE Office (J.G.E. Knight)
380 Westminster St.
Providence, RI 02903
(401)528-4571
Fax: (401)528-4539
Website: http://www.riscore.org

SCORE Office (Warwick)
3288 Post Rd.
Warwick, RI 02886
(401)732-1100
Fax: (401)732-1101

SCORE Office (Westerly)
74 Post Rd.
Westerly, RI 02891
(401)596-7761
800-732-7636
Fax: (401)596-2190

South Carolina

SCORE Office (Aiken)
PO Box 892
Aiken, SC 29802
(803)641-1111
800-542-4536
Fax: (803)641-4174

SCORE Office (Anderson)
Anderson Mall
3130 N. Main St.
Anderson, SC 29621
(864)224-0453

SCORE Office (Coastal)
284 King St.
Charleston, SC 29401
(803)727-4778
Fax: (803)853-2529

SCORE Office (Midlands)
Strom Thurmond Bldg., Rm. 358
1835 Assembly St., Rm 358
Columbia, SC 29201
(803)765-5131
Fax: (803)765-5962
Website: http://www.scoremidlands.org/

SCORE Office (Piedmont)
Federal Bldg., Rm. B-02
300 E. Washington St.
Greenville, SC 29601
(864)271-3638

SCORE Office (Greenwood)
PO Drawer 1467
Greenwood, SC 29648
(864)223-8357

SCORE Office (Hilton Head Island)
52 Savannah Trail
Hilton Head, SC 29926
(803)785-7107
Fax: (803)785-7110

SCORE Office (Grand Strand)
937 Broadway
Myrtle Beach, SC 29577
(803)918-1079
Fax: (803)918-1083
E-mail: score381@aol.com

SCORE Office (Spartanburg)
PO Box 1636
Spartanburg, SC 29304
(864)594-5000
Fax: (864)594-5055

South Dakota

SCORE Office (West River)
Rushmore Plz. Civic Ctr.
444 Mount Rushmore Rd., No. 209
Rapid City, SD 57701
(605)394-5311
E-mail: score@gwtc.net

SCORE Office (Sioux Falls)
First Financial Center
110 S. Phillips Ave., Ste. 200
Sioux Falls, SD 57104-6727
(605)330-4231
Fax: (605)330-4231

Tennessee

SCORE Office (Chattanooga)
Federal Bldg., Rm. 26
900 Georgia Ave.
Chattanooga, TN 37402
(423)752-5190
Fax: (423)752-5335

SCORE Office (Cleveland)
PO Box 2275
Cleveland, TN 37320
(423)472-6587
Fax: (423)472-2019

SCORE Office (Upper Cumberland Center)
1225 S. Willow Ave.
Cookeville, TN 38501
(615)432-4111
Fax: (615)432-6010

SCORE Office (Unicoi County)
PO Box 713
Erwin, TN 37650
(423)743-3000
Fax: (423)743-0942

SCORE Office (Greeneville)
115 Academy St.
Greeneville, TN 37743
(423)638-4111
Fax: (423)638-5345

SCORE Office (Jackson)
194 Auditorium St.
Jackson, TN 38301
(901)423-2200

SCORE Office (Northeast Tennessee)
1st Tennessee Bank Bldg.
2710 S. Roan St., Ste. 584
Johnson City, TN 37601
(423)929-7686
Fax: (423)461-8052

SCORE Office (Kingsport)
151 E. Main St.
Kingsport, TN 37662
(423)392-8805

SCORE Office (Greater Knoxville)
Farragot Bldg., Ste. 224
530 S. Gay St.
Knoxville, TN 37902
(423)545-4203
E-mail: scoreknox@ntown.com
Website: http://www.scoreknox.org/

SCORE Office (Maryville)
201 S. Washington St.
Maryville, TN 37804-5728
(423)983-2241
800-525-6834
Fax: (423)984-1386

SCORE Office (Memphis)
Federal Bldg., Ste. 390
167 N. Main St.
Memphis, TN 38103
(901)544-3588

SCORE Office (Nashville)
50 Vantage Way, Ste. 201
Nashville, TN 37228-1500
(615)736-7621

Texas

SCORE Office (Abilene)
2106 Federal Post Office and Court Bldg.
Abilene, TX 79601
(915)677-1857

SCORE Office (Austin)
2501 S. Congress
Austin, TX 78701
(512)442-7235
Fax: (512)442-7528

SCORE Office (Golden Triangle)
450 Boyd St.
Beaumont, TX 77704
(409)838-6581
Fax: (409)833-6718

SCORE Office (Brownsville)
3505 Boca Chica Blvd., Ste. 305
Brownsville, TX 78521
(210)541-4508

SCORE Office (Brazos Valley)
3000 Briarcrest, Ste. 302
Bryan, TX 77802
(409)776-8876
E-mail. 102633.2612@compuserve.com

SCORE Office (Cleburne)
Watergarden Pl., 9th Fl., Ste. 400
Cleburne, TX 76031
(817)871-6002

SCORE Office (Corpus Christi)
651 Upper North Broadway, Ste. 654
Corpus Christi, TX 78477
(512)888-4322
Fax: (512)888-3418

SCORE Office (Dallas)
6260 E. Mockingbird
Dallas, TX 75214-2619
(214)828-2471
Fax: (214)821-8033

SCORE Office (El Paso)
10 Civic Center Plaza
El Paso, TX 79901
(915)534-0541
Fax: (915)534-0513

SCORE Office (Bedford)
100 E. 15th St., Ste. 400
Ft. Worth, TX 76102
(817)871-6002

SCORE Office (Ft. Worth)
100 E. 15th St., No. 24
Ft. Worth, TX 76102
(817)871-6002
Fax: (817)871-6031
E-mail: fwbac@onramp.net

SCORE Office (Garland)
2734 W. Kingsley Rd.
Garland, TX 75041
(214)271-9224

SCORE Office (Granbury Chamber of Commerce)
416 S. Morgan
Granbury, TX 76048
(817)573-1622
Fax: (817)573-0805

SCORE Office (Lower Rio Grande Valley)
222 E. Van Buren, Ste. 500
Harlingen, TX 78550
(956)427-8533
Fax: (956)427-8537

SCORE Office (Houston)
9301 Southwest Fwy., Ste. 550
Houston, TX 77074
(713)773-6565
Fax: (713)773-6550

SCORE Office (Irving)
3333 N. MacArthur Blvd., Ste. 100
Irving, TX 75062
(214)252-8484
Fax: (214)252-6710

SCORE Office (Lubbock)
1205 Texas Ave., Rm. 411D
Lubbock, TX 79401
(806)472-7462
Fax: (806)472-7487

SCORE Office (Midland)
Post Office Annex
200 E. Wall St., Rm. P121
Midland, TX 79701
(915)687-2649

SCORE Office (Orange)
1012 Green Ave.
Orange, TX 77630-5620
(409)883-3536
800-528-4906
Fax: (409)886-3247

SCORE Office (Plano)
1200 E. 15th St.
PO Drawer 940287
Plano, TX 75094-0287
(214)424-7547
Fax: (214)422-5182

SCORE Office (Port Arthur)
4749 Twin City Hwy., Ste. 300
Port Arthur, TX 77642
(409)963-1107
Fax: (409)963-3322

SCORE Office (Richardson)
411 Belle Grove
Richardson, TX 75080
(214)234-4141
800-777-8001
Fax: (214)680-9103

SCORE Office (San Antonio)
Federal Bldg., Rm. A527
727 E. Durango

San Antonio, TX 78206
(210)472-5931
Fax: (210)472-5935

SCORE Office (Texarkana State College)
819 State Line Ave.
Texarkana, TX 75501
(903)792-7191
Fax: (903)793-4304

SCORE Office (East Texas)
RTDC
1530 SSW Loop 323, Ste. 100
Tyler, TX 75701
(903)510-2975
Fax: (903)510-2978

SCORE Office (Waco)
401 Franklin Ave.
Waco, TX 76701
(817)754-8898
Fax: (817)756-0776
Website: http://www.brc-waco.com/

SCORE Office (Wichita Falls)
Hamilton Bldg.
900 8th St.
Wichita Falls, TX 76307
(940)723-2741
Fax: (940)723-8773

Utah

SCORE Office (Northern Utah)
160 N. Main
Logan, UT 84321
(435)746-2269

SCORE Office (Ogden)
1701 E. Windsor Dr.
Ogden, UT 84604
(801)629-8613
E-mail: score158@netscape.net

SCORE Office (Central Utah)
1071 E. Windsor Dr.
Provo, UT 84604
(801)373-8660

SCORE Office (Southern Utah)
225 South 700 East
St. George, UT 84770
(435)652-7751

SCORE Office (Salt Lake)
310 S Main St.
Salt Lake City, UT 84101
(801)746-2269
Fax: (801)746-2273

Vermont

SCORE Office (Champlain Valley)
Winston Prouty Federal Bldg.
11 Lincoln St., Rm. 106
Essex Junction, VT 05452
(802)951-6762

SCORE Office (Montpelier)
87 State St., Rm. 205
PO Box 605
Montpelier, VT 05601
(802)828-4422
Fax: (802)828-4485

SCORE Office (Marble Valley)
256 N. Main St.
Rutland, VT 05701-2413
(802)773-9147

SCORE Office (Northeast Kingdom)
20 Main St.
PO Box 904
St. Johnsbury, VT 05819
(802)748-5101

Virgin Islands

SCORE Office (St. Croix)
United Plaza Shopping Center
PO Box 4010, Christiansted
St. Croix, VI 00822
(809)778-5380

SCORE Office (St. Thomas-St. John)
Federal Bldg., Rm. 21
Veterans Dr.
St. Thomas, VI 00801
(809)774-8530

Virginia

SCORE Office (Arlington)
2009 N. 14th St., Ste. 111
Arlington, VA 22201
(703)525-2400

SCORE Office (Blacksburg)
141 Jackson St.
Blacksburg, VA 24060
(540)552-4061

SCORE Office (Bristol)
20 Volunteer Pkwy.
Bristol, VA 24203
(540)989-4850

SCORE Office (Central Virginia)
1001 E. Market St., Ste. 101
Charlottesville, VA 22902
(804)295-6712
Fax: (804)295-7066

SCORE Office (Alleghany Satellite)
241 W. Main St.
Covington, VA 24426
(540)962-2178
Fax: (540)962-2179

SCORE Office (Central Fairfax)
3975 University Dr., Ste. 350
Fairfax, VA 22030
(703)591-2450

SCORE Office (Falls Church)
PO Box 491
Falls Church, VA 22040
(703)532-1050
Fax: (703)237-7904

SCORE Office (Glenns)
Glenns Campus
Box 287
Glenns, VA 23149
(804)693-9650

SCORE Office (Peninsula)
6 Manhattan Sq.
PO Box 7269
Hampton, VA 23666
(757)766-2000
Fax: (757)865-0339
E-mail: score100@seva.net

SCORE Office (Tri-Cities)
108 N. Main St.
Hopewell, VA 23860
(804)458-5536

SCORE Office (Lynchburg)
Federal Bldg.
1100 Main St.
Lynchburg, VA 24504-1714
(804)846-3235

SCORE Office (Greater Prince William)
8963 Center St
Manassas, VA 20110
(703)368-4813
Fax: (703)368-4733

SCORE Office (Martinsvile)
115 Broad St.
Martinsville, VA 24112-0709
(540)632-6401
Fax: (540)632-5059

SCORE Office (Hampton Roads)
Federal Bldg., Rm. 737
200 Grandby St.
Norfolk, VA 23510
(757)441-3733
Fax: (757)441-3733
E-mail: scorehr60@juno.com

SCORE Office (Norfolk)
Federal Bldg., Rm. 737
200 Granby St.
Norfolk, VA 23510
(757)441-3733
Fax: (757)441-3733

SCORE Office (Virginia Beach)
Chamber of Commerce
200 Grandby St., Rm 737
Norfolk, VA 23510
(804)441-3733

SCORE Office (Radford)
1126 Norwood St.
Radford, VA 24141
(540)639-2202

SCORE Office (Richmond)
Federal Bldg.
400 N. 8th St., Ste. 1150
PO Box 10126
Richmond, VA 23240-0126
(804)771-2400
Fax: (804)771-8018
E-mail: scorechapter12@yahoo.com
Website: http://www.cvco.org/score/

SCORE Office (Roanoke)
Federal Bldg., Rm. 716
250 Franklin Rd.
Roanoke, VA 24011
(540)857-2834
Fax: (540)857-2043
E-mail: scorerva@juno.com
Website: http://hometown.aol.com/scorerv/Index.html

SCORE Office (Fairfax)
8391 Old Courthouse Rd., Ste. 300
Vienna, VA 22182
(703)749-0400

SCORE Office (Greater Vienna)
513 Maple Ave. West
Vienna, VA 22180
(703)281-1333
Fax: (703)242-1482

SCORE Office (Shenandoah Valley)
301 W. Main St.
Waynesboro, VA 22980
(540)949-8203
Fax: (540)949-7740
E-mail: score427@intelos.net

SCORE Office (Williamsburg)
201 Penniman Rd.
Williamsburg, VA 23185
(757)229-6511
E-mail: wacc@williamsburgcc.com

SCORE Office (Northern Virginia)
1360 S. Pleasant Valley Rd.
Winchester, VA 22601
(540)662-4118

Washington

SCORE Office (Gray's Harbor)
506 Duffy St.
Aberdeen, WA 98520
(360)532-1924
Fax: (360)533-7945

SCORE Office (Bellingham)
101 E. Holly St.
Bellingham, WA 98225
(360)676-3307

SCORE Office (Everett)
2702 Hoyt Ave.
Everett, WA 98201-3556
(206)259-8000

SCORE Office (Gig Harbor)
3125 Judson St.
Gig Harbor, WA 98335
(206)851-6865

SCORE Office (Kennewick)
PO Box 6986
Kennewick, WA 99336
(509)736-0510

SCORE Office (Puyallup)
322 2nd St. SW
PO Box 1298
Puyallup, WA 98371
(206)845-6755
Fax: (206)848-6164

SCORE Office (Seattle)
1200 6th Ave., Ste. 1700
Seattle, WA 98101
(206)553-7320
Fax: (206)553-7044
E-mail: score55@aol.com
Website: http://www.scn.org/civic/score-online/index55.html

SCORE Office (Spokane)
801 W. Riverside Ave., No. 240
Spokane, WA 99201
(509)353-2820
Fax: (509)353-2600
E-mail: score@dmi.net
Website: http://www.dmi.net/score/

SCORE Office (Clover Park)
PO Box 1933
Tacoma, WA 98401-1933
(206)627-2175

SCORE Office (Tacoma)
1101 Pacific Ave.
Tacoma, WA 98402
(253)274-1288
Fax: (253)274-1289

SCORE Office (Fort Vancouver)
1701 Broadway, S-1
Vancouver, WA 98663
(360)699-1079

SCORE Office (Walla Walla)
500 Tausick Way
Walla Walla, WA 99362
(509)527-4681

SCORE Office (Mid-Columbia)
1113 S. 14th Ave.
Yakima, WA 98907
(509)574-4944
Fax: (509)574-2943
Website: http://www.ellensburg.com/~score/

West Virginia

SCORE Office (Charleston)
1116 Smith St.
Charleston, WV 25301
(304)347-5463
E-mail: score256@juno.com

SCORE Office (Virginia Street)
1116 Smith St., Ste. 302
Charleston, WV 25301
(304)347-5463

SCORE Office (Marion County)
PO Box 208
Fairmont, WV 26555-0208
(304)363-0486

SCORE Office (Upper Monongahela Valley)
1000 Technology Dr., Ste. 1111
Fairmont, WV 26555
(304)363-0486
E-mail: score537@hotmail.com

SCORE Office (Huntington)
1101 6th Ave., Ste. 220
Huntington, WV 25701-2309
(304)523-4092

SCORE Office (Wheeling)
1310 Market St.
Wheeling, WV 26003
(304)233-2575
Fax: (304)233-1320

Wisconsin

SCORE Office (Fox Cities)
227 S. Walnut St.
Appleton, WI 54913
(920)734-7101
Fax: (920)734-7161

SCORE Office (Beloit)
136 W. Grand Ave., Ste. 100
PO Box 717
Beloit, WI 53511
(608)365-8835
Fax: (608)365-9170

SCORE Office (Eau Claire)
Federal Bldg., Rm. B11
510 S. Barstow St.
Eau Claire, WI 54701
(715)834-1573
E-mail: score@ecol.net
Website: http://www.ecol.net/~score/

SCORE Office (Fond du Lac)
207 N. Main St.
Fond du Lac, WI 54935
(414)921-9500
Fax: (414)921-9559

SCORE Office (Green Bay)
835 Potts Ave.
Green Bay, WI 54304
(414)496-8930
Fax: (414)496-6009

SCORE Office (Janesville)
20 S. Main St., Ste. 11
PO Box 8008
Janesville, WI 53547
(608)757-3160
Fax: (608)757-3170

SCORE Office (La Crosse)
712 Main St.
La Crosse, WI 54602-0219
(608)784-4880

SCORE Office (Madison)
505 S. Rosa Rd.
Madison, WI 53719
(608)441-2820

SCORE Office (Manitowoc)
1515 Memorial Dr.
PO Box 903
Manitowoc, WI 54221-0903
(414)684-5575
Fax: (414)684-1915

SCORE Office (Milwaukee)
310 W. Wisconsin Ave., Ste. 425
Milwaukee, WI 53203
(414)297-3942
Fax: (414)297-1377

SCORE Office (Central Wisconsin)
1224 Lindbergh Ave.
Stevens Point, WI 54481
(715)344-7729

SCORE Office (Superior)
Superior Business Center Inc.
1423 N. 8th St.
Superior, WI 54880
(715)394-7388
Fax: (715)393-7414

SCORE Office (Waukesha)
223 Wisconsin Ave.
Waukesha, WI 53186-4926
(414)542-4249

SCORE Office (Wausau)
300 3rd St., Ste. 200
Wausau, WI 54402-6190
(715)845-6231

SCORE Office (Wisconsin Rapids)
2240 Kingston Rd.
Wisconsin Rapids, WI 54494
(715)423-1830

Wyoming

SCORE Office (Casper)
Federal Bldg., No. 2215
100 East B St.
Casper, WY 82602
(307)261-6529
Fax: (307)261-6530

Venture capital & financing companies

This section contains a listing of financing and loan companies in the United States and Canada. These listing are arranged alphabetically by country, then by state or province, then by city, then by organization name.

Canada

Alberta

Launchworks Inc.
1902J 11th St., S.E.
Calgary, AB, Canada T2G 3G2
(403)269-1119
Fax: (403)269-1141
Website: http://www.launchworks.com

Native Venture Capital Company, Inc.
21 Artist View Point, Box 7
Site 25, RR 12
Calgary, AB, Canada T3E 6W3
(903)208-5380

Miralta Capital Inc.
4445 Calgary Trail South
888 Terrace Plaza Alberta
Edmonton, AB, Canada T6H 5R7
(780)438-3535
Fax: (780)438-3129

Vencap Equities Alberta Ltd.
10180-101st St., Ste. 1980
Edmonton, AB, Canada T5J 3S4
(403)420-1171
Fax: (403)429-2541

British Columbia

Discovery Capital
5th Fl., 1199 West Hastings
Vancouver, BC, Canada V6E 3T5
(604)683-3000
Fax: (604)662-3457
E-mail: info@discoverycapital.com
Website: http://
www.discoverycapital.com

Greenstone Venture Partners
1177 West Hastings St.
Ste. 400
Vancouver, BC, Canada V6E 2K3
(604)717-1977
Fax: (604)717-1976
Website: http://www.greenstonevc.com

Growthworks Capital
2600-1055 West Georgia St.
Box 11170 Royal Centre
Vancouver, BC, Canada V6E 3R5
(604)895-7259
Fax: (604)669-7605
Website: http://www.wofund.com

MDS Discovery Venture Management, Inc.
555 W. Eighth Ave., Ste. 305
Vancouver, BC, Canada V5Z 1C6
(604)872-8464
Fax: (604)872-2977
E-mail: info@mds-ventures.com

Ventures West Management Inc.
1285 W. Pender St., Ste. 280
Vancouver, BC, Canada V6E 4B1
(604)688-9495
Fax: (604)687-2145
Website: http://www.ventureswest.com

Nova Scotia

ACF Equity Atlantic Inc.
Purdy's Wharf Tower II
Ste. 2106
Halifax, NS, Canada B3J 3R7
(902)421-1965
Fax: (902)421-1808

Montgomerie, Huck & Co.
146 Bluenose Dr.
PO Box 538
Lunenburg, NS, Canada B0J 2C0
(902)634-7125
Fax: (902)634-7130

Ontario

IPS Industrial Promotion Services Ltd.
60 Columbia Way, Ste. 720
Markham, ON, Canada L3R 0C9
(905)475-9400
Fax: (905)475-5003

Betwin Investments Inc.
Box 23110
Sault Ste. Marie, ON, Canada P6A 6W6
(705)253-0744
Fax: (705)253-0744

Bailey & Company, Inc.
594 Spadina Ave.
Toronto, ON, Canada M5S 2H4
(416)921-6930
Fax: (416)925-4670

BCE Capital
200 Bay St.
South Tower, Ste. 3120
Toronto, ON, Canada M5J 2J2
(416)815-0078
Fax: (416)941-1073
Website: http://www.bcecapital.com

Castlehill Ventures
55 University Ave., Ste. 500
Toronto, ON, Canada M5J 2H7
(416)862-8574
Fax: (416)862-8875

CCFL Mezzanine Partners of Canada
70 University Ave.
Ste. 1450
Toronto, ON, Canada M5J 2M4
(416)977-1450
Fax: (416)977-6764
E-mail: info@ccfl.com
Website: http://www.ccfl.com

Celtic House International
100 Simcoe St., Ste. 100
Toronto, ON, Canada M5H 3G2
(416)542-2436
Fax: (416)542-2435
Website: http://www.celtic-house.com

Clairvest Group Inc.
22 St. Clair Ave. East
Ste. 1700
Toronto, ON, Canada M4T 2S3
(416)925-9270
Fax: (416)925-5753

Crosbie & Co., Inc.
One First Canadian Place
9th Fl.
PO Box 116
Toronto, ON, Canada M5X 1A4
(416)362-7726
Fax: (416)362-3447
E-mail: info@crosbieco.com
Website: http://www.crosbieco.com

Drug Royalty Corp.
Eight King St. East
Ste. 202
Toronto, ON, Canada M5C 1B5
(416)863-1865
Fax: (416)863-5161

Grieve, Horner, Brown & Asculai
8 King St. E, Ste. 1704
Toronto, ON, Canada M5C 1B5
(416)362-7668
Fax: (416)362-7660

Jefferson Partners
77 King St. West
Ste. 4010
PO Box 136
Toronto, ON, Canada M5K 1H1
(416)367-1533
Fax: (416)367-5827
Website: http://www.jefferson.com

J.L. Albright Venture Partners
Canada Trust Tower, 161 Bay St.
Ste. 4440
PO Box 215
Toronto, ON, Canada M5J 2S1
(416)367-2440
Fax: (416)367-4604
Website: http://www.jlaventures.com

McLean Watson Capital Inc.
One First Canadian Place
Ste. 1410
PO Box 129
Toronto, ON, Canada M5X 1A4
(416)363-2000
Fax: (416)363-2010
Website: http://www.mcleanwatson.com

Middlefield Capital Fund
One First Canadian Place
85th Fl.
PO Box 192
Toronto, ON, Canada M5X 1A6
(416)362-0714
Fax: (416)362-7925
Website: http://www.middlefield.com

Mosaic Venture Partners
24 Duncan St.
Ste. 300
Toronto, ON, Canada M5V 3M6
(416)597-8889
Fax: (416)597-2345

Onex Corp.
161 Bay St.
PO Box 700
Toronto, ON, Canada M5J 2S1
(416)362-7711
Fax: (416)362-5765

Penfund Partners Inc.
145 King St. West
Ste. 1920
Toronto, ON, Canada M5H 1J8
(416)865-0300
Fax: (416)364-6912
Website: http://www.penfund.com

Primaxis Technology Ventures Inc.
1 Richmond St. West, 8th Fl.
Toronto, ON, Canada M5H 3W4
(416)313-5210
Fax: (416)313-5218
Website: http://www.primaxis.com

Priveq Capital Funds
240 Duncan Mill Rd., Ste. 602
Toronto, ON, Canada M3B 3P1
(416)447-3330
Fax: (416)447-3331
E-mail: priveq@sympatico.ca

Roynat Ventures
40 King St. West, 26th Fl.
Toronto, ON, Canada M5H 1H1
(416)933-2667
Fax: (416)933-2783
Website: http://www.roynatcapital.com

Tera Capital Corp.
366 Adelaide St. East, Ste. 337
Toronto, ON, Canada M5A 3X9
(416)368-1024
Fax: (416)368-1427

Working Ventures Canadian Fund Inc.
250 Bloor St. East, Ste. 1600
Toronto, ON, Canada M4W 1E6

(416)934-7718
Fax: (416)929-0901
Website: http://www.workingventures.ca

Quebec

Altamira Capital Corp.
202 University
Niveau de Maisoneuve, Bur. 201
Montreal, QC, Canada H3A 2A5
(514)499-1656
Fax: (514)499-9570

Federal Business Development Bank
Venture Capital Division
Five Place Ville Marie, Ste. 600
Montreal, QC, Canada H3B 5E7
(514)283-1896
Fax: (514)283-5455

Hydro-Quebec Capitech Inc.
75 Boul, Rene Levesque Quest
Montreal, QC, Canada H2Z 1A4
(514)289-4783
Fax: (514)289-5420
Website: http://www.hqcapitech.com

Investissement Desjardins
2 complexe Desjardins
C.P. 760
Montreal, QC, Canada H5B 1B8
(514)281-7131
Fax: (514)281-7808
Website: http://www.desjardins.com/id

Marleau Lemire Inc.
One Place Ville-Marie, Ste. 3601
Montreal, QC, Canada H3B 3P2
(514)877-3800
Fax: (514)875-6415

Speirs Consultants Inc.
365 Stanstead
Montreal, QC, Canada H3R 1X5
(514)342-3858
Fax: (514)342-1977

Tecnocap Inc.
4028 Marlowe
Montreal, QC, Canada H4A 3M2
(514)483-6009
Fax: (514)483-6045
Website: http://www.technocap.com

Telsoft Ventures
1000, Rue de la Gauchetiere
Quest, 25eme Etage
Montreal, QC, Canada H3B 4W5
(514)397-8450
Fax: (514)397-8451

Saskatchewan

Saskatchewan Government Growth Fund
1801 Hamilton St., Ste. 1210
Canada Trust Tower
Regina, SK, Canada S4P 4B4
(306)787-2994
Fax: (306)787-2086

United states

Alabama

FHL Capital Corp.
600 20th Street North
Suite 350
Birmingham, AL 35203
(205)328-3098
Fax: (205)323-0001

Harbert Management Corp.
One Riverchase Pkwy. South
Birmingham, AL 35244
(205)987-5500
Fax: (205)987-5707
Website: http://www.harbert.net

Jefferson Capital Fund
PO Box 13129
Birmingham, AL 35213
(205)324-7709

Private Capital Corp.
100 Brookwood Pl., 4th Fl.
Birmingham, AL 35209
(205)879-2722
Fax: (205)879-5121

21st Century Health Ventures
One Health South Pkwy.
Birmingham, AL 35243
(256)268-6250
Fax: (256)970-8928

FJC Growth Capital Corp.
200 W. Side Sq., Ste. 340
Huntsville, AL 35801
(256)922-2918
Fax: (256)922-2909

Hickory Venture Capital Corp.
301 Washington St. NW
Suite 301
Huntsville, AL 35801
(256)539-1931
Fax: (256)539-5130
E-mail: hvcc@hvcc.com
Website: http://www.hvcc.com

Southeastern Technology Fund
7910 South Memorial Pkwy., Ste. F
Huntsville, AL 35802
(256)883-8711
Fax: (256)883-8558

Cordova Ventures
4121 Carmichael Rd., Ste. 301
Montgomery, AL 36106
(334)271-6011
Fax: (334)260-0120
Website: http://
www.cordovaventures.com

Small Business Clinic of Alabama/AG Bartholomew & Associates
PO Box 231074
Montgomery, AL 36123-1074
(334)284-3640

Arizona

Miller Capital Corp.
4909 E. McDowell Rd.
Phoenix, AZ 85008
(602)225-0504
Fax: (602)225-9024
Website: http://www.themillergroup.com

The Columbine Venture Funds
9449 North 90th St., Ste. 200
Scottsdale, AZ 85258
(602)661-9222
Fax: (602)661-6262

Koch Ventures
17767 N. Perimeter Dr., Ste. 101
Scottsdale, AZ 85255
(480)419-3600
Fax: (480)419-3606
Website: http://www.kochventures.com

McKee & Co.
7702 E. Doubletree Ranch Rd.
Suite 230
Scottsdale, AZ 85258
(480)368-0333
Fax: (480)607-7446

Merita Capital Ltd.
7350 E. Stetson Dr., Ste. 108-A
Scottsdale, AZ 85251
(480)947-8700
Fax: (480)947-8766

Valley Ventures / Arizona Growth Partners L.P.
6720 N. Scottsdale Rd., Ste. 208
Scottsdale, AZ 85253
(480)661-6600
Fax: (480)661-6262

Estreetcapital.com
660 South Mill Ave., Ste. 315
Tempe, AZ 85281
(480)968-8400
Fax: (480)968-8480
Website: http://www.estreetcapital.com

Coronado Venture Fund
PO Box 65420
Tucson, AZ 85728-5420
(520)577-3764
Fax: (520)299-8491

Arkansas

Arkansas Capital Corp.
225 South Pulaski St.
Little Rock, AR 72201
(501)374-9247
Fax: (501)374-9425
Website: http://www.arcapital.com

California

Sundance Venture Partners, L.P.
100 Clocktower Place, Ste. 130
Carmel, CA 93923
(831)625-6500
Fax: (831)625-6590

Westar Capital (Costa Mesa)
949 South Coast Dr., Ste. 650
Costa Mesa, CA 92626
(714)481-5160
Fax: (714)481-5166
E-mail: mailbox@westarcapital.com
Website: http://www.westarcapital.com

Alpine Technology Ventures
20300 Stevens Creek Boulevard, Ste. 495
Cupertino, CA 95014
(408)725-1810
Fax: (408)725-1207
Website: http://www.alpineventures.com

Bay Partners
10600 N. De Anza Blvd.
Cupertino, CA 95014-2031
(408)725-2444
Fax: (408)446-4502
Website: http://www.baypartners.com

Novus Ventures
20111 Stevens Creek Blvd., Ste. 130
Cupertino, CA 95014
(408)252-3900
Fax: (408)252-1713
Website: http://www.novusventures.com

Triune Capital
19925 Stevens Creek Blvd., Ste. 200
Cupertino, CA 95014
(310)284-6800
Fax: (310)284-3290

Acorn Ventures
268 Bush St., Ste. 2829
Daly City, CA 94014
(650)994-7801
Fax: (650)994-3305
Website: http://www.acornventures.com

Digital Media Campus
2221 Park Place
El Segundo, CA 90245
(310)426-8000
Fax: (310)426-8010
E-mail: info@thecampus.com
Website: http://
www.digitalmediacampus.com

BankAmerica Ventures / BA Venture Partners
950 Tower Ln., Ste. 700
Foster City, CA 94404
(650)378-6000
Fax: (650)378-6040
Website: http://
www.baventurepartners.com

Starting Point Partners
666 Portofino Lane
Foster City, CA 94404
(650)722-1035
Website: http://
www.startingpointpartners.com

Opportunity Capital Partners
2201 Walnut Ave., Ste. 210
Fremont, CA 94538
(510)795-7000
Fax: (510)494-5439
Website: http://www.ocpcapital.com

Imperial Ventures Inc.
9920 S. La Cienega Boulevar, 14th Fl.
Inglewood, CA 90301
(310)417-5409
Fax: (310)338-6115

Ventana Global (Irvine)
18881 Von Karman Ave., Ste. 1150
Irvine, CA 92612
(949)476-2204
Fax: (949)752-0223
Website: http://www.ventanaglobal.com

Integrated Consortium Inc.
50 Ridgecrest Rd.
Kentfield, CA 94904
(415)925-0386
Fax: (415)461-2726

Enterprise Partners
979 Ivanhoe Ave., Ste. 550
La Jolla, CA 92037
(858)454-8833
Fax: (858)454-2489
Website: http://www.epvc.com

Domain Associates
28202 Cabot Rd., Ste. 200
Laguna Niguel, CA 92677
(949)347-2446
Fax: (949)347-9720
Website: http://www.domainvc.com

Cascade Communications Ventures
60 E. Sir Francis Drake Blvd., Ste. 300
Larkspur, CA 94939
(415)925-6500
Fax: (415)925-6501

Allegis Capital
One First St., Ste. Two
Los Altos, CA 94022
(650)917-5900
Fax: (650)917-5901
Website: http://www.allegiscapital.com

Aspen Ventures
1000 Fremont Ave., Ste. 200
Los Altos, CA 94024
(650)917-5670
Fax: (650)917-5677
Website: http://www.aspenventures.com

AVI Capital L.P.
1 First St., Ste. 2
Los Altos, CA 94022
(650)949-9862
Fax: (650)949-8510
Website: http://www.avicapital.com

Bastion Capital Corp.
1999 Avenue of the Stars, Ste. 2960
Los Angeles, CA 90067
(310)788-5700
Fax: (310)277-7582
E-mail: ga@bastioncapital.com
Website: http://www.bastioncapital.com

Davis Group
PO Box 69953
Los Angeles, CA 90069-0953
(310)659-6327
Fax: (310)659-6337

Developers Equity Corp.
1880 Century Park East, Ste. 211
Los Angeles, CA 90067
(213)277-0300

Far East Capital Corp.
350 S. Grand Ave., Ste. 4100
Los Angeles, CA 90071
(213)687-1361
Fax: (213)617-7939
E-mail: free@fareastnationalbank.com

Kline Hawkes & Co.
11726 San Vicente Blvd., Ste. 300
Los Angeles, CA 90049
(310)442-4700
Fax: (310)442-4707
Website: http://www.klinehawkes.com

Lawrence Financial Group
701 Teakwood
PO Box 491773
Los Angeles, CA 90049
(310)471-4060
Fax: (310)472-3155

Riordan Lewis & Haden
300 S. Grand Ave., 29th Fl.
Los Angeles, CA 90071
(213)229-8500
Fax: (213)229-8597

Union Venture Corp.
445 S. Figueroa St., 9th Fl.
Los Angeles, CA 90071
(213)236-4092
Fax: (213)236-6329

Wedbush Capital Partners
1000 Wilshire Blvd.
Los Angeles, CA 90017
(213)688-4545
Fax: (213)688-6642
Website: http://www.wedbush.com

Advent International Corp.
2180 Sand Hill Rd., Ste. 420
Menlo Park, CA 94025
(650)233-7500
Fax: (650)233-7515
Website: http://
www.adventinternational.com

Altos Ventures
2882 Sand Hill Rd., Ste. 100
Menlo Park, CA 94025
(650)234-9771
Fax: (650)233-9821
Website: http://www.altosvc.com

Applied Technology
1010 El Camino Real, Ste. 300
Menlo Park, CA 94025
(415)326-8622
Fax: (415)326-8163

APV Technology Partners
535 Middlefield, Ste. 150
Menlo Park, CA 94025
(650)327-7871
Fax: (650)327-7631
Website: http://www.apvtp.com

August Capital Management
2480 Sand Hill Rd., Ste. 101
Menlo Park, CA 94025
(650)234-9900
Fax: (650)234-9910
Website: http://www.augustcap.com

Baccharis Capital Inc.
2420 Sand Hill Rd., Ste. 100
Menlo Park, CA 94025
(650)324-6844
Fax: (650)854-3025

Benchmark Capital
2480 Sand Hill Rd., Ste. 200
Menlo Park, CA 94025
(650)854-8180
Fax: (650)854-8183
E-mail: info@benchmark.com
Website: http://www.benchmark.com

Bessemer Venture Partners (Menlo Park)
535 Middlefield Rd., Ste. 245
Menlo Park, CA 94025
(650)853-7000
Fax: (650)853-7001
Website: http://www.bvp.com

The Cambria Group
1600 El Camino Real Rd., Ste. 155
Menlo Park, CA 94025
(650)329-8600
Fax: (650)329-8601
Website: http://www.cambriagroup.com

Canaan Partners
2884 Sand Hill Rd., Ste. 115
Menlo Park, CA 94025
(650)854-8092
Fax: (650)854-8127
Website: http://www.canaan.com

Capstone Ventures
3000 Sand Hill Rd., Bldg. One, Ste. 290
Menlo Park, CA 94025
(650)854-2523
Fax: (650)854-9010
Website: http://www.capstonevc.com

Comdisco Venture Group (Silicon Valley)
3000 Sand Hill Rd., Bldg. 1, Ste. 155
Menlo Park, CA 94025
(650)854-9484
Fax: (650)854-4026

Commtech International
535 Middlefield Rd., Ste. 200
Menlo Park, CA 94025
(650)328-0190
Fax: (650)328-6442

Compass Technology Partners
1550 El Camino Real, Ste. 275
Menlo Park, CA 94025-4111
(650)322-7595
Fax: (650)322-0588
Website: http://
www.compasstechpartners.com

Convergence Partners
3000 Sand Hill Rd., Ste. 235
Menlo Park, CA 94025
(650)854-3010
Fax: (650)854-3015
Website: http://
www.convergencepartners.com

The Dakota Group
PO Box 1025
Menlo Park, CA 94025
(650)853-0600
Fax: (650)851-4899
E-mail: info@dakota.com

Delphi Ventures
3000 Sand Hill Rd.
Bldg. One, Ste. 135
Menlo Park, CA 94025
(650)854-9650
Fax: (650)854-2961
Website: http://www.delphiventures.com

El Dorado Ventures
2884 Sand Hill Rd., Ste. 121
Menlo Park, CA 94025
(650)854-1200
Fax: (650)854-1202
Website: http://
www.eldoradoventures.com

Glynn Ventures
3000 Sand Hill Rd., Bldg. 4, Ste. 235
Menlo Park, CA 94025
(650)854-2215

Indosuez Ventures
2180 Sand Hill Rd., Ste. 450
Menlo Park, CA 94025
(650)854-0587
Fax: (650)323-5561
Website: http://
www.indosuezventures.com

Institutional Venture Partners
3000 Sand Hill Rd., Bldg. 2, Ste. 290
Menlo Park, CA 94025
(650)854-0132
Fax: (650)854-5762
Website: http://www.ivp.com

Interwest Partners (Menlo Park)
3000 Sand Hill Rd., Bldg. 3, Ste. 255
Menlo Park, CA 94025-7112
(650)854-8585
Fax: (650)854-4706
Website: http://www.interwest.com

Kleiner Perkins Caufield & Byers (Menlo Park)
2750 Sand Hill Rd.
Menlo Park, CA 94025
(650)233-2750
Fax: (650)233-0300
Website: http://www.kpcb.com

Magic Venture Capital LLC
1010 El Camino Real, Ste. 300
Menlo Park, CA 94025
(650)325-4149

Matrix Partners
2500 Sand Hill Rd., Ste. 113
Menlo Park, CA 94025
(650)854-3131
Fax: (650)854-3296
Website: http://www.matrixpartners.com

Mayfield Fund
2800 Sand Hill Rd.
Menlo Park, CA 94025
(650)854-5560
Fax: (650)854-5712
Website: http://www.mayfield.com

McCown De Leeuw and Co. (Menlo Park)
3000 Sand Hill Rd., Bldg. 3, Ste. 290
Menlo Park, CA 94025-7111
(650)854-6000
Fax: (650)854-0853
Website: http://www.mdcpartners.com

Menlo Ventures
3000 Sand Hill Rd., Bldg. 4, Ste. 100
Menlo Park, CA 94025
(650)854-8540
Fax: (650)854-7059
Website: http://www.menloventures.com

Merrill Pickard Anderson & Eyre
2480 Sand Hill Rd., Ste. 200
Menlo Park, CA 94025
(650)854-8600
Fax: (650)854-0345

New Enterprise Associates (Menlo Park)
2490 Sand Hill Rd.
Menlo Park, CA 94025
(650)854-9499
Fax: (650)854-9397
Website: http://www.nea.com

Onset Ventures
2400 Sand Hill Rd., Ste. 150
Menlo Park, CA 94025
(650)529-0700
Fax: (650)529-0777
Website: http://www.onset.com

Paragon Venture Partners
3000 Sand Hill Rd., Bldg. 1, Ste. 275
Menlo Park, CA 94025
(650)854-8000
Fax: (650)854-7260

Pathfinder Venture Capital Funds (Menlo Park)
3000 Sand Hill Rd., Bldg. 3, Ste. 255
Menlo Park, CA 94025
(650)854-0650
Fax: (650)854-4706

Rocket Ventures
3000 Sandhill Rd., Bldg. 1, Ste. 170
Menlo Park, CA 94025
(650)561-9100
Fax: (650)561-9183
Website: http://www.rocketventures.com

Sequoia Capital
3000 Sand Hill Rd., Bldg. 4, Ste. 280
Menlo Park, CA 94025
(650)854-3927
Fax: (650)854-2977
E-mail: sequoia@sequoiacap.com
Website: http://www.sequoiacap.com

Sierra Ventures
3000 Sand Hill Rd., Bldg. 4, Ste. 210
Menlo Park, CA 94025
(650)854-1000
Fax: (650)854-5593
Website: http://www.sierraventures.com

Sigma Partners
2884 Sand Hill Rd., Ste. 121
Menlo Park, CA 94025-7022
(650)853-1700
Fax: (650)853-1717
E-mail: info@sigmapartners.com
Website: http://www.sigmapartners.com

Sprout Group (Menlo Park)
3000 Sand Hill Rd.
Bldg. 3, Ste. 170
Menlo Park, CA 94025
(650)234-2700
Fax: (650)234-2779
Website: http://www.sproutgroup.com

TA Associates (Menlo Park)
70 Willow Rd., Ste. 100
Menlo Park, CA 94025
(650)328-1210
Fax: (650)326-4933
Website: http://www.ta.com

Thompson Clive & Partners Ltd.
3000 Sand Hill Rd., Bldg. 1, Ste. 185
Menlo Park, CA 94025-7102
(650)854-0314
Fax: (650)854-0670
E-mail: mail@tcvc.com
Website: http://www.tcvc.com

Trinity Ventures Ltd.
3000 Sand Hill Rd., Bldg. 1, Ste. 240
Menlo Park, CA 94025
(650)854-9500
Fax: (650)854-9501
Website: http://www.trinityventures.com

U.S. Venture Partners
2180 Sand Hill Rd., Ste. 300
Menlo Park, CA 94025
(650)854-9080
Fax: (650)854-3018
Website: http://www.usvp.com

USVP-Schlein Marketing Fund
2180 Sand Hill Rd., Ste. 300
Menlo Park, CA 94025
(415)854-9080
Fax: (415)854-3018
Website: http://www.usvp.com

Venrock Associates
2494 Sand Hill Rd., Ste. 200
Menlo Park, CA 94025
(650)561-9580
Fax: (650)561-9180
Website: http://www.venrock.com

Brad Peery Capital Inc.
145 Chapel Pkwy.
Mill Valley, CA 94941
(415)389-0625
Fax: (415)389-1336

Dot Edu Ventures
650 Castro St., Ste. 270
Mountain View, CA 94041
(650)575-5638
Fax: (650)325-5247
Website: http://
www.doteduventures.com

Forrest, Binkley & Brown
840 Newport Ctr. Dr., Ste. 480
Newport Beach, CA 92660
(949)729-3222
Fax: (949)729-3226
Website: http://www.fbbvc.com

Marwit Capital LLC
180 Newport Center Dr., Ste. 200
Newport Beach, CA 92660
(949)640-6234
Fax: (949)720-8077
Website: http://www.marwit.com

Kaiser Permanente / National Venture Development
1800 Harrison St., 22nd Fl.
Oakland, CA 94612
(510)267-4010
Fax: (510)267-4036
Website: http://www.kpventures.com

Nu Capital Access Group, Ltd.
7677 Oakport St., Ste. 105
Oakland, CA 94621
(510)635-7345
Fax: (510)635-7068

Inman and Bowman
4 Orinda Way, Bldg. D, Ste. 150
Orinda, CA 94563
(510)253-1611
Fax: (510)253-9037

Accel Partners (San Francisco)
428 University Ave.
Palo Alto, CA 94301
(650)614-4800
Fax: (650)614-4880
Website: http://www.accel.com

Advanced Technology Ventures
485 Ramona St., Ste. 200
Palo Alto, CA 94301
(650)321-8601
Fax: (650)321-0934
Website: http://www.atvcapital.com

Anila Fund
400 Channing Ave.
Palo Alto, CA 94301
(650)833-5790
Fax: (650)833-0590
Website: http://www.anila.com

Asset Management Company Venture Capital
2275 E. Bayshore, Ste. 150
Palo Alto, CA 94303
(650)494-7400
Fax: (650)856-1826
E-mail: postmaster@assetman.com
Website: http://www.assetman.com

BancBoston Capital / BancBoston Ventures
435 Tasso St., Ste. 250
Palo Alto, CA 94305
(650)470-4100
Fax: (650)853-1425
Website: http://
www.bancbostoncapital.com

Charter Ventures
525 University Ave., Ste. 1400
Palo Alto, CA 94301
(650)325-6953
Fax: (650)325-4762
Website: http://
www.charterventures.com

Communications Ventures
505 Hamilton Avenue, Ste. 305
Palo Alto, CA 94301
(650)325-9600
Fax: (650)325-9608
Website: http://www.comven.com

HMS Group
2468 Embarcadero Way
Palo Alto, CA 94303-3313
(650)856-9862
Fax: (650)856-9864

Jafco America Ventures, Inc.
505 Hamilton Ste. 310
Palto Alto, CA 94301
(650)463-8800
Fax: (650)463-8801
Website: http://www.jafco.com

New Vista Capital
540 Cowper St., Ste. 200
Palo Alto, CA 94301
(650)329-9333
Fax: (650)328-9434
E-mail: fgreene@nvcap.com
Website: http://www.nvcap.com

Norwest Equity Partners (Palo Alto)
245 Lytton Ave., Ste. 250
Palo Alto, CA 94301-1426
(650)321-8000
Fax: (650)321-8010
Website: http://www.norwestvp.com

Oak Investment Partners
525 University Ave., Ste. 1300
Palo Alto, CA 94301
(650)614-3700
Fax: (650)328-6345
Website: http://www.oakinv.com

Patricof & Co. Ventures, Inc. (Palo Alto)
2100 Geng Rd., Ste. 150
Palo Alto, CA 94303
(650)494-9944
Fax: (650)494-6751
Website: http://www.patricof.com

RWI Group
835 Page Mill Rd.
Palo Alto, CA 94304
(650)251-1800
Fax: (650)213-8660
Website: http://www.rwigroup.com

Summit Partners (Palo Alto)
499 Hamilton Ave., Ste. 200
Palo Alto, CA 94301
(650)321-1166
Fax: (650)321-1188
Website: http://
www.summitpartners.com

Sutter Hill Ventures
755 Page Mill Rd., Ste. A-200
Palo Alto, CA 94304
(650)493-5600
Fax: (650)858-1854
E-mail: shv@shv.com

Vanguard Venture Partners
525 University Ave., Ste. 600
Palo Alto, CA 94301
(650)321-2900
Fax: (650)321-2902
Website: http://
www.vanguardventures.com

Venture Growth Associates
2479 East Bayshore St., Ste. 710
Palo Alto, CA 94303
(650)855-9100
Fax: (650)855-9104

Worldview Technology Partners
435 Tasso St., Ste. 120
Palo Alto, CA 94301
(650)322-3800
Fax: (650)322-3880
Website: http://www.worldview.com

Draper, Fisher, Jurvetson / Draper Associates
400 Seaport Ct., Ste.250
Redwood City, CA 94063
(415)599-9000
Fax: (415)599-9726
Website: http://www.dfj.com

Gabriel Venture Partners
350 Marine Pkwy., Ste. 200
Redwood Shores, CA 94065

(650)551-5000
Fax: (650)551-5001
Website: http://www.gabrielvp.com

Hallador Venture Partners, L.L.C.
740 University Ave., Ste. 110
Sacramento, CA 95825-6710
(916)920-0191
Fax: (916)920-5188
E-mail: chris@hallador.com

Emerald Venture Group
12396 World Trade Dr., Ste. 116
San Diego, CA 92128
(858)451-1001
Fax: (858)451-1003
Website: http://
www.emeraldventure.com

Forward Ventures
9255 Towne Centre Dr.
San Diego, CA 92121
(858)677-6077
Fax: (858)452-8799
E-mail: info@forwardventure.com
Website: http://
www.forwardventure.com

Idanta Partners Ltd.
4660 La Jolla Village Dr., Ste. 850
San Diego, CA 92122
(619)452-9690
Fax: (619)452-2013
Website: http://www.idanta.com

Kingsbury Associates
3655 Nobel Dr., Ste. 490
San Diego, CA 92122
(858)677-0600
Fax: (858)677-0800

Kyocera International Inc.
Corporate Development
8611 Balboa Ave.
San Diego, CA 92123
(858)576-2600
Fax: (858)492-1456

Sorrento Associates, Inc.
4370 LaJolla Village Dr., Ste. 1040
San Diego, CA 92122
(619)452-3100
Fax: (619)452-7607
Website: http://
www.sorrentoventures.com

Western States Investment Group
9191 Towne Ctr. Dr., Ste. 310
San Diego, CA 92122
(619)678-0800
Fax: (619)678-0900

Aberdare Ventures
One Embarcadero Center, Ste. 4000
San Francisco, CA 94111
(415)392-7442
Fax: (415)392-4264
Website: http://www.aberdare.com

Acacia Venture Partners
101 California St., Ste. 3160
San Francisco, CA 94111
(415)433-4200
Fax: (415)433-4250
Website: http://www.acaciavp.com

Access Venture Partners
319 Laidley St.
San Francisco, CA 94131
(415)586-0132
Fax: (415)392-6310
Website: http://
www.accessventurepartners.com

Alta Partners
One Embarcadero Center, Ste. 4050
San Francisco, CA 94111
(415)362-4022
Fax: (415)362-6178
E-mail: alta@altapartners.com
Website: http://www.altapartners.com

Bangert Dawes Reade Davis & Thom
220 Montgomery St., Ste. 424
San Francisco, CA 94104
(415)954-9900
Fax: (415)954-9901
E-mail: bdrdt@pacbell.net

Berkeley International Capital Corp.
650 California St., Ste. 2800
San Francisco, CA 94108-2609
(415)249-0450
Fax: (415)392-3929
Website: http://www.berkeleyvc.com

Blueprint Ventures LLC
456 Montgomery St., 22nd Fl.
San Francisco, CA 94104
(415)901-4000
Fax: (415)901-4035
Website: http://
www.blueprintventures.com

Blumberg Capital Ventures
580 Howard St., Ste. 401
San Francisco, CA 94105
(415)905-5007
Fax: (415)357-5027
Website: http://www.blumberg-capital.com

Burr, Egan, Deleage, and Co. (San Francisco)
1 Embarcadero Center, Ste. 4050
San Francisco, CA 94111
(415)362-4022
Fax: (415)362-6178

Burrill & Company
120 Montgomery St., Ste. 1370
San Francisco, CA 94104
(415)743-3160
Fax: (415)743-3161
Website: http://www.burrillandco.com

CMEA Ventures
235 Montgomery St., Ste. 920
San Francisco, CA 94401
(415)352-1520
Fax: (415)352-1524
Website: http://www.cmeaventures.com

Crocker Capital
1 Post St., Ste. 2500
San Francisco, CA 94101
(415)956-5250
Fax: (415)959-5710

Dominion Ventures, Inc.
44 Montgomery St., Ste. 4200
San Francisco, CA 94104
(415)362-4890
Fax: (415)394-9245

Dorset Capital
Pier 1
Bay 2
San Francisco, CA 94111
(415)398-7101
Fax: (415)398-7141
Website: http://www.dorsetcapital.com

Gatx Capital
Four Embarcadero Center, Ste. 2200
San Francisco, CA 94904
(415)955-3200
Fax: (415)955-3449

IMinds
135 Main St., Ste. 1350
San Francisco, CA 94105
(415)547-0000
Fax: (415)227-0300
Website: http://www.iminds.com

LF International Inc.
360 Post St., Ste. 705
San Francisco, CA 94108
(415)399-0110
Fax: (415)399-9222
Website: http://www.lfvc.com

Newbury Ventures
535 Pacific Ave., 2nd Fl.
San Francisco, CA 94133
(415)296-7408
Fax: (415)296-7416
Website: http://www.newburyven.com

Quest Ventures (San Francisco)
333 Bush St., Ste. 1750
San Francisco, CA 94104
(415)782-1414
Fax: (415)782-1415

Robertson-Stephens Co.
555 California St., Ste. 2600
San Francisco, CA 94104
(415)781-9700
Fax: (415)781-2556
Website: http://
www.omegaadventures.com

Rosewood Capital, L.P.
One Maritime Plaza, Ste. 1330
San Francisco, CA 94111-3503
(415)362-5526
Fax: (415)362-1192
Website: http://www.rosewoodvc.com

Ticonderoga Capital Inc.
555 California St., No. 4950
San Francisco, CA 94104
(415)296-7900
Fax: (415)296-8956

21st Century Internet Venture Partners
Two South Park
2nd Floor
San Francisco, CA 94107
(415)512-1221
Fax: (415)512-2650
Website: http://www.21vc.com

VK Ventures
600 California St., Ste.1700
San Francisco, CA 94111
(415)391-5600
Fax: (415)397-2744

Walden Group of Venture Capital Funds
750 Battery St., Seventh Floor
San Francisco, CA 94111
(415)391-7225
Fax: (415)391-7262

Acer Technology Ventures
2641 Orchard Pkwy.
San Jose, CA 95134
(408)433-4945
Fax: (408)433-5230

Authosis
226 Airport Pkwy., Ste. 405
San Jose, CA 95110
(650)814-3603
Website: http://www.authosis.com

Western Technology Investment
2010 N. First St., Ste. 310
San Jose, CA 95131
(408)436-8577
Fax: (408)436-8625
E-mail: mktg@westerntech.com

Drysdale Enterprises
177 Bovet Rd., Ste. 600
San Mateo, CA 94402
(650)341-6336
Fax: (650)341-1329
E-mail: drysdale@aol.com

Greylock
2929 Campus Dr., Ste. 400
San Mateo, CA 94401
(650)493-5525
Fax: (650)493-5575
Website: http://www.greylock.com

Technology Funding
2000 Alameda de las Pulgas, Ste. 250
San Mateo, CA 94403
(415)345-2200
Fax: (415)345-1797

2M Invest Inc.
1875 S. Grant St.
Suite 750
San Mateo, CA 94402
(650)655-3765
Fax: (650)372-9107
E-mail: 2minfo@2minvest.com
Website: http://www.2minvest.com

Phoenix Growth Capital Corp.
2401 Kerner Blvd.
San Rafael, CA 94901
(415)485-4569
Fax: (415)485-4663

NextGen Partners LLC
1705 East Valley Rd.
Santa Barbara, CA 93108
(805)969-8540
Fax: (805)969-8542
Website: http://
www.nextgenpartners.com

Denali Venture Capital
1925 Woodland Ave.
Santa Clara, CA 95050
(408)690-4838
Fax: (408)247-6979
E-mail: wael@denaliventurecapital.com
Website: http://
www.denaliventurecapital.com

Dotcom Ventures LP
3945 Freedom Circle, Ste. 740
Santa Clara, CA 95045
(408)919-9855
Fax: (408)919-9857
Website: http://
www.dotcomventuresatl.com

Silicon Valley Bank
3003 Tasman
Santa Clara, CA 95054
(408)654-7400
Fax: (408)727-8728

Al Shugart International
920 41st Ave.
Santa Cruz, CA 95062
(831)479-7852
Fax: (831)479-7852
Website: http://www.alshugart.com

Leonard Mautner Associates
1434 Sixth St.
Santa Monica, CA 90401
(213)393-9788
Fax: (310)459-9918

Palomar Ventures
100 Wilshire Blvd., Ste. 450
Santa Monica, CA 90401
(310)260-6050
Fax: (310)656-4150
Website: http://
www.palomarventures.com

Medicus Venture Partners
12930 Saratoga Ave., Ste. D8
Saratoga, CA 95070
(408)447-8600
Fax: (408)447-8599
Website: http://www.medicusvc.com

Redleaf Venture Management
14395 Saratoga Ave., Ste. 130
Saratoga, CA 95070
(408)868-0800
Fax: (408)868-0810
E-mail: nancy@redleaf.com
Website: http://www.redleaf.com

Artemis Ventures
207 Second St., Ste. E
3rd Fl.
Sausalito, CA 94965
(415)289-2500
Fax: (415)289-1789
Website: http://www.artemisventures.com

Deucalion Venture Partners
19501 Brooklime
Sonoma, CA 95476
(707)938-4974
Fax: (707)938-8921

Windward Ventures
PO Box 7688
Thousand Oaks, CA 91359-7688
(805)497-3332
Fax: (805)497-9331

National Investment Management, Inc.
2601 Airport Dr., Ste.210
Torrance, CA 90505
(310)784-7600
Fax: (310)784-7605

Southern California Ventures
406 Amapola Ave. Ste. 125
Torrance, CA 90501
(310)787-4381
Fax: (310)787-4382

Sandton Financial Group
21550 Oxnard St., Ste. 300
Woodland Hills, CA 91367
(818)702-9283

Woodside Fund
850 Woodside Dr.
Woodside, CA 94062
(650)368-5545
Fax: (650)368-2416
Website: http://www.woodsidefund.com

Colorado

Colorado Venture Management
Ste. 300
Boulder, CO 80301
(303)440-4055
Fax: (303)440-4636

Dean & Associates
4362 Apple Way
Boulder, CO 80301
Fax: (303)473-9900

Roser Ventures LLC
1105 Spruce St.
Boulder, CO 80302
(303)443-6436
Fax: (303)443-1885
Website: http://www.roserventures.com

Sequel Venture Partners
4430 Arapahoe Ave., Ste. 220
Boulder, CO 80303
(303)546-0400
Fax: (303)546-9728
E-mail: tom@sequelvc.com
Website: http://www.sequelvc.com

New Venture Resources
445C E. Cheyenne Mtn. Blvd.
Colorado Springs, CO 80906-4570
(719)598-9272
Fax: (719)598-9272

The Centennial Funds
1428 15th St.
Denver, CO 80202-1318
(303)405-7500
Fax: (303)405-7575
Website: http://www.centennial.com

Rocky Mountain Capital Partners
1125 17th St., Ste. 2260
Denver, CO 80202
(303)291-5200
Fax: (303)291-5327

Sandlot Capital LLC
600 South Cherry St., Ste. 525
Denver, CO 80246
(303)893-3400
Fax: (303)893-3403
Website: http://www.sandlotcapital.com

Wolf Ventures
50 South Steele St., Ste. 777
Denver, CO 80209
(303)321-4800
Fax: (303)321-4848
E-mail: businessplan@wolfventures.com
Website: http://www.wolfventures.com

The Columbine Venture Funds
5460 S. Quebec St., Ste. 270
Englewood, CO 80111
(303)694-3222
Fax: (303)694-9007

Investment Securities of Colorado, Inc.
4605 Denice Dr.
Englewood, CO 80111
(303)796-9192

Kinship Partners
6300 S. Syracuse Way, Ste. 484
Englewood, CO 80111
(303)694-0268
Fax: (303)694-1707
E-mail: block@vailsys.com

Boranco Management, L.L.C.
1528 Hillside Dr.
Fort Collins, CO 80524-1969
(970)221-2297
Fax: (970)221-4787

Aweida Ventures
890 West Cherry St., Ste. 220
Louisville, CO 80027
(303)664-9520
Fax: (303)664-9530
Website: http://www.aweida.com

Access Venture Partners
8787 Turnpike Dr., Ste. 260
Westminster, CO 80030
(303)426-8899
Fax: (303)426-8828

Medmax Ventures LP
1 Northwestern Dr., Ste. 203
Bloomfield, CT 06002
(860)286-2960
Fax: (860)286-9960

James B. Kobak & Co.
Four Mansfield Place
Darien, CT 06820
(203)656-3471
Fax: (203)655-2905

Orien Ventures
1 Post Rd.
Fairfield, CT 06430
(203)259-9933
Fax: (203)259-5288

ABP Acquisition Corporation
115 Maple Ave.
Greenwich, CT 06830
(203)625-8287
Fax: (203)447-6187

Catterton Partners
9 Greenwich Office Park
Greenwich, CT 06830
(203)629-4901
Fax: (203)629-4903
Website: http://www.cpequity.com

Consumer Venture Partners
3 Pickwick Plz.
Greenwich, CT 06830
(203)629-8800
Fax: (203)629-2019

Insurance Venture Partners
31 Brookside Dr., Ste. 211
Greenwich, CT 06830
(203)861-0030
Fax: (203)861-2745

The NTC Group
Three Pickwick Plaza
Ste. 200
Greenwich, CT 06830
(203)862-2800
Fax: (203)622-6538

Regulus International Capital Co., Inc.
140 Greenwich Ave.
Greenwich, CT 06830
(203)625-9700
Fax: (203)625-9706

Axiom Venture Partners
City Place II
185 Asylum St., 17th Fl.
Hartford, CT 06103
(860)548-7799
Fax: (860)548-7797
Website: http://www.axiomventures.com

Conning Capital Partners
City Place II
185 Asylum St.
Hartford, CT 06103-4105
(860)520-1289
Fax: (860)520-1299
E-mail: pe@conning.com
Website: http://www.conning.com

First New England Capital L.P.
100 Pearl St.
Hartford, CT 06103
(860)293-3333
Fax: (860)293-3338
E-mail: info@firstnewenglandcapital.com
Website: http://
www.firstnewenglandcapital.com

Northeast Ventures
One State St., Ste. 1720
Hartford, CT 06103
(860)547-1414
Fax: (860)246-8755

Windward Holdings
38 Sylvan Rd.
Madison, CT 06443
(203)245-6870
Fax: (203)245-6865

Advanced Materials Partners, Inc.
45 Pine St.
PO Box 1022
New Canaan, CT 06840
(203)966-6415
Fax: (203)966-8448
E-mail: wkb@amplink.com

RFE Investment Partners
36 Grove St.
New Canaan, CT 06840
(203)966-2800
Fax: (203)966-3109
Website: http://www.rfeip.com

Connecticut Innovations, Inc.
999 West St.
Rocky Hill, CT 06067
(860)563-5851
Fax: (860)563-4877
E-mail:
pamela.hartley@ctinnovations.com
Website: http://www.ctinnovations.com

Canaan Partners
105 Rowayton Ave.
Rowayton, CT 06853
(203)855-0400
Fax: (203)854-9117
Website: http://www.canaan.com

Landmark Partners, Inc.
10 Mill Pond Ln.
Simsbury, CT 06070
(860)651-9760
Fax: (860)651-8890
Website: http://
www.landmarkpartners.com

Sweeney & Company
PO Box 567
Southport, CT 06490
(203)255-0220
Fax: (203)255-0220
E-mail: sweeney@connix.com

Baxter Associates, Inc.
PO Box 1333
Stamford, CT 06904
(203)323-3143
Fax: (203)348-0622

Beacon Partners Inc.
6 Landmark Sq., 4th Fl.
Stamford, CT 06901-2792
(203)359-5776
Fax: (203)359-5876

Collinson, Howe, and Lennox, LLC
1055 Washington Blvd., 5th Fl.
Stamford, CT 06901
(203)324-7700
Fax: (203)324-3636
E-mail: info@chlmedical.com
Website: http://www.chlmedical.com

Prime Capital Management Co.
550 West Ave.
Stamford, CT 06902
(203)964-0642
Fax: (203)964-0862

Saugatuck Capital Co.
1 Canterbury Green
Stamford, CT 06901
(203)348-6669
Fax: (203)324-6995
Website: http://www.saugatuckcapital.com

Soundview Financial Group Inc.
22 Gatehouse Rd.
Stamford, CT 06902
(203)462-7200
Fax: (203)462-7350
Website: http://www.sndv.com

TSG Ventures, L.L.C.
177 Broad St., 12th Fl.
Stamford, CT 06901
(203)406-1500
Fax: (203)406-1590

Whitney & Company
177 Broad St.
Stamford, CT 06901
(203)973-1400
Fax: (203)973-1422
Website: http://www.jhwhitney.com

Cullinane & Donnelly Venture Partners L.P.
970 Farmington Ave.
West Hartford, CT 06107
(860)521-7811

The Crestview Investment and Financial Group
431 Post Rd. E, Ste. 1
Westport, CT 06880-4403
(203)222-0333
Fax: (203)222-0000

Marketcorp Venture Associates, L.P. (MCV)
274 Riverside Ave.
Westport, CT 06880
(203)222-3030
Fax: (203)222-3033

Oak Investment Partners (Westport)
1 Gorham Island
Westport, CT 06880
(203)226-8346
Fax: (203)227-0372
Website: http://www.oakinv.com

Oxford Bioscience Partners
315 Post Rd. W
Westport, CT 06880-5200
(203)341-3300
Fax: (203)341-3309
Website: http://www.oxbio.com

Prince Ventures (Westport)
25 Ford Rd.
Westport, CT 06880
(203)227-8332
Fax: (203)226-5302

LTI Venture Leasing Corp.
221 Danbury Rd.
Wilton, CT 06897

(203)563-1100
Fax: (203)563-1111
Website: http://www.ltileasing.com

Delaware

Blue Rock Capital
5803 Kennett Pike, Ste. A
Wilmington, DE 19807
(302)426-0981
Fax: (302)426-0982
Website: http://
www.bluerockcapital.com

District of Columbia

Allied Capital Corp.
1919 Pennsylvania Ave. NW
Washington, DC 20006-3434
(202)331-2444
Fax: (202)659-2053
Website: http://www.alliedcapital.com

Atlantic Coastal Ventures, L.P.
3101 South St. NW
Washington, DC 20007
(202)293-1166
Fax: (202)293-1181
Website: http://www.atlanticcv.com

Columbia Capital Group, Inc.
1660 L St. NW, Ste. 308
Washington, DC 20036
(202)775-8815
Fax: (202)223-0544

Core Capital Partners
901 15th St., NW
9th Fl.
Washington, DC 20005
(202)589-0090
Fax: (202)589-0091
Website: http://www.core-capital.com

Next Point Partners
701 Pennsylvania Ave. NW, Ste. 900
Washington, DC 20004
(202)661-8703
Fax: (202)434-7400
E-mail: mf@nextpoint.vc
Website: http://www.nextpointvc.com

Telecommunications Development Fund
2020 K. St. NW
Ste. 375
Washington, DC 20006
(202)293-8840
Fax: (202)293-8850
Website: http://www.tdfund.com

Wachtel & Co., Inc.
1101 4th St. NW
Washington, DC 20005-5680
(202)898-1144

Winslow Partners LLC
1300 Connecticut Ave. NW
Washington, DC 20036-1703
(202)530-5000
Fax: (202)530-5010
E-mail: winslow@winslowpartners.com

Women's Growth Capital Fund
1054 31st St., NW
Ste. 110
Washington, DC 20007
(202)342-1431
Fax: (202)341-1203
Website: http://www.wgcf.com

Florida

Sigma Capital Corp.
22668 Caravelle Circle
Boca Raton, FL 33433
(561)368-9783

North American Business Development Co., L.L.C.
111 East Las Olas Blvd.
Ft. Lauderdale, FL 33301
(305)463-0681
Fax: (305)527-0904
Website: http://
www.northamericanfund.com

Chartwell Capital Management Co. Inc.
1 Independent Dr., Ste. 3120
Jacksonville, FL 32202
(904)355-3519
Fax: (904)353-5833
E-mail: info@chartwellcap.com

CEO Advisors
1061 Maitland Center Commons
Ste. 209
Maitland, FL 32751
(407)660-9327
Fax: (407)660-2109

Henry & Co.
8201 Peters Rd., Ste. 1000
Plantation, FL 33324
(954)797-7400

Avery Business Development Services
2506 St. Michel Ct.
Ponte Vedra, FL 32082
(904)285-6033

New South Ventures
5053 Ocean Blvd.
Sarasota, FL 34242
(941)358-6000
Fax: (941)358-6078
Website: http://
www.newsouthventures.com

Venture Capital Management Corp.
PO Box 2626
Satellite Beach, FL 32937
(407)777-1969

Florida Capital Venture Ltd.
325 Florida Bank Plaza
100 W. Kennedy Blvd.
Tampa, FL 33602
(813)229-2294
Fax: (813)229-2028

Quantum Capital Partners
339 South Plant Ave.
Tampa, FL 33606
(813)250-1999
Fax: (813)250-1998
Website: http://
www.quantumcapitalpartners.com

South Atlantic Venture Fund
614 W. Bay St.
Tampa, FL 33606-2704
(813)253-2500
Fax: (813)253-2360
E-mail: venture@southatlantic.com
Website: http://www.southatlantic.com

LM Capital Corp.
120 S. Olive, Ste. 400
West Palm Beach, FL 33401
(561)833-9700
Fax: (561)655-6587
Website: http://
www.lmcapitalsecurities.com

Georgia

Venture First Associates
4811 Thornwood Dr.
Acworth, GA 30102
(770)928-3733
Fax: (770)928-6455

Alliance Technology Ventures
8995 Westside Pkwy., Ste. 200
Alpharetta, GA 30004
(678)336-2000
Fax: (678)336-2001
E-mail: info@atv.com
Website: http://www.atv.com

Cordova Ventures
2500 North Winds Pkwy., Ste. 475
Alpharetta, GA 30004
(678)942-0300

Fax: (678)942-0301
Website: http://www.cordovaventures.com

Advanced Technology Development Fund
1000 Abernathy, Ste. 1420
Atlanta, GA 30328-5614
(404)668-2333
Fax: (404)668-2333

CGW Southeast Partners
12 Piedmont Center, Ste. 210
Atlanta, GA 30305
(404)816-3255
Fax: (404)816-3258
Website: http://www.cgwlp.com

Cyberstarts
1900 Emery St., NW
3rd Fl.
Atlanta, GA 30318
(404)267-5000
Fax: (404)267-5200
Website: http://www.cyberstarts.com

EGL Holdings, Inc.
10 Piedmont Center, Ste. 412
Atlanta, GA 30305
(404)949-8300
Fax: (404)949-8311

Equity South
1790 The Lenox Bldg.
3399 Peachtree Rd. NE
Atlanta, GA 30326
(404)237-6222
Fax: (404)261-1578

Five Paces
3400 Peachtree Rd., Ste. 200
Atlanta, GA 30326
(404)439-8300
Fax: (404)439-8301
Website: http://www.fivepaces.com

Frontline Capital, Inc.
3475 Lenox Rd., Ste. 400
Atlanta, GA 30326
(404)240-7280
Fax: (404)240-7281

Fuqua Ventures LLC
1201 W. Peachtree St. NW, Ste. 5000
Atlanta, GA 30309
(404)815-4500
Fax: (404)815-4528
Website: http://www.fuquaventures.com

Noro-Moseley Partners
4200 Northside Pkwy., Bldg. 9
Atlanta, GA 30327
(404)233-1966
Fax: (404)239-9280
Website: http://www.noro-moseley.com

Renaissance Capital Corp.
34 Peachtree St. NW, Ste. 2230
Atlanta, GA 30303
(404)658-9061
Fax: (404)658-9064

River Capital, Inc.
Two Midtown Plaza
1360 Peachtree St. NE, Ste. 1430
Atlanta, GA 30309
(404)873-2166
Fax: (404)873-2158

State Street Bank & Trust Co.
3414 Peachtree Rd. NE, Ste. 1010
Atlanta, GA 30326
(404)364-9500
Fax: (404)261-4469

UPS Strategic Enterprise Fund
55 Glenlake Pkwy. NE
Atlanta, GA 30328
(404)828-8814
Fax: (404)828-8088
E-mail: jcacyce@ups.com
Website: http://www.ups.com/sef/sef_home

Wachovia
191 Peachtree St. NE, 26th Fl.
Atlanta, GA 30303
(404)332-1000
Fax: (404)332-1392
Website: http://www.wachovia.com/wca

Brainworks Ventures
4243 Dunwoody Club Dr.
Chamblee, GA 30341
(770)239-7447

First Growth Capital Inc.
Best Western Plaza, Ste. 105
PO Box 815
Forsyth, GA 31029
(912)781-7131

Financial Capital Resources, Inc.
21 Eastbrook Bend, Ste. 116
Peachtree City, GA 30269
(404)487-6650

Hawaii

HMS Hawaii Management Partners
Davies Pacific Center
841 Bishop St., Ste. 860
Honolulu, HI 96813
(808)545-3755
Fax: (808)531-2611

Idaho

Sun Valley Ventures
160 Second St.
Ketchum, ID 83340
(208)726-5005
Fax: (208)726-5094

Illinois

Open Prairie Ventures
115 N. Neil St., Ste. 209
Champaign, IL 61820
(217)351-7000
Fax: (217)351-7051
E-mail: inquire@openprairie.com
Website: http://www.openprairie.com

ABN AMRO Private Equity
208 S. La Salle St., 10th Fl.
Chicago, IL 60604
(312)855-7079
Fax: (312)553-6648
Website: http://www.abnequity.com

Alpha Capital Partners, Ltd.
122 S. Michigan Ave., Ste. 1700
Chicago, IL 60603
(312)322-9800
Fax: (312)322-9808
E-mail: acp@alphacapital.com

Ameritech Development Corp.
30 S. Wacker Dr., 37th Fl.
Chicago, IL 60606
(312)750-5083
Fax: (312)609-0244

Apex Investment Partners
225 W. Washington, Ste. 1450
Chicago, IL 60606
(312)857-2800
Fax: (312)857-1800
E-mail: apex@apexvc.com
Website: http://www.apexvc.com

Arch Venture Partners
8725 W. Higgins Rd., Ste. 290
Chicago, IL 60631
(773)380-6600
Fax: (773)380-6606
Website: http://www.archventure.com

The Bank Funds
208 South LaSalle St., Ste. 1680
Chicago, IL 60604
(312)855-6020
Fax: (312)855-8910

Batterson Venture Partners
303 W. Madison St., Ste. 1110
Chicago, IL 60606-3309
(312)269-0300
Fax: (312)269-0021
Website: http://www.battersonvp.com

William Blair Capital Partners, L.L.C.
222 W. Adams St., Ste. 1300
Chicago, IL 60606
(312)364-8250
Fax: (312)236-1042
E-mail: privateequity@wmblair.com
Website: http://www.wmblair.com

Bluestar Ventures
208 South LaSalle St., Ste. 1020
Chicago, IL 60604
(312)384-5000
Fax: (312)384-5005
Website: http://
www.bluestarventures.com

The Capital Strategy Management Co.
233 S. Wacker Dr.
Box 06334
Chicago, IL 60606
(312)444-1170

DN Partners
77 West Wacker Dr., Ste. 4550
Chicago, IL 60601
(312)332-7960
Fax: (312)332-7979

Dresner Capital Inc.
29 South LaSalle St., Ste. 310
Chicago, IL 60603
(312)726-3600
Fax: (312)726-7448

Eblast Ventures LLC
11 South LaSalle St., 5th Fl.
Chicago, IL 60603
(312)372-2600
Fax: (312)372-5621
Website: http://www.eblastventures.com

Essex Woodlands Health Ventures, L.P.
190 S. LaSalle St., Ste. 2800
Chicago, IL 60603
(312)444-6040
Fax: (312)444-6034
Website: http://
www.essexwoodlands.com

First Analysis Venture Capital
233 S. Wacker Dr., Ste. 9500
Chicago, IL 60606
(312)258-1400
Fax: (312)258-0334
Website: http://www.firstanalysis.com

Frontenac Co.
135 S. LaSalle St., Ste.3800
Chicago, IL 60603
(312)368-0044
Fax: (312)368-9520
Website: http://www.frontenac.com

GTCR Golder Rauner, LLC
6100 Sears Tower
Chicago, IL 60606
(312)382-2200
Fax: (312)382-2201
Website: http://www.gtcr.com

High Street Capital LLC
311 South Wacker Dr., Ste. 4550
Chicago, IL 60606
(312)697-4990
Fax: (312)697-4994
Website: http://www.highstr.com

IEG Venture Management, Inc.
70 West Madison
Chicago, IL 60602
(312)644-0890
Fax: (312)454-0369
Website: http://www.iegventure.com

JK&B Capital
180 North Stetson, Ste. 4500
Chicago, IL 60601
(312)946-1200
Fax: (312)946-1103
E-mail: gspencer@jkbcapital.com
Website: http://www.jkbcapital.com

Kettle Partners L.P.
350 W. Hubbard, Ste. 350
Chicago, IL 60610
(312)329-9300
Fax: (312)527-4519
Website: http://www.kettlevc.com

Lake Shore Capital Partners
20 N. Wacker Dr., Ste. 2807
Chicago, IL 60606
(312)803-3536
Fax: (312)803-3534

LaSalle Capital Group Inc.
70 W. Madison St., Ste. 5710
Chicago, IL 60602
(312)236-7041
Fax: (312)236-0720

Linc Capital, Inc.
303 E. Wacker Pkwy., Ste. 1000
Chicago, IL 60601
(312)946-2670
Fax: (312)938-4290
E-mail: bdemars@linccap.com

Madison Dearborn Partners, Inc.
3 First National Plz., Ste. 3800
Chicago, IL 60602
(312)895-1000
Fax: (312)895-1001
E-mail: invest@mdcp.com
Website: http://www.mdcp.com

Mesirow Private Equity Investments Inc.
350 N. Clark St.
Chicago, IL 60610
(312)595-6950
Fax: (312)595-6211
Website: http://
www.meisrowfinancial.com

Mosaix Ventures LLC
1822 North Mohawk
Chicago, IL 60614
(312)274-0988
Fax: (312)274-0989
Website: http://
www.mosaixventures.com

Nesbitt Burns
111 West Monroe St.
Chicago, IL 60603
(312)416-3855
Fax: (312)765-8000
Website: http://www.harrisbank.com

Polestar Capital, Inc.
180 N. Michigan Ave., Ste. 1905
Chicago, IL 60601
(312)984-9090
Fax: (312)984-9877
E-mail: wl@polestarvc.com
Website: http://www.polestarvc.com

Prince Ventures (Chicago)
10 S. Wacker Dr., Ste. 2575
Chicago, IL 60606-7407
(312)454-1408
Fax: (312)454-9125

Prism Capital
444 N. Michigan Ave.
Chicago, IL 60611
(312)464-7900
Fax: (312)464-7915
Website: http://www.prismfund.com

Third Coast Capital
900 N. Franklin St., Ste. 700
Chicago, IL 60610
(312)337-3303
Fax: (312)337-2567
E-mail: manic@earthlink.com
Website: http://
www.thirdcoastcapital.com

Thoma Cressey Equity Partners
4460 Sears Tower, 92nd Fl.
233 S. Wacker Dr.
Chicago, IL 60606
(312)777-4444
Fax: (312)777-4445
Website: http://www.thomacressey.com

Tribune Ventures
435 N. Michigan Ave., Ste. 600
Chicago, IL 60611
(312)527-8797
Fax: (312)222-5993
Website: http://
www.tribuneventures.com

Wind Point Partners (Chicago)
676 N. Michigan Ave., Ste. 330
Chicago, IL 60611
(312)649-4000
Website: http://www.wppartners.com

Marquette Venture Partners
520 Lake Cook Rd., Ste. 450
Deerfield, IL 60015
(847)940-1700
Fax: (847)940-1724
Website: http://
www.marquetteventures.com

Duchossois Investments Limited, LLC
845 Larch Ave.
Elmhurst, IL 60126
(630)530-6105
Fax: (630)993-8644
Website: http://www.duchtec.com

Evanston Business Investment Corp.
1840 Oak Ave.
Evanston, IL 60201
(847)866-1840
Fax: (847)866-1808
E-mail: t-parkinson@nwu.com
Website: http://www.ebic.com

Inroads Capital Partners L.P.
1603 Orrington Ave., Ste. 2050
Evanston, IL 60201-3841
(847)864-2000
Fax: (847)864-9692

The Cerulean Fund/WGC Enterprises
1701 E. Lake Ave., Ste. 170
Glenview, IL 60025
(847)657-8002
Fax: (847)657-8168

Ventana Financial Resources, Inc.
249 Market Sq.
Lake Forest, IL 60045
(847)234-3434

Beecken, Petty & Co.
901 Warrenville Rd., Ste. 205
Lisle, IL 60532
(630)435-0300
Fax: (630)435-0370
E-mail: hep@bpcompany.com
Website: http://www.bpcompany.com

Allstate Private Equity
3075 Sanders Rd., Ste. G5D
Northbrook, IL 60062-7127
(847)402-8247
Fax: (847)402-0880

KB Partners
1101 Skokie Blvd., Ste. 260
Northbrook, IL 60062-2856
(847)714-0444
Fax: (847)714-0445
E-mail: keith@kbpartners.com
Website: http://www.kbpartners.com

Transcap Associates Inc.
900 Skokie Blvd., Ste. 210
Northbrook, IL 60062
(847)753-9600
Fax: (847)753-9090

Graystone Venture Partners, L.L.C. / Portage Venture Partners
One Northfield Plaza, Ste. 530
Northfield, IL 60093
(847)446-9460
Fax: (847)446-9470
Website: http://
www.portageventures.com

Motorola Inc.
1303 E. Algonquin Rd.
Schaumburg, IL 60196-1065
(847)576-4929
Fax: (847)538-2250
Website: http://www.mot.com/mne

Indiana

Irwin Ventures LLC
500 Washington St.
Columbus, IN 47202
(812)373-1434
Fax: (812)376-1709
Website: http://www.irwinventures.com

Cambridge Venture Partners
4181 East 96th St., Ste. 200
Indianapolis, IN 46240
(317)814-6192
Fax: (317)944-9815

CID Equity Partners
One American Square, Ste. 2850
Box 82074
Indianapolis, IN 46282
(317)269-2350
Fax: (317)269-2355
Website: http://www.cidequity.com

Gazelle Techventures
6325 Digital Way, Ste. 460
Indianapolis, IN 46278
(317)275-6800
Fax: (317)275-1101
Website: http://www.gazellevc.com

Monument Advisors Inc.
Bank One Center/Circle
111 Monument Circle, Ste. 600
Indianapolis, IN 46204-5172
(317)656-5065
Fax: (317)656-5060
Website: http://www.monumentadv.com

MWV Capital Partners
201 N. Illinois St., Ste. 300
Indianapolis, IN 46204
(317)237-2323
Fax: (317)237-2325
Website: http://www.mwvcapital.com

First Source Capital Corp.
100 North Michigan St.
PO Box 1602
South Bend, IN 46601
(219)235-2180
Fax: (219)235-2227

Iowa

Allsop Venture Partners
118 Third Ave. SE, Ste. 837
Cedar Rapids, IA 52401
(319)368-6675
Fax: (319)363-9515

InvestAmerica Investment Advisors, Inc.
101 2nd St. SE, Ste. 800
Cedar Rapids, IA 52401
(319)363-8249
Fax: (319)363-9683

Pappajohn Capital Resources
2116 Financial Center
Des Moines, IA 50309
(515)244-5746
Fax: (515)244-2346
Website: http://www.pappajohn.com

Berthel Fisher & Company Planning Inc.
701 Tama St.
PO Box 609
Marion, IA 52302
(319)497-5700
Fax: (319)497-4244

Kansas

Enterprise Merchant Bank
7400 West 110th St., Ste. 560
Overland Park, KS 66210
(913)327-8500
Fax: (913)327-8505

Kansas Venture Capital, Inc. (Overland Park)
6700 Antioch Plz., Ste. 460
Overland Park, KS 66204
(913)262-7117
Fax: (913)262-3509
E-mail: jdalton@kvci.com

Child Health Investment Corp.
6803 W. 64th St., Ste. 208
Shawnee Mission, KS 66202
(913)262-1436
Fax: (913)262-1575
Website: http://www.chca.com

Kansas Technology Enterprise Corp.
214 SW 6th, 1st Fl.
Topeka, KS 66603-3719
(785)296-5272
Fax: (785)296-1160
E-mail: ktec@ktec.com
Website: http://www.ktec.com

Kentucky

Kentucky Highlands Investment Corp.
362 Old Whitley Rd.
London, KY 40741
(606)864-5175
Fax: (606)864-5194
Website: http://www.khic.org

Chrysalis Ventures, L.L.C.
1850 National City Tower
Louisville, KY 40202
(502)583-7644
Fax: (502)583-7648
E-mail: bobsany@chrysalisventures.com
Website: http://
www.chrysalisventures.com

Humana Venture Capital
500 West Main St.
Louisville, KY 40202
(502)580-3922
Fax: (502)580-2051
E-mail: gemont@humana.com
George Emont, Director

Summit Capital Group, Inc.
6510 Glenridge Park Pl., Ste. 8
Louisville, KY 40222
(502)332-2700

Louisiana

Bank One Equity Investors, Inc.
451 Florida St.
Baton Rouge, LA 70801
(504)332-4421
Fax: (504)332-7377

Advantage Capital Partners
LLE Tower
909 Poydras St., Ste. 2230
New Orleans, LA 70112
(504)522-4850
Fax: (504)522-4950
Website: http://www.advantagecap.com

Maine

CEI Ventures / Coastal Ventures LP
2 Portland Fish Pier, Ste. 201
Portland, ME 04101
(207)772-5356
Fax: (207)772-5503
Website: http://www.ceiventures.com

Commwealth Bioventures, Inc.
4 Milk St.
Portland, ME 04101
(207)780-0904
Fax: (207)780-0913

Maryland

Annapolis Ventures LLC
151 West St., Ste. 302
Annapolis, MD 21401
(443)482-9555
Fax: (443)482-9565
Website: http://
www.annapolisventures.com

Delmag Ventures
220 Wardour Dr.
Annapolis, MD 21401
(410)267-8196
Fax: (410)267-8017
Website: http://
www.delmagventures.com

Abell Venture Fund
111 S. Calvert St., Ste. 2300
Baltimore, MD 21202
(410)547-1300
Fax: (410)539-6579
Website: http://www.abell.org

ABS Ventures (Baltimore)
1 South St., Ste. 2150
Baltimore, MD 21202
(410)895-3895
Fax: (410)895-3899
Website: http://www.absventures.com

Anthem Capital, L.P.
16 S. Calvert St., Ste. 800
Baltimore, MD 21202-1305
(410)625-1510
Fax: (410)625-1735
Website: http://www.anthemcapital.com

Catalyst Ventures
1119 St. Paul St.
Baltimore, MD 21202
(410)244-0123
Fax: (410)752-7721

Maryland Venture Capital Trust
217 E. Redwood St., Ste. 2200
Baltimore, MD 21202
(410)767-6361
Fax: (410)333-6931

New Enterprise Associates (Baltimore)
1119 St. Paul St.
Baltimore, MD 21202
(410)244-0115
Fax: (410)752-7721
Website: http://www.nea.com

T. Rowe Price Threshold Partnerships
100 E. Pratt St., 8th Fl.
Baltimore, MD 21202
(410)345-2000
Fax: (410)345-2800

Spring Capital Partners
16 W. Madison St.
Baltimore, MD 21201
(410)685-8000
Fax: (410)727-1436
E-mail: mailbox@springcap.com

Arete Corporation
3 Bethesda Metro Ctr., Ste. 770
Bethesda, MD 20814
(301)657-6268
Fax: (301)657-6254
Website: http://www.arete-microgen.com

Embryon Capital
7903 Sleaford Place
Bethesda, MD 20814
(301)656-6837
Fax: (301)656-8056

Potomac Ventures
7920 Norfolk Ave., Ste. 1100
Bethesda, MD 20814
(301)215-9240
Website: http://
www.potomacventures.com

Toucan Capital Corp.
3 Bethesda Metro Center, Ste. 700
Bethesda, MD 20814

(301)961-1970
Fax: (301)961-1969
Website: http://www.toucancapital.com

Kinetic Ventures LLC
2 Wisconsin Cir., Ste. 620
Chevy Chase, MD 20815
(301)652-8066
Fax: (301)652-8310
Website: http://
www.kineticventures.com

Boulder Ventures Ltd.
4750 Owings Mills Blvd.
Owings Mills, MD 21117
(410)998-3114
Fax: (410)356-5492
Website: http://
www.boulderventures.com

Grotech Capital Group
9690 Deereco Rd., Ste. 800
Timonium, MD 21093
(410)560-2000
Fax: (410)560-1910
Website: http://www.grotech.com

Massachusetts

Adams, Harkness & Hill, Inc.
60 State St.
Boston, MA 02109
(617)371-3900

Advent International
75 State St., 29th Fl.
Boston, MA 02109
(617)951-9400
Fax: (617)951-0566
Website: http://
www.adventinernational.com

American Research and Development
30 Federal St.
Boston, MA 02110-2508
(617)423-7500
Fax: (617)423-9655

Ascent Venture Partners
255 State St., 5th Fl.
Boston, MA 02109
(617)270-9400
Fax: (617)270-9401
E-mail: info@ascentvp.com
Website: http://www.ascentvp.com

Atlas Venture
222 Berkeley St.
Boston, MA 02116
(617)488-2200
Fax: (617)859-9292
Website: http://www.atlasventure.com

Axxon Capital
28 State St., 37th Fl.
Boston, MA 02109
(617)722-0980
Fax: (617)557-6014
Website: http://www.axxoncapital.com

BancBoston Capital/BancBoston Ventures
175 Federal St., 10th Fl.
Boston, MA 02110
(617)434-2509
Fax: (617)434-6175
Website: http://
www.bancbostoncapital.com

Boston Capital Ventures
Old City Hall
45 School St.
Boston, MA 02108
(617)227-6550
Fax: (617)227-3847
E-mail: info@bcv.com
Website: http://www.bcv.com

Boston Financial & Equity Corp.
20 Overland St.
PO Box 15071
Boston, MA 02215
(617)267-2900
Fax: (617)437-7601
E-mail: debbie@bfec.com

Boston Millennia Partners
30 Rowes Wharf
Boston, MA 02110
(617)428-5150
Fax: (617)428-5160
Website: http://
www.millenniapartners.com

Bristol Investment Trust
842A Beacon St.
Boston, MA 02215-3199
(617)566-5212
Fax: (617)267-0932

Brook Venture Management LLC
50 Federal St., 5th Fl.
Boston, MA 02110
(617)451-8989
Fax: (617)451-2369
Website: http://www.brookventure.com

Burr, Egan, Deleage, and Co. (Boston)
200 Clarendon St., Ste. 3800
Boston, MA 02116
(617)262-7770
Fax: (617)262-9779

Cambridge/Samsung Partners
One Exeter Plaza
Ninth Fl.
Boston, MA 02116
(617)262-4440
Fax: (617)262-5562

Chestnut Street Partners, Inc.
75 State St., Ste. 2500
Boston, MA 02109
(617)345-7220
Fax: (617)345-7201
E-mail: chestnut@chestnutp.com

Claflin Capital Management, Inc.
10 Liberty Sq., Ste. 300
Boston, MA 02109
(617)426-6505
Fax: (617)482-0016
Website: http://www.claflincapital.com

Copley Venture Partners
99 Summer St., Ste. 1720
Boston, MA 02110
(617)737-1253
Fax: (617)439-0699

Corning Capital / Corning Technology Ventures
121 High Street, Ste. 400
Boston, MA 02110
(617)338-2656
Fax: (617)261-3864
Website: http://
www.corningventures.com

Downer & Co.
211 Congress St.
Boston, MA 02110
(617)482-6200
Fax: (617)482-6201
E-mail: cdowner@downer.com
Website: http://www.downer.com

Fidelity Ventures
82 Devonshire St.
Boston, MA 02109
(617)563-6370
Fax: (617)476-9023
Website: http://
www.fidelityventures.com

Greylock Management Corp. (Boston)
1 Federal St.
Boston, MA 02110-2065
(617)423-5525
Fax: (617)482-0059

Gryphon Ventures
222 Berkeley St., Ste.1600
Boston, MA 02116
(617)267-9191
Fax: (617)267-4293
E-mail: all@gryphoninc.com

Halpern, Denny & Co.
500 Boylston St.
Boston, MA 02116
(617)536-6602
Fax: (617)536-8535

Harbourvest Partners, LLC
1 Financial Center, 44th Fl.
Boston, MA 02111
(617)348-3707
Fax: (617)350-0305
Website: http://www.hvpllc.com

Highland Capital Partners
2 International Pl.
Boston, MA 02110
(617)981-1500
Fax: (617)531-1550
E-mail: info@hcp.com
Website: http://www.hcp.com

Lee Munder Venture Partners
John Hancock Tower T-53
200 Clarendon St.
Boston, MA 02103
(617)380-5600
Fax: (617)380-5601
Website: http://www.leemunder.com

M/C Venture Partners
75 State St., Ste. 2500
Boston, MA 02109
(617)345-7200
Fax: (617)345-7201
Website: http://
www.mcventurepartners.com

Massachusetts Capital Resources Co.
420 Boylston St.
Boston, MA 02116
(617)536-3900
Fax: (617)536-7930

Massachusetts Technology Development Corp. (MTDC)
148 State St.
Boston, MA 02109
(617)723-4920
Fax: (617)723-5983
E-mail: jhodgman@mtdc.com
Website: http://www.mtdc.com

New England Partners
One Boston Place, Ste. 2100
Boston, MA 02108
(617)624-8400
Fax: (617)624-8999
Website: http://www.nepartners.com

North Hill Ventures
Ten Post Office Square
11th Fl.
Boston, MA 02109
(617)788-2112
Fax: (617)788-2152
Website: http://
www.northhillventures.com

OneLiberty Ventures
150 Cambridge Park Dr.
Boston, MA 02140
(617)492-7280
Fax: (617)492-7290
Website: http://www.oneliberty.com

Schroder Ventures
Life Sciences
60 State St., Ste. 3650
Boston, MA 02109
(617)367-8100
Fax: (617)367-1590
Website: http://
www.shroderventures.com

Shawmut Capital Partners
75 Federal St., 18th Fl.
Boston, MA 02110
(617)368-4900
Fax: (617)368-4910
Website: http://
www.shawmutcapital.com

Solstice Capital LLC
15 Broad St., 3rd Fl.
Boston, MA 02109
(617)523-7733
Fax: (617)523-5827
E-mail: solticecapital@solcap.com

Spectrum Equity Investors
One International Pl., 29th Fl.
Boston, MA 02110
(617)464-4600
Fax: (617)464-4601
Website: http://
www.spectrumequity.com

Spray Venture Partners
One Walnut St.
Boston, MA 02108
(617)305-4140
Fax: (617)305-4144
Website: http://www.sprayventure.com

The Still River Fund
100 Federal St., 29th Fl.
Boston, MA 02110
(617)348-2327
Fax: (617)348-2371
Website: http://www.stillriverfund.com

Summit Partners
600 Atlantic Ave., Ste. 2800
Boston, MA 02210-2227
(617)824-1000
Fax: (617)824-1159
Website: http://
www.summitpartners.com

TA Associates, Inc. (Boston)
High Street Tower
125 High St., Ste. 2500
Boston, MA 02110
(617)574-6700
Fax: (617)574-6728
Website: http://www.ta.com

TVM Techno Venture Management
101 Arch St., Ste. 1950
Boston, MA 02110
(617)345-9320
Fax: (617)345-9377
E-mail: info@tvmvc.com
Website: http://www.tvmvc.com

UNC Ventures
64 Burough St.
Boston, MA 02130-4017
(617)482-7070
Fax: (617)522-2176

Venture Investment Management Company (VIMAC)
177 Milk St.
Boston, MA 02190-3410
(617)292-3300
Fax: (617)292-7979
E-mail: bzeisig@vimac.com
Website: http://www.vimac.com

MDT Advisers, Inc.
125 Cambridge Park Dr.
Cambridge, MA 02140-2314
(617)234-2200
Fax: (617)234-2210
Website: http://www.mdtai.com

TTC Ventures
One Main St., 6th Fl.
Cambridge, MA 02142
(617)528-3137
Fax: (617)577-1715
E-mail: info@ttcventures.com

Zero Stage Capital Co. Inc.
101 Main St., 17th Fl.
Cambridge, MA 02142
(617)876-5355
Fax: (617)876-1248
Website: http://www.zerostage.com

Atlantic Capital
164 Cushing Hwy.
Cohasset, MA 02025
(617)383-9449
Fax: (617)383-6040
E-mail: info@atlanticcap.com
Website: http://www.atlanticcap.com

Seacoast Capital Partners
55 Ferncroft Rd.
Danvers, MA 01923
(978)750-1300
Fax: (978)750-1301
E-mail: gdeli@seacoastcapital.com
Website: http://www.seacoastcapital.com

Sage Management Group
44 South Street
PO Box 2026
East Dennis, MA 02641
(508)385-7172
Fax: (508)385-7272
E-mail: sagemgt@capecod.net

Applied Technology
1 Cranberry Hill
Lexington, MA 02421-7397
(617)862-8622
Fax: (617)862-8367

Royalty Capital Management
5 Downing Rd.
Lexington, MA 02421-6918
(781)861-8490

Argo Global Capital
210 Broadway, Ste. 101
Lynnfield, MA 01940
(781)592-5250
Fax: (781)592-5230
Website: http://www.gsmcapital.com

Industry Ventures
6 Bayne Lane
Newburyport, MA 01950
(978)499-7606
Fax: (978)499-0686
Website: http://
www.industryventures.com

Softbank Capital Partners
10 Langley Rd., Ste. 202
Newton Center, MA 02459
(617)928-9300
Fax: (617)928-9305
E-mail: clax@bvc.com

Advanced Technology Ventures (Boston)
281 Winter St., Ste. 350
Waltham, MA 02451
(781)290-0707
Fax: (781)684-0045
E-mail: info@atvcapital.com
Website: http://www.atvcapital.com

Castile Ventures
890 Winter St., Ste. 140
Waltham, MA 02451
(781)890-0060
Fax: (781)890-0065
Website: http://www.castileventures.com

Charles River Ventures
1000 Winter St., Ste. 3300
Waltham, MA 02451
(781)487-7060
Fax: (781)487-7065
Website: http://www.crv.com

Comdisco Venture Group (Waltham)
Totton Pond Office Center
400-1 Totten Pond Rd.
Waltham, MA 02451
(617)672-0250
Fax: (617)398-8099

Marconi Ventures
890 Winter St., Ste. 310
Waltham, MA 02451
(781)839-7177
Fax: (781)522-7477
Website: http://www.marconi.com

Matrix Partners
Bay Colony Corporate Center
1000 Winter St., Ste.4500
Waltham, MA 02451
(781)890-2244
Fax: (781)890-2288
Website: http://www.matrixpartners.com

North Bridge Venture Partners
950 Winter St. Ste. 4600
Waltham, MA 02451
(781)290-0004
Fax: (781)290-0999
E-mail: eta@nbvp.com

Polaris Venture Partners
Bay Colony Corporate Ctr.
1000 Winter St., Ste. 3500
Waltham, MA 02451
(781)290-0770
Fax: (781)290-0880
E-mail: partners@polarisventures.com
Website: http://
www.polarisventures.com

Seaflower Ventures
Bay Colony Corporate Ctr.
1000 Winter St. Ste. 1000
Waltham, MA 02451
(781)466-9552
Fax: (781)466-9553
E-mail: moot@seaflower.com
Website: http://www.seaflower.com

Ampersand Ventures
55 William St., Ste. 240
Wellesley, MA 02481
(617)239-0700
Fax: (617)239-0824
E-mail: info@ampersandventures.com
Website: http://
www.ampersandventures.com

Battery Ventures (Boston)
20 William St., Ste. 200
Wellesley, MA 02481
(781)577-1000
Fax: (781)577-1001
Website: http://www.battery.com

Commonwealth Capital Ventures, L.P.
20 William St., Ste.225
Wellesley, MA 02481
(781)237-7373
Fax: (781)235-8627
Website: http://www.ccvlp.com

Fowler, Anthony & Company
20 Walnut St.
Wellesley, MA 02481
(781)237-4201
Fax: (781)237-7718

Gemini Investors
20 William St.
Wellesley, MA 02481
(781)237-7001
Fax: (781)237-7233

Grove Street Advisors Inc.
20 William St., Ste. 230
Wellesley, MA 02481
(781)263-6100
Fax: (781)263-6101
Website: http://
www.grovestreetadvisors.com

Mees Pierson Investeringsmaat B.V.
20 William St., Ste. 210
Wellesley, MA 02482
(781)239-7600
Fax: (781)239-0377

Norwest Equity Partners
40 William St., Ste. 305
Wellesley, MA 02481-3902
(781)237-5870
Fax: (781)237-6270
Website: http://www.norwestvp.com

Bessemer Venture Partners (Wellesley Hills)
83 Walnut St.
Wellesley Hills, MA 02481
(781)237-6050
Fax: (781)235-7576
E-mail: travis@bvpny.com
Website: http://www.bvp.com

Venture Capital Fund of New England
20 Walnut St., Ste. 120
Wellesley Hills, MA 02481-2175
(781)239-8262
Fax: (781)239-8263

Prism Venture Partners
100 Lowder Brook Dr., Ste. 2500
Westwood, MA 02090
(781)302-4000
Fax: (781)302-4040
E-mail: dwbaum@prismventure.com

Palmer Partners LP
200 Unicorn Park Dr.
Woburn, MA 01801
(781)933-5445
Fax: (781)933-0698

Michigan

Arbor Partners, L.L.C.
130 South First St.
Ann Arbor, MI 48104
(734)668-9000
Fax: (734)669-4195
Website: http://www.arborpartners.com

EDF Ventures
425 N. Main St.
Ann Arbor, MI 48104
(734)663-3213
Fax: (734)663-7358
E-mail: edf@edfvc.com
Website: http://www.edfvc.com

White Pines Management, L.L.C.
2401 Plymouth Rd., Ste. B
Ann Arbor, MI 48105
(734)747-9401
Fax: (734)747-9704
E-mail: ibund@whitepines.com
Website: http://www.whitepines.com

Wellmax, Inc.
3541 Bendway Blvd., Ste. 100
Bloomfield Hills, MI 48301
(248)646-3554
Fax: (248)646-6220

Venture Funding, Ltd.
Fisher Bldg.
3011 West Grand Blvd., Ste. 321
Detroit, MI 48202
(313)871-3606
Fax: (313)873-4935

Investcare Partners L.P. / GMA Capital LLC
32330 W. Twelve Mile Rd.
Farmington Hills, MI 48334
(248)489-9000
Fax: (248)489-8819
E-mail: gma@gmacapital.com
Website: http://www.gmacapital.com

Liberty Bidco Investment Corp.
30833 Northwestern Highway, Ste. 211
Farmington Hills, MI 48334
(248)626-6070
Fax: (248)626-6072

Seaflower Ventures
5170 Nicholson Rd.
PO Box 474
Fowlerville, MI 48836
(517)223-3335
Fax: (517)223-3337
E-mail: gibbons@seaflower.com
Website: http://www.seaflower.com

Ralph Wilson Equity Fund LLC
15400 E. Jefferson Ave.
Gross Pointe Park, MI 48230
(313)821-9122
Fax: (313)821-9101
Website: http://
www.RalphWilsonEquityFund.com
J. Skip Simms, President

Minnesota

Development Corp. of Austin
1900 Eighth Ave., NW
Austin, MN 55912
(507)433-0346
Fax: (507)433-0361
E-mail: dca@smig.net
Website: http://www.spamtownusa.com

Northeast Ventures Corp.
802 Alworth Bldg.
Duluth, MN 55802
(218)722-9915
Fax: (218)722-9871

Medical Innovation Partners, Inc.
6450 City West Pkwy.
Eden Prairie, MN 55344-3245
(612)828-9616
Fax: (612)828-9596

St. Paul Venture Capital, Inc.
10400 Vicking Dr., Ste. 550
Eden Prairie, MN 55344
(612)995-7474
Fax: (612)995-7475
Website: http://www.stpaulvc.com

Cherry Tree Investments, Inc.
7601 France Ave. S, Ste. 150
Edina, MN 55435
(612)893-9012
Fax: (612)893-9036
Website: http://www.cherrytree.com

Shared Ventures, Inc.
6550 York Ave. S
Edina, MN 55435
(612)925-3411

Sherpa Partners LLC
5050 Lincoln Dr., Ste. 490
Edina, MN 55436
(952)942-1070
Fax: (952)942-1071
Website: http://www.sherpapartners.com

Affinity Capital Management
901 Marquette Ave., Ste. 1810
Minneapolis, MN 55402
(612)252-9900
Fax: (612)252-9911
Website: http://www.affinitycapital.com

Artesian Capital
1700 Foshay Tower
821 Marquette Ave.
Minneapolis, MN 55402
(612)334-5600
Fax: (612)334-5601
E-mail: artesian@artesian.com

Coral Ventures
60 S. 6th St., Ste. 3510
Minneapolis, MN 55402
(612)335-8666
Fax: (612)335-8668
Website: http://www.coralventures.com

Crescendo Venture Management, L.L.C.
800 LaSalle Ave., Ste. 2250
Minneapolis, MN 55402
(612)607-2800
Fax: (612)607-2801
Website: http://
www.crescendoventures.com

Gideon Hixon Venture
1900 Foshay Tower
821 Marquette Ave.
Minneapolis, MN 55402
(612)904-2314
Fax: (612)204-0913

Norwest Equity Partners
3600 IDS Center
80 S. 8th St.
Minneapolis, MN 55402
(612)215-1600
Fax: (612)215-1601
Website: http://www.norwestvp.com

Oak Investment Partners (Minneapolis)
4550 Norwest Center
90 S. 7th St.
Minneapolis, MN 55402
(612)339-9322
Fax: (612)337-8017
Website: http://www.oakinv.com

Pathfinder Venture Capital Funds (Minneapolis)
7300 Metro Blvd., Ste. 585
Minneapolis, MN 55439
(612)835-1121
Fax: (612)835-8389
E-mail: jahrens620@aol.com

U.S. Bancorp Piper Jaffray Ventures, Inc.
800 Nicollet Mall, Ste. 800
Minneapolis, MN 55402
(612)303-5686
Fax: (612)303-1350
Website: http://
www.paperjaffreyventures.com

The Food Fund, Ltd. Partnership
5720 Smatana Dr., Ste. 300
Minnetonka, MN 55343
(612)939-3950
Fax: (612)939-8106

Mayo Medical Ventures
200 First St. SW
Rochester, MN 55905
(507)266-4586
Fax: (507)284-5410
Website: http://www.mayo.edu

Missouri

Bankers Capital Corp.
3100 Gillham Rd.
Kansas City, MO 64109
(816)531-1600
Fax: (816)531-1334

Capital for Business, Inc. (Kansas City)
1000 Walnut St., 18th Fl.
Kansas City, MO 64106
(816)234-2357
Fax: (816)234-2952
Website: http://
www.capitalforbusiness.com

De Vries & Co. Inc.
800 West 47th St.
Kansas City, MO 64112
(816)756-0055
Fax: (816)756-0061

InvestAmerica Venture Group Inc. (Kansas City)
Commerce Tower
911 Main St., Ste. 2424
Kansas City, MO 64105
(816)842-0114
Fax: (816)471-7339

Kansas City Equity Partners
233 W. 47th St.
Kansas City, MO 64112
(816)960-1771
Fax: (816)960-1777
Website: http://www.kcep.com

Bome Investors, Inc.
8000 Maryland Ave., Ste. 1190
St. Louis, MO 63105
(314)721-5707
Fax: (314)721-5135
Website: http://
www.gatewayventures.com

Capital for Business, Inc. (St. Louis)
11 S. Meramac St., Ste. 1430
St. Louis, MO 63105
(314)746-7427
Fax: (314)746-8739
Website: http://
www.capitalforbusiness.com

Crown Capital Corp.
540 Maryville Centre Dr., Ste. 120
Saint Louis, MO 63141
(314)576-1201
Fax: (314)576-1525
Website: http://www.crown-cap.com

Gateway Associates L.P.
8000 Maryland Ave., Ste. 1190
St. Louis, MO 63105
(314)721-5707
Fax: (314)721-5135

Harbison Corp.
8112 Maryland Ave., Ste. 250
Saint Louis, MO 63105
(314)727-8200
Fax: (314)727-0249

Heartland Capital Fund, Ltd.
PO Box 642117
Omaha, NE 68154
(402)778-5124
Fax: (402)445-2370
Website: http://
www.heartlandcapitalfund.com

Odin Capital Group
1625 Farnam St., Ste. 700
Omaha, NE 68102
(402)346-6200
Fax: (402)342-9311
Website: http://www.odincapital.com

Nevada

Edge Capital Investment Co. LLC
1350 E. Flamingo Rd., Ste. 3000
Las Vegas, NV 89119
(702)438-3343
E-mail: info@edgecapital.net
Website: http://www.edgecapital.net

The Benefit Capital Companies Inc.
PO Box 542
Logandale, NV 89021
(702)398-3222
Fax: (702)398-3700

Millennium Three Venture Group LLC
6880 South McCarran Blvd., Ste. A-11
Reno, NV 89509
(775)954-2020
Fax: (775)954-2023
Website: http://www.m3vg.com

New Jersey

Alan I. Goldman & Associates
497 Ridgewood Ave.
Glen Ridge, NJ 07028
(973)857-5680
Fax: (973)509-8856

CS Capital Partners LLC
328 Second St., Ste. 200
Lakewood, NJ 08701
(732)901-1111
Fax: (212)202-5071
Website: http://www.cs-capital.com

Edison Venture Fund
1009 Lenox Dr., Ste. 4
Lawrenceville, NJ 08648
(609)896-1900
Fax: (609)896-0066
E-mail: info@edisonventure.com
Website: http://www.edisonventure.com

Tappan Zee Capital Corp. (New Jersey)
201 Lower Notch Rd.
PO Box 416
Little Falls, NJ 07424
(973)256-8280
Fax: (973)256-2841

The CIT Group/Venture Capital, Inc.
650 CIT Dr.
Livingston, NJ 07039
(973)740-5429
Fax: (973)740-5555
Website: http://www.cit.com

Capital Express, L.L.C.
1100 Valleybrook Ave.
Lyndhurst, NJ 07071
(201)438-8228
Fax: (201)438-5131
E-mail: niles@capitalexpress.com
Website: http://www.capitalexpress.com

Westford Technology Ventures, L.P.
17 Academy St.
Newark, NJ 07102
(973)624-2131
Fax: (973)624-2008

Accel Partners
1 Palmer Sq.
Princeton, NJ 08542
(609)683-4500
Fax: (609)683-4880
Website: http://www.accel.com

Cardinal Partners
221 Nassau St.
Princeton, NJ 08542
(609)924-6452
Fax: (609)683-0174
Website: http://
www.cardinalhealthpartners.com

Domain Associates L.L.C.
One Palmer Sq., Ste. 515
Princeton, NJ 08542
(609)683-5656
Fax: (609)683-9789
Website: http://www.domainvc.com

Johnston Associates, Inc.
181 Cherry Valley Rd.
Princeton, NJ 08540
(609)924-3131
Fax: (609)683-7524
E-mail: jaincorp@aol.com

Kemper Ventures
Princeton Forrestal Village
155 Village Blvd.
Princeton, NJ 08540
(609)936-3035
Fax: (609)936-3051

Penny Lane Parnters
One Palmer Sq., Ste. 309
Princeton, NJ 08542
(609)497-4646
Fax: (609)497-0611

Early Stage Enterprises L.P.
995 Route 518
Skillman, NJ 08558
(609)921-8896
Fax: (609)921-8703
Website: http://www.esevc.com

MBW Management Inc.
1 Springfield Ave.
Summit, NJ 07901
(908)273-4060
Fax. (908)273-4430

BCI Advisors, Inc.
Glenpointe Center W.
Teaneck, NJ 07666
(201)836-3900
Fax: (201)836-6368
E-mail: info@bciadvisors.com
Website: http://www.bcipartners.com

Demuth, Folger & Wetherill / DFW Capital Partners
Glenpointe Center E., 5th Fl.
300 Frank W. Burr Blvd.
Teaneck, NJ 07666
(201)836-2233
Fax: (201)836-5666
Website: http://www.dfwcapital.com

First Princeton Capital Corp.
189 Berdan Ave., No. 131
Wayne, NJ 07470-3233
(973)278-3233
Fax: (973)278 4290
Website: http://www.lytellcatt.net

Edelson Technology Partners
300 Tice Blvd.
Woodcliff Lake, NJ 07675
(201)930-9898
Fax: (201)930-8899
Website: http://www.edelsontech.com

New Mexico

Bruce F. Glaspell & Associates
10400 Academy Rd. NE, Ste. 313
Albuquerque, NM 87111
(505)292-4505
Fax: (505)292-4258

High Desert Ventures, Inc.
6101 Imparata St. NE, Ste. 1721
Albuquerque, NM 87111
(505)797-3330
Fax: (505)338-5147

New Business Capital Fund, Ltd.
5805 Torreon NE
Albuquerque, NM 87109
(505)822-8445

SBC Ventures
10400 Academy Rd. NE, Ste. 313
Albuquerque, NM 87111
(505)292-4505
Fax: (505)292-4528

Technology Ventures Corp.
1155 University Blvd. SE
Albuquerque, NM 87106
(505)246-2882
Fax: (505)246-2891

New York

New York State Science & Technology Foundation
Small Business Technology Investment Fund
99 Washington Ave., Ste. 1731
Albany, NY 12210
(518)473-9741
Fax: (518)473-6876

Rand Capital Corp.
2200 Rand Bldg.
Buffalo, NY 14203
(716)853-0802
Fax: (716)854-8480
Website: http://www.randcapital.com

Seed Capital Partners
620 Main St.
Buffalo, NY 14202
(716)845-7520
Fax: (716)845-7539
Website: http://www.seedcp.com

Coleman Venture Group
5909 Northern Blvd.
PO Box 224
East Norwich, NY 11732
(516)626-3642
Fax: (516)626-9722

Vega Capital Corp.
45 Knollwood Rd.
Elmsford, NY 10523
(914)345-9500
Fax: (914)345-9505

Herbert Young Securities, Inc.
98 Cuttermill Rd.
Great Neck, NY 11021
(516)487-8300
Fax: (516)487-8319

Sterling/Carl Marks Capital, Inc.
175 Great Neck Rd., Ste. 408
Great Neck, NY 11021
(516)482-7374
Fax: (516)487-0781

E-mail: stercrlmar@aol.com
Website: http://www.serlingcarlmarks.com

Impex Venture Management Co.
PO Box 1570
Green Island, NY 12183
(518)271-8008
Fax: (518)271-9101

Corporate Venture Partners L.P.
200 Sunset Park
Ithaca, NY 14850
(607)257-6323
Fax: (607)257-6128

Arthur P. Gould & Co.
One Wilshire Dr.
Lake Success, NY 11020
(516)773-3000
Fax: (516)773-3289

Dauphin Capital Partners
108 Forest Ave.
Locust Valley, NY 11560
(516)759-3339
Fax: (516)759-3322
Website: http://www.dauphincapital.com

550 Digital Media Ventures
555 Madison Ave., 10th Fl.
New York, NY 10022
Website: http://www.550dmv.com

Aberlyn Capital Management Co., Inc.
500 Fifth Ave.
New York, NY 10110
(212)391-7750
Fax: (212)391-7762

Adler & Company
342 Madison Ave., Ste. 807
New York, NY 10173
(212)599-2535
Fax: (212)599-2526

Alimansky Capital Group, Inc.
605 Madison Ave., Ste. 300
New York, NY 10022-1901
(212)832-7300
Fax: (212)832-7338

Allegra Partners
515 Madison Ave., 29th Fl.
New York, NY 10022
(212)826-9080
Fax: (212)759-2561

The Argentum Group
The Chyrsler Bldg.
405 Lexington Ave.
New York, NY 10174
(212)949-6262
Fax: (212)949-8294
Website: http://www.argentumgroup.com

Axavision Inc.
14 Wall St., 26th Fl.
New York, NY 10005
(212)619-4000
Fax: (212)619-7202

Bedford Capital Corp.
18 East 48th St., Ste. 1800
New York, NY 10017
(212)688-5700
Fax: (212)754-4699
E-mail: info@bedfordnyc.com
Website: http://www.bedfordnyc.com

Bloom & Co.
950 Third Ave.
New York, NY 10022
(212)838-1858
Fax: (212)838-1843

Bristol Capital Management
300 Park Ave., 17th Fl.
New York, NY 10022
(212)572-6306
Fax: (212)705-4292

Citicorp Venture Capital Ltd. (New York City)
399 Park Ave., 14th Fl.
Zone 4
New York, NY 10043
(212)559-1127
Fax: (212)888-2940

CM Equity Partners
135 E. 57th St.
New York, NY 10022
(212)909-8428
Fax: (212)980-2630

Cohen & Co., L.L.C.
800 Third Ave.
New York, NY 10022
(212)317-2250
Fax: (212)317-2255
E-mail: nlcohen@aol.com

Cornerstone Equity Investors, L.L.C.
717 5th Ave., Ste. 1100
New York, NY 10022
(212)753-0901
Fax: (212)826-6798
Website: http://www.cornerstone-equity.com

CW Group, Inc.
1041 3rd Ave., 2nd fl.
New York, NY 10021
(212)308-5266
Fax: (212)644-0354
Website: http://www.cwventures.com

DH Blair Investment Banking Corp.
44 Wall St., 2nd Fl.
New York, NY 10005
(212)495-5000
Fax: (212)269-1438

Dresdner Kleinwort Capital
75 Wall St.
New York, NY 10005
(212)429-3131
Fax: (212)429-3139
Website: http://www.dresdnerkb.com

East River Ventures, L.P.
645 Madison Ave., 22nd Fl.
New York, NY 10022
(212)644-2322
Fax: (212)644-5498

Easton Hunt Capital Partners
641 Lexington Ave., 21st Fl.
New York, NY 10017
(212)702-0950
Fax: (212)702-0952
Website: http://www.eastoncapital.com

Elk Associates Funding Corp.
747 3rd Ave., Ste. 4C
New York, NY 10017
(212)355-2449
Fax: (212)759-3338

EOS Partners, L.P.
320 Park Ave., 22nd Fl.
New York, NY 10022
(212)832-5800
Fax: (212)832-5815
E-mail: mfirst@eospartners.com
Website: http://www.eospartners.com

Euclid Partners
45 Rockefeller Plaza, Ste. 3240
New York, NY 10111
(212)218-6880
Fax: (212)218-6877
E-mail: graham@euclidpartners.com
Website: http://www.euclidpartners.com

Evergreen Capital Partners, Inc.
150 East 58th St.
New York, NY 10155
(212)813-0758
Fax: (212)813-0754

Exeter Capital L.P.
10 E. 53rd St.
New York, NY 10022

(212)872-1172
Fax: (212)872-1198
E-mail: exeter@usa.net

Financial Technology Research Corp.
518 Broadway
Penthouse
New York, NY 10012
(212)625-9100
Fax: (212)431-0300
E-mail: fintek@financier.com

4C Ventures
237 Park Ave., Ste. 801
New York, NY 10017
(212)692-3680
Fax: (212)692-3685
Website: http://www.4cventures.com

Fusient Ventures
99 Park Ave., 20th Fl.
New York, NY 10016
(212)972-8999
Fax: (212)972-9876
E-mail: info@fusient.com
Website: http://www.fusient.com

Generation Capital Partners
551 Fifth Ave., Ste. 3100
New York, NY 10176
(212)450-8507
Fax: (212)450-8550
Website: http://www.genpartners.com

Golub Associates, Inc.
555 Madison Ave.
New York, NY 10022
(212)750-6060
Fax: (212)750-5505

Hambro America Biosciences Inc.
650 Madison Ave., 21st Floor
New York, NY 10022
(212)223-7400
Fax: (212)223-0305

Hanover Capital Corp.
505 Park Ave., 15th Fl.
New York, NY 10022
(212)755 1222
Fax: (212)935-1787

Harvest Partners, Inc.
280 Park Ave, 33rd Fl.
New York, NY 10017
(212)559-6300
Fax: (212)812-0100
Website: http://www.harvpart.com

Holding Capital Group, Inc.
10 E. 53rd St., 30th Fl.
New York, NY 10022
(212)486-6670
Fax: (212)486-0843

Hudson Venture Partners
660 Madison Ave., 14th Fl.
New York, NY 10021-8405
(212)644-9797
Fax: (212)644-7430
Website: http://www.hudsonptr.com

IBJS Capital Corp.
1 State St., 9th Fl.
New York, NY 10004
(212)858-2018
Fax: (212)858-2768

InterEquity Capital Partners, L.P.
220 5th Ave.
New York, NY 10001
(212)779-2022
Fax: (212)779-2103
Website: http://www.interequity-capital.com

The Jordan Edmiston Group Inc.
150 East 52nd St., 18th Fl.
New York, NY 10022
(212)754-0710
Fax: (212)754-0337

Josephberg, Grosz and Co., Inc.
633 3rd Ave., 13th Fl.
New York, NY 10017
(212)974-9926
Fax: (212)397-5832

J.P. Morgan Capital Corp.
60 Wall St.
New York, NY 10260-0060
(212)648-9000
Fax: (212)648-5002
Website: http://www.jpmorgan.com

The Lambda Funds
380 Lexington Ave., 54th Fl.
New York, NY 10168
(212)682-3454
Fax: (212)682-9231

Lepercq Capital Management Inc.
1675 Broadway
New York, NY 10019
(212)698-0795
Fax: (212)262-0155

Loeb Partners Corp.
61 Broadway, Ste. 2400
New York, NY 10006
(212)483-7000
Fax: (212)574-2001

Madison Investment Partners
660 Madison Ave.
New York, NY 10021
(212)223-2600
Fax: (212)223-8208

MC Capital Inc.
520 Madison Ave., 16th Fl.
New York, NY 10022
(212)644-0841
Fax: (212)644-2926

McCown, De Leeuw and Co. (New York)
65 E. 55th St., 36th Fl.
New York, NY 10022
(212)355-5500
Fax: (212)355-6283
Website: http://www.mdcpartners.com

Morgan Stanley Venture Partners
1221 Avenue of the Americas, 33rd Fl.
New York, NY 10020
(212)762-7900
Fax: (212)762-8424
E-mail: msventures@ms.com
Website: http://www.msvp.com

Nazem and Co.
645 Madison Ave., 12th Fl.
New York, NY 10022
(212)371-7900
Fax: (212)371-2150

Needham Capital Management, L.L.C.
445 Park Ave.
New York, NY 10022
(212)371-8300
Fax: (212)705-0299
Website: http://www.needhamco.com

Norwood Venture Corp.
1430 Broadway, Ste. 1607
New York, NY 10018
(212)869-5075
Fax: (212)869-5331
E-mail: nvc@mail.idt.net
Website: http://www.norven.com

Noveltek Venture Corp.
521 Fifth Ave., Ste. 1700
New York, NY 10175
(212)286-1963

Paribas Principal, Inc.
787 7th Ave.
New York, NY 10019
(212)841-2005
Fax: (212)841-3558

Patricof & Co. Ventures, Inc. (New York)
445 Park Ave.
New York, NY 10022

(212)753-6300
Fax: (212)319-6155
Website: http://www.patricof.com

The Platinum Group, Inc.
350 Fifth Ave, Ste. 7113
New York, NY 10118
(212)736-4300
Fax: (212)736-6086
Website: http://
www.platinumgroup.com

Pomona Capital
780 Third Ave., 28th Fl.
New York, NY 10017
(212)593-3639
Fax: (212)593-3987
Website: http://www.pomonacapital.com

Prospect Street Ventures
10 East 40th St., 44th Fl.
New York, NY 10016
(212)448-0702
Fax: (212)448-9652
E-mail: wkohler@prospectstreet.com
Website: http://www.prospectstreet.com

Regent Capital Management
505 Park Ave., Ste. 1700
New York, NY 10022
(212)735-9900
Fax: (212)735-9908

Rothschild Ventures, Inc.
1251 Avenue of the Americas, 51st Fl.
New York, NY 10020
(212)403-3500
Fax: (212)403-3652
Website: http://www.nmrothschild.com

Sandler Capital Management
767 Fifth Ave., 45th Fl.
New York, NY 10153
(212)754-8100
Fax: (212)826-0280

Siguler Guff & Company
630 Fifth Ave., 16th Fl.
New York, NY 10111
(212)332-5100
Fax: (212)332-5120

Spencer Trask Ventures Inc.
535 Madison Ave.
New York, NY 10022
(212)355-5565
Fax: (212)751-3362
Website: http://www.spencertrask.com

Sprout Group (New York City)
277 Park Ave.
New York, NY 10172
(212)892-3600
Fax: (212)892-3444
E-mail: info@sproutgroup.com
Website: http://www.sproutgroup.com

US Trust Private Equity
114 W.47th St.
New York, NY 10036
(212)852-3949
Fax: (212)852-3759
Website: http://www.ustrust.com/
privateequity

Vencon Management Inc.
301 West 53rd St., Ste. 10F
New York, NY 10019
(212)581-8787
Fax: (212)397-4126
Website: http://www.venconinc.com

Venrock Associates
30 Rockefeller Plaza, Ste. 5508
New York, NY 10112
(212)649-5600
Fax: (212)649-5788
Website: http://www.venrock.com

Venture Capital Fund of America, Inc.
509 Madison Ave., Ste. 812
New York, NY 10022
(212)838-5577
Fax: (212)838-7614
E-mail: mail@vcfa.com
Website: http://www.vcfa.com

Venture Opportunities Corp.
150 E. 58th St.
New York, NY 10155
(212)832-3737
Fax: (212)980-6603

Warburg Pincus Ventures, Inc.
466 Lexington Ave., 11th Fl.
New York, NY 10017
(212)878-9309
Fax: (212)878-9200
Website: http://www.warburgpincus.com

Wasserstein, Perella & Co. Inc.
31 W. 52nd St., 27th Fl.
New York, NY 10019
(212)702-5691
Fax: (212)969-7879

Welsh, Carson, Anderson, & Stowe
320 Park Ave., Ste. 2500
New York, NY 10022-6815
(212)893-9500
Fax: (212)893-9575

Whitney and Co. (New York)
630 Fifth Ave. Ste. 3225
New York, NY 10111
(212)332-2400
Fax: (212)332-2422
Website: http://www.jhwitney.com

Winthrop Ventures
74 Trinity Place, Ste. 600
New York, NY 10006
(212)422-0100

The Pittsford Group
8 Lodge Pole Rd.
Pittsford, NY 14534
(716)223-3523

Genesee Funding
70 Linden Oaks, 3rd Fl.
Rochester, NY 14625
(716)383-5550
Fax: (716)383-5305

Gabelli Multimedia Partners
One Corporate Center
Rye, NY 10580
(914)921-5395
Fax: (914)921-5031

Stamford Financial
108 Main St.
Stamford, NY 12167
(607)652-3311
Fax: (607)652-6301
Website: http://
www.stamfordfinancial.com

Northwood Ventures LLC
485 Underhill Blvd., Ste. 205
Syosset, NY 11791
(516)364-5544
Fax: (516)364-0879
E-mail: northwood@northwood.com
Website: http://
www.northwoodventures.com

Exponential Business Development Co.
216 Walton St.
Syracuse, NY 13202-1227
(315)474-4500
Fax: (315)474-4682
E-mail: dirksonn@aol.com
Website: http://www.exponential-ny.com

Onondaga Venture Capital Fund Inc.
714 State Tower Bldg.
Syracuse, NY 13202
(315)478-0157
Fax: (315)478-0158

Bessemer Venture Partners (Westbury)
1400 Old Country Rd., Ste. 109
Westbury, NY 11590
(516)997-2300
Fax: (516)997-2371
E-mail: bob@bvpny.com
Website: http://www.bvp.com

Ovation Capital Partners
120 Bloomingdale Rd., 4th Fl.
White Plains, NY 10605
(914)258-0011
Fax: (914)684-0848
Website: http://www.ovationcapital.com

North Carolina

Carolinas Capital Investment Corp.
1408 Biltmore Dr.
Charlotte, NC 28207
(704)375-3888
Fax: (704)375-6226

First Union Capital Partners
1st Union Center, 12th Fl.
301 S. College St.
Charlotte, NC 28288-0732
(704)383-0000
Fax: (704)374-6711
Website: http://www.fucp.com

Frontier Capital LLC
525 North Tryon St., Ste. 1700
Charlotte, NC 28202
(704)414-2880
Fax: (704)414-2881
Website: http://www.frontierfunds.com

Kitty Hawk Capital
2700 Coltsgate Rd., Ste. 202
Charlotte, NC 28211
(704)362-3909
Fax: (704)362-2774
Website: http://
www.kittyhawkcapital.com

Piedmont Venture Partners
One Morrocroft Centre
6805 Morisson Blvd., Ste. 380
Charlotte, NC 28211
(704)731-5200
Fax: (704)365-9733
Website: http://www.piedmontvp.com

Ruddick Investment Co.
1800 Two First Union Center
Charlotte, NC 28282
(704)372-5404
Fax: (704)372-6409

The Shelton Companies Inc.
3600 One First Union Center
301 S. College St.
Charlotte, NC 28202
(704)348-2200
Fax: (704)348-2260

Wakefield Group
1110 E. Morehead St.
PO Box 36329
Charlotte, NC 28236
(704)372-0355
Fax: (704)372-8216
Website: http://
www.wakefieldgroup.com

Aurora Funds, Inc.
2525 Meridian Pkwy., Ste. 220
Durham, NC 27713
(919)484-0400
Fax: (919)484-0444
Website: http://www.aurorafunds.com

Intersouth Partners
3211 Shannon Rd., Ste. 610
Durham, NC 27707
(919)493-6640
Fax: (919)493-6649
E-mail: info@intersouth.com
Website: http://www.intersouth.com

Geneva Merchant Banking Partners
PO Box 21962
Greensboro, NC 27420
(336)275-7002
Fax: (336)275-9155
Website: http://
www.genevamerchantbank.com

The North Carolina Enterprise Fund, L.P.
3600 Glenwood Ave., Ste. 107
Raleigh, NC 27612
(919)781-2691
Fax: (919)783-9195
Website: http://www.ncef.com

Ohio

Senmend Medical Ventures
4445 Lake Forest Dr., Ste. 600
Cincinnati, OH 45242
(513)563-3264
Fax: (513)563-3261

The Walnut Group
312 Walnut St., Ste. 1151
Cincinnati, OH 45202
(513)651-3300
Fax: (513)929-4441
Website: http://
www.thewalnutgroup.com

Brantley Venture Partners
20600 Chagrin Blvd., Ste. 1150
Cleveland, OH 44122
(216)283-4800
Fax: (216)283-5324

Clarion Capital Corp.
1801 E. 9th St., Ste. 1120
Cleveland, OH 44114
(216)687-1096
Fax: (216)694-3545

Crystal Internet Venture Fund, L.P.
1120 Chester Ave., Ste. 418
Cleveland, OH 44114
(216)263-5515
Fax: (216)263-5518
E-mail: jf@crystalventure.com
Website: http://www.crystalventure.com

Key Equity Capital Corp.
127 Public Sq., 28th Fl.
Cleveland, OH 44114
(216)689-3000
Fax: (216)689-3204
Website: http://www.keybank.com

Morgenthaler Ventures
Terminal Tower
50 Public Square, Ste. 2700
Cleveland, OH 44113
(216)416-7500
Fax: (216)416-7501
Website: http://www.morgenthaler.com

National City Equity Partners Inc.
1965 E. 6th St.
Cleveland, OH 44114
(216)575-2491
Fax: (216)575-9965
E-mail: nccap@aol.com
Website: http://www.nccapital.com

Primus Venture Partners, Inc.
5900 LanderBrook Dr., Ste. 2000
Cleveland, OH 44124-4020
(440)684-7300
Fax: (440)684-7342
E-mail: info@primusventure.com
Website: http://www.primusventure.com

Banc One Capital Partners (Columbus)
150 East Gay St., 24th Fl.
Columbus, OH 43215
(614)217-1100
Fax: (614)217-1217

Battelle Venture Partners
505 King Ave.
Columbus, OH 43201
(614)424-7005
Fax: (614)424-4874

Ohio Partners
62 E. Board St., 3rd Fl.
Columbus, OH 43215
(614)621-1210
Fax: (614)621-1240

Capital Technology Group, L.L.C.
400 Metro Place North, Ste. 300
Dublin, OH 43017
(614)792-6066
Fax: (614)792-6036
E-mail: info@capitaltech.com
Website: http://www.capitaltech.com

Northwest Ohio Venture Fund
4159 Holland-Sylvania R., Ste. 202
Toledo, OH 43623
(419)824-8144
Fax: (419)882-2035
E-mail: bwalsh@novf.com

Oklahoma

Moore & Associates
1000 W. Wilshire Blvd., Ste. 370
Oklahoma City, OK 73116
(405)842-3660
Fax: (405)842-3763

Chisholm Private Capital Partners
100 West 5th St., Ste. 805
Tulsa, OK 74103
(918)584-0440
Fax: (918)584-0441
Website: http://www.chisholmvc.com

Davis, Tuttle Venture Partners (Tulsa)
320 S. Boston, Ste. 1000
Tulsa, OK 74103-3703
(918)584-7272
Fax: (918)582-3404
Website: http://www.davistuttle.com

RBC Ventures
2627 E. 21st St.
Tulsa, OK 74114
(918)744-5607
Fax: (918)743-8630

Oregon

Utah Ventures II LP
10700 SW Beaverton-Hillsdale Hwy., Ste. 548
Beaverton, OR 97005
(503)574-4125
E-mail: adishlip@uven.com
Website: http://www.uven.com

Orien Ventures
14523 SW Westlake Dr.
Lake Oswego, OR 97035
(503)699-1680
Fax: (503)699-1681

OVP Venture Partners (Lake Oswego)
340 Oswego Pointe Dr., Ste. 200
Lake Oswego, OR 97034
(503)697-8766
Fax: (503)697-8863
E-mail: info@ovp.com
Website: http://www.ovp.com

Oregon Resource and Technology Development Fund
4370 NE Halsey St., Ste. 233
Portland, OR 97213-1566
(503)282-4462
Fax: (503)282-2976

Shaw Venture Partners
400 SW 6th Ave., Ste. 1100
Portland, OR 97204-1636
(503)228-4884
Fax: (503)227-2471
Website: http://www.shawventures.com

Pennsylvania

Mid-Atlantic Venture Funds
125 Goodman Dr.
Bethlehem, PA 18015
(610)865-6550
Fax: (610)865-6427
Website: http://www.mavf.com

Newspring Ventures
100 W. Elm St., Ste. 101
Conshohocken, PA 19428
(610)567-2380
Fax: (610)567-2388
Website: http://
www.newsprintventures.com

Patricof & Co. Ventures, Inc.
455 S. Gulph Rd., Ste. 410
King of Prussia, PA 19406
(610)265-0286
Fax: (610)265-4959
Website: http://www.patricof.com

Loyalhanna Venture Fund
527 Cedar Way, Ste. 104
Oakmont, PA 15139
(412)820-7035
Fax: (412)820-7036

Innovest Group Inc.
2000 Market St., Ste. 1400
Philadelphia, PA 19103
(215)564-3960
Fax: (215)569-3272

Keystone Venture Capital Management Co.
1601 Market St., Ste. 2500
Philadelphia, PA 19103
(215)241-1200
Fax: (215)241-1211
Website: http://www.keystonevc.com

Liberty Venture Partners
2005 Market St., Ste. 200
Philadelphia, PA 19103
(215)282-4484
Fax: (215)282-4485
E-mail: info@libertyvp.com
Website: http://www.libertyvp.com

Penn Janney Fund, Inc.
1801 Market St., 11th Fl.
Philadelphia, PA 19103
(215)665-4447
Fax: (215)557-0820

Philadelphia Ventures, Inc.
The Bellevue
200 S. Broad St.
Philadelphia, PA 19102
(215)732-4445
Fax: (215)732-4644

Birchmere Ventures Inc.
2000 Technology Dr.
Pittsburgh, PA 15219-3109
(412)803-8000
Fax: (412)687-8139
Website: http://www.birchmerevc.com

CEO Venture Fund
2000 Technology Dr., Ste. 160
Pittsburgh, PA 15219-3109
(412)687-3451
Fax: (412)687-8139
E-mail: ceofund@aol.com
Website: http://
www.ceoventurefund.com

Innovation Works Inc.
2000 Technology Dr., Ste. 250
Pittsburgh, PA 15219
(412)681-1520
Fax: (412)681-2625
Website: http://
www.innovationworks.org

Keystone Minority Capital Fund L.P.
1801 Centre Ave., Ste. 201
Williams Sq.
Pittsburgh, PA 15219
(412)338-2230
Fax: (412)338-2224

Mellon Ventures, Inc.
One Mellon Bank Ctr., Rm. 3500
Pittsburgh, PA 15258
(412)236-3594
Fax: (412)236-3593
Website: http://
www.mellonventures.com

Pennsylvania Growth Fund
5850 Ellsworth Ave., Ste. 303
Pittsburgh, PA 15232
(412)661-1000
Fax: (412)361-0676

Point Venture Partners
The Century Bldg.
130 Seventh St., 7th Fl.
Pittsburgh, PA 15222
(412)261-1966
Fax: (412)261-1718

Cross Atlantic Capital Partners
5 Radnor Corporate Center, Ste. 555
Radnor, PA 19087
(610)995-2650
Fax: (610)971-2062
Website: http://www.xacp.com

Meridian Venture Partners (Radnor)
The Radnor Court Bldg., Ste. 140
259 Radnor-Chester Rd.
Radnor, PA 19087
(610)254-2999
Fax: (610)254-2996
E-mail: mvpart@ix.netcom.com

TDH
919 Conestoga Rd., Bldg. 1, Ste. 301
Rosemont, PA 19010
(610)526-9970
Fax: (610)526-9971

Adams Capital Management
500 Blackburn Ave.
Sewickley, PA 15143
(412)749-9454
Fax: (412)749-9459
Website: http://www.acm.com

S.R. One, Ltd.
Four Tower Bridge
200 Barr Harbor Dr., Ste. 250
W. Conshohocken, PA 19428
(610)567-1000
Fax: (610)567-1039

Greater Philadelphia Venture Capital Corp.
351 East Conestoga Rd.
Wayne, PA 19087
(610)688-6829
Fax: (610)254-8958

PA Early Stage
435 Devon Park Dr., Bldg. 500, Ste. 510
Wayne, PA 19087
(610)293-4075
Fax: (610)254-4240
Website: http://www.paearlystage.com

The Sandhurst Venture Fund, L.P.
351 E. Constoga Rd.
Wayne, PA 19087
(610)254-8900
Fax: (610)254-8958

TL Ventures
700 Bldg.
435 Devon Park Dr.
Wayne, PA 19087-1990
(610)975-3765
Fax: (610)254-4210
Website: http://www.tlventures.com

Rockhill Ventures, Inc.
100 Front St., Ste. 1350
West Conshohocken, PA 19428
(610)940-0300
Fax: (610)940-0301

Puerto Rico

Advent-Morro Equity Partners
Banco Popular Bldg.
206 Tetuan St., Ste. 903
San Juan, PR 00902
(787)725-5285
Fax: (787)721-1735

North America Investment Corp.
Mercantil Plaza, Ste. 813
PO Box 191831
San Juan, PR 00919
(787)754-6178
Fax: (787)754-6181

Rhode Island

Manchester Humphreys, Inc.
40 Westminster St., Ste. 900
Providence, RI 02903
(401)454-0400
Fax: (401)454-0403

Navis Partners
50 Kennedy Plaza, 12th Fl.
Providence, RI 02903
(401)278-6770
Fax: (401)278-6387
Website: http://www.navispartners.com

South Carolina

Capital Insights, L.L.C.
PO Box 27162
Greenville, SC 29616-2162
(864)242-6832
Fax: (864)242-6755
E-mail: jwarner@capitalinsights.com
Website: http://www.capitalinsights.com

Transamerica Mezzanine Financing
7 N. Laurens St., Ste. 603
Greenville, SC 29601
(864)232-6198
Fax: (864)241-4444

Tennessee

Valley Capital Corp.
Krystal Bldg.
100 W. Martin Luther King Blvd., Ste. 212
Chattanooga, TN 37402
(423)265-1557
Fax: (423)265-1588

Coleman Swenson Booth Inc.
237 2nd Ave. S
Franklin, TN 37064-2649
(615)791-9462
Fax: (615)791-9636
Website: http://
www.colemanswenson.com

Capital Services & Resources, Inc.
5159 Wheelis Dr., Ste. 106
Memphis, TN 38117
(901)761-2156
Fax: (907)767-0060

Paradigm Capital Partners LLC
6410 Poplar Ave., Ste. 395
Memphis, TN 38119
(901)682-6060
Fax: (901)328-3061

SSM Ventures
845 Crossover Ln., Ste. 140
Memphis, TN 38117
(901)767-1131
Fax: (901)767-1135
Website: http://www.ssmventures.com

Capital Across America L.P.
501 Union St., Ste. 201
Nashville, TN 37219
(615)254-1414
Fax: (615)254-1856
Website: http://
www.capitalacrossamerica.com

Equitas L.P.
2000 Glen Echo Rd., Ste. 101
PO Box 158838
Nashville, TN 37215-8838
(615)383-8673
Fax: (615)383-8693

Massey Burch Capital Corp.
One Burton Hills Blvd., Ste. 350
Nashville, TN 37215
(615)665-3221
Fax: (615)665-3240
E-mail: tcalton@masseyburch.com
Website: http://www.masseyburch.com

Nelson Capital Corp.
3401 West End Ave., Ste. 300
Nashville, TN 37203
(615)292-8787
Fax: (615)385-3150

Texas

Phillips-Smith Specialty Retail Group
5080 Spectrum Dr., Ste. 805 W
Addison, TX 75001
(972)387-0725
Fax: (972)458-2560
E-mail: pssrg@aol.com
Website: http://www.phillips-smith.com

Austin Ventures, L.P.
701 Brazos St., Ste. 1400
Austin, TX 78701
(512)485-1900
Fax: (512)476-3952
E-mail: info@ausven.com
Website: http://www.austinventures.com

The Capital Network
3925 West Braker Lane, Ste. 406
Austin, TX 78759-5321
(512)305-0826
Fax: (512)305-0836

Techxas Ventures LLC
5000 Plaza on the Lake
Austin, TX 78746
(512)343-0118
Fax: (512)343-1879
E-mail: bruce@techxas.com
Website: http://www.techxas.com

Alliance Financial of Houston
218 Heather Ln.
Conroe, TX 77385-9013
(936)447-3300
Fax: (936)447-4222

Amerimark Capital Corp.
1111 W. Mockingbird, Ste. 1111
Dallas, TX 75247
(214)638-7878
Fax: (214)638-7612
E-mail: amerimark@amcapital.com
Website: http://www.amcapital.com

AMT Venture Partners / AMT Capital Ltd.
5220 Spring Valley Rd., Ste. 600
Dallas, TX 75240
(214)905-9757
Fax: (214)905-9761
Website: http://www.amtcapital.com

Arkoma Venture Partners
5950 Berkshire Lane, Ste. 1400
Dallas, TX 75225
(214)739-3515
Fax: (214)739-3572
E-mail: joelf@arkomavp.com

Capital Southwest Corp.
12900 Preston Rd., Ste. 700
Dallas, TX 75230
(972)233-8242
Fax: (972)233-7362
Website: http://
www.capitalsouthwest.com

Dali, Hook Partners
One Lincoln Center, Ste. 1550
5400 LBJ Freeway
Dallas, TX 75240
(972)991-5457
Fax: (972)991-5458
E-mail: dhook@hookpartners.com
Website: http://www.hookpartners.com

HO2 Partners
Two Galleria Tower
13455 Noel Rd., Ste. 1670
Dallas, TX 75240
(972)702-1144
Fax: (972)702-8234
Website: http://www.ho2.com

Interwest Partners (Dallas)
2 Galleria Tower
13455 Noel Rd., Ste. 1670
Dallas, TX 75240
(972)392-7279
Fax: (972)490-6348
Website: http://www.interwest.com

Kahala Investments, Inc.
8214 Westchester Dr., Ste. 715
Dallas, TX 75225
(214)987-0077
Fax: (214)987-2332

MESBIC Ventures Holding Co.
2435 North Central Expressway, Ste. 200
Dallas, TX 75080
(972)991-1597
Fax: (972)991-4770
Website: http://www.mvhc.com

North Texas MESBIC, Inc.
9500 Forest Lane, Ste. 430
Dallas, TX 75243
(214)221-3565
Fax: (214)221-3566

Richard Jaffe & Company, Inc,
7318 Royal Cir.
Dallas, TX 75230
(214)265-9397
Fax: (214)739-1845

Sevin Rosen Management Co.
13455 Noel Rd., Ste. 1670
Dallas, TX 75240
(972)702-1100
Fax: (972)702-1103
E-mail: info@srfunds.com
Website: http://www.srfunds.com

Stratford Capital Partners, L.P.
300 Crescent Ct., Ste. 500
Dallas, TX 75201
(214)740-7377
Fax: (214)720-7393
E-mail: stratcap@hmtf.com

Sunwestern Investment Group
12221 Merit Dr., Ste. 935
Dallas, TX 75251
(972)239-5650
Fax: (972)701-0024

Wingate Partners
750 N. St. Paul St., Ste. 1200
Dallas, TX 75201
(214)720-1313
Fax: (214)871-8799

Buena Venture Associates
201 Main St., 32nd Fl.
Fort Worth, TX 76102
(817)339-7400
Fax: (817)390-8408
Website: http://www.buenaventure.com

The Catalyst Group
3 Riverway, Ste. 770
Houston, TX 77056
(713)623-8133
Fax: (713)623-0473
E-mail: herman@thecatalystgroup.net
Website: http://
www.thecatalystgroup.net

Cureton & Co., Inc.
1100 Louisiana, Ste. 3250
Houston, TX 77002
(713)658-9806
Fax: (713)658-0476

Davis, Tuttle Venture Partners (Dallas)
8 Greenway Plaza, Ste. 1020
Houston, TX 77046
(713)993-0440
Fax: (713)621-2297
Website: http://www.davistuttle.com

Houston Partners
401 Louisiana, 8th Fl.
Houston, TX 77002
(713)222-8600
Fax: (713)222-8932

Southwest Venture Group
10878 Westheimer, Ste. 178
Houston, TX 77042
(713)827-8947
(713)461-1470

AM Fund
4600 Post Oak Place, Ste. 100
Houston, TX 77027
(713)627-9111
Fax: (713)627-9119

Ventex Management, Inc.
3417 Milam St.
Houston, TX 77002-9531
(713)659-7870
Fax: (713)659-7855

MBA Venture Group
1004 Olde Town Rd., Ste. 102
Irving, TX 75061
(972)986-6703

First Capital Group Management Co.
750 East Mulberry St., Ste. 305
PO Box 15616
San Antonio, TX 78212
(210)736-4233
Fax: (210)736-5449

The Southwest Venture Partnerships
16414 San Pedro, Ste. 345
San Antonio, TX 78232
(210)402-1200
Fax: (210)402-1221
E-mail: swvp@aol.com

Medtech International Inc.
1742 Carriageway
Sugarland, TX 77478
(713)980-8474
Fax: (713)980-6343

Utah

First Security Business Investment Corp.
15 East 100 South, Ste. 100
Salt Lake City, UT 84111
(801)246-5737
Fax: (801)246-5740

Utah Ventures II, L.P.
423 Wakara Way, Ste. 206
Salt Lake City, UT 84108
(801)583-5922
Fax: (801)583-4105
Website: http://www.uven.com

Wasatch Venture Corp.
1 S. Main St., Ste. 1400
Salt Lake City, UT 84133
(801)524-8939
Fax: (801)524-8941
E-mail: mail@wasatchvc.com

Vermont

North Atlantic Capital Corp.
76 Saint Paul St., Ste. 600
Burlington, VT 05401
(802)658-7820
Fax: (802)658-5757
Website: http://
www.northatlanticcapital.com

Green Mountain Advisors Inc.
PO Box 1230
Quechee, VT 05059
(802)296-7800
Fax: (802)296-6012
Website: http://www.gmtcap.com

Virginia

Oxford Financial Services Corp.
Alexandria, VA 22314
(703)519-4900
Fax: (703)519-4910
E-mail: oxford133@aol.com

Continental SBIC
4141 N. Henderson Rd.
Arlington, VA 22203
(703)527-5200
Fax: (703)527-3700

Novak Biddle Venture Partners
1750 Tysons Blvd., Ste. 1190
McLean, VA 22102
(703)847-3770
Fax: (703)847-3771
E-mail: roger@novakbiddle.com
Website: http://www.novakbiddle.com

Spacevest
11911 Freedom Dr., Ste. 500
Reston, VA 20190
(703)904-9800
Fax: (703)904-0571
E-mail: spacevest@spacevest.com
Website: http://www.spacevest.com

Virginia Capital
1801 Libbie Ave., Ste. 201
Richmond, VA 23226
(804)648-4802
Fax: (804)648-4809
E-mail: webmaster@vacapital.com
Website: http://www.vacapital.com

Calvert Social Venture Partners
402 Maple Ave. W
Vienna, VA 22180
(703)255-4930
Fax: (703)255-4931
E-mail: calven2000@aol.com

Fairfax Partners
8000 Towers Crescent Dr., Ste. 940
Vienna, VA 22182
(703)847-9486
Fax: (703)847-0911

Global Internet Ventures
8150 Leesburg Pike, Ste. 1210
Vienna, VA 22182
(703)442-3300
Fax: (703)442-3388
Website: http://www.givinc.com

Walnut Capital Corp. (Vienna)
8000 Towers Crescent Dr., Ste. 1070
Vienna, VA 22182
(703)448-3771
Fax: (703)448-7751

Washington

Encompass Ventures
777 108th Ave. NE, Ste. 2300
Bellevue, WA 98004
(425)486-3900
Fax: (425)486-3901
E-mail: info@evpartners.com
Website: http://
www.encompassventures.com

Fluke Venture Partners
11400 SE Sixth St., Ste. 230
Bellevue, WA 98004
(425)453-4590
Fax: (425)453-4675
E-mail: gabelein@flukeventures.com
Website: http://www.flukeventures.com

Pacific Northwest Partners SBIC, L.P.
15352 SE 53rd St.
Bellevue, WA 98006
(425)455-9967
Fax: (425)455-9404

Materia Venture Associates, L.P.
3435 Carillon Pointe
Kirkland, WA 98033-7354
(425)822-4100
Fax: (425)827-4086

OVP Venture Partners (Kirkland)
2420 Carillon Pt.
Kirkland, WA 98033
(425)889-9192
Fax: (425)889-0152
E-mail: info@ovp.com
Website: http://www.ovp.com

Digital Partners
999 3rd Ave., Ste. 1610
Seattle, WA 98104
(206)405-3607
Fax: (206)405-3617
Website: http://www.digitalpartners.com

Frazier & Company
601 Union St., Ste. 3300
Seattle, WA 98101
(206)621-7200
Fax: (206)621-1848
E-mail: jon@frazierco.com

Kirlan Venture Capital, Inc.
221 First Ave. W, Ste. 108
Seattle, WA 98119-4223
(206)281-8610
Fax: (206)285-3451
Website: http://www.kirlanventure.com

Phoenix Partners
1000 2nd Ave., Ste. 3600
Seattle, WA 98104
(206)624-8968
Fax: (206)624-1907

Voyager Capital
800 5th St., Ste. 4100
Seattle, WA 98103
(206)470-1180
Fax: (206)470-1185
E-mail: info@voyagercap.com
Website: http://www.voyagercap.com

Northwest Venture Associates
221 N. Wall St., Ste. 628
Spokane, WA 99201
(509)747-0728
Fax: (509)747-0758
Website: http://www.nwva.com

Wisconsin

Venture Investors Management, L.L.C.
University Research Park
505 S. Rosa Rd.
Madison, WI 53719
(608)441-2700
Fax: (608)441-2727
E-mail: roger@ventureinvestors.com
Website: http://www.ventureinvesters.com

Capital Investments, Inc.
1009 West Glen Oaks Lane, Ste. 103
Mequon, WI 53092
(414)241-0303
Fax: (414)241-8451
Website: http://
www.capitalinvestmentsinc.com

Future Value Venture, Inc.
2745 N. Martin Luther King Dr., Ste. 204
Milwaukee, WI 53212-2300
(414)264-2252
Fax: (414)264-2253
E-mail: fvvventures@aol.com
William Beckett, President

Lubar and Co., Inc.
700 N. Water St., Ste. 1200
Milwaukee, WI 53202
(414)291-9000
Fax: (414)291-9061

GCI
20875 Crossroads Cir., Ste. 100
Waukesha, WI 53186
(262)798-5080
Fax: (262)798-5087

Glossary of Small Business Terms

Absolute liability
Liability that is incurred due to product defects or negligent actions. Manufacturers or retail establishments are held responsible, even though the defect or action may not have been intentional or negligent.

ACE
See Active Corps of Executives

Accident and health benefits
Benefits offered to employees and their families in order to offset the costs associated with accidental death, accidental injury, or sickness.

Account statement
A record of transactions, including payments, new debt, and deposits, incurred during a defined period of time.

Accounting system
System capturing the costs of all employees and/or machinery included in business expenses.

Accounts payable
See Trade credit

Accounts receivable
Unpaid accounts which arise from unsettled claims and transactions from the sale of a company's products or services to its customers.

Active Corps of Executives (ACE)
A group of volunteers for a management assistance program of the U.S. Small Business Administration; volunteers provide one-on-one counseling and teach workshops and seminars for small firms.

ADA
See Americans with Disabilities Act

Adaptation
The process whereby an invention is modified to meet the needs of users.

Adaptive engineering
The process whereby an invention is modified to meet the manufacturing and commercial requirements of a targeted market.

Adverse selection
The tendency for higher-risk individuals to purchase health care and more comprehensive plans, resulting in increased costs.

Advertising
A marketing tool used to capture public attention and influence purchasing decisions for a product or service. Utilizes various forms of media to generate consumer response, such as flyers, magazines, newspapers, radio, and television.

Age discrimination
The denial of the rights and privileges of employment based solely on the age of an individual.

Agency costs
Costs incurred to insure that the lender or investor maintains control over assets while allowing the borrower or entrepreneur to use them. Monitoring and information costs are the two major types of agency costs.

Agribusiness
The production and sale of commodities and products from the commercial farming industry.

America Online
An online service which is accessible by computer modem. The service features Internet access, bulletin boards, online periodicals, electronic mail, and other services for subscribers.

Americans with Disabilities Act (ADA)
Law designed to ensure equal access and opportunity to handicapped persons.

Annual report
Yearly financial report prepared by a business that adheres to the requirements set forth by the Securities and Exchange Commission (SEC).

Antitrust immunity
Exemption from prosecution under antitrust laws. In the transportation industry, firms with antitrust immunity are permitted under certain conditions to set schedules and sometimes prices for the public benefit.

Applied research
Scientific study targeted for use in a product or process.

Asians
A minority category used by the U.S. Bureau of the Census to represent a diverse group that includes Aleuts, Eskimos, American Indians, Asian Indians, Chinese, Japanese, Koreans, Vietnamese, Filipinos, Hawaiians, and other Pacific Islanders.

Assets
Anything of value owned by a company.

Audit
The verification of accounting records and business procedures conducted by an outside accounting service.

Average cost
Total production costs divided by the quantity produced.

Balance Sheet
A financial statement listing the total assets and liabilities of a company at a given time.

Bankruptcy
The condition in which a business cannot meet its debt obligations and petitions a federal district court either for reorganization of its debts (Chapter 11) or for liquidation of its assets (Chapter 7).

Basic research
Theoretical scientific exploration not targeted to application.

Basket clause
A provision specifying the amount of public pension funds that may be placed in investments not included on a state's legal list (see separate citation).

BBS
See Bulletin Board Service

BDC
See Business development corporation

Benefit
Various services, such as health care, flextime, day care, insurance, and vacation, offered to employees as part of a hiring package. Typically subsidized in whole or in part by the business.

BIDCO
See Business and industrial development company

Billing cycle
A system designed to evenly distribute customer billing throughout the month, preventing clerical backlogs.

Birth
See Business birth

Blue chip security
A low-risk, low-yield security representing an interest in a very stable company.

Blue sky laws
A general term that denotes various states' laws regulating securities.

Bond
A written instrument executed by a bidder or contractor (the principal) and a second party (the surety or sureties) to assure fulfillment of the principal's obligations to a third party (the obligee or government) identified in the bond. If the principal's obligations are not met, the bond assures payment to the extent stipulated of any loss sustained by the obligee.

Bonding requirements
Terms contained in a bond (see separate citation).

Bonus
An amount of money paid to an employee as a reward for achieving certain business goals or objectives.

Brainstorming
A group session where employees contribute their ideas for solving a problem or meeting a company objective without fear of retribution or ridicule.

Brand name
The part of a brand, trademark, or service mark that can be spoken. It can be a word, letter, or group of words or letters.

Bridge financing
A short-term loan made in expectation of intermediateterm or long-term financing. Can be used when a company plans to go public in the near future.

Broker
One who matches resources available for innovation with those who need them.

Budget
An estimate of the spending necessary to complete a project or offer a service in comparison to cash-on-hand and expected earnings for the coming year, with an emphasis on cost control.

Bulletin Board Service (BBS)
An online service enabling users to communicate with each other about specific topics.

Business and industrial development company (BIDCO)
A private, for-profit financing corporation chartered by the state to provide both equity and long-term debt capital to small business owners (see separate citations for equity and debt capital).

Business birth
The formation of a new establishment or enterprise. The appearance of a new establishment or enterprise in the Small Business Data Base (see separate citation).

Business conditions
Outside factors that can affect the financial performance of a business.

Business contractions
The number of establishments that have decreased in employment during a specified time.

Business cycle
A period of economic recession and recovery. These cycles vary in duration.

Business death
The voluntary or involuntary closure of a firm or establishment. The disappearance of an establishment or enterprise from the Small Business Data Base (see separate citation).

Business development corporation (BDC)
A business financing agency, usually composed of the financial institutions in an area or state, organized to assist in financing businesses unable to obtain assistance through normal channels; the risk is spread among various members of the business development corporation, and interest rates may vary somewhat from those charged by member institutions. A venture capital firm in which shares of ownership are publicly held and to which the Investment Act of 1940 applies.

Business dissolution
For enumeration purposes, the absence of a business that was present in the prior time period from any current record.

Business entry
See Business birth

Business ethics
Moral values and principles espoused by members of the business community as a guide to fair and honest business practices.

Business exit
See Business death

Business expansions
The number of establishments that added employees during a specified time.

Business failure
Closure of a business causing a loss to at least one creditor.

Business format franchising
The purchase of the name, trademark, and an ongoing business plan of the parent corporation or franchisor by the franchisee.

Business license
A legal authorization issued by municipal and state governments and required for business operations.

Business name
Enterprises must register their business names with local governments usually on a "doing business as" (DBA) form. (This name is sometimes referred to as a

"fictional name.") The procedure is part of the business licensing process and prevents any other business from using that same name for a similar business in the same locality.

Business norms
See Financial ratios

Business permit
See Business license

Business plan
A document that spells out a company's expected course of action for a specified period, usually including a detailed listing and analysis of risks and uncertainties. For the small business, it should examine the proposed products, the market, the industry, the management policies, the marketing policies, production needs, and financial needs. Frequently, it is used as a prospectus for potential investors and lenders.

Business proposal
See Business plan

Business service firm
An establishment primarily engaged in rendering services to other business organizations on a fee or contract basis.

Business start
For enumeration purposes, a business with a name or similar designation that did not exist in a prior time period.

Cafeteria plan
See Flexible benefit plan

Capacity
Level of a firm's, industry's, or nation's output corresponding to full practical utilization of available resources.

Capital
Assets less liabilities, representing the ownership interest in a business. A stock of accumulated goods, especially at a specified time and in contrast to income received during a specified time period. Accumulated goods devoted to production. Accumulated possessions calculated to bring income.

Capital expenditure
Expenses incurred by a business for improvements that will depreciate over time.

Capital gain
The monetary difference between the purchase price and the selling price of capital. Capital gains are taxed at a rate of 28% by the federal government.

Capital intensity
The relative importance of capital in the production process, usually expressed as the ratio of capital to labor but also sometimes as the ratio of capital to output.

Capital resource
The equipment, facilities and labor used to create products and services.

Caribbean Basin Initiative
An interdisciplinary program to support commerce among the businesses in the nations of the Caribbean Basin and the United States. Agencies involved include: the Agency for International Development, the U.S. Small Business Administration, the International Trade Administration of the U.S. Department of Commerce, and various private sector groups.

Catastrophic care
Medical and other services for acute and long-term illnesses that cost more than insurance coverage limits or that cost the amount most families may be expected to pay with their own resources.

CDC
See Certified development corporation

CD-ROM
Compact disc with read-only memory used to store large amounts of digitized data.

Certified development corporation (CDC)
A local area or statewide corporation or authority (for profit or nonprofit) that packages U.S. Small Business Administration (SBA), bank, state, and/or private money into financial assistance for existing business capital improvements. The SBA holds the second lien on its maximum share of 40 percent involvement. Each state has at least one certified development corporation. This program is called the SBA 504 Program.

Certified lenders
Banks that participate in the SBA guaranteed loan program (see separate citation). Such banks must have a good track record with the U.S. Small Business Administration (SBA) and must agree to certain conditions set forth by the agency. In return, the SBA agrees to process any guaranteed loan application within three business days.

Champion
An advocate for the development of an innovation.

Channel of distribution
The means used to transport merchandise from the manufacturer to the consumer.

Chapter 7 of the 1978 Bankruptcy Act
Provides for a court-appointed trustee who is responsible for liquidating a company's assets in order to settle outstanding debts.

Chapter 11 of the 1978 Bankruptcy Act
Allows the business owners to retain control of the company while working with their creditors to reorganize their finances and establish better business practices to prevent liquidation of assets.

Closely held corporation
A corporation in which the shares are held by a few persons, usually officers, employees, or others close to the management; these shares are rarely offered to the public.

Code of Federal Regulations
Codification of general and permanent rules of the federal government published in the Federal Register.

Code sharing
See Computer code sharing

Coinsurance
Upon meeting the deductible payment, health insurance participants may be required to make additional health care cost-sharing payments. Coinsurance is a payment of a fixed percentage of the cost of each service; copayment is usually a fixed amount to be paid with each service.

Collateral
Securities, evidence of deposit, or other property pledged by a borrower to secure repayment of a loan.

Collective ratemaking
The establishment of uniform charges for services by a group of businesses in the same industry.

Commercial insurance plan
See Underwriting

Commercial loans
Short-term renewable loans used to finance specific capital needs of a business.

Commercialization
The final stage of the innovation process, including production and distribution.

Common stock
The most frequently used instrument for purchasing ownership in private or public companies. Common stock generally carries the right to vote on certain corporate actions and may pay dividends, although it rarely does in venture investments. In liquidation, common stockholders are the last to share in the proceeds from the sale of a corporation's assets; bondholders and preferred shareholders have priority. Common stock is often used in firstround start-up financing.

Community development corporation
A corporation established to develop economic programs for a community and, in most cases, to provide financial support for such development.

Competitor
A business whose product or service is marketed for the same purpose/use and to the same consumer group as the product or service of another.

Computer code sharing
An arrangement whereby flights of a regional airline are identified by the two-letter code of a major carrier in the computer reservation system to help direct passengers to new regional carriers.

Consignment
A merchandising agreement, usually referring to secondhand shops, where the dealer pays the owner of an item a percentage of the profit when the item is sold.

Consortium
A coalition of organizations such as banks and corporations for ventures requiring large capital resources.

Consultant
An individual that is paid by a business to provide advice and expertise in a particular area.

Consumer price index
A measure of the fluctuation in prices between two points in time.

Consumer research
Research conducted by a business to obtain information about existing or potential consumer markets.

Continuation coverage
Health coverage offered for a specified period of time to employees who leave their jobs and to their widows, divorced spouses, or dependents.

Contractions
See Business contractions

Convertible preferred stock
A class of stock that pays a reasonable dividend and is convertible into common stock (see separate citation). Generally the convertible feature may only be exercised after being held for a stated period of time. This arrangement is usually considered second-round financing when a company needs equity to maintain its cash flow.

Convertible securities
A feature of certain bonds, debentures, or preferred stocks that allows them to be exchanged by the owner for another class of securities at a future date and in accordance with any other terms of the issue.

Copayment
See Coinsurance

Copyright
A legal form of protection available to creators and authors to safeguard their works from unlawful use or claim of ownership by others. Copyrights may be acquired for works of art, sculpture, music, and published or unpublished manuscripts. All copyrights should be registered at the Copyright Office of the Library of Congress.

Corporate financial ratios
The relationship between key figures found in a company's financial statement expressed as a numeric value. Used to evaluate risk and company performance. Also known as Financial averages, Operating ratios, and Business ratios.

Corporation
A legal entity, chartered by a state or the federal government, recognized as a separate entity having its own rights, privileges, and liabilities distinct from those of its members.

Cost containment
Actions taken by employers and insurers to curtail rising health care costs; for example, increasing employee cost sharing (see separate citation), requiring second opinions, or preadmission screening.

Cost sharing
The requirement that health care consumers contribute to their own medical care costs through deductibles and coinsurance (see separate citations). Cost sharing does not include the amounts paid in premiums. It is used to control utilization of services; for example, requiring a fixed amount to be paid with each health care service.

Cottage industry
Businesses based in the home in which the family members are the labor force and family-owned equipment is used to process the goods.

Credit Rating
A letter or number calculated by an organization (such as Dun & Bradstreet) to represent the ability and disposition of a business to meet its financial obligations.

Customer service
Various techniques used to ensure the satisfaction of a customer.

Cyclical peak
The upper turning point in a business cycle.

Cyclical trough
The lower turning point in a business cycle.

DBA
See Business name

Death
See Business death

Debenture
A certificate given as acknowledgment of a debt (see separate citation) secured by the general credit of the issuing corporation. A bond, usually without security, issued by a corporation and sometimes convertible to common stock.

Debt
Something owed by one person to another. Financing in which a company receives capital that must be repaid; no ownership is transferred.

Debt capital
Business financing that normally requires periodic interest payments and repayment of the principal within a specified time.

Debt financing
See Debt capital

Debt securities
Loans such as bonds and notes that provide a specified rate of return for a specified period of time.

Deductible
A set amount that an individual must pay before any benefits are received.

Demand shock absorbers
A term used to describe the role that some small firms play by expanding their output levels to accommodate a transient surge in demand.

Demographics
Statistics on various markets, including age, income, and education, used to target specific products or services to appropriate consumer groups.

Demonstration
Showing that a product or process has been modified sufficiently to meet the needs of users.

Deregulation
The lifting of government restrictions; for example, the lifting of government restrictions on the entry of new businesses, the expansion of services, and the setting of prices in particular industries.

Desktop Publishing
Using personal computers and specialized software to produce camera-ready copy for publications.

Disaster loans
Various types of physical and economic assistance available to individuals and businesses through the U.S. Small Business Administration (SBA). This is the only SBA loan program available for residential purposes.

Discrimination
The denial of the rights and privileges of employment based on factors such as age, race, religion, or gender.

Diseconomies of scale
The condition in which the costs of production increase faster than the volume of production.

Dissolution
See Business dissolution

Distribution
Delivering a product or process to the user.

Distributor
One who delivers merchandise to the user.

Diversified company
A company whose products and services are used by several different markets.

Doing business as (DBA)
See Business name

Dow Jones
An information services company that publishes the Wall Street Journal and other sources of financial information.

Dow Jones Industrial Average
An indicator of stock market performance.

Earned income
A tax term that refers to wages and salaries earned by the recipient, as opposed to monies earned through interest and dividends.

Economic efficiency
The use of productive resources to the fullest practical extent in the provision of the set of goods and services that is most preferred by purchasers in the economy.

Economic indicators
Statistics used to express the state of the economy. These include the length of the average work week, the rate of unemployment, and stock prices.

Economically disadvantaged
See Socially and economically disadvantaged

Economies of scale
See Scale economies

EEOC
See Equal Employment Opportunity Commission

8(a) Program
A program authorized by the Small Business Act that directs federal contracts to small businesses owned and operated by socially and economically disadvantaged individuals.

Electronic mail (e-mail)
The electronic transmission of mail via phone lines.

E-mail
See Electronic mail

Employee leasing
A contract by which employers arrange to have their workers hired by a leasing company and then leased back to them for a management fee. The leasing company typically assumes the administrative burden of payroll and provides a benefit package to the workers.

Employee tenure
The length of time an employee works for a particular employer.

Employer identification number
The business equivalent of a social security number. Assigned by the U.S. Internal Revenue Service.

Enterprise
An aggregation of all establishments owned by a parent company. An enterprise may consist of a single, independent establishment or include subsidiaries and other branches under the same ownership and control.

Enterprise zone
A designated area, usually found in inner cities and other areas with significant unemployment, where businesses receive tax credits and other incentives to entice them to establish operations there.

Entrepreneur
A person who takes the risk of organizing and operating a new business venture.

Entry
See Business entry

Equal Employment Opportunity Commission (EEOC)
A federal agency that ensures nondiscrimination in the hiring and firing practices of a business.

Equal opportunity employer
An employer who adheres to the standards set by the Equal Employment Opportunity Commission (see separate citation).

Equity
The ownership interest. Financing in which partial or total ownership of a company is surrendered in exchange for capital. An investor's financial return comes from dividend payments and from growth in the net worth of the business.

Equity capital
See Equity; Equity midrisk venture capital

Equity financing
See Equity; Equity midrisk venture capital

Equity midrisk venture capital
An unsecured investment in a company. Usually a purchase of ownership interest in a company that occurs in the later stages of a company's development.

Equity partnership
A limited partnership arrangement for providing start-up and seed capital to businesses.

Equity securities
See Equity

Equity-type
Debt financing subordinated to conventional debt.

Establishment
A single-location business unit that may be independent (a single-establishment enterprise) or owned by a parent enterprise.

Establishment and Enterprise Microdata File
See U.S. Establishment and Enterprise Microdata File

Establishment birth
See Business birth

Establishment Longitudinal Microdata File
See U.S. Establishment Longitudinal Microdata File

Ethics
See Business ethics

Evaluation
Determining the potential success of translating an invention into a product or process.

Exit
See Business exit

Experience rating
See Underwriting

Export
A product sold outside of the country.

Export license
A general or specific license granted by the U.S. Department of Commerce required of anyone wishing to export goods. Some restricted articles need approval from the U.S. Departments of State, Defense, or Energy.

Failure
See Business failure

Fair share agreement
An agreement reached between a franchisor and a minority business organization to extend business ownership to minorities by either reducing the amount of capital required or by setting aside certain marketing areas for minority business owners.

Feasibility study
A study to determine the likelihood that a proposed product or development will fulfill the objectives of a particular investor.

Federal Trade Commission (FTC)
Federal agency that promotes free enterprise and competition within the U.S.

Federal Trade Mark Act of 1946
See Lanham Act

Fictional name
See Business name

Fiduciary
An individual or group that hold assets in trust for a beneficiary.

Financial analysis
The techniques used to determine money needs in a business. Techniques include ratio analysis, calculation of return on investment, guides for measuring profitability, and break-even analysis to determine ultimate success.

Financial intermediary
A financial institution that acts as the intermediary between borrowers and lenders. Banks, savings and loan associations, finance companies, and venture capital companies are major financial intermediaries in the United States.

Financial ratios
See Corporate financial ratios; Industry financial ratios

Financial statement
A written record of business finances, including balance sheets and profit and loss statements.

Financing
See First-stage financing; Second-stage financing; Thirdstage financing

First-stage financing
Financing provided to companies that have expended their initial capital, and require funds to start full-scale manufacturing and sales. Also known as First-round financing.

Fiscal year
Any twelve-month period used by businesses for accounting purposes.

504 Program
See Certified development corporation

Flexible benefit plan
A plan that offers a choice among cash and/or qualified benefits such as group term life insurance,

accident and health insurance, group legal services, dependent care assistance, and vacations.

FOB
See Free on board

Format franchising
See Business format franchising; Franchising

401(k) plan
A financial plan where employees contribute a percentage of their earnings to a fund that is invested in stocks, bonds, or money markets for the purpose of saving money for retirement.

Four Ps
Marketing terms referring to Product, Price, Place, and Promotion.

Franchising
A form of licensing by which the owner-the franchisor- distributes or markets a product, method, or service through affiliated dealers called franchisees. The product, method, or service being marketed is identified by a brand name, and the franchisor maintains control over the marketing methods employed. The franchisee is often given exclusive access to a defined geographic area.

Free on board (FOB)
A pricing term indicating that the quoted price includes the cost of loading goods into transport vessels at a specified place.

Frictional unemployment
See Unemployment

FTC
See Federal Trade Commission

Fulfillment
The systems necessary for accurate delivery of an ordered item, including subscriptions and direct marketing.

Full-time workers
Generally, those who work a regular schedule of more than 35 hours per week.

Garment registration number
A number that must appear on every garment sold in the U.S. to indicate the manufacturer of the garment, which may or may not be the same as the label under which the garment is sold. The U.S. Federal Trade Commission assigns and regulates garment registration numbers.

Gatekeeper
A key contact point for entry into a network.

GDP
See Gross domestic product

General obligation bond
A municipal bond secured by the taxing power of the municipality. The Tax Reform Act of 1986 limits the purposes for which such bonds may be issued and establishes volume limits on the extent of their issuance.

GNP
See Gross national product

Good Housekeeping Seal
Seal appearing on products that signifies the fulfillment of the standards set by the Good Housekeeping Institute to protect consumer interests.

Goods sector
All businesses producing tangible goods, including agriculture, mining, construction, and manufacturing businesses.

GPO
See Gross product originating

Gross domestic product (GDP)
The part of the nation's gross national product (see separate citation) generated by private business using resources from within the country.

Gross national product (GNP)
The most comprehensive single measure of aggregate economic output. Represents the market value of the total output of goods and services produced by a nation's economy.

Gross product originating (GPO)
A measure of business output estimated from the income or production side using employee compensation, profit income, net interest, capital consumption, and indirect business taxes.

HAL
See Handicapped assistance loan program

Handicapped assistance loan program (HAL)
Low-interest direct loan program through the U.S. Small Business Administration (SBA) for handicapped persons. The SBA requires that these persons demonstrate that their disability is such that it is impossible for them to secure employment, thus making it necessary to go into their own business to make a living.

Health maintenance organization (HMO)
Organization of physicians and other health care professionals that provides health services to subscribers and their dependents on a prepaid basis.

Health provider
An individual or institution that gives medical care. Under Medicare, an institutional provider is a hospital, skilled nursing facility, home health agency, or provider of certain physical therapy services.

Hispanic
A person of Cuban, Mexican, Puerto Rican, Latin American (Central or South American), European Spanish, or other Spanish-speaking origin or ancestry.

HMO
See Health maintenance organization

Home-based business
A business with an operating address that is also a residential address (usually the residential address of the proprietor).

Hub-and-spoke system
A system in which flights of an airline from many different cities (the spokes) converge at a single airport (the hub). After allowing passengers sufficient time to make connections, planes then depart for different cities.

Human Resources Management
A business program designed to oversee recruiting, pay, benefits, and other issues related to the company's work force, including planning to determine the optimal use of labor to increase production, thereby increasing profit.

Idea
An original concept for a new product or process.

Import
Products produced outside the country in which they are consumed.

Income
Money or its equivalent, earned or accrued, resulting from the sale of goods and services.

Income statement
A financial statement that lists the profits and losses of a company at a given time.

Incorporation
The filing of a certificate of incorporation with a state's secretary of state, thereby limiting the business owner's liability.

Incubator
A facility designed to encourage entrepreneurship and minimize obstacles to new business formation and growth, particularly for high-technology firms, by housing a number of fledgling enterprises that share an array of services, such as meeting areas, secretarial services, accounting, research library, on-site financial and management counseling, and word processing facilities.

Independent contractor
An individual considered self-employed (see separate citation) and responsible for paying Social Security taxes and income taxes on earnings.

Indirect health coverage
Health insurance obtained through another individual's health care plan; for example, a spouse's employersponsored plan.

Industrial development authority
The financial arm of a state or other political subdivision established for the purpose of financing economic development in an area, usually through loans to nonprofit organizations, which in turn provide facilities for manufacturing and other industrial operations.

Industry financial ratios
Corporate financial ratios averaged for a specified industry. These are used for comparison purposes and

reveal industry trends and identify differences between the performance of a specific company and the performance of its industry. Also known as Industrial averages, Industry ratios, Financial averages, and Business or Industrial norms.

Inflation
Increases in volume of currency and credit, generally resulting in a sharp and continuing rise in price levels.

Informal capital
Financing from informal, unorganized sources; includes informal debt capital such as trade credit or loans from friends and relatives and equity capital from informal investors.

Initial public offering (IPO)
A corporation's first offering of stock to the public.

Innovation
The introduction of a new idea into the marketplace in the form of a new product or service or an improvement in organization or process.

Intellectual property
Any idea or work that can be considered proprietary in nature and is thus protected from infringement by others.

Internal capital
Debt or equity financing obtained from the owner or through retained business earnings.

Internet
A government-designed computer network that contains large amounts of information and is accessible through various vendors for a fee.

Intrapreneurship
The state of employing entrepreneurial principles to nonentrepreneurial situations.

Invention
The tangible form of a technological idea, which could include a laboratory prototype, drawings, formulas, etc.

IPO
See Initial public offering

Job description
The duties and responsibilities required in a particular position.

Job tenure
A period of time during which an individual is continuously employed in the same job.

Joint marketing agreements
Agreements between regional and major airlines, often involving the coordination of flight schedules, fares, and baggage transfer. These agreements help regional carriers operate at lower cost.

Joint venture
Venture in which two or more people combine efforts in a particular business enterprise, usually a single transaction or a limited activity, and agree to share the profits and losses jointly or in proportion to their contributions.

Keogh plan
Designed for self-employed persons and unincorporated businesses as a tax-deferred pension account.

Labor force
Civilians considered eligible for employment who are also willing and able to work.

Labor force participation rate
The civilian labor force as a percentage of the civilian population.

Labor intensity
The relative importance of labor in the production process, usually measured as the capital-labor ratio; i.e., the ratio of units of capital (typically, dollars of tangible assets) to the number of employees. The higher the capital-labor ratio exhibited by a firm or industry, the lower the capital intensity of that firm or industry is said to be.

Labor surplus area
An area in which there exists a high unemployment rate. In procurement (see separate citation), extra points are given to firms in counties that are designated a labor surplus area; this information is requested on procurement bid sheets.

Labor union
An organization of similarly-skilled workers who collectively bargain with management over the conditions of employment.

Laboratory prototype
See Prototype

LAN
See Local Area Network

Lanham Act
Refers to the Federal Trade Mark Act of 1946. Protects registered trademarks, trade names, and other service marks used in commerce.

Large business-dominated industry
Industry in which a minimum of 60 percent of employment or sales is in firms with more than 500 workers.

LBO
See Leveraged buy-out

Leader pricing
A reduction in the price of a good or service in order to generate more sales of that good or service.

Legal list
A list of securities selected by a state in which certain institutions and fiduciaries (such as pension funds, insurance companies, and banks) may invest. Securities not on the list are not eligible for investment. Legal lists typically restrict investments to high quality securities meeting certain specifications. Generally, investment is limited to U.S. securities and investment-grade blue chip securities (see separate citation).

Leveraged buy-out (LBO)
The purchase of a business or a division of a corporation through a highly leveraged financing package.

Liability
An obligation or duty to perform a service or an act. Also defined as money owed.

License
A legal agreement granting to another the right to use a technological innovation.

Limited partnerships
See Venture capital limited partnerships

Liquidity
The ability to convert a security into cash promptly.

Loans
See Commercial loans; Disaster loans; SBA direct loans; SBA guaranteed loans; SBA special lending institution categories Local Area Network (LAN) Computer networks contained within a single building or small area; used to facilitate the sharing of information.

Local development corporation
An organization, usually made up of local citizens of a community, designed to improve the economy of the area by inducing business and industry to locate and expand there. A local development corporation establishes a capability to finance local growth.

Long-haul rates
Rates charged by a transporter in which the distance traveled is more than 800 miles.

Long-term debt
An obligation that matures in a period that exceeds five years.

Low-grade bond
A corporate bond that is rated below investment grade by the major rating agencies (Standard and Poor's, Moody's).

Macro-efficiency
Efficiency as it pertains to the operation of markets and market systems.

Managed care
A cost-effective health care program initiated by employers whereby low-cost health care is made available to the employees in return for exclusive patronage to program doctors.

Management Assistance Programs
See SBA Management Assistance Programs

Management and technical assistance
A term used by many programs to mean business (as opposed to technological) assistance.

Mandated benefits
Specific treatments, providers, or individuals required by law to be included in commercial health plans.

Market evaluation
The use of market information to determine the sales potential of a specific product or process.

Market failure
The situation in which the workings of a competitive market do not produce the best results from the point of view of the entire society.

Market information
Data of any type that can be used for market evaluation, which could include demographic data, technology forecasting, regulatory changes, etc.

Market research
A systematic collection, analysis, and reporting of data about the market and its preferences, opinions, trends, and plans; used for corporate decision-making.

Market share
In a particular market, the percentage of sales of a specific product.

Marketing
Promotion of goods or services through various media.

Master Establishment List (MEL)
A list of firms in the United States developed by the U.S. Small Business Administration; firms can be selected by industry, region, state, standard metropolitan statistical area (see separate citation), county, and zip code.

Maturity
The date upon which the principal or stated value of a bond or other indebtedness becomes due and payable.

Medicaid (Title XIX)
A federally aided, state-operated and administered program that provides medical benefits for certain low income persons in need of health and medical care who are eligible for one of the government's welfare cash payment programs, including the aged, the blind, the disabled, and members of families with dependent children where one parent is absent, incapacitated, or unemployed.

Medicare (Title XVIII)
A nationwide health insurance program for disabled and aged persons. Health insurance is available to insured persons without regard to income. Monies from payroll taxes cover hospital insurance and monies from general revenues and beneficiary premiums pay for supplementary medical insurance.

MEL
See Master Establishment List

MESBIC
See Minority enterprise small business investment corporation

MET
See Multiple employer trust

Metropolitan statistical area (MSA)
A means used by the government to define large population centers that may transverse different governmental jurisdictions. For example, the Washington, D.C. MSA includes the District of Columbia and contiguous parts of Maryland and Virginia because all of these geopolitical areas comprise one population and economic operating unit.

Mezzanine financing
See Third-stage financing

Micro-efficiency
Efficiency as it pertains to the operation of individual firms.

Microdata
Information on the characteristics of an individual business firm.

Mid-term debt
An obligation that matures within one to five years.

Midrisk venture capital
See Equity midrisk venture capital

Minimum premium plan
A combination approach to funding an insurance plan aimed primarily at premium tax savings. The employer self-funds a fixed percentage of estimated monthly claims and the insurance company insures the excess.

Minimum wage
The lowest hourly wage allowed by the federal government.

Minority Business Development Agency
Contracts with private firms throughout the nation to sponsor Minority Business Development Centers

which provide minority firms with advice and technical assistance on a fee basis.

Minority Enterprise Small Business Investment Corporation (MESBIC)
A federally funded private venture capital firm licensed by the U.S. Small Business Administration to provide capital to minority-owned businesses (see separate citation).

Minority-owned business
Businesses owned by those who are socially or economically disadvantaged (see separate citation).

Mom and Pop business
A small store or enterprise having limited capital, principally employing family members.

Moonlighter
A wage-and-salary worker with a side business.

MSA
See Metropolitan statistical area

Multi-employer plan
A health plan to which more than one employer is required to contribute and that may be maintained through a collective bargaining agreement and required to meet standards prescribed by the U.S. Department of Labor.

Multi-level marketing
A system of selling in which you sign up other people to assist you and they, in turn, recruit others to help them. Some entrepreneurs have built successful companies on this concept because the main focus of their activities is their product and product sales.

Multimedia
The use of several types of media to promote a product or service. Also, refers to the use of several different types of media (sight, sound, pictures, text) in a CD-ROM (see separate citation) product.

Multiple employer trust (MET)
A self-funded benefit plan generally geared toward small employers sharing a common interest.

NAFTA
See North American Free Trade Agreement

NASDAQ
See National Association of Securities Dealers Automated Quotations

National Association of Securities Dealers Automated Quotations
Provides price quotes on over-the-counter securities as well as securities listed on the New York Stock Exchange.

National income
Aggregate earnings of labor and property arising from the production of goods and services in a nation's economy.

Net assets
See Net worth

Net income
The amount remaining from earnings and profits after all expenses and costs have been met or deducted. Also known as Net earnings.

Net profit
Money earned after production and overhead expenses (see separate citations) have been deducted.

Net worth
The difference between a company's total assets and its total liabilities.

Network
A chain of interconnected individuals or organizations sharing information and/or services.

New York Stock Exchange (NYSE)
The oldest stock exchange in the U.S. Allows for trading in stocks, bonds, warrants, options, and rights that meet listing requirements.

Niche
A career or business for which a person is well-suited. Also, a product which fulfills one need of a particular market segment, often with little or no competition.

Nodes
One workstation in a network, either local area or wide area (see separate citations).

Nonbank bank
A bank that either accepts deposits or makes loans, but not both. Used to create many new branch banks.

Noncompetitive awards
A method of contracting whereby the federal government negotiates with only one contractor to supply a product or service.

Nonmember bank
A state-regulated bank that does not belong to the federal bank system.

Nonprofit
An organization that has no shareholders, does not distribute profits, and is without federal and state tax liabilities.

Norms
See Financial ratios

North American Free Trade Agreement (NAFTA)
Passed in 1993, NAFTA eliminates trade barriers among businesses in the U.S., Canada, and Mexico.

NYSE
See New York Stock Exchange

Occupational Safety & Health Administration (OSHA)
Federal agency that regulates health and safety standards within the workplace.

Optimal firm size
The business size at which the production cost per unit of output (average cost) is, in the long run, at its minimum.

Organizational chart
A hierarchical chart tracking the chain of command within an organization.

OSHA
See Occupational Safety & Health Administration

Overhead
Expenses, such as employee benefits and building utilities, incurred by a business that are unrelated to the actual product or service sold.

Owner's capital
Debt or equity funds provided by the owner(s) of a business; sources of owner's capital are personal savings, sales of assets, or loans from financial institutions.

P & L
See Profit and loss statement

Part-time workers
Normally, those who work less than 35 hours per week. The Tax Reform Act indicated that part-time workers who work less than 17.5 hours per week may be excluded from health plans for purposes of complying with federal nondiscrimination rules.

Part-year workers
Those who work less than 50 weeks per year.

Partnership
Two or more parties who enter into a legal relationship to conduct business for profit. Defined by the U.S. Internal Revenue Code as joint ventures, syndicates, groups, pools, and other associations of two or more persons organized for profit that are not specifically classified in the IRS code as corporations or proprietorships.

Patent
A grant made by the government assuring an inventor the sole right to make, use, and sell an invention for a period of 17 years.

PC
See Professional corporation

Peak
See Cyclical peak

Pension
A series of payments made monthly, semiannually, annually, or at other specified intervals during the lifetime of the pensioner for distribution upon retirement. The term is sometimes used to denote the portion of the retirement allowance financed by the employer's contributions.

Pension fund
A fund established to provide for the payment of pension benefits; the collective contributions made by all of the parties to the pension plan.

Performance appraisal
An established set of objective criteria, based on job description and requirements, that is used to evaluate the performance of an employee in a specific job.

Permit
See Business license

Plan
See Business plan

Pooling
An arrangement for employers to achieve efficiencies and lower health costs by joining together to purchase group health insurance or self-insurance.

PPO
See Preferred provider organization

Preferred lenders program
See SBA special lending institution categories

Preferred provider organization (PPO)
A contractual arrangement with a health care services organization that agrees to discount its health care rates in return for faster payment and/or a patient base.

Premiums
The amount of money paid to an insurer for health insurance under a policy. The premium is generally paid periodically (e.g., monthly), and often is split between the employer and the employee. Unlike deductibles and coinsurance or copayments, premiums are paid for coverage whether or not benefits are actually used.

Prime-age workers
Employees 25 to 54 years of age.

Prime contract
A contract awarded directly by the U.S. Federal Government.

Private company
See Closely held corporation

Private placement
A method of raising capital by offering for sale an investment or business to a small group of investors (generally avoiding registration with the Securities and Exchange Commission or state securities registration agencies). Also known as Private financing or Private offering.

Pro forma
The use of hypothetical figures in financial statements to represent future expenditures, debts, and other potential financial expenses.

Proactive
Taking the initiative to solve problems and anticipate future events before they happen, instead of reacting to an already existing problem or waiting for a difficult situation to occur.

Procurement
A contract from an agency of the federal government for goods or services from a small business.

Prodigy
An online service which is accessible by computer modem. The service features Internet access, bulletin boards, online periodicals, electronic mail, and other services for subscribers.

Product development
The stage of the innovation process where research is translated into a product or process through evaluation, adaptation, and demonstration.

Product franchising
An arrangement for a franchisee to use the name and to produce the product line of the franchisor or parent corporation.

Production
The manufacture of a product.

Production prototype
See Prototype

Productivity
A measurement of the number of goods produced during a specific amount of time.

Professional corporation (PC)
Organized by members of a profession such as medicine, dentistry, or law for the purpose of conducting their professional activities as a corporation. Liability of a member or shareholder is limited in the same manner as in a business corporation.

Profit and loss statement (P & L)
The summary of the incomes (total revenues) and costs of a company's operation during a specific period of time. Also known as Income and expense statement.

Proposal
See Business plan

Proprietorship
The most common legal form of business ownership; about 85 percent of all small businesses are proprietorships. The liability of the owner is unlimited in this form of ownership.

Prospective payment system
A cost-containment measure included in the Social Security Amendments of 1983 whereby Medicare payments to hospitals are based on established prices, rather than on cost reimbursement.

Prototype
A model that demonstrates the validity of the concept of an invention (laboratory prototype); a model that meets the needs of the manufacturing process and the user (production prototype).

Prudent investor rule or standard
A legal doctrine that requires fiduciaries to make investments using the prudence, diligence, and intelligence that would be used by a prudent person in making similar investments. Because fiduciaries make investments on behalf of third-party beneficiaries, the standard results in very conservative investments. Until recently, most state regulations required the fiduciary to apply this standard to each investment. Newer, more progressive regulations permit fiduciaries to apply this standard to the portfolio taken as a whole, thereby allowing a fiduciary to balance a portfolio with higher-yield, higher-risk investments. In states with more progressive regulations, practically every type of security is eligible for inclusion in the portfolio of investments made by a fiduciary, provided that the portfolio investments, in their totality, are those of a prudent person.

Public equity markets
Organized markets for trading in equity shares such as common stocks, preferred stocks, and warrants. Includes markets for both regularly traded and nonregularly traded securities.

Public offering
General solicitation for participation in an investment opportunity. Interstate public offerings are supervised by the U.S. Securities and Exchange Commission (see separate citation).

Quality control
The process by which a product is checked and tested to ensure consistent standards of high quality.

Rate of return
The yield obtained on a security or other investment based on its purchase price or its current market price. The total rate of return is current income plus or minus capital appreciation or depreciation.

Real property
Includes the land and all that is contained on it.

Realignment
See Resource realignment

Recession
Contraction of economic activity occurring between the peak and trough (see separate citations) of a business cycle.

Regulated market
A market in which the government controls the forces of supply and demand, such as who may enter and what price may be charged.

Regulation D
A vehicle by which small businesses make small offerings and private placements of securities with limited disclosure requirements. It was designed to ease the burdens imposed on small businesses utilizing this method of capital formation.

Regulatory Flexibility Act
An act requiring federal agencies to evaluate the impact of their regulations on small businesses before the regulations are issued and to consider less burdensome alternatives.

Research
The initial stage of the innovation process, which includes idea generation and invention.

Research and development financing
A tax-advantaged partnership set up to finance product development for start-ups as well as more mature companies.

Resource mobility
The ease with which labor and capital move from firm to firm or from industry to industry.

Resource realignment
The adjustment of productive resources to interindustry changes in demand.

Resources
The sources of support or help in the innovation process, including sources of financing, technical evaluation, market evaluation, management and business assistance, etc.

Retained business earnings
Business profits that are retained by the business rather than being distributed to the shareholders as dividends.

Revolving credit
An agreement with a lending institution for an amount of money, which cannot exceed a set maximum, over a specified period of time. Each time the borrower repays a portion of the loan, the amount of the repayment may be borrowed yet again.

Risk capital
See Venture capital

Risk management
The act of identifying potential sources of financial loss and taking action to minimize their negative impact.

Routing
The sequence of steps necessary to complete a product during production.

S corporations
See Sub chapter S corporations

SBA
See Small Business Administration

SBA direct loans
Loans made directly by the U.S. Small Business Administration (SBA); monies come from funds appropriated specifically for this purpose. In general, SBA direct loans carry interest rates slightly lower than those in the private financial markets and are available only to applicants unable to secure private financing or an SBA guaranteed loan.

SBA 504 Program
See Certified development corporation

SBA guaranteed loans
Loans made by lending institutions in which the U.S. Small Business Administration (SBA) will pay a prior agreed-upon percentage of the outstanding principal in the event the borrower of the loan defaults. The terms of the loan and the interest rate are negotiated between theborrower and the lending institution, within set parameters.

SBA loans
See Disaster loans; SBA direct loans; SBA guaranteed loans; SBA special lending institution categories

SBA Management Assistance Programs
Classes, workshops, counseling, and publications offered by the U.S. Small Business Administration.

SBA special lending institution categories
U.S. Small Business Administration (SBA) loan program in which the SBA promises certified banks a 72-hour turnaround period in giving its approval for a loan, and in which preferred lenders in a pilot program are allowed to write SBA loans without seeking prior SBA approval.

SBDB
See Small Business Data Base

SBDC
See Small business development centers

SBI
See Small business institutes program

SBIC
See Small business investment corporation

SBIR Program
See Small Business Innovation Development Act of 1982

Scale economies
The decline of the production cost per unit of output (average cost) as the volume of output increases.

Scale efficiency
The reduction in unit cost available to a firm when producing at a higher output volume.

SCORE
See Service Corps of Retired Executives

SEC
See Securities and Exchange Commission

SECA
See Self-Employment Contributions Act

Second-stage financing
Working capital for the initial expansion of a company that is producing, shipping, and has growing accounts receivable and inventories. Also known as Second-round financing.

Secondary market
A market established for the purchase and sale of outstanding securities following their initial distribution.

Secondary worker
Any worker in a family other than the person who is the primary source of income for the family.

Secondhand capital
Previously used and subsequently resold capital equipment (e.g., buildings and machinery).

Securities and Exchange Commission (SEC)
Federal agency charged with regulating the trade of securities to prevent unethical practices in the investor market.

Securitized debt
A marketing technique that converts long-term loans to marketable securities.

Seed capital
Venture financing provided in the early stages of the innovation process, usually during product development.

Self-employed person
One who works for a profit or fees in his or her own business, profession, or trade, or who operates a farm.

Self-Employment Contributions Act (SECA)
Federal law that governs the self-employment tax (see separate citation).

Self-employment income
Income covered by Social Security if a business earns a net income of at least $400.00 during the year. Taxes are paid on earnings that exceed $400.00.

Self-employment retirement plan
See Keogh plan

Self-employment tax
Required tax imposed on self-employed individuals for the provision of Social Security and Medicare. The tax must be paid quarterly with estimated income tax statements.

Self-funding
A health benefit plan in which a firm uses its own funds to pay claims, rather than transferring the financial risks of paying claims to an outside insurer in exchange for premium payments.

Service Corps of Retired Executives (SCORE)
Volunteers for the SBA Management Assistance Program who provide one-on-one counseling and teach workshops and seminars for small firms.

Service firm
See Business service firm

Service sector
Broadly defined, all U.S. industries that produce intangibles, including the five major industry divisions of transportation, communications, and utilities; wholesale trade; retail trade; finance, insurance, and real estate; and services.

Set asides
See Small business set asides

Short-haul service
A type of transportation service in which the transporter supplies service between cities where the maximum distance is no more than 200 miles.

Short-term debt
An obligation that matures in one year.

SIC codes
See Standard Industrial Classification codes

Single-establishment enterprise
See Establishment

Small business
An enterprise that is independently owned and operated, is not dominant in its field, and employs fewer than 500 people. For SBA purposes, the U.S. Small Business Administration (SBA) considers

various other factors (such as gross annual sales) in determining size of a business.

Small Business Administration (SBA)
An independent federal agency that provides assistance with loans, management, and advocating interests before other federal agencies.

Small Business Data Base
A collection of microdata (see separate citation) files on individual firms developed and maintained by the U.S. Small Business Administration.

Small business development centers (SBDC)
Centers that provide support services to small businesses, such as individual counseling, SBA advice, seminars and conferences, and other learning center activities. Most services are free of charge, or available at minimal cost.

Small business development corporation
See Certified development corporation

Small business-dominated industry
Industry in which a minimum of 60 percent of employment or sales is in firms with fewer than 500 employees.

Small Business Innovation Development Act of 1982
Federal statute requiring federal agencies with large extramural research and development budgets to allocate a certain percentage of these funds to small research and development firms. The program, called the Small Business Innovation Research (SBIR) Program, is designed to stimulate technological innovation and make greater use of small businesses in meeting national innovation needs.

Small business institutes (SBI) program
Cooperative arrangements made by U.S. Small Business Administration district offices and local colleges and universities to provide small business firms with graduate students to counsel them without charge.

Small business investment corporation (SBIC)
A privately owned company licensed and funded through the U.S. Small Business Administration and private sector sources to provide equity or debt capital to small businesses.

Small business set asides
Procurement (see separate citation) opportunities required by law to be on all contracts under $10,000 or a certain percentage of an agency's total procurement expenditure.

Smaller firms
For U.S. Department of Commerce purposes, those firms not included in the Fortune 1000.

SMSA
See Metropolitan statistical area

Socially and economically disadvantaged
Individuals who have been subjected to racial or ethnic prejudice or cultural bias without regard to their qualities as individuals, and whose abilities to compete are impaired because of diminished opportunities to obtain capital and credit.

Sole proprietorship
An unincorporated, one-owner business, farm, or professional practice.

Special lending institution categories
See SBA special lending institution categories

Standard Industrial Classification (SIC) codes
Four-digit codes established by the U.S. Federal Government to categorize businesses by type of economic activity; the first two digits correspond to major groups such as construction and manufacturing, while the last two digits correspond to subgroups such as home construction or highway construction.

Standard metropolitan statistical area (SMSA)
See Metropolitan statistical area

Start-up
A new business, at the earliest stages of development and financing.

Start-up costs
Costs incurred before a business can commence operations.

Start-up financing
Financing provided to companies that have either completed product development and initial marketing or have been in business for less than one year but have not yet sold their product commercially.

Stock
A certificate of equity ownership in a business.

Stop-loss coverage
Insurance for a self-insured plan that reimburses the company for any losses it might incur in its health claims beyond a specified amount.

Strategic planning
Projected growth and development of a business to establish a guiding direction for the future. Also used to determine which market segments to explore for optimal sales of products or services.

Structural unemployment
See Unemployment

Sub chapter S corporations
Corporations that are considered noncorporate for tax purposes but legally remain corporations.

Subcontract
A contract between a prime contractor and a subcontractor, or between subcontractors, to furnish supplies or services for performance of a prime contract (see separate citation) or a subcontract.

Surety bonds
Bonds providing reimbursement to an individual, company, or the government if a firm fails to complete a contract. The U.S. Small Business Administration guarantees surety bonds in a program much like the SBA guaranteed loan program (see separate citation).

Swing loan
See Bridge financing

Target market
The clients or customers sought for a business' product or service.

Targeted Jobs Tax Credit
Federal legislation enacted in 1978 that provides a tax credit to an employer who hires structurally unemployed individuals.

Tax number
A number assigned to a business by a state revenue department that enables the business to buy goods without paying sales tax.

Taxable bonds
An interest-bearing certificate of public or private indebtedness. Bonds are issued by public agencies to finance economic development.

Technical assistance
See Management and technical assistance

Technical evaluation
Assessment of technological feasibility.

Technology
The method in which a firm combines and utilizes labor and capital resources to produce goods or services; the application of science for commercial or industrial purposes.

Technology transfer
The movement of information about a technology or intellectual property from one party to another for use.

Tenure
See Employee tenure

Term
The length of time for which a loan is made.

Terms of a note
The conditions or limits of a note; includes the interest rate per annum, the due date, and transferability and convertibility features, if any.

Third-party administrator
An outside company responsible for handling claims and performing administrative tasks associated with health insurance plan maintenance.

Third-stage financing
Financing provided for the major expansion of a company whose sales volume is increasing and that is breaking even or profitable. These funds are used for further plant expansion, marketing, working capital, or development of an improved product. Also known as Third-round or Mezzanine financing.

Time deposit
A bank deposit that cannot be withdrawn before a specified future time.

Time management
Skills and scheduling techniques used to maximize productivity.

Trade credit
Credit extended by suppliers of raw materials or finished products. In an accounting statement, trade credit is referred to as "accounts payable."

Trade name
The name under which a company conducts business, or by which its business, goods, or services are identified. It may or may not be registered as a trademark.

Trade periodical
A publication with a specific focus on one or more aspects of business and industry.

Trade secret
Competitive advantage gained by a business through the use of a unique manufacturing process or formula.

Trade show
An exhibition of goods or services used in a particular industry. Typically held in exhibition centers where exhibitors rent space to display their merchandise.

Trademark
A graphic symbol, device, or slogan that identifies a business. A business has property rights to its trademark from the inception of its use, but it is still prudent to register all trademarks with the Trademark Office of the U.S. Department of Commerce.

Translation
See Product development

Treasury bills
Investment tender issued by the Federal Reserve Bank in amounts of $10,000 that mature in 91 to 182 days.

Treasury bonds
Long-term notes with maturity dates of not less than seven and not more than twenty-five years.

Treasury notes
Short-term notes maturing in less than seven years.

Trend
A statistical measurement used to track changes that occur over time.

Trough
See Cyclical trough

UCC
See Uniform Commercial Code

UL
See Underwriters Laboratories

Underwriters Laboratories (UL)
One of several private firms that tests products and processes to determine their safety. Although various firms can provide this kind of testing service, many local and insurance codes specify UL certification.

Underwriting
A process by which an insurer determines whether or not and on what basis it will accept an application for insurance. In an experience-rated plan, premiums are based on a firm's or group's past claims; factors other than prior claims are used for community-rated or manually rated plans.

Unfair competition
Refers to business practices, usually unethical, such as using unlicensed products, pirating merchandise, or misleading the public through false advertising, which give the offending business an unequitable advantage over others.

Unfunded accrued liability
The excess of total liabilities, both present and prospective, over present and prospective assets.

Unemployment
The joblessness of individuals who are willing to work, who are legally and physically able to work, and who are seeking work. Unemployment may represent the temporary joblessness of a worker between jobs (frictional unemployment) or the joblessness of a worker whose skills are not suitable for jobs available in the labor market (structural unemployment).

Uniform Commercial Code (UCC)
A code of laws governing commercial transactions across the U.S., except Louisiana. Their purpose is to bring uniformity to financial transactions.

Uniform product code (UPC symbol)
A computer-readable label comprised of ten digits and stripes that encodes what a product is and how much it costs. The first five digits are assigned by the

Uniform Product Code Council, and the last five digits by the individual manufacturer.

Unit cost
See Average cost

UPC symbol
See Uniform product code

U.S. Establishment and Enterprise Microdata (USEEM) File
A cross-sectional database containing information on employment, sales, and location for individual enterprises and establishments with employees that have a Dun & Bradstreet credit rating.

U.S. Establishment Longitudinal Microdata (USELM) File
A database containing longitudinally linked sample microdata on establishments drawn from the U.S. Establishment and Enterprise Microdata file (see separate citation).

U.S. Small Business Administration 504 Program
See Certified development corporation

USEEM
See U.S. Establishment and Enterprise Microdata File

USELM
See U.S. Establishment Longitudinal Microdata File

VCN
See Venture capital network

Venture capital
Money used to support new or unusual business ventures that exhibit above-average growth rates, significant potential for market expansion, and are in need of additional financing to sustain growth or further research and development; equity or equity-type financing traditionally provided at the commercialization stage, increasingly available prior to commercialization.

Venture capital company
A company organized to provide seed capital to a business in its formation stage, or in its first or second stage of expansion. Funding is obtained through public or private pension funds, commercial banks and bank holding companies, small business investment corporations licensed by the U.S. Small Business Administration, private venture capital firms, insurance companies, investment management companies, bank trust departments, industrial companies seeking to diversify their investment, and investment bankers acting as intermediaries for other investors or directly investing on their own behalf.

Venture capital limited partnerships
Designed for business development, these partnerships are an institutional mechanism for providing capital for young, technology-oriented businesses. The investors' money is pooled and invested in money market assets until venture investments have been selected. The general partners are experienced investment managers who select and invest the equity and debt securities of firms with high growth potential and the ability to go public in the near future.

Venture capital network (VCN)
A computer database that matches investors with entrepreneurs.

WAN
See Wide Area Network

Wide Area Network (WAN)
Computer networks linking systems throughout a state or around the world in order to facilitate the sharing of information.

Withholding
Federal, state, social security, and unemployment taxes withheld by the employer from employees' wages; employers are liable for these taxes and the corporate umbrella and bankruptcy will not exonerate an employer from paying back payroll withholding. Employers should escrow these funds in a separate account and disperse them quarterly to withholding authorities.

Workers' compensation
A state-mandated form of insurance covering workers injured in job-related accidents. In some states, the state is the insurer; in other states, insurance must be acquired from commercial insurance firms. Insurance rates are based on a number of factors, including salaries, firm history, and risk of occupation.

Working capital
Refers to a firm's short-term investment of current assets, including cash, short-term securities, accounts receivable, and inventories.

Yield
The rate of income returned on an investment, expressed as a percentage. Income yield is obtained by dividing the current dollar income by the current market price of the security. Net yield or yield to maturity is the current income yield minus any premium above par or plus any discount from par in purchase price, with the adjustment spread over the period from the date of purchase to the date of maturity.

Index

Listings in this index are arranged alphabetically by business plan type, then alphabetically by business plan name. Users are provided with the volume number in which the plan appears.